ELIZABETH JANE HOWARD

Born in 1923, Eilizabeth Jane Howard was awarded the John Llewellyn Rhys Memorial Prize for her book *The Beautiful Visit*. Her subsequent novels were *The Long View*, *The Sea Cha... After Julius*, *Odd Girl Out*, *Something in Disguise*, and *Getting ...ight*. She has also written fourteen television scripts, a biography of ...ina von Arnim with Arthur Helps, a cookery book with Fay Mas..., two film scripts, and has edited two anthologies and published a b... of ghost stories. She is currently working on the Cazalet Chronicle the first two volumes, *The Light Years* and *Marking Time*, are already available in paperback from Pan.

ELIZABETH JANE
HOWARD

THE
BEAUTIFUL VISIT
AND
SOMETHING
IN DISGUISE

PAN BOOKS
in association with Jonathan Cape

The Beautiful Visit was first published in 1950 by
Jonathan Cape Ltd
© Elizabeth Jane Howard 1950

Something in Disguise was first published in 1969 by
Jonathan Cape Ltd
© Elizabeth Jane Howard 1969

This two-volume edition published 1993 by Pan Books Ltd
a division of Pan Macmillan Publishers Limited
Cavaye Place London SW10 9PG
and Basingstoke
in association with Jonathan Cape Ltd

Associated companies throughout the world

ISBN 0 330 33434 4

This two-volume edition © Elizabeth Jane Howard 1993

The right of Elizabeth Jane Howard to be identified as the author
of this work has been asserted by her in accordance with the
Copyright, Designs and Patents Act 1988.

1 3 5 7 9 8 6 4 2

A CIP catalogue record for this book is
available from the British Library

Printed and bound in Great Britain by
Cox & Wyman Ltd, Reading, Berkshire

THE
BEAUTIFUL VISIT

To Robert Aickman

I woke because the fur wrapped round me had slipped off my feet, which were cold. As I moved to cover them, there was a loud creak and I discovered that my waist was encircled with a heavy leather belt. This was not at all usual, and drawing the fur up to my chin I lay back again to think. If it came to that, I did not usually sleep in a fur rug. Lying there, the ridiculous thought occurred to me that I had just been born. She was born with a girdle round her waist, they would say, to account for her misadventures. This is the kind of absurd notion one has when half awake; but for some minutes I lay still, waking; enjoying the exquisite detachment and emptiness of my mind.

It was not dark nor light, but a very fresh early grey air, and above me I could see small round windows, uncurtained. *Round* windows! I looked down again and saw, a few yards away, a pair of shining black boots which appeared never to have been worn. I was on the floor. I stretched out my left arm to touch it, and I was wearing a heavy gauntlet. The floor seemed to be shivering, or perhaps it was I who shivered. Listening, I heard a faint indescribable sound, an unhurrying rush, a sound of quiet, continuous, monotonous movement. I imagined the noise one makes walking through long dry grass; a little water spilt on to stone from some height; the distant drum-like murmur of a crowd ceaselessly conferring. Surely I must be the only person in the tremendous silence lying outside the small sound I could hear. I felt alone, warm and alone, in a desert or in outer space.

At this, my mind pricked up its senses and drawing the fur closely round me, I sat huddled on the floor and stared at the two round windows which were now a perceptibly paler grey.

After a moment, I rose stiffly to my feet and went to a window. There was nothing to be seen but a limitless wash of sea, breaking, and glinting where it broke, like steel. Above it was a paler empty stretch of sky, divided from the sea by a straight, faint, silver line. This whole round picture quivered, dipped a little, sustained the decline, and then rose again so that the original proportions of two-thirds sea, one-third sky were visible. This, very generally speaking, was where I was: but why? where was I going? and how did I come to be here at all?

I walked softly to the door, opened it, and looked out. There was nothing but a dim narrow passage: I hesitated a moment, then closing the door again, stood with my back to it, surveying the cabin where I had been sleeping. Catching sight of the boots again, I drew back the fur and looked down at myself. I was not reassured by my clothes, but clothes in which one had slept all night are not very re-assuring. There was a perfectly good bed in one corner. Why had I not slept in that? I went to look at the bed. Lying in the middle of it were two fat marbled exercise books.

I remembered everything: remembered who I was and felt imprisoned with the knowledge that I was not free and new and empty as I had been when I woke on the floor. I stared at the two books which contained my life. I took them and sat beneath one of the windows, intending only, I think, to glance at them for the contrast they provided to my present circumstances. After all, I had little idea what would happen next. My life loomed before me, as wide with chance as it had been the day I was born.

CHAPTER ONE

I was born in Kensington. My father was a composer. My mother came from a rich home, and was, I believe, incurably romantic. She married my father, despite the half-hearted protestations of her family, who felt that to marry a musician was very nearly as bad as to marry into trade, and far less secure. I imagine their protestations were half-hearted, because she was, after all, their seventh daughter; and if they had been at all vehement in their disapproval I cannot imagine my mother sticking to her decision. At any rate, her family, after attending the wedding (there are pictures of all my aunts looking sulky, righteous, and incredibly tightly laced, on this occasion), washed their hands of her, which was far the cheapest, and from their point of view, the most moral attitude to adopt. It was certainly the cheapest. My father was not a good composer, he was not even successful; and my mother had no idea of money (or music). She had four of us in as many years, and I was the fourth. We would all wear passed on clothes until our nurse would no longer take us near the shops, and our contemporaries laughed at us; and then suddenly, in the drawing-room, would hang rich fiery brocade curtains; or perhaps there would be a party, and we would have new muslin frocks with velvet sashes; worn for that one occasion, and outgrown long before the next. I always remember my mother as pretty, but ceaselessly exhausted by her efforts to keep the increasing number of heads above water.

We had the usual childhood, with governesses, and interminable walks in Kensington Gardens. We soon learned that most people's fathers were not composers, and we boasted about ours to the other children we met on our walks: affected a knowledge and love for music which we did not feel, and held prearranged conversations about it for the benefit of these richer and generally more fortunate friends. We were intelligent, and they were impressed. It all helped us to bear the lack of parties, seaside holidays and expensive toys.

Eventually, of course, my two brothers went away to school, and I was left at home with my sister. In all the years we grew up together, only two things stand out in my mind. The first was our poverty. I do not think we were exactly poor, but we had, as we were continually told, a position to keep up. I think the situation was complicated by the fact that my father and mother had quite different positions in mind; with the result that we oscillated hopelessly just out of reach of either.

The second was music. Music dominated our lives ever since I can remember. We were forced to listen to it for hours on end in silence; sometimes for a whole afternoon. My garters were often too tight; I used to rub under my knees, and my father would frown, and play something longer, and even less enjoyable. He was a tired, disgruntled little man; ineffectually sarcastic, and haunted by a very bad digestion, which made him morose and incapable of enjoying anything. I think even he got sick of music sometimes, but not until he had left it too late to start anything else: and my mother, I think, would have been finally shattered if he had presented her with any alternative.

Occasionally, his work would be performed; we would all go and there would be desperate little parties in the Green Room afterwards, with a lot of kissing, and frenziedly considered praise.

We were all made to learn the piano; but I was the only one who survived the tearful lessons with an enormous woman, who lisped, adored my father, and ambled into unwieldy rages at our incompetence. Also the chill, blue-fingered hour of practice before breakfast, choked the others' less dogged aspiration. After some years, my father suddenly added another hour on to this practice, and began to superintend it. He used to stand over me while I raced through easier passages of Mozart, or perhaps exercises of

Bülow, asking me difficult questions which were larded with sarcastic similies I was far too resentful and afraid to comprehend.

I remember us getting steadily poorer. There were eventually no parties, except at tea-time, when my mother would perforce entertain her more distant relations, who patronized her, and suggested alterations in the household which she had neither energy nor means to allow.

The house smelt of dusty carpets and forgotten meals; of grievance and misfortune. There was cracked white paint on all the window sills, and there were slimy slips of soap in the basins. The drawing-room degenerated to a dining, living and schoolroom; with the remains of furniture for all three purposes. There were yellowing pictures of us on the mantelpiece; languid, and consciously cultivated. The glass bookcase with cracked panes held rows of dull dark volumes which nobody wished to read. I remember the sunlight, sordid and unwelcome on my mother's sofa; and her head drooping over the arm. Her hair was always parted in the middle, strained back, and escaping in brittle strands round her ears. She seemed perpetually struggling with an enormous round work basket, writhing with grey and brown socks which gaped for attention. I can remember no colour that I can describe: no change of tempo. In the studio, the pianos stopped and started with monotonous regularity when my father resorted to teaching. For several years there was a great jar of dusty crackling beech leaves. I remember odd ends of braid round the piano stools, which shivered when pupils banged the door, as they invariably did. It was a very heavy door. Upstairs there were wide draughty passages covered with small faded mats over which one slid or tripped. My mother's bedroom was filled with huge and reputedly valuable pieces of furniture: but her remnants of jewellery winked sadly in worn white velvet; her silver-topped brushes were always tarnished; there were innumerable bent hairpins in cracks between the floorboards; and the whole room was impregnated with the brisk improbable smell of my father's shaving soap (there was always a soft grey foam on his brush). There were a great many gilt mirrors about the passages, all spotted and blurred with damp, like the passages themselves. We had a tiny garden, surrounded by black brick walls, filled with straggling grass and silent fleeting cats. I do not recall anything else very much.

My elder sister put up her hair, and began going down to dinner. The boys were always away, and I did not, in any case, like them very much. I was horribly lonely. I read everything I could lay my hands on, which was little; grew too fast; and, above all, longed for something to happen.

My sister began going to church a great deal and I found a purple Bible with silver clasps in her bedroom. She was out and I was amusing myself with her room and private things. There were a crucifix, a rosary and a few books on religious subjects smugly bound in red and gold. Was she a Roman Catholic? I didn't know anything about her; if I caught her eye at meals or in the evening she would smile, remotely gentle, and go on eating or sewing, delicately withdrawn. Her speech was carefully non-committal and she didn't talk to me much beyond asking me if I was going to wash my hair or telling me to help our mother.

I opened the drawers of her dressing-table. Her underclothes were beautifully embroidered, all white and folded, made by herself. Her boots were polished, with no broken laces. Above them in the wardrobe her dresses hung wasted with waiting; with no one to take them out into the air. They were chiefly white, mauve, dark blue and grey, with shoulders flopping sulkily off the hangers. The mauve was pretty: I had never worn mauve. It had hundreds of little buttons made of itself. I took it out of the wardrobe. It swayed a little, and suddenly I was unhooking my skirt, tearing my blouse under the arms as I wrenched it over my head, my long hair catching on the hooks, and then standing in my petticoat looking down at my ugly black shoes and stockings. I laid hands on the mauve frock. The buttons were awfully difficult to do up. I couldn't manage the one in the middle of my back at all. I twisted like a flamingo and heard the taut cotton cracking. Just about to crack I hoped. Not actually torn. I turned to a long thin mirror by the bed. My petticoat was not long enough and there was a line like a let-down hem. The dress fitted me. How clean and trim and old. I looked into the glass and said: 'I love you, Edward,' several times. My hair was wrong; he would laugh. I rushed to the dressing-table, the tight mauve skirts primly resisting, and succeeded after some agonizing moments with hairpins in twisting a bun at the back of my head. 'Good afternoon, Lavinia,' I said, advancing on the mirror. 'Good afternoon.' And I curtsied. At that moment my sister came into the room. I saw her face in the mirror. I turned round quickly so that she should not see the gap with the undone buttons. I was very frightened and afraid the gap would make her more angry. I hated her for coming in. No harm, I kept repeating to myself, only one frock, no harm.

'I hate my clothes,' I said. 'I didn't choose this house. I can't start life in it. This is so pretty.'

She shut the door, and began taking off her gloves from slim smooth white hands, fingers unpricked because she always wore thimbles when she worked.

'Will you take if off now? I don't want it too crushed,' she said.

I was struggling with the buttons when she glided forward and I felt her fingers regularly neat, releasing them, down to my waist. I pulled the dress over my head. She took it from me in silence and replaced it on its hanger in the wardrobe. I reached for my skirt and she said, 'Have you been trying on all my clothes?'

She saw the drawers open. I bent over my skirt ashamed. She sat down and talked. She would not have minded me trying on her clothes with her there, she said. But did I not feel it a little wrong to come to her room when she was out, to play with her private possessions? 'If I had known you were going to do that I should have asked you to wash your hands.' And she laughed pleasantly.

I looked at my hands. They were grey and clumsy. I felt they had only become dirty for her to see.

'We must try and remember that things don't matter.' She

was leaning forward. 'I know jealousy is hard. I have suffered from it myself' (with a weary reminiscent little smile). 'But there are other things so much more important and so little time to set sufficient values. Life is hard for us all in different ways.'

She talked for a long time in the same quiet assured un-emotional voice. There was a lot about God and trying to live a good life, peace of mind, acceptance of what was given, examples, final reward, and back to not prying un-asked into other people's things: and an absolute passion of disagreement grew in me.

'I split the frock,' I said.

'That is a pity. But I expect it can be mended. I am not angry. It's quite all right.'

'I've got to go. I promised to sort the laundry,' I said. I couldn't bear her voice any more.

'Well we'll say no more about it. Agreed?' And she rose suddenly and kissed my cheek. I left her room quickly and ran into mine. 'Don't forget the laundry,' I heard her voice daintily energetic as I shut my door.

My passion broke and I sat on the floor clutching my knees and repeating her words so that I could fight them more clearly in my mind. Things must matter. Everything existed because someone had once thought it important. Nobody gave me this house, nobody could love it; if you were peaceful you never wanted to change. I wanted every single simple thing to be different. I should not mind people looking at my clothes if they were nice. There *wasn't* anyone to help. If helpful people didn't care about beautiful stuffs and colours, sounds and more people, then they weren't any use to me. But there was nobody to help me here. Hot resent-ful tears fell down into my hands. Everything was dirty, dusty and grey; no clear colour; no piercing sound; and at tea everything would be the same. Nobody worth their salt ever had much peace of mind. I wasn't jealous of her. Good Lord no. And I repeated 'Good Lord' aloud in a pompous self-satisfied manner enjoying its rounded scorn. It was a mistake to put me in this house. I wasn't suited to it. I couldn't even cry any more, but my nose was hot and full: horrid. I got up to search for a handkerchief and rooted for hours among bits of string; postcards; a broken watch; a ring out of a cracker; a musty lavender bag, all dust and spikes; a shoelace; elastic; a ninepenny Nelson; a little pink china pig with a chipped ear; a balloon, soft, and curiously unpleasant to touch; an envelope bursting with stamps; a penwiper; and, at last, a handkerchief, grey, but folded. I shook it out, and it smelt of dolls' houses and the water out of their tea cups. I blew my nose and sat down.

'I am against everybody,' I said.

Nothing changed.

'Everybody and everything. I don't like it, I'm going to change.' The gaping drawer reminded me. A lot of those things were too childish to keep. I had outgrown them. I would throw away everything I hated. Everything in my room.

But it was tea-time.

Two days later I was still in the midst of my private revolution. My room was chaotic and each night when I went to bed the bloated waste-paper basket reminded me of more to purge. The family took no notice of me, which was comforting as there would only have been an incredulous banality about their comments. I eventually made my room unsentimentally bare; hardly belonging to me, and only resentfully part of the house. All the books and toys that had verged on grown-up possessions were gone, and it took me no time to find a handkerchief. That was not as enjoyable as I had expected; but I persevered and sorted my clothes into heaps of the unwearable, mendable, and usable. The mending took several days; I got bored and relegated many garments to the first heap.

The next thing was to find new people. I started walking in Kensington Gardens by myself, watching the people, and trying to find someone to suit my needs. This accomplished, I intended taking the person home to tea with me. The Round Pond seemed the most likely spot, because people stopped to feed the birds, or watch the yachts, or simply the minnows. I was afraid to speak to anyone. Each day I resolved to take the plunge but I was determined that it should be thoroughly done and there was a private rule that the person had to be taken to tea. I saw one girl: very pretty, carrying a little blue book, and gazing at the swans. She sat down on a seat and I watched her, fascinated. She had enormous brown eyes with very long lashes and moth-like eyebrows. She opened the little blue book, and a stupid duck which was walking on the grass and gravel, moved, hasty and eager, like a shop attendant, thinking about bread I suppose. It waited, then walked to the water and slid in, swimming smugly away as though it never hurried greedily up to seats at all. The girl stopped reading and looked up pensively. The sun was setting, and gold was slipping uncertainly off the trees and water and her hair. It was very calm; the yachts were lying on the pond, with their sails shivering still; and the gardens were blue in the distance with the tree trunks dark, like legs seen from a basement window. On the Broad Walk a leisurely stream of perambulators rolled homewards; stiff gaiters to unbutton and peel off fat frantic legs and square white feeders to be tied round hundreds of warm pink necks. A clock struck four, and the swans arched their necks for the sound to pass through. A minnow floated on its side in the water, its mouth opening: it was going to die. The girl shut her book and walked away, and I had not spoken to her. I imagined her walking back to a neat beautiful home with friends all coming to a wonderful tea. She did not walk towards my gate. 'She would never have liked me,' I said. 'She would not have come home.' The thought cheered me for the loss of her. She was only a speck among the trees already. It didn't matter, there were so many people. It was just a pity to let anyone go. All the way home I imagined her walking with me, telling me many new and exciting things about how to live, so that tea with the family would be a waste of her. It was cold by the time I reached home; the lamps were being lit in the streets, and the piano sounded in petulant bursts as I stood on the door step. My father was giving a lesson. My sister was wearing her mauve frock.

After tea I darned black stockings and ironed my hair ribbons.

The next day I went to the Round Pond half hoping, half expecting to see the girl with the blue book. It was a fresh, cold day and she was not there. I stood in front of the water: a little tufted duck dived and came up gleaming with secret pleasure. Beside me was a tall old man, very neat and black, with a stick.

'Water water everywhere nor any drop to drink,' he said suddenly. I turned to him.

> 'The very deep did rot: Oh Christ!
> 'That ever this should be!'

he went on rapidly with great emphasis.

'I know it all by heart,' he said. Then suddenly: 'Do you know where that came from, young lady?'

'Coleridge. *Ancient Mariner*,' I mumbled. My governess had read it with me.

'Quite right. Exactly right. Not many young people nowadays know that sort of thing. Great poetry. I know it all by heart.' And he walked away lifting his hat. A dog ran after him sniffing, but he took no notice and walked faster.

Nothing else happened that day. I told my family at tea about the old man, and they received it with the expected mild surprise. My father had written a choral work which was to be performed at Christmas, and they were all absorbed with being a composer's family.

We went to a concert that evening. We always contrived to look poor, cultured, and apart at these functions. The programme was chamber music, mostly Schubert and Brahms. I could never listen to chamber music for more than an hour; after which I began to count people's heads; still, bald, hatless, swaying, thrown back, shrunk forward between the shoulders, sunk on the hands, erect, anguished, emotional, ecstatic; my father stern and bored, and my mother acquiescently rapt; my sister prettily still; and I, I wondered what I looked like. I shut one eye and squinted. No good. There were red plush and gold paint; fat naked little boys in biscuit-coloured relief. The platform was a pale blue semi-circle, with the players impressively still, driving their instruments with a delicate force and deliberation. We went to see the players afterwards. They were dazed and friendly, their hands wrung and their faces stretched with answering good-will.

Going home was the nicest.

CHAPTER TWO

I still walked in the Gardens, but I did not feel any less lonely.

One windy day there were kites between the Orangery and the Pond. I went to the slope and stared upward at three of them. They were half proud, half fearful; soaring with wild little tugs at their strings. I watched their joy at a moment's release in the dropping wind's fantasy; their floating in the second's calm before they were off again; sinuous and wild, and captive all the time. I looked down, too far of course, to the ground and saw muddy tufted grass and a pair of black boots. Enormous boots. A boy. An old boy; nearly as old as I. His suit was dirty, his breeches tight, his sleeves too short, and his wrists red and bony. He was very intent on his kite; his eyes were screwed up with the sky and staring cold; his dark hair ruffled up by the wind into a square crest. He had a large Adam's apple which reminded me of five notes and then down a fifth on a piano. I stood a little nearer and stared again at the kite because he was so intent upon it. I was suddenly possessed of a desire to have been flying it with him; for his winding in to be by our mutual consent, because we had other things to do, planned together. The kite was almost in; it was pink and yellow, with ribs dark and delicate against the sky; and he was winding fast, his fingers hard and capable against the string. His eyes came down to earth, and he glanced at me just as the kite hit the ground with a thin papery thud.

'Can I look at it?'

'What?'

'Your kite. Can I look at it?'

'If you like.' He watched the kite in my hands indifferently.

'Did you make it?'

'No.' I knew he wished he had.

'Do you often fly it?'

'No.'

I gave it back to him.

'I've stopped because of the wind,' he volunteered.

'It's dropping.' My mouth was very dry.

'I'm going home now. Good-bye.' He started off, the kite perched in his arms. 'I'll be here tomorrow if you want to see it fly properly.' He was going.

'I say,' I called. 'I say. Would you like to come home to tea?'

He stopped. It was up to him. I saw his eyes faintly curious and defensive, and I longed for him to come.

'What's your name?'

I told him.

'How old are you?'

I told him.

'All right,' he said; and we set off down the Broad Walk.

'Will your family wonder where you are?'

'Oh no. I shouldn't get any tea anyhow. They're against me at the moment. I don't agree with them.'

I digested that in silence.

'My father's a doctor,' he added as an explanation.

'I see,' I said. 'What school do you go to?'

'I don't. I've been expelled.'

I didn't know what to say.

'How awful.'

'It jolly well is. I didn't like it much there but it's worse at home.'

'Why did they?'

'Partly because of God.' He stopped and transferred the kite from one arm to the other. 'And partly because of games.'

'I didn't know they could expel you for them.'

'Oh well it wasn't just them. They just started it. I was a bad influence anyway,' he said with some pride.

'How do you start being an influence?'

'Why?' He stopped and regarded me again suspiciously. 'I

don't think it would be easy for you. You might be a good influence of course. Girls always want to be that. But I shouldn't advise you to try. It's no good deliberately trying to influence anyone. My English master taught me that. It's about all I learned at school. You mustn't try and change other people. It's never good for them in the end. At school they want the masters to change everyone. And they want the boys to be sure of being everyone. He wouldn't and I wasn't and so he left and I was expelled.'

'Where is he now?'

'Edinburgh. With his family. They aren't pleased. I get letters from him. I'll show you if you like. You seem sensible.'

'Oh I am,' I said.

'We'd better sit down. Letters are too difficult standing up.'

We sat on a black bench. He took a crumpled envelope out of his pocket, and unfolded the letter. The writing was slanting and very difficult.

'– decision is not simple. Man's ultimate purgatory could be fraught with endless decisions; the consequences unknown and terrible even with knowledge – ' a blank which I couldn't read, ending with – 'and he spent twenty years deciding that, incomplete though it is – ' unreadable again – 'therefore assess yourself freely with sincerity and courage and tackle the main problem of what you want to be; once you are at all sure, nothing should stop you. Until then it is just strife for the sake of self-expression, a grisly means to achieve no positive end. I hope – '

The boy didn't turn over the page but folded it away back into the envelope and his pocket. 'The rest is just about writing and what to read,' he said.

I was paralysed. It was the first time I found myself facing something about which I had never thought, and was quite incapable of judging even generally, good from bad.

'He means, if you are going to change be sure why, and know what you want to change into, or else it would be like throwing your clothes away and being naked.'

'But if you want to change,' I said. 'If you want everything to be different, it's because the old things are dreary and dead and *anything* else would be new to you.'

'Not necessarily good though.'

'Supposing you wanted them new at all costs? Surely sometimes anything different would be better?'

'To think or to do?'

'I can't separate them,' I said.

He looked at me rather scornfully. 'I don't think you can. But don't you see by renouncing anything blindly without substitute you expose yourself to any fool or foolishness.'

'But supposing you hate everything that is in you,' I cried desperately, 'and you've never had a chance to know anything else, you only know you must change, what do you do then? You have to throw things away.' A litter of fairy books and dolls' clothes flung across my mind.

'You can read can't you?' he demanded fiercely. 'And talk to people. Learn, listen, and find out, and then choose.' And he went on in stern little spurts of energy and knowledge, serious, even sententious, but it didn't seem that then; only marvellous and rather frightening that one could be my age and know so much, and then be so fierce, and excited and serious about it.

My thoughts were like shillings in a pool, glittering and blurred, shimmering to the groping finger and always deeper and more elusive, until you think that perhaps there isn't a shilling at all, it seems so far out of reach. I floundered and the words wouldn't come. He forced me relentlessly into corners, and I felt the back of my neck getting hot, and warm little shivers down my spine. I didn't tell him about myself lest he should scorn what then seemed to me such childish endeavour. He raced on through religion, came triumphantly to blasphemous conclusions. Education was stabbed with a ferocity I had never before encountered; until it lay a bewildered mess of Latin, historical dates and cricket stumps. And then the older generation was subjected to a vitriolic attack: such remorseless contempt, such despairing anger, such a thunder of criticism was broken over their meek, bald and bun-like heads that I was dumb at the death of so large a body; trembling with anxious rapture of choice and the still distance of freedom.

He stared at the gravel, his talk calming. The kite lay between us on the bench, its paper stretched between the struts, breathing and rucked a little in the breeze. I had not attempted to argue or deny, I was quite incapable of either; it just seemed to me that my solitude was at an end; and his talk, his spate of words were rushing, like liquid, into my mind.

'What about *your* parents?' he said, suddenly lifting his head.

'Oh they – I have the same trouble.'

'Do they stop you doing things?'

'No, not exactly. There's nothing for them to stop.'

'What does your father do?'

'He writes music.'

'Oh, that should make it simpler for you.'

'I don't think it does. Anyway I don't think he thought much about it being simple for anyone when he started. There isn't much money and my mother's always tired.'

'I'm cold,' he said and rose to his feet. 'You're cold too,' looking down on me. It was an impersonal remark but I blushed and rose with a murmuring denial. It was blue grey, and the Gardens were nearly empty. We walked home almost in silence, and apprehension superseded the excitement I had known on the bench with the letter and the kite.

Lights were showing from houses, but mine was dark. I noticed the paint bubbled and peeling off the plaster, and the windows powdered and dull with dust.

We went in to tea.

'Do you always keep your door open?'

'Yes. It saves so much time.' My teeth were chattering and I didn't want to talk.

'I like that.' He put the kite on two chairs in the hall.

'Do you want to wash?'

He looked surprised, and urged me on down the passage.

The dining-room was terribly near. I prayed that they wouldn't all be there. They would put down their cups and their bread and look up, all towards the door, at him, and at me, and back to him again, and there would be a stealthy concert against speaking first, an awkward calm, which I must clumsily break. I opened the door. They put down their cups.

'He's come to tea,' I said, and turned to him blocking their sight. 'I can't remember your name.'

'Michael Latham,' he muttered as though it meant nothing, and he had learned it by heart.

'Come and sit down, Michael. Milk and sugar, Michael?' My mother wielded the tea-pot.

My father resumed his reading of *Blackwood's Magazine*. Michael stared at him. My sister lowered her eyes and scraped strawberry jam neatly with her knife. I could think of nothing to say. There was an exhausted pupil swallowing tea with a pale film; it was cold, and he had been too nervous and depressed to drink it, until he had felt sure that attention was diverted from him and his tremendous, thick, white hands. Michael ate an enormous tea, punctuated by monosyllabic replies to my mother's and sister's small inquisitive advances. He seemed fascinated by my father, watching him timidly and bending his head abrupt and shy if my father turned a page or stirred his tea.

How to escape and where? My brothers always seemed to manage it when they had friends to tea. They clattered with one purposeful rush to their large bedroom, where they remained for the evening. If, for any reason, I had ever gone into their room, they were always to be found standing in a conspiratorial group, quite silent and apparently doing nothing, frozen like animals at an unavoidable intrusion; hostile, scarcely breathing, with some secret purpose deep in their minds. I could not take Michael upstairs; I knew that for some reason my parents would not like it.

'Are you going to use the studio?' I asked my father. The pupil wriggled and hid his hands with a desperate little grin.

'I have to play something over once. Why?'

'I thought that if it was empty it would be a good place for us to go,' I said.

'Do you want somewhere to play?'

'No. It doesn't matter.'

'Well I want somewhere to play and I can't move my toys about as you can.' And he went on reading.

I saw Michael furiously kneading his bread, with shining eyes. There was a meek little silence; my mother was filling the tea-pot and we were all eating our tea, regardless of anything but our little personal movements.

I knew that if we were to escape I must get up and know where we were to go.

Better get on with it. I rose to my feet and in the same instant I heard Michael say, 'Could I hear you play, sir?'

My father looked up, a little pleased. 'Certainly, if you like.'

My heart thudded and I felt very cold. There was a general movement and I found myself in the studio, my father at the piano, with Michael and the pupil in appreciative attitudes. He played for two hours, and then Michael left. He stopped being shy with my father, thanked him with a great jerk of enthusiasm, and shook his hand twice very quickly. I walked with him down the steps to the gate.

'Well thank you,' he said. 'I loved hearing your father play. You never told me how good he was. I wish my family were like that.'

I was silent.

'Music whenever you like and no one minding who you bring home. Marvellous. Thank you very much. Good-bye.' And he went off with his kite.

I walked slowly back up the path. I would go upstairs, and perhaps I would cry a little because it finished a feeling more quickly and it would be easier to start again. It would be better to stay alone for a bit in order to know how to talk about it at dinner. I was tired; my legs felt heavy and the sides of my forehead ached. In the hall I met my sister who smiled discreetly, as though she knew the secret wrong thing, and suggested I lay the table for dinner. So I did. The girl who cooked helped me with fat pasty sighs, pushing her mauve fingers through her greasy hair and saying 'Yes Miss' while she smeared boards and tables with a grey stringy cloth. I filled the water jug from the cold tap in the scullery which roared out in an angry gush, leaving me with little round cold drops on my arms and chin; wiped the jug with a cloth; and carried it into the dining-room, where it left a little dim damp rim afterwards hidden by a cork mat. I edged the blue glass mustard pot out of its silver frame, rinsed the malevolent brown crust with my fingers, half expecting it to sting; and mixed the fresh yellow powder to an appealing cream. Then I shook the leather strap on which hung an assortment of Swiss cow bells, which wrangled among themselves, dreary and at the same time fierce, dying away into one surprisingly clear sweet note as they settled into a trembling silence.

There was only just time to tear with a comb at my hair before we sat down. They wanted to know all about him. How I had found him. Where he lived, what his father did, and whether he had any brothers or sisters. The worst of it was that they behaved quite nicely, especially my father, whose comments on his intelligence were unbarbed with sarcasm. I was surprised to find how little I knew of Michael, but I took a secretly spiteful delight in evading any question the answer to which I knew. They asked if he was coming again, and I realized that unless I went to watch his kite tomorrow I could not secure him. I said I didn't know and the talk frittered away to our usual subjects.

I was not alone until I went to bed, and by then I did not want to cry, I did not even feel sad; there was only an exhausted irritation about the whole episode culminating in a dreary uncertainty about whether to see him tomorrow. I had wanted him so desperately to bring his life to me, and he had identified himself with mine; I had thought he would bring a new air into the house, and he had merged with my family until I was again alone.

'I won't go tomorrow.' The thought gave me a queer little

tinge of pride. 'He may come again by himself. Or he may not.'

Two tears came out of my eyes. I fell asleep and dreamed that I was having tea at Michael's house, which had pink and yellow walls. His father wrote me two hundred prescriptions in very slanty handwriting, which we administered to an enormous shy man and I kept putting my tongue out at Michael, until he burst into tears and washed all the bottles with a grey cloth.

CHAPTER THREE

Michael did not come again, and I had no chance to mind, or to renew my search for anyone else, because a week later I was asked, or rather my sister was asked, to stay with a family who were spending the Christmas holidays at their home in the country. The family were some distant connection of my mother's, and my sister did not want to go. My mother wrote refusing for her, and received a telegram a day later which said: 'Send another daughter.' Telegrams in my family meant that you had died or missed a train, so it caused a stir. My father surprisingly decreed that I should go; so my mother worried over collars and stockings and my sister looked generously aloof. I was at first excited, and then appalled at the enormity of the adventure, never having stayed anywhere by myself before. And now for a whole ten days I should be surrounded by people I did not know, with new rooms, food, furniture, and country. I knew guests at parties had to do what was planned for them, although they were given the mockery of a choice; they had to pretend to enjoy it; their time was never their own until they were in bed in their new room.

Whenever I could consider the visit calmly, I realized, of course, that this was my chance, the chance for which I had longed; to get right away from my family and see new people and a different life. I was to go in a week from the telegram. As the days fled by I was less and less able to think calmly about it, and prayed that something, anything would happen to prevent it.

My mother took me shopping and bought me a red dress with black braid; a dark blouse; half a dozen stiff collars; a long thin jersey; and a pair of thick shoes. I was very quiet and did not argue over her choice of colours. She looked at me once in an unusually penetrating manner, and then led me to another part of the shop where she bought a beautiful frock, of rose-coloured silk, with knife thin pleating round the hem and foaming soft lace at the neck; a perfectly grown-up dress. She said that now I was sixteen I must put up my hair.

The dress fitted without any alteration, and my mother seemed gently pleased. She smiled and said would I like it? 'There is sure to be a party and I want you to look nice,' she said.

The pleasure of the frock, its glowing colour, its delicate silky polish under my fingers, its grace and beautifully fitting silk, was so sharp that my eyes were liquid; I felt myself blushing deeply and couldn't speak for enchantment.

'I don't think we need try any more,' my mother was saying to the assistant, and they went out of the little room. When they came back, I was still standing, staring at myself in the dress. When I had taken it off, the assistant swung the frock with a delicious rustle over her arm.

'Thank you. It's beautiful. The most beautiful frock. Thank you.'

They both smiled. I had never seen my mother so much alive, and I felt a little thrill of sympathy as a cord between us: as though we had some private vague plan. I must glitter and be decked and the reason was clouded and hidden: only they knew a little, I not at all. The assistant went away for wrappings and a pair of pink shoes: we were left alone, with the frock on the counter between us.

'Yes, it's a pretty frock. I hope you have a good time in it,' said my mother.

She seemed almost wistful. Suddenly I thought of red carpets under glass porches; men in top hats with dark green silk umbrellas helping her out of carriages to the golden luxury of a house filled with lights and tiny little pink ices and a great shining hard floor on which to dance in a rose-coloured frock – all the things I imagined she had had before she married my father. She fingered the frock and I could feel her looking ahead for me into those ten days, and beyond, as though I were a pebble to be dropped into water

29

and she an exhausted outside ripple from the pebble before. I was filled with a pity and distaste for her life, and the ten days suddenly became significant and timeless. I touched the frock: there was a heavy sweet taste in my mouth and the resistance of panic mounting to a recklessness so that I couldn't bear to be silent.

'I can't go. I don't want to go. Don't make me. Say I'm ill. I *am* ill. I shall be ill if I go. I can't be ill in a strange house. It wouldn't matter if you said I couldn't go. Please mother I can't go away' ... My voice stopped. I was crying tears on to the frock, soaking little dark pink circles; and in a minute the assistant would come back. I felt a handkerchief soft in my hand; I smelt lavender water, and the warm sweet smell of my mother: which made it much worse. I couldn't speak, or stop crying: and then I was in the fitting-room again, sitting on a round chair, blowing my nose, and feeling incredibly stupid and sad. My mother was treating me as a child; holding my shoulders, and seeming beautiful and necessary again; saying that she understood, but of course I must go, and things were nice once you had started them, and I should soon be back, and so sad that it was over. Now I must stop crying and come home and be pleased about my frock. So I stopped and we went home. I didn't feel less terrified about going away, only a little relieved that my mother knew, and I was not entirely alone with my fears.

CHAPTER FOUR

I was not ill. The morning arrived when I came down from my room with its bare dressing-table and my small trunk packed and strapped in the middle of the floor; and was enjoined to eat a good breakfast.

My father took me to the station. I know I felt faintly apologetic in the midst of my apathy; he disliked trains; they made him nervous. He found me a corner seat in a second-class carriage which possessed a large old lady who looked at me with inquisitive kindness, assuring my father of her protection.

'Well,' said my father. 'You know where you have to get out?' I nodded.

'Got something to read?' I shook my head. There was a lump in my throat.

'Well, you can amuse yourself looking out of the window. Your luggage is at the back of the train.' He edged out of the carriage, and looked up the platform, at the clock, I guessed.

'Don't wait,' I said. I wanted him to very much, but he nodded, offered me his pale grey face to kiss, almost smiled, and was gone.

I opened my bag, containing a new leather purse, my ticket, one sovereign, and sixpence for the porter; shook out my handkerchief and blew my nose. It had begun. I stared out of the window and wondered whether everyone in the station had travelled alone and how much they had minded. The old lady suddenly offered me a pear drop which I accepted. It was rather common to eat sweets in a train in the morning but I was afraid she would be hurt.

The old lady asked me where I was going, and what did I do at home, and whether I liked animals; and then told me about herself. She told me nearly her whole life, because the train started quite soon, and she never stopped talking. Her life was very dull; mostly about how animals loved her and how much her sister disapproved, because her sister was very religious, and didn't believe that animals had souls and went to heaven. It all seemed pretty dull to me, or else she never told me the interesting bits. She had always lived in one house; and now she was left with her sister, whom I don't think she liked; their father having been a clergyman who died of a stroke when he was quite old. That was a horrible bit: she described his face and muttering with no one able to understand a word he said. They had nursed him devotedly, until one day when he sat up, said 'Thank God,' and died.

We were in the country by then. There was fine drizzling rain, so that houses looked remote, mysterious and too small; and the cows in the fields lay and waited like sofas on a pavement; patient, uncomfortable and somehow rakish. The train stopped four times, but it was never my station, and the old lady didn't get out; until I began to think that she didn't have a station, but simply lived on pear drops in a train and told people about animals.

The old lady eventually said that my station was next. I tidied my hair, and looked in my purse to see if the sixpence was still there.

The train stopped, and I got out. The old lady said I was sure to enjoy myself, young people always did, and settled herself back in her corner seat.

I collected my trunk and it was wheeled outside the small station by a porter. I could see no one to meet me at all. It was cold and still raining; and I began to feel very fright-ened again. The rain dripped off the scalloped edges of the platform roofs and gathered in sullen little puddles on the gravel; the tree trunks looked black and slippery like mac-kintosh. The porter asked me where I was going. I told him The Village, whereupon he said They thought the train came fifteen minutes later than she do, they'll be along, well miss he'd be leaving me. So there was nothing for it but to give him the sixpence and wait.

They came at last, a boy and a girl, in a pony trap.

'How long have you been waiting?'

'Not very long.'

'Mother's fault again. She's hopeless about trains. She simply makes up the time they arrive and it's always wrong. Last week we were half an hour early.'

The boy shouted:

'Joe. I want a hand with this trunk. Here I'll find him.' He disappeared.

The girl smiled encouragingly.

'Get in. It's no drier, but at least there's a seat.' I climbed up clumsily and sat beside her.

'My name's Lucy,' she said. 'What's yours?'

I told her.

'It was jolly nice of you to come. I hate staying with people, don't you?' For a moment I was outfaced.

'I've never done it before, but I thought I would hate it.'

She flicked the whip across the pony's back. 'You won't by tomorrow. Keep still you. We have great fun these holidays. Lots of people. We're having a dance on Christmas Eve. I hope you've got a frock.'

'Yes, I did bring one.'

'Good. How old are you?' I told her. 'I'm just sixteen too. Can you skate?'

My heart sank. 'No. I'm afraid not.'

'Well you needn't. I hate it, it hurts your ankles.' She stretched out a long thin boot. 'But Gerald adores it.'

'Is he your cousin?'

'My brother. I have two sisters and two brothers but the whole place is full of cousins.'

'Is there any ice for skating?'

'Not yet. But Gerald says there will be. He's always right about things he likes. He's awfully good at it. He simply skims about. Lovely to watch.' She turned her thin, pale pink face to me eager and friendly. 'What do *you* like?'

'I don't know yet.'

'Oh well,' she said cheerfully, 'there's lots to do. The great thing is not to mind doing it till you've tried. Here comes Gerald.'

33

My trunk was hoisted in and we set off; Lucy driving, with Gerald a watchful critic.

'I shall tell mother about that train. She really ought to know better. Can you skate?'

'No,' I said. 'But I'd love to learn.'

Lucy gave me a brilliant smile; I smiled back, and it was delightful.

'Look where you're going, Lucy.'

'Gerald thinks only men can drive and talk. Women are so lucky to be allowed to drive at all that they certainly shouldn't speak or enjoy it. Their poor little minds aren't capable of thinking about two things at once. *Don't* Gerald.' They were laughing, the trap was all over the road, and I felt much happier.

'It's easy,' I thought, 'staying with people is easy;' then thought of the house and unknown family and shivered a little because I was wet.

'Cold?' said Lucy. Large drops of rain slipped down her face and thin arched nose, and watered her silky-gold strands of hair. Her eyes seemed almost transparently wet, so darkly grey, clear and alive.

'Of course she's cold. We're all cold *and* hungry. Hurry up Lucy, think of lunch.'

We trotted through a silent streaming village, into a drive, with an elegant iron gate swung back and embedded in brilliant soft grass; round a gentle curve edged with iron railings, to the sweep before the house: a square cream-coloured house, with large square windows and green shutters; a magnificent cedar tree like a butler, old, indispensable and gloomy; and curls of smoke, the colour of distance, creeping sedately up out of the squat mulberry chimneys.

We walked slowly past the house through an arch into a cobbled courtyard, surrounded by buildings, which smelled of moss and leather, hot wet animals, and a curiously pungent clean smell that I afterwards learned was saddle soap. A white-haired man limped out of a loose box and took the pony's head. He looked very fierce, until I realized that one eye stared out sideways unwinking like a parrot. Gerald helped me out. 'Parker will bring your trunk.'

We walked back through the arch, pushed open the green front door, and were in the large hall. I shall never forget the smell of that house. Logs, lavender and damp, the old scent of a house that has been full of flowers for so many years that the very pollen and flower pots stay behind intangibly enchanting – candles and grapes – weak aged taffeta stretched on the chairs – drops of sherry left in fragile shallow glasses – nectarines and strawberries – the warm earthy confidential odour of enormous books and butterfly smell of the pages, a combination of leather and moth – dense glassy mahogany ripe with polishing and the sun – guns and old coats – smooth dead fur on the glaring sentimental deers' heads – beeswax, brown sugar and smoke – it smelled of everything I first remember seeing there, and I shall never forget it.

We hurried along a passage into the drawing-room. It was very full of people. Lucy took my hand, and led me up to a thin delicate woman who was sitting bolt upright in a tall thin armchair, doing an intricate and incredibly ugly piece of embroidery in a wooden frame stuck with nails and festooned with strands of coloured wool.

'Here she is. This is my mother,' said Lucy. Lucy's mother had a pair of mild blue eyes and a blue-veined hand with rings that dug into my fingers.

'You are Mary's eldest daughter?' she said. As I had never heard my mother called Mary I kept politely silent.

'No, Mother, she came last week.'

'Ah yes. Then *I* know who you are.'

'And you were quite wrong about the train, Mother.'

'Nonsense. Here she is. How could I have been wrong?'

A gong boomed.

'Lunch?' said Lucy's mother. 'Come with me. Wash your hands, people. Mind the jigsaw.'

A boy got up from beside its fragments. 'That is Mary's eldest son,' said Lucy's mother triumphantly, as she rose

35

from her chair, scattering little balls of wool, heavy decorative thimbles, and tiny crumpled white handkerchiefs over the carpet.

We went to lunch, after washing our hands in a flower sink in the passage. We sat at an enormous table with a bowl of Christmas roses. At first, I had a confused impression of boys and girls, with Lucy's mother carving cold mutton neatly and fast at one end, and an oldish man, who came in last with a glass of sherry, at the other. Then I began trying very hard to sort them out; their brown hands, freckles, fair heads, dark eyes. In a moment we seemed to have reached the fruit pie (with too much sugar on it); streaks of clear crimson juice round hectic shining mouths; small hands crushing nutcrackers, the nut escaping with a teasing bounce; chairs scraping back; and older hands crumbling bread in the ensuing peace. The first meal, a ceremony I had been dreading for weeks, was over, and when I counted the meals that remained, as I had so miserably counted them many times before, it was already with an entirely new and welcome regret that they could be so easily numbered.

CHAPTER FIVE

After lunch I was taken to my bedroom, which was small, square, and white, with dark wood and a gorgeous carpet, a Lord Mayorish carpet, rich, and somehow vulgar. There was a second door in one corner.

Out of the window I could see a wide gravel path, flower beds, a long slanting lawn drifting into distant long grass down the slope to a lazy winding river, with reeds, and moorhens in an ungraceful hurry. Rising beyond the river were a field or park, picked out with big casual trees; and a copse at the top of a gentle crest, held together, it seemed, by railings, like an elastic band round a bunch of twigs. Above this a grey sky was framed on either side by scarce bony trees, which were distorted high up, with dense dark jagged nests.

'Rooks,' said Lucy behind me.

'How did you know I was looking?'

'I didn't. But you would have asked me. People always ask what they are. Come out. You'd better get some thicker shoes.'

'I'd better unpack.'

'Nanny'll do it. Just get your boots out.' We struggled over the trunk.

'Are you awfully rich?' I asked as it opened.

'Good heavens, I don't know. Papa wouldn't tell me, because he won't give me a new saddle unless it's a side saddle. I would like to ride like a boy, but it's not delicate. Life for women is terribly unfair, you know.' She sat on the floor holding her knees, earnestly sad.

'Is that what it is?'

'How do you mean?'

'Well, things haven't felt right to me for some time now. Years really,' I added, feeling old and extravagant about my life. 'But I didn't think of it being worse for women.'

'Of course it is!' cried Lucy energetically. 'Who gets the best ponies? The boys. Or they get a horse and we have to rattle about on little grass-fed creatures with no wind. If Papa has an expedition and only a few may go, it's always the boys. They're always allowed to learn things first. Fishing and driving; and they shoot, but Papa says I may not. And their clothes are so much more suitable. When I was fourteen I cut off my hair and there was a fearful row . . .'

'Right off?'

'Up to here,' she placed her fingers just below her ears. 'It was very uneven. I did it with Nanny's cutting-out scissors. But of course I had to grow it again. And everyone laughed. Except Gerald. He thought I looked jolly fine.'

All my clothes and possessions seemed strange and far away; belonging to my home and London, and even to the train; but not to me and this house. Boots at the bottom, of course. I plunged.

'And chocolate pudding,' burst Lucy. 'They always get second helpings of that. Girls aren't supposed to mind about food. Except fruit. It's all right to like fruit. Sometimes I can hardly bear it. Still, we do go to bed at the same time. And Gerald says I have beautiful hands. He'd trust me with his own horse, he says.'

'Has he got one?'

'Not yet. But he would. Look, I'll get Nanny to come and do your clothes.'

Lucy was amazing, I thought. She seemed to have done so many things and yet she was no older than I. Perhaps it was living in the country. She came back with Nanny, who shook hands with me and called me Miss.

'We're going for a walk, Nanny.'

'Change your shoes, then.'

'They're changed. I didn't change them for lunch.'

'All that mud over the carpet. How many times have I told you . . .'

'Hundreds of times, Nanny. I forgot. She still thinks I'm seven.'

'Well, you behave like seven. You're the worst of the lot,' said Nanny adoringly.

'I'll change them for tea like anything. I'm afraid we've rumpled the trunk. Come on,' she added to me.

'Let her get her coat on. Whatever will the poor young lady think?'

'Oh, is that your frock? How lovely!'

'Leave go of it, Miss Lucy. Run and get your jacket. Be quick now. You'll have to be back before tea because I've that blouse to try on.'

'Nanny, you simply ruin my life.'

'Anyone would think I was cruel to her.' Lucy had gone for the jacket. 'I've put your stockings in the drawer.'

'Nanny, could I wash?' Her eye, which had looked at Lucy with such loving despair and pride, and at me so calmly shrewd and appraising as if she could assess my manners at meals by the way I parted my hair and tied my laces, was instantly active and commanding. I could see her managing all the little crises of countless children with tremendous certainty and devotion, keeping life easy and natural and safe, always watching, now that they were grown up, for the rare casual moments when they might need her a little. I began to realize Lucy and the house, and understand the security and affection which shot through the air like light.

'Of course, Miss, I'll take you. Miss Lucy should have thought. There you are. The other's that little door on the right,' and she padded tactfully away.

We went downstairs.

'I know,' said Lucy. 'We'll take Elspeth.' She opened a door and we entered a library with enormous leather chairs.

'Elspeth.' No sound. '*Elspeth.*' There was a faint scuffle. We crossed the room and by the window in one of the enormous chairs was a girl crumpled up and weighed down by a great book with coloured plates. She shook her hair back.

'Elspeth. You are hiding. Come out. Leave your old caterpillars.'

'Oh, don't.'

'Why?'

'Don't tell them about there being caterpillars. They think it's just butterflies. They say caterpillars aren't nice for girls.'

'Oh, they won't know. Come out, we're going to the wood.'

'I'd rather stay.'

'You can't read all day. We might build a house. They'll find you here and send you out anyway, so you'd much better come with us.'

'Oh all right.' She got up and the book slid to the floor with a fat, heavy bang. 'Oh!'

'You haven't hurt it.'

'I have! Oh I have. There's a page crumpled.' Her eyes filled with tears and spurted out.

'Don't cry on the leather anyway. Remember what happened to Gerald's stamp album. The marks all went puffy and dull.'

'Put it away for me. I can't stop.' Lucy put it away.

'Look here,' she said severely. 'You can easily stop. I've smoothed the page.' She went close to Elspeth. 'You look *stupid*. Your face will go puffy and dull like leather.'

Elspeth took the antimacassar off the back of the chair and wiped her face. 'I've stopped,' she said calmly.

'Well get your coat and hurry up.' Elspeth went.

'Now we'll *have* to build a house. She loves them,' said Lucy.

'What kind of a house?' It sounded rather childish. I didn't think I'd enjoy it much.

'Oh, a log house. You'll see.'

Elspeth came back and we set off. It had stopped raining; there was a grey stillness, and my nose felt cold immediately.

Elspeth must have been about fourteen, although her face was older. She was very bony, with thin clear skin stretched over the bones, making her look taut and breakable. She walked beside us with a little hop without speaking except when Lucy asked her a question to which she replied 'No', very firmly, thereby shattering any further advances. But her silence was not so much unfriendly as absorbed, so that it didn't spoil anything.

When we left the lawn for the long grass, little silver drops leapt from each blade as our shoes shuffled through. The river was very still as though the last moorhen hurrying across had cleared the scene for some exciting action. I could hear the rooks now, fluttering about their messy nests. We turned left, and walked under their trees. There was a damp velvety path covered with leaves, either slimy and curled as though each had died in a separate little agony; or older and rotted to delicate silvery skeletons. The path was edged with ragged rhododendra, massed, and hiding the sudden rustle of some bird. We were in single file, Lucy, and me, and Elspeth hopping very slowly behind. We came to a wooden bridge over the river, mossy and overgrown; there were brown lily leaves in the water, and the noisy uneven drip from the trees disturbed the grey of the river. The other side of the bridge we were in grass again.

'Where are the others?'

'Gone to fetch Deb,' said Lucy.

'Who is Deb?'

'My sister. She's been staying with cousins. She's very beautiful.'

'Have they all gone to fetch her?'

'Only Gerald and Tom. And Elinor. The others are in the house. Aunt Edith has a cold and my mother doesn't go out much in winter. Papa will be riding. He likes best to ride by himself. Do you ride? Oh I suppose you don't. What do you *do* in London?'

'Not very much.'

'Your papa is a painter, isn't he?'

'He writes music.'

'All the time?'

'No. Every now and then. He teaches it, too.'

'You cannot teach people to write music, can you?'

'No,' said Elspeth.

'Elspeth, you don't know anything about it.'

'I do. A girl at school wrote a song. It just came. No one taught her.

'She wasn't a proper writer. One song!' said Lucy scornfully.

'He doesn't teach people to write it. He teaches people to play it,' I said.

'Can you teach people to write it though?'

'I don't know,' I said truthfully. I felt embarrassed. Of course I should have known.

'You can't teach people anything that matters,' said Elspeth surprisingly.

'Of course you can, Elspeth.' Lucy was very shocked. 'Books and things. People always learn like that. Think of schools. You ought to know that. You're always reading.'

'It saves a certain amount of time. I couldn't get enough species together in my head unless there were books.'

'She's showing off. You read lots of fairy tales.'

'I don't.'

'You do.'

'I hardly ever read them. I read books out of the library.'

'Don't be silly. It doesn't matter what you read anyway.'

'It does matter what I read.'

'The trouble with you is,' said Lucy very gravely, 'that you take yourself far too seriously for your age. You simply can't go about being so old *and* crying. Do *you* read a lot?'

'Well, a bit,' I said cautiously.

'You don't read just to talk about reading anyway. I hardly ever read. It depends whether you need it. I like moving about.'

We were quite close to the wood which was striped with different trees; dark, aloof and inviting.

'I never like starting a wood,' said Elspeth.

There was a small iron gate. We went in. It did feel rather like going into a place that easily might belong to someone who resented our feet and our voices. A blackbird flew low, chattering dramatically.

'Where are we going?'

'To the middle,' said Lucy. 'There's a clearing with a bank.'

I looked up at the sky streaked with branches and suddenly thought of Michael and his kite. He would like Elspeth and scorn Lucy, and he was the kind of awful person whom it was difficult not to believe, so perhaps it was a good thing he wasn't there.

'Is Rupert coming?' asked Elspeth.

'He's coming for the dance. Just for Christmas; otherwise he has to work.'

'Who is Rupert?'

'Rupert Laing. His father was at school with Papa. He always comes in the holidays.'

'He sounds mysterious and rich.'

'Why?'

I didn't know why I'd said that. How silly. How very very silly.

'How odd. He is mysterious. I don't think he's rich. You'll see. He looks into the back of you, and he makes very silly jokes.'

There was a silence. Rupert was finished. To me he was just an appalling embarrassment and Lucy and Elspeth had explored his character and whereabouts sufficiently to leave him alone.

'Here we are,' said Lucy.

It was a clearing, a hollow, filled with Spanish chestnut suckers, reddish brown, with shining sharp bumps. We sat down on the rubble of leaves and moss.

'Now,' said Elspeth.

'All right,' said Lucy. 'But you can't expect a house every time you go for a walk.'

Elspeth rolled on the ground clutching her knees; then leaped up and walked slowly, darting down for a silvery stick. One was too long and she bit it. It snapped in half, and she bit it again in a rage and stamped it into the leaves.

'It wouldn't have been strong enough,' said Lucy. 'I'll help.' And she, too, joined in the collecting. I sat, feeling miserable and stupid. I had no idea what they were doing.

'We collect sticks,' said Lucy.

'We collect special *useful* sticks,' said Elspeth, pouncing in time to her words. I smiled foolishly and sat still. They put eight sticks upright and firm in the ground, two and two in a square. Then they laid thinner sticks in between to make walls, which crept up slowly with uneven ends. I stared at the ground, a tear dropped on to a leaf, tap, and it overbalanced; oh horror, I was going to cry, and for no reason I filled my hands with earth and squeezed, ground the tears out of my eyes; tap, tap, tap, they seemed endless. It was terrible to be sixteen and cry in a wood.

'You're crying,' said Lucy, concerned, and they both came and stood in front of me looking down. 'What's the matter?'

I looked up and snatched bravely. 'I'm a bit homesick, that's all.'

'Oh,' said Lucy. She squatted. 'Bad luck. You needn't be. Have you got a handkerchief?'

'Yes.' Really, I couldn't use other people's handkerchiefs. Elspeth stared. I blew my nose.

'Poor you,' said Lucy. 'Do you want to go home?'

'Only a bit.' I didn't at all, but once you cried you had to sound brave about it.

'Bad luck,' said Lucy again, very helpless. 'Would you like to go back to tea?'

'You'd better finish your house first. I'm all right.'

'Will you help us then?'

'You'll have to show me what to do,' I said patronizingly.

'I'm never homesick,' said Elspeth.

'You don't get the chance to be,' said Lucy fiercely.

I got up.

'Promise you won't tell the others I cried.'

'I promise,' said Lucy. 'Go on, Elspeth.'

'Honour bright,' said Elspeth carelessly, and turned away.

It was a beautiful house. The walls were about a foot high, with a gap in one wall for a door. There was the intricate job of constructing a flat roof which did not imperil the shaky structure. We laid slender strips across, then bark and moss on top of them. Elspeth wanted leaves; but they would not lie flat, and snapped and crumbled maliciously weak, so we gave them up, and between the twigs crammed smoky dry moss in wedges. We scraped the ground flat round the house and Elspeth started to make a fence; but got bored, and found a slug. It was under a bit of loose bark, and was grey and oily, with a brilliant orange front. 'If I look at it long I shall be sick.'

'Don't be silly, Elspeth. Don't look at it.'

'It's moving,' said Elspeth, horrified.

'I can't think why you mind them if you like caterpillars.'

'Caterpillars are dry.' She loved watching it really. 'Anyway, it's such a slimy shape.'

'Better kill it,' said Lucy.

'No, don't kill it. It's a horrible poor thing.'

'They eat the vegetables.'

'It couldn't walk as far as the vegetables. Ugh, it doesn't walk. It crawls. It sort of slimes along. Lucy, there are probably lots of them. I may have sat on one. Have I, Lucy?'

'Oh, my goodness! An enormous one!' Lucy examined her skirt in mock horror, then turned her round.

'Don't cry, baby, of course you haven't. Can't you take a joke?'

'Can't always risk a joke.'

'The house is finished,' I said. I had been patting and poking the roof. It was beautiful, and it looked so useful and necessary that I wanted to have it and take it away. It was finished and we stood round it. Even Lucy was touched by its complete sweetness.

'The best we've ever made,' said Elspeth.

They had done it before. It was so new to me that I couldn't bear to think of that. I suggested we go, and we left the house to its first night's adventure.

We were through the gate again, on the grass, staring at the misty dusk ahead and the little orange sparks glowing from the house down the slope.

'Let's run,' said Elspeth.

We took hands and ran down the slope; past when we were breathless, until our running became almost frightening, although enjoyable because we were together. The ground was uneven, and I watched it (I was not as used as the others to running on a field). When I looked up, the bony trees were high above us; the river gleamed like a wide snake asleep; the windows were paler gold broken by their frames; and the black creeper clinging to the house made it seem a wonderful place to receive us for the end of the day. We were panting, Elspeth had not run all the leaves out of her hair, and the lights shone in our eyes.

Upstairs, Lucy showed me her room. There were two beds and a coat lay at the end of one.

'Deb's back,' said Lucy joyfully.

I did not see Deb until tea. She was beautiful, and it was obvious that they all adored her. She sat between Gerald and her mother, and I saw him turn the plate round so that the cake with the large cherry was nearest her. She took it so easily that I knew she had always had the cherries. Elspeth told her about the house; Elspeth's father about a horse; and she turned from one to another radiant; recounting her visit with a kind of brilliant modesty, infecting us with her success and happiness, and enriching all their tales with her attention and concern so that one watched her, wholly enchanted. She was quite beautiful; triangular eyes with flecks of green, shining dark hair, a thin pointed mouth, pointed eyebrows to match, and a skin so milky pale that if you were to touch it it would hardly be there. I could not take my eyes off her. I sat and watched her neck twisting (she wore a tight gold chain round the hight collar of her blouse), and neat head above it. I sat and watched until my fingers were cramped in the handle of my tea-cup and Lucy leaned forward and said '*Isn't* she lovely!' in a warm rush. Everyone laughed. Her mother said 'Nonsense.' I flushed. Deb sat quite still, half smiling and not at all shy.

After tea, we all went to the morning-room which everyone left in a joyful state of confusion. The jigsaw was still on the floor, half completed; it was very big, and Toby, the fat little boy, would allow no one to touch it but himself. He was very slow and immersed in fitting pink roses all over a thatched cottage. When Lucy found the door, he growled and crossed the room with his hands in his pockets in a solemn rage, and one tuft of hair sticking straight up from the crown of his head.

Lucy's mother said, 'Don't dear,' calmly. She was embroidering a hideous peacock with exquisite deliberation; admiring Elspeth's butterfly transfers, crooked and smeared in a large scrap book; reminding Gerald and Lucy about the names of ponies (they were absorbed with an old collection of plaited horses' hair kept, with labels attached, in a weak cardboard box); advising Deb over colours for her cross stitch, who, I noticed, listened charmingly and never took the advice; hearing Elinor's poem that she was learning, and being quite unruffled when the recital always stuck in the same place; then talking to me, asking me about my mother, and my sister and brothers, what I did, and which I liked best, town or country; making everything I'd done seem important and interesting, so that I could not imagine why it had all seemed empty before.

'I think it is very brave of you to come,' she said. 'Come along, darling, finish the roses.' Toby came and smiled a beautiful slow smile, shook himself like a puppy, and fell on the floor beside his great work. 'He does it over and over again. No, darling, a *host* of golden daffodils. Start again to yourself. And are your brothers all at the same school? That must be nice. Punch he was called, Lucy dear. The funny pink pony with a brindled tail who used to flybuck.'

'Strawberry roan,' they chanted, and Gerald wrote another little ticket.

'All right, Toby, I won't do it but you should try and finish the edges first. And do you play the piano? You must play to us some time. Not today; wait until there are a lot of us and then we can dance. We all want to hear you. Well, darling, call it a Tortoiseshell, and do another with more water for a Painted Lady. Will you ring the bell, dear? I want to speak about Aunt Edith's sarsaparilla. No, Toby, that bit is lost. Blue, Deb, like the other side; or red like the border; you'll find them both in my Indian Bag.' Deb abstracted a thread of green with a charming smile.

Feeling completely part of the great warm untidy room I asked if after all I might play the piano. Of course I might. I played a rather scratchy piece of Scarlatti, and remember feeling faintly shocked when no one paid the slightest attention. Elspeth had just upset her transfer water and was mopping it up with a skein of pale blue wool, and Elinor was half-way through the daffodils, still holding her breath for the last verse. However, I found it much nicer from the playing point of view; it was much more enjoyable to approve and criticize oneself, to play back, as it were, only to one's own ears. I stopped after a bit. There was a great dark picture above my head, with the canvas gleaming like oily water at night. It was of a man, surly with health, in a pink coat, holding a riding crop with both hands and leaning forward a little. He looked irritable and impatient, as though sitting anywhere but on a horse was a woman's job; and now he was dead, I felt he was very dead, and condemned to listen to any music I cared to make, with only the welter of mainly feminine ploys beyond as relief. A maid came and drew the curtains all round the bay window and at my side by the piano. She moved on tip-toe and answered Lucy's mother about sarsaparilla with a kind of gasping lightness as though it were only respectful to use the very edge of herself, her toes and fingers and the front of her throat. She was very neat and pretty.

Deb rose from her work and strolled over to me. 'Come and change for dinner with me,' she said. She was leaning over the piano, provocative and friendly, with a 'come and see what I've got' look.

Lucy heard.

'The bell hasn't gone,' she said. Their mother laughed.

'You know how Deb loves to potter. Run along.'

As if Deb would run. No, she would glide unhurried, preferably, I thought, down smooth paths banked by pinks and delphinia, or glassy floors flocked with people less beautiful than she making a wide lane for her, she accepting it. We left together, with a little laughing demur at the door which ended in my holding it for her and turning the glass knob carefully, shutting us out together. Half-way down the passage she stopped and dabbled her fingers in a large Chinese bowl.

'Lavender,' she said stretching out her fingers to me. I

copied her. We went straight to the room with the two beds.

'I have to share it with Lucy. Sit down, I'll show you my jewellery. Wait, I'll shut the door.'

She sped to it. I sat and watched the room in comfort. Lucy slept there, but I could now see that it was certainly not shared; it was Deb's room. The pictures, the large pink roses flopping over the white chintz curtains; the dressing-table delicately shrouded in muslin with petulant frills, topped by a slender elegant rosewood mirror; the fat white beds, and heavy jug and basin with kingfishers on it; all assumed a pretty significance, unique and personal to Deb; Deb's possessions, Deb's elegance, and her rich careless charm. She was kneeling by a little cabinet with two doors which swung back to disclose a pile of shallow drawers of blushing yellow wood. There were eleven, and I knew the first six were hers.

'Which belong to Lucy?'

'Those at the bottom. I have one extra.' And she smiled very sweetly.

They were stiff to pull and the knobs were too dainty for use. I was very pleased at being right about the drawers. It is a wonderful feeling to guess anything about a person and hear aloud that you were right. It made me feel stronger with Deb. Suddenly the drawer flew open almost too far so that it swayed and disclosed rows of pink and yellow shells neatly placed on flat cotton wool.

'Wrong drawer,' said Deb crossly.

The jewel drawer slid open with ease; she dropped down to it and then, straightening casually, flung a handful of jewels in my lap, so suddenly that they weighed my skirt down between my knees. She rose, leaving the drawer bare and gaping like someone who has had a great surprise.

'Look at them,' she said impatiently, seeing me. 'I'm going to change my dress.' She opened her wardrobe, and ran her hands through her frocks in a nervous and affected manner.

There were a pearl brooch shaped in a crescent; a turquoise heart; a locket on a golden chain. There were a string of corals; a topaz brooch with elaborate gold work round it; a large and beautiful ring with garnets and pearls and a minute turquoise in the middle; a golden cross on another chain; and a thin wavering bracelet with moonstones. There was also a brooch with a miniature of a lady, placid and fragile, with grey powdered hair, a fresh complexion, a tiny little dark red mouth, and pale blue eyes which looked out with an air of sprightly indifference.

'I don't like that one,' said Deb. 'An aunt left it to me. It's a clumsy old thing. I don't take it away when I stay in houses. Do you enjoy paying visits?'

'This is the first I've ever paid.'

'Well, are you enjoying it? I do. I enjoy *all* the times I stay away. More and more I enjoy it,' with a voluptuous little sigh.

'Do you always go by yourself?'

'Usually. Do you? Are you enjoying yourself now?'

'Oh yes. Much more than I thought.'

That pleased her, and she began unpinning her hair as though it were a direct reward.

'You seem to have had a lovely time,' I said.

She paused, her face full of a thousand unknown moments, smiled a little, shook herself, and turned to receive my curiosity.

'There was a dance,' she said. I did not perceive the significance of this remark, but I gave an understanding smile of encouragement.

'Do you dance much in London?' she asked abruptly.

'No, not much.' I felt that I could hardly afford never to have danced at all.

'Do you know why I am unpinning my hair?' I shook my head. 'In a minute I shall tell you. There.' And suddenly there it was; pouring down her back; flocked and tumbling, swinging round each shoulder; clinging to her head but escaping in tendrils round her ears. She seized a white brush.

'Now,' she said. 'I'll tell you. If you are interested. You are interested, aren't you?' with a questioning dart at me.

'Yes,' I said. 'Oh yes, I am.' She laughed; of course she knew I was. 'Will there be time?'

'We can have more talks,' she said, settling comfortably

down to her monologue. 'Something very exciting has just happened to me. We have always lived here and as you can see nothing would be likely to happen here that could afford one any real amusement. That is why I have always longed to go away and one is only allowed to do so in order to pay visits. And even then ... but this time ...' She broke off holding the brush against her head.

'You must listen and not watch me. But – am I beautiful? I don't want you to say so unless you think I am. *Am* I?' She leaned forward a little. She was sitting on the floor holding her knees, her face tilted towards me. I complied. There was such compelling charm, such charming desire, that I had no alternative, although I was embarrassed into inadequacy. She seemed satisfied, however, and leaned back with a little sigh.

'You don't know how important it is for me yet. It all happened in this last fortnight. I was staying with cousins. Very distant cousins of Papa's. We had an awfully jolly time.' She paused again, forcing me to an unbearable impatience. She had the quality of making one feel that anything she said was almost unbearably interesting. 'We rode a great deal. I don't know why it was so pleasant. New people, I suppose. And it was a lovely house. I had met Roland before but we hadn't noticed each other. It is extraordinary how one does not realize at once about the most important person in one's life. Everyone adores him; but I – this is the point, and a very great secret, only I must tell someone – I love him. I told him.'

'Was he pleased?'

She opened her lovely eyes, incredulously.

'Of course. We both love each other. I shall marry him, but my parents don't know yet. We aren't going to tell them. Roland agrees that there should be some secrecy about anyone's love. Don't you think so?'

'I don't know much about it.'

'I'll tell you. We decided at the dance. Before, I hadn't been so sure that Roland really loved me. But half-way through a dance he suddenly waltzed me away and into the

hall, threw a man's coat round my shoulders and we stole out
through a door in the passage, and down a path with a high
hedge. I was shivering, but I wasn't cold. Then he took my
face and kissed me. I wasn't frightened at all. I watched the
leaves black against the moon. I put my arms round him and
then there was a cloud across the moon and I couldn't watch
the leaves. He's wonderful. He said that he loved me and
asked me to marry him. He is sure our families would approve, we are such very distant cousins, and I think so, too,
although of course they will say we are too young. Isn't it
extraordinary that they can say that when they haven't the
faintest notion how much we love each other? Roland has
got to get settled in his job.'

'What does he do?'

'He works in the City. He hates it, and as soon as he has
thought of something else he's going to do it, if it doesn't
make our future uncertain. But I shouldn't mind what he
did as long as I could be with him. Do you know he tried to
pull down my hair? Isn't that odd? He said it would seem
more possible, more real to him, if he saw my hair down, I
should seem to belong to him more. That reminds me.
Look.'

She had a pair of golden scissors, shaped in some curious
way like a stork. I can only remember the wings and neck
impossibly graceful and twisted.

'Cut some off for me. He wants it. I can't cut it myself. I
can't cut hair.'

I was terrified.

'I've never cut hair. Couldn't you get Nanny to do it?'

'She'd want to know why. What are you thinking of? This
is a secret.'

I took the scissors.

'Why does he want it?'

'To keep, of course. People always do that. Didn't you
know?'

'Have you some of his hair?'

'No. No, I haven't. Roland's hair isn't the kind one keeps.

It's too thin – fine,' she added. And then honesty got the better of her and she said, 'Besides it isn't a very interesting colour. *Please* cut it for me.'

'How much do I cut?' I still felt nervous.

Deb seemed nonplussed. 'I don't know. I've never actually done this before. How much do you think he would like?'

'All of it, I should say. Growing.' I was holding a lock, feeling rather proud to be with her.

'Silly thing,' she laughed, delighted. 'Cut what you like.' I grasped the lock firmly and hacked away, the little scissors protesting, squeaking weakly until they collapsed on air with a final gasp.

'There.' I held it up.

'Yes.' She seemed doubtful. 'It's left a funny end and I don't know whether he'll want quite so much. Still it will be a surprise.' She folded it away in crumpled tissue paper and pushed it into one of the shallow drawers. 'Good. I knew you'd help me.' A bell rang. 'Time to dress.'

'What shall I wear?' I had never changed for dinner in my life, and I suddenly felt rather tired, and afraid of new things.

'Oh, a frock. I shall wear this.' She pulled out a mass of dull green silk. 'See you at dinner.'

In my room, I wrenched off my clothes. My hands were cold and I began to worry about the way to the dining-room and always being called Mary, and Nanny noticing my hair, newly washed and utterly out of control. There was a gleaming brass jug standing in my basin, the steam very white and noticeable in the cold room. Better warm my hands. The jug was very heavy and I slopped some water on the marble washstand and nearly chipped the basin.

I washed my face and neck and hands, using an un-yielding new cake of soap, rubbed myself dry, first with a rough scratching bath towel, and finally with a fragile slip of linen with embroidered initials that became bumpy as the cloth grew wet. I stepped into the red frock with black braid. I should be late, and they would all have gathered in the drawing-room, or worse still, be sitting in their places at table, all waiting for me to come into the room. Thank goodness Nanny was coming; I could never have managed all the buttons up the back. I pulled my hair down, and was breaking the teeth of my comb when Nanny came in. She started by fastening my buttons with huge cold fingers and ended by doing my hair with an impeccable parting and a bun so tight that the hairs were strained and tweaking behind my ears. She noticed that I had a hole in one of my stockings, so I changed them. My shoes were rather tight and slippery. Nanny cleaned my brush with the comb and clicked her tongue over the broken teeth, but I was still immeasurably grateful to her. She was a perfect woman. She sent me down tidy and assured and luxurious. She would draw the stocking together, and I need have no fears about being late. I think she must have been understanding enough to have encompassed the world she served, Deb and Lucy's world, and that house and their friends, and wise enough never to venture further so that she always remained mistress of every situation she encountered. Dressing for dinner held the same importance for her as it did for me. She was infinitely kind.

Dinner was long and gay, ending with oranges and nuts and a sip of port because I had never tasted it before. It burned my tongue, but it was a beautiful colour. Deb smiled at me, sweetly conspiratorial. I told Gerald about Michael although he wasn't very interested except in the expelling part. He told me much more about his school than my brothers had ever vouchsafed about theirs. He was very anxious to assure me of the narrowness of his own escape from expulsion, and my interest and surprise must have pleased him, as he grew bright red and very friendly.

After dinner we played charades. I'd played them before, but this was different. I was picked by Gerald to act. We jostled out into the hall, which was flickering with a dying fire; and everyone talked simultaneously with choleric speed, decrying and applauding each other's efforts without apparently interrupting their own flow of ideas; collecting walking sticks, summer hats, overcoats, and Nanny's glasses the while. I could think of nothing, my self-conscious apprehension rose in my throat, and my heart bumped against my new red dress as I took refuge in weak general approval.

It was not so terrible. I was to be a shop assistant, which entailed an apron, secured from a maid who giggled and resisted at first, investing our designs with a delicious mixture of wickedness and importance. I was to arrange the hats on the piano, and Gerald was to bring Deb, his wife, to choose one; and at one point I must implore her to observe the back, so they told me again and again. Gerald went to clear the scene, and we heard the impatience of our audience through the door. He came back. Deb was not ready, but finally floated down the stairs in a long white fringed shawl with her hair miraculously different. I was pushed forward. Nervously, I arranged the hats and waited. Nothing happened, and I was deeply conscious that my audience now knew as much of the situation as I did. In a minute I should forget the bit about the back of Deb's head. I surveyed the hats. 'That looks stylish,' I said aloud, and felt the quickening of attention in the room. Emboldened, I selected an old straw hat with artificial roses pinched together, and tried it on. At that moment Gerald and Deb came in and from then on the whole charade went with a swing. The audience guessed it, of course, but nobody cared as long as enough people dressed up, and the waits between the scenes were not interminable.

We went to bed at eleven o'clock, general good-nights being exchanged in the drawing-room. Lucy took me up to my room and left me tired and happy. I had just undressed when there was a tap on my door.

'Oh,' she said. 'About the wood. I mean what you said in it. Of course I haven't told anyone, but are you all right now?'

'Yes, quite all right, thank you.'

'I just wanted to know.' We were both rather embarrassed.

'Well, good, I just wanted to know,' she repeated, and then

55

clumsily, she kissed me, my ear and a good deal of hair.

'Good night,' she said, and smiled, brightly sweet.

'Good night,' I replied.

Having fumbled with the gas lamp, which shot up like a train coming towards me, then subsided, I felt my way into bed.

The sheets were cold and different; there was a knife edge of air cutting through the crack of window and it was very silent. Lying there, I reviewed the day which had begun with getting up, my trunk bumping corners down the stairs, and a choking tasteless breakfast (travellers' pride, someone had said). My father's rough blue cheek; the carriages upholstered like short thick grass; my mouth sore from the pear drop; rain; cows; people, black purposeless specks since I never saw them achieve their destinations; the gate open, the door shut, the hedge reached; arriving, waiting for the trap; cold, damp and apprehension, Lucy, Gerald, the whip making a greasy line on the pony's heavy coat, Lucy's smile, laughing; then the house, and the parrot's eye of the groom. Lucy's mother; the smell, oh yes the smell; lunch, a gleaming table and Deb; Nanny, and the darling little house. I dwelled on that until it became almost animate. I had enjoyed it so much. Perhaps we should go and see if it were still there; whether it had stood the weather and the night and the silence – of course it would be noisy in a wood I supposed, rather frightening. I remembered running in the dusk, and the sparks of windows, orange, like the slug. Deb, and her cherries at tea, what a secret I knew, all about an engagement; her hair, her jewels. There must be stars in the sky, should I look at them? I remembered the high hedge and the moon. What extraordinary things happened to other people!

Still, I notice them, I notice a good deal more than some people, and something exciting must happen to me. Lucy kissed me, she must like me. I love it: I want this time to last. I don't care if nothing else happens; I'll have this as my loveliest time. Really, it's only a beginning, I'm sixteen. I want everything, every single thing.

In the dark, almost asleep, I embraced the wonderfully welcome unknown; slept, hugging every change, and all the time I had, with this one lovely day, slipping out of my body into my mind.

CHAPTER SIX

That was the beginning of the best Christmas that I remember. I think one of the most delightful aspects of the house was that it was made up of fascinating ceremonies and expeditions. They made every day and moment taut with excitement or sprawling with pleasure: the house accepted me, and the people unfolded like tulips.

The mornings were exquisite: beginning with pure white mist on the ground, which had been secretly inlaid with sparkling hard frost, glittering and twinkling like stars in a morning sky, as the palely elegant sun rose and devoured the drops, broke the ice-like paper on the river, and touched the copse to red with its spidery rays. Porridge poured down our throats like molten lead, heating us for the day. Other people's breakfasts seem so infinitely richer than one's own; even their marmalade seems rarer, and the toast is a different shape. Then there were things like honey and mushrooms and pears that I had never before eaten for breakfast. And what were we going to do today? Lucy's mother always asked.

'Picnic.'

'Silly, far too cold.'

'I'm going to ride. Gerald, shall you ride?'

'I don't know. Where's this ice?'

'Papa, who is to have Tufty?'

'Someone has to get holly for the church.'

'It's not a good year for holly.'

Elspeth opened her eyes wide. 'It's an excellent year for holly.'

Well *you* find it. *You* find enough for the pulpit and all the windows.'

'Papa, who is to have Tufty? Gerald had him last time.'

'Elinor, run up and ask Aunt Edith whether she'd like half a pear. Wait a minute, take it.'

'Who's going to the village?'

'The vicarage children are pining to play French and English.'

'*Papa*. Please may I ride Tufty? In a snaffle. I won't hurt his mouth. May I? Papa, please.'

'I'll take you.'

'Oh!' Lucy was delighted.

'And what's Toby going to do?'

'Balloons,' he answered, and plunged into his milk.

'What about the vicarage children?'

'Gerald can ride Golden Plume.'

'Oh!' Lucy was rather dashed. 'Gerald, you lucky thing. May I tomorrow?'

'You're having Tufty ... When creeping murmur and the something dark. Seven letters.'

Lucy's mother paused. 'Whispering. No. I don't know, dear. I never can do the Double Acrostic. It's a quotation ... Now,' she summed us all up. 'Gerald and Lucy are riding. Gerald, run and tell Parker. Elspeth's going to get holly, and you're all going to play French and English with the vicarage children before tea. I can't help it, my dears, think of their poor mother. Pouring, darling, pouring dark.' And so on.

I spent the day with several of them. I watched Lucy go off for her ride, radiant, on a wicked black pony who sidled about like a crab with a grin; and then collected holly with Elspeth, who talked much more when one was alone with her. Climbing a gate she stood on the top bar, apparently quite comfortable, and slashed at the holly, throwing down branches to me.

'What are you going to do when you're grown up?' was her opening gambit.

'I don't know.'

'Don't know! You'll have to think soon, won't you? You're nearly grown up now.'

'Yes.' I must think I supposed. 'What are *you* going to do?'

'I shall keep a small *zoo*,' she said stretching out for a

59

branch, 'and – hold my legs, will you? – I shall write a great many books. They will be about different things.'

'What sort of things?'

'Mostly about people. I want to find out where they start being different. Now you' – she sat down on the gate swinging her legs – 'now you're quite different from Lucy. And Gerald and Lucy are more alike than any of us. And I'm different again.'

'What about Elinor?'

'She's a wishy-washy little thing,' she said impatiently. Elinor was far older than Elspeth, at least fifteen, so I was impressed. 'She is so careful to be the same as other people. She can't think beyond her school. And she does her Holiday Task. Poetry.'

'Perhaps she likes poetry.'

'She doesn't know anything about it. It's the Task. In the summer holidays it was painting blackberries. Well, she did it. So that they'll be pleased with her at school. She just wants to be a mother and have babies.' This seemed to me a lot to want, but Elspeth was so scornful that I didn't dare say so. 'And if you ask her who she wants to marry, she doesn't say a pirate or a lord or anything interesting like that, she simply says a nice man. Well, I *ask* you. She says she wants to live in London because they have nice clothes. I said, now that *you've* come she can see there's nothing in that, is there? You don't have specially nice clothes. I mean, they're all right, but not feathers and things.'

'You could have feathers if you wanted them. You don't like Elinor.'

'Not much, I like older people. I like people to be ahead of me.'

'What about Deb?'

'Deb.' Elspeth considered her. 'Well, she's different. I mean you can't decide about Deb. Because the moment you start, you think, well, she's beautiful, so it means you can't count the bad things she does much, and the good things seem better. Deb wants what she thinks is everything, but she can't see very far. So really they're fairly dull things and she'll get them, I should think. Now you'd want far harder things.'

'What?'

She considered me wisely, with her head a little on one side.

'I don't *know* you.'

'Do you like me?'

'I think so, you're rather pretty. Good heavens, I didn't mean to embarrass you.'

'It's all right,' I mumbled, feeling a fool. It had been such a very stupid question. No one had ever said anything like that. 'You're cold,' Michael had said, and now, 'You're pretty, rather pretty.' Some awful fascination led me on. I gripped the gate.

'Elspeth, in what way am I pretty?' It must be an important thing to know, because Deb had minded so much. 'It's not as silly as it sounds. At least, I've never thought about it before, but it seems suddenly to matter. I don't know many people. So I haven't asked anyone else. I don't do things very well. I want to start, and if I were pretty – rather pretty – it ought to help, oughtn't it? I mean a person should have something interesting or nice about them. I play the piano a bit, but not well enough to count. I seem to have so much *less* than other people. It's an awful feeling, because you have it by yourself just as much as with other people. So in what way would you say I was pretty?' I stopped. Everything I had said sounded inexpressibly foolish.

Elspeth regarded me a moment in silence. Then in a clear voice with a hint of scorn in it she said, 'You're really worrying about whether you'll get married. *I* don't know whether you will. It seems such a queer thing to worry about. But I've noticed that quite sensible girls do. Boys don't. It just happens to them.'

'I don't think I am.'

'Well then you're worrying about whether people will like you. That's silly too. You shouldn't mind so much. *Deb* doesn't.'

I was stung. 'She does. She minds very much.'

Elspeth looked at me curiously.

'*Does* she?' she said softly, and jumped off the gate in silence. We picked up the branches and in a bewildered way I almost hated Elspeth. Why had she said that Deb didn't mind? Why was she so sure? Giving me her advice! Of course I had asked for it. She was only a child, much younger than I. She was in her own surroundings, that was all; she was at ease, but where would she not be? In my limited experience I could think of nowhere. Of course she read books . . . Supposing that was important. No, Lucy didn't read. She had said so. What was it?

'What's the time?' Elspeth broke in. 'I wish *I* had a watch. It's practically the only thing I want. I've asked for one for Christmas. Come on, lunch.' Her hands were covered with scratches and full of holly. 'It *is* lovely, isn't it?' she said. She looked purely delighted.

'Sorry I asked you such silly questions.'

'That's all right. I enjoy it really. They say I'm pompous, but I don't care. It comes out of me like that.'

'Do you always live here?'

'Yes, at present. My mother is dead.' She said it easily, looking at me, but her eyes suddenly went quite flat.

I didn't say anything, and seconds later she turned her head a little towards me, gratefully, as though she were acknowledging my silence.

Walking along a track up a hill, we came upon a cottage. It was yellow, with a low untidy thatch, and it had two stunted elms beside it. A woman stood in the open door. She wore a vast blue-flowered overall. Her hair was done in a hard bun at the back. She was holding a large baby with a grey face and pale curls and *he* was holding a painted horse by its tail, loosely, so that the head swung against the woman.

'Hello, Mrs Druid,' said Elspeth. At this, three more children suddenly appeared from among the cabbages. They stared.

'Good morning, Miss,' said Mrs Druid.

'We've been collecting holly.'

'I see you 'ave.'

'For the church.'

'Ah,' said Mrs Druid.

'How's George?' said Elspeth. Mrs Druid shook the baby gloomily.

'Better than he should be. He 'ad a ball of wool yesterday. Didn't you, George?'

George became convulsed over her shoulder and the horse flapped wildly.

'He eats things,' said Elspeth regarding him with respect.

'It was only a little ball. Last week he eat arf a page of Druid's paper, didn't you, George?'

George hung motionless like seaweed.

'He ate a lot of soap once and she couldn't wash any of them,' said Elspeth to me. One of the children giggled and fell over a hen.

'It didn't upset him at *all*,' said Elspeth with awe.

'Can't keep 'is dinner down though,' said Mrs Druid unexpectedly. 'Just picks at it. Still we can't 'ave everything. Can we, George?' She laughed comfortably and pulled his legs down like the weights of a grandfather clock.

'Oh well,' said Elspeth. 'I hope he'll grow out of it.'

'We're getting used to it,' said Mrs Druid, and she laughed again.

'Well, good-bye,' said Elspeth.

Mrs Druid banged George enthusiastically on the back by way of farewell and disappeared into her cottage. The three children ran like rabbits to the gate and watched us up the hill. They were still there when we descended the other side, out of sight.

'It's always worth stopping to see her,' said Elspeth.

'Doesn't he get frightfully ill?'

'Good Lord, no. He's not like other people at all. That's why I always talk to her.'

When we got back, I found Toby squatting on the top landing, beside four balloons, tied to the banisters by long pieces of string. He could let them down to the ground floor and then haul them up. He looked very pleased and secret and didn't speak at all. Lucy called me. She was sitting in the day nursery, with her feet in a tub. Nanny was rubbing her arm with some stuff out of a bottle.

'I fell off twice,' she said. She looked white but triumphant.

'Goodness, did it hurt?'

'Oh yes.'

'Of course it did. You should have had a good cry before you got on again. You're not a boy you know.'

'That doesn't make the slightest difference, Nanny. Can I take my feet out?'

'I don't hold with your riding a pony with tricks like that. You might have broken a bone and then where would you have been, with the dance coming on and all?'

'Nanny, never *mind*.' Lucy was very near to tears. 'You go on down,' she said, and I went.

The vicarage children came at half-past three. They were very punctual and clean and pugnacious. There were two boys and a girl. They had ordered the game and they lost no time in organizing it. They picked sides with various agressive comments on our potential running powers. I had never played the game before. After ten minutes' confusion I had a stitch in my side and had not managed to collect either a handkerchief or Lucy, now quite cured of her falls, and prisoner.

The vicarage children charged and shouted and hurled insults and won the game. It was agreed that we should play something else, and while Gerald and the elder boy were deciding, the other two children chased each other and fought, with panting fury, any of us who stood in their way.

Eventually, no other game determined, we reverted to French and English. This time, however, Gerald forced them to pick the sides evenly. It was quite an effort, although he was at least three years older than the elder boy. Our tea bell rang, just as I had distinguished myself by a spectacular capture of Gerald, who yelled 'Well done!' as he roared back to his side. I felt proud, and was just settling down to enjoy the game.

' 'Fraid we must go,' said Gerald.

'Mother said we could stay to tea as soon as we were asked,' said the girl, eyeing Lucy firmly. Good heavens, I thought, they must be awful indoors. They were the sort of children that one only visualized in the open. The training of generations rose to aid Lucy and she answered gallantly enough.

'Well, of course, do come to tea.' We all moved towards the house.

'Although, you know,' I heard Elspeth say to one of them, 'we don't really want you to tea in the least. Lucy was only being polite.'

Whether we wanted them mattered not at all, I realized. They all washed at once, turning on and off the taps with wet grey hands, leaving the soap with black cracks, and a high-water mark all round the basin which Elspeth cleaned with the nail brush in silent indignation. Elspeth was a very particular child.

At tea they ate an enormous amount; the girl spilt her milk; and the boys had an argument. Lucy's mother was admirable. After the opening courtesies, she took no further notice, and even told one of them to leave a chocolate biscuit for his brother. When we left the table, the floor was thick with crumbs round their places.

'Still, it was a nice rest for their poor mother,' said our charitable hostess. She asked me whether I had written to my mother. 'Don't you think it would be a good idea?' she said. I felt myself blushing, and she showed me to a desk with pens and ink in silver stands, and pale grey paper with the address upon it in white.

'Dearest Mother . . .' What could I tell her? She had hoped I would have a good time. How far her hopes were excelled already! Strangely, my happiness made her further removed; it was harder to write than I had thought possible.

'I am arrived here quite safely. Everyone is very kind, and Mrs Lancing sends you her love. It is very cold. This morning I went picking holly for the church with a girl called Elspeth. Last night we played games and this afternoon the vicarage children came to tea.'

65

I thought a bit and then added, 'There is going to be a dance so I shall wear my frock, so thank you for buying it for me. I am having a lovely time. Your affectionate daughter.'

That night I had a very real and frightening dream. I was dancing in my pink frock, dancing quite safely with Elspeth. At the end of a passage stood Michael; much taller than he really was, with his arms out like a tree. The nearer I danced to him the larger he was and the further away he seemed. Then I noticed Rupert whom I had never seen, on a hill. I was so frightened of Michael that I picked up my skirts and ran cold and breathless nearer and nearer to Rupert, until I was quite up to him; and then I was in a wood, with no light to be seen, groping and stumbling in the dark, with Michael's laugh outside. I felt that the whole wood was Rupert, although I could not find him. The branches clung to me like arms and the leaves smothered me like a face, but I still called desperately for Rupert, pushing him away in my struggle. I must move on, get somewhere, but I did not know where I was going. When I woke, my heart was pounding in the silent room, and perspiration streamed down between my breasts. I lay stiff and still until the blackness of the window softened to a deep grey, bringing with it a faint sense of relief. I was freezing cold. I unplaited my hair, pulled it round my shoulder for warmth, and slept.

Christmas began to make itself felt. There was a tremendous expedition to the nearest town for the purpose of buying presents. Lucy's mother became the source of all secrets, all desires and inventions were exposed to her, and she sat giving gentle practical advice, smiling at everything, laughing at no one, keeping all secrets equally well. I accompanied Deb on the expedition. She spent nearly all her money on a watch chain for her Roland, and we packed and dispatched it together. That accomplished, she seemed to have no further interest in either her plans or mine; buying all her presents with careless speed, and giving me perfunctory advice in my schemes. She did not play games like the rest of them, and I found her more difficult. Occasionally, she collected me for some confidence or other, but she neither expected nor desired any return on my part.

Gerald tested the ice every day with growing confidence. I had one fateful riding lesson with Lucy and Parker. It was all right while the pony walked, but when it was clicked and encouraged to trot, I bit my tongue and lost a stirrup. Nothing was said about the venture, but it was mutually agreed that one could not learn to ride in ten days unless one showed some aptitude.

We suffered several visits from the vicarage children whose names I found were inappropriately enough, Vivian, Cecil and Bunty. They were aggressive and awe inspiring. They wore heavy clasp knives on leather belts round their waists, and always one of them was suffering from some frightful self-inflicted wound. They came through hedges, instead of over gates, and they usually entered any building by the first floor. One of them was always stuck at the top of a tree, while the other two pelted him with chestnuts or stones, in a heartless endeavour to get him down at all costs. They were permanently and terribly hungry; and they ate almost anything, from cow cake to frost-bitten blackberries. They ran everywhere, and only stayed in one place in order to fight. Their favourite pastimes were frightening each other, and giving other people terrible shocks. I think they were curiously devoted, or at any rate dependent, one always needing the others to carry out some complicated scheme. I cannot imagine how their poor parents existed under their rule. It must have been like living with a minor storm, on the brink of revolution, with a cloud of locusts.

Parcels kept arriving by post. There was mistletoe in the hall, under which Elspeth solemnly kissed me. Nanny ironed all our best clothes. Nobody was allowed into the library, which someone said was piled to the ceiling with presents. Great curly chrysanthemums stood in the hall, yellow and white, and smaller bronze-red ones, rambling and ragged, all smelling sweetly burnt.

Three days before Christmas the ice bore. Gerald broke

the news at breakfast, and immediately after we were wrapping up for skating. I had learned in that short time to like any new venture, since new ventures were no longer initiated by me as a desperate resort against boredom and solitude. Gerald had brought a broom with which he carefully swept a large slice of the river, while we sat on the banks surveying the green-grey ice. Lucy helped me put on a pair of skates. They seemed tight; although she assured me that that gave one support.

'Now,' she said. 'Hold on to me and walk.'

I staggered down to the edge of the river. Lucy embarked and held out her hands. 'You'll soon get used to it.' Kind Lucy! My gratitude made me brave. Of course I sat down pretty hard in a moment, though the others skimmed about like butterflies. Seeing Deb coming across the grass, with some difficulty I got to my feet. Lucy took my arm and soon I was lurching along, she urging me to take long steps, and supporting me when I lost my balance.

Learning to skate is much the same for everyone: it is enough to say that before the morning was over I was able to move up and down the river with quick uneven steps alternating with a drunken roll, that I fell down with painful regularity, and that getting to my feet with nothing to help me presented its usual problems. My ankles ached badly, and it became sad to see the others racing about, cutting figures and dancing together. I was encouraged by Deb's very reserved enjoyment; she glided about for an hour with Gerald, then repaired to the house. I sat on the bank and watched them all. Elspeth seemed intent on speed; she shot up and down the swept strip, her knees bent and her face thrust forward, so that I could almost see the air being cut away by her, like the pictures of steamers with a white wave in front. Elinor was very little more advanced than I, or so it seemed. She painstakingly cut a figure of eight, over and over again. Lucy and Gerald were the best; they leapt about and he showed her complicated steps and turns, they laughed a lot, and once they collided and stood holding each other's elbows, when their laughter died, they looked at each other, and rubbed noses to make it easy and usual again. Lucy's mother came to watch with a bag of peppermints. She fed us like birds because our gloves were too thick to manage for ourselves. 'Don't get cold,' she said to me. She came back again later, bringing Toby, who skated like a duck in a hurry, quickly and easily from side to side. He said he didn't like it, but he stayed.

After lunch I packed my presents with Deb, whose parcels were all small and neat, wrapped in white paper and tied with silver cord.

'What will you do when you go back to London?' she asked.

'Just be at home. There's nothing much to do there.'

'Oh!' She glanced at me incuriously.

'It's awfully dull there. It's not a bit like being here. There's so much to do.'

'Yes, but that's only because it's different. Think of doing them for years.'

'I should like it. There are more people here. I mean you do things together.'

'I like one person at a time,' she answered absently, smoothing a piece of tissue paper.

'You like parties, too.'

'Yes, I like them well enough. If I were in London I should have many more.'

You would, of course, I thought. London would change for you, never present itself in an everyday manner for you. But that would be the same wherever you went.

'Surely you meet a lot of people there?'

'Oh well, musicians and people who like music.'

'I should love that. What are they like?'

'They are my parents' friends,' I answered stiffly, as though it was impossible for me to explain my parents' friends.

'Well?' She was impatient. 'Are you not old enough to like them?'

'I don't notice them.' I was ashamed and irritated and it was not even true. 'They don't talk to me much.'

69

'Of course, I suppose they wouldn't.' She had the half re-sentful respect the world has for an artist, that I already knew so well.

'Do you like music?' I asked.

'I like waltzes. Chopin,' she added as if to excuse her frivolous choice.

'Oh, but other kinds of real music. Don't you like that?'

'I don't know what you mean, real music. I like songs and music for dancing. But I don't see the point of the other kind.' I looked smugly shocked. 'Well, can *you* tell me the point of it? What *is* the point?'

'To – to listen to – and enjoy.'

'How do you enjoy it, if you don't see the point of it?' she persisted, mischievously intent.

'Well, flowers,' I said lamely. 'They haven't much point and you enjoy them.'

'They smell,' she said indignantly. 'And they are pretty colours.'

'I don't suppose musicians care much for flowers,' I said, uncertainly, but it served my point to say so.

'But flowers are useful. You can wear them and they make rooms look nice. There's nothing useful about music.'

'I suppose people have special enjoyments, and they don't need them to be useful. It's just luck if you like beautiful things.'

'I adore beautiful things,' she said.

'Not all . . .' I began.

'But I just like to like them. I don't want to have to be clever to like them.' She threw a little parcel on the heap and touched her hair.

I realized then how self-consciously I admired the things I thought it right to admire. We were silent for a time and I was sorting desperately the things that I *knew* I liked. I did not get very far, because I liked everything about that house and nothing about mine; and yet many things were the same. I dismissed the whole problem because Deb interrupted me with some comment on our activity.

When we went to tea, I met Toby on the stairs. He was

very warm and smelt of toast. There was a huge chocolate cake and everyone was hungry from skating. I sat next to Elinor, who left her icing to the end, and ate it very thoughtfully. Everyone was gay and peaceful. Suddenly in the middle of tea the door opened and two young men appeared.

'Rupert!' cried Lucy.

There was much confusion, people got to their feet, with littles cries of delighted surprise, and there was a spasm of excitement. I had leisure to observe, and watched Rupert because I had a natural curiosity about him. The other young man might have been his shadow. Rupert walked forward, kissed his hostess's hand, straightened himself and smiled faintly.

'How did you come, my dear boy?'

'We motored. Ian had a motor. By the way, this *is* Ian.'

'How long did it take?'

Gerald wore a keenly professional look.

'Well we had a puncture or so.'

'Who drove?'

'I drove and the wretched Ian sat and mended tyre after tyre.'

'Introduce me to Ian,' said Lucy's mother calmly.

'Mrs Lancing. The Lady of the House, and my, our. admirable hostess. This is Ian Graham.'

'Have you come to stay?'

The young man was dreadfully embarrassed and Rupert had turned away to shake hands with Lucy's father. Ian was thin and fair. He blushed, and murmured something, rubbing his hands which were white with cold.

'We're delighted to have you. Sit down. Elspeth ring for some more tea. Sit by me,' this to Ian. 'Now I must introduce you. This is my husband. This is Deborah, my eldest daughter, Lucy, Elinor, and Elspeth, who is their cousin. Toby, my youngest, Gerald ...' She continued round the large table. Rupert followed these introductions with a jerk of his eyes; to Deb he threw a mocking smile of admiration, and then when Mrs Lancing stopped he came to me, and by reason of her silence, he stared a little. Ian seemed too confused to speak. He was very shy and kept looking at his hands.

'And who is that?'

'Good gracious I forgot.'

I was duly introduced, Mrs Lancing explaining that I had been sitting too close to her, thus stalling the flood of shame in me that Rupert's faintly insolent remark had induced. They sat down.

'How do you come by a motor car?' Mr Lancing rarely spoke.

'Well Ian is my only rich friend. We bought it this morning, because I don't like trains and he's very fond of me. And of course once we'd bought it, he had to come too, and I knew you'd like him so that was that.'

'Why didn't you drive if it was your motor car?'

'He doesn't like cars,' said Rupert calmly as he slashed a piece of cake.

'Rupert how selfish of you. You are so selfish. Give Ian some cake.'

'He doesn't like cake either.'

'Stop telling us what he doesn't like. It's horrid for him.'

The tea arrived.

'Deborah,' said Rupert lovingly. She arched her neck and looked at him inquiringly.

'Sweet Deb, how do you manage to keep it up?'

'Keep what up?'

'Your beauty.'

She was defiantly silent.

'Rupert, stop it,' cried Mrs Lancing. 'You are an impudent boor.'

He grinned sweetly.

'Well it's true. Ian don't you think she . . .?'

'It's no use,' said Lucy's mother. 'Every year when you go away I resolve never to have you again and then you write me such an enchanting Collins that I find it impossible to deprive myself of the chance of another.'

'Ho, you shouldn't do things for gain.'

'You shouldn't speak with your mouth full,' said Elspeth severely.

'When you reach my age you can do the most awful things and no one will stop you. They merely shudder and hold up their hands.'

Toby suddenly shuddered and held up his hands, so funnily that everyone laughed. He relapsed into a silent little boy and took no notice.

'What awful things have you been doing?'

'Nothing much. Why haven't you got a dog in this house? It's all wrong, I found myself in that hall, and nobody knocked me down, or licked my face. I was awfully disappointed.' His narrow eyes screwed up. 'But the chrysanthemums smelled a treat. Ian was at Cambridge with me,' he added suddenly.

'I should have thought people stopped you doing things far more when you were old,' said Elspeth.

'Oh no,' I said. 'Only then you don't want to do them.'

Rupert looked at me.

'Well, well,' he said softly.

'We've been skating,' said Gerald after a pause.

'There's going to be a dance.'

'I say how marvellous.' Ian choked in his tea.

'Pat him on the back. He's very young.'

'Awful chap,' spluttered Ian.

'Oh I'm beyond the pale. Far beyond it,' said Rupert gravely, and for a moment he looked sad and obsessed. 'I hope you're surprised to see me,' he said, after a moment.

'You're conceited too.'

'I suppose you think we've all been *gasping* for you,' said Lucy cheerfully.

'I didn't say pleased. You're all so kind that I imagine you pleased about anyone. I prefer to engender surprise. Shock. Startlement.' His angular eyebrows shot up and he looked fiercely at Toby who grinned resentfully.

'Ha,' said Rupert. 'I really annoyed him.' He said it with a sort of satisfaction.

CHAPTER SEVEN

Two days later I was in the library with Elspeth. There was a smell of books seldom opened, or perhaps it was Elspeth's hair. I remember we were kneeling on the window seat and there was a little snow on the ground outside. Rupert put his head round the door.

'Come for a walk?'

Elspeth wriggled. 'You come here and talk.'

'No, I want a walk. And I didn't mean you.'

'All right.' I scrambled off the seat.

Elspeth caught my skirt. 'You don't want to go.'

'Why not?'

She pursed her lips. 'We were looking at books.'

Suddenly I did not want her to come too.

'Hurry up,' said Rupert. I ran to change. When I was ready he was still standing in the door and Elspeth was sulking, and trying not to laugh. I said good-bye to her and she did not answer whereupon Rupert slammed the door.

'Silly little creature.'

We strode up the drive, our feet barely marking the speckled ground.

'She's clever.'

'Only compared with the other people in the house.'

'Of course she may prove intelligent later on,' he said after a pause, then glancing at me. 'Don't look so shocked. Does intelligence mean so much to you?'

'I don't know,' I said truthfully.

'Oh I hoped you knew. I hoped you would say that intelligence was the distinction you needed and admired in your friends. That you would throw away beauty, charm and riches for so precious a commodity as intelligence. What would you say it was anyway?'

'What?' This was going to be a startling walk.

'Intelligence.'

'Untrained knowledge?'

He threw back his head and laughed loudly. 'What a damn silly thing to say. But she doesn't rise,' he said in mock surprise a moment later. I felt he was teasing, provoking me into a reply, but I was better able to hold my ground with silence. We strode on up the hill, with the snow flakes slipping down towards us, dark against the milky sky, and suddenly shining white as they fell into our landscape.

'Do you like all this?' I indicated the country before us.

'Yes,' he said. 'But I couldn't live in it for long. I am drawn to the Metropolis. The lights, music and the people. There isn't enough to do here.'

'Much more than in London, I think,' I said warmly.

'What? One can farm, or be a gentleman of leisure and I have neither inclination nor means.'

'What do you do in London?'

'Nothing now. I was to be a doctor.'

'Were you expelled?'

'No I left,' he answered quite seriously, as though I had used the right word.

'Why did you leave?'

'That's the trouble. I don't know, I never stop anything merely for something else. Hence these awful gaps, when I come to sneer and vegetate in the country, with a crowd of people who give me the benefit of the doubt through sheer ignorance.'

'Where do you live?'

'I did live in a horrible room in Gloucester Road. Last week I left it in the morning in a fog and I shan't go back now.'

'Have you left all your things there?'

'Some of them. I didn't want them you know.' He seemed amused.

'I have been throwing things away too.'

'And where do you intend going?'

'Going?' I repeated. 'I hadn't thought. I just want to do something.'

'You do. What do you want to do?'

'I don't know.'

'Ah,' he said. 'We neither of us know.' His comfort in the fact communicated itself to me.

'What could I do?'

'Come and keep house for me.'

'Oh *no*.'

'What vehemence. You asked me what you should do. I imagine like most girls you have made a passionate resolve to be needed. You've thought of being a nun, a nurse, the wife of a blind man. Surely my housekeeper is the next step? Or is there someone else? Have you dedicated yourself to some other aimless youth?'

'I want to help myself.'

'Hooray!'

'I don't like being teased. I was serious.'

'I knew you were. I like teasing people.'

'Well you shouldn't.'

'I only tease people I like.'

'You shouldn't do just what you like to people.'

'Not to do what I like to people would be pretending. If you're to housekeep for me I should see you every day and however much I liked you I couldn't keep up the pretence. That would be like marriage.' He said the last with such extraordinary bitterness that I was startled into continuing the conversation which I had before begun to regret.

'What do you mean "like marriage"?'

'I forgot. You probably think that married people love each other.'

'I hadn't thought anything about it.' Suddenly I was remembering my father padding away to his studio after meals, and my mother settling with a whimpering little sigh, to her darning. 'I thought they ceased to consider it.'

'They pretend,' he said fiercely after a moment, 'so hard that there isn't time for anything else.'

'They have their house, children, work. I don't think they consider it,' I said.

'Do they honestly love each other then?'

'No.'

'Do they admire each other?'

'No.'

'Enjoy each other's company?'

'Not much.'

'Like each other?'

'Oh, I don't know.' I felt inexpressibly sad.

'Poor little thing. That's why you're so concerned with doing something. You get away. They're finished. You can't do anything for them.'

At once the whole universe rocked for me, leaving what had been an accepted supposition an abyss of uncertainty and fear. The shock of realizing that Rupert knew I had been speaking of my parents, breaking down as it did such necessary reserve, paralysed me. It did not occur to me that he was generalizing out of personal bitterness; that therefore this awful statement could be fought, could be disproved or rejected. (I was at an age when if anyone said something with sufficient certainty I was forced to believe them and suffer accordingly.) I looked at Rupert; he was only one person. He was still striding along with his head bent; a little cut on his cheek, furtive and crimson. The cut made me feel surer. Suddenly I could speak and my own voice gave me courage.

'There's no need to marry anyone unless you love them. Of course there might be mistakes, but that's nothing to do with pretending. A great many people may be utterly content. You don't know all the people. Enough people then,' I added, feeling his laugh about to break.

We had turned off the lane into a bridle path, edged with dead blackberries, mottled hips and crackling grass stiffened by frost.

'Let's see who's in the best position to generalize. How many married couples do you know intimately?'

I was not be caught again. 'Not many. How many do you know?'

'Not many. But I'm older than you so that my "not many" means more. Therefore I am better able to judge about marriage than you, and until you're my size of mind you must accept any statement I care to make.'

'People aren't an even age. I am older than you in some ways.'

'Darling little creature, I was teasing you. Still able to quarrel about who's the oldest. Not very old yet,' he said in mock despair.

'I don't believe you about marriage.'

'I was warning you.'

'I don't want to be warned. I *shall* love someone and I *shall* marry them. I will manage myself,' I said sullenly.

'Hooray, you have thought everything out.'

The path was now skirting a wood, a copse. The older trees were felled and lying in reckless attitudes, their bark blistering and ragged like wallpaper.

'I'm tired,' I said.

He glanced at me. 'We won't argue any more. I won't tease you.'

'I'm tired. Really,' I repeated, some instinct telling me how to get the better of him.

'Right.' He lifted me in his arms, over a ditch, and into the wood where he seated me on a log.

'How old are you?'

'Sixteen.'

'Ah yes. Sixteen, and there you sit, cold and tired and teased past all endurance.'

I looked up at him. He seemed kind. I was still aching and wondering what I should think alone, with my thoughts uncoloured by his interruptions.

'Nothing is certain,' I said rather shakily.

'What a desperate little remark. Yes, we need to believe some things.'

'You don't leave much.'

'There are too many things for belief,' he said sadly. 'The world's too full. It has extended beyond any single mind. There are so many Gods, so many people, so many ideas, so many creeds and convictions. We have simply to choose.'

'How do we do that?'

I felt him groping along my thoughts with the fingers of his mind. 'Don't try to find out what is generally right. That's mere condonement, *not* personal acceptance, which means feeling, thinking and knowing until that belief will live with you from sheer love.' He seemed to be telling himself. He finished suddenly. He sat down and pulled out a pipe. 'And now, may I smoke this?'

I nodded, I did more or less understand him, and felt calmer.

'Your family are musicians aren't they?'

'My father.' I stared at his long bony hands loosely clasped round his knees.

'I've heard some of his work. Influenced by Schumann isn't he?'

'Everyone says that.'

'I'm sorry.' He was mocking again.

'Everybody is influenced by someone.'

He bowed and a long lock of hair fell over his face.

'I should like to come and see them.'

'No you wouldn't.'

'Yes, I shall accompany you on your day off, to visit your family.'

'No.'

'But what deadly secret have you to hide that you are so positive?'

'No secret.' I stared again at his hands. 'I'll come and see you.'

'You will?'

'Wherever you are living.'

'You *want* to be my housekeeper?'

'Rupert, I ...' Did he really mean that? What did he expect me to say?

'I suppose it would be rather improper.' I looked up at the sound of his voice and found him watching my face. 'Did you think I was furtively asking you to be my mistress?'

I had very little idea of what being a mistress implied, but I felt the blood rushing to my face; a wild desire to escape and stop everything or be someone else. He took both my hands in his: I looked down at them warmly folded, and then back to his face again, and still I couldn't speak. He stared at me intently; and there was such a depth of honesty in his eyes that my self-consciousness melted as my face cooled, and I was unafraid.

'That wasn't very kind of me. Of course you didn't. I'm afraid you can't even be my housekeeper. But you shall come to tea, or whenever you haven't anywhere else to go, and want to come. I'll tell you where I am, when I know, so that you won't forget.'

'I won't.'

'Now I'm going to kiss you to finish things off because we must go home.'

He took my face in his hands and bent his head. I put my arms round his neck; his hair felt silky at the back.

'What a convulsive little gesture,' he said and kissed me. His lips were cool and firm; and when he stopped, my mouth felt strange, separate and alive.

He held out his hand, pulled me to my feet, and we set off out of the wood, back down the mysterious dead path to the road.

The snow was falling more thickly, into our faces, but I did not mind it. I was in an unquestioning exhilarated mood where I needed no more or less of the road and snow and company than was provided.

Half-way home we found a young cat, almost a kitten. It followed us desperately, falling behind and then running round our feet, its ears flattened with dislike of the weather. Rupert insisted on buttoning it into his coat in spite of my saying that cats always found their way home.

'Nonsense,' he said decisively. 'Almost as silly a saying as the one about the English always being kind to animals.'

I felt rebuffed and faintly jealous. The cat was secure and drew the warmth of Rupert's presence away from me. Instantly my mood deserted me. I felt really tired; my legs ached, my boots rubbed my heels, and my skirts were heavy and dank.

The village appeared, its street ribbed with wheel tracks,

and my knowledge of Rupert slipped away as we approached it.

'Nearly home,' said Rupert cheerfully. 'We'll have an enormous scorching tea. You'll feel rested, warm and tired and full of food. It's the best part of a walk.'

Numb with a lack of reality I turned towards the house.

CHAPTER EIGHT

I remember lying rigid on my back having been sent to rest on the afternoon before the dance.

Nanny had drawn the curtains, and padded away to mull the afternoon suitably for the others. Telling me to have a nice rest, she shut the door. There ensued the most still and lasting silence. This is how to lie I thought when one is dead. Stiff and narrow amid complete silence. A cock crowed and I jumped out of bed and drew back the curtains again. I remember Rupert had looked at us at lunch, at Deb, at Lucy and at me, agreeing that we should rest, and the thought flitted across my mind, that we were to emerge from the artificial dusk of our rooms to dance a few hours in the light, like butterflies, for his pleasure.

I became very sad lying there because I could not imagine what was to happen after the dancing, when I went home. My pride would never let things be the same; so there would be decisions to make, life to be wielded, and too many people drifting with time to watch. I thought of my sister; she had refused this visit; she had no desire for anything new: she could sew and read and go to church, and for walks, and stay the same size, and complete herself within that tiny sphere. I wanted things before I knew what they were. I wondered what Rupert would do when he went back to London. I had not asked him. There were so many things I had wanted to ask him, but had not dared or had forgotten. The time I had spent with him had been choked with talk, and yet now it felt so short. Of course one would not have had one's fill of anybody in a single afternoon. Perhaps he would not want to talk to me again. I numbered on my fingers the few days left. Christmas could not count, it needed the day for itself. I tried to imagine Rupert with my father. They would talk about music, of course; my father's face would light up, and he would use boyish exclamations coined in his youth. Rupert would be perfectly at home. I would sit and watch them both and occasionally Rupert would smile at me. But the house! I could not bear Rupert to see the house. He was fastidious. The dirt and decay would not please him. I could never let him come there. I would not see him at all. I must wait for him to invite me. It was not possible to collect people just because you wanted them. If you were a woman, you must wait until they came to you.

The doctrine vaguely dissatisfied me: I got out of bed again to look for a book and found *The Wide Wide World*. It was full of very interesting information, and religion, and a little girl cried on nearly every page.

The house was warm and polished, with clusters of flowers in pots, which were scrubbed like sand to the fingers. The dining-room had long tables with white cloths to the floor; lines of glasses, and heaps of little spoons tangled and gleaming like fishes. The great room where we were to dance was lined with chairs, the floor bare, waiting to be furnished with people.

'Roland is coming,' said Deb.

'And I shall have Rupert,' I thought to myself with a little arrow of excitement. 'It will be quite different from the wood. I shall wear my beautiful frock and it is a dance.' And all the while I dressed I was conscious of a new delight in preparing myself for a single person's approbation.

I had bathed and was drawing my heavy bronze silk stockings up my legs. They unrolled with a beautiful smooth precision over the bony whiteness, collecting my limbs in elegant silken lines. I pointed my toe. Really they were a good shape. It was perfectly sensible to admire them, since nobody else would see them. I pulled down my petticoat. I was to brush my hair for Nanny to put it up. Deb having invited me to her room I planned to ask her for a piece of jewellery to wear on my frock. I dipped my finger in water and smoothed my eyebrows until they were finely narrow like Deb's. When I looked in the mirror, a new face looked back, with little shadows lying on the bones, and enormous eyes startled with excitement. I felt very beautiful then; the fear of being newly grown up and not knowing things slipped away because I could praise my own appearance from perfect intimacy with its shortcomings. The pink frock was laid out on the bed, with the pointed pink shoes beside it. I scratched the soles with scissors, and my finger suddenly blossomed a thin line of blood, with a drop on the pink strap of the shoe. I rubbed the strap with my flannel. It would not show, but the little moist circle was disquieting.

Nanny did my hair superbly with a narrow plait over the top of my head and the rest drawn waxen smooth. I raised my hands in bewildered delight.

'Don't touch it now,' Nanny said. 'Are you wearing any ornament in it?'

Despair engulfed me. 'I haven't got anything,' I stammered. Impossible, of course, I must wear something; it looked so stiff and bare. Deb swept into the room.

'You never came to see me.' She looked at my head and hopeless face below it. 'That's lovely, Nanny. It suits you. Wait a minute. Nanny, fetch my roses like an angel. The little pink ones.' When they came she fastened them into the edge of my plait. 'There,' she said. 'Three little pink roses.' Our eyes met, amused and grateful. 'All right?' she said. 'Nanny my stockings again,' and flung something misty across the room. So those were the stockings one wore for dancing. Mine were hopeless thick things – still they would not show. How absurd I had been. Nanny had disappeared. Deb was particularly charming to me. 'Let's put on your frock. Have you a locket?'

'No.'

'Come into my room. I'll lend you one.'

I rustled after her feeling gracious and at least twenty years old in my dress. She slung the turquoise heart on a chain, and fastened it round my neck where it lay brilliantly in the hollow of my throat.

'Now sit on a chair while I dress.'

She looked wonderful of course, and she loved to be

watched. I recollect yards and yards of pale yellow in an enormous skirt trimmed with green velvet ribbons. 'He likes green,' she said complacently as she fastened that colour neatly round her white neck. I watched her fasten green leaves in her hair, green velvet round her wrists; slip her feet into green slippers; tweak her shoulders, stroke her skirts and preen, and smile at me in the glass, all with a calm contented efficiency. This was really her life.

'Find out what Nanny is doing. I don't want her to come in here suddenly.'

Nanny was doing Elspeth's hair.

'Elspeth always cries when her hair is done. It takes ages.' From the back of a drawer she took a box of powder and carefully powdered her nose. 'Have some.' I leaned forward. 'I'll do it for you. Shut your eyes.' A fine dust descended on me, gathered in the corners of my eyes and mouth. She put the powder away. 'There it is if we want it,' she said with a gleam and again I had the feeling of a conspiracy. She pinched her cheeks and bit her lips and the colour flowed into them. Then she took a minute handkerchief gritty with lace, and shook out two little drops of lavender water. This time I was not included.

'Women can't wear the same scent,' she said, half apologetically. 'How do I look?'

'Wonderful.'

'You are awfully pretty too,' she said generously.

We rose from our chairs, shook out our skirts, and descended.

Dinner was an unsubstantial affair; a dream of half-eaten dishes and desultory anticipation. Nobody's mind came to the surface; nobody wanted to eat, but it was too old and established a custom to be foregone. Elspeth sat next to me absently eating nuts. She was in crimson velvet, with puff sleeves showing her childish arms with a little stream of delicate blue veins in the crook running down to her wrists. Her evening was darkened with the knowledge that she was to go to bed at half past ten. 'Although I sleep very little nowadays,' she said with scornful eyes and a quivering mouth.

Before the meal, we had been into the morning room, where Rupert was admiring Mrs Lancing's pearls and Aunt Edith sat in black velvet with a marvellous white silk shawl the fringes of which caught in her chair. Mrs Lancing had admired us, and Rupert had said 'Beautiful,' very firmly, with his eyes on Deb.

After the meal we were finally inspected by Nanny, Deb again powdered her nose, and we stood in the drawing-room, at one end of which the orchestra was now grouped, surrounded with hothouse ferns. There were sounds of the first people arriving. Lucy waltzed me across the room to the entrance where Mrs Lancing stood, with Deb frowning at us. The first announcement sounded absurd in the empty room when everyone could see who the arrivals were. Two plain girls wearing queer short dresses of peacock blue and hair tied back with enormous bows of the same colour, advanced nervously to be introduced.

'Their mother believes in Freedom of Movement,' muttered Lucy viciously in my ear. Rupert came in announcing himself in a loud unnatural voice which made the footmen shuffle sheepishly.

Then scores of guests arrived: girls in white and pink, and blue; boys in Eton suits; men, very young in evening dress; mothers, in lace and pearls; fathers, military men, with stiff legs and walking sticks; red-faced men curiously light on shiny black feet, good riders, sportsmen, all prepared for a festivity that would become the ladies, the objects of their chivalry, tolerance and affection; thin spare men of uncertain age laughing with nervous goodwill and rubbing their hands. (Surely men couldn't be shy?) Amid the hum of conversation Gerald handed out programmes with tiny pencils and tassels. I was introduced to a number of men who booked dances. I wondered when I should dance with Rupert and whether Roland had arrived: yes that must be Roland, tall and fair and close to Deb. I left four dances free for Rupert. He would of course forget to book them; would see me standing, and assume that we had planned those dances. He would put his arm round me; we should glide away in silence, and perhaps look at each other a moment later to acknowledge our understanding.

Upstairs, Nanny would be hovering with pins and combs and a needle, ready for any feminine emergency. And elsewhere supper was prepared; the slices of lemon floating sideways in the jugs of cup; the trifles quivering on their plates: everything was ready. The first dance. And the second. Learning the things one said; the general form of the conversation; dancing with good dancers and with bad, abandoning oneself to the delight of the movement, or admiration, tentative and clumsy ('those roses are ripping'): or the choking flood of panic when one could not interest one's partner with any of the opening remarks so newly learned – the floor, the orchestra, skating, Christmas, the hospitality of the Lancings. Dreary little pools of silence, broken by an apology ('So sorry.' 'My fault.'). The fifth dance. Rupert dancing with Deb, then with Mrs Lancing herself. Elspeth being sent to bed with a jelly. Rupert, his arms folded, leaning against the wall talking to another man. Dancing with Roland, and Deb smiling her approval. An uneasy little conversation on Deb's beauties. The sixth dance.

I went upstairs to tidy my hair. One could not walk into the room and say 'Rupert take me in to supper,' as Deb had done. Lucy was standing impatiently while Nanny whipped up a frill on her skirt. 'Who's taking you in to supper?'

'I don't know.'

'Oh.'

Poor Lucy was so kind that she was easily unhappy.

'It's all right,' I said carefully.

'You've had lots of partners haven't you?' said Lucy with an eager reassuring smile.

'Oh *yes*. I'm having a lovely time. Are you?'

'Of course,' she said simply. 'It's a dance.

'Down you go,' said Nanny. We went.

'I think Roland is rather unhappy,' whispered Lucy. 'I shall talk to him,' and she sped away, her coffee-coloured skirts flying round her neat ankles. Why was not Deb having supper with Roland? Why had it not been I who had smiled up at Rupert so affectionately, and commanded him to take me in to supper? Only a third of the evening gone.

Mrs Lancing introduced me to a sturdy young man in spectacles. Mr Fielding. 'You both like music,' she said firmly and left us.

'What sort of music do you like?'

'Oh, different things. What do you like?'

'Oh, any music really.'

'What about a little supper?'

'That would be lovely.'

We had supper. Gerald was hilarious with several men friends and a girl in yellow who giggled at everything he said and ate a great deal. Mr Fielding politely supplied me with food. Music died a natural death between us and we had nothing further to say to one another. Deb and Rupert were not there. How strange. Lucy and Roland were discussing the feeding of ponies for hunting. The cup was very cool and a little bitter, and I was desperately thirsty. A clock struck eleven. Mr Fielding was joining in the general conversation. I murmured something about a handkerchief and left him. In the hall I paused. My face was burning hot and I longed to cool it. I opened a door leading on to the garden and slipped out. There was a watery moon galloping across the sky. I heard footsteps, a low laugh, a murmured protesting denial, and then silence. The moon slipped thinly behind a feathery cloud and out the other side, rakish and gleaming. I stood a moment uncertain, then shut myself into the house again, and after wandering round the hall, seated myself half-way up the stairs.

They came in by the same door, as I had known they would, he holding it for her, she with his coat round her shoulders. All exactly as she had told me.

I was above them and they did not see me, but Lucy and Roland came out of the supper-room facing me.

'Hullo,' said Lucy, but Roland saw Deb.

'I was looking for you,' he said and moved forward uncertainly.

'Were you?' said Deb. 'Well here I am, come and give me a drink.' She sounded sharp and a little nervous. As she moved to Roland she saw me, through the banisters and tilted her head. I saw a spot of colour on her cheekbones, her eyes narrowed, sparkling through the black fringe of lashes, and a tendril of hair curling down her neck. 'You there, too?'

'I was having a rest.'

She nodded, and went away with Roland. I could feel Rupert watching me and rose to my feet. He met me at the bottom of the stairs.

'May I have the honour of dancing with you?'

Dust and ashes; I swallowed.

'There isn't any dancing, they're having a rest too,' said Lucy cheerfully. 'But I expect they'll start soon,' she added kindly. 'I'm going to have an ice,' and she went.

'Would you like an ice?'

'No thank you.'

'Would you like to go on resting here? Hullo, you've got Deb's turquoise heart.'

My fingers clutched the heart, there was an ache in my throat. I nodded.

'Does that mean you *would* like to sit here?'

I shook my head and turned away. He caught my wrist and a large tear fell on his hand.

'I cannot allow you to turn away from me in tears,' he said, and pulled me back.

He looked hard at me for a second and fumbled in his pockets. 'Damn, I never have one.' He smoothed my cheeks with his fingers and then licked them, and seeing my surprise he said seriously, 'I like your tears very much. Now, I'll decide what to do, since you can do nothing but cry.'

We went to the dance room. It was almost empty. The orchestra were sitting waiting their appointed time to start again. Rupert left me and talked to them.

'We are going to dance by ourselves. Now, if you've a handkerchief I think you'd better use it.'

'I haven't.'

'You people who weep never have,' he said.

89

We danced in silence and alone. He was a very much better dancer than I, which afforded me a peculiar delight. People joined us in the end and when it was over Rupert said he was starving and I must come and watch him eat. 'I shall sup off cold chicken and tears.' He piled a plate and said, 'Now we sit on the stairs. Take this, and I'll join you.' He returned with a pink ice. 'For you. Now, are you happy?'

'I don't know.'

'You shouldn't say that. When people ask you whether you're happy, they don't require a serious answer. Unless you are a person who takes happiness very seriously.'

'I do.'

'I'll ask you in five years whether you meant that.'

I spooned my ice in silence.

'But I think you meant yourself,' he added, 'which is a very different thing.'

I wanted to change the subject. 'Doesn't Deb look beautiful tonight?'

'Now, now, none of that,' he said sharply. 'I've given you every chance to recover gracefully from your tears.'

Again I had the naked sensation of having my mind laid bare for his understanding.

'You see,' he said. 'If one is unhappy for a good reason one does not mind exposure so much. But if one suffers because one is young and absurd, silence and secrecy are preferable, and should be supported.'

'Am I young and absurd?'

'You are young and absurd.'

I stared ahead of me, my hands in my lap, finding it easier now that he said that. A wave of gratitude to him loosened my tongue.

'It was silly of me to mind.' He was silent. 'You see I went into the garden and I knew it was you. It was silly of me to mind,' I repeated.

'It was very silly of you.'

'I should have realized that it didn't make any difference.'

'To what?'

'To, to what you said on the walk,' I said weakly.

'I cannot understand how a moment's moonlight dallying in the garden with Deb is connected with anything I said to you on a walk.'

'I thought you didn't care.'

'Care?'

'About me,' I faltered. This was getting worse every moment.

'But I don't.' He sounded thoroughly startled. 'Listen. We had a very nice walk, and I enjoyed your company. You are not only young and absurd, which is enjoyable but commonplace; you are other things. Deb is other things too and she is enjoyable in a different way.' I could see he laughed at his own choice of words. 'But neither of these minor, these very minor events deserve the complications with which you would honour them. You are both charming and I enjoy you both, and perhaps you enjoy me which makes it better still, but we none of us need to make things larger than they are. In fact you must not be a creator of situations.'

'You didn't mean what you said?'

'Of course I did. I was, if I remember, extremely earnest, and dictatorial. But I am a talker. I talk like that all the time. You mustn't let the idea of a young girl going into a garden getting kissed under a moon and instantly becoming engaged to be married get too strong a hold on you. You've been reading the wrong sort of books. And as you cannot prevent Deb being more beautiful than you, you must accept it and not damage yourself by jealousy in so ridiculous a manner. And now if you dare to cry I shall shake you and be so unkind that you're irritated into stopping.'

There was a pause while I struggled with my feelings: shame, astonishment and chagrin, but strangely no resentment towards him. He had, I suppose, an innate understanding for what was bearable and what was not, and the gift of saying brutal things with a mixture of honesty and ease that took the sting out of them.

'You liked being kissed didn't you?'

I nodded.

'Good, that was honest. Some things can be very nice when

91

they happen once. It isn't necessary to ensure that they are repeated indefinitely before one can begin to value them.' I recognized this gentle piece of mocking and felt calmer.

'Do you know how old I am?'

I didn't know.

'I'm twenty-three.'

I had not imagined him as any particular age, but had felt sure he was more. I took a deep breath. 'Remarkable,' I said ironically.

'I always planned to be remarkable at twenty-three,' he answered. 'So you can laugh. Come and do it in front of a lot of people. I am sure they would be surprised.' And we went back to the dance.

People began to go at twelve o'clock and by half past the dance was finished. We were left supping warm milk, and exclaiming contentedly over the success of the evening.

Upstairs, Deb drew me into her room.

'I shall not marry Roland after all. It would be the greatest mistake. I'll tell you about it tomorrow if you like. Sleep well.'

CHAPTER NINE

I don't know why I should have expected life to be different at home, but I did. I had imagined so strongly that it would be, without any clear idea what form the change would take, that for a few days I lived in my imagination, the food tasted new, and even my father's pupils were more interesting. Gradually, the exhilaration of my holidays ebbed away. I had written a stilted little letter to Mrs Lancing, expressing my gratitude, which set the seal on the visit, and finally finished it in my mind. My sister showed no curiosity about my adventures, and to my mother I remained unduly silent. One of my brothers began teaching at a preparatory school in Kent and the other was at a Training College. They were shadows. I knew they thought us very dull and they avoided bringing their friends to the house.

I determined to educate myself, and joined a library. The young lady who attended to my needs overawed me. I had approached her with a tentative inquiry hoping that she would assign me some particular book, and thus relieve me of the responsibility of choosing. But she flung out her arms in different directions and said Travel, Fiction, Biography and Religious with a detached generosity which it was impossible to refuse. I thanked her and walked away. Travel, I thought; I should know about other countries; it would widen and improve my mind. I selected *Ten Weeks in Northern Italy* by May something or other, illustrated by the author. I returned to the assistant and laid it uncertainly on the counter.

'You're allowed three books you know,' she said.

I hastened away. A biography. I searched until my neck ached and the names of the books before me had no separate meaning. In the end I chose the Memoirs by a lady-in-waiting at some obscure Ducal court in Germany. I chose it because it was bound in crimson leather with gold lettering and the colour pleased me. And then in a nervous little rush I seized *Wuthering Heights*, the first book that caught my eye from the rows of fiction. With these, I returned to my assistant, not a little pleased with myself. While she was writing my name and address, I asked her stupidly whether the books were good.

'I don't know,' she said. 'You've serious tastes, haven't you? I should think that would be interesting.' She flicked back the cover of the Memoirs. 'But that other's classic, isn't it?'

'Do you read much?'

'I like a nice novel. But by the time I finish here I'm ready for a good time. I like a bit of fun in the evenings myself.' She was called away by an old gentleman. 'Back in a minute.'

She had a fleeing bouncing figure as though she were set on springs. The wide belt at her waist pulled her in, so that it seemed she must spring out above it. She wore a white blouse with a black ribbon at the neck, and a black ribbon at the back of her head. Her hair was very light brown, almost green, and sprang out round her face in enormous puffs. She had large pale blue eyes set rather close together, and a mouth that reminded me of two little sausages. When she came back to me she smiled, and showed unexpectedly neat teeth with a gold stopping flashing a signal of friendliness. She had great good humour about her. I remember her so well because we became close friends. We did not talk any more that day; she was busy and I was shy, but I was attracted by the ease with which she did her work, and the evident satisfaction she had in her appearance.

Ten Weeks in Northern Italy was written in the form of letters to her father by a very religious woman. The book was adorned with uneasy little pen drawings and filled with watery raptures over the beauties of the landscape and buildings. After two chapters, I wondered how it was possible to see so much in so short a space of time. The Italians were regarded as odd and amusing and I gathered that they were chiefly there to be admired for their picturesque appearance. Were all Italians picturesque, I wondered? Why did they not talk at all? I supposed that the author knew no Italian. I left the book after the third chapter, with a confused impression of mountains, churches and lakes.

My mother made some efforts at that time to introduce me to people of my own age. There was a cousin called Mary who was very short sighted and sang. We never had much to say to each other. I went to tea with her. She enjoyed the luxury of a sitting-room into which we self-consciously shut ourselves and talked about music and my father's works, and her ambitions. I chiefly remember the cloying hygienic smell of the lozenges she sucked, and the persistence with which one stuck to my handkerchief where I had hidden it.

I read the Memoirs to the end, feeling guilty about Northern Italy. They were very dull, and chiefly concerned the sayings of the Duchess and the occasional events which took place in her life; which apart from the birth of an incredible number of children, were very few.

I went back to the library several times and talked to Miss Tate. She recommended me a good novel; about a nun in olden times, she said. I enjoyed it enormously. The nun had a unique capacity for combining a truly noble spirit and the power to get what she wanted. She finally turned out not to be a nun at all, and fainted into the arms of a crusading knight, where she remained during the last two pages of the book. I was much affected by the story but I felt sure that my enjoyment proved of how little use the book was to my education.

I asked Miss Tate to have tea with me in a teashop. I was afraid to ask her home lest it be a repetition of Michael. She talked a great deal about her life at home. Her father was a draper, hence the selection of ribbons she wore on her white blouses; and her brother was in the army. She told me at first that her mother was dead, but later said that she had run off with a conjurer, and nobody knew where she was.

'Wasn't your father terribly unhappy?'

'I expect he was put out at first, but he has his life all right, just the same. There's the shop and he plays bowls. He's president of his club. Mother went off when I was ten so I don't remember her much and auntie came and brought us up, till she and father had a quarrel. She left then, and took all the spoons with her. Father was put out, they were a wedding present from his sister and auntie went right back to Bexhill and never said a word. Still it was nice while it lasted.' She very often finished a story with some gay enigmatic phrase of this kind, throwing back her head and laughing afterwards, her gold stopping glinting and a tear in the corner of her eye. She asked me perfunctorily about myself and seemed impressed that my father wrote music. She condoled with me easily about the dullness of my life and gave me the impression that she thought I was too good for it, that I had a devil up my sleeve which would betray itself to her own admiration. 'Go on now,' she would say, 'I bet you laughed.' And 'If only they knew.' She asked me if I had ever been in love, and I lied and said once but that he had gone away. I remember a sincere pang as I said this for something unknown. I asked her about herself and she bridled and said she liked a bit of fun, no harm in it; and for some extraordinary reason I imagined her putting on her stockings. In spite of her appearance she had a delicate regard for her health and suffered from a series of unaccountable headaches, turns and suffocations which always manifested themselves at some crisis in her life. 'I felt awful,' she would say rolling her eyes. 'I didn't know how I was going to get through. Still you never know till you try.' She would cram fat white hands into gloves, fumble with the buttons, and be getting along, leaving half a cake on her plate. Through her I became acquainted with Charlotte M. Yonge and Dickens.

I wrote twice to Lucy and once to Deb, but received no reply.

It was early spring and my sister was engaged in organizing a stall for a Church Bazaar. The promise of a long but peaceful summer loomed ahead.

One day Miss Tate (whose other name was Agnes) said, 'Why don't you take a job? Or do you like it as you are?'

'No,' I said. 'I'd love to work.'

'*I* like it. Then you know where you are. When to work and when to play. Still they say all work and no play makes Jack a dull boy,' she laughed.

'What could I do?' I stared hopefully at her. She was so gay and sure, I depended on her exuberance.

'Well, you might come here. Or wouldn't you like it?' She was very well aware that we lived in different ways and generally treated me with a kindly concern, never feeling very sure that I could do things for myself. She liked and expected ineptitude.

'Oh yes. Is there a place for me?'

'The other girl left last week. Trouble at home.' She rolled her eyes. 'Oh dear, some people. But Mr Simmons, he's our manager, he's on the look out.'

'Where is he?'

'Better ask your parents first. You don't want trouble.'

'They won't mind,' I said defiantly.

She eyed me protectively.

'You ask first. Don't want any nastiness, not with summer coming on.'

'Summer?'

'My father stops me going out in the evening if he's put out.'

'I don't think mine would do that.'

'You haven't gone against them,' she said wisely. 'You talk it over. It's nine to six, three-quarters of an hour for lunch. Saturday afternoon off. Two pounds a week. I'd show you round. You'd soon pick it up, with an education.'

Two pounds! An enormous amount of money.

'What a lot.'

'Don't make a mistake. Depends how far you have to make it go. You tell me tomorrow. Bye-bye.'

I went home with a beating heart. As soon as I was out of the shop I realized the wisdom of her remarks about my family. It would be terrible to have started and be ignominiously hauled back. Two pounds. I would even be able to buy flowers. But supposing my father refused to allow me. I wondered how Agnes spent her money. Perhaps she had to buy her clothes with it. Well I could pay for my clothes and surely my parents would be pleased. They could not object to my earning some part of my living. We were desperately short of money. My mother had darned my stockings herself, when I was out, to make up for not buying me new ones; and when I had thanked her she had flushed and promised to afford them in a month. Perhaps if I earned enough money we could even paint the house bright shiny cream like the others. I must choose a moment when my sister was not there. We sat through tea and cleared it away. My father went to his studio. My sister sat firmly in the room embroidering a boot bag. I had decided to approach my mother alone. The opportunity did not come, and I grew more and more nervous and despairing of success.

My sister went to bed very early after supper: I think she read in her bedroom. But fate persisted against me and my father for once did not go to his studio, but elected to play patience with me. For twenty minutes we played; I growing more and more distrait and stupid. Finally I dropped a whole pack of cards on the floor.

'What is the matter with you?' asked my father. I knelt, fumbling and groping to pick them up, and then I knew I must have courage to tell them.

'I should like to start ...' My voice was cracked and squeaky. I began again with a deep breath. 'I have been thinking that perhaps it would be a good thing if I had a job, work of some kind.' There was a short silence. They looked at me expectantly.

'Well,' I said. I remember sketching a feeble little gesture with my hands as I waited for their reply.

'And what work would you consider taking up?' My father was at his dryest and most sarcastic. I hated him then.

'Of course I know that I cannot do anything. I haven't been taught.' I was speaking to my mother. The irony of placating her with my uselessness escaped me at the time. 'But I thought there are things I could do, learn to do, that aren't very difficult, if you had no objection to my trying.'

'You have plenty to do at home,' said my father.

'No,' I said. 'I haven't.' The firmness of my voice surprised us all. 'There is a vacancy in a library near here. I thought I might apply for it. Two pounds a week. The hours are from nine until six with three-quarters of an hour off for lunch, and half a day on Saturday.'

'How did you find all that out?'

'Somebody told me.'

'Have you been making friends with people who work there?'

'One of them.' I stared at my father defiantly. 'I should like it very much. I could earn enough money to buy my clothes.' My mother winced. 'Or to buy anything we wanted,' I added ashamed that I had hurt her.

My father laughed. 'My dear little girl, it's out of the question. Poor though we are, I could not think of you slaving in a shop in order to relieve us.'

'It wouldn't be slaving. I should love it. Oh please let me go. I'm tired of doing nothing. I'm tired of trying to fill up my life with little events, and remaining so useless. I should like to earn money and feel that I could do a proper job like other people.'

'That is all very well, but I'm afraid that the job cannot be in a library.'

'Why not? What is the difference between working there, and anywhere else?'

'There is a difference,' he reiterated stubbornly. 'But perhaps we might find other work for you. Why do you not help your sister with her stall?'

'Oh *that*. That's not what I mean. It is done for fun. For charity. In a few weeks it would be over. I want a real job that would go on, where I could earn money.'

'I'm afraid I cannot allow you to work in a library.' He appealed to my mother. 'Don't you agree?'

'I think it would probably be a mistake.'

'You see, dear,' he went on awkwardly to me, 'the girls who work there are different from you. They would resent your coming there, they would feel that you did not need the money and they would naturally resent it. It would not be fair.'

99

'But we do need it.' I was terrified of crying and the fear made me reckless and cruel. 'We do need money. Our house is never painted. We never have new curtains or enough clothes. We're always having to consider before we buy things. We only have one servant and the house is too big for her to keep it clean. We don't have holidays unless someone asks us to stay. Tom and Hubert never bring their friends back here because it's so dull and they can have better times somewhere else. We used to have parties with candles on the table and fruit in a big dish. And concerts when people came. Soon no one will ask us to stay because they'll have forgotten we exist. I'm getting older; I want to know things and see more people. This is something for me, not you, you needn't think about it.'

'You are overwrought. Go to bed now and we'll talk about it in the morning.'

'You won't, you won't.' My voice was shaking and I was crying. 'You'll forget, on purpose. Just because you've got some silly class prejudice you'll try to stop me going.'

'You are being very thoughtless and unkind. We have done the best we can for you, and you are making the worst of it. I think staying with your rich friends in the country has had a very bad effect on you.'

'I am sure we could find a nice place where you could work,' said my mother, and I saw how she was suffering from the situation and how desperately she wanted it to stop before I could say more things that would hurt her and enrage my father.

I went to my room without a word, and sitting on my bed I heard the low hum of my parents' voices below, rising and falling for a good two hours. I undressed. I was still and cold and I knew that I had lost. The thought of complete rebellion never entered my head.

My mother came into my room that night, and bent over me.

'Are you all right, dear?'

'Yes.'

'Father was upset. He is very tired these days.'

I reached out my arms and hugged her, so fiercely that she was almost frightened although a little pleased.

'I didn't mean it about the clothes. I just said it because I wanted to go so much.'

The chance had slipped from my fingers on to the floor finally into the past. She sat on the edge of my bed and promised that she would find me something to do, stroking my hair nervously all the while. She said that she understood how I felt, that she had been like that, and one of those unaccountable tales came out that one's parents sometimes tell one, utterly inconsistent with the idea one has of them and fascinating for that very reason. I loved her very much and she lulled me into acquiescence through the content I had in that feeling. But I went to sleep pondering on the doctrine of 'You shall not do what you like,' wondering how many more people lived under its grey sinuous rule.

CHAPTER TEN

The next morning my father treated me as though the night before had never happened; and I was grateful to him.

I also had leisure to reflect that he was after all not deliberately trying to thwart me, that he was obeying a code laid down by generations; and in a flash of understanding I realized how poverty must strengthen it.

Agnes's sympathy fell sweetly on my ears when we had lunch together. She never stored things up as I did, but felt most thoroughly and strongly any feeling she had until it was finished, and had no false pride about admitting the change of her mood. 'Oh, I felt like that yesterday, but least said soonest mended,' she would say and I profited by the buoyancy of her nature.

A week later, I started taking two children out for walks in Kensington Gardens every afternoon. They lived in a large crimson house in our road, and were part of a big family. My mother had met them, in the midst of various charitable functions. The two mothers arranged the walks. I went to see the other mother, who said that she must pay me for the time and trouble. I became proud and stupid and refused the offer saying that I liked walks and it was no trouble. I think I had a subconscious desire to make the job of my parents' choosing unsatisfactory to myself, to render it amateur and ladylike and so nurse a grievance.

'Nonsense, my dear,' she said. 'I shall have to pay a governess. You can talk French to them if it makes you feel any better about it.' I thought of the endless limitations of my French and we both laughed. It was finally arranged at the rate of two shillings an afternoon. The children were a boy and a girl aged seven and five. Their names I remember were William and Anne. I grew fond of them and nervously proud of my responsibility. Of course it was boring at times:

William would become without warning exceedingly unmanageable, throw stones at the ducks and put his boots in the water, or throw them at me if I attempted to pull him away from the edge. Anne was a good little thing, content to walk sedately telling me the most astonishing lies.

'Are you tired?' I asked her one day.

'Not much. But I walk seven miles you know every morning.' She also said she had hot strawberries for tea every day. I believed her in the beginning; the little pink face with the candid blue eyes, and the quiet convincing calm of her manner made her difficult to disbelieve: until one day when she announced that Nanny slept with a big axe in her bed to chop off their heads if they were naughty; and that some being called Mr Sykes rode her tricycle round the nursery at night.

'That cannot be true,' I implored William aghast.

'Oh no. She just says that.'

'It is quite well true.' She shrugged her minute shoulders and walked on, quelling any moral reasoning upon which I might have embarked.

On wet days I played with them in their schoolroom. The Victorian house had large rooms with high ceilings, and dark flamboyant wallpapers, except in the children's quarters, which were in pale green paint. The schoolroom had 'Scenes from History' pictures stuck in a frieze on the walls and glazed. I remember officers, standing almost bolt upright on their horses (which were invariably rearing), as they urged on their men to relieve some fort or other; the picture being decorated with little orange sparks surrounded by puffs of smoke which represented the shells bursting. There were the Crusaders; the Battle of Bosworth; the Battle of Hastings, with Harold staggering, an arrow exactly in the middle of his eye; the signing of Magna Charta; Canute in an enormous chair with the waves rippling delicately over his big pointed feet; Agincourt; Henry VIII surrounded most improbably by all his wives at once; Queen Elizabeth prancing over Raleigh's cloak; Charles II hiding in an oak tree in bright sunlight; Nelson dying, ghastly pale by the light of a flickering lantern – I have forgotten the rest, but I was fascinated at the time. The children, of course, had grown up with them, and never looked at, or even saw them. The elder children were at schools, but there was a baby in long white lace clothes, and a child of three, both in charge of a Nanny. The family was well-to-do; the father having managed some industry in the north, and settled in London when his fortune was made. They had wonderful teas, I remember.

On Sundays the children walked with their parents, and I was free. I met them once on a Sunday and was for some reason incredibly embarrassed; they seemed like different people although they were perfectly friendly.

I planned to give my mother a length of silk for a dress, as thick and heavy as it was possible to buy. I knew that I could not bear to buy clothes for myself after my cruel outburst on the lack of them. After one visit to the shop I realized that it would be another month before I had the necessary sum.

My family never inquired about Agnes Tate, and as I did not bring her home the friendship prospered on the few hours allotted to it. (Agnes had only her lunch hour to spare.) I had met at the library a young man with pale hair and a lisp. I had not liked him, his voice and his choice of words being too intellectually effusive for my young Spartan mind, but he had been kind about books, selecting, encouraging and asking my opinion, in a manner which I later realized could only be described as woman to woman.

Agnes had laughed at me with careless admiration. We had to be very careful not to talk too much while she was working, as it displeased Mr Simmons, who would sidle towards us like a crab, scratching his right ear where he kept his pencil.

And then something happened in the middle of this calm. We were sitting in the park, Agnes and I, eating cherries.

'Why don't you come out on the spree one night?' she said. 'With you?'

'With me and some friends. Unless you like to bring anyone yourself.'

I knew she meant a man and there was no one to take.

'I'd love to,' I said guardedly. 'Where would we go?'

'Might go to a show and have a bit of supper. Or walk in the park. You leave that to me.'

I was rather frightened. 'I haven't anyone to bring.'

'Don't you have any friends?'

'They're in the country, except you.'

'Oh *me*. I meant men friends. Funny idea keeping them so far away. Tell you what. I'll ask my friend to bring a friend.'

'I don't need one. I could go with you.'

'Go on, you are awful. Wouldn't my friend be pleased! He works in a big place. He'll find someone.'

'What about my family?'

'Tell them you're going to a concert. Something fancy.' She imitated someone playing the violin. 'That'll fetch them. They won't know.' A sense of adventure seized me.

'I'll tell them I'm going out with a friend I met in the country.'

'That's it,' she said and looked at my watch. 'Oo, I must be getting back. I'll let you know.'

Two days later she said it was all right for Thursday night, if that suited me. We were to meet in the Gardens at seven o'clock under Queen Victoria's statue. 'Arthur is bringing a friend,' she said. 'They work together. I said you wanted a bit of fun and didn't get out much. His friend's older than Arthur, he knows his way about.'

I was filled with vague misgivings.

'What'll you wear?'

'I don't know. What shall you wear?'

'I'll wear a skirt and my new piqué. And I shall take a coat. I trimmed my straw last week and father'll lend me some gloves. Don't dress too fine,' she added, rather anxiously.

'I haven't got anything fine. Would a cotton frock be all right?'

'What's it like?'

'Pale green. Trimmed with white. I haven't a hat though.'

'I'll lend you one. I'll bring it tomorrow. You'll have to put something on it.'

'Oh Agnes, you *are* kind.'

'You'll have me embarrassed next. You'd better get a green ribbon to match. It's a dove straw.'

'What are we going to do?'

'Arthur doesn't know yet. He's asking his friend. It's much better to let the men plan. After all, they pay.' The financial aspect had not occurred to me.

'Will it cost very much?' I faltered. Surely it could not be right to let a completely unknown man pay for my supper.

'They can manage. After all they choose to do it. They get something out of it too. Arthur's friend hasn't got a friend and he wants to meet you. I told Arthur what you were like.'

What had she said I wondered.

'Is Arthur in love with you?'

'Goodness me what a leading question,' she giggled. 'We've passed an evening in the park from time to time.'

Passed an evening in the park. And we were meeting in the park. Still Agnes would be there. It must be all right really. I went home planning what to tell my parents.

She gave me the hat next day, and I spent an anxious half hour choosing ribbon. Wide green petersham, and, as an afterthought, a strip of artificial daisies. I showed them to Agnes, who approved.

'Tell you what. I'll trim it for you. I like doing it.'

I was filled with gratitude.

It was Tuesday evening. I told my mother that a girl I had met at the Lancings' had asked me to a concert and supper.

'Did she write to you?'

'No, I met her, quite by chance in the street.'

My mother was appeased and I was delighted with my easy success.

Wednesday passed in a fever of anticipation. Agnes brought me the hat and told me that Arthur's friend was called Mr Harris, Edward Harris, and that we were going to a musical. I had no idea what a musical was, but did not dare display my further ignorance.

'Then we'll have supper,' she said. 'Arthur says they're going to do it in style.'

On Thursday I took the children up to Queen Victoria's statue and sat beneath it, hardly able to believe that in a few hours' time I should be there under such different circumstances. The day was very fine and hot with a threat of thunder. Suppose it should rain. The afternoon crept by loaded with doubts and fears. I took the children back, and was unusually helpful to my mother in order to pass the time.

'Where is your friend staying?' she said suddenly.

'I am meeting her in the park.'

'If you do not know where she lives, you may need a cab home. Have you money?'

'No – yes.'

'Which do you mean?'

'I have money.' My mother said nothing, but when I went to my room, I found three shillings on the dressing-table. I brushed my hair and wished that I could wear my pink frock. There was a little sick feeling of excitement, and I found it impossible to stop shivering as I stared at the frock, my shoes, a handkerchief and the hat. I must conceal the hat; put it on when I was away from the house. My mother would be sure to ask where I had bought it, and then when it disappeared mysteriously after this evening, she would want some explanation. It was oppressively hot. I had no face powder. I tried some talc in the bathroom but it turned me a greenish white, and meant washing my face again.

At a quarter to seven I slipped out of the house, calling good-bye to my mother. Her voice, shouting, 'Don't be late', floated away from me. At the corner, I put on my hat and fastened it by two immense hatpins with white heads. Then lifting my skirts I ran up Victoria Road, until the heat and my age reminded me to stop. It would be better to let the others arrive first. Ten to seven ... I had plenty of time. I walked along, alternately feeling the back of my hair, tucking in any stray wisps, and looking down at my frock. An old man who was airing his dog, watched me anxiously. I felt his eyes on the back of my head after I had passed, and looked round. He was standing facing me. I should never have turned back. When he saw me he stared at the pavement, grunted and continued his walk. I hastened up the Broad Walk, emptier than in the day time, but sprinkled with couples, slowly pacing, their faces turned to each other. There was a tall ragged boy pulling a cart on iron wheels. He looked at me and grinned. 'Don't be late for 'im. 'E mightn't wite.' I flushed angrily. Horrid little boy.

I arrived at the statue at two minutes to seven. There was no one there: I was early after all. I sat down and smoothed my gloves, beset by anxiety. Suppose Agnes had been laughing at me and had never intended to come.

Seven o'clock struck. There was one yacht becalmed on the pond. People were beginning to drift towards the entrance of the park. Agnes was too good-natured to deceive me so cruelly. Would they come from the right or the left? I must not look too eagerly for them. Two minutes past seven. Time slept. I watched the sky, a golden blue, the white-edged clouds scalloped like lace, the great trees heavy with green, the biscuit-coloured paths stretching in every direction and accentuated by the low black railings over which William loved to jump, the coarse green grass worn bare in patches, the line of pink may trees planted each side of my bench and filling the air with a rich common sweetness . . .

'Hullo,' said Agnes.

I looked up. She was standing before me, a young man on either arm. She introduced us. 'You were day-dreaming,' she said. 'Make room for us.'

They sat down, Arthur one side and Edward on the other. 'We're going to Gilbert and Sullivan. *The Mikado*. You know.'

'How lovely.'

The two young men seemed tongue-tied, Arthur blushing whenever Agnes looked at him and Edward staring straight in front of him with his arms folded. Edward was obviously older than the others, and was possessed of a fine black moustache and grey eyes which caught mine from time to time. Once he took out a purple silk handkerchief with which he blew his nose, whereupon Agnes jumped and said he gave her such a fright. We laughed and the situation settled itself. Agnes talked to Arthur and I was left to Edward. We both made strenuous efforts, but we were desperately shy. He, I think seeing my awkwardness, replied to my questions with patronizing little bursts to prove that it was more than his own. I asked him about his job and whether he liked it, and he said it 'was all right for the time being'. He asked me whether I had ever seen *The Mikado*, and was pleased when I said no; assured me that it was quite amusing, and said that he knew a nice little place for supper afterwards.

Agnes and Arthur giggled and chattered and provided an enviable contrast to our stilted efforts.

'Well, we ought to be going,' said Arthur. He was a fair spry man, very young, with a fresh complexion. We started walking. Agnes told them how she and I had met, and we all laughed and said how lucky it was. Edward offered me his arm in a friendly manner and I felt gratified that everything was going so well.

We stopped an omnibus and went on top, as the evening continued so finely in our favour. It was cool and refreshing and we admired the Albert Memorial. Edward, becoming more expansive, told me about Kew Gardens and Richmond, and the fair on Hampstead Heath. Knightsbridge was alive with hansom cabs like upright beetles, trotting towards Piccadilly.

'I like to see a bit of life,' said Agnes, and we all agreed with her. Here I was, going to an opera. I had always been promised a Gilbert and Sullivan but the promise had never been fulfilled and I had no conception of what form the entertainment would take.

We had jostled off the omnibus, nearly too late, and were now walking four abreast. Arthur bought a rose from an old flower seller; and Edward, after a moment's hesitation, selected a little bunch of violets and presented them to me. They were soft and cool and smelt faintly of purple mist. From that moment I was really happy. I had never been given flowers, and the violets were perfect to me. I turned on Edward, stammering with gratitude, and embarrassed the poor man considerably, although the others laughed with pleasure to see me so easily pleased. Edward took my arm rather more firmly and said it was nothing, nothing at all, and they suited me. 'You're rather like a violet yourself, I should say.' He then choked so badly that he had to use the purple handkerchief. We arrived at the theatre with time to spare and watched the people pouring into the building. Edward said that you could tell where they would sit by their clothes. Agnes pointed out real lace and well cut gowns with professional discernment. The carriages drove to the entrance; a footman alighted and let down the steps; the gentlemen, in black and white, sprang out to assist the ladies, who stepped down, settled themselves on the pavement like birds, and walked proudly in talking and laughing.

'I should love to go in a carriage like that,' said Agnes to me. I did not tell her that I had, and that sitting with one's back to the horse made one feel sick, but enjoyed the illusion and freedom of the spectacle, leaning on Edward's arm.

We were seated in the pit. 'Lovely seats,' Agnes whispered excitedly to me as we settled ourselves and broke the seals on the two programmes. Edward leaned over me to share mine. Our shoulders pressed together. Once he looked at me, I smiled, he went on looking, and I felt that he admired me, thought I was pretty. I smiled again recklessly disarming. He leaned over the violets pinned on my frock. 'Do they smell?' I lowered the programme into my lap. He sniffed and murmured something softly that I did not hear. The lights went down and the orchestra struck up with the overture.

The curtain went up noiselessly and at a tantalizing speed and I heard myself gasp with excitement and delight. Edward covered my hand with his own, large and hard, and irresistibly comforting.

We took the air in the interval. It was dusky, and we walked in couples, up and down outside the theatre, saying very little. My head was full of tunes, glorious racy tunes, that came to the expected and desired ending, with pleasing and reassuring certainty. The acting was wonderful. Several times a song had been sung again which made me feel that I had seen the whole act twice.

Agnes and I repaired to a cloak-room to preen. It was crowded and presided over by an old woman who exulted in the overcrowdedness with a blowsy delight. 'They must think we're fairies,' I heard Agnes say, and we giggled. She lent me some face powder and I returned rejuvenated with gritty eyelashes.

It was unbearable to find the opera at an end, the singers standing in a line, bowing, and giving one a final chance to take an agonized farewell of their charms.

We reeled into the street, discussing what we had liked best, and Edward leading the way to our supper place. Arthur hummed one of the tunes and Agnes supplied the words. 'For he's going to marry Yum-Yum, Yum-Yum.' We marched in time.

I had not left the theatre, or the scene, the black-haired women with fluttering hands, the large fat man who followed the Mikado himself, the exotic and improbable colour which had pervaded the whole evening – I was in a dream, with only Edward's presence between me and reality. He did not talk, and I assumed that his mood was like mine; that our consciousness of each other was only a recognition of our mutual feeling. I wanted to walk for ever in silence, on his arm. We stopped. I had never been in a public house in my life. Edward pushed open the swing door marked 'Saloon Bar', and we entered. It was full of people. Edward spoke to the man behind the counter, who nodded, raised the flap, and ushered us to the back of the room, through a pair of deep red curtains, into a passage, and finally into a much smaller room, with a table and a large window looking on to the street. 'They know me here,' said Edward, and I think we were all impressed. We sat down. The window had coarse net curtains which showed the dark shapes of people passing in the street. The ceiling was encrusted with a repeated pattern of fruit and flowers and painted pale green. I sat with my back to a brown marble fireplace, obviously not used as there was a screen of brown paper pasted over the grate. Green paint glistened half-way up the walls, and above it extended red wallpaper with a frieze of convolvulus and pears round the top. We sat at the table, which was spread with a newly ironed cloth spotted with a few blurred and yellow stains.

'And now,' said Arthur. 'Bring on the bubbly.'

'Oo,' said Agnes. 'You do go on.'

What was bubbly? I asked. They shrieked with laughter, tilting back their chairs. It made the evening that I did not know.

A waiter came, a small man, fatherly but obsequious. He carried the menu, a sheet of paper on which was written the choice of food in a large round hand; he could not have written it himself with those gnarled stubby fingers. Edward studied it very grandly, reading aloud the items. Steak. Fried plaice. He hurried over the half portion of lobster saying it was the wrong month, with a certain amount of relief. Mixed grill. Saddle of mutton. Cold beef.

'I'd like a steak,' said Agnes. 'I need nourishing.' I agreed to a steak. I was not hungry and did not care what I ate. 'Four steaks,' repeated the waiter scribbling on his pad. Then cocking his head on one side he remained motionless while the vegetables were discussed. He had waxed whiskers; the shadow of them on the wall was enormous, the end of one point stabbing a pear on the frieze. Agnes ordered a stout with her food. Edward turned inquiringly to me. After my ignorance about the champagne I could hardly ask for lemonade; I tried to appear deep in thought. 'Have a stout?' suggested Edward and I knew he was not deceived. 'That's the ticket,' cried Arthur. The waiter scudded away and we could relax. There was a little silence while we smiled vaguely at each other, savouring the evening.

'Good show that,' said Arthur.

'Wonderful,' I said. It had already slipped into the past. I felt something pressing my foot under the table. Edward caught my eye and smiled, a warm secretive smile. We were both back in the dark, holding hands, alone together in some magic way, despite the crowds of people round us. A little tremor ran through me.

'Cold?' said Edward. His voice was elaborately casual. I shook my head.

The waiter returned with four brimming glasses on a tray. He dusted the table and the liquid swayed in the glasses but did not spill. Three very dark, the colour of a black kitten in the sun, and one brown for Edward. He set them before us, and murmuring confidentially to Edward that the steaks wouldn't be long, he disappeared. There was a thin layer of rich froth on top of my glass. It looked delicious.

'Here's to all of us,' said Arthur, and raised his glass.

I took a gulp and swallowed it quickly. It was horrible.

'All right?' asked Edward.

'Lovely.' How could anyone like it? How would I even finish it? I determined to watch Agnes and drink when she drank.

'I knew you'd like it,' Edward said complacently.

'What would you like most in the world?' asked Agnes dreamily, a moment later gazing into her glass.

'A motor car,' said Arthur promptly. 'With you in it. Driving to Brighton with you.' She flushed and he took her hand.

'Clerks'll never have motor cars,' said Edward scornfully. 'Be lucky to drive in a cab.'

'Everyone'll have motor cars, you mark my words.'

'Only the rich,' said Edward gloomily. Agnes drank again and I raised my glass. There was so much of it.

'Perhaps I won't always be a clerk.'

'Perhaps there'll be an earthquake and we'll all have different jobs.'

'Cheer up, Mr Harris,' cried Agnes. 'This is a party, see.'

'Call me Edward,' he said, and was friendly again.

'Well go on, what would you like?'

'Like?'

'Most in the world.'

'Most in the world,' he repeated slowly looking at me. I buried my face in my glass again. 'I dunno. I'd like to travel, see things, see if everyone has the same social system where a quarter of the population are a bit of all right, and the other three-quarters don't have time to want anything. I'd like to know if it's reading does the trick; or I'd like to know if it's work makes people happy, or if it stops them thinking anything, or knowing what they want. I'd like to find out how many people do what they like; or if they just think it's better to do what they don't like. Smoothes their conscience or something. Things like that.'

'Gloomy aren't you?' said Agnes. 'There's ever such a lot of fun if you take it.'

'I'd like a farm as well.'

'That's better,' said Arthur approvingly. 'She meant what would you like to *have*.'

'Who's she? The cat's mother?' We all laughed. Only a quarter of my glass gone.

'I should like a big house in town and one in the country,' said Agnes. 'And a carriage, and black horses, and lots of gentlemen sending me flowers. And a lot of clothes the latest fashion, from Paris. And a little dog, you know a tiny one that shivers, and furs, and a diamond bracelet, and everyone taking their hats off to me, and a lady's maid, French, and I'd send her to the library, for novels, and boxes of chocolates with pink ribbons, and people taking me out to shows every night, and dancing.' She set down her glass, flushed with excitement. 'I'd marry a foreign count in the end, who'd kiss my hand.'

'Crikey,' said Arthur. He looked unhappy. She looked at him affectionately.

'Go on,' she said. 'That's only what I *want*.'

The waiter brought our steaks, pink and golden with dark edges. There was a little watercress on the top of each, and a rich pile of fried chips on each plate. There were a dish of fresh young beans and two bottles of sauce.

'Everything all right, sir?'

Edward said it was, and the waiter ran away beaming.

'What do *you* want?' said Edward. I had been so fascinated by the others that I had not thought.

'I don't know,' I said foolishly.

'Come now,' they cried, 'that's dull, think a bit, you must want something.'

'Or have you got everything?' said Edward keenly.

'Oh no.' I had not by any means got everything. I wanted so much without knowing precisely what it was. 'Well, I'd like to write a book,' I was startled to hear myself say.

'She's always reading,' Agnes said to the others, showing me off.

They seemed so impressed that I decided to let it stand although I was very much afraid they would ask me what I had written.

'I want to find out about people; feelings.' None of the words felt quite right. 'Living,' I said. 'About living. I would like to be famous. At least I would like to be really well known by someone.' That was absurd. 'I would like to be older and well – wiser I suppose. I don't want things ever to be the same, at least nothing I know. If I found the right things I'd want them for ever. Really I want to be older and know things. Be absolutely certain of them. Now, I don't know much, and I try to make it fit for everything and of course it doesn't. I'd like to be wise enough for anyone's size of mind.' I looked at them, hopelessly incoherent.

'Your steak's getting cold,' said Edward kindly.

'Anyway you want to write a book,' said Agnes.

Heavens, she had finished her stout. I took a deep breath and gulped mine down until the glass was empty except for a drift of bubbles slipping down the inside. I felt hot and light-headed and the stuff didn't taste so bad. We ate our meal, Agnes telling stories of the people who came to change their books.

When he saw that I did not eat much, Edward took my knife and fork and insisted on cutting my meat. I flirted with him, and felt Agnes's approval. She had taken her rose off her dress. The bud was limp, with one petal curled back. She put it in water. 'Looks mopey, poor thing,' she said. 'I love flowers.' Her large blue eyes devoured it hungrily.

I could not finish my plateful but the others did not mind,

seemed rather to admire it as an evidence of my dainty appetite.

We had cold apple tart; and finally little glasses of port, four brilliant red jewels winking on our empty table. Edward smoked a pipe. Did I mind? Mind! I was fascinated. He puffed away, content and well fed. We all agreed that it was a nice little place.

'I wonder what it would be like to be an actress.'

'Wonderful,' I said. The port slipped down my throat like burning balm. It was very sweet and sticky and much nicer than stout. Edward offered me another and I accepted.

'Aren't you a one!' said Agnes admiringly. 'I can't drink any more. I'll have a red nose.' She squinted down it.

'I shouldn't like you to be an actress,' said Arthur firmly.

'Why not?'

'I just shouldn't like it.'

'That settles it,' she said cheerfully. 'I'll have to turn down the offers. Lots of money in it though, I should think.'

'Awful life,' said Edward gloomily, and we all felt glad we were not on the stage.

What a lot Edward knew. I felt sleepy, and all their voices seemed to come startlingly separate out of nothing. They talked and I drank my second port in silence. I did not want it when it came, but I could not be rude when I had asked for it. She got what she asked for, I remembered people saying, and this was what she asked for. Not so terrible as they had made it sound. A wreath of convolvulus and pears swayed suddenly down to hit the top of Agnes's head. My own head was too heavy. 'For he's going to marry Yum-Yum, Yum-Yum,' crawled through my head. Agnes and Arthur were swaying slowly in time to the words. 'She's nearly asleep,' I heard Agnes say, and with a start I realized that my head was on Edward's shoulder and his arm round my waist. I sat up, blinking the blur of lights out of my eyes. 'I'm so sorry.' How awful. What would he think?

'We'll be going upstairs. It's time to go now,' said Agnes.

Edward stood up to let me out and I got carefully to my feet, holding the table as I squeezed past. The floor was a long way down and every time I stepped it was like going downstairs. Agnes took my arm and led the way to a tiny cloak-room.

'How awful of me to go to sleep.'

'It was the port,' she said. 'We're going to see if we can get a cab.'

'What about the bill?' I was very pleased with myself for remembering the bill.

'They're paying it now. Like some powder?' I took it. 'I should wash your face first,' she advised. She had innate tact. She must have known how the cold water would clear my head and revive me but she said nothing. I dried my face and looked in the glass. Agnes was combing her hair over the puffs.

'Been a lovely evening, hasn't it?'

'Lovely,' I said, too emphatically. 'Very nice,' I repeated more guardedly.

'There, now you'll be all right.' She had put on her hat. Where was mine?

'Edward's got it,' she said. 'The pins stuck in his neck.'

We joined the others. They had our coats on their arms and Edward helped me into mine. 'You mustn't get cold.'

'Mind my violets.'

'They'll be all right.' He squeezed my arm.

We went out through a side door into the grey airless street. I stumbled a little until I was used to the light. My head was aching and I could not loosen my tightly arranged hair because Agnes held my other arm. We found a cab and got in. 'Where to?' said the driver. 'Victoria Road,' said Agnes. She knew I lived there. 'We'd better drop you on the corner,' she said. I nodded forgetting that in the dark she could not see. 'All right?'

'Yes,' I said. It was very stuffy and smelt of damp leather and mildew. Arthur lowered the windows. We were off.

'Aren't we nobs, going home in a cab,' said Agnes. 'Laugh at the buses we can.' Dimly I understood that the cab was unusual and for my benefit.

'It's very kind of you,' I murmured.

Edward bent down. 'What was that?'

'Kind of you,' I murmured again. Agnes and Arthur were very quiet. I said something about how quiet they were, and there was a little suppressed giggle from Agnes and some movement in the dark.

'Put your head on my shoulder again,' said Edward. 'I like it.'

How kind he was. My hat was in his lap. I saw the straw gleaming like a neat round nest in a fairy tale. I leaned against him. He put his arm round my shoulders and clasped my wrist. His hand was very hot. We jolted on in silence while I wished that someone would speak, but felt too tired and weak to begin. I sighed, and slowly his hand edged up to the back of my neck, his face loomed over me for a second, so that I saw his eyes in the grey blur, and then his mouth was on mine; his moustache soft and dry in contrast. There was a feeling of a very long time or perhaps none at all: still he was kissing me, with warmth and deliberation, and I lay in his arms unresisting, half stirred. He was not a person to me any more, he was a kiss, the part of myself that I wanted to feel alive. He stirred over me and the hat slipped to the floor with a papery rustle. My neck was aching and I pressed against his hand until I was supported by the corner of the cab. He let me go and then gathered me into his arms again more fiercely, his hands hard on my bones through the thin dress. My arms being limp at my sides, he took them and pressed them round his neck. There was a little chuckle in the dark from Agnes, some whispered protest, and still Edward's mouth urgent, harsh and warm. I was stifled, could not breathe, almost ceased to exist. I was no longer stirred but endured him with a breathless acquiescence with no thought or hope or desire for an end. The jolting slowed into a walk.

'I think we're nearly there,' said Agnes, and her voice sounded small, crushed and unreal.

Edward released me, bent down, picked up my hat, and placed it on my lap. The stopping, the practical neatness of his gesture bred in me a sudden panic, a horror of him and myself, and I had only one thought, to get out of the cab, away from him, from all of them, into the air with no part of my body touching anything but only my feet on the hard familiar pavement. I must have leaned forward groping for the door, for Edward put his hand on my arm and drew me back.

'Don't be in such a hurry. We've not stopped yet.'

I bent my head stiffly over the straw hat in my lap. I felt very sick. I remember the clop of the horse's feet running down slowly like a clock, and the jolt when we finally pulled up into silence. Edward got out, and I followed, my legs shaking so that I could hardly stand.

'Aren't you going to say good night to *us*?' said Agnes with a plaintive emphasis that made the others laugh.

'Good night,' I said, 'and thank you very much. I've enjoyed it most awfully.'

'So have I,' said Edward softly. He was standing close to me.

'Good night,' I said. I could not look at him.

'Say good night to me,' his voice demanded softly. I backed away. 'Why you little witch!'

'Please,' I said. 'I can't.' His arms were round me again and I lifted my face in an agony of surrender and dislike. He let me go abruptly and turned to the cab.

'Hammersmith,' he said, and there was a hurt significance in his voice.

'Thank you for bringing me home,' I called weakly as he was getting back into the cab.

He turned and I felt that he smiled. 'It was nothing. I shall see you again.' And they drove off.

I stood and watched them out of sight, and then hearing, hardly able to realize the relief of being alone. A dry hot breeze ruffled my face; stirred the great trees in the park opposite me and reminded me where I was. A quarter past the hour struck from some distant church clock. The houses round me were dark. It must be very late. I turned shakily and walked back to my home, where a single light gleamed. They were waiting up for me. The memory of my deception and the mood in which I had left the house a few hours before flooded back. I must not think of what had happened. I must get safely to my room. I tapped on the front door and a minute later my sister opened it, with a candle in her hand. She stood aside for me to come in.

'It's after twelve.' Her wrapper fell about her like the folded wings of a moth. 'Where have you been? I was listening and I didn't hear a cab.'

'They dropped me on the corner,' I said, very weary, and started to climb the stairs. I heard her bolt the door and follow me almost noiseless on her bare feet.

'They? Who?' she whispered. We were passing my parents' room.

'I'll tell you about it tomorrow,' I said. She seemed satisfied and pausing at the door of her room she kissed my cheek.

'How hot your face is,' she observed. 'Good night.'

'Good night.'

There was another candle burning on the low table by her bed, before a statue. Goodness, Purity, I thought and stumbled into my room.

I lighted a candle and automatically started to undress. Now I was alone all the nausea and panic crept back. I lived again those minutes lying in the dark; forced to remember every sensation, up to the moment when my sister had finally touched my burning face with her lips. I wrenched off the frock which his hands had crushed. It lay on the floor and I could not bear to touch it again. My mouth was bruised and dry. I remembered the uneasy fluttering and burning of my whole body when I had wanted him to go on kissing me; how I had not cared what he did; how I had lain passive under his mouth and hands, only half conscious of a slow uncertain crescendo within myself. He had kissed me and I had accepted it, and even liked it. In the mirror over my washstand I stared at my face. It was flushed with hectic ringed eyes. My mouth looked rough and pinched.

Suddenly I bathed my face; plunging my arms up to the elbows in the cold water jug, washing Edward from my body, rubbing him off my mouth until it ached. Agnes: had that happened to her? 'I like a bit of fun.' Of course it had. But it was different for Agnes. Arthur was her friend. To me Edward had been a complete stranger. Though he was the first man who had tried to make love to me, I had accepted it with no thought of propriety or his feelings. In bed that night, I still rubbed my mouth again and again with the corner of the sheet.

CHAPTER ELEVEN

The next day I faced the questions and comments of my mother and sister. I had insane gusts of wanting to tell them, or one of them; in order to be scolded and reassured. But most of the time I realized that my adventure was beyond their horizon; that they would be even more shocked, disgusted and unhappy, than I had made myself. And so, pale and heavy eyed, I evaded their probings and promised to help my sister with her stall as a sort of retribution. How fortunate that my parents had refused to allow me to work in the library with Agnes! I took a dreary satisfaction in their refusal having turned out for the best. I was not fit to choose what I did, since I had so easily sunk to such depths of immorality on the first provocation.

I had a great shrinking from seeing Agnes: I knew that I could not endure meeting Edward again, and I had no idea what her reaction would be, although I was afraid that she would be angry with me for an entirely different reason.

It was about then that I got a postcard which said: 'This is where I live. Just the place for you, and I should like to see you here. I believe we called it tea? No matter. I am a very bad painter, and shall expect to see you. Come whenever you like. R.' I put it carefully away beneath clothes in a drawer. Nothing was said about it, although I was sure my sister had read it, for she always read postcards. He must have found my address through the Lancings. I felt a stab of homesickness for the Lancings. They had answered none of my letters and it was impossible to go on writing to a collective silence. The postcard comforted me. He, at least, had not forgotten.

A week had passed since my evening with Agnes and I felt that I could no longer shirk seeing her. I went to the library, choosing the busiest hour in the morning. She was there, and looked just the same, trim and neat and gay.

'Where have you been? Somebody's been asking for you,' she began, and my heart sank.

'There's been a lot to do at home,' I said lamely.

'Well when would you be free?'

'I don't know. You see my parents were furious that I was so late.'

'What a shame! Never mind, we needn't be so late. We can sit in the park. Or what about a Sunday? Edward suggested Kew.' I felt a shudder of the familiar sick feeling I associated with Edward.

'I can't, Agnes. Truly I can't.'

'What's the matter then? Changed your mind?'

'Yes,' I said. 'That's it. I've changed my mind.'

'Well!' She was obviously suspicious and ready to be hurt. 'What's the matter with him?'

'I . . . I wouldn't want to marry him,' I said with desperate simplicity.

She went into gales of laughter, covered her mouth with her hand and said: 'Who said anything about marriage? You *are* a queer one. Don't you like a bit of fun?'

'Look,' I said, 'I'll explain to you. Not here. We could have lunch and I'll try and explain.'

She looked at me for a minute, and then said slowly: 'No, don't do that. I don't think I'd like it really. I'll tell him you've gone away.'

'Thank you. It's very kind of you.'

'I must get back to work,' she said. She was very flushed.

'How's Arthur?' I said.

'He's all right.' She blew her nose on a tiny handkerchief. She was going away to a customer.

'When shall I see you?'

'Oh, we can make an arrangement next time you come. I must get back. Bye-bye.'

I left the shop perturbed and anxious. I wanted badly to explain to her, and yet somehow I knew she was right, that I

123

should not be able to do so without hurting her and myself. For the first time I realized how painful people could be to each other, against both their will and intentions. It made me unbearably sad for the rest of that day.

CHAPTER TWELVE

For several weeks I concentrated on the children and my sister's stall for the Bazaar. The routine steadied and comforted me. In the morning I sewed under my sister's direction. We became better friends sitting in the window of the large dilapidated dining-room with material spread all over the table and linen bags full of scraps on every chair. She was wonderfully neat with her fingers, and her ingenuity and patience in contriving pretty and useful objects out of nothing, made me admire her, and feel less cruelly objective.

I remember asking her one day whether she would like to get married.

'If it comes my way,' she answered mildly, snipping off a thread. She had scissors like Deb's; and in a way she reminded me of her then, so neat and calm and assured. She had much hair and drooping shoulders.

'Do you think things do come one's way?' I asked.

'I'm sure they do. Our lives are very easily filled.'

'But what would you *like?*' I persisted. 'Would you like children?'

She blushed faintly. 'Of course. Two boys and a girl. I should call them Anthony, Richard and Margaret. I should like to live in the country as it would be better for their health.'

So she too had dreams, was not entirely composed of the divine resignations which I had confused with emptiness of mind.

'Go on,' I said. 'What else? What would your husband be like?'

Her face darkened a moment in the effort of concentration, and she said, 'I'm not sure. Fair, I think, but I don't know.' She gave it up.

'But you can't plan your children without a husband.' I was shocked.

She gave me a startled look and said, 'I have not planned them. That's only what I think sometimes. What do *you* want?'

'I want to write a book and get married.' That was the second time I had been asked, the second time I had answered. 'I'm not sure about children,' I went on hurriedly. 'I'd want to be sure of being married first.' It was her turn to be shocked.

'When you are married you expect to have children.'

'Oh well,' I said. 'I'd have them later. I like one thing at a time.'

'You are not likely to have twins.' She smiled at her joke. I don't think she ever laughed. I think she liked my helping her, and her ascendancy over all household matters. She had no one to whom she could show this talent, which obviously meant very much to her.

I went with her on the day that her things were sorted and priced by the Bazaar committee, comprised almost entirely of women. The Bazaar was to take place in a vast house, dark with panelling and draughty along mosaic floors. The stalls were placed round the edges of three large rooms. Two workmen were hammering a small platform, on which the Princess who was to open the Bazaar must stand. The noise was terrific. The hammering and shouting of the men; the excited babel of the women exclaiming over their handiwork; the heat and the rustle of endless tissue paper; and the buzz of bluebottles round the lead-encrusted windows made the scene one of indescribable confusion. There was also an inexplicable smell of bananas and turkish delight.

My sister seemed happier arranging her stall by herself, so with a murmured excuse I slipped away to wander round the rooms. The stalls were made of wooden trestle tables with large white cloths sweeping down to the floor, the corners pinned neatly back. Two women were struggling, scarlet-faced, with a huge pumpkin which they were trying to set up in the middle of their table. The pumpkin wobbled and finally rolled, ponderously juicy, to the floor. There were wails of dismay.

There were packing cases filled with tiny pots of jam; I read Apricot and Strawberry on the labels. A thin earnest creature with a hook nose and brilliant black eyes was painting signs on strips of shiny white paper in one corner of the first room. 'This Way to the Teas'; I read. 'Bran Tub sixpence.' 'Jumble' (in black and yellow). There were little streams of bran like chicken food and the tub had red and green crêpe paper tied round it. There were heaps of raffle tickets on tables; pins and labels, and gaunt pairs of scissors attached to some piece of furniture by string so that one had to crouch to cut anything. Tricks of that kind were what the feminine mind calls 'Organization', I learned. There was a tray of lavender bags belonging to an odious little girl of about fifteen, who was trying to sell in advance to the kind, harassed stall holders. An anxious young curate was engaged in trying to disentangle the lines of a bunch of fishing rods: 'Isn't it dreadful, Mr Beard? I packed them so carefully.'

In the third room I found a woman writing in a notebook. 'Three dozen, no four dozen teaspoons (eighteen Lady Bellamy) in brackets what *can* that mean?' Everyone appealed to Lady Bellamy, who flitted to and fro on incredibly thin elegant feet with a silver pencil pointing outwards in her hand, ordering, directing and admiring her host of followers.

The shadows lengthened on the street outside as the hours passed with no appreciable inroad made on the confusion. A curious way to spend a hot June day. I helped as much as I could, but it was difficult when one knew nobody's names and the help depended very much on a thorough knowledge of them. I carried things to people, counted, sorted, pinned labels, tied parcels, wiped cups and saucers; and simply stood holding one end of string, or with my finger on a knot. By the evening I was more exhausted than I had ever been before in my life.

The following day was the Bazaar itself, of which nothing need be said except that the sum raised was two hundred pounds odd, and that considering the time, energy and patience employed, I think every penny was earned many times over. It did occur to me going home afterwards that it would have been simpler to have had a collection for the money, but seeing my sister's tired, satisfied face I was not sure.

I had bought nothing at the Bazaar. There was at last enough money to buy the material for my mother's dress. My sister, who now knew of the plan, accompanied me to the shop for the purpose of helping to choose. I was faced with bales of material and choice seemed unbearable. There were three possible reds and I was at last able to decide only when on presenting them to my sister she rejected them all on the ground that red was an unsuitable colour.

'Grey,' she said. 'Or a good dark blue would be far more becoming.'

Instantly I was determined on red. I wanted to make my mother rich and gay and full of colour.

'The blue wears better,' said the shopman, sticking his head out and staring at me. My sister agreed that one did not get tired of dark blue as one did of red.

'You don't get tired of it because you never really like it,' I said. 'You can't have any feelings about dark blue. I'll have this one.' And I selected the richest red.

'She never *wears* red,' moaned my sister wringing her hands over the stuff.

'How many yards?' asked the assistant pausing and blinking his eyes.

'Six,' said my sister.

'I'll take seven,' I said grandly.

'Can you afford it?' whispered my sister in a frenzy.

'Of course. I've got enough for the trimming as well.'

I showed her a bulging purse, from which a half-crown fell out.

'Dear oh dear,' said the assistant, darting after it. I could not take my eyes off the silk.

'Could we have a snip to match the trimmings?' I heard my sister ask. She was being very kind. I had completely disagreed with her and she was still being kind. I squeezed her arm.

'What's all that for?' she asked.

'I'm excited. Let's choose the trimming.'

'Why not let Mother do that herself?'

'It's my present. I shall choose all of it.'

'Well you have to pay first.'

'You do it,' I said and handed her the purse. I could never count change and I felt slightly sick at the amount of money I was spending.

We chose a pale tea-coloured lace, ruffled at the edges with a coffee ribbon to draw it up. When it was over I had five shillings left.

'When shall you give it to her?'

'After supper. In the evening.'

'Can you wait till then?'

'Of course. You could,' I retorted.

'We're not the same about waiting,' she replied quietly, and for a second I wondered what she meant.

The day went slowly and I tortured myself with the fear that my sister had been right, that my mother would not like red, or would not want a frock. After tea my mother began discussing my clothes. My father was trying to read the paper, a thing he never did well, as his arms were short, and the paper crumpled and folded the wrong way when he tried to turn the pages. He grunted and battled miserably and finally left us with some withering remark about the way women took no interest in outside events but thought only of clothes.

'You should have money enough to buy a couple of nice cotton dresses.' I could see that she was anxious at having shown no interest in the paper and embarrassed about the money I earned. She could not get used to the idea. I mumbled something about the frocks I possessed doing quite well, and she looked up in relief. 'Ah, you're saving your money like a good careful girl,' she said.

After supper I gave it to her. 'What is it?' she asked nervously, smiling into my eyes.

'It's for you, a present.'

She gave a little gasp and bent over the string; then looked up uncertainly: 'From you?'

I nodded.

'You shouldn't,' she murmured enraptured.

I had never known how much presents meant to her and my heart beat wildly with a painful excitement. Her fingers trembled over the string until I could no longer bear it. 'I'll help.' We laughed and the string was undone. I sat back on my heels and watched her unfold the brown and white paper until she could see the red silk. She stared at it a moment unbelieving, touched it with her fingers, gave it a little pat, then suddenly lunged forward and shook it out in beautiful rich folds.

'Red,' she cried. 'Red,' and rubbed it softly against her face.

'It's silk,' I said. I was anxious that she should miss none of its beauty.

She became quickly aware of me again and said, 'Is this from you? All this red silk?'

'Seven yards,' I said. 'For a dress. You do like it, don't you?'

She turned her head away from the stuff. 'Darling, it's a wonderful present. You shouldn't have done it. You must have spent so much. All your money. It's magnificent.'

'These are the trimmings.' I gave her the second parcel. I wished now that I had put them together; I found it hard to watch her, she made me feel her pleasure almost too sharply. But she undid the trimmings quite quietly, and laid them on the stuff.

'Do you think they will look all right?' I said falsely. I was sure that they were perfect.

'I haven't worn red for years,' she said, with a hint of doubt.

'Would you have preferred dark blue?'

'No. I – like this very much better. Thank you, darling. It is very sweet of you.' She put her arms round me and kissed me, once, and then again, as though it wasn't enough.

'Will you have it made up soon?'

'I'll have it done in time for Daddy's concert.' She only said Daddy when she was happy and unselfconscious. The present was a success.

'She likes red,' I told my sister triumphantly.

'I shan't know you,' was my father's comment to her. He was unaware of the quick little look of pain that she gave him.

A few evenings later, I believe it was a Sunday, I was repairing music for my father on the dining-room table. My mother was mending as usual and my sister was leaning over me sorting the battered sheets of Brahms. It had been very hot all day and now there was a faint breeze swaying the tassels on the old green curtains. My father came in with an evening paper which he read in unusual silence. There was an organ grinder in the street outside, stopping and starting again with a violent animation as though he could never have stopped.

'Anything in the paper, dear?' asked my mother dutifully.

'Some Archduke or other has been murdered at ...' he paused, 'at Sarajevo. That's it. Sarajevo.'

'Oh dear.'

The organ grinder stopped and there was peaceful domestic silence.

CHAPTER THIRTEEN

I do not think I was very concerned about the growing unrest in Europe. Indeed I do not think anyone was seriously disquieted.

I clearly remember my father's agitation over his concert, or rather the concert where his Symphonic Variations were to be performed: his fits of indigestion and depression affected us all. One followed very closely upon the other, infecting the household with nerves and despair. As the work had never been published, the parts had to be copied; and, when the time grew near, he became anxious at the prospect of too little rehearsal. We all suffered the mixture of anxiety and irritation that prefaces a first performance of any kind. The weather was oppressive.

On the morning of the concert, I upset a vase of water on my father's piano. I shall never forget the frightened fluster for dry cloths, and his almost venomous rage. When the damage had been as much repaired as was possible, and I was creeping out of the studio, he called me back. He was standing by the piano, his fingers tapping the damp blotched case. He did not look at me.

'How came you to be so incredibly careless?'

'I'm very sorry, Father.'

'I don't understand it. You have always been brought up to respect a piano. You must have known that it was courting disaster in attempting to slide a heavy vase full of water across it.'

As there had already been an inquest on how I had done it, and why, this was almost more than I could bear.

'I didn't do it on purpose, Father.'

'I can't understand it,' he repeated still drumming his fingers. His hand looked yellow in the light. I was starting to go when he turned on me with a kind of concentrated ferocity and said, 'Purpose. What do you know about such a thing? Whether you ruin my piano or not is surely a business entirely within your control. You're not a fool. If you had cared enough this wouldn't have happened. What do you mean by "Purpose" – yours or God's?'

'I didn't mean to do it. That's what I meant. I didn't want ...'

'You didn't care,' he accused. I could hear his breath coming in sharp little gasps. I remembered his concert and it saved me from losing my temper.

'I honestly think the piano will be all right.'

'Sit down. I must make you understand this. What you do, what you are, is entirely a matter for you to decide. You are responsible for your future. Nothing else. No one else. If you care to do things, or not to do them, it is possible ...' He was walking about the room picking up small objects, a pencil, a postcard, and throwing them down on a different table. 'You do not seem to me aware of this. Some people think that we are controlled by some destiny or fate. It's utterly untrue. Utterly untrue. Whether we succeed, or fail, our perseverance and the direction we pursue is us. We finish by living the life we have made for ourselves.' His voice stopped suddenly and I realized that he was torturing himself, revealing even to me his own tragedy of failure, a failure because he saw it like that, and a tragedy because to be a failure made him so unhappy. I knew that he needed me to go up to him, touch him, perhaps kiss him; to say something, that would give him some false assurance that I had not understood him, to comfort and deceive. But the old familiar sick hatred for my surroundings and the people trapped in them with me, rose with such violence that I left the room without a word.

My mother's frock was not ready in time for that evening. I remember the concert well: it was the last time I ever went to a concert with my family.

The hall was full, and my father's work was received with a polite, rather uncertain attention. Afterwards, while he was standing on the platform stiff and small in his old evening clothes, I thought of the water on the piano and almost believed that he was right and I had spilt it on purpose. It was a terrifying idea.

We went afterwards to the house of some friends and drank coffee and ate cakes and everyone congratulated my father all over again. The curtains were not drawn; every window was open and even then it was not cool. There were thunder and forked lightning. Otherwise it was still, but in that smoky room people talked about music and exchanged endless personal reminiscences and anecdotes. My father played for a heavy Irish woman who sang, and nobody seemed to mind the ominous rumbling or the brilliant tongues twisting across the sky.

The party broke up very late. My father herded us together and said that we would walk. 'We can pick up a cab by the park,' he said and we all knew, my mother and sister and I, that even if there were a cab we should do no such thing.

The walk was over two miles. As we reached the park there was a tremendous burst of thunder: a few seconds later the rain began, with great angry drops slamming down on to the pavement, and above, branches of the trees swaying from the impact. Instinctively, we covered our heads and started to run. In a few minutes the futility of running became obvious; we had still most of our journey before us and neither my mother nor father was strong. We cowered under an enormous plane tree, hoping, I suppose, that the rain would abate.

'There may be a cab,' gasped my mother.

The drops from the tree gathered and fell with a metallic drip, and beyond the tree it roared. Soon the leaves would be beaten down and we should be no drier where we were.

'It will stop,' said my father, unusually sanguine.

It did not stop. There was another streak of lightning; for a second the sky was lit and we could see the raging clouds hurtling down from their heights. Then thunder, louder than before; I can remember it almost shaking my spine, and the crescendo of rain that followed. The street was empty of anything but the bouncing rain drops, collecting torrents in the gutter.

'We'd better walk,' said my father.

'We'll catch our deaths,' said my mother.

My father shrugged his shoulders and pulled his coat round his chin. There was more thunder and my sister turned to me, her eyes glittering. I knew she was frightened and took her arm as we set off. After a moment's hesitation, my father took hold of my mother and then recoiled with a little grunt saying, 'You're soaked. You'd better have my coat.'

'No dear.' My mother's cloak of old stamped velvet clung round her legs, the ruffles on the shoulders damply flattened.

'Don't be a fool, Evelyne,' said my father irritably as he ripped off the cloak and thrust her arms into his overcoat. 'Can't have you dying of pneumonia.'

We were by a street lamp, and I remember her wan little smile. So, with her cloak over his arm we walked home.

We arrived after one o'clock. My mother suggested warm milk, but there was no milk.

'Tea then.'

But my father, who looked exhausted, snorted and said we'd be far better in bed. He left the room and we heard him sneezing on the stairs. My sister quietly and efficiently filled hot water bottles and we went to bed.

CHAPTER FOURTEEN

Next morning my father was in bed with a feverish cold. He remained there for two days, refusing to see a doctor; and on the third day came down to his studio in his dressing-gown.

He was still feverish and very cross and would not eat the meals we brought in to him, but flew into a rage if we asked how he was feeling or suggested any remedy. He smoked until he began to cough. He was restless, and possessed of a violent desire to tidy all his music and the studio. He pulled everything out of the cupboards and shelves on to the floor; broke a plaster bust of Brahms which nearly fell on his head; and filled the studio with old photographs of people he could not remember. The dust made his cough worse. He would not let anyone help him and became wilder and less approachable as the confusion in his room grew. He left cups of tea, and Bovril made with milk, until they were quite cold and had a film or skin and dust on them. He tore the dead flowers out of the vase I had used, and thrust them head downwards into the bulging waste paper basket with the slimy green stalks in the air and dripping on to the rug. He burned papers in the stove until the air was clouded with crisp black ash. He did not touch the piano. This went on for three days and my mother was almost beside herself. Whenever any of us went into the studio he would demand some piece of music; accusing us in a hoarse strained voice of taking it or losing it or throwing it away. There was a terrible mad feeling in the house, as though we were to expect anything to happen however fantastic or bad.

On the third afternoon my mother gave me his tea to take to the studio, imploring me helplessly 'to try and persuade him to go to bed'. We had already asked her why she did not send for a doctor but she evaded us; she was clearly terrified of my father and utterly unable to manage the situation.

He was scrubbing the mark I had made on his piano, with a curtain which he must have ripped off the pole.

'Here is your tea, Father.' He muttered something and did not look at me.

'Will you come and drink it while it's hot? You have been working so hard, Father.'

He looked up and I saw that his cheeks were a brilliant pink.

'You'll spoil the curtain anyway. I'll fetch you a duster when you have had your tea.'

'Come and look at it. It's *worse*. The damp spreads across the varnish.' He hung over the stain and drawn by some new fear I went to him. He began scrubbing it again furiously. I touched him; he seemed to have forgotten me, when suddenly he whipped round, seized my arm and shouted, 'You did this. You're responsible for this. It's getting worse, I can't use the piano. I can't work unless I have order and you've made that impossible for me. You must have done it on purpose. Look at this room. Haven't I been trying to arrange it for weeks. Look what I've tried to do. You're all against me – all of you . . .' A frightful fit of coughing shook him. It went on and on until he could not see, but hung over the piano still gripping my arm, coughing, an intolerable dry agonizing cough, until I could feel the wracking tearing pain in his lungs, through the frantic grasping of his fingers in my arm. Gradually he stopped; shivered, and whimpered a little, his hair over his face. I pushed back his hair automatically; his forehead was dry and burning. My sister had heard the shouting and was at the open door. Together we led him upstairs. He did not seem to notice us at all.

He collapsed in bed, and my sister went for the doctor. I went back to the studio; I think with an idea that I might tidy some of the chaos. It was impossible. There were letters in grey ink, sheets of music paper with a few bars scrawled in the middle, yellow photographs of singers with bands round their heads and opulent shoulders twisted into coy or smug angles. There were tiny morose men with cellos, and a fat creature with a flute, all of them scrawled with ink that had spurted over the shiny surfaces. To dear Alfred; With kindest remembrances to dear Alfred; To my dear friend – Alfred. Profuse and forgotten affections sprawled over the grey pictures with their faint yellow gloss. There were programmes, with 'First Performance' in brackets under the announcements of my father's works. All the machinery of music lay rampant; even the curtain rail was loose and unbalanced, pointing down across the window, with the rings of the remaining curtain slipping off if anyone slammed a door or a cab passed in the street. There were whole shelves full and untouched. He seemed only to have cleared the less accessible cupboards high up by the picture rail or down by the skirting board. There were ragged press cuttings, unnaturally thin and flat, of concerts I had never heard: it was all a generation beyond me. He seemed to have no present; only a long uncertain past about which I knew nothing; except for the bowls filled with light grey ash and the little contorted stubs of cigarettes. And so while I vainly attempted to arrange his possessions, I sought for some purpose in his life that would comfort me; some joy he had had which I could imagine; some faith or reason which had warmed his heart. I ended by sitting on the floor staring at the rail across the window. My sister came in with a tray on to which she collected the cups and bowls of ash.

'The doctor has come.' She stopped to take a bowl out of my hands. 'Pneumonia. Isn't it odd that he should have said that to mother in the street? Do you remember?' she persisted, pressing the unnecessary drama at me.

'Of course. Is it bad?'

'Yes, it's acute pneumonia of the right lung. We shall have to fight, he will need very careful nursing.' Her face was lit with her energy and resolve. She was one of those people who are most themselves when faced with illness.

'For what purpose?'

'For what purpose?' her shocked voice repeated. 'So that he shall recover.' She set down the tray and came to me. 'I don't think you understand. It's serious. He may die. It would be terrible. Mother would be all alone. I have tried to keep the danger of his illness from her. He will need constant nursing until his crisis. But I can do it. You must help Mother, it is a terrible shock to her. He is delirious.'

I felt the tears spring out of my eyes and put out my hands. 'I don't want him to die.'

'Now you mustn't do that. You must pull yourself together. There's going to be quite enough to do without your giving way. Think how much worse it is for Mother.'

'Or him,' I sobbed.

'He doesn't know anything about it,' she said quickly. 'We must pray for him,' she added seriously.

There was nothing more to say. I got up and followed her, feeling in some curious way deeply ashamed of both of us.

She nursed my father devotedly, until, indeed, there was very little for either my mother or me to do. She sat up with him every night, only consenting to lie down for three hours in the afternoon. She supervised his broths and medicine; cleaned his room, and was always freshly competent for the frequent visits of the doctor. My mother and I sat dumbly in the living-room, starting up almost guiltily if we were called by my sister to perform some minor task.

I think my mother was paralysed all through that time: stripped bare of her daily round, dreary and uneventful as it was, she was revealed in all the unbalance and inadequacy of pure despair, unrelieved by even the warmth of a burning affection for my father. She was simply dependent on him. He was part of her structure, and the possibility of his no longer being in the house was appalling. She was always ready to acknowledge the superior qualities of her daughter. 'Oh no, I am sure he would rather your sister did that.' Her humility was almost unbearable to me. She did not even claim her share of anxiety or grief, effaced herself and her emotions: but I would see her drop her mending and stare ahead, her eyes dull and desperate in her bewilderment, and I imagined two little questions stabbing her mind, 'Will he die?' and 'What shall I do?' just as I found myself endlessly asking, 'What was the use? Have we been worth it to him?

Was there any alternative for him? Does he care what happens to him now?'

I sat with him, one stifling hot night, having persuaded my sister to go to bed for the first time since he had been ill.

He lay on his back, his head propped with pillows, because breathing was a continuously painful effort to him. Occasionally he dozed. I sat in the dim light, acutely conscious in the silence of his irregular rasping breaths, until I leaned forward while each separate gasp was achieved, and the minutes hung heavy and single in the airless room. Then some unknown dream or imagined sound would force him awake, exhausted and querulous. What time was it? he would ask.

The hours struck by the church clock, an eternity apart; ten; eleven; and twelve. I remember him raising himself at the last and asking 'Is it nearly over?' and my not knowing what to reply. He waited a moment then leaned back; an expression of peevish fear like a child flitted across his face. 'Midnight,' he murmured. 'No, it's only just begun.'

'Would you like me to read to you?'

He made a little gesture of indifference with his fingers on the sheet. I searched for a book; those in the room were all about religion (my sister's design). I found a copy of the *Imitation of Christ* bound in white vellum with a rich golden cross, and opened it at random.

'On the contempt of all temporal honour,' I read.

'Oh that,' he said. 'I don't want to consider my death you know.' I looked up startled, and found his eyes alive and appraising.

'Of course not,' I fumbled. 'You're going to get well.'

'I didn't mean that,' he said, and we were silent again, conscious of the chance lost between us.

Part of the night I had an insane desire to tell him that it had been a good thing to devote his life to music, or to have made me, or any of his children; but my own uncertainty loomed before me so immensely that I was prevented. Snatches of his music and aspects of my sister and myself raced through my mind, but they did not help me even privately to any kind of reassurance; and finally I was forced to believe in my separate distant brothers who were expected home at any moment. My sister had written to them, with the result that Tom, the schoolmaster, was coming for one night and Hubert, the embryo accountant, for a week.

And so the night wore wearily away, and I wondered whether it was any comfort to my father to believe that it was as long for me as for him.

He swallowed his medicine, patiently cynical of its properties, and breathed his way painfully through the hours. He did not complain, which made his obsession with time, which was no longer any use to him, more deeply touching.

Gradually a shallow light showed in the window; the street lamps lost their power and stood useless and squalid in the pale grey air; and I was able to tell him that the day had really begun, as though it held some magnificent promise. He slept then, his head on one side, and his short, strong, somehow elegant fingers curved in a little with content.

In the middle of breakfast, my younger brother arrived. He walked straight in, kissed us all in the right order, inquired after my father, and without waiting for a reply, told us that war had been declared on Germany.

'At midnight. Exactly at midnight. We are at war,' he repeated, almost as though he were asking us whether we really were. He was in a state of profound excitement. My mother received the news as a fresh personal tragedy; my sister was indignant (surely something could be done?). I think she minded the deflection from what was, to her, the main issue. To me it meant precisely nothing. I remembered the clock striking twelve, and wondered why, if it had been such an important moment, it had not seemed so then.

'Who will win?' I asked innocently. My brother shot me an exalted, terrifying glance.

'We shall, of course,' he said. 'Thank God, I'm eighteen. They'll need all the men they can get.'

'Oh, Hubert,' said my mother.

'We must keep it from Father,' said my sister, her voice elevating us to more spiritual matters.

141

Then they started to tell Hubert about father. Hubert walked about the room with folded arms, raising his eyebrows and frowning; asking intelligent questions with a kind of suppressed energy, as though he were really meant for something else.

I went to sleep.

CHAPTER FIFTEEN

Two days later my father died. He died at two o'clock in the morning; none of us had been to bed and we all saw him die. His head just slipped sideways, and my sister in a choked voice said he was dead, although his eyes were open, which seemed very terrible to me. 'Take Mother,' she commanded. We led her away, Tom and I, one limp hand for each of us, and I put her to bed, unresisting and quite silent.

When I went back to my father's room, my sister would not let me in, but told me to go to bed. My brothers kissed me and asked if I would be all right. In my room I sat a long while without crying. Eventually I groped in my chest of drawers until I found Rupert's postcard. I did not read it; just stared until the writing was blurred and my eyes ached. Then I put it carefully away and slept.

The funeral was a slow practical nightmare. Processions of wreaths with shiny cards; piles of letters; and four and a half inches in *The Times* (which considering the war was rather good, said my sister complacently). The house, converted from the silent dread of illness, became crowded with people and their expressions of sorrow. As my mother pointed out, unconscious of the irony, one never knew how many friends he had, until he was no more with us. My sister managed everything with admirable propriety and control. On the afternoon of the funeral, we were all sitting round the dining-room table waiting for the kettle to boil, when the bell rang. My mother began to rise, but my sister motioned her back and went into the hall. She returned with letters and a large cardboard box. 'For you, Mother. I wonder what it is,' she added in the tone with which one encourages a child. 'The letters are all for you, too.'

'Nothing for me?' Hubert relaxed in his seat impatiently. He behaved all the time as though he were waiting for something. Tom continued to read the newspaper, which was blaring with headlines.

I watched my mother undo the string, and remembered that it would be the frock, the red frock she had had made from my material. My heart warmed at the prospect. The lid of the box fell open, and there under the tissue paper lay my present, glowing and beautifully folded. My mother lifted it out by the shoulders and turned to me. 'There, darling, it's come at last,' she said, as though it were mine.

My sister was leaning over her chair. 'It will have to be dyed,' she said. 'What a pity. But it will come in very useful.'

My mother lowered her head, and I saw her hands fall slack on the red.

'What?' I cried. 'It will ruin it. You *can't!*'

'It will have to be dyed,' repeated my sister gently, looking at me.

There was a terrible emotional solicitude hovering in the air. Everyone was very still, watching my mother.

'It is very good material. It won't be spoiled,' said my sister.

At last my mother raised her head, her face covered with tears. She saw us all watching; her shame at being seen to cry broke her shadowy dignity, and she sobbed holding the stuff to her face.

'He never even saw it. He said I won't know you. I can't help it. He didn't see it once.' Her fingers raked in among the silk with an awful comfortless energy.

Swiftly my sister leaned forward, put her arms under my mother's, and lifted her to her feet. 'You are tired. You need a rest. Come and lie down and I will bring you some tea.' With gentle force she led my mother from the room.

I sat like a stone, with grinding pain in my heart for her at the very beginning of her grief; with years ahead, and the poor commiseration by which she was now surrounded contracting until it was just a casual memory, half forgotten and finally vanished. One's own sorrow, I thought then, how bearable, how understandable; but the misery of another

144

person, a separate being, how unimaginably terrible, of what unseen quality, unknown duration, inconceivable anguish! Nobody would feel my mother's suffering even for the years left in her life.

'She's wonderful with Mother,' said Tom, indicating my sister with the newspaper.

Hubert acquiesced moodily and suggested fetching the kettle; at least tea could be made to happen.

'Hey, what are *you* for?' said Tom, and I fetched it.

When I returned, they were both discussing the future, or rather their futures.

Hubert shocked us all by announcing that the chief reason for his anxiety was that he had volunteered for the Army, which meant his immediate departure.

'If they won't have me, I shall lie about my age.'

Tom seemed deeply concerned and implored him to reconsider his decision. 'After all,' he said, 'there's Mother.' It was all exceedingly dangerous and meant putting a terrible strain on her just at this moment.

'She's got you and the girls. I've made up my mind. I've given the matter a great deal of thought.' He frowned deeply, with his eyes sparkling. 'If Father were alive, I should have done it, and it's far too important a business to forgo simply because of Mother.'

'She may not have me. I may feel I should join up.'

'Good Lord, no! This war will be over in a few weeks, or months at the outside. They won't have time to start on schoolmasters. They'll need them where they are.'

'You might not like the Army, Hubert,' I cried.

Both brothers smiled kindly.

'It's not a question of what I should like,' replied Hubert gravely. I noticed his eyes still sparkled.

I poured out the tea. My sister came and fetched cups for mother and herself and retired with them filled.

The brothers were deep in speculations on modern warfare. I wondered desperately what was going to happen to me. The thought started quite casually, like the beginning of rain, but it quickly increased until my mind was full of it, and the need to disperse it amongst the others became too great to overcome.

I remember asking them what I should do. What could I do? I repeated. They both looked at me in astonishment.

'Do? You mean about the war?'

'About anything. About me chiefly.'

'The best thing you can do is to keep the home fires burning.' Tom patted my knee. 'Men do the fighting. All you have to do is to keep yourself fascinating for when we return.'

I think it was coming from one of my brothers that made it such a watery jest.

'But I can't just do nothing.'

'What do you want to do?'

'I don't know. Couldn't I teach or something? If what you said about your being needed is true, surely they will need women for teaching.'

'But you haven't been educated for teaching. It's a serious profession. You didn't go to a school. You haven't passed any examinations.'

'Good thing, too.' Hubert sighed deeply and stared into the fire.

'There's Mother, you know,' I was reminded. 'She will need looking after.'

'*She* does that all the time. There won't be enough for me to do.'

'If Mother sells the house and moves into a smaller one, you will have plenty to do with the move.'

'Tom, you don't understand. That won't last. That's like a – like a Bazaar.'

'Well, you'll get married one day. That's what happens to most women, unless they have some kind of vocation.'

'*She* won't,' said Hubert, and they fell to rapt contemplation of my sister's chastity.

I looked from one to the other in despair. Did they seriously consider me so different from themselves? Did they think that I could live without any of the support they deemed so necessary and admirable? That to prepare meals

146

and clothes and beds in which to sleep was for a woman an end in itself. I stared from Tom's pale moustache to Hubert's shaven cheek and hated them. That was all they need do, trim their moustaches and shave. Their clothes were mended; they did not cook their food or pull back the sheets each morning. They were able to use the means of living as a means: for me they were assumed to be an end.

'It isn't as though you were artistic,' said Tom kindly.

'As though she were what?' Hubert wiped his mouth and put the handkerchief back in his pocket.

'As though she had anything to do with Art.'

'Oh. Good Lord!' he added as an afterthought.

I got up and went to the door.

'What about the tea?' called Tom.

'Clear it yourself.'

I remember feeling inanely proud of that petty little retort. It gave me the courage to lock my door and find the postcard in my top drawer. Some street in Chelsea. I had never heard of it. I must have a suitcase. I crept out into the passage, up the rickety flight of stairs which led to the box-room. The door was stuck; even the paint had melted in the heat. The door yielded, and I had the sense to shut it, for fear of any noise I might make selecting my case. It had been a servant's bedroom, and had white paper striped with watery roses, hanging loose in triangles. The cistern in the passage made horrible furtive noises. I should not have liked to sleep in that room. It was unbearably hot, and the small window was tightly shut. I struggled with the sash until there was a pain in my chest. The sash opened, and a large bluebottle fell out. I turned to survey the trunks. They were all too big and very dirty. There was the black one I had used for my beautiful visit. I unstrapped it almost without thinking, and inside, under the tray, was a small worn case. It had a label marked Bruges on it. It would do. I strapped the trunk and tried to shut the window, but it was jammed. I looked right down into the garden with the weedy square bed in the middle, spattered with nasturtiums. Hubert's bicycle was leaning against the wall. Soon I should be away. I should never come back. The thought provoked action. I slipped down and into my bedroom, locking the door carefully. I packed my best clothes and a hairbrush and looked round. There was nothing else that I wanted; I had no precious possession. There was a photograph of my father looking tired and pensive. Perhaps I had better have something like that, although the frame would make my case heavier.

It was finished. I felt almost light headed with calm. I would leave them all. At that moment the whole thing seemed so simple that I could not understand why I had not thought of it before. One just packed a case and walked out of the house. My mind stopped at that point, but I felt no need to consider any further. I washed my hands and put on a coat. A door slammed downstairs and I heard my brothers coming up. They passed my room and I stood motionless until my ears almost hurt with listening. I heard them go into Tom's bedroom and shut their door.

I seized the case and ran down the stairs, out of the house, down the path, out of the gate, and down the road until I was breathless and had to stop. Then an irrational fear of pursuit spurred me on again until I was two streets away. After that I walked, aiming for Gloucester Road; changing hands as the suitcase established its weight. The familiar streets fell away and I became more conscious of adventure. I passed a little girl skipping in a front garden. She did not notice me, but skipped violently, intent on achieving a 'double through', with her pigtails flying up each time she jumped. Her feet on the stones interrupted my plan until I was listening to them as they grew fainter in the distance behind me. I passed the shop where we had bought hoops and tops as children. It was a stationer's, but specialized in a few rare and delightful toys. A faint regret made me stop just past the shop and put down the suitcase. I was in sight of Gloucester Road and a bus lumbered by. Where was I going? I realized that I had neither the postcard nor money. Neither. Not a penny, and I could not remember the address.

Sixteen? six? twenty-four? Any of those numbers seemed probable: indeed, each, when considered separately, invited approval. Four sixes make twenty-four, I murmured frantically aloud. But I had read the postcard many times. I was almost sure that it was sixteen. Perhaps it was simply that my cousin had lived at number sixteen. It could be six. I shut my eyes and tried to see the squat fat handwriting on the postcard. I knew it by heart, but not the number. Not the number. And I had no money. I was trembling and desperately hot. I picked up the suitcase and put it down again. One could not appear at a strange house with no money. I felt foolishly in my pockets. My fingers were merely speckled with stuff like powdered glass. Of course there was no money there. I must think. I could not go on. I could not go back. A man walking on the other side of the street looked at me curiously. Dizzy with chagrin, I staggered up the side streets to the park.

I sat down on the nearest empty seat, with the suitcase beside me. It must look very strange to be sitting there with a suitcase. I pushed it under the bench and out of sight. It was a relief to be still. I was utterly bewildered at my blunderings. That other people or circumstances should prove hostile was bitterly reasonable; but that I should be subject to such an attack from within was beyond my horizon, and I could only feel humiliated and ashamed. If it had not been for my ridiculous and unbusinesslike rush, I should have arrived at the studio by now. Rupert would be painting and there would be a bowl of fat summer roses with loose petals on the table. The room would be very still and golden with the evening light; there would be an unfamiliar smell of paint and another person's house. We would drink milk and I would provoke his admiration by the strength and simplicity of my achievement. Fantastic conceptions of how it would all be, flowed through my mind; all impossibly good and delightful. I remembered my nervous pride in the boxroom ('I shall never come back!'), my headlong rush out of the house. Surely I had hardly given myself time to think. Leaving one's home was not so simple it seemed, even when one knew where to go. *Was* it number sixteen? Nobody must know of this abortive attempt. I kicked the suitcase further under the seat. For a moment I was tormented by the thought that other people would have walked, would have found the house by asking at all three numbers. But then I could not have carried the case. It was too heavy for me I decided, and the irony of accepting another weakness escaped me. Perhaps I would take a lighter case. Or perhaps I would pack more belongings and go in a cab. On my way downstairs I had remembered something left out. Hardly remembered. A fleeting thought. It could not have been more than that, or surely I should have thought of the postcard.

I would go home. They would be having supper. There would be cold rice pudding in the pie-dish with blackberries painted on it. I had a peculiar rush of affection for that dish. My brothers would read or play chess and my sister would sew as usual. I wondered whether my mother was better, whether her tears had relieved her, or left her dry and exhausted as tears did me. A sensation which was not hunger, nor fatigue, nor loneliness, but perhaps a blend of all three overcame me. I rose slowly and reached for the case. As I walked out of the gardens, I saw an old woman sprawled back on a seat, underneath which was a parcel wrapped in newspaper. I quickened my steps and still the suitcase did not feel heavy.

CHAPTER SIXTEEN

I excused my shame at the misadventure by making practical arrangements which would conceal my plan from the
family. I packed a case with much more care and looked up
Beechley Street on a map. I told my mother that I was going
to see a friend in Chelsea, implying that Rupert was a
woman; and she acquiesced quite readily. Tom had gone
back to his school, and Hubert was so obsessed with his own
impatience that he took very little notice of me. I feared my
sister most, and to her I embroidered the story most cunningly with a long account of this girl's exhaustion from
having nursed an aunt who had recently died. I said that I
did not want to tell my mother all this, for fear it would
distress her. The whole business was arranged with detailed
deceit, and was quite undramatic. I finally left at three
o'clock, in a cab procured by Hubert, with the family gathered round the door to say good-bye.

A faint disappointment claimed me as I waved farewell
and settled back in the cab. This was not really the way to
do it. But it was the way that things happened. I was conscious of disliking being overpowered by circumstances, of
romance being drained out of the adventure, leaving it as it
appears now, tawdry, practical and highly probable. The
only pleasant element left was one of surprise. I had not told
Rupert that I was coming. This seemed satisfactory to me,
and the feeling mounted as we trotted away from Kensington.

I asked the man to put me down at the corner of the street.
Somehow I did not want to appear to have arrived in a cab. I
paid the driver out of the money I had been given, and
walked down the street with my case. It was warm, still and
deserted, except for several cats packed between the spikes of
railings, or perched on narrow window-sills, with the most

belying air of comfort. 'Those artists of position', somebody had once said to me.

I walked past a little row of houses followed by a large block with wide windows, studios I imagined, and next to them an uneven stretch of buildings, all colours and shapes, mostly fat and low, with gay painted front doors immediately on to the street. Here it was at last. A pale green door with a gargoyle knocker. I put down the case and paused. Did one simply say, 'I have come to stay'?

Someone across the road was playing Saint-Saëns on a gramophone. Surely Rupert would understand when he saw the case. Did people often do this kind of thing? Was it generally expected amongst friends? Was one expected to know the friend very well before doing it? Even these speculations were not very practical; but they made my own inexperience painfully clear to me and I realized bitterly how foolish it had been to rejoice in the surprise I was about to spring. He had said, 'Come whenever you like,' but it was hardly the same thing as coming without warning of any kind. However, I could not go back now. The dignity and authenticity of my departure rendered return impossible. I need not stay very long. And then what? I must have hesitated for several minutes before I lifted the grinning creature's head and let it fall. It fell with such violence that it rebounded, and knocked twice; and I recoiled from the noisy peremptory object. I waited, my thoughts congealing in the silence that followed; even the music had stopped, somebody having taken off the record in the middle. Perhaps Rupert was out. Better knock again. Better count ten first. Very slowly. Somebody had put a waltz on the gramophone now. I counted with my heart beating time as fast. Out: perhaps he was out. Perhaps he was away. What should I do? Almost in a panic I knocked again. Faintly I heard steps. Soft shuffling steps. He must have slippers on, I thought, and my heart was light again. I heard someone fumbling with the door, then it opened, and a girl stood there, staring at me. Her eyes were brown and beautifully set. Her hair was hanging down her back. She was dressed in a flowered wrapper, edged with innumerable ruffles, and feathered mules on her bare feet. We must have stared at each other with equal astonishment for some seconds, a silence from which she recovered first, for she said quite pleasantly: 'And what can I do for you?'

She was almost the first person I had ever heard speak with a foreign accent and I was charmed into smiling.

'Is Mr – ? Does – er – Rupert live here?' Absurd that. But I could not remember his name. 'Rupert Laing' (that was it). 'Does he live here?'

Her eyes narrowed a little as she looked down at the case, and up my body again to my face; but she flattened herself against the narrow wall of the passage and answered that he did, down there, indicating the passage in her voice, without turning her head. I stepped inside, starting down the passage while she shut the door and followed me. We went through a door with stained glass to its waist and out into a little garden, a courtyard, paved, but without flowers, and through another green door, straight into a large studio, with skylights half covered by grey blinds.

'Will you wait here?' the girl said, moving unhurriedly to another door at the far end of the room. 'Do sit down,' she added with great courtesy, so that the phrase seemed new, and the invitation a peculiar honour.

The place was in the utmost confusion. I found a chair with no back and a coffee cup on the seat. I put the cup carefully on the floor and sat down. Flame-coloured sunlight streamed down through the strips of windows (which were also partially covered by blinds) and added to the confusion by vast livid zigzags on the rush matting and black rugs. In one corner was a bed, unmade but strewn with brilliant shawls and scarves. A half empty glass of milk lay on the floor at the head beneath a scarlet corner of fringe, the silken ends of which were poised just above the milk. There was an easel, and canvases were propped against the walls. Three huge orange jugs perched about the room. The paint-work was black, but the walls were a dead pale grey, which, suffused with the violent and restricted sunlight, gave the room a conflicting quality of warmth and cold, of heat and of chill, half midday, half evening, the twilight of some tropical scene. I remembered the girl's black mass of coarse shining hair hanging down her back; it completed the disorder before me, and I had just time to wonder what Rupert would be like, when he entered.

He came through the door at the far end of the room, and stood in a patch of sunlight. I saw him screw up his eyes for a second, as he looked about for me. The moment before a person sees you presents a rare and fleeting aspect of that person, which vanishes after the meeting. It was the first time I had felt it, and I saw him for the first time, tired and defensive and somehow drained.

'It's I, Rupert,' I said.

'Yes, I see you now,' he replied and moved a trifle uncertainly towards me. Then he was standing over me. There was a short silence, and I felt more and more that this was a strange thing to do and less and less able to account to him for my having done it.

'You said I could come when I liked.'

'Yes, of course I did. Do you never warn people when you like?'

'I've never done it before.'

'Of course. You're the person who is always doing things for the first time. Of course.' He bent his head a little to scratch it and saw the suitcase.

'My father's dead,' I said foolishly.

'I'm sorry,' he answered, preoccupied.

I knew he was going at any moment to ask me terrible, practical questions about that case, which pride and resentment rendered me incapable of answering. This was not at all what I had imagined.

'I'm not particularly sad about it,' I said stiffly.

He began to stare at me in a penetrating manner, when the girl re-entered the room. She stood quite still at the door, but Rupert heard her and turned.

'Get some tea,' he said. She nodded. 'Make some toast. Take half an hour over it. I want to talk.'

She moved a step further into the room, standing in the

patch of sunlight (it had narrowed a little now, I noticed), and staring at me inquiringly.

'Go *on*,' he shouted.

'You won't go out?'

'*No!* For the tenth time, I won't go out.'

She nodded again and withdrew.

'Who is she?'

'Her name's Maria.'

'Does she live here?'

'Yes. Does that surprise you?'

'I thought she must live here,' I answered carefully.

'Oh! You did,' he seemed amused, and unhelpful. 'Now, what's the matter?'

'Nothing. I just thought I would come to tea with you.'

'Bringing your suitcase?'

'No – I'm going somewhere else. I had to bring that.'

'Where are you going?'

'To friends.'

'And this was on your way?'

'This was on my way.'

He looked at me again and then said, 'Right. Help me collect some of these cups or we shan't have enough for tea. Wait a minute while I fetch a tray.'

A curious feeling of relief swept over me. I did not then worry at all about the result of my lying, but relaxed now the questions had come to an end. I collected every cup, mug and glass I could see and there were a great many of them.

'Hey! We don't need all those,' he cried. I had ranged them on a papier mâché table. 'Maria can clear them up tomorrow.'

'Does she work for you?'

'No,' he laughed. 'She just lives with me. I suppose it comes to much the same thing though,' he added as though discovering something. 'I don't pay her, you see. She loves me.'

'As though you were married?' I felt intensely curious. The idea was utterly new to me.

'That is a very embarrassing question and one which is not usually asked.'

'Do you love her then?'

'Now you are being very childish and ought to be ashamed of yourself.'

Instantly I felt very impertinent and ashamed and blushed hotly. He took the tray I had filled and kicked open the door.

'Do recover before I return. I keep forgetting how sensitive you are.'

I recovered, slowly and painfully.

Rupert returned and began unwinding the cords which rolled back the blinds so that the windows were clear, and light coloured the room evenly.

Then he said: 'Come and sit on the bed and wait quietly for toast. You must not mind Maria. She is not at her best today, and anyway, she'll try and resent you. She is a – ' he hesitated, and his voice softened – 'a childish creature. She is not very happy today, and she's bad at that.'

'Oh.'

'Perhaps you are not very happy either? Am I surrounded by unfortunate women perhaps?'

I remained silent. I think I was a little afraid of him. Eventually I said:

'Do you like being a painter?'

'More than becoming a doctor, but otherwise not so much as I thought. Doctoring is a disillusioning business. They take years to disillusion you, because they are so scientific about it, of course. Now painting – with painting you can produce a picture in, say, a couple of days, and within half an hour of its completion your friends will flock round it telling you they don't like pink, or nobody has shoulders like that. It is all over in a trice. The most extraordinary thing about painting is the way everyone who sees any picture assumes you are showing it to them solely for the purpose of benefiting by their destructive criticism. They are positively exasperated if they do not at once give vent to some eager ignorant disapproval. After the faint praise, of course. There is very little variety in that.'

'What do you do with them?'

'Take no notice of them. And that is a lonely business. You see one cannot really *afford* their taking no notice of you. It does not make for better painting. I am certain that even the people who survived it would have painted better if they had been needed instead of endured or ignored. People are kind to lovers. All the world loves a lover, they say. It's because they know it won't last. I suppose it is a tribute to the artist when people are hostile to him.'

'Are they hostile?' I was thinking of my father.

'Perhaps hostile is a bad word. They perpetrate a kind of wilful indifference which is just as bad.'

He continued in this strain for some time. At first I thought that he was merely trying to put me at my ease – to avoid any personal subject which might force me to reveal my situation (about which I was sure he had doubts); but then I realized that he was simply obsessed with artistic problems and his own uncertainty, and glad to have a new listener to whom he could talk about them. He finished by saying: 'The other point about people being kind when they know things can't last, is people being lenient about somebody when they know he can't do any more.'

There was a knock on the door.

'Oh, heavens!' He leapt up to open it.

Maria stood there with a tray. She wore a black skirt with a white blouse; but her hair still hung down her back. Rupert seized her hair with both hands, one on each side of her face.

'Listen, Maria. You are not to start being jealous and knocking.'

'There was the tray in my hands.'

He shook her head.

'You know that is not why you knocked. We were talking.'

'*You* were talking,' she interrupted.

'*We* were talking. Weren't we?' He turned to me, his hand on her hair. 'You wouldn't have enjoyed it. You wouldn't have understood one single word.'

This statement was calculated to calm her; as even I could see.

She was trying to frown, to glower at him, but her hair was strained back from her forehead too hard; it was not possible, and only her brows met.

'Will you be reasonable? I shall introduce you from here and if you are not polite and kind, you'll be sorry.'

He introduced us. I was terribly embarrassed; but Maria seemed quite unmoved by the situation. She accepted the introduction with dignity, continuing to frown at Rupert.

'What were you talking about? I *should* have understood,' she added like a child.

He shook her head impatiently again. 'About art. About life.'

'Oh, that,' she said and shrugged her shoulders, so that the tea-cups rattled violently; after which she smiled a magnificent smile. She had the kind of face which seemed correctly arranged when smiling: I remember her small, exceedingly white teeth, and her upper lip curved above them.

'Please may I put the tray down?' He was looking at her; he nodded slowly, running his fingers down to the ends of her hair, and finally releasing her.

We had tea. There were two boiled eggs for Rupert, and one for me. Maria said she was not hungry, whereupon Rupert looked at her with an exasperated anxiety and tried to feed her with egg. She sat on the floor. At the beginning of tea she watched me, but in the end she watched Rupert. I noticed that she treated him with a kind of restrained but agonized attention, that she hated him to see her watch him, anticipated a glance from him and dropped her eyes or turned her head; but even then, I felt her desperate concentration. It was as though his voice touched her, and was unbearable; as though she knew how breathing felt to him; how the eggshell felt to his fingers; these and countless other minute sensations were as if shared by her all the time. At first I thought that he was unaware of this, but as the meal progressed I was less sure. I think in the end we were all affected by it. Apparently we talked easily. We talked about the Lancings: Rupert had not been to see them again, although he had had lunch with Deb and her mother when they were shopping in London; about my family (most superficially); about Rupert's painting (that was when I was acutely sensitive to Maria); about the war (this most vaguely, I being unable to contribute through ignorance, and Maria being vehemently averse to the subject).

'You think wars should be fought, not talked,' I remember Rupert saying to her, when the restraint suddenly loomed enormous before us, filling the room.

'Not talked,' she said.

After tea she lit a cigarette and smoked it very slowly. Almost everything seemed different I reflected. I watched her fascinated, until Rupert asked me whether I would like one, which I hastily refused. When she had finished, Rupert got up off the bed. 'Go and buy something for the pancakes. Enough for all of us. Will you do it now?'

'Won't you come?'

'No. Do it now, or the shops will be closed.'

She left the room without a word. We stacked the things on a tray.

'I'll take this out. I shan't be long,' he said.

'When are we having pancakes?'

'For supper.' He kicked the door and went.

The room was very peaceful. I wondered idly why Rupert had assumed I was staying to supper, but only for a moment. I heard a murmur of voices through the door, and envied Maria, with an abstract impersonal envy, for the kind of life she led. Perhaps, though, it was very painful. She seemed unhappily obsessed with Rupert. He had said she was not happy today, and that she was bad at it. It was strange to be here, not half an hour from my home and yet surrounded by so complete a change. Some of the things Rupert had said came back into my mind, and then, inevitably, I was forced to consider what I should do on leaving this place. It would be worse in the evening. I struggled to enjoy the time I was spending, and still had left to spend. For a long while I stared miserably at the rush matting, going over the insoluble crisis again and again. This unprofitable occupation was broken by Rupert.

'She's gone to buy mushrooms,' said Rupert. He pulled out his pipe and sat on the floor leaning against the bed. 'Now I think you had better talk. You are not an accomplished liar, which is the only possible excuse for being one. You can stay here tonight if you want, but don't bother about lies, because there isn't enough time.'

I was completely silent, shivering and picking the edge of the fringe.

'Has somebody let you down badly? Was this a last resort?'

'No.'

'Poor creature. Were you so desperate then? Had to get away somewhere?'

I nodded.

'Is that yes or no? I can't see.'

'Yes.'

'Your father died – when?'

'Just over two weeks ago.'

'And that was what made you decide to do this?'

'No – not exactly. It's more complicated.'

'I am not asking you from idle curiosity. I might be, but I'm not. Can you go back to your family?'

'I suppose so. Not for a few days. I said that I was going to stay with a friend.'

'Did you tell them it was me?'

'Oh no. They wouldn't have liked it. I said it was a girl who was very tired from nursing someone who'd just died.'

'Very sensible of you,' he said approvingly. 'So that you can go back if you like.'

'Yes.'

'I feel that you are going to cry at any moment,' he said after a pause. 'So I shall just sit here and go on talking to you and asking you questions and we'll both take no notice of you. Why do you hate it at home so much?'

I began to tell him, starting with my brothers at tea, and working backwards. He did not listen in complete silence which would, I think, have frightened me, but threw in small practical questions, which kept my balance for me. In a short time I did not want to cry. I told him nearly everything, the only large exception being Agnes and Edward and *The Mikado*. That I could bear to tell no one, and I was able to persuade myself that it was quite irrelevant.

I came to an end and waited. I think I was certain that he would present me with some solution. At those moments, waiting for someone to speak is rather like the moment before opening a book which one had long desired; or the second at a concert before some new work begins; or the ten seconds before somebody kisses you; or the minute before you open that person's next letter: the almost inevitable disillusionment is far away, indeed it is blessed for the contrast which at that moment it presents. I waited trustfully, expectantly, joyously for that solution; and during those seconds I experienced the complete calm of peaceful certainty.

He had twisted round on the floor facing me and now he suddenly knelt, took my hands and kissed them. Then I thought I knew that he would not be able to help me; and my heart sank down into my hands so that they were heavy and lifeless as he held them.

'Now you will see how very little use people can be to each other,' he said. 'Practically speaking, I'm let out of it. I'm going away tomorrow. Joining the Army.'

'The *Army*?'

'Yes. This war you know. It's going to take up a great many people's time.'

'The Army!' I repeated, dazed. It seemed fantastic. Everyone was in it. Everyone.

'Yes. We can talk about that later. The point is that even if I were continuing here, it would be very difficult for me to be much help. Don't misunderstand me. I think I see your difficulties most clearly, and I am the last person to underestimate them. A purpose in life. I find that hard enough for myself, but for another person, a woman, why it's almost impossible.' He fell silent, staring at my hands.

'Some work,' I said. 'I thought I might be able to do a job of some kind.'

'You might. You might even earn your living. For what?

There is little purpose in earning your living simply in order to go to sleep for the next day's work. And there's very little purpose in marrying someone in order not to earn your living.'

'But I should like it.'

'To marry or work?'

'To work. And marry some day,' I added truthfully.

'Work isn't an end in itself. I know that is a platitude, and so no one really believes it. People are beginning to think of work as an end. I think they may even consider this war as an end. What do you consider the end of a war?'

'To win it?'

He gave my hands a little shake.

'Nobody wins a war nowadays. There is no end to it. War is becoming a compulsory amateur affair. Look at me. I shall be an amateur. That means somebody who does it for the love of the thing. It's not amateur. It's simply compulsory. Once you drag everybody into something, there's no end to it. They muddle along until they're all either dead, or so clearly dying that they can see their own end. Then it stops. It doesn't end.'

'I don't know anything about war.'

'You will,' he said tiredly, and dropped my hands.

I was afraid that he was going to talk and forget me and I was not ready for it. 'I think I should like almost any job as a contrast.'

'Would you?' He looked at me gently. 'I believe you would. What do you want to do?'

'Everyone asks me that. I don't know. But I think that what you said was all very well for people who have a choice, or a talent or something like that, but no use to me. I haven't got any choice, because I don't know what jobs there are, and I haven't any talent that I can see.'

'What, no talent? No talent at all? And you a young lady. Do you not sing?'

'I hate you when you're like that. You won't be serious.'

'I am frequently very serious.'

'Only about yourself, or other things. You won't be serious

about my affairs. You think I'm a child. I wouldn't have come if I'd realized . . .'

'If you'd realized how little I could help you. Well, if it's any comfort to you, I don't think anyone else would be much better. Also, and again if it comforts you, I do think you'll get what you want, because at least you do really seem to want it. You are prepared to take some trouble. Now, let's be practical. You have three possibilities that I can see. One is to go home. From there your chances of getting work that you'll be allowed to do are lessened; but you'll be clothed and fed, which can't be underestimated. Another is to try and get some work which means that you'll be living away from home. It limits the work again, because either you'll have to keep yourself or else persuade your family to make you an allowance which gives them some control over what you do. Considerable control. The third is to stay here with Maria if she'll have you, and find your feet a bit. You'll have to do something for your keep as she won't be able to earn enough. My money goes on keeping this place, as the war is not a paying proposition for those who fight it. The third possibility depends very largely on Maria. All right?'

I nodded. 'What does Maria do?'

'She's a model. No you couldn't do that,' he added seeing my face. 'You aren't nearly flamboyant enough to be popular. It would take a good painter to paint you and they are in a minority. Maria gets plenty of work because she's Spanish.'

'And beautiful.'

'And beautiful, too,' he repeated softly.

'How long have you known her?' I wanted to digest the possibilities before further discussion, and I knew he would need very little encouragement to talk about Maria.

'Three months. We met three months ago. She broke the heel of her shoe in the Underground, and when she calmly kicked off the other shoe, put it in her bag, and walked into the street I followed her. It was all very like a play. She was married to a horrid little man who imports wine,' he went on dreamily. 'He told her a lot of lies about England and married her. Then he brought her back to a semi-detached villa in Lewisham with a semi-detached family who hated her. That was last winter. She was cold and homesick. She hated the family, and wouldn't clean the house. One day she left with a man who sang ballads on the Halls. She went to see him nearly every night and persuaded him to take her. She told him she didn't love him as soon as they had left Lewisham and he was nice about it. He told her the address of an Art School, where he thought she would find work. Of course she got it. Now she lives with me. And tomorrow I go away and leave her. She's very unhappy about it. We haven't had time. She's *very* unhappy,' he repeated with emphasis, and I could feel his grief and resentment.

'Are you sorry?'

'Of course I am. I'm very sorry for both of us. It's worse for me although she may feel it more. It's far worse for me.'

'Now you are being sorry for yourself.'

'Well? What of it?'

'I thought you said it was a bad thing for people to indulge in self-pity.'

'I never said any such thing. A little straightforward self-pity never did anyone any harm. It's reasonable and necessary, if you're to feel anything at all. It's when people start eliminating self-pity that they go wrong. They might simply say "this is very bad and I'm unhappy about it," but in fact they nearly always say "of course I'm not sorry for myself, but . . ." and then a host of excuses and justifications, if possible vilifying someone else concerned. Does my dogmatic and self-assertive nature strike you?' he asked suddenly.

'I – I don't know.' I was caught off my guard.

'It should. Tonight I am feeling peculiarly defensive. Isn't it odd? Men will consider deeply before they buy a tie or choose a meal; but when it comes to throwing aside their purpose in life, possibly life itself, they do not think at all. They consent to being marshalled, controlled, exposed to unimagined shock, mutilation and death, with barely a tremor, and their reasons for complying, if indeed they have any, would compare most shamefully with their reasons for doing almost anything else. And I am one of them.'

'But surely you don't have any choice?'

'What is that? Ignorance or patriotism? It could easily be both.'

'I mean, you would feel you had to fight in the end, wouldn't you?'

'Oh! Oh, I see. I don't know. But I like to preserve the fragile illusion of personal freedom. You see how I cheat myself. I haven't thought beyond that, at all. There hasn't been time. So I choose to join the Army before public opinion joins me to it.'

'And you go tomorrow?'

'Yes. In the afternoon. Late afternoon,' he added as though the question and the assurance were painfully familiar.

'Where do you go?'

'Can you keep a secret? I go to my family for the night. They live in Norfolk. I have not told Maria. Although a Spaniard she left all her family for that wine importer. She wouldn't understand. My father has not recovered from my giving up medicine. I think this decision will go far to reassure him. If I'm killed it would be better for him to think kindly of me. So I go.'

'Have you a mother?'

'No. She died. I have a father, and an aunt who will knit scarves and revel in the potential crisis.'

'What?'

'My death,' he answered impatiently. 'Oh don't look so anguished. I may not be killed, and you may all live to be sorry.'

Maria came back. Her basket was stuffed with bread and mushrooms and eggs and she seemed very pleased.

'Everything has been bought,' she announced and kicked the door open.

'Come and see the kitchen,' said Rupert.

Once there he became very gay. He sat on the small square table and proceeded to admire Maria for all the things she had bought, whilst I sat primly on a chair and watched them. She said she must peel onions, whereupon he rolled up her sleeves and then changed his mind and peeled them himself. She started to pull her sleeves down again, but he turned round suddenly, the tears from the onions already on his face, saying in a melodramatic manner, 'No don't. I want to remember your arms.'

Immediately Maria burst out crying; he hesitated a second, and then dropping the knife on the draining board, walked over to her, pulled her arm from her face and seated her on the edge of the table.

'Maria, I was not serious. You know I was not serious.'

'I cannot laugh about it. I shall die if you go. It gets worse. I have a terrible pain in my heart about you.' She looked up at him frightened and imploring. 'I have never had that. It won't go. I think I shall not be able to bear it.'

'I shall be back soon. They will give me leave in three months.'

'It is that you go. It is not the time. Don't go tomorrow. Go the next day. No one will notice one day more.'

'It is not the time?' he said, repeating her.

She looked at him speechless and desperate, and for a moment, I, who had sat silent and horrified, could exactly feel her passionate resistance to his reason. It was soon over; he took her hands and led her out of the room without a word.

He returned alone to finish the onions, and for some time we did not speak. He seemed gloomy and uncommunicative and I was afraid and could think of nothing to say.

'Can I help you?' I ventured at last.

'No. She'll come back and do the rest. Women do feel like that,' he added abruptly, as though to reassure himself, 'only she says it.'

'Do women feel very differently from men?'

He looked at me and I saw his bewilderment.

'Sometimes. The devil of it is that you never know when. Come and help me wash up the tea, and we'll discuss your problems again by way of a change.'

So we did. From him I learned that jobs were advertised in newspapers; that the war would probably involve a greater choice of work for women; and that one could live on seven and six a week as far as food was concerned. Presently Maria returned, to begin cooking pancakes with skill and concentration, as though nothing had happened; only perhaps her eyes looked more beautiful and her sleeves were rolled down. Rupert explained that I was staying the night. She accepted this quite calmly. They showed me my room, a narrow strip with a bed and pictures stacked against the walls and space for nothing else. Rupert must be a prolific painter I thought, as I edged my way and started to unpack. The evening cooled. My open window looked out on to another back garden with a studio at the end of it, and I watched the sun sink behind the chimney pots, which were black against the delicate sky, uneven like ogre's teeth. I was cold and hungry. It was half past eight.

We finally ate supper in the studio. The pancakes were crisp and thin and filled with mushrooms deliciously spiced.

'She only cooks pancackes,' said Rupert fondly.

'But I make many kinds.'

'You do indeed. I'm proud of your pancakes.'

'At home my mother cooked with charcoal. It was much better.

'With nothing else?'

'She made a hole – there was a hole,' she corrected herself, 'in the ground with flat stones on it and the charcoal underneath. Great care was needed to help the oven heat. But it was much better.'

'One day, we'll go and see,' said Rupert, and she shot him a brilliant grateful glance.

After dinner, when we had carried our plates back to the kitchen, we drank a thin, sharp, flame-coloured wine. I was very cautious about it, refusing more than one glass. Maria lit candles in silver branched candlesticks. They were old candles, and had burned unevenly, so that the flames quivered in the air on either side of their silver stems; like someone balancing with outstretched arms on a rope. Rupert made a drawing of Maria which he threw away before either of us could see it. 'I don't really want to draw you,' he said, and frowned at me, twisting the charcoal round and round in his fingers.

'Draw her,' ordered Maria. 'And for a change, I watch.'

'Oh no you don't. You sing. You entertain us.'

A deadlock ensued as Maria would not sing. Eventually I was placed primly on a chair, 'as you were in the kitchen', with my hands in my lap (a most unromantic position I secretly considered). Maria spread herself on the floor against the bed with some sewing, saying that she would sing if the spirit moved her, or words to that effect.

Rupert started to draw, then said that the paper was not wide enough, and he must have a board. He ambled about the room, pulling things from shelves and out of drawers; creating further confusion, alternately swearing and whistling under his breath until he had procured what he needed. I sat all that time tremulously still, my neck beginning to ache with the effort, but not daring to move lest he should swear at me. Returning to his original position, about four yards away on a low stool, he started again. There was silence except for Maria's thread pulled through her material and the occasional squeak of the charcoal.

'Sing the one about the fishermen,' he said after a while.

Maria sang in a small pleasant voice. It was obviously a folk song; a gay simple tune, of the type which is sad in spite of its gaiety. The Spanish words made it irresistibly compelling and attractive.

'Tell her what it is about,' said Rupert drawing hard.

'It is what the women sing when the boats go out on the first day of the season. It is to ask that their nets will be blessed, that they shall safely return, and that good money shall be made in the season and there shall not be storms.'

'It asks a good deal,' said Rupert.

'It simply asks.' Maria shrugged her shoulders.

'Did you like it? You can talk if you want to.'

'Yes. I should like to hear it again.'

'*I* am not allowed to talk when I sit,' said Maria.

'You're different. You're a professional. Besides you move when you talk.'

Maria sulked a little, but most gracefully; and sang again for us, this time a love song about a girl who was renouncing her lover and the world in order to enter a convent as her positon in the family decreed.

The evening wore away, almost unbearably sweet to me. Maria seemed less unhappy; Rupert calmer and less defensive. He did not talk to Maria as he had with me, I noticed, but accepted her presence and was satisfied, did not probe or analyse or work himself into a frenzy over his own words. There was a feeling of private achievement about them; as though they were at least partially contained in each other, and as though this very dependence were a source of joy and peace to them. I was most acutely aware of it, because I was outside and could watch it undisturbed. It was a very lovely thing to watch.

CHAPTER SEVENTEEN

I never saw the drawing. I don't know whether Rupert kept it.

He went the next day. I kept the secret of where he was going from Maria, as he later once more implored me to do. It linked me with them, gave me a responsible share in their crisis. We saw him off at a station, Maria and I, and when the train had disappeared I touched Maria's arm to go. There were so many tears in her eyes that she could not see, and she swayed a little when I touched her. All the way home in the train the tears poured down her face. It was I who bought the tickets, shepherded us through the long tunnels, and into the lifts. She did not speak at all. I do not think she realized that I was there, or where we were going. When we emerged from under ground, I had to ask someone the way to our street. Maria followed me a pace behind. At first I was anxious that I should lose her, but she seemed docile. I think she regarded me as a link with Rupert; as such I am sure she would have followed me any distance. When we reached the door, I turned to her for a key, but she shook her head and then stared at the pavement immobile, so I rapped the knocker as I had done just over twenty-four hours before. After much effort, the people above admitted us. We went back down the passage, through the garden, and into the studio. Maria flung herself on the bed, and after a moment's hesitation I left her.

There was really nothing I could do: her despair was so evident, I had never seen anyone so openly unhappy. I picked a book at random and retired to my room feeling unutterably depressed. I missed Rupert quite enough to start imagining Maria's feelings. I left both the doors open in case she should call me, but the minutes went by and there was no sound. 'Look after her,' he had said in those last self-

conscious minutes. 'I'll write when I have an address,' and he
had kissed my forehead. Had he known that she would feel
like this, I wondered? Had he known the desolation which
would break on her when he had gone? I remembered her
few tears in his presence; perhaps he did not know. And now,
quite suddenly, I was faced with the problem of how to look
after a girl from another country, whom I barely knew, who
was older than myself (I was young enough for that to
weigh heavily in my mind), and whose grief was well beyond
the limits of my experience. She will not kill herself, I
thought madly; surely she would not do that; but the
temptation to creep to the studio door and look at her
became overpowering. She lay precisely as I had left her,
face downwards, making no sound.

I went back to my room and lay on my bed (it was the only
comfortable thing to do in that narrow and congested
closet). I tried to review the situation. I did not really know
how much Rupert had said to Maria about my staying.
Perhaps she knew nothing about it and would dislike the
idea very much. It was, of course, Rupert's studio, but it
seemed to belong to her, as much, if not more. She had no
alternative. The villa in Lewisham sounded worse than my
home. But it was impossible for me to go back after one day
and night away. If I went back now I should never again
escape. Tomorrow I would buy a newspaper and find myself
a job. When I had found it, I would go home and explain to
them. I would not go home for a week; by which time my
brothers should have left, leaving only my mother and sister
to persuade. Rupert's warnings about jobs seemed absurd
and irrelevant. He had no conception of how tedious life had
been in my home, and therefore his ideas of what was stimu-
lating were vastly more ambitious than my own. I would
allow three days for finding the job, and then, consulting
Maria, I would decide about where to live. These decisions
were lighthearted, and based on profound ignorance, but
even so, they took some time to achieve.

It was late when I finally reached my conclusions, and
there was still no sign or sound of Maria. I looked in the

kitchen for food. I found two eggs, some celery, a melon and a small end of bread. Nothing else. There was coffee, but I was not very sure how to make it. I put everything else on a tray. Maria would want coffee. With great difficulty I boiled a kettle on the oil stove, with the eggs in it; taking half an hour over the business. The coffee was in a biscuit tin. I measured three teaspoonsful into a jug, and added one for luck, poured on the water and waited. It was obviously wrong. I added more and more coffee, until the jug was half full of it, and the water slopped over the top turgid with coffee grounds. It was very difficult to prepare anything in other people's kitchens I decided, faint with hunger.

Maria still lay on the bed. When I set the tray on a table, she sat up and stared at me. Her face was quite white, which somehow shocked and astonished me. I expected her to be flushed, with red eyes, but this strained even pallor alarmed me. She had not been crying then, just lying there for these two silent hours.

'I've brought a meal,' I said.

She would not eat, although I tried to make her as hard as my diffidence would allow. The coffee was appalling, but she drank it without comment. I tried to talk; she replied with courtesy to my advances, which soon came to an end, however, when I could think of nothing new to say. The evening dragged on. I do not remember anything about it except the general oppression of complete anti-climax.

She knocked on my door when I was undressing; wearing the wrapper in which I had first seen her, with her hair down her shoulders. It is how I remember her, standing in a doorway, waiting for me to speak.

'Understand me,' she said. 'I do not *at all* mind your staying here. *At all*,' she emphasized, as though aware that she had not perfectly expressed her meaning. Then, before I could reply, she had gone; shutting my door with a gentle decision which permitted no further discourse.

I lay awake for a long time that night, thinking about her and Rupert, and the love people were able to have for each other. There were my parents to consider, but whether they had ever felt deeply about each other at moments like these I could not determine. Perhaps they had not been parted, at least not for a war. Perhaps they had never really had the chance or conditions to be in love. Perhaps parents had to be too much concerned with houses and children and making enough money; so that the initial reason for undertaking all these responsibilities was lost under a morass of material emergencies. Of course Rupert and Maria were not married. I had to think very hard here, because they were to me an exception, and I felt cautious about them. Nearly everyone married, and I had always understood that this was because they fell in love; but according to Maria loving someone was a life in itself demanding all the energy and sensibility that she possessed.

The phrase 'until they've settled down' came into my mind as being one which was often applied to newly married people. Rupert had said that he and Maria had not had time; perhaps that was what he had meant. Then I had only the extremes before me; the end of my parents, and the beginning of Rupert and Maria. This settling down then, seemed an unhappy horrible affair, a disillusionment from which there was no escape or second chance. I did not want to settle down if it was like that, I decided. Perhaps it was merely a matter of selecting one's love with tremendous care. I remembered a discussion between my father and another man about what book they would take to a desert island. I remembered privately selecting my choice, and knew that now I would take no such book because I had changed. One could not manage with any one book on a desert island. Suddenly, like a shooting star in the midst of these depressing conclusions, Mrs Lancing fell into my mind. She seemed happy enough; serene, and surrounded by her devoted family. I turned over to sleep, and the star went out as suddenly as it had come; because try as I would, I could not imagine myself a Mrs Lancing.

CHAPTER EIGHTEEN

I went home. Maria accepted my departure indifferently. She seemed sunk in a kind of stupor. I never saw her again.

I only answered one of the advertisements I read, for the simple reason that it seemed the only position I was capable of occupying. Also, it was the only position that my family would allow; and that I could believe would suit my purpose. I read that a lady living in south-east England, required a young and cheerful companion; light duties, congenial surroundings, etc.; ending with a box number to which I wrote. I was subsequently interviewed in London by an enigmatic but kindly relative of Mrs Border. I had a long argument with my family, which I won through sheer patience and determination; and about three weeks after Rupert had left the studio I set out from my home for the third time in my life.

I realized in the train, that having secured permission to take this step was perhaps my most considerable achievement hitherto. My sister had unwittingly turned the scale by assuring my mother that I should be back in no time at all, and that then I should settle down. That was the phrase she used, with no idea that it was the one utterance calculated to spur me into persistence.

Two men in the compartment were discussing the probable ambitions and state of mind of the Kaiser; but it was a beautiful afternoon and I did not listen. I watched the tightly packed grey houses with gigantic sunflowers in their back gardens; the street children (who never looked at the train, I noticed, for they lived too near the railway); the factories, belching smoke and splayed with advertisement of their products. Then the beginnings of country; or rather the end of London. My thoughts began travelling ahead to the house where I was going, and Mrs Border whose company I was to be paid to keep. The country gradually arrived, and was beautiful. There were enormous patterns of corn stooks curving in lines over the fields; trees laden with leaves declining to a languid yellow; steep fields of stubble and clover; and girls picking blackberries into a blue pail. There were neat green ponds spattered with ducks; hedges sharpened with brilliant berries; rich brown and white cows muddling through a gate; and the sky a pale simple blue, even and cloudless.

What would Mrs Border be like? The relative had said she was lame; had murmured something about rheumatism. I would wheel her in a chair, I thought; she would be certain to possess a chair. I would take her for walks in the afternoons. In many ways I would make her life nicer for her. I wondered what Rupert would say to this adventure. I had not heard from him, although Maria had had a postcard just before I left the studio. She had begun to work again and had promised to let me know about them both, although she never wrote letters. Already the studio seemed distant. I did not mind: setting off to an unknown destination with a salary was an absorbing occupation.

The men were discussing the probable strength of the German navy. They did not agree about anything. They became angrier and more confidential as the stations slipped by. It was a leisurely train. About half an hour too soon I began looking at my watch, struggling with my case, and tucking away the ends of my hair.

A fly met me at the station. At this point I began to feel vaguely frightened. It was not the fly, or the journey, both of which I enjoyed; it was the curious feeling that in a matter of minutes I should be snatched away from myself, be questioned, watched, appraised, be alone with someone I did not know, and utterly subject to her approval. I began to feel sick. Just as the sickness was becoming unbearable we turned into a lane and then a short drive overhung with evergreen trees. It was like diving into a cave.

The drive ended in a small sweep before the house, which had pointed gables and was covered with creeper. The man jumped down and rang the bell, which was immediately answered by a tall elderly parlour maid. She led the way straight upstairs to a bedroom, followed by me, and the driver with my luggage. I was requested to ring when I was ready to be taken downstairs to tea, as Mrs Border was waiting for it, whereupon they withdrew on my presenting the man with a shilling for his services. I hurriedly washed my hands, and laid my jacket on the bed, but even in my nervous haste had time to be struck by one feature of the room. Its walls were covered, literally covered, with water colours, all in precisely the same kind of golden frame, six deep on the walls, with barely two inches between them. They gave the room a curiously crowded appearance, as with the sun from the window, they were reflected in each others' glass, which multiplied their already impressive numbers, and confused their colour to distraction. I rang.

Mrs Border sat in a large chair, very close to a blazing fire. The curtains were half drawn across the narrow Gothic windows and I did not immediately see her face.

'Come in, come in,' she said. 'Come and sit by the fire after your terrible journey. We'll have tea at once, Spalding.' There was only one other chair within polite conversational reach, and that was equally near the fire. However I sat on it.

'Well,' said Mrs Border. 'Let's have a good look at each other. This is the first time you've ever done anything of this nature, isn't it?'

'Yes,' I said. I was looking at her hair which was quite black and most elaborately curled with a waving fringe arranged across her forehead.

'And why are you doing it now? Quarrelled with your family or crossed in love?'

This seemed to me impertinent.

'Neither,' I said firmly. 'I wanted a job.'

'Good. How old are you?'

'Nineteen,' I lied.

'You don't look it. Well, you can take it from me that men are very queer creatures.'

Spalding brought the tea on a large Japanese tray which

176

she set on a low table between us. It was the most magnificent tea.

'You pour out,' said Mrs Border. 'I should like a quince jelly sandwich, with brown bread.' I poured the tea, and made the sandwich.

The walls of this room also were covered with water colours. I was beginning to realize that they were the work of one artist when I caught Mrs Border looking at me with small grey eyes.

'You were looking at my pictures.'

'Are they yours?'

'I own them and I painted them. I never sell them. I like them round me. After tea you must examine them more closely. Now I should like asparagus with brown bread rolled round it.'

She ate exceedingly fast.

'Help yourself to food,' she said. 'I don't like to know what other people eat; it confuses me.'

She occupied the rest of tea, which continued for a long time, by asking me about my family, and background as she called it. I must have sounded incredibly dull, because after that day she never asked me any more about myself. It was terribly hot in the room. Tea was cleared away, and we continued to sit there until she told me to look at her pictures.

'Start there,' she said, pointing to the door. I assured her that I knew nothing about painting, but she brushed this aside.

'I don't care what you know. I want to hear what you *feel*,' she said.

So round the room I went, admiring what I afterwards counted to be seventy-five water colours.

Sunsets, flowers, churches, buildings, the sea and bits of the room I was in. Many subjects were repeated again and again, particularly the sunsets. The pictures were bad. But apart from avoiding this elementary and final criticism, I could think of nothing to say. There was something almost lovable in her assurance of their quality. Finally, hot and embarrassed, I was allowed back to my seat.

Mrs Border then proceeded to tell me a little about herself, and the life she now led. She lived very quietly, she said; because of her lameness and her unfortunate life she had few friends. I gathered that her uncle had left her the house, or lived in it before her, or bought it for her, and that except for one or two relations to stay, she saw nobody. Very different from what it once had been. Her narration was larded with obscure hints about her past; occasionally, I had the impression that she invited questions, but I was so conscious of my new position that I dismissed this as absurd. Except for going to church three times a year – she would go more often, she assured me, but for the present vicar, of whom she disapproved – she went abroad very little, except to London every two or three years to shop. But her lameness made these visits increasingly exhausting, and also rendered a companion necessary. She was, she said, quite content with her painting and other ploys. She waved her hand vaguely when she said this, and for the first time I noticed an utterly silent and motionless parrot on a perch. I could not think why I had not seen him before. His stillness was as noticeable as the shuffling and squawking I should have expected from such a bird.

'Was he asleep?' I asked interrupting her.

'No. But he only talks at night. He's a night bird, aren't you, Iago?' The bird rolled its curious double eyelids at her but did not move.

We sat there until seven o'clock, when Mrs Border retired to prepare for dinner. I offered, rather timidly, to assist her, but she answered that she did not wish me to begin my duties that evening, leaving me in considerable apprehension as to what my duties would be when they did begin.

Alone, I walked to the windows. They were narrow and upright; fashioned to admit as little light as possible. The light was dying already. Colour had almost left the garden into which I looked. I could, however, faintly discern a brick wall edged with flower beds, a gravel path and a lawn. The size and shape of the garden could not be seen.

I was startled by the maid, Spalding, who made up the fire,

and then drew the curtains, with a purposeful gesture which depressed me. She did not speak, and I could think of nothing to say, although then I should have been grateful for the utmost banality.

I was standing uncertainly in the middle of the room when a shrill little gong rang. I followed Spalding meekly across the passage to the dining-room.

Mrs Border was already seated at the end of a small and elaborately laid table. She was clad in plum-coloured silk and a white cashmere shawl. I apologized for my lateness.

'Dinner is at a quarter past seven,' she replied affably.

We began a long meal, with exceedingly hot soup which Mrs Border drank with alarming speed. Game, sweet and a savoury followed. I found it difficult even to simulate hunger. The room was papered deep red which alone would have produced an illusion of heat; but seemed now to collect the warmth of the fire and throw it back at one from all sides of the room.

We repaired at length to the drawing-room, where we played backgammon until ten o'clock, when hot milk was brought to us by Spalding, which I was emboldened to refuse.

'A little weight wouldn't do you any harm,' observed Mrs Border, and I had the uneasy feeling of my body being appraised by someone I barely knew.

When she had finished her milk, she rose from her chair announcing bed for both of us. She stood for some time, holding on to the tall arm of the chair, and biting her lips as though in pain. I offered to help, but she refused, saying that she was only stiff and needed a few minutes to recover.

Eventually we journeyed slowly out of the room, the door of which was to be left open to afford us light. I stood at the foot of the stairs.

'Up you go,' she said. 'I don't like people behind me on the stairs.' I went, and stood interminably at the top, while she hoisted herself up, step by step.

'Breakfast will be at eight-thirty for you. I have it in my room. When you have finished, I shall require you to come and see me. I think that is all. Good night.' She passed to her room and shut the door.

The windows in my room were tightly closed. I was hot and exhausted from the hours of confined and unfamiliar surroundings. I opened them and leaned out on to the gravel sweep before the house, hemmed in with dark motionless trees. It was still, with no colour or sound; almost secretly quiet with perhaps thunder high in the sky above, which, even now, might be descending, crushing the clouds into rain. I don't know why it should have seemed important but I remember well the certainty in my mind that it would rain, and I was so strung up with the oppressive atmosphere inside the house, that I slept with this notion as a relief.

I woke very suddenly later in the night. It is well known how some grief or fear at the end of a dream can start one into instant wakefulness: the dream is forgotten, and one is left only with the shock of sudden consciousness, and the feeling that something is about to happen, that the shock is only a prelude. I woke like that; every nerve expectant and tense.

All was silent: and then I distinctly heard the most dreadful paroxysm of laughter. It started very high up, dying into a low strangled chuckle, as though whatever was laughing had not breath to subside. It seemed to come from downstairs in the house.

There ensued the most complete and utter silence, during which I heard the blood beating on each side of my forehead, as I lay, frozen and motionless. Whoever had laughed like that could not be sane. Seconds passed while I sought frantically for some solution, however terrible, that could explain it. I dared not move. The sound had come from downstairs; it had been muffled, although distinct; there were walls and stairs between me and it ... Mrs Border ... No, it could not be she ... One of the servants was mad, had laughed in her sleep. In a flash *Jane Eyre* leaped to my mind. The laugh of the first Mrs Rochester wandering about at night, in the dark house. I felt the sweat down my backbone; and still there was no further sound, no sound at all.

With trembling fingers I lit my candle, sinking back on my pillow as the faint misty light filled the room, and I saw my own suitcase, my hairbrush; practical everyday objects lying there to comfort me.

Then I noticed with a return of fear that my door was not shut. Surely it had been shut. It was only just open, just ajar; as though the lock had not been secured and it had sprung back of its own accord. It frightened me, and I could not get up to shut it. I lay and watched it, the long dark slim edge of the door; until the dawn broke or crept into the room, and the candle fluttered, paling in the gentle light. After which I must have slept.

CHAPTER NINETEEN

Spalding woke me with the apparently noiseless efficiency of the trained housemaid. She drew the curtains, placed a can of hot water in my basin, covered it with the towel, and retired. The moment she had left the room I jumped out of bed and tried the door. I opened and shut it. It shut quite naturally. I found this oddly comforting; and dressed with a slight feeling of shame at my fears, and relief that nobody had witnessed them. Perhaps Mrs Border would mention that one of the servants slept badly – had nightmares. At any rate, I would say nothing about it.

I breakfasted alone in the red dining-room which, relieved of its heavy drawn curtains, appeard dank and gloomy. There was a small rectangular conservatory at one end of it, which had been concealed at night by the curtains, and which now added a dense grey light to the room. It appeared to be filled with ferns. All the glass was edged with a narrow rim of alternate red and blue.

Immediately after breakfast, I was told by Spalding that Mrs Border wished me to see her in her bedroom. The door opposite mine on the landing, I was told.

She was seated in a high-backed armchair drawn close to a blazing fire that looked so established I could hardly believe it had only been lighted that morning. She wore a lace cap with ribbons tied under her chin, a wrapper, a number of shawls and at least seven rings on her hands. Her hands were very noticeable, as they were both held out to the fire, the light of which reflected the jewels as her fingers trembled. A breakfast tray in a state of abject confusion lay at her feet. The walls of the room were, of course, encrusted with watercolours, but water-colours possessed of one different characteristic from the many others I had seen in the house. They were all paintings of ruins: not always the same ruin, although there was a marked similarity. They were not precisely pleasant or unpleasant, but were very much more compelling than the other paintings; they forced one to look at them when one was in the room, and to remember them when one was not. Mrs Border never alluded to the ruins once, but I was always certain that it was she who had painted them, and surprised that she never attempted to command my appreciation of them as she so frequently did for the rest of her pictures.

I cannot always remember the exact order in which I noticed the many curious aspects of that house. On first entering Mrs Border's room, I was chiefly aware of the intense heat, and my dislike of other people's bedrooms. I stood in front of Mrs Border with my hands behind my back, in the attitude of one awaiting orders.

'Have you had enough to eat?' she asked.

'Yes, thank you.'

'Well now, what am I going to do with you all day?' She regarded me a moment, during which I felt exceedingly uncomfortable. Really her manner was very embarrassing.

'I shall shortly get up. I'm partially dressed as it is. But there are one or two little things . . .' Her voice trailed off into an unexpected silence which was broken by a coal falling out of the grate. 'Pick it up, pick it up!' she cried. 'Not above that sort of thing, are you?'

'No.'

I tried to pick up the coal, but it was red hot, and while I was fumbling for the tongs, she bent down out of her chair and picking it up in her fingers threw it back into the fire all in a moment. I looked at her in astonishment but she merely said, 'I hardly notice heat.'

There was a slight pause.

'Now, I think I'd better tell you what *I* do, and then you can fit yourself in. I shall require you here a little longer, and then, while I am finishing myself, you are to water the pots in the conservatory. I paint all the morning but I like someone in the room when I am working, provided they occupy themselves. There are usually things for you to do. In any case it is not considered good for me to be too much alone. After lunch, I rest, and you may do as you please. Then I like my tea and a little conversation. Is that quite clear?'

'Quite,' I said.

'So you see, you will not have a very strenuous time of it.'

'Oh no.'

'I expect you are fond of walking. There is beautiful country here. What sort of day is it?'

'I am afraid I have not noticed.'

'Go and see.'

I walked to the window. I observed that a little watery sunshine mottled the lawn in the garden, lay on the window sill, the top of the mirror, the dressing-table ... and then I received a very unpleasant shock. On the corner of this dressing-table stood a black wig. It was dull, yet exceedingly greasy, and elaborately arranged in curls and puffs. The parting was unnaturally white; I could see a few grains of dust lying on the coarse sleek hair stretched away from it. I must have stared at it for only a second but Mrs Border interrupted me.

'I wear a wig,' she said softly. 'I have almost no hair, and so I wear a wig.'

I stammered something, and was about to leave the window, but, rising to her feet, she moved towards some curtained recess, loosening the ribbons under her chin and saying, 'Will you lift it very gently and bring it to me? But carefully; we mustn't have it disarranged.'

I lifted the wig off its stand, carried it to her, waited until she stretched out her hands for it, then left the room as I was immediately told to do; and all the time I was filled with the most unreasonable distaste, almost horror. It was no good telling myself that it was ridiculous, even unkind, to be so repelled by something which, after all, the poor woman could not help. I was repelled, and my shame at having been so horrified induced a kind of irritation at Mrs Border herself. There was no need for me to have seen it at all. She was quite active enough to have fetched it herself. Then, as I settled down to the peaceful task of watering innumerable damp green ferns, I began to feel calmer and more ashamed of being so easily startled. Poor Mrs Border. I had read of people enduring some terrible shock or hardship which robbed them of their hair; quite suddenly it went white, or fell out. Perhaps this had happened to her and I should feel only sorry that it was so. But at the back of my mind lingered an unpleasant feeling that she had meant me to be startled, had even, perhaps, arranged it. She had never asked again about the weather.

Mrs Border painted all the morning, or rather applied herself to the business of painting, for although, as I afterwards found, it was her regular habit to paint, it took Spalding and me an hour to produce all the equipment she considered necessary. She sat in her chair while we fetched little tables, pots of water, sketch books, folios of paper, pencils that had to be sharpened to a point where they invariably broke, palette boxes, paint boxes, a most fragile and intractable easel, bundles of brushes tied together with strands of darning wool; all these had to be arranged to her eventual satisfaction. Spalding was dismissed, and I was given the task of unravelling an endless hand-knitted Shetland shawl. Mrs Border painted with great rapidity. One by one the sheets of blistering wet paper were laid all over the floor. The fire was continually replenished, cups of beef tea were brought, and, at intervals, the parrot attacked his sunflower seeds with a kind of weary but vicious dexterity.

Sitting in an overheated room, unravelling an apparently endless strand of fragile and sticky wool in a dead silence only punctuated by sudden alarming and inconsequent questions, was, I discovered, one of the most unpleasant ways of spending a morning, and I was very glad when luncheon was announced. We had what Mrs Border described as a light meal, which consisted mainly of eggs, fish and a very substantial pudding, after which she retired to rest until a quarter past four, telling me I might amuse myself.

'If you think yourself capable of it. You don't amuse me very much as yet. As yet,' she repeated tapping her stick on the dining-room floor. 'However, there's the whole winter before us and people age during the winter as you must have noticed. Run along.'

I repaired disconsolately to the drawing-room; listened until Mrs Border had thudded slowly up the stairs and shut her door; and then partly with the idea of going out, and partly as a prisoner turns to the light, I walked to the windows and looked out. It was pouring with rain; a heavy silent shower, darkening the trees, battering the life out of the Michaelmas daisies and chrysanthemums until they were sodden indistinguishable clumps, sharpening the green complexion of the lawn, and lighting on the odd pieces of slipware and bottle glass in the high garden wall until they winked and glittered.

It was too wet to go out, and I was too oppressed to care. I was about to leave the window, when I heard a tiny click, and turning round, saw the parrot sidling quickly along his perch towards me. He stopped the moment that I turned round; staring at me unblinking and motionless except for the ruffled feathers slowly settling on his neck. I moved quickly out of his reach to the fire, wondering dully whether he had been going to attack me.

The prospect seemed so depressing, I was so divided in my mind between disliking my position and fearing that I should prove unsatisfactory and lose it, that I sank on to a footstool and wept, to the accompaniment of a huge clock on the mantelpiece with a heavy metallic tick. This, not unnaturally, did not last until a quarter past four, and after considering the possibility of procuring a clean handkerchief from my bedroom and discarding it on the ground that I might wake Mrs Border, I searched for a book (there were very few in the room), chose one at random, and tried to read. It was a long and very dull novel and had an inscription inside, 'To Madgie from Dick. Christmas 1889'. Years ago.

I read for what seemed an eternity of ticks, when I heard a door shut and voices. A few seconds later Spalding announced the Reverend Mr Tyburn.

'Don't disturb Mrs Border,' he said. 'I am early, and can very well wait until a quarter past.'

Spalding looked at him disbelievingly, left the room, and was heard to mount the stairs.

Mr Tyburn introduced himself again. I told him my name, and we both stood for a moment before the fire while he warmed his hands. There was a short unavoidable silence; then he straightened himself, and, rather nervously, I invited him to sit down.

'You are paying us a visit,' he said when we had seated ourselves.

I explained my position. He coughed a little, said 'Ah yes' two or three times; then plunging at the subject which he thought most likely to interest me (or, at least, in which he felt I ought to be most interested) asked, 'And how is Mrs Border?' adding hopefully, 'Well, I trust?'

'I don't know really how she was before.'

'Of course,' he replied. 'Naturally. Most suitable that you should be here to keep her interested in things. Not good for people to be too much alone.' He turned to the fire again.

We continued a rather desperate stilted conversation for another ten minutes or so, from which I gathered there were several beautiful walks; that the village was small and straggling (he seemed to resent this); and that the church was in an advanced state of decay (he seemed proud of that). At exactly a quarter past four Mrs Border appeared.

'*You* are punctual at any rate!' he began apologetically, rising out of his chair.

'One of us must be punctual, or there would be no point in time,' she said settling herself.

'Of course,' he murmured as tea was brought.

During this meal she questioned him minutely as to the affairs of the parish; closing his replies either with some alarming contradictory statement, or with a significant silence, implying strong disapproval. He sat there, patient, nervous and conciliatory, with crumbs of shortbread all over his knees, and a cup of cold tea balanced on them. Every now and then he made desperate efforts to bring me into the conversation, and she waited until he had, so to speak, finished with me; then resumed her examination of his business.

After tea she suddenly sent me to post a letter, remarking that the air would do me good, and I escaped.

Outside it was still very oppressive, and I walked down the drive with great warm drops from the trees falling portentously on to the back of my neck. I had been told to turn to the right at the bottom of the drive and to follow the lane until it forked, when the post box would be found a little way up on the left.

On the way back I came across a tall, bony, elderly woman collecting sticks. She walked along the grass verge in little bursts of haste, intermittently swooping down upon a stick which she put in a rush bag, and exclaiming continually to herself until we drew level, when she ceased speaking, stopped, and stared at me in a burning and penetrating manner until I was past her, when she broke out again in some eager but inaudible speech.

When I returned the vicar had left. Mrs Border was seated alone, with her hands spread out to the fire.

'That man's a fool!' she remarked on seeing me. 'The whole parish going to rack and ruin. Wearing out that church of his with tourists and services, until, mark my words, it will be nothing but a ruin. He hardly ever comes, did he ask you anything about me?'

'He asked if you were well.'

'He wouldn't have cared,' she retorted. 'Perhaps you had better read to me. Third book from the right on the bottom shelf.'

It was some novel set in India and had a religious background. I do not know clearly what it was about, because I was told to start half-way through the book; the place, I remember, was marked by a parrot feather.

After dinner when we were seated over the hot milk which I no longer had the courage or heart to refuse, Mrs Border asked me whether I should have behaved as the heroine had behaved (she had, for some reason unknown to me, written a long letter refusing to marry the man to whom she was engaged, and with whom, judging by the subsequent description of her failing health and declining spirit, she was deeply in love); and whether I considered that either she or her fiancé would abide by her decision? I replied that I didn't know why she had written the letter, but that, as it was a novel, I was sure that she would change her mind.

'And what makes you think the girl would behave so differently in a novel?'

'Because I don't think things turn out so conveniently in real life.'

'What, never?'

I hesitated a little, 'Not always.'

'You *have* been crossed in love,' she cried triumphantly.

Blushing deeply, and disliking her not a little, I denied this, and prepared to continue reading, but the page was uncut.

'Mantelpiece, to the right of the paperweight and behind the peacock feathers,' she said instantly.

I cut the uncut page, and began looking for others following it, when she said: 'And what do you think of my knife?'

It was a metal knife, the handle a cobra's hooded head adorned with two red stones for eyes. It was not beautiful and I did not know what to say about it.

'Strange, isn't it?' she said watching the knife in my hands. 'I expect you wonder how I came by that.'

I looked up inquiringly. She was in a gentler mood, and seemed to be thinking deeply. There was a short silence, then she held out her hands for it and said: 'It belonged to my beloved husband. I expect you wonder how he came by an Indian paper knife,' she added a little defensively.

I had *not* wondered, but she seemed to invite a respectful curiosity, so I murmured something and waited.

'He was serving in India you see. He was in the Army.'

'Were you with him?'

'Not out there. I was never out there,' she said hastily. 'He was sent out shortly after we were married. Three months, I think it was. Yes, only three months.'

There was a curious uncertain suspension about everything she said, and also a sense of impending tragedy which I found irresistible.

'He was sent out very suddenly, but he swore that I should join him. We had such a wonderful time. He was everything to me, absolutely everything; everything I had dreamed and imagined in a man. He promised that as soon as he was settled and had found somewhere for me to live I should follow. He wrote to me almost every day, and I waited and hoped and wrote to him. After he had been away a month (it seemed an eternity to me), he said that he had found a home for me, and that I might join him as soon as things were more settled. He said that the situation where he was stationed was very unsettled. He wanted to be absolutely sure that there was no likelihood of trouble to which I might be exposed. Always devoted, you see.'

She had stopped speaking, and stared at the paper knife. I waited a moment for her to continue, but she seemed to have forgotten me, and after a long pause I ventured rather timidly, 'Yes?'

'He was stabbed,' she said. 'Stabbed in the back one night on his way back to the barracks. He had been dining with friends and he left alone at about eleven o'clock. He was found next morning a few yards from their home.' She recounted it all very quietly and without expression, almost as though it were a dream, and I felt tears starting in my eyes at the thought of her dreadful grief.

'I am so . . . How terrible for you.'

'It was terrible. No one will ever know what I suffered. I was ill for a long time. For weeks I lay, unable to think of anything else but my great happiness which had so suddenly, so cruelly been taken from me. No one understood. It was simply another young tragedy to them. To me it was my life in ruins. It is very hard for a young person to understand that. You are too young to have suffered. Really suffered,' she repeated unsteadily. 'Or do you imagine,' she continued, 'that you also have suffered?'

'Nothing like that,' I exclaimed. My own anxieties and griefs contracted as I spoke, until I should have been ashamed to admit them at all. She drew in her breath deeply and looked at me, almost as though she were pleased with this admission.

'Well my dear,' she said kindly, 'let us hope you never will.' And there the conversation ended.

The days proceeded, each one seeming so long, so packed with ponderous detail, with monotony and rain and loneliness, that it was sometimes hard to believe that there would be another exactly like it. It was an existence only broken for me by the brief illusion of liberty when at night I retired to my bedroom to undress and sleep. Then, while I shed my clothes, I could enjoy the respite of being alone, without the strain of possible interruption, of a meal, of being told how to spend my time, of being observed while I spent it.

I was frightfully, almost unbearably lonely during that time. I think it was only my comparative inexperience, and perhaps, too, a certain pity for Mrs Border, that made it at all tolerable. I suppose I always thought that something would happen. I know that in my room at night I would repeat endlessly to myself that I was earning my living, that Rupert was away, and that my home was equally monotonous.

The outstanding feature of that house was the sense of complete isolation one experienced when inside it. The affairs of the world, the war, even the village were utterly outside the house, which was fraught with its own daily routine, little tempers and accidents, domestic arrangements and confidences, heat and time and Mrs Border.

Since her revelation to me I was less afraid of Mrs Border. I successfully evaded the question whether I liked her, by a welter of conventional and very conscious emotion about her unhappy life. I felt that my association with her was a precarious and temporary affair, based on mutual ignorance of our natures, on mutual and perhaps tragic need, with an impenetrable gap of generation: she felt that her life was over; I felt that mine had not begun; and in each case we were surprised, and a little resentful that this should be so. I had to be sorry for her, because a great deal of the time I found her repellent, overwhelming, not a little frightening, even sinister. This last aspect, however, did not at first intrude itself. Everything that happened was new to me and for that reason often had very little other significance; it was not until I had thoroughly settled down that I had time and leisure to be afraid.

My fears were precipitated about two weeks after my arrival by my again hearing the ghastly paroxysm of laughter in the middle of the night; again followed by complete silence. I lay petrified as before, and then eventually managed to light a candle. My door was shut, but this time I lay waiting for it to open, to reveal some tall and hitherto unseen figure, dangerous and insane, or ghostly. I imagined the click of the releasing lock, the little blow of air, and the doorway filled with this apparition, quite silent now, but smiling at the remains of the terrible laughter. I imagined the figure pausing, watching me, and then slowly advancing into the room, while I lay, unable to move, even perhaps unable to scream. So I continued the remaining hours of the night, watching the door; my mind a riot of horrible thoughts, until, as before, the grey light suffused the room and relieved me.

The next morning it was hard to believe that I had been so much afraid; the very routine, dull and distasteful (as, for instance, the ritual which took place in Mrs Border's bedroom), belied my fear. I was called; dressed, and breakfasted in the red dining-room which reserved its utmost gloom for me in the morning; repaired to Mrs Border's bedroom (always an inferno of heat and confusion), where she instructed me in my duties for the day, or simply talked at me about what she intended doing herself; and then was dismissed, sometimes having been told to fetch her wig, sometimes without it being mentioned. I found this last particularly unnerving, as I dreaded the office, and the uncertainty of whether or no I would be called upon to perform it somehow made it worse. During the morning I would mend her thick stockings; water the plants in the conservatory; feed the parrot; polish her sticks (she had a number of them, all already highly polished); and fulfil numerous requirements attendant upon her painting. She would often demand painting water, saucers, even criticism (the amateur variety, which it was usually wise to resolve in heartfelt approval). Paper had to be cut to the requisite size with the paper knife, and a significant silence prevailed while I cut it. Flowers had to be arranged: I spent nerve-wracking and wearisome hours moving one flower and then another, and filling the vases to the brim with hot water, a practice upon which she always insisted although the water slopped over if anyone slammed a door.

All these things contrived to make the two frightful nights I had had seem quite unreal and exaggerated. If the servants had ever seemed in the least communicative and human, I might perhaps have confided in them; in Spalding at least, as I saw very little of the cook. But throughout my time there I never got beyond the trivialities which Spalding apparently considered essential to our respective positions in the house. I might, I suppose, have recounted something of my private experiences to my mother or sister, but our correspondence was mutually on the family basis where nobody writes anything which anybody wishes to read. I wrote one stilted and inaccurate letter to Rupert, which I addressed to his studio; but I received no reply, and felt discouraged and too cut off for any further efforts in his direction.

In the afternoon, Mrs Border invariably rested, and if it rained, which it usually did, I read the few books at my disposal (there were no newspapers at all). On the rare occasions when it was dry I went out, trying in vain to discover the walks which Mr Tyburn had assured me existed. I trudged up and down tortuous little lanes sunk low between hedges, and once I actually encountered Mr Tyburn himself.

He was coming out of a cottage. Before he saw me I watched the goodwill slowly ebb from his face as he hastened down the path until, when he reached the gate, it was entirely replaced by a weary and distracted expression which I now saw he must commonly wear. Then he caught sight of me, his face lighted up, and he stood collecting something suitable to say as he waited for me to reach him.

'Are you going up the lane? *I* am going up the lane,' he began, presenting me with a delightful coincidence.

I assented. We trudged up the hill together for a few moments without speaking, then he suddenly said: 'How does she occupy her time these days?'

I was rather at a loss.

'She paints a good deal you know.'

'Of course. And do you paint also?'

'Oh no.'

'I suppose one needs a dexterity of hand and a vivid imagination. Never tried myself. I haven't the time. Oh no.' He laughed cheerlessly. 'Mrs Border produces a remarkable quantity of work. Remarkable.'

'And she does it all out of her head,' I said almost proudly.

'Just so,' he said uneasily. 'Of course one can have too much imagination you know.'

'Not for painting surely?'

'Not for painting of course. Painting is an art. Perhaps for other things . . .' He broke off and glanced at me anxiously: he seemed confused and searching for something to say. 'Have you managed to get her out at all?'

'Well no, I haven't. But the weather has been so bad. She rests in the afternoons,' I added painstakingly. (The thought of suggesting to Mrs Border that she do anything was very alarming.) Nevertheless, although it had not previously occurred to me as strange, I realized that since I had known her she had not once been out of the house, and I began perforce to wonder why not. I was interrupted from this anxious speculation by Mr Tyburn who had sighted a cottage into which he seemed to consider he might reasonably escape.

'Ask her whether a visit would be acceptable next week,' he said, thankfully backing into a fuchsia hedge. 'Dear me, sorry to leave you of course, but I have more business here. I hope yours will be a pleasant walk.' And he disappeared.

At tea-time Mrs Border was in such an unapproachably fractious mood that I did not dare mention meeting Mr Tyburn. We ate muffins and seed cake, and I read to her, frequently interrupted by her commanding me to put more coal on the fire, adjust a screen at her back, or move her footstool further from her chair. She retired earlier than usual to change for dinner, and I was left in the over-heated room with the dreary prospect of playing all the evening with her a game that I disliked, but which I invariably won, with all the consequent bad feeling I had learned to expect from this.

At dinner, however, she seemed in a much happier frame of mind. I had noticed that she always appeared more gracious when wrapped in her white lace shawl. We had a long leisurely meal, during which she expatiated on painting, illustrating her views by many examples of her own work, which she compared favourably (and with an absolute assurance I could not but admire) with many specimens by what I had been taught to call the Old Masters.

From her I learned that 'they' had invariably fallen into a selection of traps from which she personally had escaped. They had painted solely for money; they had indulged in a variety of unpleasant subjects (she was particularly firm on this point); they had copied and even helped each other; they had painted pictures which were too large or too inaccessible; they had painted too much or too little; and, above all, their personal habits and private lives left so much to be desired that in a decent society they would never have been allowed to paint at all. 'They would have been better employed mending roads. The roads abroad are dreadful,' she finished grimly.

As I knew nothing about painting or painters, but very much more of Mrs Border's disposition when disagreed with, I accepted these widespread recriminations whole-heartedly, with the consequence that by the time we were seated again in the drawing-room in front of the backgammon board, she was thoroughly mellow. When I had successfully contrived to let her win a game, I gave her Mr Tyburn's message.

'Where and when have you been meeting Tyburn?'

I told her.

'That man. Messing about in lanes.'

'He seemed to be working very hard,' I ventured timidly.

'Doesn't know the meaning of the word. The only one I know who did his job properly worked himself to death. That's more like it. Died before he was forty. He was a very good man.'

'Did he really die of overwork?' I asked with some interest.

'The doctors called it lung trouble, but I naturally knew more about it than they did.'

She paused, ruminated a while, and then heaving a deep sigh, said, 'Ah well, he was not the only one to suffer, poor man.'

I waited silently, feeling sure that if I did so there would be further revelations; and there were. She made some trifling remark to the effect that surely I wasn't interested in the tragedies of life; and then with the very little encouragement required proceeded.

He was devoted to his work. I never knew another such man. He would hardly allow himself sufficient time for his meals. He was out and about at all hours of the day and night, never thinking of himself, and never thinking that I, who perhaps needed him most, was so much without him. He was never very strong, and naturally, in time (so short a time!) his health was affected. You cannot imagine what I suffered, watching his slow but certain decline, week by week. He did not give up until three months before the end. Then (he was terribly ill with a dreadful cough), we prevailed upon him to rest, but it was too late. All the nursing in the world could not save him by then. He faded slowly away and in three months he was dead. He died when I was not there. I was not with him at the end,' she repeated; she seemed very much distressed by this.

'Were you . . . did you care for him very much?'

'He was my husband. He was my life,' she said simply.
I was aghast.
'What a terrible life you have had!'

'You see that? You see that it *has* been terrible? He was so anxious about me. I tried to conceal my feelings, but he knew, he knew what I was undergoing. He had said he would have to leave me, but I had never really believed it. I clung to every shred of hope, until there was no more left. None at all. Every dream I had had shattered. No one realized what he had meant to me. I don't think he realized himself. Afterwards I cánnot remember very much, I was so paralysed with grief.'

I felt so passionately sorry for her that I could not speak for a moment, but she remained so still, so broodingly silent, that I felt I must say something.

'It seems so desperately unfair. Most people don't seem to have one tragedy, and you have it twice.'

'Twice?' She looked up suddenly.

'Your husband in India and then this,' I faltered. I was a little afraid of her.

'That is over, and I do not wish to think or speak of it,' she cried sharply, and then, seeing my startled expression, added more gently, 'It was an entirely different experience. I was young then but this was the end of my life. You are too young to understand, but to contemplate them both at one and the same time is more than I can bear.'

I tried to say how sorry I was. She dismissed the apology kindly enough, and announced another game before we retired for the night. I was so much upset by this dreadful tale that I was scarcely able to play. She reprimanded me in tones of gentle but courageous reproach; winning the game easily, and eventually even allowing me to help her from her chair, which I was more than eager to do.

I remained awake for many hours that night, bewailing her appalling tragedies; justifying her present eccentricities and tempers; reproaching myself for the lack of sympathy and imagination I had privately used towards her. One could not possibly live through such terrible times and remain totally unaffected. It explained her retired life, her painting and probably much else. It explained the wig. That night I concentrated entirely on what my new knowledge of her explained.

CHAPTER TWENTY

The real difficulty is in attempting to explain how it all ended. It is hardly enough simply to say that Mrs Border and that house got slowly more and more on my nerves. I should have to add that nothing (or nothing very much) happened to induce any hysteria on my part. How did I stand it as long as I did, and why should I suddenly find the situation and atmosphere so hard to endure? I was very proud, I suppose, and obstinate; I did not want to go back to my family confessing failure. I think, however, that the monotony was a chief cause of my increasing nervous anxiety; paralysing and detailed monotony, where the trouble lay not so much in nothing happening, but in the endless succession of tedious and insignificant events, repeated day by day and week by week, until leisure and freedom became a kind of mirage. Eventually I ceased to feel free even when I was alone out of doors. The knowledge that I could only escape from the house so far as the distance it was possible to walk in an hour and a half, added to my sense of confinement and depression. I ceased to go out very much.

Then one day Mrs Border announced that her brother was coming to stay. She seemed in a high state of excitement and displeasure at the prospect; making endless arrangements in the house which she interspersed with vituperative remarks about his character; 'Dull dog, my brother, never has a word to say for himself,' or 'Dead lame, and stupid as an ox; can't think what he does with his time,' and, most frequently: 'Cannot imagine why he's coming at all. Haven't had anything to say to each other for twenty-five years.'

Nevertheless I was set to clearing a spare room of Mrs Border's paintings (they were stored there, I discovered, in hundreds, even thousands). The room, being a small one, contained a mere thirty-seven framed specimens. The un-

199

framed paintings filled every drawer, every shelf, and at least three dozen large cardboard boxes. They were all signed, quite illegibly, by a scrawl which I could not with any effort of imagination construe as Border. Spalding and I were directed to remove this quantity of genius to the library, which was on the ground floor. I do not know why it was called the library; it contained no books, but boxes of parrot seed, piles of thick white paper, and walking sticks bracketed to the walls. It had a dark green wall paper and black paint; smelled of damp and was unutterably gloomy – the very last place where one would wish to read.

The evening before her brother was due to arrive, Mrs Border favoured me with some startling revelations of his life and character.

'Whole career ruined by women,' she opened unexpectedly.

As we had been in the middle of discussing arrangements for meeting his train, I was thoroughly unprepared for this remark, and said nothing.

'Can't help himself. Perfectly all right for months until he meets some chit of a girl and then there's an outbreak. Loses his head completely. Spends pounds. Careers all over the world making a fool of himself.'

'Is he not married?'

'Not all relationships with the opposite sex end with marriage, you know,' she said bitterly. 'Oh dear me, no. That isn't what most men want at all. My brother, for example. He was not above attempting all kinds of unpleasant things with women who were already married. Ruined his career. It finished him in the Army. Frightful scandals wherever he went. One can't have that kind of thing. He did marry some woman once, a widow, a throughly irresponsible creature, but she left him. I always said that if *she* couldn't stand it, and Heaven knows she was disagreeable enough, nobody would. I was perfectly right. Nobody has. Can't *think* why he's coming here at all.'

'He must be rather lonely,' I ventured.

'Well he won't find himself any less lonely here,' she said

grimly. Then, after a moment's thought, 'A great many young women have considered Hilary to be lonely or *appeared* to consider him so.' She said this so deliberately, and looked at me in so pointed a manner that I felt myself blushing, and at the same time inclined to laugh at the absurd implication.

'Well,' she said, having eyed my discomfiture, 'mark my words. Don't believe a *word* they say, *any one* of them, and never remain too long alone in their company. Unprincipled lout!' she exclaimed, striking her stick on the floor. And leaving her brother at that, we retired to bed.

I woke suddenly during that night, horribly frightened. This time, however, I was certain that I had wakened *after* the laughter; that it had immediately preceded the dead unnatural silence which then obtained. To make matters worse, I found but one match which extinguished itself before I had managed to light my candle from it. Briefly I saw my room in the second's wavering light; then I was forced to lie listening, listening through the dark hours, tense and exhausted with fear. I might, I suppose, have reflected that although I had heard these strange sounds several times now, nothing very alarming had resulted and therefore have learned to be less afraid: but the experience was so unpleasant in itself that each time I expected some horrific sequel; acquired, so to speak, a habit of anticipating something more and worse. I decided that night that I must tell someone what I had heard, if only to have my fears confirmed. The thought of telling Mrs Border seemed so frightening in the dark, that I was forced to discard her as even a possible confidante; indeed I found myself becoming distinctly afraid of her at the mere idea. Then who? Her brother? Mrs Border's description of him made me far from sure that such a confidence to him would be received in a manner conducive to my peace of mind. After much disjointed thought I was forced to fall back (rather uncertainly) on Mr Tyburn. He would, I felt, be discreet and reliable; and possibly reassuring. As soon as I had determined on Mr Tyburn, I spent the rest of that sleepless night persuading myself that I could find no better or more suitable person to tell; these reassurances being punctuated by long periods of almost animal fear, when my mind froze, and straining my eyes towards the bedroom door I simply listened.

I rose at length before I was called, with aching eyes and head, my resolution wavering, shivering in my mind. The practical difficulties were enormous. I was only able to go out if Mrs Border approved my going, or alternatively when she rested in the afternoon. Today, however, she would be unlikely to rest, as her brother was arriving shortly after three. I could say that I required stamps, but in all probability she would tell Spalding to buy them, and then make some embarrassing remark about my eagerness to escape, which I should not, in this case, feel able to countenance.

The problem, however, like so many minor problems (after one has exhausted oneself with anxiety on their behalf), solved itself.

Mrs Border remarked, after breakfast, that she would be unable to take her usual rest, owing to her brother's inconsiderate hour of arrival, adding that I had better take a good walk in the afternoon as she preferred to meet him alone.

'Do you good. You look peaky. You may return for tea. I haven't much to say to him.'

I walked down the drive with a beating heart after lunch, rehearsing what I should say to Mr Tyburn. The whole business had, by then, assumed an urgency, a state of crisis, which I supposed he would resolve, without any clear idea of how he could possibly do so. It was not until I reached the little grey mouldering church with the gaunt unsuitable vicarage beside it, that the frightful thought of Mr Tyburn being contained in neither of these edifices, but out visiting, occurred to me.

I resolved to try the church first, as, if he were there, he would, in all probability, be alone, and nobody would know that I had come. The thickly studded door of the church opened loudly but easily and I went in. A heavy smell of chrysanthemums, baize and damp prevailed, but the church was quite empty. I stood for several minutes, undecided, when the silence was broken by the sound of a door, and shortly afterwards Mr Tyburn appeared from behind the pulpit carrying a bundle of pamphlets. He began moving among the pews with a decorous but purposeful haste, distributing them, and every now and then clearing his throat as though he were about to speak. He saw me, and smiled understandingly, as he mouthed some inaudible greeting. Then he conscientiously took so little notice of me, that I was certain he thought I had been on the point of slipping on to some hassock to pray. As soon as I realized this, it became exceedingly embarrassing not to kneel down to his expectations. After considering the situation, I selected a pew already loaded with pamphlets and knelt in it. He acknowledged this with a quick movement of the head, and began working steadily in the opposite direction. There followed an anxious interval; however, when I judged the pamphlets to be exhausted, I rose to my feet and succeeded in running him down at the main door by which I had entered the church. I was not a moment too soon; his hand was on the latch, he had opened the door by the time I reached it, and I had no choice but to precede him outside. He shut the door, cleared his throat and bade me good afternoon. He had a heavy cold.

'Out on one of your walks I take it.' he added as we walked down the path. I agreed, and murmured something about trying to meet him.

'Ah, yes. Dreadful weather we're having. Going to rain again. Yes, I distinctly felt a drop.'

We had reached the vicarage gate. He hovered uncertainly. I took the plunge.

'Could I possibly come inside for a few moments?' I asked.

He glanced at the sky and his face brightened.

'Ah, yes, shelter,' he said. 'Of course.' And led the way.

I followed him up the gravel path to the house. It was built of bright dark red brick, and the front door, which was ajar, was badly in need of another coat of chocolate-coloured paint. The hall was pitch dark; but undeterred, he conducted me into a small room, possessed of a cold fug and a kind of bare untidiness. An enormously fat, old and matted spaniel rose to its feet and lumbered towards us. It smelled strongly, and its eyeballs were covered with a blue film. Mr Tyburn patted it absently.

'Poor old girl. She hears quite well,' he added, with which excuse for the dog's continued existence he motioned me to a chair, sneezed violently, and began poking up the damp uncertain fire, which hissed and proceeded to go out faster than ever. Mr Tyburn sighed and seated himself.

'And how is Mrs Border?' he began. He was a man not lightly shaken from his duty.

'Her brother arrives this afternoon for a visit,' I replied.

'Of course. So you have absented yourself for a while. Very right. I'm sure they must have a great deal to say to one another. Perhaps she would rather I did not come tomorrow?'

'I don't know,' I said. 'She didn't give me any message about it. You see she – I didn't know I was going to see you.'

'Ah,' he said musing. 'Then I wonder ...' He was interrupted by a knock at the door. It opened and what I imagined to be the housekeeper stood there. 'Mr Tickner,' she said. Mr Tyburn rose to his feet.

'Of course. Will you excuse me a moment? I don't think the shower has quite stopped. I shall only be a few moments.' And he left the room.

The spaniel rose again and staggered snuffling after him. On finding the door closed, she stood motionless, pressing her nose against it; then laboriously resumed her corner.

I stared out of the dreary room at the grey sky. The rain had not stopped, but seemed rather to be settling down for the evening. The church clock chimed, and I realized with a shock that it must be a quarter to four. I should have to return. It occurred to me that Mr Tyburn had not grasped that I wanted to see him, and the longer I sat there, the more I shrank from my original intention of telling him about the strange sounds in Mrs Border's house in the night. The notion seemed, as I sat there, to be utterly absurd. What could he possibly do about it? I should only succeed in embarrassing him. But then, if I did not tell him, who should I tell? I sat there feebly struggling with this dilemma until he reappeared.

'I am afraid I shall have to ask you to forgive me,' he said, advancing into the room, and almost falling over the dog which had risen to greet him, 'but I have to go out. Most unfortunate. Perhaps you would like to remain until the rain stops?'

'Thank you, but I am afraid I shall have to go. I don't think it is going to stop.'

He peered at the window.

'I fear not,' he agreed.

He reached for his mackintosh which hung on a peg by the door, and blew his nose. 'We can go together,' he said, trying to make the best of it, and we went.

He wheeled an old bicycle from the black depths of the passage. I opened the door and we hurried to the gate.

'I hope you don't catch anything in this damp as I have foolishly done. I have an appalling cold,' he added unnecessarily. He mounted the bicycle. 'Very damp place. The last man died of a consumption, but I expect Mrs Border has told you that sad story.' And he sped away, waving to me, and then clutching his hat on to his head.

I hurried back, digesting this new piece of information as I went. It had not occurred to me that Mrs Border's husband, her second husband, had lived and died there. It explained her knowledge of the parish; her disapproval perhaps of things being done in a different manner; possibly even her refusal to go to church, which must contain many painful memories. Had she, then, lived in the large dreary house? It was not until I was almost running up the drive (it was raining heavily by then), that Mr Tyburn's remark struck me as at all strange. I was so afraid of being late for tea that I dismissed this strangeness with the rather hasty supposition that Mr Tyburn found that situation, as he seemed to find most situations, embarrassing.

When I had changed, I found Mrs Border opposite the profusely laid tea table.

'You are late. This is my brother. I've told him all about you,' she said almost malevolently.

I apologized and sat down.

Mrs Border and her brother discussed the war during tea. She did most of the talking, while he sat, refusing food, and topping her very general arguments with a few military observations of which she took no notice whatsoever.

He was a very tall man with a soft melancholy voice, melancholy brown eyes, and a curious small round hole in his face just above his moustache. He sat very upright stirring innumerable cups of tea; with one leg stretched stiffly out before him. Mrs Border took no notice of me; but several times I caught her brother's eyes fixed on me in a mournful and inquiring manner. As soon as I could decently be supposed to have finished my tea I was sent to pick flowers from the conservatory for the table.

When I returned, I found the Major standing with his hands behind his back in gloomy contemplation of the parrot. Mrs Border was not in the room.

'They live to the most appalling age,' he remarked, making his way slowly to the fire. I noticed that he had a pronounced limp.

'Has Mrs Border had him long?'

He did not seem to hear. 'Bit quiet here for you I should think,' he observed a moment later. 'No fun, eh? No parties.' Then, with sudden animation, 'Those were the days!' He sighed deeply, and repeated, 'Those were the days. Why, I can remember . . .' He broke off gazing at me sadly. 'Oh well. Even youth gets older, doesn't it?' He leaned forward a little with his stiff bony hands on his knees. 'Or doesn't it?' And then distinctly, and very slowly, he winked.

I thought of Mrs Border's confidence the night before; the wink seemed an awful confirmation of everything she had said. I could make no reply. But he seemed not really to expect one, as after a second he sighed again and leaned back in his chair.

'Has – has Mrs Border had the parrot long? I mean is he very old?' I asked, for want of anything better to say.

'Supposed to have been a young bird when I bought him. Bought him off a ship's steward in Liverpool. Just back from India. Thought I'd better bring Madgie something. Clean forgotten when I was out there don't you know, and had to rake round a bit for one or two little things. Must have been twenty-five years ago. Never liked them myself. Madgie's devoted to it though. Never left her through all her illnesses and everything. Devoted to it. Extraordinary.'

Mrs Border appeared in dining attire. 'What were you two talking about?' she exclaimed.

'About the parrot, Madgie, about the parrot,' he answered patiently. 'Getting on now, poor old chap.'

'He's lasted better than you,' she retorted and led us in to dinner.

After this long and exceedingly uncomfortable meal (Mrs Border was argumentative and fractious, and the Major, bored and almost silent, stared at me in the same gloomy and abstracted manner), we spent an even longer and more uncomfortable evening, in the course of which I remarked that I had seen the Vicar, and that he was coming to tea. This precipitated an avalanche of questions from Mrs Border. I explained about the rain, and his kindness in offering me shelter. I could see she was very angry and I felt so guilty about my private intention (although I had failed to carry it out) that I began to wonder whether she suspected it. The matter was eventually dropped on a very high note of tension. She suddenly announced that she was going to bed and motioned me to follow her. The Major had so thoroughly unnerved me by his staring that I could hardly say good night to him. Mrs Border glanced at us both; I could almost see her suspicion breaking new ground. However, she said nothing until we were up the stairs. Then, after I had waited for her to reach the top she laid her hand heavily on my shoulder. 'It is not at all wise to conceal anything from me,' she said softly, watching me. 'I have a very active imagination you know. I am sure you would not like me to imagine the wrong thing.' And before I could think of replying she had gone, and the door of her room was shut.

My first impulse on reaching my room was to burst into torrents of tears; but they had hardly begun when I heard the shutting of a door below and sounds of the Major hauling himself stiffly up the stairs to bed. I lay choking back my sobs for fear he should hear them, listening while he ascended the flight, paused and stumped slowly to his room. And then I did not want to cry. The events of the day swarmed upon me, disordered, unreal and incomprehensible, a horrible collection of darting inconsequent fears which I could no longer resolve or escape. I thought of Mrs Border's behaviour in the passage; indeed her behaviour throughout the evening, the whole day, and many days before that: her extraordinary confidences; her horrible greasy wig; her solitude and her spite. I thought of Mr Tyburn's curious parting remark; of his obvious embarrassment on the occasions when we had dutifully discussed Mrs Border; of the inexplicable laughter in the night; of the fact that Mrs Border had not once been outside the house during the weeks I had known her. I remembered what she had said about her brother, and what her brother had said to me. I found myself quite unable to remember anything which did not confuse and terrify me. I sat for hours striving to arrange this disjointed flood, these innumerable significances, but without any success, until, shivering, I rose to my feet, groped for my pocket book, and drew from it one pound and fifteen shillings. I had known the money was there, but it comforted me to hold it in my hands. I sat on the bed again, clutching the money as some sort of talisman to a solution. I did not attempt to undress or sleep until the night was over. It was very early morning when I suddenly realized that my fingers were cramped round the money, and that for a very long time I had not thought or felt at all. Then, a little sick with cold and fatigue, I took off my blouse and skirt and slept.

When I descended for breakfast the next morning, I found the Major already seated at the table. He said, 'Good morning,' and made as if to rise to his feet, but I slipped quickly into my place in order to save him the trouble. Spalding brought a newspaper and two letters for the Major, which she placed before him, and then retired to fetch my breakfast. He hardly noticed the newspaper but seized his letters (one I remember was a very large pale mauve envelope), then looked round vaguely, as though he expected something else.

'There were only two,' I said.

'Two?'

'Two letters.'

'Ah yes. Observant young lady. Very observant. I was looking for the thing to open 'em if you take me.'

'It is on the mantelpiece in the drawing-room. I'll get it,' I said quickly.

'Wouldn't trouble you. Don't like messing the thing up though. A knife I suppose.' He looked about for a knife and upset the salt. 'Damned uncivilized mess, I beg your pardon, damned uncivilized.'

Spalding reappeared with my breakfast.

'Clear that up would you and get me the paper knife,' he said, settling to the newspaper. Spalding cleared the salt, then fetching the paper knife she put it beside him and left the room. I suddenly realized how hungry I was, and had begun on my bacon when he put down his paper.

'Hullo,' he said. 'She's still kept this old thing.' He had picked up the knife and was staring at it distastefully. 'Never liked it.'

'It's Indian isn't it?' I faltered.

'Did she tell you it was Indian?'

I nodded.

'No more Indian than you are. No, I bought that at the same time as the parrot. Said I'd brought 'em back with me all the way from India, don't you know, to keep the peace. Clean forgot when I was out there. Memory like a sieve, always have had. Our Colonel had nine sisters and he never forgot one of 'em. Nine!' said the Major with increasing animation. 'He used to bring 'em shawls. Awful business. Good-looking gals, couldn't tell t'other from which. Never remembered Madgie, never.' He slit open a letter.

'Mind you,' he said, 'I wouldn't put it past Madgie to have

known all the time it wasn't really Indian. She'd just tell that little story to impress, you know. Remember when I was wounded. She made a fine thing out of that. Got it in battle saving people's lives. No such thing. A damned native, I beg your pardon, a damned native drove a knife into me when I was walking back one night. Nothing very gallant about that. Been a nuisance ever since. This climate if you take me.'

This burst of confidence ceased as suddenly as it had begun; he fetched out his spectacles and proceeded to read the mauve letter.

I was no longer hungry. The nightmare had begun again, or rather it had never left me. As soon as possible I excused myself and returned to my room. I had only one idea in my head now. All attempts to understand the situation were at an end; I cared not at all for any of them and was obsessed by one problem alone.

I was interrupted by Spalding telling me that Mrs Border was waiting for me.

CHAPTER TWENTY-ONE

That frightful day dragged slowly on; and not for one minute was I alone or free, until, by late afternoon, I began to feel, in an hysterical despair, that I was being watched, being kept. I do not think I was alone in feeling on edge. It was true that I had not slept for the best part of two nights, but Mrs Border and her brother seemed to me almost equally and as much wrought up. They had a number of minor arguments in the morning, during which I was not allowed to leave the room; and at lunch, when the Major in a frenzy of boredom suggested that I go for a walk with him, Mrs Border, quivering with suppressed anger, reminded him that the Vicar was coming to tea and that she was forgoing her rest on his behalf. Then we waited tea for the Vicar, and he did not come. So the day dragged, with the feeling of an imminent crisis drawing nearer and nearer (Mrs Border refusing to allow either the Major or me out of her sight), until I was almost beside myself with fear and frustration.

After tea the Major announced that he would take a turn in the garden. This remark was received in dead silence. He waited a moment, as though screwing himself up to leave the room, then went; and was shortly to be seen pacing slowly round the gravel path in an Ulster and an old tweed hat.

Mrs Border had been playing patience. I was pretending to read a book. but I was so nervous at the immediate prospect of being alone with her, that I read with no idea of what I was reading. When a few minutes later I glanced up from my book, I found her exceedingly bright grey eyes fixed on me, with an unaccountable expression. I looked at my book again, then almost immediately at her. She was still watching me.

'Well, what is it? What is the matter with you?' she snapped.

'What do you mean?'

'You look ill. Why?'

'I – I haven't been sleeping very well.'

'Nonsense. What has he been saying to you about me? What did he say this morning? Or was it last night?'

'He didn't say anything this morning and we talked about the parrot last night,' I answered desperately. I was in no condition for this cross examination, and I think I was more afraid of her than I had ever been.

'I've dealt with plots and conspiracies all my life,' she said almost cunningly, after a pause. 'That is why I'll never have anything happening behind my back. Never. Catch 'em all out at the end. Come now, what is it all about?' She tried to smile at me, but her mouth was trembling so much with suppressed eagerness, and her eyes were so sharp with spite (or something worse), that she hardly ingratiated herself.

'I really do not know what you mean.'

'Has my brother ...? I was always very delicate you know, hardly able to bear the difficult times. I was frequently very ill.'

'He said something about your being ill,' I said involuntarily.

'What? What did he say? A pack of lies the whole story! None of you speak the truth as I see it!' She became very much excited.

'He only mentioned something about your illnesses when he said you were fond of the parrot. That was all,' I said, racking my brains for some means of escape. 'That was all. Perhaps I had better get ready for dinner,' I added hopelessly.

'Or join him in the garden? More talking behind my back?' she suggested.

'Naturally I would not consider discussing you with anyone,' I said, but the words died on my lips. I was no practised deceiver and of late I had considered very little else. 'I do not in the least want to walk round the garden with your brother,' I finished lamely.

'Why not? What is the harm? What has he been saying to you?'

Desperately I seized the only remaining chance of deflecting her. 'He ... I'm afraid of him. He winked at me,' I faltered, feeling dreadfully disloyal to the poor Major.

She drew a deep breath. 'Ah – I knew it. I suppose you fancy you have made a great impression. I know what you will be thinking next. Sentimental old fool! He shan't ruin your life, I'll see to that.'

'Please do not say anything. I am sure he had no intention ...'

'Are you?' she said sharply. 'Perhaps he is not entirely to blame? I know all about young girls and their ridiculous notions. Encouraging him, waiting your chance and encouraging him, that's what you've been up to. So sharp you'll prick yourself. Don't try to deceive me: I see it all.'

This was the last straw. Utterly unable to control myself at this incredible idea, I burst into fits of laughter which I could not stop. My face streamed with tears, so that I could not see Mrs Border. I ached and gasped and laughed, until we were interrupted by the Major returning from his stroll.

'Having a joke? Hope you're not laughing at me,' he remarked affably.

Cramming a handkerchief to my face I fled.

'Too late, too late,' I sobbed in my room. It was dark: I did not feel in the least like laughing any more. the day was almost over and I was faced with another dreadful night. I was by now so seriously driven by the whole situation which seemed to ramify hourly, so utterly out of my depth, and withal so despairing at my recent failure and the uncertainty attendant upon any future success, that for some time I could only weep helplessly. Eventually, at the end of my tears, I summoned the dregs of my courage or desperation, and considered the matter carefully. It would certainly be better, or safer, to appear at dinner as though nothing, or very little was wrong. For one second I visualized the scene which might be taking place downstairs, then, shivering at its possibilities, dismissed it. Whatever had happened I must remain calm, behave naturally, in fact, keep my head. In this spirit I washed my face, tidied my hair, and, wishing for the hundredth time that there was a lock on my bedroom door, planned my descent to coincide with the dinner gong.

I encountered them moving into the dining-room, and was thus spared immediate close scrutiny. We seated ourselves in silence; then Mrs Border remarked; 'Come to your senses, have you?'

She did not seem, however, to expect a reply. Murmuring something inaudible I bent over my soup.

It was impossible to tell what had taken place after I had left the drawing-room before dinner. That something had happened there was no doubt; and the general atmosphere resulting was unexpected. The tension was no less, but I had a strong impression that the Major was in the ascendancy. Mrs Border appeared defensive, almost conciliating; she talked ceaselessly in an uncharacteristically general manner, never mentioning herself; and several times she actually sought her brother's opinion. He was even more silent than before, but watchful; I felt very strongly that he was watching her, and possibly me also. He was studiously polite to me, but underneath this I was aware of a bitter resentment. I endeavoured in my new role of deception to enter into the conversation with a few indisputably harmless remarks; invariably he met them with a soft reproachful glare, coupled with a courteous agreement. It was not a happy meal.

Afterwards, Mrs Border requested me to play backgammon with her 'as we usually do'. The evening wore on. The Major buried himself in his newspaper and we played; all of us, I think, painfully aware of the ticking clock, I quite unable to keep my mind on the game so that Mrs Border continuously won. All of us were waiting for the evening to end, and with it, perhaps, the conscious suspension of our private feelings; none of us was able to order the finish of the day before its socially appointed time.

The hot milk arrived. I swallowed it, thereby achieving

heights of self-control of which I had not known I was capable. The clock struck ten; chimed half past; after which a few heavy minutes elapsed and Mrs Border released us. I put away the game, gave her her stick, and helped her out of her chair. She made great play of being in pain, drawing from her brother some inaudible exclamation of condolence. She stood clutching the high back of her chair and biting her lips.

'Are you coming, Hilary?' she asked, less peremptory than before.

'Shortly, Madgie, shortly,' he replied bristling his paper.

I said good night, and he lowered it to reply, still with the same mournful reproach. Slowly we left the room.

Climbing the stairs as usual, I stood waiting for her, wondering wearily what she would say when she reached me; but at the top she stood breathing heavily, stared at me a moment with steady, almost venomous dislike, and left me without a word.

I sat in my room waiting for the Major to go to bed. There was a little cold sweat in the palms of my hands, which I kept rubbing with my handkerchief. More than an hour passed, during which I sat mechanically listening, until I heard his heavy irregular tread, and bedroom door shut.

I selected the smaller of my two suitcases and began slowly and quietly to pack. When I had put into it everything it would hold, I strapped it and tested its weight. It was surprisingly, impossibly, heavy; I opened it again and set about lightening it, all the while preserving the utmost possible silence. The lightening process took some time, as I was torn between the necessity of a portable case, and my human desire to leave as little as possible behind me. Eventually an unsatisfactory compromise was reached; the case was heavy but not unbearably so. I pushed it out of sight under my bed. After some thought, I changed my shoes, and then packed the other case with the remainder of my things, readdressing the label to my home. This accomplished I looked at the time. It was a little after two. I was very tired and, curiously enough, at that point I could easily have lain on my bed and slept. I was very thirsty and drank nearly all the water in the glass flagon. The cold water was reviving; my senses crept back; and I began with sharpened nerves to consider the long hours which lay ahead, hours during which, however improbable, there were chances of my being discovered. This was so anxious a thought, that I peered cautiously through my curtains for light. But there was not enough for my purpose: I was afraid of losing my way, or, perhaps worse, that I should stumble and make some sound, which would easily attract attention in the black silence. It was the dead of night; a time when it was easy to feel that sleep and death had been contrived to kill these hours; that to endure them awake and alive was a private, dangerous ordeal. I lay on my bed a short while but I was afraid of sleep and rose reluctantly. I spent some time disarranging the bed to look as though I had slept in it. I counted the pictures in the room and lit my remaining candle from the little guttering pool of its predecessor. I did not consciously think of my situation at all, I was not even afraid of hearing the laughter, but simply concentrated on passing through those few dark hours as I had never concentrated on anything before.

A little after five, as the venture loomed in sight, I became more and more restless and began to be anxious lest the boards should creak, or I should be too clumsy with fatigue; lest it be still too dark in the house for me silently to find my way. This anxiety increased to a positive terror; my bones melted like the candle, the blood thudded in my head; I began to imagine myself fainting, falling down the stairs. And still there was nearly an hour before the dawn. Even if I succeeded in getting down the stairs, I reflected desperately, there remained the door, with a key to be turned and two bolts to be drawn, and then the gravel drive. I took off my shoes and tied them together, trembling that I had not realized this necessity until now. Suppose I had never realized it? I looked repeatedly through the curtains, but there did not seem to be more light. The candle was now very low. I prayed that it would last until six o'clock. I should need matches, I suddenly realized, if I was to find the bolts on the door; but how could I contrive to carry matches, with the suitcase and my shoes? I tried hanging the shoes round my neck, but the laces were too short; I was afraid that they would fall. I put the matches in the pocket of my coat, but the box was half full, and they rattled. Eventually I separated the matches from the box and put them in different pockets. It was better, but hardly satisfactory, as I was by no means sure that they would not prove necessary on the stairs, and I was without a free hand to guide myself.

The moment for which I had waited so long was nearly arrived, but now I dreaded it. At a quarter to six I dared wait no longer, as with every minute my courage crumbled away until I was on the edge of panic. I moved the cases into the middle of the room and put on my coat. I blew out the candle and gently drew back the curtains. It was barely light. My room was near the staircase, and I hoped the uncurtained window would help me down the stairs. I felt in my pockets for the box, the matches and my pocket book. I arranged the case and shoes in one hand and moved slowly towards the door. It opened easily, and pushing it wide I listened. There was no sound. I waited a moment, until my eyes were accustomed to the gloom, and then started for the staircase. The shoes bumped softly against each other; I was forced to transfer them to my free hand. The carpet in the passage was thick and rich; I made no sound. Elated by this, I proceeded to descend the stairs.

The first stair creaked loudly; instinctively I stood frozen; then realized that it would creak again when I transferred my weight to the stair below it. I waited again, my heart pounding loudly in the silence, and then moved. The second creak seemed tremendous, but the stair below it was silent, and somehow I reached the bottom with hardly another sound. The front door was only a few yards away. Leaving the suitcase I felt for the box and a match, and then, as I withdrew them, I thought I heard a sound. I listened, could hear nothing, and was about to strike the match (it was almost entirely dark) when I heard it again. A muffled indistinct murmur. Someone was awake and talking, on the same floor as I; in the drawing-room, I quickly realized; and then realized almost as quickly that it was the parrot gabbling away in the room. The shock had been so sudden, the relief so immediate, that a moment later the incident hardly remained in my mind. I turned feverishly towards the door again. There were small windows on either side of it, and I was inspired to draw one curtain on the right-hand window. I turned the key, slipped back the top bolt, and, with more difficulty, the one at the bottom.

A minute later I stood in the grey delicious air, suitcase and shoes in hand, and the door closed behind me. The gravel was damp and painful to my unshod feet, but I crossed the sweep and continued down the drive until it curved, when I turned back to look at the house. Even that last glance revealed something strange. There were no curtains over the window of Mrs Border's bedroom, which was suffused with a warm glow of flickering light. Her bedroom fire, I thought, and knew then that it must burn throughout the night. Spalding invariably lighted it before Mrs Border changed for dinner; kept it in until she retired, but certainly did not rise to clear and relight it at six in the morning. 'She never sleeps; she does not go to bed,' I thought with the old familiar dread and revulsion. Seizing the suitcase, I stumbled running down the drive, hardly caring any more what noise I made, until I reached the gate, where I put the shoes on my soaking feet.

I must have walked the best part of a mile when a milk cart overtook me, and upon it I secured a lift to the station.

An hour later I sat in a train. My feet were wet, I was very hungry and unbearably tired, but I had escaped. From what? Almost immediately I found my mind struggling feebly with this (under the circumstances) exceedingly tiresome question. Surely it was enough to relax and be thankful that I had planned and achieved the whole difficult business; but ironically I found it impossible either to relax or be thankful. In books, I found myself thinking bitterly, in books, the character would not at this point be in any doubt whatsoever. If he or she had escaped, it would be from some explicit danger or discomfort. I had escaped, but, I realized, without any clear idea of why I had done so. It was true that I had disliked and been afraid of the house and its occupants, but for what reasons? Mrs Border had never been positively unkind to me. And now, without warning, I had fled; leaving more than half my possessions behind; almost as though I had been in danger of my life. Instantly, my divided mind rushed to excuse this apparent foolishness. I have lived cut off for weeks with an old woman who wore a black repugnant wig; who never went out of doors; who had, for no apparent reason, invented two husbands. But perhaps she had *not* invented the second husband, the clergyman. I had no evidence beyond Mr Tyburn's curious remark that: 'Mrs Border will have told you that sad story.' Possibly the man to whom he alluded had not been her husband; but there might have been another consumptive clergyman who was. This seemed improbable, however, and I concluded that she had invented both husbands. But what if she had? In books, I felt again, there would have been some conclusive circumstance or event, sinister or reassuring, which would have left me in no doubt as to what I should do and why. Then I remembered the parrot, and was filled with shame that I had not before realized that he was the author of the frightful fits of laughter. He had not, of course, uttered a sound during the day, but I now remembered Mrs Border's remark about his talking at night. That was satisfactorily about to explain that, when I reflected with renewed alarm or relief (it was really impossible to be certain which) that parrots do not usually talk and laugh like human beings unless they have either been taught to do so by one person, or been so much with them that they learn to mimic of their own accord. If her brother's account of the parrot was true, Mrs Border was the only person from whom the parrot could possibly have learned to laugh as he did. It had been with her through all her illnesses, the Major had said. This, again, presented Mrs Border in an unpleasant light. Perhaps she had only laughed like that when she was beside herself with grief, or during those mysterious illnesses. Well then,

Mrs Border was eccentric, even a little mad, but did that justify the terrible night I had spent, and my subsequent flight?

A week later I received my second suitcase. Inside, on the top was an envelope. It contained a cheque for my salary. No note accompanied it. I never heard anything more.

CHAPTER TWENTY-TWO

At home it was hard to believe I had been away so many weeks. Everything in my room was exactly as I had left it. My sister had plunged herself into packing parcels for the Army. My mother helped twice a week in some Officers Club. They did not ask me many questions (I do not think they were really at all interested), and I told them nothing. My mother had sold one of the pianos.

My mother and sister as the months went by became more and more obsessed with the war: they could talk of nothing else. They did not discuss the outcome of the war (it was assumed that we were to win it), but simply food and dressings and hospitals; the gallantry of the Belgians; the cruelty of the Germans; the appalling casualty lists; the probability of further battles; and, of course, Tom and Hubert, particularly Hubert. I think they existed in a kind of dramatic vacuum about Hubert, who they were sure would be killed. Tom was at some gunnery school and seemed likely to remain there; but Hubert was in the thick of it. They awaited his letters as though his life depended on them, read each when it came as though it were the last, and generally treated him as the family God of War. However, perhaps Hubert liked it. They were probably better for him than many families were.

Then ultimately I met Ian. I had not seen him since the Lancings' years ago. I had been sent by my sister to buy tickets for a theatre, to which she and my mother intended taking Tom on his leave. I remember that it was very cold, and that I did not want to buy the tickets, being unable to go myself, as I was working for the Red Cross and there being some function which I felt bound to attend instead.

There were a great many people trying to buy tickets. When I had eventually secured them and turned from the box office, I came face to face with him. He was wearing uniform, and looked much thinner and older. I did not immediately recognize him, as he did me. I think it was the first time in my life that anyone was really glad to see me, and I felt a warm rush of gratitude to him for it.

'Yes I do perfectly well. You are Ian. Ian Graham.'

'I say, that's most awfully good of you. To remember my name I mean.'

'You remembered mine.'

'Oh *well*,' he murmured, and was about to move away with me when I said: 'What about your tickets?'

'Oh. Oh yes.' He looked at the box office and at me, hesitated, and then went to buy them. He was some time, as there were people ahead of him. I saw him cast an anxious glance in my direction, as though he were not quite certain that I should wait.

'I suppose you are awfully busy,' he said as we walked slowly out of the theatre.

'No. That is, I do part-time work.'

'What do you do?'

'I pack parcels and help in a canteen.'

'Oh yes. Everyone is doing something, aren't they? Nobody seems to have much time.' We walked on for a few minutes of indecisive silence.

'Are you on leave?'

'Yes. My first for ten months.'

'You must have looked forward to it.'

'Oh, rather.'

We reached the end of the street. He saw me hesitate and said, 'I suppose you are hurrying back?'

'I'm going home.'

'Home,' he repeated; then, frowning slightly with the effort, said, 'I suppose you wouldn't care to have a cup of tea with me somewhere?'

I answered almost automatically, 'I'm afraid I ought to go home.' There was so reason at all for me to go home, I reflected, but now I could not change my mind, I should have to go.

'Shall I get you a cab?'

'Oh, I think I shall take a bus. I go to Kensington.'

'Where do you catch your bus?'

I pointed. We crossed the street together. I considered, for one moment, the possibility of asking him to come home to tea with me, but rejected it. I hated anyone to see my home.

The first bus was full, and although he raised his stick to stop it, it lumbered by.

'No good, I'm afraid,' he said, and as he smiled at me, suddenly I felt how desperately unhappy he was. It was such an overwhelming discovery that I was almost embarrassed by it; and began talking at random to cover my dismay. I asked whether he had had a good leave. 'Ripping,' he said, and repeated himself to impress upon me that he knew the right answer. It was nearly over, I learned, only three days remaining; he had been unable to go home for it, as his home was in Scotland and had been turned into a convalescent hospital. His father was away. 'Not much point, you see,' he said politely. His father was at the War Office all day and most of the night, he added. He answered all my questions patiently, as though he had answered them many times before, and always at the end of a sentence he met my eye with a kind of deprecating reserve.

Several buses had passed us. When I had exhausted my stock of inquiries I turned again to the road, but changed my mind and said I *should* like to have tea with him.

'Would you?' he said, and the colour rushed into his face. He raised his stick, stopped a cab into which he handed me, said something to the driver, and we set off.

'Where are we going?' I asked.

'Where would you like to go?'

'I don't know.'

There was a short silence. Then he said rather stiffly, 'I have told him to drive once round the park first. I intensely dislike hiring a vehicle solely for the purpose of arriving somewhere.'

I looked at him with some surprise. He seemed entirely different. We drove round the park in complete silence, and I had a curious feeling that he was all the while passionately conducting a continuous private conversation with me of the utmost importance, although I neither knew nor could I imagine what we were talking about.

Ultimately, we arrived at Rumpelmayer's.

Inside, he indicated a table in the extreme corner of the room. As I followed him, I realized suddenly that I had enjoyed the drive in the cab and his silent company, and began to dread talking with him. Nobody can live up to their own silence, I thought, although he had at least refrained from apologizing for it.

At tea, however, he began talking of Scotland, about which he was remarkably well informed, and I entirely ignorant. He talked with an easy intimate devotion about the country, the people, their politics (he was a Scottish Nationalist, I discovered, discovering Scottish Nationalism); their literature; their predilections for law suits, and learning, and alcohol, for devils and witches, and sculpture and travel. He set out not to impress or inform, but to entertain me with his knowledge, and I think he knew that he had succeeded.

We had been drinking chocolate and the pot was empty. He was about to send for some more, when he recollected himself, frowned, and said, 'Perhaps I should tell you that it is a quarter to six.'

'Oh.'

'Will you allow me to take you home?'

'Thank you.'

We were seated again in a cab. After a long silence he said, 'Would you care to go to the theatre with me this evening?'

I answered, 'I am supposed to be working in the canteen tonight.'

There was a brief pause. I felt him collecting himself. Then he said with some effort: 'You see I have only three days left. I cannot talk to you as though it were only three days, I cannot behave to you as though it were so short a time, because it would arrange everything I said in those terms. There would not have been time to drive round the park – ' he stopped abruptly – 'a kind of emotional short-hand – ' he stopped again – 'I have never in my life – I am in love with you, and that is all the time I have.'

We did not look at each other. The cab rumbled on until very distantly I heard myself say: 'I will come to the theatre,' and turned to find him regarding me with a kind of anxious excitement.

An expression of extreme gentleness crossed his face; then he shivered and said, 'I do not know where you live.'

I told him and he told the driver. We did not speak again until we were almost arrived at my house when he said: 'May I come and fetch you at seven o'clock?'

He saw me hesitate and said quickly: 'Half past seven if you prefer. The theatre is not until a quarter to nine, but I thought we should need something to eat first. Do you like oysters?'

'I don't know.'

He thought a moment and said, 'I think you will like them, but if you do not, there will be something else. You are not doomed to oysters.'

The cab stopped outside my house. We stood on the pavement a moment while I repeated the hour at which we were to meet; and parted.

The house was quiet. I went up to my room: I had just over an hour. As soon as I shut the door it dawned on me that I had nothing to wear; he would expect me to change and I had absolutely nothing. I had only the pink frock he had seen me wear at the Lancings'. I dragged it out of its cardboard box. It presented the indescribably withered appearance that party clothes achieve when they are not worn. It was old-fashioned, girlish and jaded; utterly impossible. I pushed the box under my bed and looked wildly through my wardrobe. I should have to wear my new dark grey jacket and skirt; they were the only presentable garments I possessed, but I had nothing to wear with them which did not lower them to the drab and disreputable status of the rest of my wardrobe. I hung the jacket and skirt on the back of my door, and stared at them. The skirt was well cut, the jacket charmingly braided; the ensemble possessed a large grey tam-o'-shanter to match it; but all was lost unless I could procure a blouse.

I had known that I should probably be forced to do it, but it was with desperation bordering on despair that I eventually crept to my sister's room, knocked and then entered to find it empty. She had for some time been engaged upon making herself a new blouse to wear at the Annual Church Bazaar, but I was not even sure that she had completed it. For the second time in my life I opened her wardrobe, searched and discovered her new confection. It was an extravagant affair of soft cream-coloured lace and net, beautifully made, achieving an elaborate and fashionable air wholly inconsistent with the rest of her nature. I seized it, shut the wardrobe and fled.

I then proceeded to dress with an utter concentration I had never formerly achieved. I did not think of Ian: he did not once enter my mind. I did not even consider the canteen where I was supposed to be that evening, or worry about my mother or sister returning to discover me. I simply dressed; with a care and thoroughness, a pleasure even, which had never before seemed necessary or possible. My hair came down and went up again perfectly, there seeming not one hair too few or too many. I changed my stockings, my shoes, my camisole; then slipped into the exquisite blouse. The collar was high and boned, surmounted by a crisp frill which just touched the lobes of my ears. The sleeves were a fraction too long, but otherwise the thing fitted perfectly. I hooked up my skirt and buckled the shining black belt my mother had given me as a birthday present. I had by then achieved the dignity of a small powder box, from which I powdered my nose and forehead. I washed my hands and scrubbed my nails. I selected a pocket handkerchief, and an exceedingly pretty bag of brown and grey beads, into which I put the handkerchief and a little money. I had no scent, and no gloves fit to wear. In a moment of inspiration I remembered my mother's small round brown fur muff, which was all that remained of what once had been a cape she had been given on her marriage. I knew where it was; but a second raid was an unnerving prospect. I looked at my watch; it was a quarter past seven. Only fifteen minutes remained in which to secure the muff.

This time, however, I met my mother coming out of her room.

'I have just met someone I knew at the Lancings'. He's a soldier,' I said. Her face cleared a little. 'I've promised to go to a theatre with him, he is just going out again.'

'What about the canteen?'

'I haven't missed a single evening before. I do so want to go to the theatre. Only I haven't any gloves, I was wondering whether . . .'

'Is not that your sister's blouse you are wearing?'

'It is, it is. Please don't tell her. I'll explain to her in the morning, I really will. I haven't had a party for so long,' I said, simulating a pathetic gaiety which I hoped would divert her from the immediate situation.

She smiled, patted my shoulder, and said: 'I hope you are not going to be late, and he is a suitable young man. I won't tell your sister, unless she asks me about it.'

'Do you think I could possibly borrow your muff?'

Going to her room, she returned with it.

'It will look much better than gloves,' I cried.

She put it into my hands and said: 'You had better keep it, darling. Have you enough money?'

'Oh yes. Oh thank you.'

'Don't be too late.'

'No, no. I won't be. I promise.' I kissed her, almost hysterically; I could think of nothing to say.

'Have a lovely time,' she murmured.

'I am awfully grateful for the muff. I *am*,' I repeated and ran back to my room. She had been so kind. She had made no difficulties. She had not even asked his name. Suddenly I remembered that he would be coming; the whole evening opened out before me, and I stood inside my clothes, trembling, with my heart on the brink of the hours ahead.

I sat on my bed to wait, remembered the tam-o'-shanter,

and heard his cab. I immediately resolved to meet him on the doorstep, or at least to open the door a moment after he had rung the bell, as he would not then see more than a glimpse of the hall, which was anyway almost pitch dark with only one gas lighted. The bell rang as I reached the bottom of the staircase, and, hearing footsteps upstairs, I almost ran to open the door.

As we walked to the gate he said: 'I am so very glad you have come. It isn't kind of you, is it?'

'Why should it be kind of me?'

'You *are* kind. I thought perhaps it might be.'

He put me in the cab and we drove away. I wanted to ask why he considered me kind, but did not dare. He told me about the theatre to which we were going, and asked me if I liked plays and whether I went often. I answered truthfully that I did like them, but went very seldom. Every single thing I said to him sounded unconscionably dull; but he listened carefully, intently, and gave no sign that he considered them so. I had the impression that he was feeling for my mind, for the best in me, as though he expected to like what he found; and I began to find it easier to talk. In Knightsbridge the cab stopped.

'Will you wait a moment?' he said, and jumped out.

He returned a minute later with two small bunches of dark red roses.

'One for your jacket, and one for your delicious muff,' he said, and the cab drove on.

I sat staring at the roses in my lap, so delighted that I was unable to speak. When I looked up to thank him, I found him watching me intently and could think of nothing to say, nothing which would express this agonizing painful delight.

'There are pins,' I heard him saying, 'but I expect they are inadequate.'

'Would you pin a bunch on my muff?'

'I will try. I don't think I shall be very good at it, but I'll try.'

When they were pinned, I did thank him and said that I

loved them. 'I have never had roses before,' I added as general explanation.

'I have never given roses before,' he answered seriously.

I looked again at the little fiery patch of roses, like hot velvet on the fur; and it was as if my senses were slowly returning to me, or perhaps arriving for the first time, to pain and delight me. Then suddenly I felt bound to ask, 'Why did you do this?'

He was silent.

'So much trouble . . .' I murmured, a little afraid of him.

'I thought perhaps they might please you,' he answered at length. 'You see, I want to please you, or at least I want you not to be so unhappy.' Almost at once he began to talk about flowers and trees, and where they originally came from. England was soon a vast forest of oak, and we reached the restaurant before there was time to plant anything else. 'In any case, I don't know nearly enough about it, so your ancestors must make do with oak,' he finished, helping me out of the cab.

A moment later we were seated in a tiny room with green walls, on a red plush seat placed in an angle between them, with a narrow table before us. A pale yellow wine was brought, sharp, light, exceedingly delicious. It reminded me of Agnes and Edward, and Arthur who said: 'Bring on the bubbly.' I asked Ian whether it was champagne.

'No. Would you prefer champagne?' And he looked at me rather doubtfully.

'No, no, I would not prefer it. But you see I am very ignorant in these matters, and once some people laughed at me because I didn't know what champagne was called . . .' And I told him about the party and *The Mikado*. He listened so well that I began to enjoy the tale; to enjoy being interrupted for more detail, further description, and even an impersonation of Agnes telling one of her stories. The oysters arrived before I had finished. I stopped to eye them rather anxiously.

'Some people do not like them, and you may be one,' he said, 'but you must not decide until your third oyster. I will prepare them for you while you finish your story. I want to hear what you wanted most in the world.'

'I didn't know. I made it up and said that I wanted to write a book.'

'Do you write?'

'Sometimes.' I remember blushing.

'What else did you tell them?'

'I can't remember. About wanting to know things, I think.' I watched him squeeze lemon on to each shell. 'Then I went to sleep. It was dreadful of me. They were very nice about it.'

'And then what happened?'

'They drove me home in a cab.' I felt my face beginning to burn.

He was silent, and suddenly I told him about Edward kissing me in the cab. I had never told anyone before: it had seemed a small shameful experience; the kind of thing one hugs miserably in one's mind; at the best with the poor comfort that one knows the worst of oneself, and at the worst blushing at one's secret and unique capability for second-rate behaviour – curiosity and half-baked sensuality and the like. Now when I told Ian, it seemed a small and unimportant thing, reflecting little, revealing less.

'Oysters,' he said when I had finished, and pushed the plate over to me with a friendly smile. 'Some people swallow them.'

I looked at them with horror.

'Only experienced oyster eaters,' he said and began eating his.

'I *do* like them,' I said a minute later.

'I am delighted,' he replied.

The rest of the meal slipped away and I was startled when he said that we must go.

'The theatre,' he said, and then seeing my dismay, 'What are you thinking?'

'How fast the time has gone.'

His face clouded, then became expressionless. But he only said, 'Yes, I know.'

All the way to the theatre he was very silent, and, I

thought, but I was not sure, very unhappy, almost as un-happy as he had seemed while we had waited for the bus; but because I was almost certain of this, I did not dare to ask him why.

We sat in a box; another delight for me, as the only oc-casions on which I had ever done so in the past had been at concerts to which I had not wanted to go.

'Are you very rich?' I asked.

'Oh, enormously rich,' he replied gravely.

'Of course. Rupert said you were.'

'Rupert? Oh Rupert Laing. Did he?'

'At the Lancings', where we met. Have you seen him since?'

'Yes – as a matter of fact we trained together. He told me he'd seen you.'

'Did he tell you about my trying to run away?'

'Yes. Yes, he did tell me that. Do you mind?'

'No. What else did he tell you?'

'That you were too sensitive,' he said, staring at his pro-gramme.

'What did he mean, too sensitive?'

'Too sensitive for your own peace of mind, I think. He said that unless you could record it, or use it, he probably said express it, you would be unhappy.'

'Oh.'

'I would always try not to hurt your feelings,' he said in a low voice. 'Always. That isn't much, but many people don't attempt even that. I love you and I would like to be very gentle with you. I would like to spend a great deal of time learning about you, being with you, and loving you more. I have always believed in the importance of love, that it should be searched for, delighted in, and treated with seriousness, and now I have precisely two and a half days before I go away, and because I cannot say everything, there is nothing worth saying, and the two and a half days seem no time at all. You see?' He made a hopeless little gesture with his hands. Then the lights went down, the orchestra struck up, and we saw the first act of a musical comedy that had been running for over a year.

231

All the while until the interval, I sat trembling, wondering, trying to adjust myself to the incredible idea that the man sitting by me loved me, or thought he was going to love me. I was unwilling or unable to consider my feelings for him at all: as whenever I attempted to do so, my mind shied away in a kind of ecstasy of nervous excitement, back to his feeling for me, his caring for me or not caring; my incredulity and his conviction, his solitary imagination of me as I began to think it must be. I stared resolutely at the stage. I did not want him to divine my thoughts; which revolved in a dull complexity incomprehensible to me. I think that I must have become more sunk in apathy and unhappiness, more hopeless of experiencing any desire, even more of attaining it, than I knew. At any rate those few hours succeeded in shocking me into some sort of life. I was quickened; my heart beat, seemed almost to enlarge itself; and my locked and silent sensibilities streamed forth, an almost unbearable torrent flooding my mind.

In the interval we turned to each other. He smiled and said, 'Would you like some lemonade?'

I nodded and he left me.

When he returned with the glasses I asked, 'How long have you – when did you think . . .'

'That I cared for you? When you left the Lancings'. No, I suppose not really until Rupert talked about you. I had thought of you often, but it was not until then.'

'But *why* do you care for me?'

'Do you mind not asking me that yet?' he replied gently, then added, 'I want to say one more thing. I do not expect you to love, to care for me. I do not want you to be anxious and disquieted. I should very much like . . .' He stopped and smiled at the inadequacy of his words, 'Well, I should *very* much like you to like spending as much of my two and a half days as you can with me. That is all. I am asking you to believe in my sincerity to that extent at least, and I should like the benefit of any doubt you may have. I am very serious, and shall not abuse it.'

'You will not be unhappy if . . .'

'No. I shall not mind what you do. It will make no difference to me what you do.'

His last words gave me a sense of infinite release. I felt vulnerable, but less exposed to being hurt; calmer, and more simply at ease with him and myself. After the theatre he took me home, having arranged that I should meet him at eleven o'clock the following morning at the place where we had drunk chocolate. He seemed to know that I did not want him to enter my home, and accepted this without surprise or resentment. When we reached the house, he took my hand and kissed it, turned it over and kissed the palm, then looked at me. 'You have such very beautiful eyes,' he said. 'If you had nothing else they would be sufficient reason for loving you. Thank you for coming.'

I entered my gate, and then stood listening until I could no longer hear the cab. It was a clear night with a frost; my feet sounded sharply on the paving stones. 'It will be fine,' I thought and longed for the next day.

I put the roses in a glass of water; they seemed soft and darker, but they were not dying. I lay in the dark trying to imagine his face, but I could only remember his eyes; his eyes and his voice matched each other with an immense kindness, perhaps an affection for me. Affection, I thought, must be a very rare thing between people, since I had lived all this time without it.

CHAPTER TWENTY-THREE

The next morning I said I would be out all day, and went before my mother and sister had time to inquire or disapprove. I went straight to the place where we had had chocolate. I was early, but he was there. We drank coffee. I remember he smiled and said 'I have not seen you in the morning for nearly four years.'

'And I look the same?'

'No, entirely different. You do not look the same for ten minutes together. When I have tried to remember your face, a hundred faces appear, a hundred expressions, each of them part of you. If I see you for a whole day I shall put some of them together. Am I to see you for the whole day?'

'If you like.'

'Oh, I should like,' he replied solemnly. 'Shall we go to the country? Walk and have lunch and come back when the light goes? Do you think you would like that?'

'Yes.'

He stared at me a moment in a penetrating manner, then said, 'You *don't* think you would like it; nevertheless, *I* think you will. I'll risk it and look at you carefully now and then to see which of us is right.'

We took a cab and drove to Marylebone. I had never in my life gone anywhere so simply and suddenly, and there was, I discovered, a delicious sense of freedom, of lack of responsibility about it. I think he must have planned the day before we met, as we caught a train immediately on our arrival at the station. He stopped at a bookstall, and asked whether I wanted to read in the train. When I said that I didn't, he bought a bunch of black grapes in a round basket. He selected an empty first class compartment and handed me into it.

In the train we ate grapes, and he asked me a little about

my home. At first I did not want to tell him, fearing he would be bored; but he had, as I had already partly discovered, a great talent for listening, for making everything I said seem absorbing. I told him about my mother, and the death of my father. I explained about there being very little money, about my wanting to work in a library, and about minding children instead. Then I again suddenly felt that everything I had to say was dull and fell silent.

'You should write,' he said. 'You observe things very well.'

'Is that the most important thing about writing?'

'No, not really. But I think it is for women who write. Observation is their strong suit. They seldom write out of their pure imagination.'

'Do men?'

'Oh dear. Perhaps *they* don't. But perhaps they observe more what one does not expect them to observe. And sometimes they use their imagination. Or mix the two more cunningly.'

'Do you write?' I asked.

'No, not really. Everyone writes a little at University,' he added almost apologetically.

'Do you always live in Scotland?'

'No, not all the time. I like it best there.'

I wanted to hear about it.

'It was a castle,' he began, 'but now it has degenerated into a mere house. Fires, and battles, and countless men who could not leave well alone, have so altered it, that only from one aspect does it still resemble a castle. It stands on a very green hill – the turf is so unnaturally green that there is a story to account for its greenness – and there are peacocks and red deer and wild daffodils and, of course, a ghost.'

'Have you seen it?'

'Oh yes. Not very often. It only comes when there is some crisis in the family. Some crisis or festivity. It is quite indiscriminate. It comes into the dining-room after the women have left the table and always sits on a special chair which is kept for it. The Ghost's Chair. Once when I was small I wanted to sit on it and my father was very angry.'

'Does it, does it speak?'

'Oh no. It simply listens and then goes away.'

He went on to tell me more about his house, and as I listened I watched his face, so that I should not again forget it. He had that very fair skin which flushes easily; a large and rather bony nose; blue eyes not in any way remarkable except sometimes for their expression; and a high broad forehead with the skin very white where it stretched over the bones. Then I saw that he was watching me, and turned to the window in some confusion, wondering whether, even now, I should remember his face. We talked easily by then, as though we knew each other much better than we did; only halted occasionally by some little shock of ignorance in each other, some taste, some phrase, some feeling that we had not encountered before.

We arrived and had lunch at an hotel. It was not a very good meal (things being bad by then in the way of food) but I do not think we noticed it very much. After lunch we walked. It was a fine, still afternoon, with no wind, and a large orange sun shining flatly on the tall bare trees. We walked up a cart track and then along a chalky ridge fringed with beeches. Their elegant leaves lay thick on the ground, pink and brown; our feet shuffled sharply among them. Below us the country seemed a mysterious and endless purple haze. After some time we came to a gap in the line of trees where several had been felled, and Ian proposed that we sit on one. We had not spoken for a long while. His voice startled me out of my private thoughts, and I wondered whether he had been bored by or disapproved my silence.

' – For a little while, unless you will be cold,' he was saying.

I shook my head and we sat on a smooth tree trunk.

'You look deliciously flushed,' he said. 'You like it?'

'You were quite right. It is lovely.'

'It is very good country for this purpose,' he said. 'One can come here easily, enjoy it, and go away again without regret. You do look happy.'

'I should like to do this again. The moment I am happy I start worrying that it will be the last time. Then I think perhaps it is whatever I am doing that makes me happy, and worry about being unable to do it.'

'Perhaps you are not often happy.'

'That is my fault, isn't it?'

'Not necessarily, and in any case not entirely. It is not easy to be happy now.'

'How long will the war last?'

'I don't know. Some people say a few months and some say much longer. I don't know. I think it must end soon if we are any of us to retain our sanity.'

'Is it – is it very frightful?' I asked. I had never dared to ask anyone before.

He turned to me and I saw the anguish in his face.

'Much worse than you can imagine. We all behave most of the time as though it were a boyish nightmare, an heroic tragedy, but it is long past human enduring. It is really that. More frightful than any creature can stand. Each single thing is too loud, too bloody and frightful for the nerves and heart and brain of anyone in their senses to bear. Many of them die of it, stretched till they break by the impossible demands made on them. But most of them will return, and God knows how they will manage to live with the people who were not there. There may not be another war, but this war ends more than war. To me, it seems to end almost everything. Unless,' he added, 'unless this war creates another species inured to its exigencies. I suppose it may do that.'

'Is it all like that?'

'No. I suppose not. It is only like that where I am. Don't believe what people say. Don't believe the books that will be written, the papers that are printed, the men who were not there. Believe me. It is the only thing I know.' He looked at me and then said, 'Perhaps not the only thing. I do not really want to talk about it. And I do *not* want to distress you.'

'You haven't distressed me.'

'You look unutterably distressed.' He paused. 'You cannot imagine how glad I am to have met you at that theatre,' he continued. 'You cannot possibly imagine it. I had thought about coming back for so long and then when I came, it seemed a kind of solitary marking time, painful and pointless; until I saw you again. I had ceased to make any plans with my time; to use it at all. I walked by that theatre, and then went back to buy a seat at random.'

'But we had a box.'

'Yes, but that was afterwards. I got that while you were changing.'

'Have you no friends in London?'

'Nobody I could bear to see. I don't want to sound pathetic. Of course there are people; relations, and a few odd friends left if one looked hard enough for them. I did at first, but then I had nothing to say when we met. It cuts you off, this business, you know. When I saw you, you looked so unhappy, so thoroughly in despair that you seemed more cut off than myself. I thought then that perhaps we are not so very different from the people at home. I had always imagined you as I used to see you – in large contented houses, surrounded by numbers of happy confident people. I used to think of you like that.'

'I only stayed with the Lancings for two weeks. I have not been there again,' I said.

'You were happy then?'

'Yes. Oh yes. I didn't expect to be, but I was. And then I have no cause, no reason, to be unhappy as you have. It isn't the war with me, at least I don't think it is. It's just that – well that I go on living and I didn't see the point of it.'

'Once you think like that you are lost. Most people don't think it so young. It does not usually cross their minds at your age.'

'But it is dreadful,' I persisted, wanting him to admit it.

'Of course. The war acts for me as a kind of safety valve. One is inclined in war to wonder what is the point of all these people dying? You have reached the stage where you wonder what is the point of all these people living.'

'I'm afraid I don't think it often of other people,' I said. 'I did think it of my father, when he was dying. I wondered about him then. But generally other people do seem to me to find some reason or contentment in life. It is only I who failed.'

238

'You are failing less – today?'

'Perhaps.' I did not want to pursue the matter. 'Once I sat in a wood with Rupert,' I said. 'He was very frightening about life, and I did not much understand what he said.'

'He was probably showing off.'

'No ... Perhaps he was. I think he meant to be kind.' There was a slight pause.

'Many men,' he said, 'many men need a kind of affectionate passion, but you, more than most women, seem to me to need affection, passionately, passionately.' When he finished speaking I found myself shivering violently. I pressed the palms of my hands together in a vain effort to stop. I turned to him to ask him whether – but one could not ask any such thing. I wondered desperately whether I should ever stop shivering. Then he held out his arms, I threw myself into them; and for the first time in my life I wept bitterly about nothing, and everything I knew, before someone else.

For a long time I wept and he did not speak, but held me, bent over me silently, stroking my head a little, until gradually I ceased weeping and lay quietly in his arms. Then he said: 'Shall I give you my handkerchief?' and after a moment gave it me.

'I haven't cried for a long time,' I said.

'No,' he replied reassuringly.

I did not feel I need say any more. I felt light, exhausted and incredibly relieved. After a while, I made some slight movement, and instantly he released me. The sun had disappeared, I noticed; the sky was grey and pink; there was no sound except a bird rustling about the trees; the air smelled dry and cold. I gave him back his handkerchief.

'Are you ready to go?'

'Yes.'

'It will soon be very cold.'

He pulled me to my feet and we walked back across the ridge, on down the cart track, where we could see the very end of the brilliant swollen sun sliding away. It was already cold, and we walked fast down the track corrugated with frozen ridges. I slipped a little, he put out his hand to steady me and I asked, 'Why are there cart tracks up here?'

'Charcoal burners most probably,' he answered.

On the station platform there was a crowd of soldiers. They all looked incredibly overloaded with rifles and kit; they were pink and panting, very young, and rather self-consciously noisy. An officer stood alone at one end of the platform. He was making entries in a large black notebook and I saw Ian begin to raise his hand as we passed, and then lower it again.

'What are they doing?'

'A draft. Going to London, and then on, I should think. We'll go the other end.'

We made our way back past the officer again. His luggage was polished like toffee, I noticed. He shut his book, and stuffing it back into his breast pocket, began slowly to walk behind us towards the men. They ceased shouting to each other, but shuffled noisily with their kit, each man trying not to look at us, at each other, or the officer. Somebody muttered something and there was a burst of suppressed laughter. Ian walked faster until we had reached the other end of the platform.

We sat alone in the train, opposite one another, watching the country pass our windows. He leaned forward and said: 'I had meant to give you tea, but then I thought we should catch this train. So now I want to take you to my house in London. You shall have tea there.'

'Yes.'

All the way in the train I sat, cold and peaceful; contented just to be sitting in a train, with him opposite me; to be moving together in the freezing fading light to his house. All my life, everything contained in my experience, seemed so past and done that it might have belonged to someone else. I knew all about it, without caring in the least. I was not unhappy, not ashamed; I had no mother, no sister; I knew nobody, I was not young or old, or afraid or beautiful. I had no plans and nothing to remember or forget; I was utterly contained in each moment, so that when it slipped and I lost it, there was another isolated moment, another little separate time alone with him in the train. Sometimes I looked at him, and he gave me a small steady smile. Sometimes I felt that he observed me as I sat with my face turned to the window, but this no longer frightened me: I felt almost as if he were I, and I he. I *wanted* to be him, I realized. Perhaps *he* had no past and no future; perhaps his heart was suspended as mine; perhaps I saw with his eyes and lived in his mind. All the pity I had felt for myself I had given him to feel for me. Then the affection he had felt for me, was, perhaps, also exchanged. Suddenly I wanted to lean forward and say, 'My dear, my dear, my very dear Ian.' I leaned forward ... but perhaps he was not mine at all, not my dear; but only kind, and without any object on which to bestow his kindness.

He had leaned forward and was saying: 'My house, you know. It is shut up, and empty. No one lives there, but I want you to come to it. I thought we might get some food and eat it there.' He seemed almost to be pleading with me, as though he half expected me to refuse. But I assented. I did not at all want to join crowds of other people. I wanted to continue to be alone with him without anything changed.

His house was a tall stucco building facing a park. I remember the trees on the other side of the Terrace, but it was dusk, and we had driven about so much that I had no idea where we were. We had stopped at three places; where Ian had each time disappeared, to return at length with some packet or basket. 'There will be drink,' he had said. 'We need only concentrate upon food.'

Now we were arrived, the cab dismissed, at his empty shuttered house. He opened the door and we entered. Inside it was dark and smelled of china tea. 'I think we will go to the drawing-room,' he said. 'Give me your hand. You are awfully cold. I did not know you were so cold.' I liked to hear him talk as we climbed the stairs, and I also liked being led by his deliciously warm hand. On the first floor he stopped and fumbled for the door handle.

The drawing-room was a very large L-shaped room: the tall windows were shuttered, and when Ian had produced some light, I saw that the piano, the sofas and chairs, almost all the contents were covered with white sheets; the carpets were rolled back and the surface of the mirrors was glazed with dust.

He led me to the fireplace; set down our packets; and stripping the dust sheet from a large sofa, pulled it over to me, inviting me to sit on it. 'No, lie on it while I light the fire,' he said. The fire was already laid, I noticed.

'Does this seem an impossible venture to you?' he asked a minute later, as he knelt before the fire.

'Very nearly.' He looked at me, then looked as though he were about to speak, but said nothing. 'What were you going to say?'

'Would you let down your hair?' he replied. 'I should so much like to see you reclining on white velvet with your hair down.'

'I shall need a comb.' Instantly he handed me a small yellowed ivory comb.

'Do not watch me then.'

'No.' He turned again to the fire and began building it up with pieces of wood and lumps of coal whilst I unpinned my hair.

'Would you like another cushion?' he asked after a time.

'Yes.'

He rose and delved under the cover of another sofa, returning with a large yellow silk cushion.

'Oh yes,' he said, placing it behind my head. 'I knew you would look beautiful like that. You should be painted. Thank you for letting down your hair. Now I am going to leave you alone in the firelight while I collect things for our meal.'

'Shall I not help?'

'No. I like to think of you lying there in your dark grey skirt. You may watch the fire. I shall come back and find you.' He walked to the door, then turned back and said: 'You will not be bored or frightened by yourself? I am only going downstairs. You will be all right?'

I nodded.

242

He shut the door. I heard his footsteps descend the bare stairs; and then there was silence. I lay watching the flames, and the shadow of the flames on the gold encrusted ceiling; the richness of my white velvet sofa in the gentle restless light; the strands of my hair lying on the glowing cushion; and the way the parquet floor looked almost like plaited hair stamped on the ground. I could still detect the closed scented smell which had seemed to fill the house. I was content just to lie there watching the room. There were pictures, and a mirror hanging above the piano. I began counting the pieces of furniture, the dim white lumps placed all over the room; even in the furthest corner they could be discerned ...

I woke to find his hand on my hair.

'It really *is* an improbable venture,' he was saying.

'I didn't intend ...'

'I like you to have slept,' he said.

There was a little round table beside me with food spread on it, laid upon a knotted lace cloth. There were knives, plates and two glasses; and a black bottle wrapped in a white napkin. There were also two small steaming pots.

'I did not even watch the fire. What *is* in the pots?'

'Soup,' he said proudly. 'I bought it in a jar and I've made it into proper soup. There are biscuits. There was a little sherry. The fire is all right. I was not very long, you know, but I had to keep unlocking things. My father has a passion for locking everything. He carries an enormous ring with all the keys of all his houses on it; he is unable to unlock anything in less than half an hour.' He sat on a stool beside me and gave me some soup and a biscuit.

'Now, you are starving and you must eat, or the food may vanish.'

The soup was very hot and good.

'Any soup tastes good with sherry in it,' he said, but I think he was secretly very proud of his concoction.

'Does your father not live here?' I asked.

'No,' he said, 'he prefers to live in his club. He works incessantly, and he says he is too tired to combat a large empty house at the end of each day. So it is shut up except for a caretaker who comes in to clean it, and make sure that nothing has been stolen.'

'Have you been living here?'

'No, not really. I come here a good deal, and I spent the first night of my leave here, but it was not the same as it is now. It needs another person.' He gave me a second biscuit. 'I shall have to go and see him again.' He fell silent and I felt all his life that I did not know crowd into his mind.

He gave me a plate on which were half a cold bird, some potato salad, and sprig of watercress. He poured some wine into the glasses. Then he said, 'I shall drink to our happiness. Your happiness.' He drank.

'May I drink to yours?'

He gave me a glass of the red wine, looked at me, and then said in a bantering facetious manner which ill became him: 'You may drink to my old age. My happy and prosperous senility.'

I repeated the toast uncomprehendingly and without much enthusiasm and drank to it.

'And now let us return to this evening. We are not old, and you are not, I think, unhappy.'

'I think,' I said cautiously, 'that I am very happy.'

'Do you? Well don't think any more about it than that. Of course you know you deserve to be. You took an awful risk. You might be utterly ruined by now, in floods of tears, or white and silent and desperately bored.'

'Why?'

'Because,' he said solemnly, 'wicked men and worse still, dull men, frequently collect young women outside London theatres, feed them on grapes and oysters, and carry them off to some deserted house. I tell you this, because you do not seem to realize how fortunate you are that I am not wicked and hardly at all dull.'

'But how are the men to know about the women? Suppose they are dull?'

'In these cases that is seldom a primary consideration.'

'I knew that you were not dull – or wicked.'

'My upbringing,' he said sadly. 'The bad thing about that

244

was that although it presented a fair chance of my being dull, it made no allowance for wickedness whatsoever.'

'Tell me about your upbringing.'

'I should like to hear about yours.'

'I don't think I was brought up. I just drifted.'

'Probably a very good thing.'

'Yes, but I'm still drifting. I don't know how to stop. I have no talents, and hardly any friends.'

'I am your friend.'

'Yes, I ...'

'What would you *like* to do?' he interrupted to relieve me.

'What would you suggest?'

He thought for a moment and then said, 'I should imagine that in a better world you are well equipped simply to live. You would not need a reason for doing this. But at the present time people have all to be doing something more or less frightful in order to justify their being alive. Everyone labours under a kind of unorganized mass guilt. When they start to organize their guilt the trouble will really begin.'

'Will they?'

'After this war they might. As long as we can think the Germans are even a little worse than ourselves, and the Germans can think that they are a little better than us, we shall rub along as we are, killing each other. But when the war is over and we are forced back on to comparing ourselves with other members of the family it will not take very long before we see, or think we see, that we are all equally wicked. Then we shall organize ourselves to compensate for this feeling. Work for work's sake, and so on. I don't think you've reached that stage.' He gave me more wine, and then continued: 'I think you should write. I cannot think of anything else. Have you ever tried?'

I nodded: 'But it was no good, and I stopped.'

'Start again. I shall expect to be sent some results.'

We finished our dinner with exquisite pears. Then he asked me to play to him.

'I cannot play to people.'

He walked to the piano, uncovered and opened it, and came back to the fire.

'I am not people,' he said. 'I cannot play, and it would give me so much pleasure to hear this piano again.'

After some minutes' indecisive silence, I rose from the sofa, went reluctantly to the instrument, and played an Allemande from the English Suites. When I had finished I turned to him, but he was staring into the fire and did not move or speak. After a moment I suddenly remembered a sonata of Scarlatti and played it.

'What key is that in?'

'B minor.'

'It is most hopelessly sad. The epitome of despair. Like the beginning of the end of something. Would you play it again?'

'The end of love,' he said when I had finished it.

I played a slow movement from a B Flat sonata of Haydn, and then shut the piano.

'Who was that?'

'Haydn.'

'All people you like?' he said.

'Yes.'

'Thank you. Please come back now.'

When I was again back on the sofa he drew up his stool, and took my hand.

'I am already so much devoted to you,' he said. 'Will you remember how devoted to you I am? Will you tell me one thing? Has anyone made you very unhappy?'

'No one.'

'Good.' He enclosed my hand in both of his for a moment and then said, 'Now I suppose I must take you home.'

'I must put up my hair.'

'Oh yes. Stay here and I will fetch you a mirror.'

He returned with a mirror and ivory brush, which he placed on the table beside me. 'While you do that I must extinguish the fire.'

'What about the remains of our dinner?'

'That will vanish of itself,' he replied.

I remember that as we opened the front door, we were assaulted by the biting moonlit air, and a thin distant howling.

'The wolves,' he said. 'They often howl at night. I had forgotten them. Do you mind walking until we find a cab?'

'No. I do not mind anything,' I replied.

'Does that mean that were you in the mood for objecting, you would object to walking for a cab?'

'No.'

We discovered a cab, and began the long quiet drive to Kensington which was the very end of our entire day together.

I think it was then that I first clearly realized that the next day was his last: it was then that I began dreading it, not very sure what precisely it was that I dreaded, not even certain that I was not simply afraid that *he* dreaded it. I knew, at least, that he was thinking about it, and realized suddenly that he must often have done so since I had met him outside the theatre – very much more often than the few occasions when he had spoken about his three remaining days. Now it was one remaining day, perhaps not even that. Perhaps he had meant that he was going away in the evening. It seemed absolutely necessary to know this. I asked him.

'Very early in the morning the day after tomorrow.'

'Oh.' There was one whole day left.

'I am awfully afraid that I shall not be free until after lunch,' he said. 'My father arranged at the beginning of my leave that I lunch with him on my last day, and he is not free at any other time excepting the evening, which I would like to spend with you. I should like to meet you immediately after lunch, if you would. If you would,' he repeated, and looked at me.

'Where shall I meet you?'

'Meet me just inside the National Gallery at half past two,' he said quickly.

He must have considered the matter, I thought, as I agreed to this arrangement.

We were silent again, unable to think of anything which did not render us more silent.

'Tomorrow night,' I remember thinking, 'tomorrow night I shall drive back like this with him for the last time,' and wondered what would become of me.

'At any rate, we have decided that you are going to write,' he said, almost as though he were interrupting me.

'I shall try.'

We had reached my home. He did not kiss my hand, but helped me out of the cab and then led me to the gate.

'Will you get in?'

'Oh yes, I have a key.'

'I adored your hair. You are a kind and beautiful creature.'

'I meet you at two-thirty?'

'Two-thirty. Inside the National Gallery.'

'Yes.'

'Good night my dear,' he said and returned to the cab.

I slipped into the house and up to my room as silently as possible; stripped off my clothes and endeavoured to choose my thoughts, or at least to collect the incidents of the day and savour them. I knew that it had been a wonderful day. I *knew* this without in the least being able to count the joys, because I was filled with vague but tremendous anxieties which could not be counted. All I could count were the hours I had left before he went, and I counted them carefully while I unpinned my hair. Eight hours at least; and he had said that he adored my hair. It had seemed a strange word for him to use. No one had ever adored anything about me. It did not anyway seem a word to which he was accustomed. I adore your hair, I said to myself, hearing his voice; and experienced a sharp nervous thrill. Tonight I should be able to sleep with my last thought that I should see him tomorrow; but tomorrow night – tomorrow night was like some disastrous precipice, towards which I was inevitably propelled and on the edge of which I was inevitably forsaken. Now I should not see him until half past two, which seemed so many hours away, that the ensuing hours with him must seem long also. He does not want to go; and I think he does not want to leave me, I thought, knowing that also. Then I lay down with the false childish little hope that perhaps something which we both desired so intensely not to happen, would not happen.

CHAPTER TWENTY-FOUR

I spent a long dreadful morning, evading my family, struggling with my share, and more than my share (for I had a guilty conscience) of the family chores, watching the time, and finally attempting to eat lunch under the watchful family eyes. At ten minutes to two I escaped to my room, at two left the house, and then was so afraid of being late that I took a cab. In consequence of this I arrived early; but once more he was there.

'I am very glad that you are early, because we are going to a theatre,' he said almost at once. 'I have a cab waiting.' He took my arm and led me down the steps again.

'I am sorry to be peremptory, but I have thought this out very carefully,' he said as we drove away. 'I thought we should have tea, and then dine in my house. Is that all right?'

I nodded. The slight disappointment I had felt about the theatre dissolved as he continued the plans. I surrendered myself to the third day in his company so completely that the morning vanished; there was nothing beyond going to his house, and I was able utterly to concentrate upon the hours between.

Curiously, I can remember almost nothing about the theatre we visited. It must have been a comedy, as I remember us both laughing; on one occasion turning to each other, ceasing to laugh, and turning back to the stage again, with the play knocked out of our minds.

Afterwards we had tea. Ian had again bought me dark red roses, which smelled of more roses than could possibly be contained in the paper. 'Do not unwrap them,' he said. 'I want you to wear them in your hair at dinner.'

'In these clothes?'

'I assure you they will be perfectly suitable. You have very good hair for the purpose. Like the Empress Elisabeth. She preferred diamonds, but you will have to make do with roses for the present.'

'Did she always wear diamonds in her hair?'

'Invariably. But she wore a top hat when riding in order to conceal the diamonds.'

He proceeded to tell me about the Empress Elisabeth: of her beauty; her passion for adventure; her terror of growing old; and her incredible hair. 'Of course, being an Empress she was able to make the most of it,' he concluded as we rose to go. 'Shall we walk a little? We have now to collect our dinner.'

I agreed. We proceeded to St James's Street.

'Do you arrange about food?'

'Yes. I wake very early, and that is how I employ the time. We are going to my club first, where I am afraid you will have to wait for me.'

As I waited, I reflected that this was, after all, not so difficult as I had previously imagined it would be. We were not tense or strained, either of us; we were simply two friends spending the day – spending it perhaps in a slightly less usual manner than many friends who spent time together (I was thinking of the empty house and the private meal we were collecting); but that was all. That really seemed to be all, I repeated to myself.

It began to rain a little. We collected the rest of the food in a cab, and then drove to his house. Here the same ceremony took place as before. Ian lighted the fire, uncovered the white sofa (everything in the room had been restored to the state in which I had first seen it), and then announced that he was going to prepare the meal. I offered to help him; but he declined, and I felt certain that he did not want me to see the rest of the house. When he had left me I wandered round the room.

Hung on the wall there was a large portrait of an extremely fascinating woman. She was wearing a riding habit: her beautiful hands palely clutched the heavy folds of her skirt, as she gazed out upon the room above the severe gloss

251

of her high stiff collar, with an expression at once imperious and immature; smiling a little curling smile, which conveyed nothing of the humour in which she was painted. Possibly she was Ian's sister, although he had never mentioned a sister. But then, I really knew very little about him. I replenished the fire; then, without thinking very much, wandered to the piano and played.

I found myself totally unable to remember any piece of music completely. This was not customary with me, and I found it unreasonably frightening. For what seemed hours of panic and futility, I struggled; always breaking down at the same place or within a few bars of it; until I was eventually interrupted by Ian.

I did not hear him come into the room, which increased my alarm and mortification. I rose from the piano, wordless and shivering, and moved to the sofa avoiding him.

'You have not used your roses,' he said.

'No.'

I made no move towards them, sat with my hands stretched out to the fire, as though they were cold and I must do nothing but warm them. I felt him regarding me; my unaccountable tumult of feeling rose to the pitch of anger. I discovered that my hands were freezing. He indicated a stool where I might sit nearer the fire, and I moved to it with my back to him. 'If he imagines that I will unpin my hair and play the piano, he is wrong,' I thought viciously, longing for him to give me the chance of denying him either of these things. 'I will do nothing of the kind.' I wanted to sit there until he was as angry with me as I was with him; there was nothing else that I *could* do now, I realized quickly. It is very easy to reach a point where one's next action is so dependent on pride and so confined by emotion that one is driven on to ungraciousness and everything fast becomes intolerable. It was intolerable to sit on the stool, unable to speak, refusing the roses, and waiting for him to be hurt, but it was all I was able to do. And a few minutes ago everything had seemed simple; until he had come into the room when I was trying to remember the music.

All this while I heard him arranging things on the table. Eventually he said: 'Would you like to eat where you are?'

I felt that he was trying to accommodate me, and knew that if I were to continue hating him at all, I must comply. I turned round, and he offered me a steaming bowl as he had done the previous evening. For some minutes we sat in silence, while I attempted to drink the soup, but long before it was finished I knew that I should be quite incapable of sustaining the meal. I put the bowl on the table in order better to struggle with myself. Then I heard him set down his bowl, looked at him, and suddenly, covering my face in my hands, was shaken with sobs. He got up after a moment and led me to the sofa. I think he knelt before me, holding my hands, asking me why I was sobbing. I shook my head. I was so ashamed and so unhappy that I did not know or care why.

'Did I frighten you? Was it because you dislike anyone hearing you practise? Or because you do not want to unpin your hair?' I heard him trying all these possibilities with patient credulity, prepared to believe anything I told him. So I told him the truth; that I did not want him to go away, most passionately I did not want it. It was the only thing I knew.

'I think I had better hold you in my arms,' he said.

'No. I am dreadfully sorry.'

'Why are you sorry?'

'I cannot manage any of my feelings at all. I simply weep. I wept yesterday.'

'That was different,' he said reassuringly.

'Yes. But this is much worse. I will try to explain. I do not love you, at least, surely if I did love you I should not be so utterly unhappy. Even if you were going away, surely I should not be so much in despair?'

'I do not know,' he said after considering this. 'Perhaps not. Perhaps you wish you did love me.'

'I wish I knew you more. I do not want you to go and never to see you. I know nothing about this. I cannot compare myself, or you, with anyone or anything else. I simply want to choose more: and not be forced into your going away. Must you go?'

'Yes, I must go.'

'Well, do you really believe that you love me?'

'Yes, I know that.'

'If you stayed, I might know that I loved you. Wouldn't that be what you would want?'

'If I were staying, I should do everything in my power to induce your love,' he replied.

'But you cannot possibly stay? Even a little time?'

I saw that he began to suffer but he reiterated steadily, 'No, I must go.'

We stared silently at each other; and then, with a tremendous effort, my heart devoured my imagination of him, and my half-conscious dream of our gentle slow-moving love. I believe I only touched his hand; but it was as though our hearts touched, lay quietly together and returned to us. If he had stayed many months I think there might not have been such another moment. They are the only moments when more than one person is beautiful: when each mind is unfolded to the other like some marvellous map of a Paradise: when each also loves the self equally because it is the lover of the beloved. They are the moments of life which continue it: the vindication of all the desolate hours and days and years that each one spends searching.

He was holding my hand again now; and still we watched the glow from the first exquisite shock die in our eyes; and the lovely amiable ease which followed.

'Who is the portrait at the end of the room?'

'My mother. It was very like her, I believe.' She was killed, he continued, in a riding accident when he was a child. He barely remembered her.

We talked very quietly for a time, hardly aware of what we said, and then he rose to his feet.

'Don't leave me.'

'I was proposing to sit on the sofa with you,' he said.

I remembered the roses.

'May I have your comb?'

'Yes, of course.'

I held out my hand. He gave it me. I walked to the mirror over the fireplace, and he watched me let down my hair.

'Don't cut it, will you? At least, not yet.'

'Why do you ask that?'

'Many women have cut their hair. I am not sure that it would become you. I should have to know you better.'

'I will ask your opinion before I cut it, but it is very heavy.'

'It is very romantic and beautiful,' he answered seriously. 'Shall I comb it for you?'

'Yes.'

'Sit on this cushion and give me the comb.'

He was very good at it and I said so, with some surprise. 'Have you combed many women's hair?'

'Would it not be better for you if I had?'

I reflected. 'Yes, I suppose it would.'

'Well then, I am an extremely experienced hair comber.'

'Of course you might be instinctively good at it.'

I felt that he smiled as he said: 'Perhaps that is what I am. Now, where are the roses. I presume you intend wearing the roses.'

'As I am without a single diamond, I have no choice.'

'I should have bought diamonds as well. It is dreadful to have no choice.'

'You are not meant to give me diamonds! I didn't mean that.'

'I think I should enormously enjoy giving you diamonds. It simply had not occurred to me.'

'Give me the roses. I want to unwrap them myself.'

'Now,' he said, when the roses were finally arranged. 'Come and recline on the sofa. I think it will entail taking you in my arms. For our mutual comfort,' he added when I came.

For a long while I lay on the sofa with his arms round me. There seemed to be so very much to say, and conversation of any kind was delightful to us both. We talked, we reassured one another (I did not at first perceive his need of this), we discovered, or bred, a crowd of new perfections in one another: and all the while, time, the hours, raced, galloped, fell headlong into the night. Then, when he suggested that we eat the rest of our meal, I did ask him the time. We found that it was well past eleven. I was so appalled that I did not notice him, as the relentless situation closed in on me again with frightful force. I should have to go, in less than an hour I should have to go. I turned from any hopeless attempt to eat; determining this time thoroughly to control myself, unconsciously clinging to him until he said: 'My poor darling. We are neither of us very good at this.' I saw his eyes filled with tears, and was overwhelmed with an agony of tenderness for him, with a passionate desire that he should not feel so much or so painfully as I. I put my arms round him and kissed him; held him in my arms as though I were the lover; and for a moment the imminence of our parting ebbed away. I remember thinking quite quietly to myself when I had kissed him: 'No, I cannot bear this, really I cannot bear it. Something must happen to stop, or at least defer my going, because this is more than I can bear.'

Then, almost immediately, he said: 'I have to go very early in the morning. Would you stay here with me until I go?'

'I will stay with you.'

'What about your family? Will they not become anxious?' He was very still, watching me steadily.

'I told them I should be late, and I have a key. I don't think they will know until tomorrow morning.' I wondered why he continued to watch me, as though he were trying to understand me. I repeated almost angrily, 'They won't know until the morning, and then I shall be back.'

'You want to stay?'

'I don't want to leave you. I think I must love you very much indeed. I want to lie on this sofa all night, talking with your arms round me.'

'That is what you want?'

'Yes. Is that wrong?'

He touched my hair and then dropped his hand. 'No,' he said, 'of course it is not wrong. That is what you shall have. But first you must eat.'

We ate: the morning seemed very far away. We even discussed the plans for his departure, and they none of them seemed in the least real to me. He must leave at seven, he said, in search of a cab, but he would make tea before he left; therefore we must, if we slept at all, wake at six-thirty.

'Shall we sleep?'

'I expect not,' he said, 'but we might.'

Fetching a small clock, a kettle and two large cups; he set them on the table, which he moved away from the sofa whereon I lay.

'Should I do anything?'

'No, I will make up the fire and join you.'

He knelt before the fire, began to replenish it, and then suddenly exclaimed: 'Oh my darling!'

'What is it?' He was sitting back on his heels regarding me.

'I have a sudden access of anxiety for you. I do not want to make you unhappy. I do not want you to suffer because of me.'

'But you are not making me suffer.'

'I am in no position to love anyone,' he said. 'Perhaps you least of all.'

'But – but you do not want to go away?'

'You know that I do not want to.'

'Well then I do not understand. It is not you who are deliberately making me unhappy, but the situation, which is no more yours than mine.'

'Then you *are* unhappy.'

'Oh – not more than you. I think, perhaps less. I am simply filled with feelings I have never had before. I no longer know precisely what I feel. I do love you,' I added.

'I desire you,' he said quietly. 'I want you, because I love you so much. Most of all, I have wanted to tell you. I don't want you to answer me, but it eases my mind to tell you this one thing. I know quite well that you are not ready to love me as much as you must love me before I could possess you. But telling you makes it possible for me to love lying on the sofa with you in my arms; my beloved creature. You do not mind my saying this? In other circumstances there would be

257

no need to say it. I love you.' He turned back to the fire again.

'I suppose,' I said uncertainly, 'that it is I who am a step behind you.'

'Or a step ahead. It makes no difference.'

'Then do we never meet? Do not people ever feel the same at the same moment?'

'Sometimes they do. I think that at the beginning and at the end of love there is always a kind of dishonesty; it is inevitable, and should not be resented, even when it is painful. But in the middle, the centre, there is a brilliant pure streak, when honesty is merely another joy. Then people meet.'

All the remainder of the night we lay, wrapped in one another's arms, furthering our love, spending the precious time like gold, that we, as misers, were forced to spend. We lay with the small clock evenly distributing our hours, striking them off by a single impersonal note, so that we began each hour in trembling silence.

Very early in the morning he slept for a short while. I watched his face by the light of the dying fire. I moved to touch his head, and he woke, instantly alert, as though he never slept more deeply.

'Is it time?'

'No, no I do not think so. I am sorry I woke you.'

'I did not mean to sleep.'

We would make tea now, he continued, and talk while we drank it. He put the last pieces of wood on the fire: the room seemed cold and I looked at the time. It was a quarter to six. The roses in my hair were bruised and wilting. I unpinned them.

'I should like one,' he observed.

He produced a black pocket book, like the one the officer on the station had had, and tucked the rose away. The flames from the replenished fire leapt higher up the chimney and the kettle began to throb.

'I can see the lovely bones of your face in this light,' he said. He came to me, and traced them with his finger.

'Will you remember my face?' I asked.

'Of course.'

'I do not think it is so easy. I had great difficulty in remembering yours, even when I had just left you, and wanted to remember it.'

'Perhaps I have not a very memorable face, or perhaps you tried to remember the wrong things. But I shall remember you.'

'The wrong things?'

'I shall remember you by your square forehead: it is almost completely square; and by the ledges of bone under your eyes; the way your whole face tilts into your small neat chin; the heavy enchanting curve of your eyelid; and your enormous tears. One should not try to remember people in order to describe them to someone else. In doing this one loses everything of significance. If I said that you had long grey eyes, a white complexion, and heavy dark brown hair, no one would be very much the wiser; but I should have made a public image of you which could be anybody, and which would slowly obscure my private idea of you. All of which proves, my darling, that love should be a very private business. In communicating any of it to society, one literally gives something away, and one does not get it back.'

We made and drank the tea and then I asked Ian whether I might wash my face.

'The water will be cold. Shall I boil some more?'

'No. I want cold water.'

He took me up the stairs to another landing where there was a large bathroom, and I bathed my aching eyes in icy water, resolving, as I did so, that when the moment arrived for him to go, I would employ self-control.

The moment seemed to creep towards us in a measured remorseless manner, more calculated to destroy our sensibility than any sudden unmeditated parting. We were reduced to sitting silently by one another, he holding my hand, exchanging little shadowy words of comfort, the ghosts of our grief.

'You will write to me?'

'If you will write to me.'

'Yes, I promise.'

'You know where to write?'

'Yes.'

'Shall I come to the station with you?'

'No. I have to collect some luggage on my way.'

Eventually he rose, and went out for his cab. I heard his steps go down the stairs and the door shut, as I sat holding the sides of my forehead in my hands. He had said that he would be five minutes, perhaps longer. I remembered that my hair was undressed, and, glad of employment, put it up. Almost as soon as I finished doing this, I heard the cab. It was ten minutes to seven. He did not immediately come into the room; I imagined him putting luggage into the vehicle. Then I heard him, and turned to face the door. He came quickly into the room shutting the door, and walked over to where I stood.

'Do you mind very much if I leave you here? I should prefer it to anything else.'

I shook my head.

'You need only walk out of the house. Leave everything. I should have asked you before. You don't mind?' He was gripping my hands.

'No, I don't mind.'

He took my head in his hands, bent a little to kiss me, stared at me for a moment and went. He shut the door; again I heard him descend the stairs; the front door slam; the cab door slam more faintly. I heard the cab drive away. Then there was complete silence. I was alone. For some seconds I stood, frozen and trembling, where he had left me; my throat aching intolerably. I imagined him leaning back in the cab, watching more and more streets separate us. Then the little clock struck seven and I turned blindly to the fire with some idea of extinguishing it.

I did put out the fire, and covered the white sofa and the piano; but the sight of the table with two cups still faintly warm from their tea was almost too much for me so that I decided not to touch them. All the time I had been doing these things, I had thought that my one desire was to leave the house as quickly as possible. Now, however, when everything was done, going out of the house seemed infinitely worse than staying within it. Here, no one could see me: I was afforded some kind of protection. I moved to the covered sofa and sat on it, still shivering, and quite unable to do anything which required more initiative. Now, I thought, he will have collected his luggage and be driving to the station. I would sit there until I felt better; until the ache in my throat subsided and my legs did not tremble so much; and then I would go. It seemed to have come so suddenly in the end: he had held my hands and kissed me – and gone in a moment without saying a word. I had never asked him when I should see him again; there was an utterly unknown stretch of time between his kissing me and the next time we should meet. Why had I not asked him that simple question? But perhaps he would not have known. At any rate he would have been able to tell me the longest time that he would be likely to be away. Perhaps when he wrote – *if* he wrote. I began to be uncertain even of his writing, and felt much worse. Then I suddenly remembered that a caretaker came to the house, and began to worry that she would arrive and discover me. I must go. I looked carefully round the room in order to remember it – and then my eye lighted on the clock.

It was six minutes past seven. He had only been gone six minutes. He would not even have picked up his luggage in all this time, which was only six minutes.

CHAPTER TWENTY-FIVE

I went home and remained in my room most of the day. Being very tired, I did not want to speak to my family. When they tried to make me come down for lunch, I said that I had been dancing all night and only wanted to sleep. I do not know what they made of this tale, but they left me alone. I lay on my bed and imagined the other room – wondered whether the caretaker had been to it; had taken away the cups, and cleared the fire: wept a few unrelieving tears, and slept, imagining his arms round me.

For fifteen days I existed in a kind of double life, half of which consisted in my job of packing parcels, cutting sandwiches at the canteen, and living with my family: and half of which was centred round Ian's absence; his absence and his silence. Whenever I was alone, and sometimes when I was not, my mind revolved round the three days I had spent with him. I remembered and then elaborated and invented conversations I had had with him or might have had. I thought of everything there was to remember about him, stretching and spreading it thinly over my entire mind. I tried to imagine what he was doing; and took to reading newspapers in the vain hope of discovering. I longed for him to write to me, and speculated endlessly on the reasons for his silence. On at least two occasions I began writing to him, but found this so difficult (I was afraid to express my feelings, and nothing else seemed worth expressing) that I tore up the paper before I had covered it. Sometimes I almost hated him for not writing, or I would imagine that he had done so and sent the letter to the wrong address, or that the letter had strayed, or that he had simply forgotten my address. Sometimes I would reason with myself that it was absurd to expect a letter so soon; that for all I knew, he might be so placed that he was unable to write to anyone;

and that it was mad to mind so much about so small a thing. And sometimes I would simply weep and comfort myself with the hope that he would write the next day. All the fifteen days I fell more in love with him, and each day I grew more afraid that perhaps, after all, he did not love me. Then on the evening of the sixteenth day a letter arrived.

There is, for the first time since I last saw you, the promise of an uninterrupted hour, when I can write to you and think of you continuously, instead of having you swept from my mind by the interminable demands made on one by this life.

I should really like, my darling, to carry you off to some island on the west coast of Scotland, to begin even a small new world with you, as I do not feel that we shall either of us much like the remains of the old one. But perhaps you would not like that? Will you write to me and tell me what you would like? At least write to me. Do you realize that I have not a piece of paper with your writing on it?

I continue to imagine more about you than I knew after three days of you; until now, after twelve days without you, you are probably quite different – excepting your beauty. That is indelibly fixed in my mind.

I admire and love you for spending the end of my time with me. I do believe that I might make you happy, and sometimes I almost believe that you will allow me to try.

This letter is, after all, constantly interrupted, and none the better for it.

I want to hear about your life, but I do not want to write about mine ... and I think I am afraid, my darling, that I have rushed you, with your kindness and sensibility, very much more than I had any business to rush you. I am very much content if I may love you, and you will be my friend. A letter here would be like a little water in a desert.

You see, I began this in the most feverish confidence, and line by line I have become more apprehensive about you, until an island seems a presumptuous mirage: and a letter more than I deserve. Many people are happier if they get less than they deserve, but I am not one of them. I shall be happier when you have written to me.

I am totally unsuited to what I am doing, but so is almost everyone else. I find this has a generally paralysing effect; so that one expects not to do anything well, nor to like doing it, but to have to do it again. Any qualities I possess are drawbacks, and the qualities I am considered to have are a humiliation. The effort to retain self-respect, and at the same time the respect of many more unhappy people who are forced to believe in me and God at the same time, is a severe strain. I have not an illusion about this business, not one. I have only your beauty to sustain me, and that is not an illusion, but an unhappily distant reality. I love you and am entirely yours.

IAN

P.S. Write to me, I beg you.

He did love me. I read the letter three times to be sure of this, and then, a little ashamed of myself, read it again, in an attempt to discover anything else he felt. But except that he was unhappy and that the letter was constantly interrupted, there seemed to be nothing.

'He does love me,' I repeated endlessly, smoothing the thin paper with my fingers and imagining his hand moving along it as he wrote. I examined and adored his writing. I folded the paper and put it into the envelope. 'He does love me, and he did not forget my address.' I withdrew the letter again from the envelope, and tried to imagine the bare paper, before he had covered it with words and sent it to me. That he should be able, so far away, to tell me on a piece of paper that he loved me, and then send it to me, seemed miraculous; waiting fifteen days for such a joy a mere nothing. And this letter was now in my possession, so that never again should I have to wait with nothing to comfort me – I should never again be so desolate.

I collected writing materials, and, no longer afraid of expressing my feelings, started to write to him. I told him that I had received his letter, that I loved him, that I would go anywhere with him; and after that words poured out of my heart; everything that I wrote seemed to add to my love, although never exactly pronouncing it, so that in a frenzy I wrote and wrote, tearing the sheets and beginning again, until, very late in the night, I had completed my letter, addressed it carefully (he was a captain in some Scottish regiment I discovered), and sealed it. Then I read his letter again and slept. I think it was then, reading his letter in my nightdress, that I began to desire him. At least I lay down remembering his hands and aching to be touched by them.

I posted the letter in the morning, on my way to the large dreary house where the parcels were packed. All day I packed with a feverish exhilaration which provoked the official gratitude of the Organizer; a weary little man, whose private feelings appeared to be worn away by responsibility and lack of supplies (or what he called suitable matter) for parcels, and who seemed to consider himself solely as an institution. He did not remember who I was, or what precisely I had been doing; but he thanked me, employing the faded rhetoric he used on these rare occasions; this last implying that the parcels provided our boys with more than material inspiration in their task of ending all wars, but that they could not be inspired, materially or otherwise, unless a steady flow were maintained. 'A steady flow,' he repeated, glaring at me from watery eyes and backing away as he spoke, conscious of having achieved the personal touch so important in an institution.

This incident was of the kind recounted by my family at meals. I was not usually possessed of such a crumb, and I resolved as I walked home that I would make the most of it. It was the kind of thing that made my mother laugh: my sister never laughed. Afterwards I would escape to my room and read Ian's letter again, and perhaps I would write part of another letter to him. I stopped on my way to buy writing paper. If this new and tremendous private life was to be restricted to letters, they should at least be written with extravagant care; they must at least attempt perfection. I bought a quantity of pale green paper, a box of new nibs, and a roll of purple blotting paper. I almost ran home with them.

At dinner I told them about my day and the remark of the Organizer. My mother did laugh. My sister allowed us to treat the matter lightly for a moment, then remarked that he was perfectly right, and, to change the subject, began to speculate on the possibility of Hubert obtaining Christmas leave. With a rush of excitement that brought tears to my eyes, I thought of Ian coming back; but reflected that this was really too much to hope for, when he had so recently had leave. On the other hand, Hubert, my mother confirmed, would very likely be coming. Still, I had had a letter.

The conversation staggered on to the shortage of butter; my mother remarking that there was a very good letter in the paper about it. My sister agreed that the shortage was unfortunate, but pointed out that it was better we suffer than our men, adding rather unexpectedly, that we must remember what Napoleon said. My mother looked up inquiringly, went faintly pink and said of course, but surely things were rather different nowadays, with trenches and modern warfare. 'We must march to Berlin!' cried my sister inspired; and that seemed to settle the butter shortage. I asked, as was then my custom, whether I might borrow the paper. 'Of course, darling,' said my mother, 'you can read the letter yourself.'

'There is nothing *happening*,' complained my sister, collecting the table mats. 'I thought you might help me with the studio curtains.'

I promised that I would do so the following night. Thus ended the meal; like so many hundred meals I had eaten in this dreary despairing house, whose inhabitants all seemed so utterly cut off from each other and from anything that life seemed to me to offer on the few occasions when I had succeeded in escaping from it and them. Now that I was presented with a means of escape, I was filled with remorse: that I had not been kinder, or made more attempt to impart some energy and interest to the house; had not encouraged the people who came, to do so again; which would at least have given my mother pleasure, if no one else. I resolved to do all these things, as I shut my bedroom door and my secret life with Ian consumed me.

My room possessed a small table, on which I had hitherto kept a pile of books, a framed photograph of my father, and, while they had lasted, Ian's roses. I decided that I would write my letters on it in future, and rearranged it accordingly. I then settled down to the long delicious evening of reading and writing. I began by reading his letter again, but now that I almost knew it by heart I found myself lamenting its brevity and thirsting for more of his handwriting. Perhaps he would reply to my letter. Whether he replied or no, the desire to write to him again was overwhelming; even if I refrained from sending the letter immediately, I must write. So I wrote four pages on my beautiful green paper, addressing the envelope with joy at writing his name. Afterwards, disinclined either to sleep or to read anything which absorbed my attention to the exclusion of my love, I began casually to search in the paper for the letter my mother had enjoined me to read. It was then that my eyes fell upon the list of fallen officers, and I as casually discovered that Ian had been killed three days before.

CHAPTER TWENTY-SIX

At least I was spared any uncertainty about Ian's death. There was enough in the paper to leave me in no doubt. He must have died even before I received his letter. I supposed he must always have thought that he would be killed, and that was what he had meant when he had said that he was in no position to love anybody and did not want to cause me suffering. He had never mentioned the possibility, however, and oddly enough, it had never been in the forefront of my mind. I had lived so much cut off from the war as to be almost unaware of its perils and tragedies. I simply picked up the paper, and that is what I read. I think it was the unobtrusive and incidental manner of his death which most horrified me. He had gone out there, loving me, hating the life he felt bound to live; and then, quite suddenly, he was dead; wiped out; all his heart and life were stopped, and of no account to anyone. A little notice in the paper finished him off and the war turned to the next man.

After that, I suffered agonies from those long, tightly packed lists of unknown names. I came to imagine that no one of the people who went returned. The tragedy of somebody dying is that they only die for themselves; never for the people who love them. To those who love them they remain, poised on the last moments before the last farewell. They leave a room or a house, shut a door or a gate, and disappear; but they do not die.

That was the end of it. I never told anyone about him. The last remaining comfort was that no one should know. He had said that communicating love to anyone but the beloved diminished the feeling. I clung to this; enduring the weeks that followed, until the gradual paralysis of my sensibility (which was only sharpened by an unreasoning fear that I should forget something about him), slowly crept round my aching heart; and I was left in the nerveless insensible state which is called normal.

I worked very much harder during the next months. I worked blindly through Christmas, and the dreadful spring when our armies retreated, a time when the gallantry of our soldiers was insisted on in a way which meant, I knew by now, that thousands more of them were being killed. I threw myself into the dull and probably useless work upon which I was engaged, because I had nothing else. Sometimes when I was very tired (the food available to people like my family was patently insufficient), I would read the letter from Ian, and for a short while abandon myself to the rush of feeling it invariably induced. Once, I remember weeping helplessly because I had torn the letter a little. It seemed the last unbearable bitterness that even the paper should perish.

My family went away in the summer to stay with relatives of my mother, who, since my father's death, had relented towards her for what they considered her initial folly. I refused to go with them, and remained during the hot dusty months alone in the house, except for the servant who consented to 'live in' while the family were away. I worked all day, slept heavily at night; and weeks passed when I spoke to no one outside the house where I worked and the house where I slept.

Then the tide turned, and the almost forgotten end was in sight.

On the evening after the Armistice, my sister distinguished herself by making an unprecedented scene. I never knew the real reason for her behaviour, but remember that it started quite quietly over some minor disagreement with my mother, when I took the latter's side. She was in the habit of treating our mother as a tiresome child, and on this occasion, not her remark, but her implication, was more than I could bear. It ended, however, by her declaring passionately that no one understood her, no one; that she should like anyone to tell her what on earth she was supposed to do now; and that she wished she had never been born. She then left the room, slamming the door, and in tears; leaving my mother and me alone, staring disconsolately at one another across the dining-room table.

'Oh dear,' said my mother at last. 'I wonder if I should go after her.'

'I should leave her alone.'

'If only your father were alive.' She always said this when she meant 'if only that hadn't happened'.

'I wonder what is the matter with her?'

'Of course, her work will come to an end. I think she is rather upset about that,' my mother said. 'I suppose you will have to stop too.'

'I suppose so.' I had not considered this aspect of the Armistice.

'Anyway when your brothers return, I expect they will take you both out a bit,' she continued, as though reassuring herself.

'I shall get some other job.'

'Yes, but you never have any fun, darling. I often feel that is my fault. You ought to be out enjoying yourself tonight, like everyone else.'

'And what about you?'

'I should enjoy you enjoying yourself. I used to have awfully jolly times before I met your father.' Then, a little defensively, she added: 'And afterwards, of course. But we see so few people now that I often feel you don't have a chance.'

'A chance?'

'To be light-hearted,' she said quietly, 'and perhaps to love someone.'

'Oh . . .' I began to be afraid of being hurt. 'I suppose you mean marriage,' I said aggressively.

'I suppose I do. After all, it does give one someone to live for – I mean, it does fill one's life.'

'Do you think women need someone to live for?'

She looked up, a little startled. 'Of course. They cannot *really live* by themselves.'

'Well wouldn't anyone do? Or anything, for that matter.'

'I should not like you to live for me, and a pile of parcels.'

She said this so bitterly that I was astonished. It had never entered my mind that she could regard my wartime occupation so objectively; and I asked immediately: 'You think my packing parcels for soldiers was foolish?'

'Not exactly foolish. But often when I see people, many people that I do not even know, doing things, I find myself thinking "surely they were not born and reared merely to do that". I think one cannot help expecting the people one knows and loves to do something much more significant.'

I could not help interrupting. 'Most people seem to have been born and brought up merely to get killed.'

She eyed me thoughtfully and then said: 'Yes. And one person is usually the death of another. But when they are dead one cannot go on expecting them to do anything significant. One has to put them back where they belong, with all the other people.'

With a great effort because I was terribly afraid that she knew something about Ian, I said, 'I am not dead.'

But she answered: 'Oh no. I was thinking of your father.'

I stared at the broad expanse of table between us, and realized how very little we knew about one another. She was still speaking.

'Your father believed in music, and I believed in your father. By the time he died, I don't think he believed in anything, and now I find it very difficult to believe in him.' She screwed up her eyes as though she were trying very hard to imagine something. 'What I really mean to say is, that if something should happen, and you are presented with any kind of opportunity – I cannot think at the moment what it might be – you should take it. You should not worry about me. I do not know really what makes me think of such a thing,' she continued hurriedly, 'except that, soon after your father's death, your sister told me that she would never leave me, even to marry: and although I should feel grateful I know, and she meant nothing but good, it made me feel more useless and bereaved than anything else. Sometimes things do happen by the merest chance.'

'Bad things happen too.'

'Oh yes. But you know, I have come to feel that they do

not happen by chance.' She looked at me almost timidly. 'Do you know, since your father died I have come to feel increasingly that they are organized.' She gave a little laugh. 'That is almost like your sister, isn't it? Only she would say that I pretended to understand the things, and presumed to call them bad. I cannot believe in something I do not understand. And now, I am sometimes afraid that I never understood your father.'

'I suppose, however, that my sister would say she understood God.'

She rose to her feet. A rare smile flitted across her worn face. She looked suddenly endearing and rather wicked as she said: 'Oh undoubtedly. It is very clear that they have mutual interests.'

She had walked round the table, and now she laid her hand lightly on my head.

'Good night, darling,' she said. 'I do hope that you will soon be happier.'

She left the room, and it was almost as though she were saying good-bye to me, as she never again talked to me in this manner, although on several later occasions I tried to induce her to do so.

CHAPTER TWENTY-SEVEN

A month later I let myself into the hall, having returned from an unsatisfactory interview with a Society to whom I had applied for work of some kind, to hear the steady rise and fall of a man's voice in the studio. I immediately assumed that one of my brothers had returned without warning, and slipped upstairs to my room, resolving at least to wash my hands before encountering him. I had almost nothing in common with either of my brothers and had been dreading their return for weeks, as I knew it distressed my mother if she thought that we were not perfectly in sympathy; and with Hubert, at least, once he had settled in the house, it seemed utterly impossible to conceal from her that we were not. I had barely, however, taken off my coat, and was fetching a jug of tepid water from the bathroom geyser, when my sister sped along the passage, looking flushed and important.

'When did you return?' she cried on seeing me.

'A moment ago. Is Hubert back?'

'Gracious no. I should hope he would give us some warning.'

'Thank God for that,' I thought. 'Anyone is better than Hubert.'

Then she said: 'A man called Mr Laing has called to see you. He says he knows you. He says he met you at the Lancings' before the war. He's been wounded,' she added in tones of rapturous solicitude.

'Why on earth has he come here?' I found myself repeating as I went down to the studio. 'Why on earth come *here*? He could have written,' I thought with a sudden rush of anxiety and irritation.

I opened the studio door, and found him sitting in the leather arm-chair, drinking tea with my mother. He made some attempt to rise when I entered the room, but my mother motioned him back: I saw that one of his legs was in plaster, and that a crutch lay on the floor by the tea table.

'I told Mr Laing that you wouldn't be long,' said my mother.

'My sister told me you were here. How are you, Rupert?'

'As you see, a little the worse for war,' he replied.

'I'll fetch you some tea, darling,' said my mother and before I could stop her she had flown tactfully out of the room.

'I really think,' observed Rupert, 'that your family expect me to propose to you on the spot.'

'You'd better propose to me then. Having exposed yourself to my family, you must not disappoint them,' I said crossly. I was still annoyed at the manner of his arrival.

'All in good time,' he said, staring at me. 'You have grown up. I should hardly have known you.'

'You haven't changed at all.'

'Are you not in the least glad to see me?'

'I really don't know. Yes, I suppose I am.'

'You should be, you know. You should always be glad to see a soldier back from the wars. As I did not, so to speak, invoke the King's sympathy for my leg in the shape of a medal, I do feel entitled to a little feminine consideration.'

'I am sure my sister provided you with all you were entitled to.'

'Your mother likes me. I do think you should try and be polite to your mother's friends.'

'I did not think you were principally one of my mother's friends.'

He replied in an utterly different voice: 'I had forgotten about that. I'm sorry. I have been away so long that I had forgotten the details. I have reached the stage where I really only notice whether someone is alive or dead. Anyway I like your mother.'

'I like her. But that isn't the point.'

'No. I am sorry,' he said again. 'Will you have dinner with me tonight?'

I considered this for a moment. 'If you like.'

'I don't like your sister,' he said. 'She gave me *exactly* what I deserved about my leg. Is this where your father worked?'

'Yes.'

'Will you play the piano to me?'

'No. I cannot play the piano to people.'

'I am not people, and it is such a long time since I heard a piano.'

'*No!* I said no.'

'I wondered where your sensibility had got to,' he observed. 'I've lost mine. That is one reason why I *should* like to dine with you. Do you think your mother is going to bring you tea?'

'I don't know. I'll go and stop her. Do you want me to change?' I was glad of a chance to escape.

'Well, I cannot *honestly* say you look very nice as you are, but I doubt my being worth any very radical alteration. I seem to remember you in a pink dress.'

'That was for dancing when I was sixteen.'

'Ah yes. And now you are not sixteen, and you don't dance.'

'No.' I said patiently. 'Do you want something to read while I am away?'

'I'll find something. I am perfectly capable of rising to my feet if no one is watching and trying to help.'

I rose to go, and he said: 'I am not really so tiresome as this. At least, I do not mean to be, and do not enjoy it when I am. I shall desist with the undergraduate backchat, when I have spent a few hours alone with you. Please have dinner with me. I am sorry about appearing in the bosom of your family.'

So I had dinner with him; without any strong feeling one way or the other. He seemed to have disintegrated in the most alarming manner, and was quite incapable of concentrating on anything, even to the end of a sentence. He asked me about myself but did not listen to the end of my replies; and he talked a great deal, without hearing, or, it seemed to me, caring, what he said. He was irritable and self-conscious about his leg; and alternately boastful and depressed about his future. He continually reminded me of things we had said or done together, but he never remembered them accurately, and lost interest when, at the beginning of the evening, I tried to correct him. 'Did we?' he would say.

Drumming his finger on the table he remarked, 'My father has offered me the management of his estate, just like that. But of course, it doesn't really offer much scope. I could do it with one hand tied behind my back, and still have time to think. What's your opinion?' Without waiting for a reply he continued, 'I'm no good at painting really, and even if I were it will be impossible to make a living out of it. I should end up by drawing on pavements, though you know, I was never any good with chalk. I'm no good with anything. I've spent so many years trying to make the best of a bad job. That is enough to finish anyone. Do you remember that walk we went with Deb? I wonder how she is getting on.' We had never walked anywhere with Deb, but I did not interrupt him to say so, as he continued, 'She's married, you know. They've asked me down there for Christmas. I know, *you* come too.'

'I have not been asked.'

'That doesn't matter. I'll ask them. They always make a good thing out of Christmas. No tinned puddings for them. Please come. My first Christmas home. You remember what fun we had?'

Suddenly I became infected with the desire to go. My beautiful visit. I wanted badly to get away.

'Will you ask Mrs Lancing whether she'll have me?'

'I'll ask her now. Waiter! I want to send a telegram. Could you manage that for me do you think?'

The waiter hesitated, and then, looking at Rupert's stiff white leg, said that he would do his best. Rupert wrote out a message on the back of an envelope, and gave him money. And that is how I came to spend a second Christmas with the Lancings.

CHAPTER TWENTY-EIGHT

The day before my departure, my mother insisted that I buy at least one new garment. When I protested, she pressed on me the considerable sum of ten pounds, imploring me to spend it. My sister offered to accompany me, in order to help me choose something sensible; but this I hastily declined. I took my mother, and we purchased a new black skirt, a coffee-coloured shirt and a very superior mackintosh cape, the outside of which was dark green velveteen. We ended the afternoon with tea out; my mother seeming to enjoy the whole excursion hugely. Even I began to view the prospect of Christmas in the country with pleasure. 'You've looked so *pale*, darling,' my mother kept saying, implying, rather optimistically I thought, that never again should I look pale.

Rupert was to fetch me in a cab at eleven o'clock the following day. I packed my clothes, and began to wonder about the Lancings. My mother and sister wondered (aloud as much as they dared) about Rupert. 'Such a pity he has been wounded,' said my mother, and mechanically I agreed; wondering what else was the matter with him.

My sister implied on the eve of my departure, that I was behaving in the most dissipated and selfish manner imaginable. Either I was missing my brothers' return; or, in the event of their not returning before Christmas, I was leaving her and my mother utterly alone, as she put it. She seemed unable to decide which was worse. She did not succeed in shaking me from my purpose, but she managed to make me feel exceedingly sorry for my mother, who continued, however, pathetically anxious that I should go.

We left London shrouded in fog, which resolved to a white mist in the country. Rupert had brought innumerable papers which he strewed, half read, all over the compartment, while I stared out of the window, unable to forget the last occasion on which I had been in the train.

'I ought to be spending Christmas at home,' Rupert suddenly remarked, some half an hour after the train had started.

'Why?'

'Oh, because it is expected of me. But having done what is expected of me for more than four years, I feel entitled to a little personal choice. They talk about nothing but the war. You would think they had been through it. I can't stand it. Give me the Lancings any day. Life will be just the same there as it used to be – you'll see. Gerald was killed though,' he added. 'You remember Gerald,' he said when I remained silent.

'Yes, very well.'

'Although really they've come off better than most families. All those girls. Better to have girls.'

'Who has Deb married?' I asked, to change the subject.

'I really don't know. Some chap who lives quite near them. He has a job in some Ministry or other. Nice for Deb. She's got two children, but that won't have changed her. How I hate journeys!' he exclaimed. 'I never want to go anywhere again. Just shut myself up in a little box, and have the box moved from time to time without my being aware of it. It's all the machinery of movement that bores me.' We hardly spoke again until our arrival.

We were not met, so we took the station fly.

'She's certain to have muddled the trains, bless her,' observed Rupert; and then, stretching out his leg, he exclaimed, 'By Jove, it's good to be back. Something to come back to which won't change.'

We both leaned forward as the fly rounded the drive and revealed the house. It was very quiet, and smaller than I remembered. The shutters (still crooked) had been repainted, but not the fading stucco of the house. When we stopped, I heard the peevish rhythmic wail of a baby crying. Our driver, after glancing back at Rupert's leg, jumped down and rang the bell. 'How he must hate these glances,' I

278

thought, 'or perhaps he does not notice them'; but he said irritably, 'Go on, out with you. Don't wait patiently for me.'

We were met in the hall by Mrs Lancing herself, armed most incongruously with a hammer.

'My dears,' she said, looked at Rupert's leg, and kissed us both.

'My dears – Come along – I knew I was right about your train.' We followed her, past the bowl of lavender, to the drawing-room.

'Wretched fire – Parker will not dry out the logs,' she exclaimed; looked doubtfully at the hammer; and laid it down on a small table covered with chestnuts.

'Where is everybody?' inquired Rupert when we had seated ourselves.

'Some people are collecting holly for the church. Richard has been crying all the morning. That is darling Deb's youngest child. Alfred is writing a letter to *The Times*, but he meant to write it last week. Now I'm going to give you some sherry and hear all your news.'

Rupert proceeded to furnish her with his news, interpolating some general remarks about the war; upon which she interrupted him, saying, 'That is exactly what Gerald always said. You know, of course, that we lost him.'

Rupert began to murmur something, but she continued as though he had not spoken. 'March 1917. He was hit by a bullet, and died at once. His Commanding Officer wrote me a very nice letter. He said Gerald was killed instantaneously while attempting most gallantly to hold a position. He was killed instantaneously; no pain.' She accompanied this last statement with a little social smile of reassurance; her face contracted again, and I realized how very much older she seemed. She raised one of her hands to touch her hair: I noticed that the hand was trembling, and that her hair was grey and lifeless.

'Tell me about the others,' said Rupert cheerfully. I looked at him in some surprise; to see that he was leaning forward smiling at her, almost loving her.

She pulled herself together. 'The others. Well, darling Deb

is married – Aubrey Hurst – such a nice man, who has been doing something very clever at the Foreign Office. She has two babies. Charles, who is a lamb, and no trouble at all, and Richard, who has a very strong character. Alfred adores them. They have made all the difference to him. Of course Nanny is here with them . . .'

'How's Toby?'

'Dear Toby. He's had a horrid attack of bronchitis this term and he's growing so fast. I'm afraid he isn't too dreadfully strong, but Alfred says I worry too much.'

The door opened and a tall rather colourless girl came in.

'They've arrived,' cried Mrs Lancing triumphantly. 'You remember Elinor.'

'But I've just sent Parker to the station. You said twelve forty-five, Mother.'

'I know I did, and here they are. Even earlier!'

'Shall we try and stop Parker?' said Rupert.

'It's too late, I saw him leave.' Elinor smiled at me. 'Has Mother shown you your rooms?'

'No dear. We were drinking sherry and I was telling them about – everybody. And Gerald. They wanted to know about Gerald. But you show them their rooms. Lunch is at a quarter to one because of Toby.'

'I don't want to see my room,' said Rupert. 'I want to hear the letter to *The Times*. And more sherry.'

'You need the bandage on your leg re-doing,' observed Elinor, with more animation than she had previously shown.

'Oh no I don't. You leave my leg alone.'

'Dear Elinor can do anything!' exclaimed Mrs Lancing, rather as though she wished dear Elinor couldn't.

I had the same bedroom as before. When Elinor left me, I laid my jacket on the bed, and stared out of the window at the lawn, the river, the park and the copse. It seemed unchanged; even the rooks and moorhens jostled and slid across my view as they had done before. 'I suppose they *are* different rooks and moorhens,' I heard myself say aloud; but it was hard to believe that they were. I wondered what Deb would be like; and whether Lucy and Elspeth were in the house, but I was in no great hurry to satisfy these curiosities. I unpacked my clothes, without any anxious speculation as to their quality and quantity when compared with those of the others, and was combing my hair when there was a knock on the door, and Lucy entered. Except that she was taller, and that her hair was knotted in a tight sleek bun, she had not changed at all.

'Hullo,' she said. We stood observing one another. Then she said, 'I'm so glad you've come. It will be just like it used to be at Christmas. It was awful all through the war and one couldn't even *pretend* it was the same. The hunting's wonderful, and we're going to have a dance. Elspeth's coming, and she's bringing two strange *new* men with her. We don't know them at all. Have you got everything you want?'

While I answered her, she stood regarding me with her kind eyes and eager smile; the tip of her nose a delicate pink, as though she had been out.

'I've been exercising. Deb won't do it. Would you like to see her babies? Deb hasn't been out all the morning. Some mornings she lies in bed till the lunch bell rings, and father gets furious. He likes everyone to *scald* themselves with soup. And some mornings she is up before any of us and gets through two horses by twelve o'clock. Simply wears them out, and doesn't cool them off or anything. They come back covered with sweat. She won't say where she has been.'

'Is she as beautiful as ever?'

'*More* beautiful,' said Lucy, with a kind of triumphant despair.

She led me down the passage, stopped at a white door, and opened it. I had thought it was going to be the nursery, but it was simply a rather empty little white room.

'Gerald's room. You know he was killed – Father can't bear talking about it. It's just the same as when he had it. I wanted it for my room, but they wouldn't let me. Even his brushes.' The windows were open, and the curtains floated over the silver-topped brushes on the dressing-table. An old tweed jacket hung on the back of the door. It was very cold.

'I put flowers in here,' said Lucy. She had become very white and a tear rolled down her face.

'I thought you would like to see his room,' she said, watching me anxiously, lest I feel as unhappy as she.

I nodded. She was still the kind transparent creature who judged everyone more exactly and honestly to be like herself than anybody I had known.

In the nursery, Nanny was seated in a basket chair feeding one infant on her lap while an older and more responsible baby sat strapped in a high chair beside her, eating something brown and sloppy with a short-handled spoon.

Nanny greeted me in a courteous, but abstracted manner. It was plain that she was engrossed in her charges.

'He hasn't stopped since a quarter past eleven. I don't know what it is, I'm sure. Not a tooth in sight . . .' Then to the baby in the chair, 'Put it in your mouth, Charles.'

'Can I feed him?' said Lucy.

'Give the young lady a chair and you can finish him off. Give her the spoon, Charles, there's a good boy.'

Charles watched me to my chair; but when Lucy approached him he dropped the spoon, and seizing the bowl before him turned it carefully upside down over his head. In the commotion which followed, he remained impassive, staring at me in a gentle, reproachful manner, with broth streaming down his face.

'Showing off at meal times,' muttered Nanny, as she carried him, stern and indifferent, into the night nursery.

Richard, cheated of his bottle, began to cry. He began quietly, in the manner of the real expert, and worked himself slowly up to a shattering volume, arching his back and screwing up his toes, in spite of Lucy's frantic efforts to appease him.

Then the door opened, and Deb appeared. Her hair was elaborately dressed; she wore the most ravishing and ethereal negligée, edged with swansdown. When she saw me, she smiled, walked over to the fender, and began talking to me as though nothing was happening. She was incredibly beautiful.

'Oh, Deb – I can't stop him,' cried Lucy almost beside herself.

Deb looked at Richard.

'He's a bore,' she remarked, picked him up, and threw him over her shoulder. Instantly he stopped, and began picking at the swansdown round her neck, cramming it into his mouth, choking with laughter.

'You can always stop him. I don't know how you do it,' said Lucy, half resentful, half relieved at the peace.

Deb with her back to Lucy, met my eye for an instant. She was smiling, but there was a faintly ironical, almost bitter expression in her smile. She did not reply.

A gong boomed for lunch.

'I'll take him,' said Lucy. 'Father will be so furious.'

'Why we should have the entire household upset for a little boy I fail to see,' observed Deb.

'It is only a quarter of an hour early. He has to rest afterwards. If we have lunch later there isn't time for him to get to the Westons',' pleaded Lucy holding out her arms for Richard.

'All this resting is absolute nonsense, anyway,' said Deb, and, ignoring Lucy, dropped Richard on his back in a blue cot, where after a shocked silence, he instantly began yelling again. 'I shall now get dressed,' Deb said calmly, and left the room.

Lucy cast agonized glances at Richard, the open night-nursery door and at me. Finally she gasped: 'We'll *have* to go. Can't all be late. Father has got much *fiercer* since the end of the war,' she explained, as we sped down the broad shallow staircase, almost colliding with Rupert at the foot.

'Hullo, Rupert. Frightfully sorry.' Then seeing his leg, '*Frightfully* sorry,' she repeated.

Toby was already sitting at the table. 'I had my place laid round me,' he said, 'I've been waiting ages.' He was not fat at all now; he seemed to be about twice as tall, and his face was finely powdered with freckles. 'I say, did you fly an aeroplane?' he almost shouted at Rupert.

'I did not.'

283

Mrs Lancing arrived, to settle Rupert and me next to each other and near her. Gradually the remaining members of the family appeared. Aunt Edith supported by Elinor; Mr Lancing with a sheaf of papers in his hand – all of them except Deb. When we had been greeted and everyone was settling to the very good hare soup, Mr Lancing inquired: 'Has anyone informed Deborah that we are lunching?'

'She was kept by the babies, Papa,' Lucy said. 'Richard has been crying,' she added.

'Ah.' Mr Lancing's expression softened to one of almost professional concern. 'It is my considered opinion that the child should be fed earlier.'

'Dear, we've tried that, and it throws the whole routine out, and poor Nanny doesn't get a wink of sleep.'

'Feed him when he's hungry. He knows when he is hungry.'

'But dear Alfred, one must consider his digestion.'

'Nonsense. When I was a child I was fed when I howled. I howled when I was hungry. Nothing wrong with my digestion.' He launched forth on a long and complicated story, the gist of which was that he had even eaten Stilton cheese and herrings at the age of eleven months and thrived on them.

'Have you *ever* flown an aeroplane?' persisted Toby.

'Never once been in one.' Toby fell back.

Half-way through the second course, Deb appeared, entirely and charmingly dressed in brown.

'Hullo Rupert. 'Fraid I'm rather late.'

'You are very late, Deborah.'

'Is Richard all right now?' asked the loyal Lucy.

But Deb answered, sweetly perverse, 'I don't know. I left him when you did. I expect so.' She yawned elaborately, and began on her soup.

Rupert had sat very silent, but now he began to talk to Deb, admiring her, as he had done before, in tones of mock despair. '*Why* didn't you wait for me?' he finished.

Deb lifted her head. I noticed the faintest blush, but she replied evenly, 'You never asked me.'

'What does this dreadful Aubrey *do*?'

'Something deadly dull in an office.'

There was a chorus from the others of 'Oh, *Deb*. Poor Aubrey – Really, Rupert.'

'It *is* deadly dull,' persisted Deb. 'So, poor Aubrey, I suppose.' She seized a piece of brittle toast, and began crushing it between her fingers.

'Have you ever been in a submarine then?' asked Toby. Rupert spread out his hands and shook his head. 'What a waste.' Toby was thoroughly disappointed. 'I'm going to fly an aeroplane in the next war.'

Everyone, in the brief pause which followed, instinctively looked at Mrs Lancing, and then, baffled by her immobility, and perhaps a little embarrassed by the discovery that they were not alone in their glance, looked away.

'There isn't going to *be* another war, anyway,' Lucy explained to Toby. Mrs Lancing drank a little water. The tension snapped.

After lunch, there was the usual discussion round the table of what everyone was going to do until they met for the next meal. Toby must rest for an hour and a half before he repaired to the Westons', who, I gathered, were possessed of a fives court, in which he and the younger Westons were to roller skate. Mrs Lancing was going to finish off invitations for the dance. Elinor offered to help her.

'What about a walk?' suggested Lucy.

'Where to?' said Deb; and Lucy, taking her literally, proceeded to outline a walk. Deb yawned again, stretching her hands over her head. 'There's no point in going out.'

'I think,' exclaimed Mr Lancing looking firmly at Rupert, 'that you would be interested in my collection of letters to various newspapers. If you have nothing better to do, I propose to show them to you now ...'

This left Lucy and me for the walk.

'Would you like that?'

I said I should like it. During lunch I had hardly spoken at all, not because I had been frightened, but because I could think of nothing to say. When I had stayed with them before, I had been nervous lest I prove unable to fit in with their very different and to me extremely hectic and glamorous existence; but after this fear had shown itself to be unnecessary, I had been able to throw myself into this Lancing life-in-the-country-house-at-Christmas and I had been very happy. I had, so to speak, poured myself eagerly into their large and decorative mould. Now, I was stiffened with experience, no longer nervous, but isolated in some curious manner by the reality of my own struggles from the reality of theirs. They were not to me any longer the easy happy collection of a family I had known; but they were not, so far as I could see, aware that they had changed. Gerald's death was the only change they were aware of that I could understand, and in some inexplicable manner this merely accentuated their apparent notion of the sameness of everything else.

During our walk I asked Lucy more about her family, and she, without any hesitation, told me all she knew. Deb had married very soon after my first visit, and everyone liked Aubrey. 'They have a house about twelve miles away, but Deb wants to live in London. Aubrey doesn't like London, he says he works there and that is quite enough, so I don't know what they will do. I think she would miss the hunting. It'll be London in the end I suppose. Aubrey's terribly kind, he does anything Deb wants. She's frightfully lucky because Aubrey didn't have to leave her at *all* in the war. Deb's rather – different these days. I think she must miss Gerald.' I had never noticed any particular feeling in Deb for Gerald, or indeed for anyone except the Roland she had not married. Perhaps he also had been killed. I did not want to ask.

We had been walking across the park, up the hill to the copse or little wood: the walk I had taken with Lucy and Elspeth on the first afternoon when we had made the house out of twigs. I wondered how many hundred times Lucy had walked this way, and whether she ever grew tired of it and wanted to walk somewhere else. I reminded her of the house; she remembered more about it than I did, and suggested making another. But I shrank from making another house.

I asked about Elspeth.

'She's an heiress,' said Lucy gravely. 'Her father died and left her all his money, *and* two houses. She lives with an uncle who lets her do anything she likes. She was supposed to have gone abroad you know, but the war stopped that.'

'Will her uncle let her go now?'

'I don't know. I believe he considers her ideas folly. But she's coming. She's bringing these men for the dance. Father says she is being spoilt,' Lucy added rather unexpectedly. 'Would you like to walk through the wood?' she continued. 'I expect you'd like to see the place where we made your little house. Do you know what Deb said when she heard you were coming?'

I did not know.

'She said, were you engaged to Rupert!'

'Oh.'

'Of course, she thinks rather a lot about that sort of thing.' Lucy seemed rather apologetic.

'Well I'm *not* engaged to Rupert,' I felt bound to add.

'Of course not. Why should you be? I'm twenty-one and *I* don't intend marrying anyone for years. Elinor does though. She is younger than you, and *she* has always wanted to marry someone. Well, since she was ten. She was awfully in love with a man she looked after in the war. She is a V.A.D. you know, but he died. He was frightfully badly wounded,' her voice trembled, 'but she doesn't mind that. She says there will be an awful shortage of people to marry and she doesn't mind looking after someone who has been wounded, so she'd better marry one of them, because someone who *doesn't* need looking after won't want to marry her. I suppose there are a lot of people like that? I mean you don't think she is very unusual, do you?'

'I don't think so,' I said doubtfully. 'I don't think many people are so honest – well, candid, about it.'

'Oh, she's frightfully honest. She was Head of her School in the end. She wanted that, too.'

'What do *you* want?'

Lucy seemed rather at a loss.

'Oh – I don't know. I should like another horse, and I wish my hair wasn't so straight. I wish Gerald was alive, most of all. I wish he was alive, and everything was exactly the same. Like it was last time you came.'

'Isn't it the same, Lucy?'

'Except for Gerald it is. But somehow, *nothing* feels right without him. Such a beastly way to die!' She suddenly burst into tears. 'I must tell you! I haven't had *anyone* to tell. He had a friend who was at school with him. Peter . . .' She was crying so much now that she was unable to walk, and leaned against a tree. I made some gesture inviting her to sit, but she shook her head and struggled to speak, streaming with tears. 'It doesn't matter what his name was. I can't tell you his name. He loved Gerald; they went out together. They had an awful job to stay together. When Gerald had leave, he took me to a theatre and told me all about Peter, and asked me to write to him. He said Peter was the only person he really cared about except me. After Gerald was dead he wrote to me, Peter did I mean, and said he wanted to see me. I went to London. He was dreadfully unhappy, he *cried* about Gerald. We went for a walk; he told me about him and then cried. Then he said he had to tell me about him properly, because he couldn't bear it by himself. That letter Mummy had was all a lie. He didn't die quickly at all. He was hit by a shell in his stomach. Peter found him after the attack. He was so bad Peter couldn't move him. He tried, but Gerald just shrieked and shrieked and – there was a lot more about it. I can't tell you, it is so awful, *so awful*. Peter tried to get help, but there wasn't a stretcher. He tried to give him some water, but whatever he did he said Gerald just went on moaning, and if Peter touched him, he shrieked, and stared about, as though Peter was trying to torture him. So Peter shot him. He had to. He said if he hadn't Gerald would just have gone on in that agony until he lost consciousness, and that might have been hours later. He had to do it. He kissed him, and told him he loved him first, but he said Gerald didn't know who he was. He said when he got out his revolver, he thought Gerald understood about that, because he tried to keep still and shut his eyes – Oh, I shouldn't have told you.'

I said, 'I do not think Peter should have told you.'

'He had to,' she cried fiercely, 'it was too much for him to bear. *He's* dead now, too. So I am the only one left, and Mummy goes on and on talking about it, and Papa can't bear talking about it, and they both say I take it too much to heart. I try not to think about it, but when I'm alone I remember Peter telling me, his voice, and the exact words, and it seems as though I was there – I meant not to tell *anyone*, truly I did, but it doesn't matter with you, does it? You won't tell anyone, will you – You won't?'

I assured her that I would not. She wiped her eyes. 'Most extraordinary thing,' she said, 'when other people talk about him it feels as though my heart is trying to break out. It's like a sudden burn; that sort of pain. I don't expect you know what I mean. But I like to talk about him sometimes.'

'I do know,' I said. The contrast of her pale and tear-stained face, with the appearance she presented to her family, and indeed, until a few moments ago to me, was infinitely touching. I wanted badly to comfort her, I felt she was a creature young enough to be comforted; but the things she had told me started such horrible fears in my own mind, that I dared not say anything. I took her hand and held it in mine. I had been so stunned by the fact that Ian had been killed, that I had never until now imagined the circumstances of his death. I felt sick; my legs seemed unable to support me. I sat on the ground, pulling Lucy down with me. For one moment I considered telling her about Ian, and then I knew that it would make no difference to me to tell anyone. I looked at poor Lucy. It was she who was so unhappy with her first grief. Nothing would ever be so painful for her again; but, I reflected, I could hardly tell her that, she would not believe it. She would not even believe that she would recover at all from this. Better tell her that, though. I told her.

'I shall never forget it,' she said.

'No, but it won't hurt so much.'

She stared at me disbelievingly, and then said, 'Of course I do get better at concealing it from the others. But not to myself. Never that.'

I searched desperately about for some other consolation, eventually saying feebly, and at some length, that I was sure Gerald would hate her to continue so despairing on his account. He was so gay, I added, he would think her wrong to grieve overmuch.

Lucy said with shining eyes. 'It's perfectly true. He would hate it. I will remember that. Thank you for telling me.'

She *was* capable of being comforted. She made me renew my promise to tell no one and we continued our walk.

'I suppose,' I said casually as we walked back down the park, 'that hundreds of people died like that, or something like it?'

And Lucy answered with her eyes fixed on her home: 'Hundreds I think. Of course not everybody. I don't suppose we shall ever really know how many.' She seemed calm again, calm and almost happy. 'We're going to have tea in the nursery,' she said. 'I love that.'

It was exactly as though she had handed her grief over to me, to take care of until some little circumstance should force her again to suffer it. As we entered the house, I wondered which of the spurious and meaningless little clichés would have comforted me, and when it should have been uttered, and by whom. Comfort, of any kind, seemed the most random affair.

CHAPTER TWENTY-NINE

On reaching the house, we went straight to the library where we discovered Rupert and Deb. They were sharing a large volume of *Punch*: Deb seated in one of the leather chairs, and Rupert perched rather uncomfortably upon one of its arms. A fire burned; but there was no other light, and the room was deliciously warm and dusky.

Lucy flung herself into a chair. After a moment's hesitation, I selected another. I felt we were intruding, and Rupert, at least, made no effort to conceal it. Deb had lifted her head when we entered the room, had seen me and smiled, then continued to turn the pages of their book.

'Aubrey not back yet?' asked Lucy, breaking the silence.

'I don't know whether he is back,' answered Deb.

Rupert reached out for his crutch and rose to his feet. 'I had forgotten the mysterious Aubrey. I really think it is rather forward of you to ally yourself to a man I have not even seen.'

'None of us really saw him until after she was engaged to him,' said Lucy cheerfully. 'Good thing he's so nice. He'll probably be back for tea. He usually is.'

'He invariably is,' said Deb. I knew that she was angry with Lucy. She shut the book, let it slide to the floor, and left the room. After a moment, Lucy followed, saying she would call us when tea was ready.

Alone with Rupert, I remained very still, staring into the fire. I had a sudden desire to ask him whether he knew anything about Ian; but I could not think how to do so without arousing his suspicion, or at least his curiosity.

'You are very silent here,' he said at last. 'What do you think about all the time?'

'About them. I - I am not very used to living with a lot of people. I think it makes me dull.'

'You are not dull. Although, when one thinks about you, one cannot imagine how you escape appearing inexpressibly dull. You sit and watch everyone, and hardly say a word. You also sometimes look extremely tragic. How did you get on with Lucy?'

'Very well, I think. I like her.'

'Which is more than her sister does.'

'Has she said so?'

'Oh come, sisters don't do that. No, she has not actually said anything. She says remarkably little, don't you think?' Then, without waiting for a reply he went on, 'Are you glad you came? Are you going to like it?'

'Are you?'

'Of course. I like anything new.'

'But this isn't new. It's old,' I cried.

'Oh dear. Has the gloss worn off? Are you bored?'

'No. I wish you would not ask me these questions.'

'But seriously, do you only enjoy things or people who are entirely strange to you?'

'I don't think so. If I found the right people, or things, I don't think I should want to change them.'

'But you haven't found them? Or found them and lost them?'

I did not reply.

'Well, if you think I am the person you knew, you are wrong. I am entirely, almost entirely changed, and not even used to myself. I find the most extraordinary ideas running through my head, which have nothing to do with what I was. You know, I don't think they like each other.'

'Who?'

He said ignoring me: 'But if you want change for the sake of it, here I am.'

Before I could reply Elinor put her head round the door.

'Tea is ready. In the nursery. Who lit the fire?'

'Deb lit it.'

'Oh, Deb – she lights them all over the house and never stays in one room and it makes so much work. Servants have been very difficult,' she explained to me, as we slowly ascended the staircase behind Rupert.

The day nursery (in which I had spent very little time on my previous visit), was quite unchanged, except that it showed signs of more use. The bears and dolls, which had before sat primly in rows on the seat round the bay window, now lay on the floor in various attitudes of abject and clownish helplessness. The high brass fender was hung with innumerable white garments. The rocking horse pranced well out in the room, instead of behind the screen covered by Mrs Lancing in her youth with scraps. For the rest, it contained the same pictures: Reynolds's cherubs, Millais's Ophelia, and various Henry Ford dragons and fairies; the same cracked white paint, pink curtains, and wallpaper covered with fat blue buds and pale yellow butterflies; the same bright brown chairs and table with Nanny's sewing machine; the same yellow nursery cupboard containing everything one could possibly want for a rainy afternoon, a sickness, accidents, boredom, or yet another baby. All this had not changed: only Nanny had shrunk a little, I noticed, her hair was whiter, her face more like a walnut, and her feet, which pointed outwards when she walked, bulged more painfully in her sharp black shoes. She was folding paper napkins on to each plate laid round the table when we entered the room. Lucy lay on the floor, building a tower from some bricks which she drew from a large canvas sack. Charles sat on his heels beside her taking no notice. Nanny seemed delighted to see Rupert, whom she placed in a large wicker chair between the fire and the tower of bricks. Elinor fetched a plate of crumpets to be toasted in front of the fire. I offered to help her.

'I have to put the forks out of reach because of Master Charles,' said Nanny wrenching open one of the drawers in the yellow cupboard.

Lucy finished the tower, and called us to admire it; but immediately we turned round from the scorching fire, Charles put out his hand, and with one casual sweeping gesture reduced the tower to ruins. Lucy said he was unkind (I think she was really disappointed), but he sat quite still smiling gently at her and not uttering a sound.

'You'd better wash your hands, Miss Lucy. Take him with you. He always breaks them down, don't you, Charles?'

'I cannot think why babies are so destructive,' cried Lucy. 'Come on, Charles.'

Charles rose to his feet, and as she bent to pick him up he flung himself on her, his arms round her neck and his legs round her waist so that she was unable to stand upright.

'That's his new trick,' said Nanny, prising him off the unfortunate Lucy as though he were a limpet. He opened his mouth to howl, when Deb appeared, and he changed his mind. Brushing Nanny aside, he staggered across the room to his mother, and repeated his new trick. Deb, however, seemed perfectly equal to it, as she made no move to pick him up; and after clinging to her legs for a few moments, he gave up, wheeled round, and made for the nursery at a heavy dangerous trot. Lucy dashed after him. 'I shall never manage to wash his hands.'

We had finished toasting the crumpets and sat at the table.

'Where is your mother?' asked Nanny, the steaming kettle poised in her hands over the gigantic tea-pot.

'She has gone over to Charrington. Lady Voyle sent a message.'

'There, Miss Elinor, and you never told me. Well there is nothing to keep us is there? I am sure you won't say no to your nice hot tea,' she added kindly to me. 'To tell the truth, I'd be glad to start before Master Richard wakes up. That's right, Miss Deb, you pour out for us.'

Deb who had also seated herself at the table, made a little *moue* of horror when she discovered that she had placed herself before all the tea cups.

'The big one is for Mr Hurst. He likes a good big cup like all the gentlemen.' Nanny was clearly in her element.

'What about me?' cried Rupert. 'Aren't I a gentleman, Nanny?'

Nanny bridled and burst into a peal of dried-up laughter. 'There, Mr Rupert. So many people I was forgetting.'

'He'll have to have a mug,' said Deb.

'Anything so long as it holds a lot.'

Elinor fetched a mug from the yellow cupboard and put it in front of Rupert.

'Goosey Goosey Gander, whither shall I wander, Upstairs and downstairs and in my lady's chamber,' Rupert read out, turning the mug in his hands. 'Will you fill my mug for me?' He handed it to Deb. Their eyes met for an instant, and Deb, after a moment's hesitation, put the mug on the table.

'All in good time.' She began filling the cups.

Lucy and Charles emerged from the night nursery pink and speechless.

'He's sort of washed,' said Lucy.

Nanny stuffed him into his high chair, strapped him in, and tied a huge feeder round his neck. Then she placed a piece of bread and butter in front of him cut in fingers.

'Take no notice of him and he'll eat his nice tea,' she commanded.

We all ate our nice tea. Deb immediately asked me about London, and what I had been doing. I felt that she expected me to have led a delightful life of continuous gaiety, and was at a loss how to answer her. I explained that I had been out of London much of the time, stretching the weeks I had spent with Mrs Border into months, but that did not do.

'What were you doing in the country?' asked Lucy.

'Oh, looking after an old lady.'

'How awful! Did she die or something?'

'No, she didn't die.' For a moment my mind flashed back to the dense hot house, and my terrifying employer. I realized, with a shock, that that life was probably continuing, with my successor, whoever she might be.

'Was it fearfully dull?'

'Yes. Fearfully dull. So I left.'

'And came back to London?' persisted Deb.

'Yes, and got a very dull job.'

'Oh *work*.' She managed to convey worlds of contempt

when she said that. 'But the evenings. Did you not dance a great deal? Even Elinor had hospital dances.'

'Only for the convalescents,' Elinor put in.

'I didn't, you know. My father died, and somehow we didn't go out much after that. I used to go to the theatre sometimes.'

'Deb has a romantic view of London which she can only preserve by absolute ignorance of it,' observed Rupert. I think he thought these questions were embarrassing me, but they were not (although they would once have reduced me almost to tears).

'I do go to London. *When* I go, I have a very gay time,' Deb retorted, like a child.

'I should think it is perfectly possible to have a very gay time,' I said.

'Well! Of course I remember you were very serious about things, like music,' said Deb. 'Perhaps that makes a difference.'

'I cannot think what you *do* in London,' said Lucy, helping herself to cake.

'Hand it round, Miss Lucy,' said Nanny, who, having no interest in the conversation, was well able to preserve the proprieties of nursery tea.

'Sorry. Cake anyone?'

Charles stretched out his arms for the cake. When Lucy handed it to him, he paused, picked off a cherry, and swallowed it whole.

'Just like his mother,' said Nanny hastening to bang his back. He choked; the cherry came up intact, and bounced across the table. Lucy put it back on his plate, where he regarded it with an air of stately disapproval. Nanny chopped up a small piece of cake, whipped the cherry away, and told him to finish his tea. 'He'll get hiccups if he goes eating cherries,' she explained severely to Lucy.

Rupert suddenly began the most fantastic stories about London in war time. After a few minutes, nobody took him seriously, and there was a good deal of laughter, in the midst of which Aubrey appeared.

My first impression on seeing Aubrey, was amused admiration that Deb should have discovered, and then married, someone who seemed so exactly designed to pair with her. He was tall, dark, discreetly handsome; and, as I was very soon to discover, he invariably made the right remark at the right moment. (Afterwards, one realized that it was rather an obvious remark to make; but at the time he produced it with such a charming air of modesty and kindliness – this is only a small white rabbit, but it is all I can find in my hat, and perhaps it may please you – that one could not but be charmed.)

Now, he begged not to interrupt; managed to be introduced to Rupert and me; to salute his elder child; to inquire respectfully of Nanny after his younger; to meet Deb's eye with intimate admiration; and to seat himself at the table next to her with the kind of appetite Nanny would expect of him: he managed all this in a few moments, and then steered the conversation back to Rupert's imaginary exploits in London.

Nanny insisted on making a small special pot of tea. It was plain that she adored him, that he dazzled Elinor and pleased Lucy. It was only not plain how precisely he affected Deb.

Rupert concluded his tale by turning to Aubrey and saying, 'That was solely for the benefit of your wife, who seems to have an incomprehensible passion for London.'

'I know she has. I have quite enough of it myself, but I expect we shall all end by living there. If Nanny doesn't desert us. But she doesn't realize,' he continued, having secured Nanny's devoted denial, 'how expensive London has become for a beautiful woman, or that I am only a poor struggling minnow at the Foreign Office.' And he smiled brilliantly at Deb.

'I only want a small house.'

'Yes, darling, and a motor car, and four servants – But you shall have them all so soon as anyone will buy my very inexpensive soul.'

'You might get sent abroad somewhere,' said Deb.

'I might,' he said, anxious to agree with her.

'You easily might,' repeated Deb.

'I'm sure you would be able to go too,' said Lucy.

'The climate might be very unsuitable for the children,' said Elinor.

'Why?' Deb stared at her. 'There are surely very few places where children do not live; and Aubrey would have to be a great failure to get sent to one of them.'

'Children have to be born in places to live in them. Sometimes even that isn't enough.'

'One surely is not expected to have one's entire life arranged by children . . .'

The atmosphere suddenly became unbearable; then Aubrey cleared his throat and said: 'In any case, I think you would enjoy a year or two in London first, as you missed your season; and after that, I hope I shall be in a position to select somewhere, within reason, which would be suitable for all of us, including Nanny.'

'That's right, Mr Aubrey, we must all cross our bridges when we come to them,' said Nanny approvingly. 'Drink down your nice milk, Charles.'

After tea, we all played musical bumps, ostensibly for the benefit of Charles, who hit his head on the corner of the rocking horse, and didn't enjoy any of it. Rupert worked the gramophone, and Aubrey nearly won, being left at the end with Lucy and Deb. The latter was defeated by the gasping triumphant Lucy. It was then clear that Aubrey intended to give Lucy a good run for her money, and let her win. He did this, from his point of view, extremely well; so that Lucy was convinced that he was fairly beaten, while at the same time it was perfectly clear to at least Deb, Rupert and me, that he lost intentionally.

'I'm beaten!' he exclaimed in good-tempered distress. 'Your aunt has beaten me, Charles! Never mind, I shall win next time.' And I felt that, in the interest of family diplomacy, he probably would.

After dinner, while Rupert and Aubrey played chess, the rest of us spent the evening mending, with glue, needles, cotton and other oddments, the large and battered collection of Christmas tree ornaments. 'We *must* use the same ones,' Lucy had said at the beginning of the evening.

The whole family apparently agreed with her, for they spent, and I helped them, hours of patience and ingenuity, on a multitude of fragile tarnished objects. I remember suddenly looking up to see Lucy sticking the dry yellow hair on to the head of a fairy doll; watching her intent, and happy, and disproportionately serious, and wondering whether I had dreamed or imagined her passionate outburst in the wood. But then I felt that when I had first known her, she would not have been quite so serious about the doll, and I knew that I had not dreamed.

She had divulged her secret. I was imprisoned with mine, and the new fear which accompanied it. In the dark of my room I wept for Ian; resolving that it should be the last time I wept for him; that I would leave him dead, would not consider how he died, would not try to think of him apart from myself. For a moment I allowed myself to remember him bending his head and kissing me, then walking away; the two doors slamming; the cab, and the silence. I endured the silence until I slept.

CHAPTER THIRTY

For the week before Christmas we all ate and played and slept, and generally fulfilled our functions in the house. We saw few people outside the house, and too much of each other, since the Lancings all tended to drift together for any arrangement. We saw too much of each other because for the amount of time involved, we communicated remarkably seldom. A man will pick his friend for some common interest; the friendship will flourish largely as the interest flourishes. A woman will pick her friend for some more or less intangible sympathy, emotional or compensative; and this friendship flourishes, dependent on continuing sympathy. But a family does not pick its component parts. It is marched down the aisle, and gradually born. It becomes so used to itself, it is so dependent upon regarding itself as a whole, that its individuals must find it increasingly difficult to have any emotions unrelated to other members; because if they *do* give vent to these emotions, the family, that public private life of its own, is threatened, and re-retaliates.

The Lancings were far gone in family life. They had reached the state where the real desires and feelings of each one of them were hidden from each other one. Nevertheless I; being outside the family (in a sense, more outside it than Rupert, who wished to identify himself with it), was increasingly aware of the private underlying tensions. These were not, perhaps, very significant, the Lancings having well developed the capacity of concentrating upon the many communal diversions with which they provided themselves, but they did exist; and I, unable to throw myself into the diversions with the abandon I had previously enjoyed, had very little else to do but watch the small personal struggles of temperament against the settled environment.

It was almost immediately clear that Deb was not happy,

and that she was consequently not kind to Aubrey. Aubrey, however, seemed genuinely unaware of this. The rest of the family protected him as best they could, and pretended not to notice. Deb roved about the house, beautiful, discontented, capricious and, above all, bored. She obviously intended to appear all these things, and it was some time before I realized how unhappy she must be. Then I noticed that the more time Rupert spent with me, even if he did not spend it exclusively with me, the more distant she became; until she was so positively rude that I felt it could hardly escape notice. I think Rupert noticed it (he seemed very much attracted to her), but no one else did, or, if they did, they were relieved that she was not being rude to Aubrey. I formed the conclusion that she was in love with Rupert, or very near it, and that he was aware of this and frightened by it. It upset his notion of a jolly family pre-war Christmas. He pursued me with a kind of relentless desperation, aware that the Lancings viewed this with approval. I also began to suspect that Elinor was quietly and hopelessly in love with Aubrey. It was always she, I observed, who flew to his rescue when Deb attempted to disconcert or embarrass him, to puncture his modesty and good temper. He was more the great man with Elinor, more the possessor of brilliant inside information: he knew more than he could possibly tell her, while with Deb he knew less than he dared admit.

I reached all these conclusions amid a whirl of secrets and presents and general Christmas plans, and, much of the time, it was difficult not to think I was merely dramatizing or enlarging situations which barely existed. But then I would see Lucy breathless with tickling Toby on the sofa; or clamouring to ride Deb's devilish black mare; or pink with importance over packing her Christmas presents: I would remember her leaning against the tree, her frantic outpourings of what must have been to her the most horrible story conceivable, and the infinitely touching manner in which she had said that when other people talked about Gerald, her heart broke out. And sometimes, when Mrs Lancing mentioned Gerald (which she seemed unable to

help doing at every possible opportunity), I would see Lucy
flinch, and try to smile, or simply smile. Then the chasm
between the family and each member of it yawned suddenly.
I would watch Lucy withdraw from it, trembling over the
skates that she would once have given Gerald and would
now give to Toby; would watch her feverishly trying to
decide whether to tie the parcel in red ribbon or green;
watch the chasm close up again, as her mother approved the
red ribbon and she scrambled to hide the skates because
Toby had entered the room.

Toby suffered a little, perhaps, from being too much the
object of Mrs Lancing's passionate anxiety and care, but for
a greater part of the time he remained unaware of this, and
of almost everything else. His life was rendered full and
complicated by the fact that he considered roller skates
superior, if not necessary, as a means of transport. He and
several noisy and dangerously accomplished friends spent
hours building ramps up and down steps and staircases, rolling gravel paths, and indulging in the most appalling accidents. Sometimes, however, I would see Toby submit with
uncharacteristic docility to his hair being ruffled by his
mother; or to a long and tiresome rest, so placed that, as he
would sadly explain to anyone else present, it ruined his day.

Mr Lancing lived, so far as I could determine, an extremely exhausting life of leisure. That is to say he ostensibly
did nothing, but was perpetually occupied with the most
exacting and onerous self-employment. He, alone of all the
family, spent much of his time without them. On fine days
he would swallow his breakfast and stump into the hall,
where he would collect a large and intricate tape measure
designed by himself, an old tweed cap, a villainous knobbly
stick, and a small nervous little henchman called Salt, who
was largely composed of long drooping moustaches and
frightened faithful eyes. He would disappear for the day,
occasionally sending Salt back for sandwiches. What he actually did remained a mystery. I noticed that Salt carried a
large notebook in which be wrote down, or attempted to
write down, everything that Mr Lancing said. This, as Mr

Lancing appeared when alone with Salt to talk incessantly on an endless variety of subjects, and usually when standing or walking at great speed, was naturally a somewhat difficult task, but Salt, with a spare pencil behind one ear, stuck faithfully to the job. We would sometimes watch Mr Lancing stride off, shouting information down the drive or across the park, Salt trotting behind him, the pages of the notebook flapping. On wet days, Mr Lancing would be discovered reorganizing the gun-room or repairing inexhaustible quantities of broken wine decanters, reputed to be his own wedding presents; and Salt was nowhere to be found. Any tidying or mending Mr Lancing did involved a chaos which, temporarily, at least, almost stopped the entire household. His most peaceful days were occupied in writing immense, abusive and erudite letters to newspapers. From all these pursuits he emerged at meals, and occasionally in the evenings, calm, silent and benign. He was devoted to his grandchildren, the elder of whom he frightened horribly, largely because in its presence he insisted on impersonating a lion. Charles could hardly be expected to know this, and invariably retreated, howling, to the nearest woman. This caused Mr Lancing great disappointment. He persisted, however, certain that Charles would see the joke in the end.

CHAPTER THIRTY-ONE

Just before Christmas Elspeth arrived with the two entirely new men. The latter, called George and Nicholas, were quite unremarkable in any way; but Elspeth, with whom the two young men were evidently in love, was certainly remarkable. She was now eighteen, and where she had been precocious, was now fascinating, where she had been an oddly attractive child, was now an unusually beautiful young woman. Her once long hair was now bobbed, and lay sleek and shining on her head; her clothes were expensive, and unlike everyone else's, in their neatness and severity; and she was possessed of a high, perfectly clear, voice, which in some way crowned her distinction. Altogether she imparted a glamour, an elegance to the household, which was badly in need of stimulation. She arrived with a small quantity of luxurious luggage, and an Alsatian dog who followed her everywhere, but on whom she bestowed almost no attention. She greeted everyone with enthusiasm, and at dinner, when we were all dressed in various depressing frocks ranging from beige lace to blue velveteen, caused a minor sensation by appearing in a white silk shirt, grey tie and sleek black skirt.

'Is this what young women are wearing for purposes of education?' inquired Mr Lancing. He pretended to disapprove of her, but was in reality fascinated.

'Oh no, Uncle. It is merely what this young woman wears for amusement.'

'Are you terribly educated?' asked Rupert.

'Terribly terribly educated. It is really the result of my darling uncle worrying for years about my spare time. He has educated me so much that nobody could possibly marry me and so that I know how difficult everything is and how little I know. And now he's stuck, poor lamb. It is frightfully sad for him.'

'What *are* you going to do?' asked Aubrey. He seemed very much amused by her.

'Well, he's got a new plan. He's trying to make me very very frivolous. He keeps sending me to the most awful parties with lots of paper streamers, and buying me yards of lace and pearls and things like that. He says if only I could giggle it would help tremendously.'

And then, as though she was suddenly aware that this kind of conversation, dominated by one young girl, did not suit the Lancings, she relapsed into a vital silence. She listened to conversation about the coming dance, fixing her lovely rather serious eyes upon each speaker, occasionally producing an intelligent reason for someone else's suggestion. Long before the end of the meal I noticed that Deb did not like her, although it was clear that everyone else did.

After dinner it was suggested by one of the two men (who had not previously spoken) that we dance. Everyone was enthusiastic. As before, Rupert offered to work the gramophone and everyone remembered his leg. In the end we all flocked to the big room, rolled up the carpet and danced. Rupert did work the gramophone. The two young men immediately revealed their talent. They were virtually speechless, but extremely good at dancing. Elspeth was the only one of us capable of following and entering into their intricacies. They danced with us, but it was only with Elspeth that they could abandon all pretence of conversation and let themselves go. They danced with stern concentration: Elspeth danced with a little rapt smile. Deb, who was unable to manage the latest steps, wanted older and more familiar records, but she was in a minority, only obtaining a few waltzes which she danced with anyone but Aubrey. She spent most of the evening lounging against the gramophone with Rupert. Aubrey danced conscientiously with Lucy, Elinor and me, and once with Mrs Lancing, who came to implore us all into bed. We were, indeed, very much later that night than we had ever previously been and crept up the stairs whispering and laughing and suppressing each other.

The following day a ride had been planned, but Deb upset the arrangements by announcing that she was taking Rupert out for the day in the trap. This, as Aubrey had secured Christmas leave from the Foreign Office starting from that morning, was extremely disconcerting. He suggested that he join the driving party, whereupon Deb rose from the breakfast table and left the room without a word.

'Well, the horses will be round in half an hour,' announced Mr Lancing abruptly.

Aubrey said: 'As a matter of fact, sir, I'd clean forgotten it, but I ought to ride over to old Stebbing; so I'll join you if I may.'

Everyone looked much relieved at this fragile excuse, and then Rupert made matters worse by saying rather heavily, as we left the dining-room, 'Sure you don't mind, old man? I had no idea your leave started today.'

And Aubrey replied: 'My dear fellow, of course not. Damned bad luck you can't ride.'

Mrs Lancing and I saw the riding party off. It consisted of Aubrey, Mr Lancing, Lucy, Elinor, Elspeth, the two young men, Elspeth's Alsatian and a red setter. After much noise and confusion, shortening of stirrups and loosening of curb chains, they clattered off down the drive in the brisk golden air, and we turned to the house, I, at least, wishing very much that I was able to ride.

Half an hour later Deb's trap was brought round by Parker, who adored her whatever she did, and who plainly considered now that she was forgoing a beautiful ride in order to give a wounded man some pleasure. From a landing window I watched them depart. Deb looked particularly charming in a buff-coloured driving cap and large fur hat. They were settled in the trap. A rug was tucked round them by Parker, and they were off. I watched the red ribbon on the whip glide round the bend.

I had said that I had letters to write and an alteration to make to my dress for the dance: nevertheless, I could not help feeling bored and rather desolate at the prospect. I should have liked a drive, and to see Deb's house; although I felt that my presence in the trap would have been un-welcome and embarrassing. Really, I thought irritably, Deb does behave in the most extraordinary manner, and the cer-tainty that she is unhappy does not stop one feeling cross. In a sense, I thought, the more you know about people, the less you can possibly blame them for their behaviour; and their being irreproachable implies a hostility in fate or circum-stance, which becomes very frightening when applied to oneself. I really prefer to blame them, I concluded, as I began rather viciously to rip up the hem of an old and dull party dress.

It was a tiresome day. I broke my needle, and was forced to borrow one from Nanny, which involved a long and de-pressing conversation on the relative merits of Richard and Charles. I wrote to my mother, but found myself without a stamp. Mrs Lancing was sure that she had one, although it could not be found.

After lunch I was settling down to a book in the library, when Mrs Lancing appeared, armed with a trug and huge wrinkled gardening gloves. I was kindly forced into electing to garden with her. The gardening consisted, as I find it usually does, of weeding an interminable path, down which nobody walked, which was why, as Mrs Lancing pointed out, it was so thick with weeds. For two and a half hours we toiled with horrid little knives, with increasingly sore fingers, with aching backs, with frozen feet. Mrs Lancing weeded with relish; regarding each successful struggle with a daisy or dandelion root as a personal triumph. She was a woman who talked exclusively about what she was doing all the while she was doing it. My weeding conversation ran out in the first hour; and I was left to make miserable inadequate rejoinders to remarks like 'Got it, the brute,' and 'It is amazing the *hold* they get, isn't it?'

Eventually I was released for tea, for which everybody re-turned, except Rupert and Deb, about whom elaborately nothing was said. I had a bad headache and the depression which usually accompanies it; and after tea managed to escape, more or less unobserved, to my room with some aspirin. I took off my skirt in order to lie on my bed in the darkness.

The aspirin must have sent me to sleep, as I was awakened some time later by pent-up voices, which seemed to come from the next room.

... 'Why did you marry me, then?' I heard Aubrey say.

And Deb answered: 'What an impossible question. You ask as though I was solely responsible for everything that happens. I'm not! I'm not responsible for anything. I don't want to be. I tell you I don't want always to know what is going to happen!'

I began to wonder drowsily why I could so easily hear their voices, when I heard a rustling of paper, and starting up at the sound, saw that the communicating door to the dressing-room was ajar, was neatly edged with golden light. I could hardly get up and shut it; nor could I light my gas, since obviously neither Deb nor Aubrey had any idea that I was in my room.

Then Aubrey said, with deliberate good temper: 'Well, all I can say is, I completely fail to understand you. I give up Christmas in my own house in order that you may spend it with your family, as you have always done ...'

'Exactly!'

'Isn't that what you wanted?'

'It is what my family wanted.'

'Surely that is the same thing. However, if it is not, and you seem to me to be in such an incalculable state of mind that perhaps it isn't, why didn't you say so, and we would have planned to stay at home?'

'Because it does not make any difference whether we spend Christmas here or in your house, and I loathe all plans. You love them. You even planned to marry me. To "fall in love with me"!' It is impossible to describe the scorn with which she said 'to fall in love with me'.

'Well one cannot marry without making some sort of plan.'

'Then you did plan it.'

'Plan what?'

'To fall in love with me.'

'Don't be so ridiculous, of course not. What I cannot understand is why you persist in sulking and being positively rude to Elspeth and that other poor girl, and making everyone feel uncomfortable as you did this morning.' There was a pause, and then he added: 'Do you want Richard's golliwog to go into his stocking, or is it a separate present?'

'In his stocking.'

Then he said: 'I don't mind your taking Rupert out, but I cannot see why you had to wait until today, that is all. You knew my leave started today.'

'I like Rupert. He is different.'

'Yes, but ...'

She interrupted. 'I thought marriage meant *more* freedom, not less. I didn't know it meant years of plans, and having children, and sitting by myself all day.'

Aubrey answered gently: 'It doesn't necessarily mean that.'

'It does necessarily mean that. It means that I know what I shall be doing in five, ten, twenty years' time.'

'If you know that, it means that you also know you will be surrounded by at least three people who love you.'

'Is *that* all there is to choose?' she cried passionately.

'You don't really love me,' he replied sadly.

'It is you who do not love me. You don't want to be loved. You want to be looked after, cared for. You think that that is what I want – I think you think that is love.'

'Isn't it? Listen my darling. Just before I married you I was offered a job, abroad and much less well paid but with the prospect of greatly increased responsibility, far more than I have now. I didn't take it, because of you.'

'Did you *want* to take it?'

'Oh yes. Of course.'

'With much more responsibility and less pay?'

'It would have led to something better, far more quickly than my present work is likely to do.'

'Well why didn't you take it?'

309

'Because I had other responsibilities. You, and now the children.'

'But don't you see that regarding me principally as a responsibility, you cannot love me?'

'No, I do not. How can I make you understand? I chose you. Because I loved you. I loved you more than my career. Now do you see?'

'I do not think that loving someone can be compared with anything at all,' said Deb. She sounded very unhappy.

'I don't believe that you mean serious love. You mean flirting, and being admired. You are furiously jealous of the other girls, because they can do this without censure.'

Deb answered wearily, 'I expect I do.' And then, gaining spirit, 'And what if I do? If I am so beautiful, are you to be the only man to tell me so? There seem to me enough certainties in our life without that one.'

'What do you mean, certainties?'

She answered: 'Whatever we do I know that at the end of every day you will empty your money out of your pockets and spill it over the dressing-table and undress. You will open the window, draw back the curtains, and made some remark about the night. Then you will climb into bed with me and we shall lie side by side in the dark. Then either you will say that you have had a frightful day and kiss my forehead, or you will make love to me. It all happens like that.'

There was a long silence, and then Aubrey said: 'Do you love Rupert then? Do you think he would be so different if you were married to him?'

'I do not want to discuss Rupert.'

'But I want to talk about him.' He seemed angry now.

'Do you think he is in love with me?' she asked.

'Of course he is. Any man would be in love with you. Are you in love with him?'

There was a pause, and then she said: 'No, I am not in love with him. He will marry that silent creature in the end; and she will be the you, and he will be the me. She will want security and affection, and he will want excitement, uncer-

310

tainty and love. I know much more about people than I did. But there is far less to know than I imagined.'

Her voice broke a little and I think she was crying because a minute later he said: 'I cannot bear you to be so unhappy. You are so beautiful and I *do* love you, my darling. I am sorry about Rupert. I should not have asked. I cannot bear to see you cry. My darling Deb.'

She said: 'Kiss me. Don't try to comfort me. Kiss me now ...'

There was a short silence, and seconds later he murmured something. I heard them move about the room. Then he said: 'The children's stockings! We did not finish them – No darling, we must do that first ...'

She gave a little choked laugh, or sob, and I heard her running past my door down the passage.

'Oh damn,' Aubrey said. A few moments later he put out the light and left the room.

As soon as they had gone, I lit my light to examine the door. It had always been shut; without trying it I had assumed that it was kept permanently locked, but now I saw there was no key. But why it should have been open on this particular occasion, I was unable to determine until I remembered that on several evenings lately Toby and his friends had been engaged upon some noisy and frightening game in the dark, which had involved the top floor landing and many of the rooms. I concluded that they must have opened all the doors and removed the keys.

At least neither Aubrey nor Deb had known I was there. I was no sooner congratulating myself upon this, than I became beset by serious misgivings. Perhaps, when I first heard them, I should have announced my presence, either by telling them, or by lighting my light. Or perhaps I should have attempted to creep out of my room without being heard. The last idea seemed impossible, as even if I had managed to get off the bed and open the door without their hearing me, I could hardly have wandered about the landing without a skirt. No, there was nothing else to have been done; embarrassed though I was at the prospect of facing Deb and Aubrey at dinner, I felt that to have faced them when I woke, at what was obviously not the beginning of their scene, would have been, for all of us, unbearably embarrassing. The whole situation was one which I simply had never experienced before, and I was at a loss how to deal with it. It was easier to feel sorry for Aubrey, but, without knowing precisely why, I felt more sorry for Deb, in spite of the fact that she did not appear to like me very much. At least Aubrey knew what he wanted, even if he was not getting it; while she, like I, was consumed with an aimless desire for something just beyond her own imagination. Then I remembered her weary certainty that I should marry Rupert, and a wave of irritation overwhelmed me, which was quickly followed by panic at the prospect itself. How could she be so sure that he would ask me? Why did I not know whether I wanted to marry him or not? 'I suppose that, if he is going to ask me, it will be at the dance,' I thought. 'I shall be wearing my horrible dress, and I shall be expecting it, and what could be worse. The fact that I hate my frock, in which I shall look dowdy, and that everyone else seems to be expecting the proposal, far outweigh the rest of the situation (a dance, Christmas and an eligible young man asking me to marry him). Perhaps they are all wrong, and he will not ask me,' I concluded. But that was not a very invigorating alternative.

CHAPTER THIRTY-TWO

At dinner, Rupert sat next to me, but I could think of nothing to say to him. Mrs Lancing asked whether the babies' stockings had been filled, and Aubrey answered, No, they were not quite finished.

After dinner someone suggested that we play a game in the dark. Mr and Mrs Lancing agreed to being shut in Mr Lancing's study for the evening, in order that all lights on the ground floor might be turned out. The game, which was so complicated that no one really understood the rules, was then inadequately explained by several people at once, who did not appear to agree with one another, and the lights were turned out. I was rather afraid of the dark, and having no idea of what I was supposed to do, groped and crept my way to the library.

The door of the room was wide open, and after entering I stretched out to shut it and thus cut myself off from the rest of the party, when my hand struck someone, who must have been standing stiff and motionless behind the door. I gave a little gasp of terror, and the next moment I was seized, felt arms thrown round me, and was passionately kissed on my mouth. The kiss continued until I had ceased to be terrified; indeed the dark, the man's suddenness and intensity shocked me into a kind of irresponsible excitement. For seconds I clung to the unknown, as though he were the most dearly loved and desirable creature in the world. Then, with an abrupt movement, he disengaged me. I thought he had stepped backwards, but he cannot have done so, as when I instinctively stretched out my hands, I felt nothing but the smooth leather spines of the books on the shelves.

As soon as I realized that he had left me, I began to wonder who he was, and then, who he thought *I* was. It could not be Rupert, I realized, as he was incapable of such silent mobility. I decided to retreat from the library altogether. If I was not to know who had been standing behind the door (almost as though he had been waiting for someone), then I would not give myself away by remaining foolishly for everyone to see when the lights were turned up.

So I left, encountering nobody else; nor, at the end of the game, could I determine who it had been. We were supposed to give some account of our movements; but no one, man or woman, admitted to having been in the library, and I followed suit. The game appeared not to have been a success, and we did not play it again. After a little desultory conversation (among the men the topic was where they had all been in 1914, and among the women what they were going to wear for the Christmas dance), we broke up. Elspeth and Deb, Lucy and even Elinor, it appeared, all had new confections for the occasion; but when I was asked, I was forced to admit that I had only the blue dress they had already seen.

It was no use caring, I reflected drearily in my room: I would somehow never achieve their easy innocent glamour. It would take very much more than a Christmas dance in the country to transform me. I fell asleep, wondering what it would take. It is curious that I should have wondered that: I certainly had no idea of how to set about procuring the circumstances necessary to effect the transformation, although I had some dim idea that I should, by now, know something of the ingredients. However, beyond the fact that they must be new, I had no very clear thought. Perhaps they must simply be new, I concluded, very drowsy.

Christmas was spent in the traditional manner; we were exhausted with presents before midday, and exhausted with food after it. The tree stood mysterious and glittering in the hall; the dining-room was littered with red ribbon and crumpled tissue paper; and secrets exploded all over the house, with little shrieks of delight and excitement. Charles was given a stuffed monkey which plainly frightened him even more than Mr Lancing impersonating a lion; but otherwise there were no regrets. They were very kind to me.

After lunch we walked. I wanted to walk with Elspeth, but she was so hemmed in by her men and her Alsatian that I soon gave up the attempt. She was always friendly, but, unlike the others, did not seem to recall my previous visit, and behaved all the time as though she were someone else, almost as though she were playing some part for the benefit of the Lancings – as though anywhere else she would be really quite different.

I had avoided Deb as much as possible since overhearing her, but she seemed almost to be seeking my company; she spoke to me more often – once, even, asked my opinion.

After an early tea, embellished only by the Christmas cake, which defied description, in its icy unapproachable magnificence, we retired, as I remembered we had done before, to our rooms, to rest and then to dress.

I was interrupted by a hurried tap on my door, which opened to reveal Deb. She *did* know I was here last night, I thought, with a sinking heart. She was very pale.

'Will you come to my room?' she began, and then added nervously, 'Do come.'

I followed her along the landing to her room. It was empty. She motioned me to the chaise-longue before the fire.

'I wanted to ask you something extraordinary . . .' she said, and then stopped. She was standing before me, twisting the heavy gold wedding ring round and round her finger. She did not look at me.

'Yes?' I stared at her timidly.

'Don't think that I am being patronizing or anything so absurd,' she began again in an arrogant manner, and then, catching my eye, she smiled, and slipped, with a rustling movement, on to her knees. 'Will you promise to do something for me? And will you promise now, before I tell you what it is?'

'But it might be something I could not possibly promise.'

'Against your principles? You look so serious that I always imagine you to have principles. *I* have none. I was not sneering at you. I am sure you think I was, but I was not. One must make some impression on everybody. But this is for

315

your good. To help you. It is nothing really, the smallest thing ...'

'You said it was extraordinary ...' I interrupted.

'Extraordinary for me to ask, but nothing for you to promise. Don't you trust me? Do you think that I dislike you?'

'I did not think that you liked me very much,' I said.

'I suppose not. I feel as though I don't *know* anybody you know, and that makes it difficult to like them. Or perhaps as though I knew everyone, but no one very well. I even know what I am going to do, so I find myself monotonous. Nothing ages women like monotony you know.' She delivered the last remark like someone in a play, who did not really believe what was said. I realized that she was saying anything that came into her head, in order to put off revealing what it was I had to promise. 'You always sound as though you have a very dull life. I am really sorry. I know what a dull life means, and I also know how little one can do about it. Now do you see that it cannot possibly harm you to promise?'

I promised.

'You said last night that you had only your old blue dress to wear tonight. Well, now you are to wear this.'

She rose to her feet, went to her wardrobe and drew out of it the most extraordinary dress. It is impossible to describe the very few garments one ever comes across that suit one. It was certainly not fashionable, but I knew instantly, as Deb held it before me, that dressed in it I should become more myself than I had ever been.

'I have never worn it, and I think it will become you,' she was saying.

'Were you not going to wear it tonight?'

'Oh no. I am wearing my wedding dress. It has been altered slightly, so that everyone will know it is my wedding dress which has been altered slightly. Will you put this on? The bodice will be very tight. I have lengthened the sleeves for you. You see now, why it was better to promise.'

'Yes, I do see.'

To my astonishment the dress fitted well. I looked remarkable in it. I really did: I think even Deb was surprised.

'It is extraordinary what a difference clothes make,' she said, 'but I cannot wear that colour. Your complexion is just right.'

There was a pause, a slight feeling of anti-climax while we surveyed me in the dress. Then she began unfastening it. Why was she doing it, I wondered, why should she care in the least what I wore for the dance? She seemed to think it very important, but why? I felt I must know why.

'Don't you think it is important?' she countered.

'I cannot see why it should be so for you.'

'Sometimes one knows when certain occasions are going to be significant,' she said. 'One cannot prepare when one does not know, but this is different.' I stared at her. 'Of course it is. You know perfectly well what I mean. But when I was in your position, nobody knew but I, and there was nothing I could do. Aubrey proposed to me in the waiting-room of a railway station. We were both afraid my train was leaving without me, and the whole thing was hurried. No point in caring about the accessories. But this is different. I thought I would help to make it a wonderful time.'

I started to speak, but she interrupted me. 'That is not all. I am afraid you must think very poorly of me. I am sorry. There is something, perverse, I suppose, about me, that cannot bear the steady arrangements, the forgone conclusions. I want to alter things; then I know I can't really, and wish that I had not tried. But I have not really tried to take him away from you. I have made no difference at all. I think I minded that. I thought it meant that nobody would ever care for me, but I was wrong. It is simply that life stops when one is married, and one ought to take care that it stops in a very good place. I thought perhaps that the least I could do was to help make it perfect for you. I thought perhaps this would help. You are too serious to consider such aspects; it takes frivolous people like me to do this sort of thing well.' She was very breathless, and stopped speaking suddenly, not as though she had finished, but as though she could not bear to go on talking, uninterrupted.

317

'Did Rupert tell you he wanted to marry me?'

'No, no, he didn't say anything about it.'

Deliberately, in order to gain time, I resumed my seat. 'Why do you think that he wants to marry me?'

'Oh don't be so tiresome! He brought you down here. It is obvious.' She was standing by the fire, her arm on the mantelpiece, and now she kicked a red coal as she spoke: 'I knew it the first day that you arrived.'

'But not that I wanted to marry him.'

She swung round, genuinely startled. 'But you *must* want to marry him . . . You must!'

'Why?'

'He cares for you. He needs someone who understands about his being a painter. You surely know about that. He will want to lead an adventurous life, and one cannot do that successfully alone. At least men cannot. He has had a bad time, I think, but he is awfully talented and all that sort of thing, and you could probably make him a tremendous success. He needs that. I thought perhaps you met many people like him, but you don't, do you? He is the only one. Heavens, if it is obvious to me, of all people . . . Anyway, what will happen to you, if you don't marry him? You surely do not intend spending the rest of your life doing those dreary jobs, do you? With all your family. Don't pretend you haven't thought about that.'

I had *not* thought much about it, but it was useless to say so, and in any case I immediately began thinking about it. 'I cannot understand why you should so much want us to marry.'

She made a gesture of indifference, but there was something strained about it. 'Of course I do not care what you do. But if you *are* going to marry him I thought . . .' Her voice tailed away.

'Yes?'

'That it ought to be,' she searched for a word, 'well, that it should matter very much. That it should be memorable. Aubrey said . . .' She cleared her throat. 'Aubrey said that I did not care for other people. He meant that I didn't care for

318

him, that I was heartless. And there is nothing I can do about it. I only care for things that people do not think important. Doing the small things really well; the things most people think are not worth doing at all.' She stopped.

'Does Aubrey know about this?' I indicated the dress hanging beside her.

'Of course not. No one knows. Naturally I should not have made you promise to wear it if anyone knew.'

'Are you very unhappy?' I asked.

She turned her head towards me quickly, as though she hated me. Her eyes were full of tears. 'Why do you ask that?'

'I'm sorry. I shouldn't have asked.'

'No, I am not unhappy, or happy. I am nothing at all . . .' A pulse in her throat began to beat violently. She seized the dress from its hanger and crammed it into my arms.

'Take the dress, take it. That is why I wanted to see you. Take it now. No one knows that I have it. I shall hate you, if you tell them. I shall hate you,' she repeated.

At last I began to understand her. I took the dress without a word, as I knew she wanted it taken, and fled from the room. I just heard the gentle subsidence of her skirt sinking to the floor as I shut myself out.

I had no sooner reached my room than the dressing bell sounded. I laid the dress on my bed, and then sat beside it in an agony of indecision. I had tried to pretend that I knew what I should say to Rupert; but Deb, unwittingly, had shaken up the inertia of my mind on this point, until it was now a shattering, urgent uncertainty. I felt my life depended on it, but for the life of me I did not know what to say. It seemed useless to pretend any longer that Rupert was *not* going to ask me to marry him. Wrong though Deb was about some things, I felt she was right about this. I began feverishly to count the times when Rupert had shown the slightest sign of preferring me to anyone else. I gathered these up like a few little bare bones, and I thought I could remember them all. He had sought me out, brought me here, had said that I was not dull; and several times I had caught him looking at me, with tired watchful eyes, as though he had wanted (but not very much) to know what I was thinking. That was all, and really it did not argue any very pronounced attachment. But perhaps he was reserving his feelings for this evening.

There was a knock on my door, and Mrs Lancing's maid appeared to inquire whether I wanted any help. I accepted her aid gratefully, because we could then concentrate together on my appearance; I need not think of anything else. As I put on the beautiful dress, I did think of poor Deborah and her gesture; but my mind shied away from her despair, because, in some way, I could not help relating it to Rupert, about whom I did not wish to think. 'You look a picture, Miss,' said the maid, when I was finished.

Even this casual routine remark warmed me. I sent the maid away in order that I might collect myself in peace. I had meant to come to some decision, but my unusual appearance so fascinated and overwhelmed me, that I simply stood foolishly before my mirror, abandoning myself to a detailed and intimate appraisal of my charms. I seemed to myself to have infinite possibilities ... Then the second bell rang.

CHAPTER THIRTY-THREE

I sat through dinner with the extraordinary conviction of being someone else. I found it easy to talk; to amuse them; even to astonish them. They admired the dress, they all admired it, and some of them asked why I had kept it so secret. Rupert said nothing. When I had entered the drawing-room he had been stretched out on the sofa, admiring the other women, and drinking sherry. He had not immediately looked at me, as I advanced rather nervously, wishing that he would turn round and say something before everyone would notice what he said. Lucy had spoken to me; he had turned his head, and ceased to smile. He had not said anything at all, but simply stared without speaking, while I walked to the fire and accepted my sherry; and then, when I had turned towards him with the glass in my hand, looked away, whereupon conversation, which had virtually ceased, began again.

After dinner the women clustered upstairs for a final prink, before awaiting the first guests. Following Deb as we ascended, I accidentally trod on her stiff white satin skirt, from which the train had been cut a little (although it was still much longer at the back than was usual or fashionable); and she turned to see that it was me. I apologized. She shook her head, signifying that it was of no importance. I have a final picture of her there, half-way up the red staircase; very pale, all eyes, and throat, and dark massed hair; trembling a little from the cold, and with nothing left to say to me.

When I came down again, I found Rupert waiting for me in the hall.

'Will you, as I am unable to dance, allow me to take you in to supper?'

'Yes. I cannot bear to think of supper now, but yes.'

'You are not compelled to eat,' he observed.

He had dispensed with his crutches, and was using a heavy but elegant stick, given him that morning by Mr Lancing. We walked to the big room together, at the door of which Lucy met us with a bundle of dance programmes. Rupert declined one but Lucy insisted.

'Of course you must. You can write down all the people you are going to talk to.'

'Give me your programme then,' said Rupert to me. 'I shall enter your one sedentary appointment in it.'

'May *I* come and talk to you, Rupert?' said Elspeth.

She was rather unexpectedly wearing yellow chiffon. Rupert and she continued talking, while I was swept away by Mrs Lancing, who always felt that it was a mistake for people who knew each other, to talk together at parties.

'Here is someone you *don't* know!' she announced triumphantly. 'Mr Fielding. He is devoted to music.' And she abandoned us.

I remembered that I had met Mr Fielding before, but he did not seem to recollect me; and on the point of reminding him, I restrained myself. I must have altered beyond recognition, I reflected with sudden pleasure.

'I don't know why Mrs Lancing thinks I like music. I don't. Never have. Are you very musical or something?'

I assured him earnestly that I was not, and he seemed relieved.

'That's something anyway,' he said, and then, aware that he had not said what he meant in the most tactful manner, added, 'I say, I didn't mean that. "Things that might have been expressed differently," what? That's a ripping dress. I mean it,' he added, anxious to reassure me. 'Look here, shall we set the ball rolling? Someone has to make a start.'

So we danced. There were twelve dances before the supper interval; and I was never without a partner. It was very odd, I reflected; on my previous visit I had been overwhelmingly anxious to be a success, had been disposed deeply to enjoy it if I were, or passionately to despair if I were not; but now, I floated through the evening with the utmost ease. I seemed not to *be* myself, but simply a successful reflection of all my partners. This, I found, generally speaking, constituted success.

I discoursed eagerly about fox hunting with one partner; and as vehemently deplored it with the next. I adored London; I loathed it. I agreed that dancing had disintegrated into something utterly ungraceful; I wearied of the old waltzes and longed for even further developments of ragtime. I was devoted to animals and interested in their welfare; then thought that far too much fuss was made of them which could be better devoted to people. Many of my partners considered me intelligent, and frankly said so. When I thought at all, it was about Rupert and the supper interval, which was divided from me by fewer and fewer dances, and which I had begun to dread.

When the moment finally arrived, Rupert was nowhere to be seen, and glad of a few minutes alone, I slipped away from the dancing, along the passage to the library, which was not being used that night, except as a depository for men's coats. A light was on in the room, but I entered it without thinking. I found a fire burning, Rupert seated on a stool before it, and a small table covered with supper for two people beside him.

'I'm sorry, I didn't know you were here,' I said foolishly.

'Has the supper started? I meant to come to fetch you on the stroke of eleven. Now, in fact,' he said, as the clock struck.

'Yes. I came here . . . I just came.'

'Very good thing. Shut the door, and come and eat.'

'Is that for us?'

'Of course. I made it for us. Wild with jealousy, I have limped about preparing a pathetic repast. Are you touched?'

'You meant to amuse, not touch me,' I replied moving uncertainly towards him.

'And I haven't done either. Do I ever?'

'Amuse or touch me?'

'No don't answer yet, until you have had some wine.' He poured it into two glasses.

'What is it?'

'Champagne – especially good champagne for us.'

At last I was drinking champagne, I thought, and remembered the two occasions when I had not.

'*Now* what are you thinking?'

'Nothing. I have never drunk champagne before,' I said.

The whole situation, the firelight, the little table, the slightly unexpected seclusion, was a shock to me, and I was uncertain whether I could sustain it.

'Do you feel like eating?'

'Not very.'

'Nor do I.' He suddenly drained his glass. 'I have the uneasy feeling with you that while I am quite ignorant of what is in your mind, you know exactly what I am going to say. Do you?'

I raised my eyes to him. 'I think I know what you are going to say; but I have not the smallest idea why you are going to say it.'

'Isn't that rather coy of you?'

'It wasn't meant to be,' I said, and in my embarrassment drank the rest of my champagne.

'Well, perhaps I had better attempt some sort of explanation; although I may as well warn you it will be neither explicit nor particularly illuminating. You have always, to me, ever since I first met you, seemed possessed of a potential capacity for life which I am quite without. I did not value this when I met you here, because I did not know myself how much I was without it; nor when you ran away to my studio, because then I was obsessed with my own problems. I just thought you over sensitive but delightful. It seemed to me that you wanted to get away from your home much in the spirit that I wanted to stop being a doctor. Things were simple for me then; not pleasant, but simple. I stopped being a doctor because the dazzling alternative was being a painter. I then found that this in turn produced the less dazzling alternative of becoming a soldier. That is how I saw it then, you understand. I was sorry for you when you came to the studio, but I felt quite unable to do anything about you;

and also slightly afraid that you would depend on me if I did. Painting was not at all what I had expected it to be, and so becoming a soldier did not seem, on the face of it, too bad a prospect. It took me about a year to discover how much I hated the whole thing; and by then I couldn't get away from it. I mean *I* couldn't. I hadn't the initiative to walk out, or the kind of desperate strength of mind to stop a blighty one. I just hung on, and lost my self-respect. At first I thought we should win quickly; then not for a long time; and finally that we should lose, but long after it didn't matter. I didn't care in the least. Nearly all my friends got killed, or worse, and then I had this leg trouble. Weeks and weeks of cheerful quiet and filthy smells, in a hospital. In hospital I began to think about you, and wondered whether, in order to escape your home, you had become a nurse. That would finish her, I thought, just about as much as soldiering's finished me. If you do a job for months and years which shatters the sensibility without in any way strengthening the intellect (and most people do that, war, or no war), you really are not worth more than the creature comforts a government or an employer accords you; down to the shortest possible telegram announcing your death, or everyone getting drunk for a night because you have survived. Anyhow, for some weeks I lay in bed, thinking a little about you, and concluding, quite wrongly, that you had probably been reduced to the same state as I. I suppose I wanted to think that. That is why I arrived at your house. I didn't expect you to mind. I talked to your mother, who didn't seem to know anything about you, but was obviously very relieved to see me. She seemed to regard me as the answer to a mother's prayer. Then you appeared. I couldn't understand you then, and I don't now. At first, I thought that *you* had been very unhappy, and then I changed my mind. You would not have come here for Christmas, where you had not seemed to enjoy yourself very much before, if you were very unhappy. Then I thought that perhaps, although you had not lost your sensibility, you had begun to lose hope about escaping from

325

your dreary home. And then I began to see the least I could do about it. And now we are sitting here, and I am asking you to marry me.'

There was a silence; during which I wondered where to begin. I felt he had not told me anything at all, anything, at least, that I wanted to hear. And a good deal of what he thought about me was simply wrong. No point in telling him that.

'Well?' he asked.

'I am afraid I still don't see why you want to marry me.'

'I told you my explanation would not be very illuminating. You do not seem very surprised, by the way.'

'Did you expect me to be surprised?'

'No,' he said, after a moment's thought. 'No, I suppose not. Well, if you can think of anything more to ask me, I'll try and answer honestly.'

'What do you propose to do, if I marry you?'

'I have considered that very carefully. I shall give up painting and accept my father's offer. It means living with him, but it is a large house and there would be plenty of room. I very much doubt my ability to earn enough money for two people as an artist; and in any case, after staying here, I am sure it is better to live in the country. Life is much simpler, safer too, I think. And better for children. Do you know Norfolk at all?'

'Not at all,' I answered politely. We really might have been two complete strangers conversing in a train.

'It is very flat where we should live. On the edge of a salt marsh. The country stretches flat to the sky, and green, greener than any other part of England. There are small ridges beside the dykes, and windmills standing about, and long narrow roads running dead straight; but otherwise, it is simply miles and miles of soft wet green marsh, with geese in winter, and cows all the year round. To the people who know it well, it is the most beautiful county of all.'

'I don't know it,' I repeated. I was not in a frame of mind receptive to the emotional appeal of landscape.

'I thought you minded so much about painting,' I added. I

remembered his outburst to me in the studio; it was almost impossible to believe that this was the same man.

'Oh yes,' he laughed shortly. 'I expect I was very fluent and intellectual about art when we met before. That should have warned you. Good artists are seldom good at talking about it; they simply get on with the job. Perhaps they have a larger share of animal intuition than most, but very little intellect. If they start talking about it, start relating it to life in any more than the grand, emotional, or intuitive manner, there is trouble at once. They start analysing their work, and find that there is nothing there. And then they are confounded.'

'Of course there are exceptions,' I said.

'Of course there are exceptions. There are, fortunately, always exceptions. They are the only thing which prevents anyone knowing everything about anything. I was talking about the kind of artist which I might have aimed at being. And you see, it's no good. I've done too many other things and talked too much. I'm not single-minded enough. My mind is too divided.'

'So you would not paint anyway?'

'What do you mean?'

'I mean you would not paint whether I married you or not.'

'Oh I see. No. No, you need have no fear that you are corrupting a fine artist into a breadwinner. None of that. Have some more champagne?'

'Thank you. But you still have not, so far as I can see, produced a single reason for wanting to marry me, more than anyone else.'

'Isn't the fact that I am asking you, and not, shall we say, Elinor, sufficient reason?'

'I don't think it is. Why not Elinor? Why not Maria?'

'Maria died of tuberculosis nearly two years ago. It's all right,' he continued, as I was about to interrupt. 'It was probably the best thing that could have happened to her. She could never have gone back to her family, and she was the kind of woman who loved the kind of man who left her. She found someone else about four months after I joined up. She would have been all right until she had begun to get fat, and then she would have had a bad time. Her family would never have taken her back after the wine importer, as she would no longer have been marriageable.'

I remembered Maria, and how much she had loved Rupert, and how much he had loved, or seemed to love, her; and suddenly felt frightened. But I said nothing.

'Elinor? Well not Elinor, because she would marry anyone who asked her. I should not feel that she had any particular feeling for me.'

'I think that is how I feel.' I was almost surprised at the boldness of my own voice.

'There is one other point,' he said, as though he had not heard me. 'And that is *your* position. You don't like living with your family ... I take it that you have not changed in this respect?'

'I have not changed,' I answered steadily.

'You have made several abortive attempts to get away from them. I remember you once wrote to me from Sussex where you were being companion to some boring old woman. You have not discovered some great career for yourself?'

'No.'

'Well, here I am, offering you a peaceful life, independent of your family.'

'But you used to be so much against marriage.'

'You do remember things, don't you? I was. I was against marriage, against democracy, and I did not believe in God. That is all very well until one is, say, twenty-five or thirty. One can seriously imagine that there are better alternatives to all three propositions until then. Until then, living is rather like beginning to learn a foreign language. It is exciting, and not nearly so difficult as one imagined; and then, quite suddenly, one either has to go and live in the country where the language is spoken, or one has to sweat for hours, learning declensions of verbs until one is blind with fatigue, and knowledge of the language seems hopelessly unattainable. I prefer to live in the country. That is to say, I prefer to marry, in a church, and become a Liberal.'

There was a silence, which he broke by saying: 'But *you* were not against marriage?'

'No. But I never thought of marrying someone I didn't love.'

'I was waiting for that. I know you do not love me.'

'More than that, you do not love me.'

'Really, I think I am the best judge of that.'

'I think *I* am the best judge of it.'

'You attract me,' he said angrily, 'and I like talking to you. Also, I've told you, I don't know what you are thinking all the time, and with most women, one knows exactly what they are thinking. I *want* to marry you. I tell you it would be a success.'

'Not unless I felt at least some of those things for you.'

'Don't you? Don't you feel any of them?'

'None of them,' I said.

'Why did you run away to my studio then?'

'Really, your own opinions have changed so much since then, that you can hardly blame me for any alteration in mine. Besides, I had nowhere else to go.'

'I think you would have married me then. If I had swept you into my arms, and said "Darling be mine", you would have been mine.'

'I was seventeen then. And I had never been in love.'

'Are you in love now?' he asked quickly, and I saw he flushed.

'No.'

'But you have been in love. Poor thing. Did it all end badly?' He was eager and gentle now. I did not reply. 'Well, could you not accept me as a second best?' he said, and for the first time it occurred to me that he really did badly want to marry me.

'I am afraid I could not do it in such very cold blood.'

He winced at this, but continued: 'A great many marriages start like this. More than you would think. It is not necessarily a bad way to begin. We are both honest with one another. We neither of us have any very brilliant alternative ...'

'I am sorry, Rupert, but I could not do it. I do not want to marry you.'

We had been sitting opposite one another over the table of untouched food, and now he slumped on his stool a little. I thought he had accepted my refusal, but after a moment he drew a deep breath, and said: 'Look here. I am serious about this. If you like, I didn't know how serious I was until just now. Also, if you like (and this is very honest of me), I did not expect you to refuse me. Will you think it over? Perhaps you have not thought seriously about it, and really need more time. I'll ask you again in London.'

'I do not want to be asked again, in London or anywhere else.'

'But damn it, I love you! I've banked everything on your marrying me! I've thought of very little else since we have been here!'

'I don't believe it.'

'Well what do you expect me to do? It is no good my making violent love to you. I should think you would be awfully difficult to make love to ...'

'It would not make the slightest difference,' I said, quite uncertain what difference it would make.

'Of course it would make a difference, but the wrong kind, I thought, with you. What *do* you want? Would you marry me if I remained a painter, and lived in disreputable squalor?'

'No.'

'Would you simply live with me in disreputable squalor?'

I shook my head. I could think of nothing more to say.

'I suppose I've done this very badly,' he said. 'There must be *some* way of proposing to you which you would feel constrained to accept.'

'If I loved you, it wouldn't matter much what you said; and as I don't love you, it doesn't matter what you say either.' But I could see that he did not really believe I should refuse him in all circumstances; that he was still considerably startled at my refusing him at all. The picture he had drawn of my life was certainly accurate, but the idea that I would marry him simply because I could think of nothing better to do, touched my pride, and I resolved, there and then, that I *would* find something to do. Anything, I reiterated to myself.

'Are you having to determine not to marry me?' asked Rupert.

'I was determining something else. I think I will go now.'

'May I say, gratuitously, that you look positively enchanting in that frock?' I did not reply. Then he said: 'By the way, do you remember my rich friend Ian? He asked after you, when we were at camp together. You know he was killed of course.'

I rose to my feet. 'I read it in the newspaper.'

'The title has gone to his rather unpleasant cousin. All the best people were killed. You know you will eventually have to make do with some realistic chap like me.'

I was sure that he knew something and hated him, but his face was expressionless. He, too, rose to his feet. I turned to the door.

'No, don't go yet,' he murmured, and seized my arm. I knew that he desperately wanted to kiss me; remembered Deb's envious romantic plans for us, and was suddenly filled with extreme revulsion, partly because of her, and partly because I was certain that he had meant to probe me about Ian. We stared at each other, until he dropped my arm and said: 'I am very sorry. That was unpardonable of me. Please stay and have supper with me. I won't talk any more about it . . .'

'I'd rather go.'

He watched me for a minute, and then stooped, picked up our two glasses, and flung them into the grate.

'Most people get more out of their first champagne,' he said.

I left the room.

CHAPTER THIRTY-FOUR

Two days later I left the Lancings, and went back to London
alone. They were very kind to me right up to the end, although I think they had begun to sense that I was not one of
them or ever likely to be. I told them I had to go because of
the imminent arrival of my younger brother. I put the lovely
dress back in Deb's room, with a note thanking her. She gave
no sign afterwards that she had received it, and her behaviour to me was utterly commonplace. Mrs Lancing asked
me to come again. Lucy begged me not to go. Rupert
wavered between extreme silence in my company (arguing
embarrassment or hostility), and various efforts to secure it.
He repeated his intention of again asking me to marry him
when in London.

Lucy and Elinor accompanied me to the station.

'There is a compartment with a woman in it,' said Elinor
as the train drew in.

Lucy flung her arms round me with anxious vehemence. I
knew we were both thinking of her revelations in the wood,
that she wanted to ask me for the last time to tell no one,
that I wanted to assure her I would not; but we neither of us
said anything.

'Do come back. Or it would be lovely to see you in London.
Come every year,' she said, and I answered: 'Thank you. You
have been very kind and I've enjoyed myself tremendously.'

In the train I waved to both of them until the train had
begun to hurry and they had begun to turn away.

And that was the end of my second visit.

CHAPTER THIRTY-FIVE

My mother opened the door to me and said: 'Well, darling?'
And that was only the beginning of it; I did not immediately perceive what she meant, but five minutes with my sister left me in no doubt. (I escaped my sister in rather less than five minutes, unable to bear the exasperating vulgarity of her inquisition.) They had both clearly been certain that Rupert had carried me off for Christmas with the express intention of proposing to me. The worst of it was that they were right. It was the kind of point on which I was very bad at deceiving them, although I did what I could. I wrote to Rupert asking him never to arrive in my home, particularly without warning. I quelled my poor mother by preserving an obstinate and forbidding silence on the subject of my visit. I think she was rendered more sympathetically silent by my sister's persistent and increasingly hostile curiosity. My sister, I reflected, after three days of unrequited tension, was certainly very odd about the whole affair. She followed me about the house, appearing suddenly in my room for no ostensible reason; her conversation at these and other times consisting in discourses alternatively on her hard life, and my selfish ingratitude and want of confidence in those nearest me. As we none of us had anything whatever to do, she had ample opportunity for this kind of thing. In front of our mother she contented herself with a series of repetitive and double-edged remarks about marriage, and other peoples' friends.

For about a week I racked my brains for something to do. Eventually I hit upon the not very brilliant notion of part copying for orchestras. I told my mother that I was going to do this; she looked at me sadly and acquiesced. 'Don't try your eyes, darling,' was all she said.

The work, with my father's connections, was easy to acquire. I copied slowly, but with extreme neatness: however, people underpaid me, and were satisfied.

Two weeks after I had begun this work I received a letter from Rupert. I came in and found it lying on the hall table. It suggested that we meet somewhere and 'discuss matters'. I was reading it in my room, when, without any warning, my sister entered.

'You have had a letter from him!' she cried. 'He never comes here, but you meet him, and he writes to you!' She was panting as though she were hardly able to breathe, and as she finished speaking she put one hand to her side.

I stared at her in some astonishment.

'What has it to do with you?'

'Why don't you tell us about him?'

'Do you mean whether he asked me to marry him?'

She nodded, but her eyes never left my face.

'I do not understand . . .' I began.

But she interrupted me: 'You go off with him to those people at a moment's warning, leaving me here doing what I can to make poor Mother's Christmas brighter for her, and then you come back without saying one word. It's *awful* for her. Simply selfish and unkind. I know you meet him. This copying you do is just a blind. You're too jealous to have him here. Afraid of what he might think. It's wicked of you. We all go on day after day as though nothing were happening, and it *is* . . . it must be, only you won't say. How can you be so deceitful!'

'He has asked me to marry him,' I said. I was very angry. 'I have refused him. I have asked him not to come here because I don't like it.'

'But he has asked you to meet him elsewhere!'

'Did you open this letter?'

She stared at me without replying, but a slow painful colour suffused her neck and then her face.

'You opened my letter?' Suddenly I was so angry that I could not see her standing in front of me. I lunged forward. I think I must have struck her. I realized that my hand hurt and I could see her fallen back upon the door, supporting herself by its handle. There was a broad white mark across her face; she seemed scarcely to breathe at all, and the letter lay on the floor between us.

Before I could say anything, she began talking, so quietly that at first I could hardly hear her. I don't think she cared whether I heard, it was simply her own mind let loose, she barely knew herself what she said.

'I thought when he came, that he would want to marry you. He sat in Father's chair with his poor leg, and I felt so sorry for him. You went away with him, and I steeled myself to face your coming back ... engaged. I am older than you, and Mother has no one. If you married and went away I should be left. Then I thought that he might have friends and, and ... but if you do not marry him you've no right to prevent me from doing so. I've nothing to look forward to now my war work has ended. If *you* married, you would go away and leave us; but if I married, I should take Mother with me and it would all be exactly the same as before. It would be so much more ... *sensible* if I married.' She rambled on, explaining herself, and giving herself away, unconscious of her dishevelled unattractive appearance, which had never, perhaps, been so dishevelled before.

When she had nothing more to say, I took her hand and led her to the only chair in my room. Then I sat on the bed facing her. She was pushing the hairpins back into her thick slippery hair, and staring at me with a haggard, somewhat vacant expression.

'You cannot,' I said patiently, 'simply marry someone because you see them and want to be married. You do not know this man. You might not like him.'

'I have not had a chance with him. I have never had a chance.'

'But he might not like you. He might not in the least want to marry you.'

She flushed again. 'You've set him against me!'

'Don't be foolish. We have not discussed you.'

'I suppose you are so sure of him,' she said. 'I suppose you do mean to marry him in the end.'

'No, I do not. I don't want to marry for the sake of marrying.' As soon as I said this and heard how smug it sounded I felt rather ashamed.

'How do you know that he doesn't?' she asked suddenly. It was the first acute remark she had made. I was taken off my guard and said lamely: 'I *don't* know.'

'Well, why won't you help me? It's not very much to ask. If you really don't want him yourself, why shouldn't you at least ask him here so that I have a chance to see him again?'

I was trapped. I had already said that Rupert and I had not discussed her, so I could hardly say now that the only remark he had made about her had been far from flattering.

'I'll think about it.'

'You are trying to put me off,' she said and began to cry.

'He might not want to come here now he knows that I won't marry him.'

'The letter,' she sobbed, 'you know what he says in the letter. Oh I wish I were dead! Everything happens to you and nothing to me. It is you who go off and find people and do things, and I can't. I'm not made that way. I thought I could lose myself in work, but now there is no work, and Mother does not need all I have to give. I'm sick of this house that is too big for us and trying to find things to do. I want a nice little home: with Mother, of course; and children, and everything arranged by me.' She pulled out a little handkerchief embroidered by herself, and wiped her eyes. 'Do you know, I have never even had a letter from a man? Of course Hubert used to write to me sometimes. But even he doesn't seem very anxious to come home, and he is only a brother, after all. Men don't recognize the lasting qualities in women. You are hopeless in the house and yet he wants to marry you! How can you refuse him!' she added inconsistently. 'What do you mean to do instead?'

'I don't know.' I was becoming very tired of this question, because even on the rare occasions when other people were not asking it, I was asking myself, and I never had any satisfactory reply.

My sister stared at me morosely. 'You must be mad,' she said at last.

'I am sorry I struck you,' I said awkwardly.

'Oh. Of course I forgive you,' she replied. She did not apologize for opening my letter.

Nor was that the end of it.

My sister and I avoided each other for the rest of that evening (she had left the room when she had forgiven me, still pressing the embroidered handkerchief to her eyes); but next day she resumed her attack. When was I going to ask Rupert to tea? Why had I not already asked him? Why did I not at least *ask* him? In the end, worn down by a series of little urgent private scenes with her I gave in, and wrote asking Rupert to tea. She posted the letter herself, and was then unaccountably irritable for the rest of the day.

Rupert accepted the invitation; my sister made various absurd and pathetic preparations; and I dreaded the whole thing so much that I felt sick when I thought of it. One preparation of my sister's consisted in manoeuvring our mother out of the house. She did this by the simple expedient of telling our mother that *I* did not want her there; but I only discovered this afterwards.

Rupert was due to arrive at four o'clock, but at half past, when he still had not appeared, we received a telegram to the effect that he was unable to come.

My sister, who seemed in the most alarming state of nerves, broke down completely at this. She wept, became hysterical, and finally accused me of conspiring with Rupert against her. After a useless interminable scene, I got her to her room with aspirin and lavender water and a handkerchief round the lamp. My mother returned and, when my sister did not come down for dinner (she had locked her door and would not answer me when I tried to fetch her), I learned why my mother had gone out.

I had been thinking very hard since the end of the scene with my sister, and after dinner I took the plunge and told my mother what I intended doing. She listened to me carefully, and made no objection, which was worse, of course,

337

than even the most selfish or unreasonable opposition. She even offered me a little, a very little, money, which was, I am sure, more than she could afford. I explained that I was out of sympathy with my sister, and that I thought the situation was likely to get worse. My mother did not understand me. She suggested hopelessly that perhaps things would be better when my brothers came home, although she admitted that Tom would go straight to his school and Hubert showed no signs of appearing at all. Then she reverted to worries about money. One by one she enumerated my own fears, and one by one I pretended to explode them. She believed me. By the end of the evening she was quite full of light-hearted admiration for the scheme, or pretended to be.

I fell asleep stretching thirty pounds over twelve months so thinly that the weeks showed through, and I had to make shillings of the pounds.

CHAPTER THIRTY-SIX

The end of it was that I found, after much searching, a room in which I could live by myself. The search took several days, partly because I had no idea how to start anything of the kind, and partly because even when I had learned something about it, there was the problem of finding a respectable room that I possibly dare afford.

I began by crossing Kensington Gardens to Bayswater and searching the streets at random for houses with signs about letting rooms. I did find one or two, but their landladies were expensive and disproportionately suspicious. One of them, who raised my spirits by being much cheaper, scratched herself furiously while I told her what I wanted, and then, withdrawing her hand from the small of her back, laughed so much that she broke two exceedingly dirty milk bottles which had been propped on her doorstep. She kicked the pieces of glass into the area and slammed her door.

As I neared Paddington station there were more and more houses with rooms to let. I became very used to ringing the bell at some gaunt house, to the door being opened (generally by a pasty-faced girl with half her wits about her and a cold), to explaining what I wanted, to the girl shouting 'Mum!' or 'Auntie!' or 'Vi!', to the appearance of some woman who was invariably too fat or too thin, and to whom I must explain all over again what I wanted, and then either to being turned away, or to being shown some attic which was damp, dirty or dark, and very often all three, and finally to the long silent descent of the house after I had fabricated some excuse for declining the room – and then the street again.

The first day was utterly abortive; on the second I discovered the invaluable assistance of local newspapers; on the third, the still more invaluable assistance of newspaper shops. It was in one of these that I found, approximately, what I was looking for.

I was scanning the rows of miscellaneous advertisements stuck to his window with stampedge when the shopkeeper himself beckoned to me.

'Thought I might help you. I know them cards off by heart,' he began. 'What is it, a little dawg, or yer Mum's tiara?'

I told him, and he whistled.

'Don't know London, do you?' he said. 'You want somewhere quiet, and respectable, *and* cheap. I know. Just come off the train you 'ave.' He nodded knowingly. 'Now, let's see, what 'ave we? We got everything 'ere,' he said after a minute's fruitless search in a large greasy blue book. 'Ah! Here we have it. Mrs Pompey. Number sixteen.' He scribbled something on a card and pushed it across the counter. 'Schoolmaster's widder. You say I sent you. Williams is the name. Tell 'er 'er ad's lapsed. Turn left outside the shop, keep straight on down and then right turn. Orlright?'

I thanked him gratefully.

'You can get yer papers 'ere,' he called cheerfully as I shut the door.

Number sixteen was in the middle of a terrace of tall thin houses, but was quite noticeable, being painted a rich apricot cream with a black front door. (The door was newly painted.) There was nothing to say that rooms were to be let. However, I rang the bell. Mrs Pompey answered the door. She was a little woman with no neck and a strong Scottish accent. I explained who had sent me, and what I wanted, while she surveyed me keenly.

'What do you want to pay?' she said.

I nervously stated my maximum figure.

There was a short silence.

'It's not very much, is it?' she said.

I added another two shillings to my price.

'I have one room I might let you have at that,' she said. 'Will you step inside while I close the door?'

I stepped into a hall which was pitch black when she shut the door.

'Will you follow me up, then?'

One floor from the top she halted and unlocked a door. At the same moment a loud bell rang twice from somewhere below us.

'Perhaps you'd step inside and be looking round you a minute. I shall be back.' And she hastened away.

The room was small, rectangular and clean. It was not very light, although possessed of a fair-sized sash window. The window, I discovered looked squarely out on to a sooty brick wall of a neighbouring house, which stood but three yards away, and which was broken only by olive green drainpipes. There would never be very much more light, I realized, although the afternoon was a dull one. I turned to the rest of the room. There was a black iron and brass bed, covered by a flaming slippery counterpane. The walls were covered in streaky buff paper which was heavily laced with mauve wistaria clinging to a darker buff trellis. There were a small gas fire and ring, a washstand with huge pitcher, a large highly polished wardrobe with an oval mirror set in its door, a comfortless armchair bristling with horsehair and little vicious round buttons, a stained oak chest of drawers. There were two pictures on the walls, one of which was entitled 'First Love'. I did not have time to examine the other before Mrs Pompey entered the room.

'Well, have you decided?' she began. She was a woman, I discovered, who went straight from one point to the next, wasting no time at all.

I started. I had been surveying the room with a minute, objective interest, but I had forgotten the purpose for which I was surveying it.

'You will see there is a gas ring, and the bathroom is across the passage. I change the linen once a week and you have your own keys. No visitors after seven, and one hot meal a day for an extra consideration. This is a respectable household and I wouldn't take gentlemen if they paid me.'

I did not feel that she would take anyone who did *not* pay her. However, I said nothing.

'What is your opinion?' she pressed after a moment.

I looked wildly round the room. It was not in the least what I had imagined, but I had searched for three days now, and did not seem likely to procure anything better.

'I should like to take it, please.'

'One month's rent in advance, and when would you be coming in?' she said instantly.

'Tomorrow. I have to fetch my things.'

And so the bargain was concluded. In the end I obtained the room and the meal for the original price she had agreed to. I paid the rent, and she hastened away for a receipt, while I waited in the dark hall.

I left with the keys, and strong, but very mixed feelings. By the time I had reached home, however, the situation settled itself into a romantic attitude of escape and a new life. I told my mother that I had a clean and cheap room with a respectable landlady, and that I was leaving the following day. I was so intent upon concealing my anxieties and fears that I succeeded in sounding merely callous about the whole thing; but my mother tried to enter into the spirit of it, helping me to pack, bringing me little pots of jam, and encouraging my optimism (assembled for her benefit) as much as she was able. My sister absented herself from these preparations in a marked manner. She had made one remark to the effect that I should soon return, after which she had ignored me.

'You will come back if you are ill?' asked my mother when we said good night.

'I'll come back anyway, in two days' time, for tea,' I replied. Her face brightened.

No, it was not really an escape, I reflected, but it was a new life.

CHAPTER THIRTY-SEVEN

I left my home at three o'clock the following day. By half past three I was back in the room facing the brick wall, with the door shut, and my trunks beside me. I found the speed with which I had effected this a little disconcerting. It did not seem very adventurous to leave one's home and reach the new destination in merely half an hour. The room was exactly the same as when I had left it except that there was a coarse white net cloth on top of the chest of drawers, rather like the cloth I had at home. I tried to think that that was far behind me, but half an hour did not seem very far. I decided to unpack and arrange all my belongings.

It took me about an hour to do this. I discovered that the wardrobe door swung open with a creak if I did not wedge it with a piece of paper, and that almost none of the drawers would open or shut unless I employed great ingenuity or strength or both. The first real trouble presented itself when I realized that I had no table on which to do my part copying. I should have to speak to Mrs Pompey. I would go and buy the food and other necessities required before broaching Mrs Pompey, I thought.

I bought bread, sausages, butter, margarine, apples and milk, in the street containing the newspaper shop. I did not feel able to run to the luxury of a newspaper, but I had decided to keep a diary, and, remembering that the man sold stationery, resolved to buy an exercise book from him for this purpose. He was very cheerful, and asked if I was fixed up, and whether I had reminded Mrs Pompey about her ad? I promised to remind her that evening, and he sold me a fat exercise book. 'Going to write yer life?' he remarked, expertly tying the string. 'That'll be something for us all to read. My eye!' He rolled them both skywards. 'Come back when you get to Vol. Two.'

After him, and a brief interlude with Mrs Pompey, who produced a small table, I did not speak to anyone for the rest of the day.

I cooked my supper, started the first page of my diary, and then, although it was only nine o'clock, went to bed. I could think of nothing else to do. The light was not strong enough for copying, and I was disinclined to read. The bed had noisy springs, but was quite comfortable.

The next day I rose, made myself toast on the fire (which required an alarming number of pennies to keep it alight), and settled down to work. I was interrupted, however, by an old woman who intended 'doing' my room. She was amiable, but so inquisitive that I fled, walking about the streets for nearly an hour, by which time I deemed my room should be clear of her. It was. It was also clear of three shillings which I had left on the writing-table with the intention of getting them changed into pennies for the fire. I was somewhat discouraged by this, and searched anxiously through my things to see whether anything else had disappeared. But she seemed to have the simple immediate kind of mind that takes only money.

I copied until a quarter to one, when an absurdly dignified gong rang. I ate stewed rabbit and semolina pudding in a room with seven tables and four other lunchers. They muttered occasionally to each other, but they mostly ate, with gloomy concentration, the not very appetizing food. Then, one by one, they left in a portentously silent manner, as though they had something important to do but the remainder of us must not be disturbed. After lunch I automatically went to my room. What should I do now? The thought of copying even more music was intolerable, as was the alternative of darning my stockings. I wrote to my mother; and then, as an afterthought, to Lucy, asking for Elspeth's London address.

Friends were essential to this sort of life. I wondered what they were doing at home. I could walk over and see them. I resisted this idea with some difficulty, and posted my letters instead.

There were sausages again for supper. The bathroom geyser required a shilling, and took even longer than the one at home. I wrote the diary again, and was disappointed in the shortness of the entry and its repetition of the day before.

A week passed, in which the only events were a self-conscious visit to my home, and a friendly but very short letter from Lucy containing Elspeth's address.

Even after a week I realized that the money I made from part copying, and the money my mother had given me, were not going to be enough. The food, and most of all, the fire, raced through a third as much again as I had calculated to spend on them.

I went to the newspaper shop and asked the proprietor to put a card in his window to the effect that a young lady would teach music on pupil's own piano. We worded it together, and he told me how much to charge. 'Can't be much in these parts,' he said, shaking his head wisely. 'You won't get them to pay for it. I should say five bob a lesson is about the mark, or maybe half a crown.' We settled on three and six.

I wrote to Elspeth asking whether I might come and see her. There was no reply. I went every day to the newspaper shop, but nobody seemed to want piano lessons. Then one night after I had eaten my bacon, and tried to write the listless monotonous diary, I broke down and simply wept. It did not seem to matter how hard I tried, life continued blank and impenetrable like the black brick wall outside. I seemed to have no friends. Elspeth did not reply, and even Rupert seemed to have given me up. I had no talents and no money. I was not starving. I had what unsympathetic listeners would call a good home. And a young man had asked me to marry him. I flipped through the pages of my diary with their sparse uninteresting information, tore the written sheets from the book and threw them away in fragments. What was the use of writing the same thing day after day all through this thick book? Then I remembered the newspaper man telling me to come to him when I got to Vol. Two. If I

had always kept a diary, there would have been Vol. Two by
now, and after all, things had not always remained exactly
the same. They had not, I remembered more sharply, as an
engine whistled at Paddington, and I recalled my first
journey to the Lancings, to whom my father had seen me
off. One could not keep a retrospective diary, however, and it
was just my luck that I should choose this moment to begin.
Then I suddenly wanted to write about my first journey to
the Lancings, diary or no diary.

And that was how I came to write this book.

CHAPTER THIRTY-EIGHT

I wrote the book. I continued to live in my room in Paddington; to copy music, and to eat my lunch in the dim room on the ground floor, crowded with cruets, with sauce, and with tables, in fact with anything but people. I bought food; collected shillings and pennies for the geyser and my fire respectively; went home to my mother once a week (she did not ask to see my room, and I did not invite her); mended my clothes; and occasionally went for walks when I had music to return, as the concentrated confinement was making me more than usually pale. Every hour when I was not occupied in the above employments, I wrote.

I began by writing about the first visit to the Lancings, and then realized the necessity of describing my home which provided such violent contrast. After the earlier part was completed, I related every incident subsequent to the first visit, that seemed in the least worthy of narration. I found the whole business incredibly arduous, but I was no longer lonely or bored. I only stopped to consider whether I had remembered the things that had mattered to me at the time; the right things, and enough of them. When I began, I found this difficult; but after one painful month my past life consumed me, and I had no trouble in projecting myself back into each experience as its turn came.

I told no one about my writing. Even Mr Williams, the newsagent, with whom I had become very friendly, when selling me a second fat exercise book, laughed about my 'life' because, of course, he did not really believe in it. I began to write every afternoon except on the day that I went home; continuing until eleven or twelve at night, with a break for the inevitable sausages or eggs or bacon. I ate them in rotation by now, but I had ceased to notice them very much; I had ceased to notice anything. It is only now that I realize

347

how difficult it is to live, observe and feel; and to write. Living and writing at once were almost impossible to me. For five months I did not live at all; that is to say, almost nothing happened to me, and when it did, I made no effort to enjoy whatever it was, I hardly noticed it, and resented what I did notice. I simply wrote. It was a curious business. I had no very clear idea of why I was writing, or even, as the months went by, how I was to end the whole thing. This last point became for some time a very real problem. Everything connected with the book had by then become real, and everything else a drab boarding-house dream. The underlying problem in my life became the end of my book; the most immediate problem, my increasing lack of money.

Several weeks after I had begun writing, Mr Williams hailed me from his shop as I was passing (I had ceased asking him about the advertisement, which indeed I had forgotten).

'Lidy with too many daughters wants you to call. Any afternoon this week. Here's the address. 'Tisn't far. What ho! looks as though yer luck's turned, hey?'

I agreed that it probably had, and hastened home for my music. Now I was faced with it, the prospect of teaching little girls the piano was rather appalling. I had lived without a piano for some time, and had not practised seriously for years. Also, if there were a *great* many daughters, my writing time would be seriously depleted. However, I had paid for the advertisement, and I needed money.

Having selected several pieces like Somervell's Rhythmic Gradus, 'The Harmonious Blacksmith', a little very early Mozart, and some Czerny, I set off that afternoon to Mrs Garth-Jackson's house. It was, I discovered, another boarding-house, of the more genteel and expensive variety. It had a chinese lantern in the hall, and an intricate piece of furniture bracketed to the wall, which pigeon-holed all the inmates' letters in alphabetical order. There was also a smell of soap and burnt rock cakes which assailed me the moment the door was opened by a stolid young woman of about eighteen who conducted me to a room leading off the hall, and then abandoned me. There was a piano in it, an extraordinarily ancient Erard.

Mrs Garth-Jackson had an exceedingly thin stiff nose, like a placket jammed between two pale grey buttons which were her eyes. When she smiled, which she did all the while she was talking, she displayed bulbous ingrown teeth, which were so large and so numerous that they seemed almost to be falling out of her mouth. She wore a hideous overall spattered with huge orange flowers, and over this, to show, I suppose, that she wore real clothes underneath, a large lapis lazuli and mother-of-pearl cross on a silver chain.

'I am Mrs Garth-Jackson,' she began. 'You must excuse my greeting you like this, but I have everything to do myself, and all my large family have home-made food. Today is my baking day and you couldn't have caught me at a worse moment, but never mind. Do sit down. Be at home. Now then. I have three daughters who all require lessons, but I'm afraid I cannot run to the figure you are asking as I am a war widow.'

This did not seem a very promising start. However, I smiled, wanly sympathetic, and she continued: 'One of the things I rescued from the Wreck, was the dear old piano which nobody has played on since I can remember. So all we need is a nice sing-song in the evening with one of the girls officiating.'

I summoned enough courage to ask: 'Have your daughters received no previous tuition?'

'Dear me no. Of course I see that if you had been contemplating *advanced* tuition your price was perhaps not so ... but these girls are right at the *beginning*, and only the most elementary teaching is necessary. That *does* make a difference, doesn't it?' She smiled harder than ever.

Panic stricken, I attempted to consider the difference it made. But she allowed me no time for this.

'You look very young to be a teacher of any kind. What are your qualifications?'

I explained, as impressively as possible, about my father. She seemed satisfied, but not impressed, and continued to talk about her daughters.

'You will find them eager to learn, and not, I fancy, ungifted. Their great-uncle used to play the viola; so you see there is music in our family, too. They are available any afternoons that you wish, but perhaps it would save your time and my money if you taught them together, shall we say for an hour and a half at the figure you mentioned?'

She was still smiling, with her eyes boring into my face as she exploded this last awful suggestion. I was about to grasp weakly at the only straw in sight, when she continued: 'I see you have brought music with you. Quite unnecessary, as a matter of fact. I have got something suitable for each of them.'

I found my voice. 'Have they any knowledge of musical notation?'

Mrs Garth-Jackson laughed.

'No idea of notes from A to Z. That is your job, isn't it?' Here is the music. I will fetch the girls while you peruse it.' She laid three thin leaflets on my lap and hurried purposefully out.

The leaflets contained three songs: 'Tipperary', 'Roses in Picardy', and one I had never heard of called 'Moonlight on My Dreams'. I stared at them aghast. I was still staring at them in a kind of petrified trance, when the three Miss Garth-Jacksons followed their mother into the room. The daughters were all alike, and exactly like their mother. The first shock, however, was in respect of their age. They all looked, in spite of their girlish and identical clothes, considerably older than me. I realized by their expressions, that if Mrs Garth-Jackson had not constantly smiled, she would have looked morose and stupid. On the whole, I still wished she would not smile. Meanwhile four sharp noses were directed at me, and three pairs of pale grey eyes stared with expressionless intensity into mine.

'This is Muriel; Mildred; and my youngest, Mabel. Now as I think we were agreed upon terms, supposing you begin now, and when I have finished my weary round of household duties, I shall be able to join you, and I hope also profit.'

The next moment I was left facing the unprepossessing and silent trio. Divested of Mrs Garth-Jackson's smile, the atmosphere became frankly gloomy, even desperate. Stiffening my sinews, however, I began, with assumed confidence, which did not for one moment deceive any of us, to examine the extent of their knowledge. This was easy. They knew nothing, and, I felt, cared less. I realized with horror that teaching them the names of the notes was going to be no easy task. Nevertheless, I began to attempt this.

I opened my book of Czerny and they shuffled up to the piano. The situation was made worse by the fact that some of the notes of the piano never sounded at all, many others were erratic, and all of them were out of tune. With every minute I felt my pupils grow more bewildered and hostile. They never spoke to me, but muttered an occasional disparaging remark to each other. My position was only relieved by their apparently despising each other more thoroughly even than me, although they clearly had no very good opinion of me. In half an hour I had made no progress at all. Their minds did not exactly wander; quite simply they did not seem to have any minds. I endeavoured to remain bright and patient, but I was clearly very bad at teaching. I could not remember when I had learned this particular aspect of the subject myself. I seemed always to have known it. So I dare say my methods were hopeless.

Mrs Garth-Jackson's reappearance, which I had formerly been dreading, came as a relief.

'What *have* you been doing?' I haven't heard a sound,' she began.

'We haven't been learning the songs you said,' announced, I think, Mildred, but I was so bemused by their noses that I am not very sure.

'Although I know all the chunes,' said another daughter.

'We *all* know the chunes,' said the third crushingly.

That was the beginning of the end. In vain did I try to

351

explain the elementary principles that must be grasped before any playing might proceed. I was too depressed to be very persuasive.

Mrs Garth-Jackson succeeded in getting rid of me as a charlatan and without paying me. I went with all the dignity I could muster, inadvertently leaving Czerny behind me. I withdrew my advertisement and gave up all thought of teaching anybody anything which I could not remember learning myself.

I resolved to cut down my meals, at least until I had finished writing.

CHAPTER THIRTY-NINE

I discovered that exercise and fresh air made me hungry. Sitting in my room and drinking a quantity of cold water, however, did not. I was far from starving, but subsisting mainly on the monotonous tepid luncheons provided by Mrs Pompey, reinforced by bread, apples and cocoa in my room, required a certain adjustment of the mind if one was occupied in successively copying music, writing and, worse still, worrying about a book.

One afternoon, however, having some music to return, I decided to walk back to Paddington. It was a beautiful day; one of those rare single perfect days, with balmy air and exquisite colour; the whole inlaid with a seductive, but treacherous sense of timelessness. Tomorrow it would probably rain, but it was impossible to think so today.

I turned reluctantly from the edge of the Park towards my sunless room, and the copying which lay before me. The door of my room was unlocked. I pushed it open – and there was Elspeth.

As I opened the door she rose from the chair in which she had been sitting. She was dressed in a costume of vivid yellow, which seemed to illumine the room. I think I gasped: tears of amazement started into my eyes.

'I have been waiting for you,' said Elspeth. 'You must have thought me so rude in not answering your letter that I decided simply to come.'

I shut the door. Curiously, seeing someone, a friend in this room for the first time, where I had spent so many solitary hours, my loneliness rushed out on me, enveloping me.

Elspeth said: 'Can we light your fire? I cannot make it work.'

'It needs pennies.' I went to the little box in which I kept them, on the mantelpiece.

'Have you been waiting long?' I asked when the fire was alight.

'Not very long. Your landlady put me in here. Is this where you live?'

'Yes.'

She stared at me thoughtfully for a moment, and then said:

'I have been abroad. Uncle does not forward letters. So you see, I have only just had yours. I got back two days ago.'

'I am very glad to see you,' I said. 'Shall we have tea?'

'On the bed there is a paper bag full of meringues,' she observed.

I made tea. We talked about the Lancings, and she a little about Paris. There was a kind of constraint upon us; neither of our minds was employed in our conversation, as we wondered about each other, our eyes occasionally meeting in a spasm of amiable curiosity.

When the tea was poured she said suddenly: 'Tell me why you are here? Has something dreadful happened since I saw you last?'

'No. I couldn't bear living with my family any more, so I left.'

'But why here?'

I looked at her shining trim head with small ear-rings glinting at the edge of her hair (her actual ears were invisible), and answered carefully: 'I have very little money. I couldn't afford anywhere else.'

'Do you work?'

'I copy music. I don't earn very much.'

'Are you not very lonely? What happens when you've finished copying music?'

'Nothing. I get some more.'

'So much music as that?' She made an extravagant little gesture with her fingers. 'What did you dislike so much about your home?'

I tried to tell her, but somehow, since I had written about it, I had no more to say on the subject, and found it difficult even to be convincing.

354

'I see,' she said. I do not think she did. 'But what do you intend doing? You surely cannot copy music all your life?'

I was becoming hardened to this question and countered: 'What do *you* intend doing?'

Her clear serious eyes widened a moment but she answered casually: 'Oh, I have some sort of plan.'

'Well I have none,' I said flatly. I knew from experience that this kind of conversation only made me thoroughly unhappy for long afterwards.

'I remember you once said that you would write books and keep a small Zoo,' I added.

'How do you remember that? I remember thinking it, but I do not remember telling you.'

'I was thinking about it the other day. Well, are you doing either of those things?'

'Good heavens, no. At least, not at the moment.' The corners of her mouth flitted upwards and then down again as though she were smiling alone to herself.

'You see?' I said. 'It's no good planning anything. Anyway, what could I plan?'

'I suppose you could earn more money. That would make a difference.'

'It would certainly make a difference. But I am not trained to do anything. I have no vocation or talent, or whatever it is people need.'

'How did you learn to copy music?'

'That doesn't count. I was brought up on music. It is like words; only a little more complicated.'

'And do you do it all day?'

'Yes.' I did not want to tell her about the book.

'All the time?'

'Almost all of it.'

'That's better,' said Elspeth calmly. 'I am afraid I know that you don't.' She indicated my writing-table with the back of her head. I saw that my second vast exercise book lay open upon it, and felt violently angry and stupid.

'I have not touched it. You must have left it there. Generally you lock it up, but today you forgot.'

'How do you know that?'

She leaned back a little in her chair.

'That is what people do. The locking up and the forgetting.'

'Do you write?' I asked politely.

She frowned. 'I cannot. I have done enough of it to know that I cannot. It is a bad situation.'

I did not know what she meant, and did not reply. Suddenly she leaned forward and said, very charmingly: 'Do *you* find it difficult? Will you tell me about it?'

I stared at her, hopelessly incoherent. 'I haven't finished,' I said at last.

'It's about you, I suppose?' Elspeth said.

I nodded.

'What are you going to do with it?'

'Do with it?'

She laughed. 'Extraordinary creature. You don't plan anything, do you? Look here, I want to read it. I read very quickly and shall not lose it,' she added.

'My writing . . .' I began faintly. I suddenly felt sick at the thought of anyone reading it. There were all kinds of things.

'Am *I* in it?' asked Elspeth sitting bolt upright.

'Yes. So you are.'

'So I am,' she smiled delightedly. 'I'll read it in one day, or perhaps two. Yes?'

I hesitated, knowing she would win. 'It isn't *finished*,' I said again.

'We'll invent an ending,' said Elspeth. 'If I have time we will. I shall have to be quick because of . . . Why it might make you famous!'

I had the feeling that she said this to prevent herself saying something else. We did not talk about it any more. Nor did we again mention the Lancings. I felt that for quite different reasons we had neither of us liked staying with them and that we neither of us wanted, by discussion, to find out how different our reasons for not liking it were.

She left in a short while, carrying the exercise books, with the promise that she would return with them two days later.

She left me in a tumult; about her and about the book. I lay for hours that night imagining myself an accepted and successful author. Gigantic fantasies rioted with wholly improbable simplicity; clear unpractical dreams filled me to the brim; my ambition was as boundless, as limitless, as my illusion, and I indulged them both in the privacy of my dark room for hours and hours.

CHAPTER FORTY

The next day, of course, I had to battle with the depression which results from any orgy of private and imaginative optimism.

In thinking of Elspeth reading my books, I fell to thinking of Elspeth herself. I realized that I knew almost nothing about her, since on each of the three widely spaced occasions when we had met, she had seemed an entirely different creature. Nor could I, except by the wildest unsatisfactory conjecture, connect these three people, although they all had something in common. She had on all occasions given the impression of being only partially contained in the immediate situation, as though the most vital part of her was withdrawn, intensely active, but withdrawn. If she had some private life of which I was ignorant, it did not seem dependent upon her environment. I felt she carried it about with her; and since ignorance is conducive to envy, I envied her.

Her appearance was also perplexing. She had dressed on this last, and the previous occasion with an extreme, but elegant, severity, although her face, her habitual expression of grave preoccupation had altered remarkably little, I realized, since she was fourteen. She had looked too old for her age then; now she appeared, not precisely too young, but imbued with a curious mixture of sophistication and youth. The effect was certainly startling, but it was impossible to be sure whether or not it was conscious.

In spite of the feeling I had so strongly about her divided nature, I felt that there was no situation to which she would prove unequal, possibly *because* of her essential division. She had, I felt, what many people call (and I can think of no better way to describe it) some secret purpose in her life.

Fortunate Elspeth, I thought, having successfully

simplified her situation without knowing anything about it.

I spent the whole day alternately resolving to put Elspeth and the books out of my mind, and impatiently waiting for her return and her conclusions. I spent an almost sleepless night in the same condition.

She arrived exactly when she had said she would. She was carrying a small suitcase. I had prepared tea for us, and proceeded to dispense it, confidently expecting that she would of herself broach the subject of my book. But she seemed wrought up and unusually silent. It had been raining, and she arrived buttoned to the chin in an unusually long and heavy mackintosh, although she was bareheaded.

'I had better hang it somewhere,' she observed, after standing restlessly in it for some moments. She was wearing an equally businesslike shirt and tie; together with a beautifully cut grey costume, the skirt of which reached to her ankles.

'I'm so sorry.' I unwedged the piece of paper in the wardrobe door, and produced a hanger.

'Do you always have to do that?' she asked.

'Use the paper? Yes. Otherwise it swings open.'.

'Bore for you,' she remarked and flung herself into a chair.

'Do you know what struck me most forcibly about your book?' she said suddenly after a very long silence which I had not known how to break. I drew a deep breath; she was coming to the point.

'No? How should I?'

'It struck me so much that I thought you might also have noticed it,' she replied, ignoring the tea I had placed beside her.

I waited.

'It is that after repeated efforts to shake off your family atmosphere and environment, you have finally succeeded in eloping with it . . . in carrying it off, and bringing it here.'

'This is not in the least like my home!' I cried.

'No? It is considerably less comfortable, and much more solitary. Otherwise it seems to me to be very much the same.' She said this almost aggressively, but her eyes looked calmly out of her pale serious face, and I saw that she really meant what she said.

'What I want to know,' she continued, 'is whether, if presented with the opportunity, you would be prepared to leave all this behind, and *really* get away? Would you, do you think?'

I struggled hard to adjust my mind to the new and brutal conclusion she had put forward.

'I suppose *if* the opportunity really arose, yes,' I said slowly, my dreams of authorship rapidly fading under her practical and unexpected attack.

'But you do not believe in the opportunity?'

'I find that difficult,' I admitted.

'Is that because you really want an unadventurous kind of life, or because you simply haven't had the chance to try anything else?'

'You've read the book,' I said stiffly.

'What sort of shape do you believe the world to be?'

This question really shook me so much that I answered quite simply: 'Round.'

'Entirely round? Spherical?'

'Er . . . yes. I haven't thought much about it.'

'My uncle has thought of almost nothing else for the last twenty-five years,' said Elspeth.

There was a short silence.

'I am beating round the bush, but there *is* a bush,' she said at last. 'It is not so much that I believe in *it*; but I believe in *him*, and he is too old to find out for himself.'

'Could you explain a little more about it?' I asked.

'The point is that I am not talking nonsense. This has something to do with that book you have written. I should not have said anything if I had not read it. First of all: do you think you would be prepared to leave all this for something utterly different? I cannot say very much more than that until I know myself.'

I looked round the drab crowded room.

'Don't you think I should be foolish to refuse?'

'*I* think so. Now look.'

She picked up her plate, turned it in her hands, and put it down.

'No,' she said. 'It would be easier if I get my suitcase.'

Thereupon began a most improbable exposition. It was her uncle's theory, she said, and although a few people upheld it, they were totally unprepared, or unable, to do anything to promote it. Her uncle was rich, he was old, he was infirm, and above all he was obsessed with his idea. He left it to her, and she was determined to do everything in her power to prove or disprove the thing. She required someone who was able to record her findings, accurately, and at the same time, with imagination. 'The two are indivisible. I have discovered that,' she said. I must divulge the idea to no one, but she thought that I would fulfil this particular position admirably. 'There will also be a lot of hard work,' she said. 'Harder, I think, than you have ever known.' She looked at the exercise books. As soon as she had finished speaking, she rose to her feet and announced that she was going.

'Write to me about it,' she said. 'There is not very much time left. I should be glad to know as soon as you have made up your mind.'

So she left me.

It was not a difficult decision. It was really one of those decisions which are instantly decided; until the sheer size of it forces one to rally a few faint objections, in order to flatter one's initial judgement. I knew, the moment Elspeth had gone, that I would gladly leave this room. I could assure myself with a kind of triumphant self-pity that I had no ties beyond it, or, if I had, they were ties I could easily break. I wanted just then to think of myself spinning away round the earth, unbreakable and separate from anything that I touched. Round the earth was, perhaps, hardly the way to describe this desire.

I wrote to Elspeth that night.

CHAPTER FORTY-ONE

Two weeks later we left. The days were so hectically crowded with practical preparation and emotional spilt milk, that I was not able to record them. I spent most of the mornings and afternoons ordering things, choosing things, buying things, fetching things, and having things altered. There were to be three of us; but the third was not to join Elspeth and me until something obscure had been arranged between Elspeth's uncle and some mythical eccentric elsewhere. Elspeth displayed remarkable ingenuity and intelligence, together with her customary incomplete presence of mind whenever I saw her. The whole business was transacted efficiently, and with a comfortable disregard for money which made even the suppliers of our varied and incongruous requirements treat us with astonished awe.

I spent the evenings alternately with Elspeth and my family. The family evenings were extraordinarily difficult. I had been pledged to a complete silence on the real reason for my departure, which made the venture frivolous, incomprehensible and almost disastrous to my mother. I told her I was going to write: she looked suddenly anxious and said: 'Not music, darling?' I answered: 'No, only words,' and she seemed faintly reassured. She did not feel that composing music was a very happy career, she said: for a woman, she added. She was unhappy about my going: I felt helplessly sorry for her, but I knew that I should go. How long would it all *take*? she would inquire at intervals. I did not really know.

Eventually, the day before we were to leave London, I left my room in Paddington, and walked with a single light suitcase out into the street. Although I was leaving my room for ever, I felt quietly unreal about it, as though my departure were merely imaginary (I had come very close to my imagination during the recent months), as though there were no real question of my leaving at all, in spite of Mrs Pompey's brisk decisive farewell.

I went home to sleep the last night in my old room. Having kissed my mother and sister (my sister seemed to feel that the solemnity of the situation required this), I lay awake in this earlier bed that I knew so well, with the unknown prospect of the journey flooding my mind. In spite or because of the knowledge that I must rise at six o'clock the next morning, I slept very little.

I quelled the alarum-clock almost as soon as it rang, but a minute later my mother stood in the door of my room, shivering in a faded pink dressing-gown.

'I was awake anyway,' she said. 'I will get tea.'

This was the worst time to attempt any kind of social departure, I reflected, struggling into the garments the arduous labours ahead of me required. It was the time when memory is sharp, everything is remembered, but there is nothing to say. The worst possible time.

When my mother returned with a tray she gasped faintly and said: 'Darling! Are you going like that?'

For a second we both looked at my clothes, and then, both aware of the hopelessness of any argument or explanation, looked away. She had always prepared me for any previous journey, I knew we were both remembering.

We said the things we had said the night before; of course they did not console her. When she had asked whether I should come back soon, and I had reassured her, she said: 'We shall hardly know you.'

Would she have felt like this if I had been marrying? I wondered. No, she would regard my marriage as a logical continuation, she would comfort herself with that. She would not regard this venture as either logical or lyrical; nor could it seem a continuation of anything at all.

We drank the warm metallic tea from the thermos. I swallowed a piece of bread and butter to please her. The cab arrived. The man blustered silently with my trunks in the hall while my mother hovered miserably on the stairs, catching cold and trying not to cry, not to utter one word against me.

Kissing her, saying good-bye, was a curiously formal affair. I felt very like saying: 'Thank you for having me', the kind of thing one says after a long disappointing visit. I simply kissed her again and went. The feeling was no more than a shadowy echo of what I had felt before embarking on a fortnight in the country. But this was not a fortnight in the country.

In a few racing silent moments my home was left behind; the little span when there was no present, and I was strung between the last moments of my family and the enormous mysterious future, was endured in the cab, until, meeting Elspeth, it began to be my present again.

The journey by rail to the ship took ten hours. I had to read most of the time, a manuscript of technical and, in consequence, chiefly incomprehensible notes.

I imagined that on arrival we should board our (unexpectedly small) vessel and relax. I was utterly wrong about this. The boarding itself took three hours with all our equipment, and the suspicious hostility of all customs officials to be contended with.

On board, a great deal of unpacking was necessary. I was given a cabin to myself with a good small table for writing.

Elspeth is next door, which is a good thing as she seems to know much more about every aspect of travelling than I. I found we had missed dinner, but were provided with sandwiches and soup. Elspeth has gone to bed, and I am writing this, although I am too exhausted to do more than make notes now.

Tomorrow, however, I shall start my new book. I am so tired that I cannot see the lines on the paper, but I have finished the second exercise book from Mr Williams. I am very cold, and work on the floor, wrapped in Elspeth's magnificent rug.

The new book in which I am to write has no lines.

I have opened it and written the title across the first page.

I am calling it 'The Four Corners of The Earth'.

SOMETHING
IN DISGUISE

For my brother, Colin Howard

Contents

Part One: April

1. Wedding

When Oliver saw his sister in her bridesmaid's dress he laughed so much he could hardly stand.

'I've never looked my best in pink.'

'Oh shut *up*, it's not as funny as all that.'

'You look like a sort of elongated Shirley Temple. Or a chimpanzee at a Zoo tea-party : yes – more like that, because of your little hairy arms peeping out from all that dimity, or whatever it is –'

'Organza,' she said crossly; 'and it's quite pale on my arms.'

'What is? Your fur? Don't worry about that. Lots of men love hairy women, and if they turn out not to, you could always fall back on another chimpanzee in a sailor suit. Turn round.'

'What for?' she asked when she had done so.

'Just wanted to see if the back was as funny as the front.'

'Is it?'

'Not quite, because one misses your face. Do keep that expression for the wedding photographs.'

'You are being beastly. *Anyone* would look awful in it. *You* would.'

'Let me pop it on. I bet I could bring tears to your eyes. The tragic transvestite : a sort of leitmotif for Colin Wilson. Come on, Lizzie. I'll go mincing down to Daddo, and send his old blood coursing through his veins –'

'Get dressed, you fool. The whole day's going to be quite awful enough without you doing a thing to make it worse. It is poor old Alice's day, after all.'

'I haven't had any breakfast.'

'Well you won't get any now. You'll get buffet lunch in –'

she looked at her man's watch strapped by black leather round her wrist – 'just over an hour and a half.'

'You'll have to take that watch off. You might as well be carrying a tommy-gun. I promise I'll be nice to Alice. I *like* Alice. I like *Alice*,' he added going to the door. 'And May. And you. I shall always remember the first time I saw you like this.'

'You're not going to see me like it any other time. Really be nice to Alice.'

'Really being nice would entail a kind of Rochester wedding. Finding that Leslie had a mad wife shut up in one of his building estates –'

'Who's Shirley Temple?' Recognizing *Jane Eyre* reminded her that she didn't know that one.

'An infant prodigy who looked her best in pink. Honestly, you don't know *any*thing.' He slammed her door so that it burst open. She shut it, and turned sadly to the pointed satin court shoes that had been half-heartedly dyed to match. They'd be too uncomfortable to wear in ordinary life anyway.

*

Alice sat in front of her stepmother's dressing-table wondering whether she could improve her hair. She couldn't, she decided : it had been back-combed with such obsessional care by the local hairdresser, that any interference with it now would probably be disastrous. 'My wedding morning,' she thought, and tried to feel momentous and festive – somehow more worthy. It was April; the sky was overcast in slate, and livid green trees waved wildly in the gusty wind. Ordinarily, by now she would be feeding the dogs which Daddy would not have in the house, and cleaning out their horrible kennels that smelled like animal public lavatories however often you cleaned them. It wasn't at all a nice day from the weather point of view. 'I'm leaving home,' she thought; but even that seemed a bit hopeless as they'd only lived there for two years and she'd never liked it anyway. Daddy had bought the house when he married May : it was large and ugly, and Alice knew that secretly May didn't like it either – she was always too cold, she said. 'I *want* to leave,' she thought more vehemently. Then she thought what a good man Leslie obviously was, and that she would miss May who'd been much nicer to her than her other stepmother – nicer even than her own mother who'd always seemed to be what Daddy called failing. He loathed ill health.

She opened her dressing-gown to see whether her skin had subsided from pink to white after her bath. May had insisted on her using this room with its bathroom attached; had insisted also upon giving her the last remaining bath salts, had offered to help her dress, or keep out of the way – in fact was behaving with effortless, model kindness. It was amazing that anyone could be so practical about feelings when they weren't at all about things. 'Weren't at all *what*, Alice?' Daddy would say, with his pale bulging eyes fixed upon her (when she was little she had thought he did it to bully, when she was a young girl she had thought it was because he was stupid – now she thought it was a bit of both); 'Practical, Daddy,' she would always have replied in a small uninteresting voice used only on him. Oliver and Elizabeth hated him. It was only affection for their own mother, May, that prevented them from being rather horrible to poor old Daddy. As it was, Oliver called him Daddo – in quotes –and gave him earnest, frightfully unsuitable Christmas presents which he then kept asking about. He'd made him a Friend of Covent Garden, for instance, and given him a whole book of photographs of ballet dancers and books about pygmies and Kalahari Bushmen which said how wonderful and civilized they were when Oliver must know perfectly well that Daddy thought black men and ballet dancers were the *end* .. Elizabeth was not so bad, but she thought that everything her brother did was all right, and they were always having private jokes together and May just laughed at them and said, do be serious for a moment, not really wanting them to be at all.

I must be. I'm getting married. I must get dressed. She got up from the dressing-table and slipped off her multi-coloured Japanese kimono. All her underclothes were new. Her skin had now reverted to milky-whiteness. She was tall, big-boned and an old-fashioned shape. She had, indeed, the heavy brows, beautiful eyes, slightly Roman nose and square jaw that were typical of du Maurier. Modern underclothes did not suit her – the gaps were not alluring, but faintly embarrassing – they embarrassed *her*, at any rate. She suffered intermittently from hay fever, mastitis and acne, and anti-histamine, unboned bras and calamine lotion fought an uneasy battle with the anxieties of her nervous, gentle temperament. Today it was the mastitis that was giving her trouble; her brassière was too tight, but it was the one she had worn for fitting her dress – she couldn't change it now. All the dressing and undressing in marriage must be so difficult – if one hated doing it even in shops when trying on clothes, what would it be like in a bedroom with a man, an audience of one? And the *same* one at that? Not that she meant . .. Poor Alice had an unfortunate capacity for confounding herself – even when alone, even with what could fairly be described as innocently random thoughts: she conducted a great deal of her spare and private time (and there had been a good deal of that because she was rather shy) with some anonymous, jeering creature who seemed only to exist in order to trap her with some inconsistency, some banal or lewd or plain dotty remark which it waited for her to make. *She* was the last person in the world to want hundreds of men watching her take off her clothes ... Sneering, incredulous silence.

She walked over to her wedding dress which hung stiffly with the long sleeves sticking out, not looking as though it could fit anyone. The trouble with satin – even cut on the cross – was that it fitted you as long as you didn't move at all; the moment you did, great rifts and creases and undercurrents of strain determined themselves: this had happened at every fitting, and an angry woman in mildewed black, who combined a strong odour of Cheddar cheese with the capacity to talk with her mouth bristling with pins, had stuck more pins into the dress (and Alice) with no lasting effect.

The veil would conceal a certain amount. It had been carefully arranged in an open hat-box which now lay on May's bed, but on approaching the box, she discovered that it was entirely full of her cat, Claude, who lay in it like a huge fur paperweight. She mentioned his name and he opened his lemony eyes just enough to be able to see her, stretched out a colossal paw and yawned. He was an uneasy combination of black and white : on his face this gave him an asymmetrical and almost treasonable appearance. His pads were the bright pink of waterproof Elastoplast, and between them, the thick, white fur was stained pale green. He'd been hunting, she told him as she lifted him off her veil, and he purred like the distant rumble of a starting lorry. He was heartless, greedy and conceited, but the thought of going to Cornwall (the honeymoon) without him made her feel really sad. She had not liked to ask Leslie whether he could live with them in Bristol, and, indeed, it had crossed her mind that even if Leslie agreed, Claude might not. His standard of living in Surrey was exceptionally high – even for a cat – as apart from two large meals a day that he ate primly out of a soup plate, he procured other, more savage snacks such as grass snakes and rabbits, that he demolished on the scullery floor at times convenient to himself. Enough of him, she thought, putting him tenderly on the bed. He got up at once, shook his head – his ear canker rattled like castanets – and chose a better position eight inches from where she had put him. Her veil was quite crushed and spattered with his hairs – he moulted continuously in all his prodigious spare time. 'What on *earth* am I doing?' she thought as she hung the veil on the back of a chair. 'Starting a new life without Daddy, I suppose.'

There was a whimsical fanfare of tapping on the door, and before she could answer, Leslie's sister, Rosemary, came in. She was dressed from head to foot in pink organza : it was she who had chosen the bridesmaids' dresses. Pink, she had said, was her colour, and it certainly provided a contrast to the dark, wiry curls and the mole on the left side of her face. She was older than Leslie, unmarried, and with a robust contempt for all Englishmen. When younger, she had been an air hostess, and so was able to back up this contempt with many a passing romantic interlude in which men, generically described by her as continental, invariably demonstrated their superior approach to ladies. She regarded her brother's marriage to Alice with almost hysterical indulgence, and had arranged so much of the wedding that Alice felt quite frightened of her.

'Here I am!' she exclaimed. Her nails were far too long, thought Alice as Rosemary twitched the wedding dress off its hanger.

'In view of the time, I think we ought to pop this on – why – whatever *has* happened to your veil? That awful cat!'

Alice, inserting her arms into the tight, satin sleeves (it was rather like trying to put back champagne bottles into their straw casings), mumbled something defensive about Claude and at once, without warning, her eyes filled with tears. Rosemary, like many obtrusive people, was quick to observe any such physical manifestations of dismay and to rush into the breach she had made for the purpose. She would get the veil ironed; Sellotape was wonderful for removing hairs; Alice must cheer up – it would not do for her to meet Leslie at the altar with red eyes. But at least she went, leaving Alice to struggle with the tiny satin buttons – like boiled cods' eyes – that fastened the sleeves at her wrists. 'Something borrowed,' she thought miserably. She would far rather borrow Claude's hairs than anything else she could think of. If only May would come; would stop being tactful, and come, and just stay with her until it was all over ...

•

May, wearing an anonymous macintosh over her wedding clothes, was mixing the dogs' food in the scullery. Biscuits – like small pieces of rock – a tin of animal meat and last night's cabbage lay in a chipped enamel bowl, and she was stirring it with a wooden spoon. It smelled awful and did not look enough, but she did not notice either of these things because she was trying to think about the Absolute – a concept as amorphous and slippery as a distant fish and one that she feared was for ever beyond her intellectual grasp. 'The Whole,' she repeated dreamily: at this point, as usual, the concept altered from being some kind of glacial peak to an orange-coloured sphere – a furry and at the same time citrus ball; but these visual translations interrupted real understanding of the idea – were nothing, she felt, but childish cul-de-sacs, the wrong turning in this cerebral maze. She tried again. 'God,' she thought, and instantly an ancient man – a benign King Lear and at the same time Father Christmas in a temper – was sitting on a spiky, glittering chair. 'Absolute Being'; the chair wedged itself on the glacial peak. She sighed, and a bit of cabbage fell out of the bowl. A very interesting man she had met recently had told her to live in the present. She picked up the piece of cabbage and put it back into the bowl. The trouble with the present was the way it went on and on and on, and she found it so easy to live in that when the man had suggested to her that she wasn't doing it the right way, she had felt sure he was right.

It was so easy to be a vegetable, she thought, staring humbly into the bowl, and somehow or other the amount more that was expected of one must be achievable by slow degrees: it was not necessary to jump straight from a cabbage to God. It was worse than that really; babies, for instance were all right; even children – 'little children' – were spiritually acceptable; but somewhere along the line leading to adolescence people got demoted from being children to being vegetables, and often wicked vegetables at that. The Christian world blamed a good deal of this on to carnal knowledge. This seemed, to her, to be an over-simplification, because even she could think of a lot of dreary and comparatively unevolved people whose carnal knowledge seemed to her nil ... Anyway, this interesting man had said that sex was a good thing – if properly approached – but he had added that hardly anybody understood how to approach it properly. The only time she had thought about sex had been the gigantic months after Clifford had been killed, when underneath or inside her misery had continued her aching unattended body that simply went on wanting him, that seemed no more able to recognize his death than some poor people could recognize that a limb that itched and twitched was no longer there because it had been cut off. Several of her friends had lost their men in the war, but she quickly discovered that the plane on which such losses were touched upon was the empty-chair-beside-the-fire one: the empty body in the bed was never admitted in the social annals of bereavement. She hadn't 'approached' sex before Clifford, and she hadn't approached it with him. He and it had arrived together; she had loved him almost at once and remarked – breathlessly soon afterwards – how lucky it was that when you loved someone there was so much to do about it. They had had four years of interrupted, but otherwise splendid pleasure, but always with the war lying in wait – at first, hardly mattering, seeming distant and unreal and vaguely wicked as a child's view of death. After Oliver was born there were a few more months when Clifford – doing navigation courses at a Naval Training Establishment – worked harder, but was still able to get home more often than not. Home was then a two-roomed flat at the top of a non-converted house in Brighton. They were poor – a sub-lieutenant's pay and her fifty pounds a year was all they had – but Clifford had a second-hand bicycle for getting to work, she became extraordinarily good at vegetable curries and, as Clifford had pointed out, a baby was one of the cheapest luxuries currently available. Then the war had pounced: a fine spring afternoon, and he had come back early – she heard his step on the linoleum stairs and ran to meet him trembling with unexpected delight ... Next morning he left her at five, a full lieutenant newly appointed to a frigate. She had sat in the tiny blacked-out kitchen staring at his half-drunk cup of tea and wondering how on earth she could bear it. To be in love, to say good-bye for an unknown amount of time (weeks? months? years? she would not imagine further) only to know that *he* was to be put professionally in danger somewhere, and that, worse, this was fast becoming the accepted, general situation, was the beginning of the war for her. She had sat in the kitchen hating men for devising, allowing, lending themselves to this monstrous stratagem, which seemed to her then as evil and pointless and heartless as the origins of chess. Even *he* – she had sensed his professional excitement, his pride in that wretched piece of gold lace, his complete acceptance that the Admiralty could, at a moment's notice, break up his private life and send him anywhere to fight and perhaps be killed ...

He *hadn't* been killed for nearly another three years after that morning: the war had played cat and mouse with her:

after three years of sharpening her courage by a succession of these partings, of stretching her anxiety and loneliness to breaking point in the months between them, of informing her fears (it was impossible not to discover a good deal of the horrors and hazards of convoy work in the North Atlantic and that was Clifford's life), it pounced again. He never saw his daughter: he never even *saw* her, she had used to reiterate – a straw of grievance which she clung to for months because even some kind of grievance seemed to help a bit – with the days, at least. So, like thousands of women and hundreds who had been deeply in love, she settled down to the problems of bringing up two children without their father or enough money ... When they were up, and before, she hoped, they had begun to think of her as a responsibility, she had married again.

Reminiscence was not thought: it couldn't be, because it was so easy. Another interesting point the interesting man had made was that anything worthwhile was difficult; he had not actually said that if you stumbled upon some natural talent, the talent would turn out to be inferior or unnecessary, but she suspected, in her own case, at least, that this was probably so. Obedience to natural laws, he had said, was essential, *if only you could find out what they were.* Obedience and your own talents turning out to be no good had a ring of truth about it: the people who ran institutions seemed always primarily concerned with the dangers of spiritual/temporal pride in their subjects; look at nuns and the Foreign Office ...

'Oh madam! Whatever are you doing in here on a day like this!' It was Oliver doing his imitation of the horrible housekeeper who had ruled the colonel's life until May had come into it.

'I'll do it,' he continued, looking into the bowl; 'you haven't got enough there to keep a lovesick Pekinese – let alone those two great witless sods in the kennels. Give me another tin of what's-his-name and go and be gracious somewhere.'

'Thank you darling. Have you seen Alice?'

'No. Should I have?'

'I just wondered if she was all right.'

'Why don't you go and see, then? It'd be a kindness: that

ghastly Rosemary's been at her, and guess what she's up to now?'

May shook her head as she struggled out of the macintosh.

'She's made Liz iron Alice's veil. Came to her and said she couldn't find any of the servants to do it. "There aren't any, my dear," I said. "What, in a great house like this!" she said. (Christ, this stuff smells like Portuguese lavatories!) "There's Mrs Green who does for us three times a week, but she's sulking because of the caterers so she's not doing for us today." So then she went mincing off to Liz who says that ironing is dangerous because her dress is too tight under the arms. She really does look awful in it, but she's ironing just the same. We may not have servants, I told Rosemary, but the house is fraught with splendid little women. Rosemary said something about Alice being a bit weepy.'

May looked concerned : 'I'll go and see her. Where's –'

'My stepfather is bullying the caterers. You look much less awful than Liz, I must say. Who *usually* does this filthy job?'

'Alice used to. From now on it'll be me.'

'Make Daddo do it.'

'Oliver – don't call him that. Just for today. It upsets him. He's afraid you're laughing at him.'

'His fears are absolutely grounded, *I'm* afraid.' Then he looked at her again and said, 'You know what I think?' He had lit two cigarettes and put one in her mouth. 'I think you should get out. After two years of this you must know it can only get worse.'

'Please darling, shut up.'

'Right. Sorry. I just want you to know,' he added in a quavering manner, 'that vulgar and pretentious though it is, you can always make your home with me.'

'Good,' she said in a more comfortable voice, and went.

•

Herbert Browne-Lacey, May's husband, Alice's father and the stepfather of Oliver and Elizabeth, had given up the caterers in despair (the fellows didn't seem to understand a word he said to them, as though he was talking Dutch or Hindi) and was now stalking up and down the side of the lawn which was banked by rhododendrons beginning to flower. He was in full morning dress and walked slowly, holding his grey top hat behind his back in both hands: the wind was very uncertain. His feelings were sharply divided: naturally any father would feel so at the marriage of his only daughter. He was glad that she was getting married in some ways, and sorry in others. He would miss her; he thought of innumerable things: the way she made his middle-morning beef tea; her ironing the newspaper if May got hold of it first (women were the devil with newspapers and it was absolutely unnecessary for them to read them anyway), how good she was with the dogs (the long, wet walks, kennel-cleaning and feeding), her housewifely activities (the house had twenty-five rooms but Alice had helped to make it possible to do with the one char), and as for boots and the odd medal (he touched his left breast and there was a reassuring clink), why, she was jolly nearly up to his old batman's standards. Of course she was marrying a prosperous, steady young man. Leslie Mount was clearly going far; the only thing that worried the colonel was whether he had a sense of direction. Money wasn't everything ... He began to think about money. The wedding was costing far more than he had meant it to: on the other hand, he would no longer be responsible for Alice. When he had told Leslie that Alice was worth her weight in gold he had felt that he was simply being appropriately sentimental: now, he began to wonder whether there wasn't some truth in the remark. May, bless her, of course, was so confoundedly unworldly: not always impractical – she made damn good curries of left-overs, not hot enough, but damn good – but she had her head in the clouds too much of the time to recognize the value of money. She did things and bought things quite often that were totally unnecessary. Totally unnecessary, he repeated, working himself into one of his minor righteous rages. And those children of hers were totally out of hand. *They* were responsible for her worst extravagances: it would have been much better to put the boy into the army than to send him to a fiendishly expensive university, and as for the girl, what was the point of having her taught domestic science – again, at fiendish expense – if the result was simply that she sent all the housekeeping bills soaring with her fancy cooking? Money between husband and wife should be shared, in his opinion, and this meant that May had absolutely no right to squander that inheritance from her relative in Canada – an estimable old lady who had died about a year before the colonel had married May. He had forced her to buy this house with some of the money, because any fool could see that property was going to go up, but after that, he had got nowhere. She had insisted upon having her own bank account and cheque books, and could therefore scribble and fritter away any amount of capital without reference to himself. The only times when the colonel could contemplate being French – or something equally outlandish – were when he thought about the marriage laws: there was no nonsense about women being independent *there*. His rather protuberant and bright blue eyes blazed whenever he thought about the Married Woman's Property Act. Well at least he made her pay her share of the household accounts: she couldn't have it both ways. But the wedding presented difficulties. He had managed, by playing on Leslie's father's snobbery and patriotism, to wrest from him a certain share of the – in his view – totally unreasonable and iniquitous expenses of this jamboree. He was, after all, a gentleman, a soldier and he had served his country, and he had made these three points delicately clear to Mr Mount who was clearly no gentleman, but had the grace to recognize this fact, and who had been reduced to explaining and apologizing for his flat feet (a plebeian complaint if ever there was one, nobody at Sandhurst had ever had flat feet, by God!) which had precluded his serving his country in any way but building ordnance factories. There was a world of difference between that sort of job and being in Whitehall.

But the fact was that those factory-building fellows had made the money, and simple chaps like himself, fighting for their country, hadn't. Mr Mount had offered to pay half the cost of the reception, and the colonel had accepted this, because, after all, Alice *had* no relatives that they ever saw apart from himself, whereas the Mount contingent was positively pouring from

Bristol or wherever it was they came from, so Mr Mount paying half was really the least he could do. The border was looking very ragged. Alice hadn't seemed to put her heart into it these last months although he had pointed out again and again that if you wanted a decent herbaceous border you had to work hard on it in the spring. He sighed and his waistcoat creaked: he had had the suit twenty-six years after all – bought it to get married to Alice's mother, and although his tailor had adjusted it several times to accommodate the effects of time, no more adjustments were possible. Few men, however, could rely upon their figures when they were in their sixties as well as he could. The upkeep of this place was a terrible strain to him: it was so damn difficult to get anyone to do anything these days. He pulled a pleasant gold half-hunter out of his watch pocket – twenty to twelve – must be getting a move on. The watch had been left to Alice by her godfather, but it was no earthly use to a girl ... He turned towards the house and began shouting for his wife.

•

The church was Victorian neo-gothic: varnished oak, brass plaques and candlesticks, atrocious windows the colours of patent medicines, soup, syrup and Sanatogen foisted upon the building by families who had feared society considerably more than they can ever have feared God; hassocks like small dark-red ambushes lurked awkwardly on the cold stone floor; battered prayer books slid about the pew desks, and tired little musty draughts met the guests as they were ushered in. The organ, whose range seemed to be between petulance and exhaustion, kept up the semblance of holy joy about as much as a businessman wearing a paper hat at a party pretends to be a child. Even the beautiful white lilac and iris could not combat the discomforting ugliness of the place. 'Poor God,' thought May. 'If He is really present here, and many places like this, it must be like being a kind of international M.P. A hideous place with boring people not meaning what they say, except when they come to some private grievance.'

The organ came to an end, took an audibly bronchial breath

and began on what was recognizably some Bach. Alice had entered the church on her father's arm, followed by Rosemary and Elizabeth. Heads turned and turned back to the chancel steps where the vicar stood waiting for them. 'He's a wonderful looking man,' thought Gertie Mount wistfully. A kind of cross between William Powell and Sir Aubrey Smith, she decided, as the colonel glided past her and came to a majestic halt and Leslie materialized out of the gloom beside his bride. Alice handed her bouquet to Rosemary, who received it with operatic humility, and the marriage service began. Mr Mount, whose clothes seemed to him to be slowly strangling him at all key points, glanced surreptitiously at the wife. She might start at any moment, but he had a nice big clean one handy: he groped in his right-hand trouser pocket, forgot about his morning coat and dropped his prayer book. He stooped to retrieve it, but the pews were so narrow that he hit his bottom – a hard but springy blow – on the edge of the seat. This had the effect of knocking him forwards, his jaw came in contact with the pew desk and his false teeth gave an ominous lurch. He now seemed to be wedged, and was only rescued by his teenage daughter, Sandra, who hauled him to his feet and handed him her prayer book with a minutely crushing smile. She was, in his opinion, well on the way to becoming over-educated, and terrified him. He turned to Gertie for comfort: she'd begun, and he felt (more warily) for the hanky.

The vicar was asking the couple if they knew any impediment to their marriage. His voice and manner, Oliver thought, gave one the feeling that he could not possibly be real – might at any moment, in a Lewis Carroll manner, turn into a sheep or a lesser playing card: that would be an impediment, all right. He didn't believe in marriage himself.

Leslie was looking forward to the bit where he had his say, which he had practised privately on a corner of the golf course at home. So keen was he about getting on with the job that he interrupted the vicar after the first question and said 'I will' with immense resolution, but the vicar was accustomed to amateurs and simply raised his voice a semi-tone. Leslie's final asseveration was far more subdued. 'Will *what*?' muttered his

Great-Aunt Lottie peevishy. She seldom had what Mrs Mount called a grip on things, and Mrs Mount had been against bringing her all this way, but Mr Mount had said that it would be an outing for her. Gertie felt in her bag for the tin of Allenbury's Blackcurrant Pastilles, and nearly ruined her glove getting one out and thrusting it into Auntie's mumbling hairy jaws.

The colonel waited until the padre had asked the question that usually applied to fathers, nodded briskly and stepped smartly back to the front pew beside May. His actions, to Gertie, showed that of course he had the proper respect, but he was a plain man with no nonsense about him. She was sure he had a heart of gold.

'Going, going, gone!' thought Alice wildly. Leslie's hand was soft and dry, her own, damp and icy. Enunciating with care, he was plighting his troth: it did not sound like his usual voice, but then these were not things that people usually said to each other. In a moment it was going to be her turn ...

'I *hope* she's secretly terrifically in love,' thought Elizabeth hopelessly as she listened to Alice's clear, unexpectedly childish tones repeating her share of the phrases after the vicar. But how could you be, with Leslie?

'With my body I thee worship,' Sandra repeated derisively to herself: the whole thing was unbelievably old-fashioned. *She* would get married in a registry office or America or a ship, in white leather, and go away in a helicopter. And she certainly wouldn't marry anyone as old as Leslie.

Rosemary watched the ring being put on Alice's finger and felt a lump in her throat: a lot of her men friends had said she was too emotional, but there it was. *She* felt like crying, and those two, standing there, seemed quite unmoved: that was British phlegm for you. If *she* had been standing where Alice was, her eyes would be full of great, unshed tears.

The vicar, gathering speed, was pronouncing them man and wife. He's like an old horse, Oliver thought, on the last lap to the stable, or, in this case, the registry. His stomach was rumbling uncontrollably and he had the nasty feeling that it was just the sort of sound most suited to the acoustics of this church.

End of the first lap, thought the colonel, rising to his feet. He had managed, during the service, to count the guests – roughly, anyway – and on the whole he felt he had been sensible to put away two of the cold salmon trout that the caterers had been laying out. Those fellows always produced too much food because then they could charge you for it. So he had simply taken away two of the dishes and put them in the larder ...

Where Claude, who never had very much to do in the mornings, smelt it. He had known for ages how to open the larder door, but had not advertised the fact, largely because there was hardly ever anything there worth eating; but he was extremely fond of fish. He inserted a huge capable paw round the lower edge of the door and heaved for several minutes: when the gap was wide enough he levered it open with his shoulder and part of his head. The fish lay on a silver platter on the marble shelf, skinned and garnished. He knocked pieces of lemon and cucumber contemptuously aside, settled himself into his best eating position and began to feast. He tried both fish – equally delicious – and when he could eat no more, he jumped heavily off the shelf with a prawn in his mouth which he took to the scullery for further examination.

2. Flight

Elizabeth, back into her comfortable blue jeans and one of Oliver's old shirts, had taken the two salmon trout from the larder and laid them on the vast kitchen table. Her assignment was to patch up one of the fish for supper, so that the colonel need never know of Claude's depredations. Alice, before she had left, had begged both Elizabeth and May to look after him; of course they had both promised, and Alice was scarcely out of sight before May discovered the larder crime.

Taking pieces from one fish and transposing them to another was like a frightful jigsaw with none of the pieces ready made. On top of this, the fish had been overcooked so that the flakes broke whenever she tried to wedge them into position. 'I'll have to cover the whole lot with mayonnaise,' she thought despairingly. Well – at least she knew how to make good mayonnaise: at *least* she knew that.

'Isn't it nasty having the whole house to ourselves?'

It was only Oliver.

'How do you mean?'

'I mean that anywhere as large and hideous *and* otherwise undistinguished as this is only bearable when it's heavily populated.' He sat on the kitchen table. 'It must have been built by someone who made a packet out of shells or gas masks in the First World War. Do you know what the first gas masks were made of?'

'Of course I don't. What?'

'Pieces of Harris tweed soaked in something or other, with bits of tape to tie round the back of the head. What fascinates me about that is that it should have been *Harris* tweed: so hairy – a kind of counter-irritant.'

A minute later, he said,

'Listen, ducks, what are you going to do?'

Elizabeth had been separating two eggs into pudding basins.

'How do you mean?'

'Don't be so *stupid*, Liz.'

'I'm *not* being stupid – I just don't know what you mean.' She seized a gin bottle filled with olive oil.

'I said: what are you going to *do*?'

'Make mayonnaise.' She selected a fork and began to beat the eggs: her eyes were pricking. 'That's one thing I *can* do.' The feeling that she was dull, and that Oliver, whom she loved, was brilliant and would therefore suddenly realize this one day and abandon her, recurred for what seemed like the millionth time. How did he *know* about First-World-War gas masks? she thought. Why didn't she know anything surprising like that?

'I'll pour – you beat.' She wasn't very bright, but from her first moments, May had, so to speak, let him in on looking after her. She wasn't very bright, and needed him.

'You're not stupid,' he said, taking the oil bottle. 'Goodness me, how weddings make women cry. Cheer up: think of spending a fortnight in Cornwall with Leslie.'

She smiled: she would have giggled if she'd felt better.

'A pink chiffon nightdress and all the lights out and twin beds.'

'He's taken his golf clubs,' she said, entering the game.

'They can't talk about what they did last week, because they didn't have one.'

'They can discuss the wedding. To tide them over.'

'He can tell her about his future: and how he can't stand dishonesty – he's funny that way – but he's all for plain speaking. That cuts down nearly anyone's conversation.'

'But on honeymoons,' said Elizabeth hesitantly, 'don't you spend a lot of time making love to the person?'

'That's a frightfully old-fashioned way of putting it. Besides, golf takes much longer: if he plays two rounds a day, he won't have all that time.'

'Steady: don't put any more in till I tell you.'

'What happens if I put in too much?'

'It separates and I have to start all over again with another yolk.'

'Listen: what I meant just now was, you don't want to just stay here, do you?'

'I mean, there's a serious danger that Daddo will just push you into being another Alice,' he went on when she didn't reply.

'I know.'

'We can't have *you* escaping to Southport or Ostend in five years' time for a gay fortnight with a girl friend and meeting someone like Leslie: if you had to choose between dog kennels and Daddo or the equivalent of Leslie you might easily choose Leslie. Seriously, Liz, you'd be better off in London.'

'Where?'

'With me.'

She flushed with delight. 'Oh – Oliver!'

'We'll live on our wits – Edwardian for sharp practice.'

'How would we?'

'My wits then,' he said with careless affection. 'Awful people are always offering me jobs.'

'Aren't you *in* a job?'

'The accountants' office? Honestly, Liz, I couldn't stand it. I left last week.'

'Does May know?'

'*She* knows, but *he* doesn't. We've agreed not to tell him. He'd think I was going to the dogs more than ever. It's funny how keen he is on girls going to *his* blasted dogs, when he can't stand young whipper-snappers like *me* going to them.'

'What are you going to *do*?'

'I don't know: that's what's so nice. After all those years of educational regimentation I want a breather. I shall probably marry an heiress,' he added carelessly.

'You mightn't love her. I mean – you couldn't just marry her because of that.'

'Oh, couldn't I! Well – until we find her – we could always advertise as an unmarried couple willing to wash up, or something like that.'

There was a pause while she beat industriously (the sauce was now the colour of Devonshire cream) and wondered what she ought to do. Then she said, 'It's all right now: pour a thin, steady stream.'

He said, 'I know what's the trouble. You're worrying about May.'

She hadn't been, she'd started to imagine life in London with Oliver: concerts, cinemas, cooking up delicious suppers for his friends, all charming, funny, *brilliant* people like Oliver – people he'd met at Oxford ... 'Don't go: Elizabeth will you knock up something to eat?' 'I say, Elizabeth, is this what you call knocking something up? It's fabulous!' (no, wrong word – a bit cheap and unintellectual) 'It's the best pasta I've ever eaten in my life' ...

But she'd been going to end up thinking about May: May stuck here for the rest of her life, in this awful red-brick fumed-oak stained-glass barracks – every room looking like a Hall on Speech Day – even the garden filled with the worst things like rhododendrons, laurels, standard roses with grotesque flowers, hedges of cupressus, a copper beech and a monkey puzzle, cotoneaster and an art nouveau sundial; all this instead of the cosy little house in Lincoln Street where they had lived the moment Great-Aunt Edith had kicked the bucket in Montreal ... Aloud, she said, 'It's not just the house: it's *him*.'

'Daddo?'

She nodded. 'He gives me the creeps. He ought just to be poor and funny, but he isn't.'

'Well he *is* funny: he's a pompous old fool.'

'You're not a woman: you wouldn't understand.'

There was enough mayonnaise; she seasoned it and began spreading it over the fish with a palette knife.

'If she's lonely enough, she might leave him. If you stay here, she never will.'

'I could come back for week-ends,' she said anxiously.

He pushed his hand through her silky brown hair.

'I'm not my sister's keeper.'

'What are you *doing*?'

'Getting the oil off my hands.'

The next conversation about Elizabeth's future was at dinner.

*

The dining-room was, of course, large; a rectangular room

whose ceiling was too high for its other dimensions. A red-and-blue Turkey carpet very nearly reached the caramel-coloured parquet surround. The colonel had bought the carpet, together with a gigantic Victorian sideboard, a stained oak pseudo-Jacobean table and eight supremely uncomfortable and rickety chairs, in a local sale. The windows were also large, but so heavily leaded that they gave the room the air of a rather liberal prison: the top of the centre one was embellished in a key pattern of blue and red stained glass. There were four immense pictures (also bought by the colonel in another sale): one of a dead hare bleeding beside a bunch of grapes on a table; a huge upright of a Highland stag standing on some heather; a brace of moony spaniels with pheasants in their mouths; and a rather ambitious one of a salmon leaping a weir. These were hung upon panelling of highly varnished pitch pine: they were not glazed, and so, as Oliver said, wherever you sat at table there was no way of escaping at least one of them. It was twenty-five to eight, and the colonel was doling out sparse portions of the salmon trout. 'What's all this?' he said when he saw the mayonnaise.

Oliver answered immediately, 'It is a sauce made of egg yolks and olive oil and flavoured with black pepper and vinegar called mayonnaise. It was invented by a French general's chef at the siege of Mahon – hence its name; how *interesting* that you should never have encountered it before.'

The colonel put down his servers and glared steadily at his stepson.

May said, 'Herbert didn't mean that, did you dear? He meant –'

'What's it doing *here*?' finished Oliver. 'Ah, well Liz made it, with a bit of help from me. We thought you'd like a sauce with a military background.'

There was an incompatible silence while the colonel served the fish and handed plates to May for new potatoes and peas. Then he said, 'I'm all for plain English cooking, myself.'

May shot a reproachful glance at Oliver which he did not miss, and said, 'Anyway, these are the first of our own peas.'

The colonel stabbed one with his fork. 'Far too small: Hoggett is always premature. If I've told him once, I've told him a hundred times –'

'They taste delicious,' said Elizabeth. (I can't *bear* this: meal after meal of trying to make things right – of keeping them dull so that they won't go wrong.)

'Are these our own potatoes?' asked Oliver politely.

'We don't grow enough potatoes to have new ones,' said Elizabeth quickly. Oliver knew perfectly well that one of the colonel's petty tyrannies was to force an arthritic old gardener to go through the motions of keeping up an enormous kitchen garden. This meant that the colonel resented bought vegetables and prohibited the use of their own until they were so old as to be almost uneatable. He *knew* that, so why didn't he shut up? She glared at him, and his grey eyes immediately fixed upon hers with an empty innocent stare.

'. . hope Alice was pleased, anyway,' May was saying to her husband.

'Tremendous palaver – just to get a girl married: still it all went off quite smoothly. The Mounts seemed impressed with the house.'

'I'm not surprised,' said Oliver.

The colonel took his napkin out of a cracked and yellowing ivory ring, wiped a moustache of much the same colour and turned to Oliver.

'Oh. And why, may I ask, are you not surprised?'

'I only meant that as they are in the building business, they would, so to speak, look at it with a professional eye. It must have cost a packet to build – even in nineteen-twenty.'

Elizabeth was stacking the plates which she then carried to the sideboard, where waited a trifle, left by the caterers. She brought this, placed it doubtfully in front of her mother, and went for clean plates. The colonel had decided to accept Oliver's speech about the house at face value, and so he had merely grunted. Now he said, 'Ah! Trifle!'

There was a silence while they all looked at the trifle. 'Caterers' Revenge,' thought Elizabeth, as her mother began gingerly spooning it on to the plates. She knew what it would be like. Sponge cake made of dried egg smeared with the kind of raspberry jam where the very pips seem to be made of wood, smothered in packet custard laced with sherry flavouring. The top was embellished with angelica, mock cream and crystallized violets whose dye was bleeding carbon-paper mauve on to the cream.

'A classic example of plain English cooking,' said Oliver smoothly.

'When is he going to *leave*?' thought the colonel. 'Insufferable beggar.'

'What time is your train, Oliver?'

He looked at his mother and felt reproved. 'The last one is ten thirty-eight.' He cleared his throat, feeling suddenly nervous – something of a traitor. 'Liz and I thought – I wondered whether it might not be a good thing for her to come up with me for a bit. Look around, and perhaps get herself a job.'

May was clearly taken aback, but she managed to look calmly at her daughter, and asked – really wanting to know, 'What do you think, darling? Would you like to go to London?'

'I think I might quite like to.' Her eyes were on her mother's face; she frightfully wanted to find out what May really felt, but now, with Oliver doing it all so treacherously in front of him, she was afraid she wouldn't find out. May might awfully mind her going away, and not be able to say so. 'It would be leaving you with rather a lot.'

'Nonsense.' Even the colonel had found the trifle heavy going, and was again wiping his moustache. 'You must stop treating your mother as though she is a chronic invalid: she's perfectly capable of looking after herself. And on those few occasions when she is not, what am I for? Eh?' He glared round the table, looking, Oliver thought, about as jocular and useless as the Metro-Goldwyn-Mayer lion.

'Is there room in the flat at Lincoln Street?' May, who had given herself hardly any trifle, now stopped pretending to eat it.

'She can have the second-best bedroom and a fair share of all mod. cons. She can look after me when I get home exhausted from work: very good practice for both of us.'

May opened her mouth and shut it again.

The colonel took a tin of Dutch cigars from one of his capacious pockets, opened it, and offered one to Oliver. There were – as usual – two in the tin. Oliver refused. The colonel, pleased about this, lit one for himself, and said, 'Ah – the office. And how is the job, Oliver? Going well, I trust?'

Oliver said, 'As well as can be expected.'

'I could come home for week-ends.' Elizabeth was the kind of girl who blushed if other people told lies, and deflection was her form of apology.

'There comes a time,' the colonel said, 'when all young people have to leave the nest and try their wings.'

'Well, that's settled, then.' Oliver got up from the table. 'Liz joins the chicks in Chelsea. If you'll excuse me, I must go and pack. What about you, Liz?'

'Are you going to*night* darling?'

Elizabeth halted in her tracks: if only Oliver hadn't done all this at dinner; if only she could have *talked* to her mother; if only she didn't feel so guilty about wanting to go so badly ... But May got briskly to her feet and said,

'In that case, I had better come and help you pack.'

The colonel was left in the dining-room alone. He took a second tin of cigars from another pocket, extracted one, and put it in the first tin. It would be a relief to get rid of both young Seymours: have May to himself: with Alice gone, it was better to have May to himself.

*

Barely three hours later, Elizabeth sat opposite Oliver in the train. Most of the reading lights in the compartment did not work, but in any case, she did not want to read. Oliver had gone to sleep: she stared without seeing anything out of the dirty window and tried to think, but she was feeling so much that it was very difficult. Escape was the first thing she felt: a sense of freedom, but funnily, of *safety* as well; as though she had been locked up or ill-used – like girls in ordinary Victorian novels, and detective or spy stories since. Why? Nobody had ever been unkind to her; it was her fault that she could not feel at ease with her stepfather who had only ever been dull, pompous, and *obvious* really with her. Too like himself to be true — something like that. Before she had met him, she had thought that what people said about Colonel Blimp and ex-army men, particularly those who had served in India, was a sort of coarse shorthand to save them having to know or describe anybody. She couldn't think that now. It was almost as though he was a jolly good character actor toeing the popular line. Perhaps it was the house that was so ugly and nasty as to be sinister. May had said when she married him, 'He's not meant to be your father, darling, because you had a perfectly good one; he's just meant to be my husband: it would be stupid of me to try and provide you with a new father at your age. Of course I hope you like him, but you needn't feel you've got to.' But how could she — how *could* she ever have thought that she would be happy with him? And in that house? She had bought it because he wanted it. The moment she had married, Elizabeth had realized how much she was meant to be married to somebody; she wasn't at all the kind of woman to manage life on her own. And just when Oliver and she might have started looking after *her* for a change, she'd made it impossible for them. Their family life had become a kind of conspiracy; jokes, habits, any kind of fun or thinking things awful had become furtive and uncomfortable. Apart from the blissful feeling of escape (and as she was so selfish she couldn't help feeling that), she felt really worried about May. While Alice had been there, she had provided a kind of buffer for all of them. Alice was used to her father; she had become devoted to May, she had never stopped doing things for other people, or at least for her father, which stopped other people having to do them for him.

She had never got to know Alice: they had always been so anxiously, fumblingly *nice* to each other, had early set such a high standard of you-through-the-swing-doors-first courtesy that neither had never found out what the other really liked or wanted. Alice had once shown her some poetry — short, rhyming verses about nature going on whatever she was feeling: they were very dull, imbued with a kind of sugary discontent; nature-was-pretty-and-Alice-was-sad stuff. She had read them very slowly to look as though she cared, and said they were jolly good in a hushed voice to show that words were inadequate to express her feelings. And Alice had said how bad they were very fast a good many times, laughing casually and getting very pink. But really the poems, which Elizabeth could see had been meant to be a confidence, had simply put another barrier of nervous dishonesty between them. Practically their only point of contact had been Claude. She had found Alice, changed into her new pale-blue going-away suit, with Claude overflowing in her arms: Alice was crying and Claude was licking his lips and staring hopefully at the floor so perhaps they were *both* minding. Elizabeth had promised to be nice to him, and now, except for concealing the larder crime, here she was escaping. At least if I'm not famous for being intelligent, I ought to concentrate on being reliable and nice. But she had a feeling that people's natures just went on regardless of their talents; you weren't any nicer because you were stupid. Oliver, except for his dastardly behaviour to Herbert (she called him Herbert to herself and nothing to his face), was just as *nice* as she was, and although she didn't always agree with him he was far more interesting because he knew so much and could talk about it. She had tried reading books about *things*, like soil erosion and monotremes and the Moorish influence in Spain, but none of these subjects ever seemed to fit into day-to-day conversation. She had tried asking May what she ought to do about this (just after she failed Oxford and before the domestic science school), but May had said most unhelpfully that hardly anybody she knew thought. Oliver did, she retorted; he was brilliantly clever – a Second and he hardly seemed to work at all! But May had just said, 'Yes darling, I expect he is' rather absently, like someone agreeing with a boring question so that they could stop talking about it. Much though she adored her mother, Elizabeth had wondered then whether it was because she was a bit old-fashioned *and* a woman (a pretty hopeless combination when you came to consider it) that made her not set the store by intelligence that she should. She wouldn't have married Herbert if she'd cared about an intellectual life. She certainly hadn't married him for money, and at her age sex appeal was out of the question – so what was it? It was like being stuck with someone for ever who said at least one awful, obvious thing a day, like a calendar where you tore off Tuesday but couldn't help reading what it said. The most outstanding feature of her mother was how nice she was to absolutely everybody, so possibly she regarded Herbert as a challenge; perhaps, also, she was the only person who could see that secretly, deep down, Herbert was a very good man. Dull people often were, unless that was what their friends said about them to make up for their dullness. I do hope I get less dull, she thought. Living with Oliver ought to help that. She looked at him. He lay, or lounged, opposite her, legs crossed so that she could see a blue vein between his socks and his trousers. His head was thrown back, his eyes shut, a lock of his pale-brown hair was lying over his bulging forehead. Even asleep, he managed to look plunged in thought. He was wearing a very old but nice tweed suit that had belonged to their father: his only civvy suit, May had said, so he had got a good one – to last. He had lovely eyelashes that curled upwards very thickly: he said girls always remarked on them. She supposed she would be meeting his girls at Lincoln Street. I can always go home at week-ends to keep out of his way, she thought; I'll be terrifically tactful and not surprised at anything. Anyway, I *should* go home: I would hate her to feel abandoned. She started to think of her mother carrying the heavy supper trays from the dining-room all along the passage – two baize doors that were meant to stay open but never did – to the kitchen. And then doing all the things that had to be done before anybody could have an evening there, let alone go to bed. Usually Alice and she had done a good deal of it; mostly Alice, she admitted honestly. Putting all the horrible food away so that they were certain to be faced with the left-overs next day, feeding Claude, turning out lights and getting more coal for the fire in the colonel's den (wouldn't you know he'd call it that) where they sat in the evening. There was only one really comfortable chair, and you bet, he took it. Filling hot-water bottles, turning down the beds, drawing bedroom curtains: Herbert liked everything to go on as though there was a large resident staff: oh lord, and now it was just

May to be that ... She shouldn't have come or gone or whatever she'd done ...

Oliver opened his eyes.

'Dearest Liz. You look as though you've got indigestion; remorse, I bet. Cheer up. It was all my fault: that's why I did it at dinner. If we'd given them too much notice, I was afraid of Daddo working on May to stop you: he's going to wake up tomorrow and kick himself for letting all that free labour go. Cheer up: think of spending two weeks in Cornwall with Leslie.'

'I have. I am.'

They smiled at each other; then she laughed.

*

Leslie had just said, 'Excuse me, dear', and gone to the magnificent peach-tiled bathroom that was part of their suite. A bedroom and the sitting-room – where they were now sitting – was the rest of it. They had arrived at the hotel rather late for dinner in the dining-room, and so Leslie had ordered supper in their suite. The head waiter had been able to let them have consommé – hot or cold – cold chicken and mixed salad, pêche melba and cheese. Leslie had ordered a bottle of sparkling burgundy with this repast, and brandy and crème-de-menthe afterwards. (Alice had had hot consommé and crème-de-menthe, Leslie had had three brandies – he had told the waiter to leave the bottle when he had brought the weak but bitter coffee.) Hours seemed to have gone by since then, and they were still sitting at the small round table with the pink-silk-shaded lamp on it. At the beginning of the meal they had not said much: each of them had made a few desultory remarks about the wedding which the other had instantly agreed with. But when his second brandy was inside him, Leslie had become more expansive. He thought the time had come for a little plain speaking. He was funny that way, but he couldn't stand dishonesty. He looked at her for approbation of this curious and unusual trait. Alice looked seriously back.

'What I want you to know,' Leslie went on, 'is – well it's a bit difficult to put it in the right way. I'm forty-two as I think I told you –'

'Yes.'

'Well – it wouldn't be reasonable to expect me to be completely inexperienced at my age – now would it?'

'No.'

'I'm not – you see. Not at all inexperienced: quite the reverse – you might say. I've been – intimate – with quite a number of women. I've never known them *well*,' he added hastily, 'you understand what I mean, don't you Alice?'

'Yes.'

'I mean, naturally, they weren't the sort of women you'd expect me to have known well. That wasn't their function if you take me. But it *does* mean that I know a good deal about a certain side of life. That's necessary for men. For women – of course – it's different. I don't suppose – well I wouldn't expect you to know anything at all about that.' He finished his brandy and looked at her expectantly.

'No.'

'Of course not.' He seemed at once to be both uplifted and disheartened by this. 'But naturally I've got about a good deal. The war – Belgium – you get all kinds of women there –' He poured some more brandy: his forehead was gleaming. He started to tell her about Belgian women ...

*

By the time May had cleared up the supper, wedged the larder door so that Claude could not possibly open it, opened him a tin of cat food that, naturally enough, he did not feel inclined to eat although he had made it plain that he was unable to be certain about this until the food was on his soup plate, put on a kettle for hot-water bottles (the house was never really warm and May felt that she got colder there week by week), turned off some passage lights that her children had left on, and conducted a tired and abortive hunt for her spectacles, all she wanted to do was to go to bed. But Herbert, she knew, would be waiting for her. Usually Alice had played backgammon with him after dinner while she pretended to do *The Times* crossword puzzle or got on with her patchwork, but from now on there was no Alice, and Herbert needed her company. Perhaps they could just have a cosy post mortem on the wedding, which now seemed an age away.

The colonel stood with his back to the small coal fire and was gazing reproachfully at the door through which she came.

'What on *earth* have you been doing?'

'Just clearing up supper.'

'Why don't you leave that sort of thing for Mrs what's-her-name?'

May cast herself into the one comfortable chair. 'She may not come tomorrow. Tomorrow isn't her day.'

'She didn't come today, did she?'

'No. Today was supposed to be her day, but she wouldn't come because of the caterers. In any case there is far too much for her to do.'

The colonel grunted. 'The woman's getting above herself. Why don't you fire her, and get somebody else?'

May kicked off her shoes. 'Because there isn't anybody else. Who would come, I mean. We're not on a bus route, so it means nearly two miles walking or on a bicycle. People won't do that nowadays. We've plenty of room: we ought to have somebody living in – a couple.'

The colonel looked wounded: then he stalked slowly over to his filing cabinet, took an immense bunch of keys from a pocket made shapeless by them and unlocked a drawer. He was going to mix his nightcap: a small whisky and soda. They both spoke at once. Then the colonel said, 'I beg your pardon, my dear. What did you say?'

'Just that I thought I'd like a whisky tonight: a small one.'

She knew that he had strong views about what women should, or should not, drink: he particularly disliked her drinking whisky.

'Are you *sure?*' He surveyed her with as broad-minded disapproval as he could muster.

'Just tonight, darling. It's been such a day.'

He mixed her a small weak drink in silence, handed it to her, made himself one, looked disparagingly at the bottle which was only about a quarter full, put it away and locked up the cabinet. All this seemed to take a very long time, and May resisted the impulse to gulp her drink. Then, when the colonel had made his way, as it were, blindly to her chair, discovered that she was in it, and remained standing (it was *his* chair she was lounging in, and nothing else would do), he said, 'You must realize, my dear, that we cannot possibly afford a couple living in. The expenses of this house are – ah – stretched to their fullest extent; their fullest extent. A couple would land us with heavy expenses that with the best will in the world they could not justify.'

'Perhaps we ought to sell the house then, and find something smaller.' She had finished her whisky, and now wanted a cigarette, but as she only had ten a week and had already smoked two that day she knew there were none left.

'My dear May! You surely cannot mean what you say!'

'Well I did – actually.'

'Part with our *home*!'

'Only to get another one, dear.'

'You speak as though homes are a mere matter of exchange and barter.'

'Well they are really, aren't they? I mean, we bought this one.'

The colonel sat suddenly down on quite an uncomfortable chair. He was speechless, absolutely speechless, he repeated to himself. To justify this situation, he said nothing, he simply stared at her.

'Darling, don't look so appalled! It just seemed to me that with Alice gone, and my two in London, perhaps we don't need all these rooms' – she pretended to count – 'what is it? Nine bedrooms we aren't using.'

As he still kept silent, she added, 'Not counting all the other rooms.'

He perceptibly found his voice. 'My dear May, this house was an absolute bargain – dirt cheap – an absolute bargain –'

'Goodness,' May thought as she stopped listening, 'you couldn't call it that. Or perhaps I've been poor too many years to think that spending eleven thousand pounds on *anything* would be a bargain. *My* eleven thousand pounds,' she also thought, and then felt thoroughly ashamed of herself . . .

'. . . simple chap,' the colonel was saying, 'can't be said to have expensive tastes – moderation in all things – but all my life – serving my country and all that – *all* my life, I've looked forward to settling down – in a simple way – my one piece of land – a comfortable home – somewhere that I can call my own – chopping and changing difficult for a feller my age –'

The upshot of what, at their time of life, amounted to a scene was that she was forced to recognize what he said the house meant to him. Her private dream of a cottage in the country and the half of Lincoln Street that was now let being their homes vanished for ever that evening. If she would leave the management of the house to him – not upset her head about it – *he* would keep the whole thing within bounds of their income. She thought at one moment that he was trying to get her to sell the London house (because Oliver and now Elizabeth were to live in it rent free) but, strangely, he seemed most anxious that she should keep it. What it was necessary to review, he said, was their remaining free capital. Here she sensed danger : she did not want to have to discuss Elizabeth's allowance or anything that she gave Oliver with him, or indeed with anyone. She was awfully tired, she said at this point. They would both be the better for a spot of Bedfordshire, he said. But the most incongruous aspect of the whole argument or discussion or whatever one could call it was that he had been really upset; eyes moist, stuttering slightly, repeating phrases more than usual : she honestly hadn't realized that this house meant so much to him. He said, too, that he wanted to be alone with her – to have her to himself. She did not trust him enough about things : if she would leave it all to him everything would work out. He had blown his nose for a long time on one of the handkerchiefs she had given him for his birthday and this had touched her much more than anything he had actually *said* (which had left her not so much unmoved as indefinably depressed). It was the house that depressed her, but now she would just have to make the best of it.

*

Elizabeth lay in the dark in bed in the tiny top-floor back bedroom at Lincoln Street. The room had no curtains, because May had sent them to the cleaners and Oliver hadn't bothered to put them up when they came back, so light from a street lamp patterned the ceiling and some of the walls. The bed was familiar and uncomfortable – she had had it as a child; indeed, for a short time – the blissful period after Aunt Edith died and before May married Herbert – this had been her room. Now the basement and ground floor were let and they only had the first and top floors. It was wonderful to be here – with Oliver. She wondered what *sort* of sharp practice he had in mind ...

*

Alice lay very still on her back in the dark. The twin bed beside her was empty. Leslie had passed out (there was no other word for it) in the sitting-room. After a time, she had lifted his legs – unbelievably heavy – on to the other end of the sofa from his head : it hadn't seemed to make any difference to him. He was clearly alive because his breathing was so noisy. She had stood looking down on him for a bit without thinking or feeling anything very much. Any fear or excitement that had lurked in wait for the end of this day had long since gone. By the time he had finished telling her how many women he had known, he had drunk nearly all the brandy. She had left the pink silk lamp lit in case he woke up and wondered where he was, and retired for the night. No problem about undressing, she had thought with bitter exhaustion. She wished one could stop being a virgin without noticing it ...

3. Marking Time

By the end of a week in Lincoln Street, Elizabeth was thankful that she had found some sort of job. Living with Oliver, though tremendously exciting, disconcerted her : it was like having a very exhausting holiday, or the last week in someone's life, or before they were going to be caught by the police, or one's birthday every day; really she didn't know *how* to describe it. To begin with nothing ever happened when she expected it to; meals, getting up, parties, conversations, all occurred with consistent irregularity. The first day had been lovely. They had got up very late and had boiled eggs and warm croissants that Oliver had fetched from a shop, and strong coffee and then a kipper each because she had found them in the fridge and they found that eating was making them hungrier; and Oliver had had two very intelligent conversations with friends on the telephone – one about Mozart and one about the Liberal Party. Then Oliver had said, 'How much money have you got?' and they had looked at her cheque book and it didn't say because she was bad about her counterfoils, so she had rung up and the bank said eleven pounds thirteen and fourpence. 'Oh well,' Oliver had said, 'we've no need to worry.' And he had stretched out his legs – he was wearing black espadrilles over purple socks. She had suggested that she should clean up the house, it was pretty awful, really, but he had said no, no; he was going to cut her hair and then they'd go to the cinema. He'd tied a tablecloth round her neck and cut her the most expert fringe. 'Now you look much more as though you're lying in wait. For something or other,' he added. They'd cashed a cheque for five pounds and gone to *Mondo Cane* in Tottenham Court Road – a simply extraordinary film, but Oliver laughed at it quite a lot.

Then they had walked to Soho, and Oliver had made her buy fresh ravioli and a pair of black fishnet tights.

'Why?' she had said both times. 'We might have a party in which case it would come in handy,' he said about the ravioli; and, 'I haven't been through your clothes yet, but whatever you've got will look better with tights.' Then it had begun to rain, and Oliver bundled her into a taxi. Awful extravagance. She mentioned then that she thought she ought to think about getting a job, and he stopped the cab and bought an *Evening Standard*. 'I'll look through it in the bath for you,' he had said.

While he was doing this, she set about the living-room. There was so much dust in it that everything *was* actually dust-coloured. The room had been painted entirely white, but the walls and woodwork were now, as Oliver had remarked, the colours of old cricket trousers. 'I take refuge in calling it *warm* white,' he had said : 'but really redecoration does so go with being pregnant or homosexual or in love, and my emotional life never seems to reach any such peak – just tidy it up, love. That chest of drawers is for tidying things into.' He had disappeared into the bathroom for about an hour and a half where she heard him having conversations on the telephone – a frightfully angry one about D. H. Lawrence and some much friendlier ones to people called Annabel and Sukie. She cleaned away – with a carpet sweeper that didn't really work, until she found that it was entwined and choked with fantastically long auburn hairs, and a duster that was so dirty she used one of her handkerchiefs.

The party had been a success in the end, but it took a long time to start. Sukie and Annabel arrived in a Mini each. Neither of them had auburn hair. They wore clothes like string vests and feather boas and striped plastic boots, so Elizabeth was glad about her tights. Apart from their striking appearance they seemed awfully intelligent and knew all Oliver's other friends and whom they were talking about. A lot of them had been to Oxford, and some of them had gone to Spain together – apart from innumerable parties like these where they all knew all the records they were playing – and she felt rather out of it. She tried to be helpful about the food and what drink there was. Sukie had brought a bottle of Scotch, and Annabel a nearly full bottle of Cointreau which a friend of Oliver's insisted on mixing with Coca-Cola and soda. 'It's absolutely *foul*, Sebastian.' But Oliver had said nonsense; all drinks were foul till you got used to them. Afterwards she found that Sebastian had mixed them up like that – with Oliver's approval – to make them last. The Gauloises ran out after the pubs had shut, but somebody produced some sort of sticky wodge in a cold-cream jar that he said was hashish, and one or two people tried a spot of that on Annabel's nail file. By then, everybody was very friendly and there was a competition to gauge what hashish was most like. Stuff from between tremendously wide floorboards, Elizabeth had thought aloud, and all the people who had said worse than school jam and scrapings off the lids of chutney bottles agreed with her, so warmly that she blushed with her sudden notoriety. Thereafter, whenever she had said anything, people stopped talking and listened kindly for another *mot*, but she never said anything else that was any good. Nothing seemed to happen to anyone as a result of the hashish, except for someone called Roland who was sick, but he said that that was something he had for lunch. By then they were drinking Maxwell House in the whisky-Cointreau-Coke glasses, the gramophone had been changed from jazz to Monteverdi which Oliver said could be played at a mutter (people had banged on the wall and finally rung up), and a – to her – incomprehensible, but frightfully interesting argument had broken out about the time-lag of influence that philosophers had upon politics and religion. Kiyckerkgard, Neecher, Marks, Plato (at least she'd heard of *him*) were being bandied about and words like subjective and relative were in constant use. It seemed generally agreed that it was all right for things to be relative, but not at all all right for them to be subjective. She noticed that nearly everyone could squash anyone else by calling them that. She felt terribly sleepy by then and was quite glad when Annabel said she must get out of her eyelashes they were weighing her down so, and they went upstairs. They stayed in Elizabeth's bedroom, talking about eye make-up and really good second-hand clothes' shops and what it would be like to marry an Asian or African, and Annabel said how much simpler everything would be if everybody was sort of fawn-coloured, but this would probably take a million years and *they* wouldn't live to see it; and it was very cosy being with Annabel in such eugenically difficult times ... Then Annabel told her about how frightful it had been being an au pair girl in Lyons, and they talked a bit about careers, and that was when Annabel told her about this marvellous new agency. 'You just go to them and say you want a job: it doesn't matter a bit if you think you can't do anything: *they* think of that. They specialize in being a last resort for people who want someone; they say their clients are so broken down by the lack of butlers and people to arrange flowers and do typing for them that they're glad to have *anyone*. I've been exercising a cheetah for the last ten days. Fifteen bob an hour – you can get danger money for exotics, so I never do dogs and any of that domestic jazz. Daddy doesn't mind what I do as long as I don't get overdrawn.'

By the time they joined the others Elizabeth felt that Annabel was almost certainly going to be her best friend.

The conversation had changed when they got back to what it would be like nowadays being a modern master-criminal. Pretty easy, most people seemed to think, but rather dull. That was one thing where a class structure was invaluable. Oliver said: the aristocracy of the underworld ought to steal huge sums of money from people like mad, but never hurt anyone. It would only be the working classes who hit old ladies over the head and took their handbags with pensions. He was instantly accused of being a ghastly snob by someone called Tom who was reading sociology. The conversation got boring again. She went to sleep.

She woke hours later, to find Oliver carrying her upstairs. He took off her clothes, wrapped her in his dressing-gown and levered her into bed. 'Your fringe is a wow.' Sleep again.

Next day Oliver was terribly gloomy. She knew that brilliant people were far more moody than the other kind, and made him a specially good brunch, but he wouldn't eat it. He said that the party had been kid's stuff, old ropes, a nasty little canapé de vieux: he was getting nowhere; he was damned if he wanted to be reduced to writing a novel at *his* age ...

'Is that what you were thinking of doing?'

'It's bound to cross the mind. If you don't *know* anything and can't write poetry or a decent play, there's not much left, is there?'

'I suppose not,' she said respectfully. She was sitting carefully on the end of his bed trying not to move her legs which people who were *in* bed always called kicking.

'I'm too old, really, anyway. I don't want to *be* a novelist, you see. Just to write one adolescent best-seller. You have to be under eighteen for that. Even you are too old.'

'Was the *Evening Standard* no good?'

'There was nothing in it for you. I wasn't looking for me. *The Times* is the one I look in for me. It's different for girls: you just need a job; I need a career.'

'What's the time?'

'Twenty past two. I would like something like being Churchill's private secretary: I seem to have missed everything. It's this damned narrow social life I lead. It's a pity May didn't have me taught to play the trumpet or to be a dentist or something obviously rewarding like that ...'

'Have a lovely hot bath.' She was beginning to know some things about him.

'Good idea. You run it. No cold – just hot: I'm practising for when I go to Japan.'

'I know what,' he said an hour and a half later. 'I say, you *have* made this room nice ...'

She was so pleased that she looked round it to notice what he had noticed; the *Encounters* all upright, which made them look distinguished instead of merely untidy, everything clean, or clea*n*er, and she had hung the curtains back from the cleaners since last December ...

'You haven't listened to a word I was saying!'

'Sorry!'

'I think the best thing is for me to marry a very rich girl – very rich indeed. Then my natural talents will have time to develop naturally. Also, have you noticed how everybody nowadays who is supposed to have initiative always turns out to have some capital as well? And, it's much easier to develop integrity if you've got something to lose ...'

'What about the girl?'

'Eh?' He looked at her. 'Oh, she'll love me all right, don't worry.'

'But supposing you don't –'

'That doesn't matter,' he said, almost irritably. 'Rich girls are used to a pretty low standard of marriage. She'll adore *me*, and I'll be considerate and nice to her, and she'll be thankful I don't turn out to be an utter swine. That's what they usually marry – a swine in a sheepskin car coat who takes her out in a borrowed E-type.'

She said nothing. She was shocked and hoped he was joking.

●

Annabel's agency was above a greengrocer in Walton Street. It took her nearly a week to find this out because whenever she rang up Annabel, a woman who sounded as though she had been born in Knightsbridge on a horse said that Annabel was out and she had simply no id*eah* when she would be in. She laughed a lot after she said this, which was very loudly, and Elizabeth found it tremendously difficult simply to say 'Goodbye' to somebody who was in the middle of laughing like that, and not frightfully easy even just after they had stopped. So she didn't ring up much, and the curious days and nights with Oliver went by; but in the end Annabel *was* in, and she got the agency's address, put on her tidiest clothes and went to see them.

It was run by two ladies called Lady Dione Havergal-Smythe and Mrs Potts. Both seemed rather surprising people to find running an agency: Lady Dione looked about fifteen – even in dark glasses – and Mrs Potts, who was the perfectly ordinary age of about fifty – old, anyway – turned out to be Hungarian. The agency consisted of two small rooms: one in which customers or clients waited to see Lady Dione and Mrs Potts and one where they saw them. There were two telephones which rang very nearly as often as they could, so that any sustained conversation was difficult. In between two calls Elizabeth was invited to sit down which she started to do, until she realized, perilously near the point of no return, that the chair indicated was minutely occupied by a Yorkshire terrier.

'Put her on the floor, would you very kindly?' Lady Dione's voice was unexpectedly deep and authoritative, and Elizabeth felt that the kindness referred to the dog rather than to herself.

Mrs Potts was talking fluent Italian (Elizabeth, who didn't know her nationality at this point, thought that she must *be* Italian as the peevishly caressing inflections continued). Lady Dione's telephone rang again – she listened for about half a minute and then said, 'Good God! No.'

'And what can we do for *you*?' she asked, as though she was quite ready to repeat her earlier remark after Elizabeth had told her.

'I've come about a job. Annabel Peeling told me that you had them. Jobs, I mean.'

'Oh! People nearly always come to us wanting people to *do* jobs.' Lady Dione seized a very expensive-looking leather address book.

'Do give me your name. And address. And things like that.'

Elizabeth did this.

Lady Dione pushed her dark glasses on to the top of her head and said earnestly, 'What would you *like* to do? I mean – somebody wants almost anything.' Her eyes were like Siberian topazes, Elizabeth thought: her only piece of jewellery was them so she jolly well knew what they looked like. Knowing that was a bit like Oliver, she thought: but she had to be left a brooch to know anything, and that was the only thing she'd ever been left, so that showed you ...

'I can cook a bit,' she said.

'Gosh! Can you really? I mean not just *sole Véronique* and chocolate mousse?'

Elizabeth shook her head.

'Hetty! (Mrs Potts, she's Hungarian.) Miss –' (she consulted her book) 'Seymour can cook!'

Mrs Potts had stopped having her Italian conversation, and was having another in some unknown mid-European language.

'How marvellous!' she said, with only a trace of an accent (pre-war B.B.C.). 'Wait for me, Di. We must spread her very thin!'

'We must wait for Hetty.' Lady Dione took a small cigar out of her lizard handbag.

'I must say that when you said Annabel had sent you, my heart sank. That girl thinks of nothing but money and is quite ungifted. If you live on your connections – as opposed to your attractions – under the age of twenty, you are in for the most ghastly middle age.'

Mrs Potts finished her conversation, and having replaced her receiver, took it off again.

'Oh – all right,' Lady Dione did the same.

'Now. You can get three guineas for cooking up to six, and more for more. I take it you just want to do dinners?'

'What are your qualifications?' Mrs Potts's voice, though chameleon to the point of virtuosity, had a certain edge which those non-committal creatures do not, in their neutral moments, seem to possess.

Elizabeth took a deep breath.

'I spent a year at Esprit Manger, six months Cordon Bleu, and three months with Mme Germaine. Orange,' she added.

Lady Dione and Mrs Potts looked at each other in a way that made Elizabeth feel quite important. Then Lady Dione said:

'How many evenings would you like to work? Don't do more than you feel like,' she added earnestly.

Elizabeth thought. 'About four?'

'That's simply marvellous of you.' She turned eagerly to Mrs Potts. 'What do you think Hetty? I mean there are just scads of people who –'

'I think we shall be able to suit you, Miss Seymour,' Mrs Potts interrupted smoothly. 'Perhaps we could call you later in the day?'

The moment Elizabeth got to her feet, the Yorkshire terrier leapt, with one neat spring, into the chair, where it gazed up at her with burning, reproachful eyes.

'We have your telephone number, Miss Seymour?'

Elizabeth nodded. Mrs Potts had met her eye some minutes ago, and continued, Elizabeth found now, implacably to meet it. Elizabeth wondered rather uncomfortably whether Mrs Potts was perhaps a Lesbian, but then she thought no you couldn't be Hungarian *and* a Lesbian, it would be too much of a coincidence getting two minorities in one person . . .

'Right then – sweet of you to come.' Lady Dione's dark glasses were back into position. 'And do remember,' she called as Elizabeth reached the door, 'that if you don't *like* anyone we send you to, you needn't ever go again.'

'You can report to us,' confirmed Mrs Potts – with a smile as sugary and firm as Brighton Rock.

*

When she got home, she found Oliver lying on the sitting-room floor poring over an enormous sheet of paper.

'I've had a brilliant idea – a new board game based on the Battle of Britain. I'm going to call it "Dogfight": it'll make a fortune – you'll see,' he remarked. 'Get me your nail scissors, there's a duck, and I would love a Welsh rarebit.'

So she wrote to May, whom she knew would be really interested to hear about her new job, and waited to tell Oliver when he felt more like it.

*

Lady Dione rang up a few days later to say would she mind awfully doing a dinner that very night? No. Right: had she got a pencil? She'd get one. She was to go to some people called Hawthorne in Bryanston Square. 'They're quite young from the sound of her voice,' Lady Dione had said, 'just married, and she can only cook one thing she learned from Cordon Bleu. She wants you there at five thirty; dinner for six, and she'll have bought all the food. Right? Right. And the best of British luck to you,' she added, more amiably than people usually make that remark.

'Do you want me to fetch you?' asked Oliver, who was now entering into the spirit of the thing. 'I can easily borrow Sukie's car by taking her out first. Haven't been out for days.' The game was now permanently on the sitting-room floor, and he had spent hours making friends play test games which they always lost because he was still inventing the rules. But Sukie, who had spent nearly two terms at an art school, had painted him an art nouveau board and they'd spent many a happy hour making tiny little models of aeroplanes, people and bombs out of glitter wax, bits of matchboxes and tinfoil.

'It would be lovely, if it won't be too late for you: probably after eleven.'

'My darling Liz, you must stop worrying so about *time*.'

'Yes, I must.' She wanted to get on with clearing up the house, having a hot bath and eating a couple of boiled eggs before going to Bryanston Square. She nearly always had boiled eggs before any sort of adventure and she didn't want to be late for this one. 'I'll try not to worry about it,' she repeated, and escaped.

*

Mrs Hawthorne opened the door to her at Bryanston Square. She was tall and thin, and fashionable to the point of prettiness: she wore a Thai silk trouser suit, pearl encrusted sandals and such an enormously thick dark pigtail draped over one shoulder that Elizabeth guessed it must be false.

'Hullo!' she said. 'You must be Miss Seymour.' She was carrying a small, white, elegantly clipped poodle who began yapping uncontrollably the moment Elizabeth stepped inside the flat. Mrs Hawthorne shut the door saying without any conviction, 'Shut up Snowdrop – shut *up*!

'I'll put her in the bedroom: hang on a minute.'

While she was doing this, Elizabeth waited in the hall. It was a very expensive flat: very thick pale-blue carpet, and a tank full of tropical fish; William Morris wallpaper, the kind she knew you jolly well had to like in the first place, since if you cleaned it with pieces of bread it would last for ever.

'Now. Where shall we put your coat?'

Elizabeth felt she could not be expected to know the answer to that; however, she took it off and looked obliging.

'I suppose you'd better shove it in the coat cupboard.' Mrs Hawthorne made this sound so like a concession, that it was almost offensive.

'I'll take you to the kitchen.'

'You'd better, if you want any dinner,' thought Elizabeth, wondering how Mrs Hawthorne managed to make quite ordinary sounding remarks sound so rude.

The kitchen was small, but spotless, all steel and Formica and what passed with the uninitiated as teak. It looked as though it was an Ideal Home kitchen, and not as though anybody had actually ever used it.

'All the food's in the fridge.' She opened the door of a gigantic Lec. 'Potted shrimps for first course, cold duck, and stuff to go with it, and then strawberries and cream. That was absolutely all I could *get*. Oh yes – some cheese. All right? You'll find knives and things in drawers. The dining-room's through there.' She pointed to a hatch. 'I must go and cope with Snowdrop: she can't stand strangers and she loathes being shut up.'

'What was the point of *having* me?' Elizabeth muttered as she unpacked her overall. The mixture of there being virtually no cooking to do, and Mrs Hawthorne's unfriendly behaviour, was most disconcerting. 'I must be fairly stupid to mind being disconcerted so much; Oliver wouldn't,' she thought as she took the food out of the fridge. Horrible frozen peas – the worst kind: and who in their senses would put new potatoes in the freezing compartment? The duck had that wizened, false look that nearly all shop-cooked birds seem to get; the strawberries turned out to be green on their hidden sides; but the potted shrimps were comfortingly just themselves as they always are. She found a huge white loaf – like a giant's Sorbo sponge – in the bread bin and that was that. There did not seem to be any butter, or coffee. The kitchen, indeed, contained one small packet of Indian tea, a jar of lump sugar and tins of grapefruit juice and Aristodog. Nothing else. It was twenty to six: she went in search of Mrs Hawthorne.

She heard her talking on the telephone and knocked rather timidly on the door. Mrs Hawthorne told her to come in, but the moment that she did so, the poodle rushed at her in a cacophanous frenzy. Mrs Hawthorne, who was lying on a white satin eiderdown (the room was unmistakably the bedroom) said, 'Oh lord! Hang on a minute, Boffy darling, I'm being interrupted,' heaved herself off the bed and collected the poodle.

'I'm sorry to bother you, but there doesn't seem to be any coffee – or butter for the toast and the vegetables ...'

'Oh – really!'

'I could go out and get them, if you like. I don't think all the shops will be shut.'

'Oh well – do that then. That's marvellous.' She turned back, with the poodle in her arms, to the telephone. 'Boffy? Still there darling? A domestic crisis ...'

'Er – the only thing *is*, I'm afraid I haven't brought any, so could you possibly let me have some money?'

'Oh God – hang on again darling, there seems to be another one. Another *crisis* – well, she's new ...' She put the receiver down and indicated with her head. 'Over there.'

There was a small lilac purse the same colour as her suit. Elizabeth picked it up and opened it.

'No – bring it to me : I'll do it.

'Damn! I only seem to have a pound note.'

Elizabeth opened her mouth to say something about most shops having change, but she didn't because she knew she was going to croak or squeak which was what always humiliatingly happened to her voice when she was angry and nearly in tears.

'You'll have to take it, won't you? Don't be long.'

She ripped her coat out of the coat cupboard and marched out of the flat. The lift was being used so she went on marching – down the stairs. She had never met anyone so *young* and so horrible in her life. For a moment she thought of not going back; but then she realized that she couldn't let the agency down like that, on her first job too : they'd probably never give her another one. Mr Hawthorne must be horrible as well; or else terribly stupid. Perhaps the moment you earned your living, people *were* horrible to you. No wonder poor Oliver hadn't been able to stand the accountants' office if this was true. Then she remembered May and how she'd behaved to the few people who'd ever worked for her. Of course it was nonsense : there was probably nobody as nasty as Mrs Hawthorne in the whole of north-west London. It was only for one evening; she'd do her best, earn her three guineas and get the hell out. By the time she reached Edgware Road, where she knew there was a large self-service grocer, she was planning to tell Oliver all about it. Mr and Mrs Hawthorne drinking tinned grapefruit juice and eating bowls of Aristodog for breakfast, because what *else* they did for that meal she could not see. Perhaps feral-type vitamins really brought out the beast in people.

In the grocer she bought butter, coffee and a couple of lemons for the shrimps, and cashed out at a register operated by a young black man. He took her pound impassively, but when she smiled at him, and apologized for not having anything smaller, he smiled so beautifully at her that she felt warmed by it. In the middle of his smile he yawned, put up an elegant hand which hardly hid his mouth and then laughed. 'All work makes you tired,' he said putting change on to her palm. 'Work is a terrible thing.' He put the lemons into a bag then the butter into a bag, and then the coffee into a third bag. 'You have no basket?' ' 'Fraid not.' He stooped and came up with a carrier. 'I give you family hold-all bag.' There were people queueing behind her, but he placed each of the three small bags carefully in the carrier and then held it to see if the parcels were well disposed therein. The woman behind her looked sour and began to mutter. He put the carrier back on the counter, arranged the string handles for her and inclined his head. 'Ready for you now. Easy – and nice.'

She thanked him, and saw his face shut down again as the sour woman plonked her stuff on the counter and thrust her money at him saying, 'We haven't got all night, you know.'

She walked back worrying about how people nearly always seemed to be horrible to one another – just in ordinary life – so naturally there would be wars.

Mr Hawthorne opened the door to her this time. His face was a uniform pale pink, and he was very nearly bald, but he was clearly quite young in spite of this, in the same way that you could tell about pigs. In one hand he carried a cocktail shaker which he was agitating steadily all the time he opened and shut the door. 'Good evening,' he said. 'And what shall we do with your coat?'

'Last time, we seemed to think it had better go into the coat cupboard.'

'Of course.' Her accent had thrown him. Filthy snob. Anyway, she needn't be *sorry* for him.

The rest of the evening was more of a cold war against the kitchen than against the people. (She didn't see much of the guests, whose voices sounded very much like their hosts', but she reflected that nobody who wittingly went to dinner with the Hawthornes could be very nice.) The problems were much more that there was neither a bread knife nor a potato peeler anywhere to be found, and come to that, not even a sharp knife of any description. The horrible, new, spongy bread was a nightmare to cut; the potatoes were the joke kind of new that would not scrape; she found, also, that she was expected to carve the duck. Laying the dining-room table when you didn't know where anything was, and it had been made impossible for you to ask, took simply ages. Luckily, Mr Hawthorne came out to the kitchen to decant some claret, so she was able to ask him when they wanted to eat and where they wanted their coffee served. Twice the poodle escaped in order to come and yelp at her and snap around her ankles. She came to the conclusion that it was slightly off its head, as indeed she would be if she had to live cheek by jowl with Mrs Hawthorne. When she took the coffee in, they had obviously been talking about her '... hasn't had to *cook* a thing –' Mrs Hawthorne was saying as she brought in the tray), and their efforts at covering this up were rudely ineffective. When she was washing up, Mr Hawthorne came into the kitchen and said, 'Are we expected to pay you?'

No, she said, the agency : *they* would pay her.

'Because really it seems a ridiculous sum, considering how little you have had to do.'

'I was asked to come here to cook dinner. The fact that Mrs Hawthorne had bought pre-cooked food is nothing to do with me.'

'Naturally, I can *see that*,' he said, as though he was making an enormous concession because she was so very stupid. 'It doesn't take very much intelligence to *see that*. But the fact remains that you didn't have to do anything except boil a few potatoes, which I take it most of us could manage if we were really pushed to it, and you're trying to charge us four guineas.'

Elizabeth, her heart thumping, put down the (only, and wringing-wet) drying-up cloth. 'The agency are charging you, Mr Hawthorne : they engaged me on your behalf. I think you'd better take the matter up with them. My brother is collecting me in ten minutes so I must finish the washing up now.' And in case he could hear her heart thumping, she turned on the cold tap very hard which splashed them both so suddenly and so much that he retreated without saying another word.

She dried the rest of the things on her apron, wiped the draining board, turned out the kitchen lights and collected her coat. She couldn't bear to wait in the flat for Oliver, who, in any case, might be late, as watches never went very successfully on him.

He *was* late; not very, but enough to make her feel abandoned as well as miserable. He and Sukie drew up with a flourish : they looked very gay, with Sukie wearing a pink velvet yachting cap on her straight, ashy hair.

'Pop in, sorry if we're late, how was it?'

Sukie was thoughtfully in the back, so she climbed in beside Oliver just as tears began to spurt from her eyes.

'Darling Liz! Here!' He seized the remains of a packet of popcorn and started to feed her. 'It's almost impossible to cry if your mouth is absolutely full. Unless you're about two, when it all slides out like a slimy blind. Poor Liz!' He put his arm round her and gave her a hug and such a weighty kiss on the cheek nearest him that all the popcorn had to change sides, and she nearly laughed.

She told them about it, and Sukie said things like, 'The bastard!' 'Fantastic scum!' and what a good thing they were *both* so ghastly, married couples often weren't, and Oliver said he had a good mind to join the agency and get hired by them; one evening with *him* as their cook and they'd change their tune. The rest of the drive home cheered Elizabeth up completely, because Oliver thought of such awful things to do while being their cook : 'Casserole of poodle was probably a fine Siege-of-Paris dish; of course I'd say that I only cooked live food : the meal would start with their beastly tropical fish *en gelée*, and end with me advancing on lovely Mrs Hawthorne with my meat chopper asking him how he would like her done.'

They all had hot buttered rum when they got back to Lincoln Street, because Sukie had found a very pretty silver flask of her father's that she was stealing to put scent in, and it seemed a waste not to use up the rum. After it, Elizabeth suddenly felt so tired that she was being turned to dormouse stone on the spot, so Oliver told her to go to bed. Sukie must have stayed the night, because when Elizabeth woke at about six, as she always did when things were worrying her, and went down to get a drink of water, the scarlet Mini was still parked outside the house. But by the time she and Oliver got up there was no sign of Sukie, and the Mini had gone. When she mentioned tentatively to him how nice Sukie was, his face closed and he said shortly, 'She's all right. A bit dim, though. A little of her goes a long way.' 'Goodness!' she thought, 'If he thinks that about Sukie, it's jolly nice to have *me* all the time.'

4. A New Life

'And now it'll go on for ever and ever,' thought Alice. It seemed impossible that somebody could turn out to be so different all the time; surely they must sometimes have been it before – and she had simply never noticed? And it was no good saying that love was blind, because she was far from sure what love was – now. It was obviously her own fault for expecting a miracle, but she had thought that the reason that people made so much fuss about (going to bed with someone) was because it was the only certain way of having an intimate friend. All that (sex) would only be possible if you felt really close to the person all the time when they weren't (making love to you). He wasn't unkind to her: she simply felt miserably shy with him – in fact, exactly as she felt with everyone else, only now, with him, there were more, and more awful opportunities for feeling shy. For the hundredth time she went back to her meeting with Leslie: on a beach in Sitges. He and some friends were playing with a large rubber ball which had fallen near her and bounced off her back. He had come to apologize and she had sat up. She had been wearing a navy one-piece bathing suit and a huge pink straw hat (she always had to be careful of the sun on her skin). He had lingered, asked her if she would like to join in the game: she had shaken her head, smiling too much to conceal how nervous she felt and also not to seem rude. It was very kind of him to ask her. Then, a bit later, they had met in the sea, and he had asked her whether she was enjoying herself and she had said yes, although she hadn't been, much. Holidays were always difficult if you were on your own. How had he known that? He could tell. He was bronzed which made his eyes look bluer, more piercingly kind. She had had drinks with him and his friend (who'd been best man at the wedding), and then lunch.

After that, they had met every day until her holiday time was up. He had proposed to her their last evening among the flood-lights, red gravel and green hillocks of the miniature golf course. She had admired him; she was deeply flattered by his attentions to her (nobody had ever treated her like that in her life; or anything like that when she came to think of it, which during the holiday she unceasingly did); he was all masculine steadiness and assurance and she imagined that he understood her. She was nearly twenty-six and nobody had ever proposed to her before, or for that matter got anywhere near it. She had said yes and found she was trembling so much that he had given her a brandy before walking her home to her hotel. On the way back, he'd found a dark archway and kissed her in an exploring kind of way. Distaste and gratitude and the odd tremor of ner-vous curiosity. 'You're shy – you're very tense,' he'd murmured. 'Don't worry, I'll always be kind to you.' Gratitude had welled over everything else: indeed, now, when she remembered his voice saying that, she was back to her nearest point of loving him, of knowing now, that then she had thought it was the beginning of love. Perhaps if they'd gone back to Sitges for their honeymoon it would have been better? But he had said it was too early in the year; they wouldn't be able to bathe, and the golf course in Cornwall was a very good one. And the hotel, he had assured her, would be first class – nothing on the cheap and much more reliable food. She had had a couple of lessons at golf, but she was absolutely no good and uninterested in the game: so then she'd walked around with him for a day or two, and then, because she felt tired nearly all the time, she'd simply stopped walking round. 'Have a nice rest,' he had said: he seemed very much in favour of that. So she'd tried, but lying down in the afternoon simply made her feel restless and a bit guilty. (Daddy would have roared with laughter at a healthy woman mollycoddling herself.) So she used to go for walks on the cliffs above the sea, making sure that she got back to the hotel before Leslie returned from his afternoon round. Once she wrote a poem about a seagull and being lonely, and this made her feel much better for a day or two. When, at tea, she told Leslie that she had been for a walk and watched this seagull he said he was glad she had been amusing herself, so she didn't tell him about the poem. He frequently asked her if she was happy and she knew that he felt sure she was, so of course she said yes. She supposed the sex part of marriage got better as you got used to it. It couldn't possibly go on being like it was in Cornwall, because otherwise people surely wouldn't stay married even the amount that they did. Once she had rung up home, and May had fortunately answered (she'd picked the afternoon when Daddy would be having his rest) and apparently Claude was perfectly all right except that he'd given the window cleaner an awful fright by jumping on to the top of a sash window while it was open and being cleaned so that it slammed down on the man's arms and nearly knocked him off his ladder. He was marvellously agile for his weight and age, Alice thought, and he'd always liked giving people surprises. His canker was worse, and when May had managed to get a few drops in his ears, he'd gone on shaking them out for hours over all kinds of things ... Her father was fine, May had volunteered, adding, 'He keeps buying things for the lawn. You know how the moment he's stopped worrying about the Budget, he starts on the lawn.' She had not said anything about herself, and Alice afterwards felt ashamed of having forgotten to ask.

The fortnight in Cornwall had got used up: now she was packing to go. She wondered how much she would remember it when she was old. Four kinds of meals every day. Breakfast with Leslie in the dining-room: stewed prunes or corn flakes, bacon and egg or sausages and tomato, tea or coffee, rubbery toast, not enough butter and Cooper's Oxford marmalade. Leslie read the *Express* and she had *The Times*, which impressed him. In between reading their papers, people looked out of the windows and wondered aloud about the weather, which was showery enough to keep them wondering. Lunch in the Golf Club, a room which gave the impression of being a Tudor swimming bath, as it was immense, very low-ceilinged, with oak panelling and incredible clashing echoes: people laughed like horrible giants about their morning game, and a fork dropped was like the clash of spears in a Roman epic film. Tea in the television lounge at the hotel; deep chairs and little rocking tables covered with scalding silver jugs and teapots (she liked China and he liked Indian), mercilessly dainty sandwiches and very small, evil, shining cakes. Dinner in a short silk dress – a bit shivery but everyone wore them; thick or clear, turbot or sole, chicken or veal, crème caramel or ice cream and cheese. A drink in the bar with coffee, perhaps a bit more television – and bed. Leslie always let her go to the bathroom first; she undressed in there. The worst part was lying in bed waiting for him to come out in his pyjamas, because sometimes he climbed into her bed and sometimes he didn't, and whichever he did seemed wrong. Afterwards she would lie awake in the dark blaming herself variously for not having the right instincts, not being attractive enough, for not, perhaps, recognizing that this was what women had to do in return for being clothed and fed and looked after all their lives. This last was the worst, and she tried strenuously not to believe it, at the same time feeling that as it was the most despairing likelihood it was probably true. It would be better for there to be something wrong with *her* than for it to be awful for everyone – all women, at least. She was docile, passive, even brave when he hurt her, which he did a good deal at first; she tried to be affectionate, to conceal her senses of isolation and embarrassment and inadequacy, but in the end she decided that he did not seem to notice her much. One night he gently touched her breasts – which were large and painfully tender – and murmured something about them being lovely: she felt her whole body begin to respond, as though sealed eyelids had opened for the first time inside her, but then he had crushed himself upon her and the feeling vanished. She only had it once, and even by the end of two weeks she began to wonder if she had imagined it.

She had finished the packing – Leslie's and her own. Leslie was downstairs paying the bill, and just as she closed the last case, there was a knock on the door.

'Porter, madam.' He was old and short and very broad, and came sideways through the door out of habit. His ears stuck out and he leered like a horrid old version of Punch.

'Just the four. And I hope you've enjoyed your *stay*, madam.'

'I hope I have:' It came out before she could stop it, and, blushing, she stalked angrily out of the room, slipped on one of the brass studs that nailed the carpet down and nearly tripped.

'Oops-a-daisy,' he said in his mechanically fruity old voice. In the lift, he fixed his eyes on a point just below her stomach and remained unwinking and motionless as they descended. If he'd moved or said anything, she could have told him to stop staring at her, but he'd had far too much practice: the lift cage simply became charged with unclean thoughts.

In the reception hall he turned into a bustling, obsequious crab – treating all their luggage as though it was desperately heavy and very fragile – filled with atom bombs. Leslie gave him a pound.

They had lunch on the train. There was a small, brilliant slug in her watercress: she thought it looked very pretty, but it made her not want the watercress and when Leslie discovered she wasn't fancying it, he gave her an immensely knowing smile and said he wondered whether there might not be – you know – a little stranger on the way. He hadn't seen the slug. After lunch, Leslie went to sleep and she did some of *The Times* crossword – she still felt privileged to have this newspaper all to herself, instead of yesterday's scrumpled up by Daddy and with all the easiest clues done. London: Paddington station. It was very hot; the air under the glass-domed roof was thick with dust and illuminated by majestic shafts of sunlight – cosmic revelation falling upon the paltry antics of arrival and departure.

'Come *on*, dear. You're daydreaming!'

She wondered how quickly he would descend from admiring her for constantly doing something which was to him so incomprehensible, into irritation at having to keep prodding her into life on his terms. Getting used to people cut both ways. They were going to the Station Hotel – have a gin and tonic while they waited for the Bristol train. In the bar she remembered that May had said that Elizabeth had gone to stay with Oliver in London. 'I could ring her up,' she thought suddenly, feeling urgent and homesick. So she told Leslie, who was having an argument with a man at the bar about underfloor heating, and the woman at the desk put her in a telephone booth and got the number.

Oliver answered. There was a lot of talking in the background.

'*Who*? Hold on a sec while I turn the gramophone off.

'My dear Alice. No – she's out. She's cooking dinner for some Christian Scientists in Pimlico. Me? Oh – I'm doing a spot of reviewing: *Julius Caesar* on L.P.s for a friend's magazine. Just a little job. How are you? Was it foul in Cornwall? The weather, I mean,' he added.

'A bit changeable. I'm at Paddington.' She could not think of anything interesting to say. There was a short pause, then she said, 'We're off to Bristol on the six forty-eight.'

Another short pause. 'I see,' he said.

'How's May?'

'I don't know, really. She keeps saying she's coming up, and then she doesn't seem to make it. I'll give her your love.'

'And to Elizabeth.'

'Of course. Come and see us if you're in London.'

'I will. Goodbye.'

He said goodbye at once: she imagined him starting his gramophone again; immediately devoting his brilliant, critical attention to the schemes of the Roman senate. If he hadn't been so brilliant, she would have been hopelessly in love with him. He was so attractive, so entertaining; he had such an air of constantly finding life easy and amusing, of being able to do anything if only he felt like it, that even things like going with him to return the empties to the pub turned into a sort of holiday venture. But he was far, far too clever for her: also she was two years older than he was, and anyway, almost as soon as she met him, he became a kind of relation. And this last, she thought, going to pay for her telephone call, did not seem to make knowing people or being able to talk to them any easier. She thought of the Mount family – now all turned at one stroke into relations – waiting in Bristol for her to get on with them ... Her mother-in-law at least was kind.

Mrs Mount *was* kind. As they did not arrive until nearly ten o'clock, she was sure they must be very tired and hungry, in spite of them having had, as they had told her they would, dinner on the train. There was an immense cold collation laid out in the Mounts' gloomy dining-room: ham, tongue, spiced loaf, potato salad, beetroot, pickles and radishes, tinned fruit, home-made caraway seed cake and bakewell tarts and some pastel coloured junkets. There was tea, coffee, whisky and pale ale. Mr Mount said it was quite a feast, whereupon Mrs Mount described it as just a snack. Rosemary, dressed in ski pants and smoking through an exceptionally long holder, rolled her eyes knowingly at Alice and said that she was sure Alice knew what parents were. Sandra, wearing white tights, an imitation lizard skin tunic and silver plastic boots, said nothing at all. She was so staggered by her own appearance that she was entirely taken up with looking at herself in various mirrors, or watching the others seeing her for the first time and willing them to be amazed. But, 'You look smart, Sandra,' Leslie said kindly, spoiling it all. It was just as well he was so frightfully stupid and tasteless; it knocked out any possibility of incest, which otherwise appealed to her as the simplest and wickedest way of shocking everyone at once.

Alice, who was really tired and had eaten a large dinner on the train to fortify herself against this homecoming to her in-laws' house, looked frantically at the plate that Mrs Mount had heaped up for her. She said that she was not very hungry and looked at Leslie for support, but he quelled her by saying that he could always fancy Mother's food, however much he had eaten elsewhere. The room was very hot: her hay fever had started with the country air and the anti-histamine pills always made her feel stupid, but some, at least, of the food on her plate had to be eaten; some questions – about Cornwall, the hotel, her family's health and so on – answered. Leslie was soon engaged upon business gossip with his father while Mrs Mount told her which shops were reliable in Whiteladies Road, Rosemary told her about a hairdresser whose favourite client she was – he was Italian and need she say more? Sandra stared at her and asked whether she had ever learned judo or been to America. Halfway through the meal, there was a scratch on the door which Mrs Mount then opened, and a huge, heavy dog waddled in. It lay down at once between two electric fires and immediately began to snore. At intervals, and in comparative silence, it emitted offensive, and seemingly endless smells. Mrs Mount, Alice discovered, was the sort of person who, when she found that you did not eat what was put in front of you, simply gave you a huge plate of something else. This did not strike Alice as especially kind, but obviously Mrs Mount thought it was: she knew everybody knew that she was kind and she was the sort of person who always said things and always did them, too.

At last she felt that she could perhaps go up to their room and unpack. Mrs Mount said she'd pop up and show her the way: Rosemary said she would come too – she longed to see Alice's nightgowns. Sandra followed in their wake – partly because she had been sent to bed and it was the easiest way of pretending she wanted to go up anyway. Before they left, Mrs Mount put Alice's plates of largely unfinished food in front of the dog who gulped up everything without otherwise moving at all – it was a kind of living Hoover, Alice thought with weary disgust.

The room – the guest room as Mrs Mount explained, no good putting Alice in Leslie's old bed – had been done up specially for Alice. New paper, new curtains and bedspread: Rosemary had chosen it, as Mrs Mount was a weeny bit old-fashioned. Two walls were ochre-coloured and two were a rather muddy turquoise. The carpet was a mixture of these colours – speckled like a thrush but not in nearly such good taste. The room contained a three-piece suite and a small double bed covered with a slippery old-gold eiderdown which Alice knew would be possessed of reptilian agility in the night. On the dressing-table was a colour photograph of a very fat little boy leaning against a lamp-post. 'Leslie when he was little,' said Mrs Mount, 'a present for *you*, dear. For years I've been saying it was high time he got married. He was such a lovely little boy.'

Sandra made retching noises, and that was the end of *her*, since Mrs Mount, in an entirely different tone of voice, ordered her to bed that minute. She went – kicking her boots against the skirting board before she remembered that they were her new birthday boots – bought with Great-Aunt Lottie's money.

Rosemary, with unspeakable energy, had started to unpack one of Alice's suitcases. Alices hated this so much that she wanted to scream, but instead she smiled and protested inside. Mrs Mount, laughing indulgently, said *she* knew when she was in the way, she'd be popping off, and leave the girls together. This she did.

'At last!' cried Rosemary. 'Old people never know when they're not wanted, do they? Now! Let's put our feet up, and tell me all about it.'

Alice went on unpacking, or tried to, but at the same moment as she realized that she couldn't think of anything to say to Rosemary – something that would make her shut up or go away – the back of her neck felt icy cold and she couldn't see anything properly. She heard herself asking for the bathroom, and the next thing she knew was that she was alone in it, having been violently sick. She sat down on the edge of the bath, shivering, and too weak even to wash her face. She noticed that she had bolted the door, and then heard Rosemary's voice.

'Are you all right? Alice!'

'I just want to go to bed.' Then, with a further effort, she said 'Please leave me alone, Rosemary.' It was amazing that she had bolted the door. Her face was wet with tears and sweat – like a bit of Kipling. She did not care what Rosemary did now: she would not come out until Rosemary had gone. The worst of it was that although she wished that she was not there, in Mrs Mount's bathroom in Clifton, Bristol, she could not really think where she wanted to be. Not in Surrey, certainly: look at the lengths she'd gone to to get away from there. Before that, there had been furnished rooms: in Earls Court, in Stanmore, in Finchley, in Stoke Newington. Before that, the house in Westdown Road, Seaford, that had belonged to her first stepmother – twenty years ago, she could hardly remember it; she'd been six, and they'd just come back from India. No – India had been two years earlier; she must have been four then. All she could remember about India was the spicy smell of her Indian nurse, the wailing at her mother's death, delicious fruit drinks and an old man who seemed always to be watering the garden of their bungalow. Coming back to England it had been funny not having to wear a hat, and people's feet made an awful lot of noise so that she'd been afraid of being trampled on, which she'd never felt with Indian people. She couldn't want to be in India if that was all she could remember of it. The trouble was that all these places had Daddy looming over them so much that it had made them nearly the same. In fact, everything she could remember seemed to be years and years of being alone; the only child; being nearly always bored and sometimes frightened; being in the way, or at least out of place; wondering what to do with herself and hearing other people openly speculate about this problem – punctuated by terrifying occasions when she was suddenly dispatched without warning to some new school, or to some acquaintances of Daddy's: agonizing afternoons of answering a battery of dispassionate questions, choking on bread and butter, having to drink milk, or tea with horrible sugar in it, and Daddy coming to fetch her talking in a kind of public genial voice which he never did at home ... The schools were worse, though, because they went on for longer and sometimes she had even to live in them. By the time she was sent off in this manner she had become used to hours and even days alone, and to live in a regimented but alien crowd was torture to her. Introspective children who are neither pretty nor very clever are simply a baffling nuisance to overworked staff; the children immediately recognized her as easy prey for bullying, and in the end too dull even to be worth those attentions. She longed for a friend, but had no idea how to make one; she blushed very easily, and her asthma ruined every summer term; school food brought out the worst of her acne; and the difficulty she found in communicating – with anyone at all – made her seem far more obstinate even than she was. May was the first person whom she had really not been in some measure afraid of, and by then she was twenty-three. Oliver and Elizabeth had seemed so wonderfully lucky and glamorous that to become related to them was an almost celestial privilege. At first she had planned that Elizabeth would become her greatest friend and Oliver might become – anything. She had actually shown some of her poems to Elizabeth, but

69

watching Elizabeth read them, she'd seen pretty quickly that poetry didn't mean much to her: she'd been impressed, of course, but she hadn't understood it. Her feelings about both of them – Oliver and Elizabeth – had soon settled to a kind of fearful admiration, and she had turned, with some relief, to May. At first she had thought that Daddy's third marriage was going to release her from unpaid bondage into the freedom of a job and money of her own. But when Daddy had insisted on May buying that enormous house, she had realized that for someone not used to looking after Daddy anywhere, let alone in a mansion, the combination would be too much for any one person, and certainly for May, who was not really a practical person at all. So she had stayed at home to help, until she had slowly begun to feel that Daddy really wanted her to make a life of her own. He had even offered to send her on a cruise to meet people. She had refused that point blank; the thought of being stuck on a ship with a lot of strangers getting on with one another seemed like being the only prisoner in a social concentration camp. She had compromised with Spain, once she had found that May thought she ought to have a proper holiday: Sitges and Leslie had been the result, and here she was. So it was idiotic to say that being here was worse than being anywhere else, really – it was just strange, and goodness knows she was used to strange places. She got up from the edge of the bath and washed her face in cold water, and then making sure that she was leaving the bathroom as she expected Mrs Mount would wish to find it, she went back to the bedroom. Rosemary was nowhere to be seen. She undressed behind the door, in case Leslie should come in, and climbed into bed. She had been right about the eiderdown. If only Claude was here, he would pin it down. The last thing she thought of before going to sleep were the lovely times when she would wake in the night with a feeling of claustrophobia and a dead weight on her chest, open her eyes to find two luminous orbs a few inches from her face and hear the grumbling mutter of his purr starting up as he realized he'd made her uncomfortable enough to wake her up. Perhaps *he* felt lonely, too.

•

Alice and Leslie were only staying with the rest of the Mounts until they could move into their new home. This was a luxury bungalow built by the Mounts on a new housing estate beyond Clifton. Leslie had shown Alice the plans, but she found them so difficult to understand that she was completely unprepared for the – nearly completed – article when she saw it. Leslie took her the next morning, after a huge Mount breakfast (the Mounts went to work on nearly everything you could think of to be on the safe side). The point about the bungalow, Leslie explained, was that they were building forty-nine others that were structurally the same, which brought down the costs quite a bit, but, on the other hand, as this one was to be theirs, he had added a number of features to it which would certainly make it a one-off job with a distinction of its own. What sort of features, Alice had asked, really not knowing what features of a building might be. Spanish-style touches, Leslie had answered. She glanced at his profile – he looked complacent and mysterious.

The housing site was a large one, and the sense of devastation which any building enterprise brings to the surrounding land was probably at its worst, since all the bungalows had been begun, and many of them were in varying stages of completion. From the distance they looked like white mini-bricks put on a ploughed field; as they got nearer, Alice saw that the third-of-an acre plots had been marked out with barbed wire and chestnut palings. Here and there were drunken remnants of the original hedges that had marked the fields. A concrete mixer was working; scaffolding was being noisily disassembled; there was a bonfire burning what looked like giant's rubbish; and the perky cackle of transistor radios filled up the cracks of silence between the crashes, thuds, hammering and tip-up lorries changing gear as they were ponderously manoeuvred in the rutty, makeshift roads. A great many men were standing about watching the man loosening the bolts on the scaffolding with a ring spanner, and several men were vociferously directing a lorry loaded with tiles which seemed to have got stuck.

Leslie drove to one end, or corner, of this battlefield where one of the most finished of the bungalows crouched.

'Here we are,' he shouted.

Getting out of the car, Alice stepped immediately into a heap of very wet sharpsand. 'Look out!' cried Leslie, as people usually do after you haven't. She stood on one leg and took off her other shoe: the sand was like damp sugar; several men had stopped watching a man unloading tiles from a wheelbarrow and were watching her. Leslie came up and held her arm. 'Bad luck!'

'Never mind. Let's go and see the house.'

At this moment a small man in a hat turned up at a kind of fast hobbling walk – like someone pretending to run in a comedy.

'Good morning, Timpson.'

'Good morning, sir.'

'This is the new Mrs Mount.' Leslie said this as though there were dozens of them.

'Good morning, madam.' He had a ferrety little face and all his gestures were exaggerated by dishonesty. Now, he looked at his hand, wiped it on his trousers and held it out to Alice with an expression of such humility that it was almost aggressive. His hand wasn't in the least dirty.

'Mr Timpson is our foreman. I've brought my wife to see our new home.'

'Definitely.' He held his hand out again – this time as though warding off a blow. 'Don't tell me. I know. All ladies are impatient. I'll tell you frankly – it's a miracle what we've performed in the time. Forty-seven – no I'm telling a lie – forty-eight weeks ago this place was just a field with animals in it. Now – and have we had our troubles – you wouldn't recognize the place. Fifty lovely homes in the twinkling of an eye.'

They were walking up what Alice supposed would eventually be the path to her front door. When they reached it, Mr Timpson clapped a hand to his head: this seized up any other movement he had been on the point of making. 'Don't move, sir! Isn't there a lovely little old custom that slipped our memory?'

Leslie and Alice stopped too, and looked at him.

'I may be wrong,' cried Timpson: he was now mincing sideways up to Leslie, 'but,' he put a hand shielding his mouth from

Alice and spoke even louder, 'don't we carry the bride over the threshold the first time she enters her domain? Correct me if I'm wrong.' He clapped his hand over his mouth and looked roguishly ashamed.

'Quite right,' said Leslie, and turned to Alice.

Alice, as we have said, was a big girl: she was quite simply the wrong size to be carried at all – except by Tarzan, or in an emergency like the house being on fire. But Leslie, though not much taller than she, was stocky and determined. He picked her up and carried her, her handbag thumping painfully against his thighs as he staggered into the bungalow.

'Easy does it,' cried Mr Timpson having seen that it hadn't. He had also seen one of her suspenders as her skirt had got rucked up, and Alice loathed him more than ever. She was blushing and didn't know where to look so as to avoid Mr Timpson's horrid little eyes, so she looked down, straight on to the enormous bottom of a man in blue dungarees who was hitting what looked to her like random bits of floorboard with a tiny hammer.

'Move for the lady, George,' said Mr Timpson in a voice which bordered on being quite different from any he had used before.

Alice looked at Leslie to see if she could tell what he thought about Mr Timpson, but she couldn't. In fact, Leslie couldn't have minded him, she thought resentfully as they got back into the car half an hour later, since Mr Timpson had been allowed to accompany them throughout their tour of the bungalow, which was not very large, and except for workmen and loose doors and tools and things was empty. She had seen it all in about five minutes, but Leslie and Mr Timpson stood interminably in each room talking about sub-contractors, the Government, the Electricity Board, fibre-glass insulation and Marley tiles. Mr Timpson always agreed with Leslie, so perhaps that was why they talked so much, Alice thought. The Spanish-style features turned out to be the threat of a good deal of wrought iron, tiles on the floors, which she thought would be slippery and cold, and an all-black bathroom, which did not strike her, among other things, as particularly Spanish. There was also an eye-level grill in the kitchen. There were two bed-rooms, one large and one small, a large sitting-room, a sort of study, a small dining-room with a hatch through to the kitchen, one bathroom and two lavatories. Her future home. In the car, Leslie asked her what she thought of it, and she said she was sure it was going to be very nice.

5. The Garden of England

May woke first, as she always did (the alarm-clock was beside her bed as Herbert was a light sleeper until, he said, about six-thirty in the morning: it was most important to him to get those vital two hours of real rest). For this reason, May never slept very well for the hour or so before the alarm went off, as she had to quell it at its first buzz, or, as Herbert pointed out, it defeated its object. He liked to sleep until the strong Indian tea was actually steaming in a huge cup at his bedside. Usually she stopped the clock before it had a chance, but on this particular morning she woke with such a feeling of excitement that she forgot. Today was probably going to be one that she would remember all her life. Herbert was going to London, to see his stockbroker, lunch at his club and look in at Lords, and *she*, nefariously – she hadn't dared tell him – was having a very interesting man to lunch; possibly, she thought, one of the most interesting men in England – if not the world. He was not coming alone; dear, kind Lavinia was bringing him; but then, without Lavinia she would never have heard about, let alone met Dr Sedum. Lavinia was a second cousin – somebody she had vaguely known as a child, and then met again when they were grown-up and going to parties together. They had never *seemed* to have much in common and after Lavinia had married a Texan millionaire and she had married Clifford their ways had entirely and naturally parted. Lavinia's husband was now dead and so she had returned to England, an older and richer woman ...

The alarm went off, and May clutched at it, and then turned fearfully to see whether it had woken Herbert. It didn't seem to have done.

She put on an old cardigan and then her dressing-gown. The

house was always its coldest early in the morning, and anyway, she was a cold person. The floors of the wide, dark passages were polished oak, which, as Herbert had pointed out, obviated the need for carpets. The staircase was also oak – no carpet there, either, which made it slippery and a nightmare to negotiate with heavy trays. The hall, with its huge, heavily-leaded window – too large to curtain – was somehow always freezing, even in summer, and dark, too, because here the oak had crept up the walls to a height of about nine feet, making any ordinary furniture look ridiculous. There was also a tremendous stone fireplace in which one could have roasted an ox; and, as Oliver had pointed out, nothing less would have done either to warm the place or to defeat the joyless odour of furniture polish. 'It really is a monstrous house,' she thought, and recognized this to be what Dr Sedum had described in one of his 'talks' as a mechanical pattern reaction – something to be avoided if one was to evolve. But later on in the same talk he had said that we were all liars because we were incapable of responding consistently to our environment, and then she didn't know what to think. When she had asked Lavinia after the Time, as meetings were called in the League, Lavinia had said that one could not start at all, until one had perceived the Paradox. She had only been to one Time, and when Lavinia had said that she must not try to walk before she could fly, she realized that she had a long way to go.

The moment she got into the kitchen, Claude hoisted himself wearily out of the vegetable trug by the Aga and set about his usual process of tripping her up until she had provided him with his early morning milk. This morning, she gave in to him at once; she wanted nothing to interfere with the clockwork routine which was to conclude with Herbert catching his train to London. She had told him she was having a cousin to lunch several days ago, but he had been deep in some gardening manual, and she had not been sure whether he had heard.

Two hours later she waved to Herbert as he lurched down the drive in the old Wolseley. Alice had washed the car once a week before she had married, but it was one more of those things which May simply didn't seem to get time to do. A final wave – he would not have seen her, but he liked all his expeditions to be taken seriously – and she heaved at the huge iron-studded front door until it shut with a prison-like click. There was a terrific amount to do before Dr Sedum and Lavinia arrived, but she was so exhausted with anxiety and the feeling that she was doing something exciting and momentous behind Herbert's back that she fled to the kitchen for a cup of coffee and a cigarette (Herbert did not like her to smoke in the mornings). 'I'll make a list,' she thought. She always resorted to lists: they proved that she had a great deal to do, and to some extent, as she crossed things off, they proved that she was doing them. Mrs Green was coming this morning: she began with a list for Mrs Green. She had decided to entertain her guests entirely in what was called the morning room: by dint of transporting most of the electric fires (the ones that were in working order, anyway) she could manage to get it tolerably cosy by one o'clock. There was a reasonable round table there; it wobbled rather on its pedestal if one cut bread or made any other emphatic movements of that nature, but was otherwise suitable for lunch. The room was sternly bare: Herbert had not put much furniture there as he did not use it, but she could collect bits and pieces from other rooms. Anyway, Dr Sedum probably appreciated austerity as long as it did not make him *too* uncomfortable. Lunch was to consist of roast spring chicken, new potatoes and peas (safe food, surely, for such an occasion) and crème caramel, which she had got very good at as Herbert had been used to it in India. Mrs Green could do the vegetables and clean the room; she would prepare the chicken, make the room as warm and nice as possible and put on her blue suit. She wrote 'half past twelve' at the bottom of the lists and set about everything.

By twelve she thought she had done everything, but the list had mysteriously disappeared, so it was impossible to be sure. The room looked much better, and was noticeably warmer than the rest of the house, although she had only been able to plug in two heaters because that was all the plugs there were. Mrs Green had polished the food trolley and altogether entered into

77

the spirit of the occasion; they had lugged two heavy armchairs in and laid the round table. She had picked some lilac from the garden and arranged it in the scullery while Mrs Green kindly did the dogs' food. A lot of earwigs fell out of the lilac, but Claude was at hand to dispatch them which, with a good deal of unnecessary strategy, he did. It was a lovely day, cold but sunny, no sign of rain which was an excellent thing, because rain sometimes stopped Herbert going to Lord's, and then he came home earlier rather grumpy.

Her blue suit had been her best for so long now that even putting it on induced a mechanical sense of festivity. With it she wore a jersey made by Alice in a paler blue which toned very nicely. It was awful to feel pleased that Alice was not here, but really, it was a blessing; with Elizabeth she could have been quite frank – simply told her to beat it, she wanted a private lunch – but with Alice this would have been pretty well impossible. Alice would have been hurt, would have had to be included in lunch, and then the whole thing would have been spoiled, since people in the League were not allowed to talk about it to people outside. Of course, *she* wasn't actually in it yet, but she knew that they were considering her; the lunch was probably a kind of *test* ...

She saw them arriving from her bedroom window in Lavinia's Bentley, and it was such a long way down to the front door that she was a bit breathless by the time she succeeded in getting it open.

'May! How nice!' Her cousin managed to make this sound like some graceful coincidence. Dr Sedum – an enormously tall man – loomed gently behind her : he was smiling in a temperate sort of way.

'It's lovely to see you. Do come in.'

'Of course, you've met Dr Sedum.'

'Yes.' May found she was getting breathless again. 'It's most awfully good of you to come.' She wasn't quite sure whether to shake hands, but Dr Sedum spread his out in a gesture denying all goodness, so she thought probably better not. She led the way to the far end of the hall, through the oak door, down the wide passage (she'd put the lights on) and through a baize door, after which a narrower passage culminated in the morning room.

'You certainly have room to turn round here,' exclaimed Lavinia, walking to the bay window where the round table was set. 'Isn't it frightfully difficult to get enough staff?'

'I expect it would be, but we don't try. Wouldn't you like to take off your coats?'

'And have some sherry?' she added, moments later. She felt tentative about this, not knowing whether the kind of person Dr Sedum was drank.

'That would be delightful.' She had forgotten how very quietly he spoke; so quietly, that it was impossible to hear, unless one gave him one's whole attention and watched his face. She had bought a bottle of Bristol Cream in case drink was the thing. Dr Sedum now produced a gold cigarette case and offered her a cigarette.

'You look surprised,' said Lavinia as she accepted her sherry. 'We are not supposed to deny ourselves the good things in life.' She sat in one of the armchairs and turned expectantly to Dr Sedum, who shook his head benevolently.

'That would be too easy. There would be an entirely false sense of achievement. The interest begins when one can say to oneself: I am smoking a cigarette, I am drinking sherry, and have a clear understanding of the *senses* that those activities bring.'

May, who had taken a sip of sherry and a puff of her cigarette and thought 'how nice' on each occasion put down her glass with the small thrill of humility and excitement that she had so often felt before when she did not understand something that seemed crystal clear to other people. 'Oh please explain to me,' she said.

Dr Sedum shook his head again: his large, round, pale blue eyes were fixed upon her face. 'On our way here, we stopped to ask the way. A man, wheeling a bicycle – an ordinary man – replied, "I'm a stranger here myself." '

May waited for him to say more, but he didn't. Instead he drank some sherry, still watching her as she gazed at him. Even sitting down, he seemed to tower above her, but his smile made her feel that if anyone could help her understand anything it would be he. It was rather difficult to drink her sherry after that, so she was glad when Lavinia said:

'I think it's so brave of you to embark on a house this size these days.'

'Oh – it wasn't me who was brave. It was Herbert: my husband. He simply insisted that I – that we buy it. It's ridiculous really; Alice, my stepdaughter, is married, and my two are in London leading their own lives so we rattle about here like two peas in a pod, I don't mean a pod – you know what I mean.'

She stopped. Lavinia had a fringe – just like when she was small, she noticed; only then the rest of her hair had been cropped very short, had been thick and silky, and now it hung in rather greasy strands over the collar of her velveteen dress. Dr Sedum had almost no hair: none at all on the top of his head, which was smooth and the same texture as a close-up photograph of a wax pear. There were also coarse, reddish tufts at the sides just above his ears. It was extraordinary how, when you *knew* about people, their appearance took on an entirely different meaning.

Dr Sedum had finished his sherry, but as he was probably the only person she had ever met with a clear understanding of how to drink it, one expected him to finish first. She offered more; it was accepted, and she wondered when the serious talking would begin. Not until she'd got lunch actually on the table by the feel of things. She filled up Lavinia's glass, and then her own. There was an astonishingly long silence at the end of which Dr Sedum and Lavinia smiled at each other, and Dr Sedum said,

'That was good; very good.'

'I think Harvey's are a very reliable brand.'

A low rumbling broke from Dr Sedum, that, as she got used to it, May recognized as his compassionate chuckle: she had heard him use it when people asked questions at the one Time she had been to. She felt herself beginning to blush.

'I'm sorry – I thought you meant the sherry. I think I'd better get lunch now.'

'I won't offer to help you.' Lavinia made this sound like a really imaginative and generous concession.

Which May thought, as she started the journey to the kitchen, it was, on the whole, because it would have been frightfully rude to leave someone like Dr Sedum all by himself.

•

The colonel lowered himself into a chair at his favourite corner table. He was feeling quite peckish, and looking forward no end to a damn good lunch. Henry, the head waiter, limped forward:

'Would you care for anything to drink, Colonel?'

'Oh yes, Henry, I should certainly care. A large pink gin.'

'With soda, sir?'

'With soda.'

It was early, and the dining-room was almost empty: very few people lunched before one, and at these times, Henry always gave any early member his personal attention. His reputation in the club stood very high; Henry was 'wonderful'. This simply meant that he remembered what each of them liked to drink and smiled obsequiously at all the monotonous badinage that went on and on and on about it. 'Henry must have seen a lot: he must know a thing or two' was another thing people far too often said about him. In fact he hardly ever saw anything: men behave differently in their clubs, but they all manage to behave differently in the same way: and all Henry ever saw was a lot of Old Head Boys having a (bit of a) spree. His varicose veins were awful, and he only stayed because he had first pick of the batches of fresh and buxom Irish girls who streamed across the Channel to earn their living and lose their virginity. The staff said he was a terror with the girls: the girls giggled and whispered about him in their attic bedrooms at the top of the building, and told one another fearful lies about his disgusting and manly ways, and the junior waiters held tremulously revolutionary meetings about him in their local. The older waitresses treated him like any other member, as though he was rather mad and failing in health. The Kitchen loathed him, though this held them together as nothing else could do, and the committee regarded him as a tradition.

While Henry was seeing to his drink, the colonel picked up the business-like typewritten menu. Potted shrimps, fresh asparagus, *paté maison* and *oeufs en gelée*: damn difficult to choose. A young waitress with rippling red hair, and a real figure, came to clear away the spare place.

'Good morning.'

'Good morning, sir.'

'Haven't seen you before. What's your name?'

'My name is Maureen, sir.'

She wore high-heeled shoes and definitely naughty stockings.

'From Oiled Oiland are you?'

'From Dublin, sir.'

She had bent to pick up the mitred napkin and put it on her tray. 'There is something about a starched apron stretched across a decent pair of breasts that brings out the worst in me,' he thought, delighted with himself.

He watched her walk languorously across to the sideboard with her tray : good from the back, too. He turned to the second course. Salmon trout, game pie, roast saddle of lamb, grilled kidneys and bacon ...

'Here you are, sir. No ice for you, isn't it, sir.' It was Henry with the drink. 'I'll send Doris to you for your order.' Two members had entered the dining-room and stood waiting for their table and to tell Henry that he didn't look a day older.

The colonel sipped his drink and felt in his inner breast pocket for his spectacles. He was wearing a lemon yellow carnation, that looked very well against his fine, black-and-white houndstooth check. Now he could see the menu with no trouble at all, and by God, it made a nice change from poor old May's efforts : all one wanted was good, simple food, produced at regular intervals with no fuss. He decided upon potted shrimps and game pie. Doris, standing by the sideboard, realized that he'd decided and padded over to him. She wore sensible, low-heeled shoes with double straps, thick, fawn cotton stockings and a very great deal of uncompromisingly heavy make-up. Her uniform made her look as though she'd be a wonderful old girl in an emergency.

'Ready to order, sir, are you?'

'Why not, Doris, why not? Tell me – what is your opinion of the game pie?'

'It's very nice, sir.'

'Then I'll risk it. Now, as we both know perfectly well what garden peas are, what other vegetable would you recommend?'

'I'd have the broccoli, sir – it's fresh.' She'd told him at least fifty times that the peas were frozen, but he'd got it into his head that they were tinned and there was no shifting him.

'And what to start with, sir?'

'A few potted shrimps would do.'

'Thank you, sir. I'll send the wine waiter.'

When he had ordered his usual, half a bottle of club claret, he started to review his morning's work. 'Lawyers all the morning – you know how it is,' he murmured to himself, in case he met any members he knew who would ask him what he was doing with himself these days. He didn't – not even the member who had suggested this particular firm to him as very decent chaps. It had been a ticklish business. Because what he'd wanted to know didn't sound right, somehow, as something to walk in and ask a total stranger about. He'd had to sort of lead up to it – hedge the whole thing a bit. He'd been wanting to make his will, he said, and old so-and-so had put him on to *you*. They'd had a brief talk – well, exchanged a few remarks about their supposedly mutual friend (whom he had only met twice) at the end of which he decided that the lawyer barely knew who they were talking about. So much the better: he didn't like the idea of his private affairs getting about, and although these chaps were supposed to be discreet – how could you tell? Well – about his will. He didn't, of course, want to leave his wife in a jam, and although he was in the best of health, it was as well to be on the safe side. The lawyer (his name was Mr Pinkney) who had been trained for years to agree with this view, agreed with it. He'd have to make a list of his securities and so forth; there would be a pension of course, but apart from that … but the thing was, that their house, their home in Surrey, happened to be in her name – so legally he supposed it was hers anyway, whether he kicked the bucket or not? And he fixed the lawyer with a look of piercing, frank anxiety. Yes, of course, the house (freehold or leasehold? Freehold? So much the better) was certainly the property of his wife – he'd be very happy to look at the deeds of course, but from what the colonel was telling him there would seem to be no doubt upon this point. The colonel relaxed almost theatrically – that is to say that if you had been up to a hundred yards away from him at the time you would have seen that that was what he was doing. It depended, Mr Pinkney went on rather more warmly (nice old chap – simply didn't know the first thing about business; you got it again and again with these retired servicemen), on the size of the colonel's estate. One might reach a position where, if things were not carefully arranged, his wife might not have sufficient income to *live* in the house, in which case, although it was a realizable asset, she might be placed in some temporary embarrassment ... She wouldn't *want* to live in the place without him, the colonel said: far too big for her – she'd be lonely in it. That reminded him of another, small point: supposing *she* were to die – would the house then naturally belong to him? Trifling point, but as he was here, he might as well clear up everything he could. Had his wife made a will, Mr Pinkney inquired? He believed she had made one years ago – before she married him. All wills made prior to marriage become invalid upon that ceremony, and it was necessary to make fresh ones. Of course, if Mrs Browne-Lacey did *not* make another will, her estate would naturally go to her husband – and vice versa. Unless, of course there were children on either side by previous marriages? What would happen then? asked the colonel – a trifle sharply (Mr Pinkney must understand that all this legal jaw was quite difficult for a plain, simple, ordinary man to follow), he hadn't quite grasped what Mr Pinkney was driving at about children ...

Mr Pinkney had explained. Having established that there were no children of the present marriage, nor likely to be, he had gone carefully into the respective situations of Alice and of Oliver and Elizabeth. The colonel had thanked him heartily for making everything so clear, had got to his feet saying that the whole matter needed thinking about, but that he would be in touch when he had done his sums, and had finished by giving Mr Pinkney one of his handshakes (Oliver had once described them as Tarzan pretending to be a Freemason).

By now he was well into the game pie and wondering whether he would have room for cheese. There was no need to worry about *Alice*; she would never cause any trouble, and in any case, as he had explained to Mr Pinkney, she had married a man of substance. The trouble, which he had *not* mentioned to Mr Pinkney, was clearly May's children. She was besotted with them, and really he wouldn't put it past her either to leave them so much of her estate that the house had to be sold to realize the cash for them, or, and possibly worse, to leave them the actual house. And it was now clear that if she *didn't* make another will, they – in fact he meant Oliver – would start kicking up if they didn't get what they thought was a fair share of the great-aunt's money. Elizabeth would almost certainly get married, but who knew what the feller might turn out to be like? One of those grasping fellers with a legal mind, or else one of those damn pacifist wallahs who wouldn't use birth-control. It really wasn't fair at his time of life that he should have to sit here worrying whether he would have a roof over his head. He wouldn't have cheese – just a brandy with his coffee. Lucky to be able to afford *that*.

* * *

•

'One of them is cherry brandy and the other's orange curaçao.' May looked from Dr Sedum to Lavinia. She looked both anxious and triumphant; she was very proud of herself for remembering the two miniature bottles she'd given the children in their stockings at Christmas, but she was worried lest both drinks might prove too *frivolous* for Dr Sedum. The coffee – made the way that Elizabeth had taught her – now stood on the trolley. It *was* such a pity there was no brandy, but she'd said that once – before she'd remembered the miniatures.

'Which are *you* going to drink?' inquired Dr Sedum.

'Oh neither. I don't like it – them. At least, sometimes I do, but not today.' (It was frightful the way she caught herself out telling a lie to Dr Sedum – it showed what she was like. 'I expect I only noticed it because he was here, and really I tell thousands of lies without noticing'.)

Dr Sedum turned to Lavinia: she did not mind which she drank. Impartiality – in Dr Sedum's case, a touch roguish – seemed to be the code; May, without meaning to, suddenly imagined Oliver being there, but dismissed him at once. Oliver wouldn't really understand Dr Sedum, who was simply trying to . . .

'. . . enter into the spirit of the thing.' He was smiling again.

'I'm afraid there isn't much spirit in two miniatures.' May heard herself saying this as though someone else had said it.

The drinks were poured, and people lit cigarettes. Now, perhaps Dr Sedum would talk. He did.

At the time, she knew that it was absolutely fascinating – although of course, very difficult. Afterwards, they had got to their feet, put on their coats, stood silently eyeing one another (a kind of mystical weighing up, she had felt, although *she* was naturally not up to this process; she knew she wasn't fit, as they so obviously were, to weigh anyone) and then walked quietly to the Bentley, where Dr Sedum most *humanly* had wound a rather ugly woollen muffler round his throat before getting into the front seat beside Lavinia – all without a single (unnecessary) word; oh yes, as they drove off, he raised his hand in a manner which reminded her, before she could stop herself, of the queen mother. Then, after they had gone, almost at once, as she turned to the huge prison front door, she had started trying to sum up all those breathtaking things he had been saying. About one's identity and not actually having one – it being all a desperate egocentric invention. Only, on the other hand, everybody had what he described as a true personality buried out of sight of conscious understanding. How did one find it then, she had asked? A very good question, he had answered. The trouble with very good questions seemed to be that their very quality guaranteed their not being answered. There would be a pause, and then – he had so much to give – he would say something quite different. There were certain people, he had said, who were searching for something very difficult to find, who did not *want* or expect the search to be an easy one. Not for them the panacea of some universal dogma and a set of rules, penalties and rewards. There were a few people who understood that there could be no rules, no penalties and no rewards. A rule only manifested itself after one had broken it : the person paying a penalty was the last one to discover what it was, and to be aware of a reward was to understand a failure in oneself. There was no such thing as cause and effect, simply a chain joined upon itself and one had the choice of being a bead upon the chain, or the chain itself. What happened when one became one of those things? But this, alas, turned out to be another good question. It was not possible either to take or to give anything to anyone : the hysteria of that kind of practical morality had to be discarded. People were not able either to give or to take – they simply were; the problem was how to discover *what* they were. It was sometimes necessary to demonstrate the impracticability of giving and taking by going through these motions : many people embarking upon the precious and mysterious search had to be initiated in this manner. One could not understand the emptiness of any gesture until one had made it. Then he had talked about the Unconscious Self and Emotion – not as she, May, and indeed most people defined that word, but something that none of us were, initially at least, capable of feeling (that was when she realized that it had a capital E); indeed, most people went through their lives without being aware of its existence; 'Like me,' she had thought – she was indeed, she felt, like most people in every respect. What did one do with this Emotion when one got hold of it? A good question : one had then to make it continuous. It sounded awfully tiring, she had thought, and then felt thoroughly ashamed of herself for being so feeble. While she was thinking this, Dr Sedum had gone on speaking, but so quietly that she hadn't been able to hear, let alone understand what he had said. Then he suddenly rose, and suggested looking at the house. She had thought that he meant he wanted to go to the lavatory, but she had turned out to be embarrassingly wrong. He had wanted to see the whole house, and so, uncomfortably, she had showed both him and Lavinia. 'Some white elephant,' Lavinia had remarked at the end of their tour. 'Oliver, my son, said a real white elephant couldn't possibly be more trouble and would be far more interesting.' Neither of them had smiled, and she had realized that darling Oliver would seem incurably frivolous to them. Back in the morning room, Dr Sedum had murmured that it was always easier to set out on a journey lightly appointed, and then, Lavinia having reminded him that *he* had an appointment in London, they all got up from the chairs they had returned to. That was roughly it. But she couldn't pretend to herself that she under*stood* much of it. They had said that they would get in touch with her very soon, so at least she hadn't been rejected out of hand. That was something. She walked dreamily back to the morning room in order to set about the frightful task of returning it to its usual state of barren, underfurnished drabness. She was immensely *interested*, she repeated to herself, but not yet actually *enlightened*.

*

Hilda had one of those awful beds that squeaked. As he leaned forward to pull on his socks, the colonel shifted his weight to allow for or avoid the noise, and failed. He'd got one sock on before he realized that it was inside out. Damn, he thought. It was extraordinary how everything invariably combined to irritate him after one of these sessions. He would set about them feeling quite jolly and serene : ring up Hilda, who seemed always to be free and always glad to see him – 'Pop along' to her place (remember to ring her flat bell in the rhythm of 'Colonel Bogey' – it always made her laugh) and there you were; Bob's your uncle, all that kind of thing. Hilda was the good old-fashioned sort; properly dressed to start with, but nippy enough getting out of it all – or whatever combination of all you fancied – and then there was a nice cup of tea and Bourbon biscuits afterwards ... here she was, with the tray, before he'd even got his *socks* on dammit.

'Here we are, then.' She put the tray down on a small bamboo table by the window, and with her back to him, peered into the dressing-table mirror to make sure that none of her mascara had smudged. She knew it hadn't, but men never liked you to watch them dressing. She had slipped into her embroidered kimono affair that a very nice regular had brought her all the way back from the Far East ... which reminded her that she was just in time to adjust the hands on the cuckoo clock to stop the poor little chap from coming out and shouting cuckoo four times for four o'clock. A very nice gentleman had brought it all the way back from Switzerland: her flat was full of these foreign tokens, each one with its own story if truth would out.

'How's the tea coming along?'

'It should be perfect now.' If only he'd get up off the bed, she could fold it up and return everything to normal. 'Come and have it in this nice chair.'

When he was well into his second biscuit, she filled up his cup and said, 'Bogey!'

'What is it?'

She'd been dreading this moment ever since he'd rung up.

'I'm afraid everything has got a weeny bit dearer.'

He put his cup down in slow motion and turned to stare at her.

'How do you mean "everything"?'

His pale blue eyes bulged like glass marbles: he knew perfectly well what she meant. Oh well! If he was going to dig his toes in, she would have to put her foot down.

'I mean things like tea and biscuits —' (he started to push his cup away) 'and the rent, Bogey dear.'

'Same for all of us. Cost of living only goes *up*: never comes *down*.'

'Don't I know it.'

'Oh, I don't suppose you do. Women never have any head for the practical aspects of life. Leave that to the men.'

There was a brief unsatisfactory silence while she told herself there was no sense in losing her temper, and he wondered what devil in him made him come and see her at all. Something pretty primitive and deep-down and uncontrollable. Her figure wasn't what it was.

'Well there it is, I'm afraid.'

'There *what* is?'

'It's another thirty bob: on top of the usual. I can't help it, Bogey – I've kept it down as long as I could.'

'I thought you were *fond* of me.'

'It has nothing to do with how I feel.'

'I looked on you as much more than a –'

She stared at a biscuit. Eventually, he said,

'Some prices may be going up, but you're not getting any younger, you know.'

Her hands held on to each other for comfort, but because of the kimono sleeves he couldn't see them. He got heavily to his feet, feeling in his pockets, counted out the notes and then slowly sorted four half crowns which he put on top of them on his biscuit plate.

'There y'are m'dear: all present and correct.' Unwilling jocularity, or perhaps he was sorry about what he had just said and didn't know how to make amends. He walked slowly to the door, opened it, and said,

'Seriously, Hilda, chaps like me – living on a pension and all that – you don't want to price yourself out of the market, do you, old girl?'

She shut the door after him and went to the bathroom to fetch poor Siegfried – she always had to put him out of the room when she had customers, or else he chirped and sang all through everything. She took off his cover, dear little chap, he put his head on one side and made an experimental cheep. As she picked up his cage and carried it carefully back to the room, she realized she was crying: a tear splashed through the bars on to Siegfried's cage sand, making an enormous blob like ink in advertisements. She knew she wasn't getting any younger.

•

May heard the Wolseley coming up the drive and hurried to the front door. The house was – not exactly frightening – but more and more depressing to be alone in: towards the end of a day, one could easily feel quite frightened at how depressed one had become, and things like turning on the wireless often made it worse. She missed Alice: if only the dogs were allowed into the house, or if Claude was less self-contained and spoke more – really, Lincoln Street with Oliver and Elizabeth had been so cosy ...

'There y'are m'dear, all present and correct.' He put his old Burberry on the carved eagle's shoulders of a lectern and bent to kiss her cheek and pat her shoulder as he always did.

'Did you have a pleasant day?'

She had to ask him again, as he seemed not to have heard her. 'Fair to middling.'

After the shepherd's pie and tinned figs, which they consumed in his den, he suggested that he make her some coffee. So she loaded and fetched the tray with all the apparatus – test tubes and spirit lamps, filters and, of course, the actual coffee. As the muddy brown liquid churned up and down, he asked,

'Did that cousin of yours make it for lunch?'

'Yes! Oh yes. She brought a friend with her: it was very interesting.'

There! Now there was hardly any concealment: although she knew that there was, really: the very idea of Dr Sedum and what he stood for would make Herbert simply furious. At the thought of Herbert thinking her underhand, she blushed.

Herbert said he was too tired to play backgammon and had the notion that a spot of early Bedfordshire would do no harm. She knew that she would not sleep so soon after the coffee, so she said she would watch the television for a bit. She switched on the vision without sound to see whether it would be funny, or she would like it, but this seemed to clear the way for the only thought she had been trying to not to have, and having ever since Dr Sedum and Lavinia had left: that if she had not married Herbert she would now be living in London with darling Oliver and Elizabeth (if they wanted her to, of course) within easy reach of Great Possibilities (Dr Sedum and his Ideas); and finally, and perhaps worst of all, that she seemed to have less and less in common with Herbert who was (quite honestly) both exacting and dull. Oh, this was really *shocking* of her! She

turned up the sound on the television to drown her guilty protestations ... a *good* man ... deep depression sweeping south-
wards ... simple and straightforward ... unusually heavy frosts
for the time of year ... A *good* man.

Part Two: August

1. First Sight

By the beginning of August, Elizabeth had cooked fifty-two dinners: Oliver, on the other hand, had gone to eleven interviews and had actually taken two of the jobs, but neither of them had turned out to be right. One of them had been in a very new book shop that concentrated upon selling poetry and giving customers cardboard cups of Nescafé, and he had quite quickly had a row with the shop's manager: 'In one morning, he said that Tibetans were probably better off under Chinese rule; all Americans were suffering from vitamin deficiencies from eating so much frozen food; and the French were the only people with literary taste. I'll Robbe-Grillet you, I said, and that was that.' The other job had been as a courier, taking a lot of nice, middle-aged women to the Costa Brava, which he said he could not go on doing because they simply hated it when they got there, and group dysentery and disillusionment wore him to a thread. 'Dogfight' had not yet been sold, although Sukie had driven him patiently all over the suburbs to places where stony-faced men bought and manufactured games. He had had to write out the rules in frightful legal jargon so that nobody could understand them, at least, certainly neither Elizabeth nor Sukie could, and Sukie said he'd simply managed to make the game sound complicated and boring. He quarrelled with Sukie rather a lot, and alternated bouts of depression with fractious, manic energy. Elizabeth would come home weary from clearing up some dinner party to find that he had made a great Indian feast by collecting dishes from the nearest curry restaurant. Or he would take her out and make her spend far more of her earnings buying clothes for herself than she felt she could afford. For about three weeks he gambled, with, she felt, horrifying success: he spent these sudden gains on a pair of wine coolers he bought in an auction at Sotheby's.

'How much did they cost?' she yelped just after she had fallen over them in the narrow hall.

'Forty-two pounds.' He switched on the hall light. 'Aren't they a marvellous sight?'

'What *are* they?'

'Wine coolers. How vulgar of you to ask how much something that you don't know what it is costs.'

She gazed at the fluted tubs of some impassively dark wood delicately inlaid with brass. The lids were fluted as well, and crowned by a handle made of a carved, rather angry crouching swan. She touched one of them. 'That part is nice.'

'See?' He lifted a lid. 'They've got their linings. What did you *think* they would be for?'

She frowned. 'Well, I suppose some Indian could keep the ashes of his best elephant in one of them. What on earth made you spend all that money?'

'You remember David Broadstairs? Well, he's starting an antique business on a Thames barge. He asked me to keep my eyes open for anything nice, so I have – I did. He'll sell them for me at the most enormous profit, you'll see.' Then he added sadly, 'He's got a terrifically rich sister, but she looks like an old-fashioned Channel swimmer and she couldn't even pass her "O" levels. I do think God's sense of justice goes too far at times. I'm off to see our mother in Surrey now.'

'You never told me!'

'I've told you the moment I saw you after I knew. She sounds as though she needs a visit.' He kissed her lightly on a bit of cheekbone, and was gone. She opened the door after him and called:

'When will you be back?'

'Late tonight, probably – why do you want to know?'

'People ringing up – you *fool*.' He whipped round in the street and charged straight at her so that she had to clutch him not to fall over.

'Let's get this clear: *you're* the fool: *I'm* the whiz kid: you're younger than me: I'm far heavier and stronger and my sense of chivalry died when I saw matron at school during a fire practice. O.K.?'

'O.K.' She was nearly in tears at being called a fool but she was laughing. She scratched what looked like some egg off his corduroy jacket, and a lot came off under her nail, but the mark looked exactly the same.

'Why can't I go with you?'

'Because it's nicer for May if we spread her children out.' He kissed her. 'You smell like a delicious clean cow. If Sukie rings, tell her I'm out with Shirley MacLaine: no – tell her, and I mean this, tell her I've gone away with Ginny Mole: she'll believe *that* all right, and it'll be more likely to choke her off.'

Then he really did go.

Back in the silent, empty little house, Elizabeth made herself a large mug of iced Nescafé, kicked off her sandals and lay on the battered old sofa wondering whether she ought to read a serious book as she was having some free time by herself. London in August wasn't very nice: or perhaps nowhere felt so good if Oliver wasn't there. She ought, as he pointed out, to make some friends of her own, but somehow, what with her job (and she had to have that because between them they needed more money than May socked them) *and* Oliver and his friends and life, there never seemed to be any time. But she had to face it: the job wasn't getting her anywhere – just as Oliver not getting a job wasn't getting *him* anywhere: the trouble was that Oliver didn't mind – after the courier job he'd said that he simply wasn't one of life's travellers, and that Stevenson's remark was a horrible mixture of austerity and showing off; personally, he, Oliver, was one of life's arrivers and wasn't going to let his life degenerate into a hopeful mystery tour. She hadn't liked to ask who Stevenson was (either a friend of Oliver's, or else someone dead and famous, because whichever he was she'd get snubbed) ... Well, she couldn't read a book, because she had awful leather patches to put on the elbows of Oliver's tweed jacket: she'd promised to do the sewing if he got the leather, thinking he'd never get it, but he did, at once. 'And what's more, it's very distinguished.'

'What *is* it?' And she had gazed with discomfort at the strip of stiff, wrinkled hide that still had tufts of dark and pale fur attached to it.

'The hind leg of a man-eating tiger. Annabel's father shot it in Bengal and had it made into one of those *snarling* rugs, but he doesn't take much notice of it nowadays, so Annabel cut off this bit for me. If he *does* notice, she'll say it got moth.

'He was a frightful tiger – full of cheap bangles and beads: just get on with your sewing and *don't* get soppy about the wrong things,' he added. 'You can't be sad about *every*one who's dead.'

Now, she'd no sooner started getting on with it, when the telephone rang, and a voice that was clearly Sukie trying to pretend to be someone else, asked for Mr Oliver Seymour.

Elizabeth explained that he was out, and the person – Sukie – rang off before she could say when he'd be back. A moment later, it rang again and Sukie, sounding pretty desperate, said, 'I know it's you. Are you *sure* he's out?'

'Yes, of course I am. All day.'

'When, when will he be back?'

'He wasn't quite sure.' The trouble with loyalty was that it always seemed to include a good deal of hard-heartedness to whoever you weren't being loyal to. There was a pause, then Sukie said,

'The awful thing is, I think Oliver's tired of me: I can't *bear* to think it, but I can't help thinking it.'

'Oh – poor Sukie!'

'What do you think?'

'Well –'

'Is there someone else, do you know?'

'I don't –'

'Because he keeps on talking about one of the most boring people I've ever met in my life and I couldn't help wondering.'

'Sukie, I really don't –'

'Has he mentioned someone called Ginny to you?'

'Only just.'

'Well he never stops mentioning her to me. She's one of the most boring people I've ever met in my life.'

There was another pause, during which it was quite clear to Elizabeth that Sukie was crying. Unable to stand this, she said,

'As a matter of fact, Oliver has gone to see his mother – our mother.'

'Honestly?'

'Honestly: he told me just before he left. Probably back to-night.'

'Really and truly? You swear you're not making this up?'

'Sukie, I absolutely promise.'

'Oh! Elizabeth! Do you think that means there is some hope for me?'

Before she could stop herself, Elizabeth had said, 'No I don't. Oh look here, Sukie, you'd better come round: it'd be much better than talking on the telephone.'

So Sukie came round in a flash, and they had a long talk about Life and not being possessive and whether young marriages turned out well on the whole or not and what jealousy did to people's character and how much being brilliant had to do with being cold, and whether young, and particularly young *brilliant* men ever really knew what they wanted and when neither of them could think of any more ways of discussing Oliver, Elizabeth made some more iced Nescafé and then Sukie helped her wash her hair. Sukie was very good at this, rinsing Elizabeth's hair until it squeaked, and saying kindly that if Elizabeth took more trouble with it, it could be one of her best features, and that hundreds of people spent thousands of pounds having artificial red-gold lights put into their hair. It was just one more of those days when knowledge of soil erosion, mono-tremes and the Moorish influence in Spain (or indeed anywhere else) would not have proved of the slightest use ...

About four o'clock they were just looking through an evening paper in case there was a film worth seeing, when the telephone rang.

'Is that by any chance Miss Elizabeth Seymour?'

'Yes.'

'You won't remember me. I was a guest at a dinner party cooked by you in Eaton Square last week. Artichokes vinai-grette, trout with almonds and cream cheese tarts: that one.'

'Oh yes; I remember.' There had been eight people in all, so that meant he could be any one of the three male guests.

'I was the tall, nearly bald one with thick glasses. The thing is, I'm in rather a mess. I wonder if you could help me out?'

Elizabeth waited.

'I've suddenly been presented with the necessity of having dinner at home without staff of any kind. I wondered, if, by any chance, you happen to be free to help me out?'

'How did you find me? I usually work through an agency.'

'So I was told. But they seem to be permanently engaged: so I rang the Mountjoys – the Mountjoys of Eaton Square – and they gave me your number. I'm really rather desperate or I wouldn't have gone to such lengths. I've never liked the telephone.'

'Well – I usually do work through the agency, and they would expect –'

'Oh, I'll pay them anything they expect, and I'm quite prepared to pay you more. I have a rather vulgar attitude to money in fact. I've found it's the best attitude to have. So don't worry about that aspect.'

'How many people do you want me to cook for? I *am* free, as a matter of fact,' she added hurriedly.

'Oh, what a relief! Just for two. A Mrs Cole and myself: I've ordered some of that very thick steak and some sort of pâté to go with it. Mrs Cole is something of a carnivore.'

'Do you want any kind of savoury or pudding?'

'A savoury would be delicious. Could I leave that to you? Have you got a pencil to write down my address?'

'No: hang on a minute.' She couldn't find one, but Sukie kindly produced her eyeliner and an advertising page of the *Evening Standard*. The address turned out to be in Pelham Place (walking distance from Lincoln Street, jolly good thing), but when he produced his telephone number, the eyeliner broke, and she had to repeat it aloud while Sukie kindly arranged bunches of matches on the carpet.

'And what's your name, please?' she remembered to ask before he rang off.

'John Cole. Tremendously in keeping with my appearance, I'm afraid you'll find. Goodbye.'

'What on earth could he mean by that?' Elizabeth said as she put the receiver down.

'By what?' Sukie was cramming the unused matches back in the box. 'You must admit I'm a marvellous secretary: full of resources.'

'Saying his name was John Cole and it was tremendously in keeping with his appearance.'

'No idea. It's a pretty dull name.'

'That's it, then. He said he was nearly bald and wore thick glasses.'

'Poor old thing,' said Sukie absently. Then she turned the awe-inspring contents of her handbag on to the hearth-rug and found a pencil.

•

Elizabeth walked to Pelham Place. Sukie had offered to drive her, but she felt like walking, and also her hair wasn't quite dry. She had managed to get Sukie to go, on the grounds that it would be rather obvious for Oliver to find her in Lincoln Street, supposing he got back before Elizabeth did. The talk with Sukie had left her feeling far more contented with her lot or life than she had been feeling before Sukie rang up. It was much luckier to be Oliver's sister than one of his mistresses: to begin with, he was far kinder to her than he seemed to be to people like Annabel or Sukie, and to go on with, whatever he was, he couldn't really stop being it, which made the whole situation feel far more secure and free.

She arrived at the house at Pelham Place at about seven o'clock. It was one of those stucco, non-committal houses where you couldn't be sure what kind of person might live. A long time after she had rung the bell, she realized that the front door was open – and walked in. She could hear a gramophone, and a bath running: the kitchen, with luck, would be on the ground floor, and if not, certainly in the basement. The gramophone was playing Mozart: one up to him, she thought, but she had got fairly professional in her expectations of her employers. Few of them had turned out as awful as those first ones in Bryanston Square, but, on the other hand, none of them had struck her as people one was sorry not to be having dinner *with* (instead of actually cooking their dinners). The kitchen *was* in the basement, but so was the dining-room, so *that* was all right. It was a comforting mixture of Formica and Elizabeth David – hygienic, but well-equipped. The dining-room had rather old-fashioned Cole's wallpaper (perhaps *he* made it) and the traditional amount of damp – or mildew. She unpacked the materials for the savoury, put on her overall, and started looking for everything else.

John Cole materialized in that kind of twilight that you never notice until somebody else brings your attention to it. He was holding two glasses in his hands. 'Do you like champagne?' is what he eventually said. He *was* very tall, and his spectacles winked in the reflection from the street lamp outside the basement window.

'Now I would.' Elizabeth took the glass and drank gratefully.

'Your overall is so dazzling that I can't see your face in this Stygian light.' He switched on some lights. 'I hope you are managing to find everything. My resident couple left rather suddenly. This afternoon in fact. Would you like some more of that?'

'Well – a little more. It's very good.'

'Ostentation combined with stinginess have given champagne an unfairly bad name.' He had opened the huge fridge and extracted an unopened bottle. 'Chuck me that cloth, would you? Have you ever drunk decent champagne at a wedding, for instance?' He was untwisting the wire from the neck of the bottle.

'Sorry, I thought when you said "more" that we'd be finishing a bottle.'

'That's all right. *I'm* not stingy – ostentatious, but not stingy. And I wanted some more myself. Hold it out.'

He drew the cork and filled her glass to the brim. After he had replaced the bottle in the fridge, he leant against one of the teak draining boards and said, 'Would it be all right with you if I stay and drink with you while you do your stuff? I've had a pig of a day, and if I go and sit upstairs by myself I shall fall asleep.' There was the briefest pause, then, before she had replied, he added, 'I *could* say that I'd be a help if you couldn't find anything, but that would be a complete lie. I haven't really the faintest idea where anything is.' Another slight pause, before he said, 'But if you hate people being about when you are at work, I should quite understand.'

Elizabeth said, 'Oh no! It's – it's much better having someone to talk to. Do stay.'

'I will.' She found she was looking at him exactly when he began to smile: this made him look more different from when he wasn't smiling than anyone she had ever seen. She smiled briefly back – even across the room she had to look up at him: he was extraordinarily tall. For a second, the whole evening suddenly seemed festive and momentous, as though something very good was certainly going to happen. Amazed by this, she continued to look at him, or rather in his direction, but seeing only herself now. '*You're* the fool,' Oliver had said only a few hours ago, and a feeling like that simply showed how right he was. She saw herself – a pair of little white dwarfs reflected in his glasses – and then she saw him again, shoulders slightly hunched, head a little to one side, at the end of his smile – 'staring casually,' she thought, if that made sense. Her forehead felt burning under her fringe. She got her pad with pencil attached out of her bag, and started to write out the menu in full in order to check off her materials.

'What time would you like to have dinner?'

They both looked at their watches.

'I should think in the neighbourhood of half-past eight. The trouble is that I can't be sure when my guest will arrive.'

'And of course you will want time for – a drink before dinner.'

'No.'

She glanced at him, surprised, and then told herself that it was none of her business: but then, it was, a bit.

'I don't think I can start to cook your steak until your guest has actually arrived –'

'There's some caviare to start with. Here.' He opened the

fridge and indicated the largest pot of caviare that she had ever seen.

'Right. Do you like onion and egg and chopped parsley – all that sort of thing?'

'None of that sort of thing. Mrs Cole and I eat it in porridge bowls with spoons: I say, you're lagging behind a bit with that champagne: if it's too warm chuck it away; the hallmark here is seasoned vulgarity.'

'Mrs Cole and I.' Of course, he had mentioned a Mrs Cole earlier. She was fitting greaseproof paper round the small soufflé dish she had brought: it did seem a curious way of referring either to your wife or your mother – but that really *was* none of her business . . .

'Is Mrs Cole your wife' (How could I. Don't tell me, I don't want to know.)

'Mrs Cole is my wife.'

(Oh. Is she indeed: well I don't see why you had to be so secretive about it.) 'Oh.'

'To be exact, she *was* my wife: she isn't any more; we're divorced.'

(Well that's something. *What?* in that case why did you ever say she was your wife and why on *earth* are you taking all this trouble to have her to dinner?) 'Oh.'

'Do *you* like caviare?'

'I've never had enough to be sure: by itself, I mean. It's nearly always *on* things. Now I'd better lay the table. Is the silver in the dining-room?'

'Let's go and see. It's possible, I suppose, that Colonel Grzimek has walked off with it; or motored, which was more his style. Isn't it odd,' he went on as he opened the dining-room door for her, 'how one always speaks of servants in the past tense the moment they have left? There's a nasty streak of egocentricity there, all right.

'I maligned the colonel. There is the silver: all of it, by the look of things.'

He was towering over the sideboard on which there was a large rosewood canteen systematically stuffed with spoons and forks.

Elizabeth, suddenly remembering Daddo, couldn't help beginning to laugh and then going on. He looked at her while she did this with approval and interest.

'What an extraordinarily involuntary noise that is. The idea of a colonel being a butler amuses you? Well, he almost certainly wasn't one. He was Romanian (there I go again, no doubt he still is), and it was his way of showing me that he was too good for the job. There is something comfortingly international about military rank. He also said his wife was an ex-opera singer. He almost certainly wasn't married to her, and she showed no signs of even retrospective musicality, but she was a damn good cook. She did everything. She cleaned *his* shoes, while he cleaned mine.' By now he was sitting in the carver at the head of the table, while Elizabeth laid a place in front of him.

'Where shall I put Mrs Cole?'

'A very good question. It's no good putting her at the other end, because she won't stay there. There, I should think, would be as safe a compromise as any.'

'If they were so good, why did they leave?'

'I wanted them to come out to the villa and the colonel said that somebody had insulted him in Monaco in 1936 and there had been a little trouble; and then he said *I* was insulting him and after that he sulked for two frightful days (a really effective sulker; the bathwater and the champagne became exactly the same uninviting temperature). Then he simply left . . .

'No doubt,' he added, following her back to the kitchen, 'his loss will prove a blessing in disguise. That is how they usually come, I find. You get misfortunes in plain clothes as it were, but not your average blessing.'

Elizabeth, rather dazed by the way in which he seemed to be talking about a lot of things she didn't know about all at once, absently gulped the rest of her champagne.

'I'm interrupting you : I'll go. Let me fill your glass, and leave you to it.'

'It's all right, so long as you don't expect any intelligent response.' She was doing the part of a soufflé that you can do ahead of time. The steak was out and ready; the watercress (the only concession to greenery in the entire meal) was waiting, washed, in the salad basket.

'Do you want your steak *on* pâté *on* toast?'

Before he could answer, the front door rang without stopping for what seemed like ages.

John Cole said, 'I'll go. There's an intercom by the door there. I'll tell you when we want to start on the caviare. Don't, for God's sake, go before I've seen you.' He went.

He's dreading it, Elizabeth thought : perhaps he's still in love with her? Yes. No. If he isn't, she must be very awful for him not to take her *out* to dinner. Surely that would have been the answer?

Voices : a contralto treacle; John Cole's. Door shutting; the woman laughing – a husky, but high-pitched laugh – another door shutting, and silence.

Silence for what seemed ages, but Elizabeth, who timed it, knew that it was no more than twenty minutes. She hummed and hawed about cooking the steak, and something told her not to until both the Coles were safely in his dining-room. But this didn't seem to be going to happen. She fidgeted around the kitchen, fiddling with the soufflé mix, turning the steak in its salt, oil and lemon juice, swinging the basket of watercress. Eventually she sat down, combed her hair and put on a spot more lipstick : her fringe was too long again – it was getting, as Oliver had said, like one of those intensely reliable dogs. Seeing herself for long always made her feel shaky and depressed. She decided to have a proper look at the dining-room.

The paper was like the passages at Convent Garden – broad stripes – only here it was two different fairly dark greens. The walls had several pictures that looked, at first sight, to be French Impressionists, and on closer examination (and bearing the champagne and caviare in mind) stayed being them. The damp patches, the marks on the lime-coloured carpet, the rather low, smoky ceiling, all gave the impression that the room had been decorated years ago – pictures and all – and then simply left. Was this the work of Mrs Cole?

The moment Elizabeth thought this, she heard Mrs .Cole's

voice; continuous and, even at a distance, seeming too loud. She slipped back into the kitchen : the voice got louder.

They seemed to be taking a very long time to come downstairs. She put the steaks under the grill; got the caviare out of the fridge and then, her heart beating out of sheer curiosity, made for the dining-room.

Mrs Cole was sitting at the table, but not at the place set for her. She had dragged (at least Elizabeth supposed it must have been she who had dragged) a chair and placed it tremendously near her ex-husband's place.

'Cavvers – goody-goody-goody gum-drops!'

Mrs Cole's voice was naturally rather high, but with a good deal of husky interference which gave her a much wider vocal range than most people. At any rate, her voice certainly made you look at her. Elizabeth looked, and then immediately looked away, because she found Mrs Cole's enormous, pale blue, rather protuberant eyes fixed upon her.

'Is this a little chum of Jennifer's?'

'It is not.' He pushed the caviare over to her while Elizabeth fetched the silver porringers from the sideboard.

'He's a *sodding* awful liar, isn't he?' Mrs Cole laid a thin, white, heavily freckled arm upon Elizabeth's overall. 'You know all about where Jennifer is, don't you, darling?'

'I'm afraid I don't –'

'Miss Seymour has kindly come in to cook dinner. She's never even *met* Jennifer. Come on, Daphne, stop needling, and have some nice caviare.'

Without letting go of what had become her grasp of Elizabeth's overall (the skinny arm culminated in a hand that was shaped like the foot of some bird of prey), Mrs Cole started to dig her spoon into the pot. 'Vere is the wodka?' she asked. Drops of caviare dripped from her shaky, laden spoon and rolled about the table. When some of it was in the bowl, she stabbed at it petulantly. 'No cavvers without wodders,' she said in a sort of voice that a large doll, if it could talk, would talk. She was altogether like a huge, old doll, Elizabeth thought. Even her hair had a very wide parting in it – like doll's hair – and she wore it in a long, permanently-waved bob – like Rita

Hayworth in ancient films. Mrs Cole's head and the shoulders of her black crêpe dress were showered with dandruff, and well over and above her Chanel No. 5, Elizabeth could detect the odour of cheap raspberry jam that so often accompanies this condition.

John Cole, without answering, took out a bunch of keys and left the room. The moment that they were alone, Mrs Cole's grip on Elizabeth's arm tightened, and just as Elizabeth was going to pull herself away from this rather surprising and horrible person, she said,

'While he's away – quick! write down her *number* – I only want to *see* her.' She had let go at last, and was fumbling desperately with her bag. '*You* look for me, darling, any old scrap will do – I just want to give her my love.' And for a moment Elizabeth found herself looking down into the huge, heavily made-up doll's face, whose eyes were of such open agony that she felt her hair prickling with shock. She would do *any*thing to stop someone looking like that.

The bag, which had seemed quite small, was crammed with dirty, broken, spilt things – loose aspirins coated with brown face-powder, a miniature bottle of Gordon's gin, a grey elastic sanitary belt, a screwed-up packet which could contain no smokable cigarette, a little Disney-type dog made of pipe cleaners, a chiffon handkerchief with a swansdown puff attached, some cloakroom tickets, pencils (broken), Biro (top off), a tube of something that was oozing out at the bottom ...

John Cole was back. He carried a bottle of vodka in one hand, and two very small glasses in the other. Elizabeth, who had been burrowing, as directed, into Mrs Cole's handbag, saw his face, and felt herself beginning to blush. Mrs Cole looked at her with hatred, but there was something helpless about it, and Elizabeth, now feeling treacherous in both directions, put the bag back on the side of Mrs Cole's chair. Her ears were burning, and the steak needed basting.

'What a one you are for locking things up. It would have been awful being married to you when the Cru*sades* were on. One would have been *hobbling* about in a chastity belt ...'

When Mrs Cole was trying to be horrible she had a kind of

old-fashioned drawl ... Who on *earth* was Jennifer? None of your *business*, you fool. She basted the steak with its juices, finished her glass of (now rather warm) champagne and tried not to hear their voices next door. The trouble was that you could. You couldn't hear absolutely everything they said unless you tried very hard indeed – and possibly you couldn't then – but without trying at all, you could hear enough to make it very difficult not automatically to try. Mostly it was Mrs Cole, who seemed to be talking a good deal, but he was also answering, or arguing with her. Sometimes she shouted, or almost cried out, and once Elizabeth thought she was actually crying, but then she realized that it had been a laugh turning into a paroxysm of coughing.

The steaks were done; the toast fried; the pâté put into position. The watercress was in a silver bowl in which (she had to admit) it looked its best. Now what? Did she wait until rung for, or march in with the next course? Perhaps this was why most cooks in the old days had had such fiendish tempers and took to drink. Hours seemed to have gone by. She decided to march.

The candles on the dining-room table had been lit, which made the rest of the room seem darker. Mrs Cole sounded as though she was in the middle of some rambling accusation. John Cole, who, elbows on the table, almost looked as though he was blocking his ears with his hands, gave a brief affirmative nod as she came in: clearly she had done the right thing. She put the tray on the sideboard, and went to clear the caviare bowls. '... but that's what you *always* do, always assume the worst instead of the best, not like me, I always assume the worst instead of the best ...'

They had neither of them eaten much caviare. Mrs Cole's helping seemed to be absolutely everywhere except inside her and the original pot was nearly full. The vodka bottle, on the other hand, was nearly empty. It stood at Mrs Cole's right hand, and as Elizabeth cleared away her bowl, she grabbed the bottle, emptied it into the tumbler which had been meant for water, and sank it.

John Cole said, 'Daphne –'

Mrs Cole said, 'Merry old soul indeed! Christmas; celebrations – fun; coming off your high horse; the trouble with you, Jack, is that you're nouveau riche – that's not like art nouveau getting fashionable with time like bead dresses and bobbed hair: the riche are always with us, and far too many of them are nouveau – they've never been popular for one very good reason – they suffer from moral over-compensation – like cork legs or being a Lesbian – they can't help regarding riches as a kind of drawback they're going to surmount. Nobody goes about saying "he's marvellous, in spite of being nouveau riche." But that's what they want. They all want it. They don't realize that however riche you are, there are some things that money can't buy. Like stopping being nouveau.'

At this point, her head sunk gently forward until it was enjoined with the steak Elizabeth had placed before her. There was a profound and continuing silence. Both John Cole and Elizabeth gazed at Mrs Cole until they looked at each other. Mrs Cole's arms lay on the dark, polished table like pieces of Arctic coastline, each side of her head. It became clear that any move that was to be made was not going to come from her.

Then John Cole said, 'I must take her home: oh dear, oh damn!'

'Shall I –'

'No. You could help me get her upstairs, though. People like this are a dead weight. Hang on a minute here, while I get the car out.' And he left the room in such haste that the candle nearest the door nearly blew out.

He was pretty callous about her, Elizabeth thought, because whatever someone was like, you couldn't help feeling sorry for them if they were being like Mrs Cole was now. Nobody would pass out with their forehead in a lot of hot gravy unless they had got past caring about anything. Except drink and Jennifer whoever-she-was. She went to the kitchen, damped a clean drying-up cloth and tried to lift Mrs Cole's head out of her plate in order to clean it up a bit. This operation, she quickly found, needed three hands: one, at least, for Mrs Cole's head (which was surprisingly heavy), one for wielding the damp cloth, and one for removing the plate of steak. She got the plate out of the way, but dropped the cloth and then lost control of Mrs Cole's head which rolled forward again almost as though it had nothing to do with the rest of her. She groaned and started to breathe rather noisily, but she must be better off lying on the cloth. 'Poor Mrs Cole!' she thought rather uncertainly. She was very glad when *he* returned.

They carried her upstairs; Elizabeth leading, backwards, with the feet. One of her shoes fell off and apart from her smeared make-up and the gravy she seemed also to have lost an earring, but she looked so absolutely awful by now that Elizabeth rather hoped that neither of them would start worrying about the ear-ring. They'd both begun saying things like, 'Mind the head: can you manage the feet?' so they were hell-bent on trying to pretend she wasn't anyone. The front door was wide open, and so was the car door. Luckily, it was a very large car, but even so, it seemed to Elizabeth that they had, rather heartlessly, to stuff her into it.

Before he got into the car, he said, 'I beg you not to go before I get back. I'll only be about twenty minutes.'

So she went back and tidied up: cleared the food out of the dining-room (it seemed such an awful waste of steak that she put it all on a dish in case John Cole knew a dog). She licked the caviare pot spoon not to waste that, and it was delicious: she put the pot firmly in the fridge before tackling the washing up – not much of *that* anyway. Now that it was almost over, she felt very sad: it seemed awful that people should either have lives with nothing happening in them (like hers) or lives where whatever it was that happened was quite so squalid and frightening (like Mrs Cole). *He* might be all right – fall into neither of these categories – but then he was a man, and she had a sinking feeling that most of the *ordinary* bad things happened to women rather than men. Men were probably saved up for heroic death (like her father) or glamorous danger (like Oliver when he'd borrowed someone's quick motor and sneaked into a race at Brands Hatch – all that kind of thing). Perhaps men were largely responsible for the things that happened to women – perhaps *he* was the reason why Mrs Cole had taken to drink! Perhaps Jennifer was her own child, and John Cole wouldn't let her see her own daughter – was, in fact, not only nouveau riche, but wicked, it was simply his glasses that misled one ... And Daddo! she thought, with exactly the same hectic alarm; supposing *he* was wicked and just masquerading as stupid and dull! There was absolutely no reason, she went on, wildly, why on earth stupid people shouldn't be wicked: it was far more likely, when you came to consider it. It was supposed to be far easier to be wicked than to be good, and Oliver had said that one of the hallmarks of stupid people was that they always did what they thought was the easiest thing: the fact that it often turned out not to be that was neither here nor there ...

The front door slammed: why hadn't she *left*? She seized her bag and basket, turned out the kitchen lights, and almost ran up the basement stairs, straight into John Cole at the top.

She ran into him with such force that if he had not caught hold of her shoulder, she would have lost her balance and fallen back down the stairs.

'Steady.'

'I'm going home now.'

'Hang on a minute.'

'I've got to go – honestly.'

But a strand of her hair seemed to have got caught in one of his waistcoat buttons: she jerked, and tore the tangled hairs out by their roots with half a dozen little dwarf mandrake screams of agony. Tears filled her eyes.

'Steady,' he said again, but more seriously.

He took her upper arm and walked her through the nearest door.

'Don't *frog*march me!'

He laughed. 'I couldn't be doing that: you have to be four to one for that. I'm leading you to the nearest comfortable chair which is what one does to girls in your condition.' He pushed her gently into it, and took the basket from her.

'There you are. I say, that's little Red Riding Hood equipment. Had you suddenly decided that I was a good old-fashioned wolf – look here, what *is* it?'

For the moment she sat down, tears began spurting from her eyes. For a few seconds she glared unseeingly at him, too offended with herself even to search for a handkerchief. He went to the other side of the room and came back with a tumbler so heavy that her hand shook with surprise at its weight.

'The male equivalent of a nice cup of tea,' he said.

'I don't like whisky.'

'As a matter of fact, it's brandy. Brandy and soda. I should have said the male nouveau riche equivalent of a nice cup of tea.'

She drank some, and then said, 'It's simply that things seem awful to me sometimes – nothing, really. Nothing to do with you,' she added, meaning to sound worldly, rather than rude. She gave him the glass to hold while she found her handkerchief, and then blew her nose in what she hoped was a practical and finishing-off manner.

'Have some more brandy. I'm going to have some too.' He handed her back her glass and went away again. It was a very large, dimly lit room, with two fireplaces and windows to the floor each end of it: it smelt of flowers and she was glad that it was dimly lit.

When he came back with his glass, he sat on the arm of a huge sofa near her chair and said, 'We've both had rather an awful evening. It's not surprising that you feel awful.'

'What about Mrs Cole?'

'Don't worry about her. *She's* all right.'

'She's *not* all right! She clearly wasn't at all all right!'

'She was stoned, of course. There's nothing unusual about that.'

Elizabeth was clutching her tumbler so hard that if it hadn't been made of plate-glass windows it would certainly have broken. She took a gulp of brandy for courage and said, 'She was extremely upset about someone called Jennifer.' She was watching him narrowly for a reaction.

'There's nothing unusual about that. She's been upset about Jennifer for years.'

'Our daughter,' he added a moment later: and now it seemed

to be the other way round – to be he who was watching her. Staring down at it, she was turning the glass round and round in her hands, and even with her fringe it was possible to see from the rest of her face that she was frowning. At last she said, 'Do you mean that she doesn't *know* where her *own* daughter lives?'

'That's right.'

'Who stops her knowing? You?'

'Yep.'

'That's monstrous!'

'Of course, sometimes my security slips up, but not if I can help it.'

'No wonder she is so dreadfully unhappy.'

'Yes, it's not a situation that makes for happiness –'

She got to her feet and looked wildly for somewhere to put her glass.

'I'm going home now.'

'You said that before.' But he rose to his feet and stood towering before her as he took her glass.

She looked defiantly up at him. 'Now I really *am*.'

He stood quite still watching her face. Then, with neat and gentle movements, he took off his glasses, folded them and put them in a pocket: without the glasses, he looked more simple, more serious, and inquiring. He put his arms round her, drew her towards him and put his mouth upon hers. They stayed like that for a long time, motionless and utterly silent.

Then they were both sitting on the sofa: he was holding one of her hands in both of his and speaking quite calmly – as though nothing had happened.

'You see, it's not only Daphne we have to consider: there's Jennifer, too. It got a bit much for her having her mother turn up without warning dead drunk, falling all over the place at Speech Days and sometimes just any old day – anywhere. You know how conservative children are: well poor old Jennifer kept turning out to have a mother not like anybody else's mother. I had to put a stop to it. Daphne suffers from gusts of sentimental passion for Jennifer and there is nothing children hate more than that. Do you begin to see, at all?'

She nodded: she felt like two people: one inside, and one sitting on a sofa, talking. She said, 'But she can't always have been like this? She must somehow have *got* like it?'

'I don't know when that was. She'd been on the drink long before I met her. When I married her she came off it, because, poor girl, she thought I was going to love her in the way she wanted. But the trouble with alcoholics is that they can't love anyone back, you see: they're too taken up with themselves, and whether people are reassuring and loving them enough, and nobody ever can, so then they feel let down and switch the situation so that most of the letting down will be done by them. That's roughly it, I think. But it's an impossible situation for children: if you have them, you have to try and protect them from bad luck on that scale. I divorced her.'

He had put on his spectacles again, and was observing her, she found, when she looked up.

'Years ago.'

'How old is Jennifer?'

He reflected. 'Twenty in September.'

'I'm twenty.'

An expression she had not seen before crossed his face: then he said, 'That's why I explained this to you. I'm forty-five.'

There was a silence while they looked at each other. Then he took off his glasses again with one hand and put them on a table behind the sofa. 'I want to kiss you,' he said, and there ensued another unknown quantity of time and by the end of it she was lying on the sofa in the crook of one of his arms.

'Now is the moment for me to examine your face,' he said, 'I'm sorry to seem so fidgety, but that means putting on my spectacles.'

'Who cuts your hair?' he asked when they were on.

'My brother.'

'Good Lord!'

'He's not actually a hairdresser.'

'I can see that.' He pushed the hair out of her eyes. 'Anyway, with a forehead like that, it's a crime to have a fringe or bang or whatever it's called. Is it my imagination, or is your hair not perfectly dry?'

'It mightn't be. I'd just washed it when you rang up.'

'*Really* – may I call you Elizabeth? Well, *really*, Elizabeth!'

'It's all very well for *you* –'

'I was waiting for that.'

'How do you mean?'

'Some disparaging allusion to my baldness. Would it help if I told you that what hair I *have* got is incredibly greasy? A little of it goes a hell of a long way; you should be thankful it is so much on the decline.'

'I only meant that you *know* when you are going to work, so you needn't get caught out washing your hair.' She sat up. 'Could I have my brandy?'

'In a minute; you're quite perky enough without it. Let me see your eyes.' He peered very close into her face and she could see two little Elizabeths – like Polyfotos – one in each lens.

'What marvellous, translucent whites you have – like a very young child. Or – let me see – thinly-sliced whites of hard-boiled egg – in case you think the young child stuff is a bit Dornford Yates.'

'Who's he?'

'When we have more time, I'll show you. True to form, I have nearly all of him in first editions upstairs. I'm afraid I've got to take off my glasses again.'

'I'll take them off.'

She leaned towards him as she did this and he kept perfectly still. He was staring at her mouth.

At last he took her head between his hands and began kissing her and this time it was different: it was not enough, and she could not bear it to stop. She clung to him and kissed him – the first time *she* had ever actually kissed in her life; afterwards, she flung her arms round his neck and rubbed her face against his to make the touching go on ...

'I'm going to take you upstairs,' he said. He took her by the shoulders and pushed her a little away. 'Elizabeth : you've never done this before, have you?'

She shook her head. 'It's a kind of love – isn't it?'

'At first sight,' he said.

2. Côte d'Azur

Oliver loved the whole business of flying, and always managed
to get a window seat where the view was not obscured by the
aeroplane's wings. It was wark, as one would expect at half past
midnight, and by the lack of lights below, he guessed that they
were flying over the English Channel. He stretched out his legs,
threw back his head, shut his eyes and waited for France. He
was on his way to Cap Ferrat, to stay with Elizabeth and the
fabulous John Cole. Elizabeth had been there a fortnight already : a week ago she had rung him at Lincoln Street – in the
morning – and said how soon could he come? Not for at least a
week, he had replied : he didn't want to sound as though he
had nothing better to do as most people who habitually haven't,
don't; also Ginny had gone to Eden Roc the day before Elizabeth rang, and the last thing he wanted her to think was that he
was chasing her. So he had spent an awful week by himself in
London, not getting down to anything more than ever. He'd
been to a sale at Simpson's and bought himself some rather
stunning bathing shorts. Darling Liz had left him every penny
she possessed, but he had thought that if he lived on corned
beef it was fair to buy the shorts. The ticket had been sent
to him with Mr Cole's compliments : a perfectly charming old-
world chauffeur (Scottish) had brought it. He had saluted Oliver
and then said, 'Your sister has expressed the wish for a picture
of her father which lies on the table by her bed here. If you will
entrust me with it, I will have the office send it out.' So Oliver
had fetched it for him, and the man had saluted again, and said,
'I hope we shall see you in France, sir. Your sister sent her love
and seemed very well when I last saw her this morning.' And
then he had popped into a silver Rolls-Royce before Oliver
could reply.

Liz really was extraordinary. As far as he could make out (and that surely must be, in her case, the whole way), she had lived a kind of schoolgirl, virginal existence, and then, suddenly, he had got back from seeing May in Surrey to find her not at home which she continued to be all night. When eventually she returned (shortly after he had started seriously to worry), she had been quite different from anything he had ever known her be; excited and dreamy; partly treating him as though he ought to know everything already; partly behaving as though *he* had incurred some minor tragedy; quite incapable of any coherent account of herself, but unable to stop talking about it.

'Do you mean you cooked dinner for him and he seduced you?'

'Well, he couldn't eat much of the dinner. We had caviare for breakfast – not with spoons, though – to revive us because we hardly slept a wink, you can't can you, if you're in bed with people you don't know very well – it's *so* fascinating talking to them in between –'

'Now Liz. Listen to me –'

'Darling Oliver I *do*. Whatever happens. I shan't stop loving you – what*ever* happens everything will be all right. How many hours is it till seven o'clock?' But she went upstairs, without waiting for an answer.

'Isn't it amazing – the first person I meet –' she said, turning on the bath on her way up.

'He's *not* the first person you've met. He's probably about the ten thousandth person you've met –'

'You know perfectly *well* what I mean. I mean the first person I've *met*. Goodness I'm tired! I feel as though I've got roots coming out of my legs that have to be torn up every time I move.' She threw herself on her bed: he stood morosely over her.

'He asked who cut my hair,' she said looking up at him with a wealth of meaning that he couldn't fathom.

'Who *is* he?'

'He lives in Pelham Place. I said you weren't a hairdresser, of course – do you know, he's got a sunken bath *in* his dressing-room?'

'What does he *do*?'

'He's nouveau riche. He told me. He has the most beautiful hands –' she gave a little shiver and fell silent.

He had opened his mouth to tell her to stop being so silly and make sense but she had smiled at him – half triumphant, half appealing (she looked tireder and prettier than he'd ever seen her) – and then, without the slightest warning, fallen asleep. And ever since then ...

And he had not only not set eyes on the famous Mr Cole, he hadn't even spoken to him on the telephone. A few days after meeting him, Liz had announced that they were going to France. She had also said that she was going to ring him to make a plan for his joining them when she knew what the house was like, and sure enough, she had done just that, the day that he'd been giving up hope.

So here he was – in the aeroplane, just in time because he had been getting very tired of corned beef. When the stewardess appeared, he asked whether there was anything to eat. She was afraid she thought there wasn't. What about a drink? He felt in his pockets and there seemed to be enough there so he said yes – a beer. The lights of the French shore appeared below; tiny, twinkling and very yellow, and he began to feel positively excited. The stewardess came back with some beer and a packet of biscuits done up in Cellophane. Most of the other passengers were, or seemed to be asleep.

'It's these tourist flights,' she said, 'they don't issue meals if they can help it: not if it's a short flight like this one, and late-night flight at that.'

It's funny how hungry you have to feel, he thought, to want to eat assorted sweet biscuits. The stewardess was – a bit more than kindly – adjusting the table for his beer. She was the wrong age for him – he liked women of thirty-odd or not over twenty-one; besides, her eyes and her breasts were too close together, and anyway, his hands were far too full with Ginny. So he thanked her lying back with his eyes shut, and she went away. He hadn't told Ginny he was coming. He planned to ring her up – very casually – or better still, encounter her in the pool at Eden Roc ... She was the kind of girl who would wear the scantest bikini and no bathing cap – she'd come up from some dive, with streaming hair and golden waterproof skin, to find him ... Perhaps *that* wouldn't bore her. Ginny's boredom threshold was one of the lowest he'd even read about, let alone met. She combined an attention span about many things that would disgrace a teenage puppy, with a startling, and morbid, capacity to stick to some dreary point – like getting blackheads out of her legs or how many calories she had consumed that day. One of the deadly attractions of people who are easily bored is the challenge of not boring them : it tickled the vanity in a very private place. She often bored him (the other side of the coin): but just when he was deciding that he couldn't stick much more of whatever she was or wasn't being at the time, she did, or said something quietly unexpected, funny and endearing. The fact that she was so frightfully, chronically, hereditarily rich *had* to be treated by anyone of sensibility as a sort of controllable, but unfortunate disease – like diabetes. Regular injections of homespun affection, honesty, and common sense were essential to people in her position if they were not to go into a coma of indulgent self-pity or persecution mania. Blaming your parents provided some sort of domestic release : in Ginny's case she had a good choice; each of her parents had remarried four times, so there were ten people in this relation to her. She lived a kind of upper-class Esperanto : in certain places with certain people; they could come from anywhere, but they had to be able to be in approximately the same position ... It was a very small, jet-propelled and gilt-edged world. Because everybody in it was on the move, they tried to make everything the same wherever they were, and being very rich, of course they succeeded. Naturally, from time to time, they felt the need of variety : Oliver, being only twenty-four, did not at all understand that that was what he was in aid of. He provided a – not very marked – contrast to Scrabble, Martinis, massage, sun tan, water-skiing, in-jokes, and being a socialist in your spare time.

He hoped he was going to get on with – even like – John Cole. Liz – without meaning to – went on not telling him anything really about her lover, so that apart from the obvious fact that he was rich, Oliver simply couldn't imagine him at all. But the fact was that it was a damn good thing he was coming to this villa to have a look at the situation : after all, he was responsible for Liz; the nearest she had got, poor darling, to a father : nobody would dream of consulting that overblown cliché that their mother had married, and May – like Liz – was not noted for her common sense. If necessary, he must be prepared to take a very firm line with Mr Cole. The mere thought of this made him feel unutterably sophisticated and responsible – light-hearted with domestic power. He began to wonder whether he ought not set about becoming an ambassador ...

'Fasten your seat belts.' The stewardess was not leaving this announcement to chance where Oliver was concerned, and before he had come out of his doze enough to stop her, she was expertly fumbling with his belt.

'We haven't arrived?'

'In about five minutes.'

She gave him a smile, more professional than disappointed, and went her way.

He must have been asleep, then.

Two thirty, French time. He wondered who, besides Liz, would meet him.

Only Liz. She stood at the barrier, not waving, but looking intently for, and eventually at him. She wore pale pink jeans and a dark brown shirt, and her hair shone. She looked marvellous, and not at all like his sister.

When they could meet, she hugged him without speaking. They walked out of the airport building, into the warm perfumed air alive with cicadas.

'It's like somebody endlessly scratching themselves in navy blue velvet.'

She squeezed his arm and looked up at him. 'I've come alone. John thought you would prefer that.'

The warm, scented smell continued. She walked them to a white, open two-seater. 'It's *my* car,' she said, rather defiantly, 'so I'm going to drive.'

'Do you mean it is *literally* yours?' said Oliver, when they were sitting side by side with his suitcase in the back.

'Mmm. John said that if you were a kept woman on the Riviera you had to have a few obvious things and it is far too hot for mink so he said a car. And *I* said,' she continued, 'either red with white leather, or white with red leather. So there we are.

'You shall drive it tomorrow,' she ended, as they swept out of the airport on to the Corniche. Warm air and lights streamed by: the sea glittered, palms, oleander, rubbish dumps, dried-up river mouths all lay shrouded in nocturnal glamour.

Elizabeth did not speak, because she wanted Oliver to think she was a good driver, and she wasn't unless she tried. Oliver watched her thin brown hands on the wheel for a bit and then said, 'Come off it, dear. Drive more like a woman, and tell me things.'

She slowed down at once, and said, 'What things?'

'Longing to be asked,' he thought. He knew they were both very happy.

'Where did you get that watch, for a start? What's happened to the good old Gamages Commando-type object you thought you looked so sweet in?'

'It fell in the sea. John gave me this. From a shop called Cartier in Nice.'

'From a shop called Cartier,' he mocked, 'well I never –'

'Well I didn't know you knew about them.' She held out her wrist. 'Isn't it beautiful? It's a man's watch really. John agreed it suited me best. He's very good at choosing things: he says it's because he's had so much practice, but I think he probably started out good at it.'

They were driving through the back streets of Cannes, and a sudden gust of hot fish soup made him remember how famished he was.

'Liz, we couldn't stop for a snack, could we?'

'There's a snack waiting at home: supper, really – a sort of midnight feast. I *knew* you'd be hungry.'

He could tell she was pleased at being right about this.

'Has your John been cutting your hair?'

'Well – actually he did have a go, but he made it so much worse, he got a man to come and do it properly.' Then to avoid being teased, she said, 'How's May, and does she know about me?'

'She's fairly all right, and I honestly don't know. I sort of told her that I thought you might be away for some time, and just as I was trying to work out whether it would be better to say you were here on a cooking job, or come clean about it, she changed the subject. Asked me whether either of us wanted that ignoble pile in Surrey after she was dead.'

'How extraordinary! She must know what we feel about it! Did you tell her?'

'I said we both preferred Lincoln Street. And she said, "That's just what I thought, darling – such a load off what passes for my mind." '

'Has she joined some new society?'

'That's a very clever guess – how *did* you think of it?'

'John says I'm quite intelligent – *very* intelligent.'

'He must be in love with you.'

'*That* wouldn't make him say it. Anyway, has she?'

'Don't know, but now you mention it, there were all the signs. She comes to London much more, and she has that terrible, faraway, secret look when you catch her unawares. She must have,' he said a minute later, 'she's completely stopped giggling: I've noticed that always happens.'

'Do you think Herbert's joined too?'

'No – because they all cost money, don't they? He'd absolutely *hate* that – especially as there's a perfectly good straightforward Church for free. Good enough for a simple, nauseating chap like him.'

Elizabeth swerved unnecessarily to avoid the black streaking shadow of a cat. 'I think he's so awful he's probably mad or actually wicked.'

'Now you're exaggerating. He's just awful. With any luck, the marriage will quietly crumble to bits and May will stop searching for obscure comfort. Can I have one of those?'

He'd been hunting in the front pocket of the car and found the Gauloises. She pushed in the cigarette lighter, and said, 'Light me one too.'

A yellow, floodlit castle appeared on their left.

Oliver said, 'What's that?'

'Antibes. The castle is a sort of Picasso museum: beautifully done; we'll take you.'

'Is your John interested in art, then?'

'Of course he is!' Then she said, 'Sorry: but I can't help feeling a bit edgy about whether you like each other. Men are so much worse than women in this way.'

'Are they? Are they really?'

'Of *course* they are!'

He looked at her fierce profile with the short ruffled hair. 'I must say that this adventure seems to have made you very stern and knowing.'

She had turned left and they were driving down an avenue of plane trees, whose jigsaw trunks were exaggerated by the headlights.

'This is St Jean,' she said. It was really, he thought, as though she had lived there all her life.

In the gaudy little square there were still people: the sound of an accordion, cars starting up, an old man morosely smoking a pipe.

'People never all go to bed here,' she said. They had reached the sea again – molten pewter in the moonlight, and dark trees on their right with the warm pine smell. 'The villa is right at the end of the point.'

He knew by the way she wasn't describing it that it must be marvellous in some way or other.

'Will he be waiting up for us?'

'No. He's gone to bed: he thought we'd like a private supper together.'

'Nice of him.'

She opened her mouth, and shut it again.

'But of course he's nice if you like him,' he added.

'I like him,' she said, and at exactly this point they plunged through a gateway and into a drive which, with its continuing archway of dark trees, looked like a tunnel.

The house seemed strung with floodlit arches and beyond that shadowy caverns; the trees overhung it, black or glistening – according to the light. They walked through – past a terrace, into a hall, a room and on to another terrace beyond which stretched dark garden trees, a wall and the sky. There was a heated trolley with soup: another with sandwiches and drink. They ate – Oliver feeling like a foreigner in a dream. He could not tell about his sister. She had sent the servant who met them to bed – with such familiar certainty, that he found it difficult to believe that she had spent only two weeks here. As soon as he had eaten, he felt very tired; Lincoln Street seemed now as far away as it had seemed near when he had got out of the aeroplane at Nice: he longed to be asleep before he started thinking about his life which – Liz and the villa apart – didn't seem to be going too well at the moment: you couldn't keep on expecting gilt-edged stopgaps ...

'You're yawning even faster than your mouth will work,' Liz was saying. She was standing over him and pulling him to his feet. 'Just one quick look outside and then you'll sleep for hours.'

She led him outside the terrace across springy grass to a low wall. Here the garden seemed to come to an end, became a steeply declining cliff, the tops of whose trees were level with their faces. A hundred feet below spread the silver and silent sea with nothing upon it.

'The next place is Africa.'

'I know.'

'He's not conventionally good-looking.'

'No?'

'You don't need experience in loving to love. Necessarily?'

He shook his head. He had not the slightest idea.

'That's all right, then.' Then she took him back to the house.

•

When he awoke next morning he was in a large, dim room charged with the feeling of suppressed heat, cracked with streaks of sunlight and noisily inhabited by one – apparently gigantic – bluebottle. He sat up to reach for a blind cord and felt the rustle of paper which must have been tucked under his head on the pillow. The blind flew up: sun flooded the room and in his hand was a note from Liz. 'We are swimming and having long breakfast by swimming pool two terraces down. Follow rice stream, starting by french window.' There were three french windows in his room, which he hadn't noticed the previous night as being on the ground floor, but only one window had an O made of rice on the pale blue carpet. Having established that, he delved in his luggage for the stunning bathing shorts and went to the marble inlaid bathroom. The whole suite was like the most successful dentist in the world having you to stay for the night. Marble, gilt, mirrors, faded, painted furniture; hopelessly refined scenes of eighteenth century social life; nylon muslin and rayon satin in flesh tones : ormolu gryphons being door handles and bathroom taps : it was extraordinary, he thought, how things were somehow all right if somebody had once thought that this was thoroughly, entirely, the best they could do. Then he thought that perhaps he ought to become the lover of some outdoor, but mysteriously cultivated duchess, and start an interior-decorating business. Mary London and Oliver Seymour. That kind of thing. He took an extremely thick and luxurious bath towel, and made for the rice window. He knew Liz. She would make it more difficult as the trail went on. But no : she must be very anxious that he should find her before he got cross. A thin but steady stream of rice led across the coarse, green grass (that only foreigners, he thought, would call a lawn) to a corner of the wall where there was a low gate. A grain of rice was impudently perched on the latch. He put it absently into his mouth and turned back to see where he had spent the night. It was, or looked to be a large house; a great apricot-coloured nineteen-thirties' sprawl, with a quantity of doors, windows, french windows, columns, patios and at least two large terraces in view – with a good deal of bougainvillaea hanging about (in no other circumstances would purple and apricot be bearable) and a heavily tiled roof descending, in some places, to a height that he could easily reach. Just as he was going to stop looking and get on with the rice, a rat ran smartly along the gutter, paused at the corner, exuding sensibility and sharp practice, and then, having recollected whatever exciting and shady it was that had stopped him in his tracks, made off.

Oliver opened the gate and started down the path, or rather steps. Rice was no longer needed, as the way was hedged by aromatic shrubs and the rough biscuit-coloured trunks of umbrella pines: it was both hot and sombre, a charming mixture if you'd been in England for a long time. He heard a man laugh protestingly – a splash and his sister's voice. 'I hope he's not an absolute beast or bore,' he thought feeling suddenly angry and a bit frightened.

They were sitting side by side at the edge of the pool – which seemed floodlit with sun – their legs were in the water and they were holding hands. Their heads were turned to each other: he could see his sister's face but simply the back of his head. 'Nearly bald!' he thought, and was fleetingly conscious of half wanting the situation to be perfect, half wanting it to be hopeless. Then Liz saw him; her face changed, and he realized how happy she had been looking.

'It's Oliver!' she said – too loudly, and Oliver wondered whether he was deaf as well as bald.

By the time he reached them, they were both on their feet.

'Oliver: John,' she said, trying to watch both of their faces at once. 'What stunning shorts,' she added before either of them could say anything. Everybody looked at Oliver's shorts; even Oliver, and John Cole said mildly, 'They are, indeed. How very nice of you to come. Do you want to eat straight away, or would you rather swim first?'

'What we're doing,' interrupted Elizabeth rather breathlessly, 'is swim a bit and eat a bit and so on. Come and see.'

And she half dragged him to an open terrace-room built against the wall where a long narrow table was covered with a very delicious looking French and English breakfast. It looked enough for a dozen people. Oliver said he'd like some orange juice and then a swim.

She gave him his juice and said, 'He's nice, isn't he?' a question so patently silly that he squeezed her arm, feeling happy that she minded so much what he thought, and said, 'You bet.' Her hair was wet, sleeked back and held in place by a pair of dark glasses perched on top of her head.

'She looks like some science fiction reptile – or very close-up of an insect, don't you think?' he remarked as they made their way back to the pool and its owner. 'It's partly the freckles – they pop up all over the place the moment you get her out of a night club.'

'I must keep her out of night clubs then,' said John tranquilly. 'I'm devoted to her freckles.'

A telephone rang, and he got up to answer it. He was even taller than Oliver, Oliver realized, and he walked as though he had a low opinion of doorways. On either side of the breakfast table terrace were square little pavilions – changing rooms, he supposed, beginning to get the hang of what to expect – and by one of these was a telephone. He picked up the instrument, listened for a moment and said, 'Well, well well!' in tones of the mildest possible surprise.

Elizabeth said, 'Come on! Swim!' And before she could drag or push him into the water, he jumped. She followed him: she swam very well, and just as he was thinking how seldom – since they were children – they had swum together, she said, 'Do you realize that this is the first time we've been abroad together? At the same time, I mean?'

'You mean together.'

'No I don't. I mean together at the same time.'

'But if we'd been abroad together, it would have to have been at the same time.' Then he saw what she meant and reached out to duck her head under, but she eluded him. The water was so bright and light a blue that it was surprising the drops on her shoulders weren't that colour.

'Lovely water,' he said.

'John says it tastes of American prawns,' she answered, and as she mentioned his name they both looked at him. He had finished telephoning, and was looking under breakfast covers. 'He wants to eat,' she said and swam fast and splashily to the side of the pool.

During breakfast the telephone rang twice more. The first time it was London and the second time New York. With the London call, John said, 'Look here, you know how I love the sound of your voice, but twice before breakfast is overdoing it.' With the New York call he simply said, 'Dear boy, I've known all that for half an hour : London told me,' and put back the receiver.

Oliver ate a huge breakfast, and decided that he liked John : Elizabeth kept buttering croissants and then dipping them in cherry jam and *then* handing them to her lover and her brother. The coffee was wonderful : there were fresh trout, Charentais melon and raspberries with thick, rich, slightly sour cream. John ate sparingly, Elizabeth hardly at all. She perched on the end of some gaudy chaise-longue, licking cherry jam off her fingers and smiling gently as she looked from one to the other.

'Like a little marmalade cat,' John said. The sky was violet blue and the sun so sharply golden it was like some brilliant daydream, with each pair of them admiring the third so that they took turns at being part of a conspiracy and the object of conspiratorial approval.

'What happens next?' Oliver asked, after another swim.

'We've been asked to the local hotel for lunch – and swimming, of course. Up to you : it's rather like here, really, but with more people. I have to go; but you two stay here, if you like?'

'Coming with you,' Elizabeth said and then looked anxiously at Oliver.

'Fine : anything,' he said. The telephone rang again and when John had answered it, he said, 'The secretary's arrived. So up I go. Why don't you take your brother down to the sea?'

'When will you be through?'

He looked at her again. Whenever either of them did this, the whole place became rich with sexual affection, Oliver noticed.

'By lunch time,' was all John said.

'At the nauseating risk of sounding like Juliet's nurse, I should say you've fallen on your back,' Oliver remarked as they made their way down the blazing little path.

'Juliet's nurse?'

'Romeo's Juliet's nurse. Shakespeare's Romeo's Juliet's nurse.'

'All right, all right.' She was walking ahead of him. She was wearing a lemon-coloured bathing suit that fitted her beautifully, and was excellent with the bronzed hair and freckles and cream of her skin.

'Did John choose that bathing suit?'

'Yes. He likes choosing things, I told you. He's jolly good at it.'

'Do stop boasting about him.'

'I can't. You're the first person I've had to boast *to* about him, so do be fair.' A minute later she said.

'I've got a ring this colour; it looks a bit like tarnished diamonds, but it's something Portuguese called chrysolite.' Then she added, 'I'm so happy that every day seems about like a week, and I can't even imagine leaving *here*. It's extraordinary how when everything is *being* perfect, the future simply doesn't count at all – there's just what happened before, and *now* is everything else.'

Oliver was silent at this, because he had never been as happy as that, and everything she said simply made him start worrying about his future instead of not thinking at all about it, which was what he had been doing before.

Just as he was going to ask her whether John and she were going to marry, she said, 'So you see, in spite of your fears, I haven't had to fall back on a chimpanzee: John says he *prefers* women with furry arms, and he says he'll never let me be anybody's bridesmaid –'

He decided not to ask: it was a woman's question, anyway.

They had their bathe, and lay on rocks in the sun, until Elizabeth said Oliver was too new to lie about without blistering, even though she had rubbed what she described as marvellous stuff all over his back.

'Anyhow, John may be finished with letters.'

She had sprung to her feet.

'So?'

'I don't want to miss any of him,' she said.

They walked slowly back up the terraced cliff path to the villa. It was now very hot: their wet heads steamed; cicadas had reached their seemingly endless zenith; the smells of hot thyme, juniper and resin from the pines thickened the hot and dazzling air. They slipped on sharp, slippery stones as they climbed: geckos froze into gracefully heroic attitudes as they approached, and then, when they got too near, disappeared with jerky speed – like odd pieces of silent film pieced together; butterflies loitered, bees zoomed, there were no birds, no fresh water and no shade. 'A foreign land,' thought Oliver, watching his sister climbing the path ahead of him. All morning, he had been seeing her for the first time as an outsider might regard her; a sturdy body, slender still, because she was so young, but all a matter of neat, solid curves; she could never have passed as a boy.

When they reached the swimming pool, all the breakfast had been cleared away and the pool was blue and absolutely still except for one large moth trapped and drowning. Elizabeth, of course, would rescue it if she noticed it, and he hoped that she wouldn't but she did, so he helped by picking a fig leaf for the creature to rest and dry out on. 'You realize how furry they are when they're wet,' Liz said anxiously. She had gone into the pool and collected the moth on her dark glasses. 'Fig leaves are awfully prickly, do you think it minds?'

'It's about like us lying on coconut matting, but think how pleased you'd be with a piece of that if you'd been drowning.'

She looked at him gratefully. 'Of course you would.'

'Swimming pools always make me think of *The Blue Lagoon*.'

'What's that?'

'Don't you read *anything*? Or at least hear about things that other people read?'

'Now I do. John reads every day of his life. Novels as well.'

'A civilized man – not a ghastly specialist for a change,' he said, but seriously, because he meant it, and not to hurt her feelings. But she simply picked up the fig leaf, saying, 'I think I'll take this moth up with me.'

When they were on the move again, he asked, 'What novels does he read?'

'People called Henry Green, Ivy Compton-Burnett and Elizabeth Taylor. They're his three favourites. He tries a new one from time to time, but he says they never seem to be so good.'

'Have *you* tried them?'

'He reads them to me in bed sometimes. I really like it,' she added looking nervously at him to see what he thought.

'Fine, so long as it isn't all you do in bed,' he said and she stared at him with a mixture of shyness and bonhomie that was, or would be, if you weren't her brother, entirely irresistible.

'It isn't.'

•

The local hotel turned out to be Eden Roc, so Oliver realized that he might well meet Ginny before he was brown, and (worse) soon enough after Ginny's arrival there for her to think that he had followed her. Oh well, he thought while showering. Oh well, to hell with it, he thought half an hour later, when all three of them were having one drink on the terrace before setting off. John wore a pair of dark linen trousers and an unremarkable silk shirt, open at the neck, but decorated with a silk scarf. That was the trouble. He was trying to get Elizabeth to knot it, and she, of course, had not had enough practice at that kind of thing, Oliver thought, laughing inside from his kindly hide of adult experience.

'Never mind,' John said, 'I'm probably too old for this kind of thing. Too balding and paunchy.'

'You're nothing of the kind,' cried Elizabeth. 'You just don't hold yourself properly.'

'*You* hold me properly,' he replied in a low voice which was neither teasing nor intense: and over her head, met Oliver's eye seriously, and then smiled: the smile changed his face completely and Oliver realized that he might be old and not particularly good-looking, but that in his case, neither of these things mattered.

On the way to the hotel he told them about Ginny Mole – casually, but he didn't want Liz letting him down by any display of vicarious enthusiasm or too much sisterly curiosity, supposing that Ginny was lunching there and they *did* meet . . . supposing that she was lunching there which she easily might not be . .

They went through the splendid, luxuriously cool hotel and on to the western terrace. The walk down its tremendously wide and shallow steps and gravel drive to the sea, Oliver thought and then said, was very like anybody's dream of the kind that they thought interesting but their audience invariably found dull. John agreed, and then went on that if you didn't know enough people who had boring dreams like that *and* told you about them, you could always go to a French film. In fact, a lot of those films were simply made by power-conscious dreamers who had hit upon a method of mass boring people.

'Still you can always leave a film : one couldn't get away from her – jerking his head towards his sister – 'and she went through a frightful period of telling you every morning – following you about and telling you.'

'When did I do that?'

'It started when you were about ten. Morning after morning, we had accounts of your flimsy, indecisive, *interminable* sagas –'

She turned protesting to Cole, who took her arm saying, 'I like the morning after morning part anyway.'

Oliver said, 'Why *are* they so indecisive, I wonder? Other people's dreams I mean –'

Elizabeth immediately said, 'Because one's forgotten the vital part : that's why you want to tell it to people – you hope you'll automatically remember. I can even remember feeling that part of it : that something particularly marvellous had happened to me and somehow I couldn't remember what it was.'

John said, 'We must see to it that you don't *always* feel that ...'

Oliver said, 'There's Ginny! I mean,' he added a moment later as they looked in vain, 'it was someone who looked jolly like her. She came out of that gate there, and went over there.'

'Then she'll be at the pool. We'll go and have a look at it, to see if our hosts, the Dawsons, are still there.'

The swimming pool, cut out of the natural rock and slung above the sea, intensely blue and sheltered and sunny, was not thickly populated : most people had gone to change and drink and eat, but just as they were leaving, a figure rose from behind a rock whom Oliver immediately identified as Ginny.

Ginny was coming towards them on her way out, but she was

doing this so moodily, that she did not see them until the last minute when Oliver accosted her with elaborate coolth, as Elizabeth afterwards pointed out to John. She wore a bikini and sun glasses, both white. She was very small, and delicately made; a sharply indented waist, small, pointed breasts, and arms and legs that gave the impression that their owner hardly ever used them in case they broke. All flesh visible was the colour of heather honey : her hair was black and long.

'Oh Oliver,' she replied, rather as though she had known he would be there, but as an afterthought.

'What an amazing thing,' she added looking up from the minute pebble that she had been scuffing along with small bare feet.

Oliver explained that Elizabeth was his sister, and John Cole was John Cole.

'John *Cole*?' Ginny said, and pushed her huge dark glasses on to the top of her head. 'You've got a villa up the road haven't you? The one Mummy used to have when she was married to Jean-Claude?' Her eyes were like horizontal diamonds from a pack of cards and the colour of dog violets. 'You must be Jennifer's father.' She looked at him, at Elizabeth, and back to him with distinct interest.

'Come and have a drink with us,' said John easily. 'And tell me where you met Jennifer.'

'We were at Lausanne together and we would have gone to Florence only Mummy was having such ghastly trouble over my maintenance. One thing I'll never do and that is get divorced in Mexico – it may seem the simplest thing in the first place, but there's no end to the complications. I say, I can't have a drink with you,' (she had seized Oliver's wrist and twisted his watch towards her) 'I've got to change and have lunch on some filthy yacht with the most boring people in the world. Do you think if one *fined* people like that for being boring they'd get better? A hundred quid an hour and a bonus if they laughed at their own non-joke? 'Bye then.' She dropped Oliver's wrist as though it was some kind of barrier and prowled lightly away.

'Come to dinner,' called John, who had seen Oliver's face.

She lifted her right hand like someone stopping a bus by way of a reply and disappeared through the changing-room door.

'Does that mean she *is* coming, or she isn't?' asked Elizabeth as they walked up the stairs to the restaurant.

'Time will tell.' Oliver felt obscurely irritated by the whole encounter. He had been afraid that Ginny would express too much surprise at his presence – thereby implying that he had followed her to France when he was pretty sure he would have come anyway, whether she had been there or not – but her total lack of interest in his sudden appearance was far more galling. And John seemed to have run the whole thing . . .

'Hope you didn't mind my asking her,' John was saying, 'I just thought it might be fun.'

'Course not. Jolly good idea.'

They went into lunch where Mr and Mrs Dawson awaited them.

In a way, having lunch with two, to him, total strangers was a relief, Oliver thought. It was curiously difficult for him and John to stop being shy with each other: whatever refuge they might take as a team in admiring or teasing Elizabeth, the fact was that their areas of intimacy with her were necessarily entirely different, and apart from her, they had not so far anything else in common. They both knew, he felt, that Elizabeth was worrying over them in that intricately illlogical way that girls could, indeed could not *stop* doing, about people they loved. So lunch, diffused by the Dawsons, was a relief. Arnold Dawson had made a fortune out of camping sites and finally holiday camps. He came from Westmorland and had a gentle wedge-shaped face with soft blue eyes to match his accent. Mrs Dawson also came from the North Country. They were both in their fifties, but whereas middle age had polished and tidied up Arnold, it had softened and blurred Edie, whose clothes fitted her like a badly-made loose-cover, and whose dry, oyster-coloured hair rippled in an uncontrollably old-fashioned manner. She wore Marina blue, a shade of muted turquoise. The Dawsons had married the same year as Princess Marina, and Arnold never liked her to change anything. He called her Mother and constantly told the company what she did, and did

136

not, like – mostly the latter although she looked far too mild to possess so much and such varied disapprobation.

It was the kind of lunch where, having chosen your main course, you went to a vast table covered with beautiful *hors d'oeuvres* and took what you liked or wanted. 'Now Mother, there's not much here for you, that's plain, but we'll do our best.' And Oliver and Elizabeth watched him allowing her one sardine, 'You're not too keen on them, but you don't *mind* them in moderation,' two bits of beetroot, 'That's safe enough,' and half a hard-boiled egg off which he carefully scraped the sauce, 'She can't *abide* her food mucked about.'

'No, I can't see anything more,' he said after careful scrutiny. 'You'll have to make it up with the steak.' He spoke, not loudly, but with unselfconscious deliberation, and her embarrassment at his behaviour was clearly routine; he was drawing attention to her, but he had been doing that for a good thirty years: she merely plucked his arm, said, 'That's fine, dear' and smiled at the general company for support. He took her back to the table where she sat by herself while the rest of the party made their choice.

'The thing is,' Arnold said in generally audible confidence to John and Elizabeth, 'she doesn't really like travelling abroad – does it to please me, she knows I like the sun and a bit of a change. A lot of it's the food you know, but if I take enough trouble over that, and she gets her paper every day, it's not so bad. I had a yacht once but she couldn't stand it, she's so prone to sea-sickness – put her on a mill-pond and she wouldn't be able to keep anything down : I said once, Mother I don't know how you manage a bath without trouble. I fly her everywhere nowadays : she doesn't mind that so much. You can't change your ways at her age, you know, and you can't *make* ways you never had.'

Elizabeth said something faintly about the sun being nice for her anyway.

'Oh not the *sun*!' he said. 'Put her in the sun for five minutes and she's out in a rash – and that's followed by blisters which I wouldn't like to describe ... I think I'll go back if you don't mind, she's all by herself.'

'As though he was one of the best, frightfully kind, owners of a dog,' Elizabeth remarked afterwards. John Cole laughed.

'He's a born owner, anyway,' he said.

After he had asked and been told about Mr Dawson's empire of holiday camps, Oliver said, 'Perhaps he'd give me a job.'

John said casually, 'Are you looking for one?'

'In a sort of a way. The trouble is, you see, that as I know what I like, I *do* mind what I do.'

He looked up to see how this was taken and found Cole regarding him with impassive intentness. He did not reply.

*

They found out that Ginny *was* coming to dinner. On John's suggestion, Oliver rang the hotel and asked her if she would like him to fetch her.

So off he went in Elizabeth's white car in a silk shirt borrowed from John.

'It would be a frightfully good thing if he *did* find out what he wanted to do.'

Elizabeth was having a shower while John shaved, so she did not hear his reply. When she emerged, sleek and streaming, a few seconds later and said 'What?' he simply laughed. 'I must say that catching you in your odd, dry moments is almost impossible. It's like living with a seal or an otter.' Before she could say 'what' again, he wrapped her in a gigantic white towel, wiped her mouth with a corner of it and kissed her.

'Seriously, about Oliver –' she began.

'I was kissing you with the utmost seriousness. What about Oliver?'

'Well – what about him? Honestly, John,' she sat on the bath stool hugging her knees, which she always did, he had noticed, when she was settling down to some insoluble confidence, 'I don't want him turning into a lay-by – oh, you *know* what I mean : I do think it's absolutely extraordinary how men don't stick to the point –'

'Come next door –'

'Why?'

'Don't ask silly questions.'

'You're not going to carry me!' She slipped on to the floor still wrapped in her towel. He stood looking down on her for a moment, then collected the four corners of the towel and started dragging her at a surprising speed across the marble floor to the bedroom. ·

'Sometimes in my loathsome way I even have to *drag* them into bed.'

Very much less later than it seemed to either of them, he said, 'You *are* like a little cat: just as firm and graceful – just as neat and sweet and only slightly less furry –'

'You would prefer me even to Ginny?'

'Ginny?'

'Her body, I mean.'

'I thought that was what you meant. I do. I don't like girls who are all chicken bones and a mass of dangerous corners. I like firm, rounded people.' He propped himself up on one elbow. 'Are you happy, Eliza?

'You don't mind my being so much older?

'Or having been married and having a grown-up child?

'Or blind as a bat and nearly bald?

'Then you shall have a drink: anyone as broad-minded as that is bound to be thirsty.'

He picked up the house telephone and said, 'Two large Paradis, please, Gustave. What a ridiculous name that is. Like a villain's chauffeur in Sapper.'

She pulled the sheet over and watched him collecting clothes for the evening. Then she said, 'Are you? Happy, I mean, as well?'

He looked silently at her for a moment, and then said, 'Oh darling!' a word he had never used to her before.

Afterwards, Elizabeth remembered everything about that time: the comfortable, untidy room with damp towels, ticking clock and smell of gardenias; the small sunset breeze ruffling muslin by the balcony windows, and outside, a fiery sky against which small bats occurred and dropped to nowhere like huge pieces of ash. She lay on the bed until the drinks were brought, and afterwards she also remembered thinking lazily that when you were entirely happy fresh raspberry juice and champagne seem a natural drink. John padded about in a very marvellous dressing-gown, 'It's meant to blind people to my true appearance,' trying to decide what Elizabeth should wear. 'You've jolly well got to wipe Ginny's eye, that's for sure.' The coat-hangers clicked against one another. 'My bet is that she will wear white, so you'd better be in colour.'

'Why couldn't I be in white, too?'

'Because with her black hair it will look as though her mother uses Persil.'

While he was choosing, they heard Oliver returning in the car.

'Oh lord! I'm not dressed at *all*, and we never talked about Oliver!'

He threw a pleated lime chiffon dress at her. 'It won't take you long to get into this, and we've got plenty of time to talk about Oliver.'

'Have we? Really?'

'All our lives.'

He told Gustave to give Oliver and his guest anything they wanted to drink, and sat on the end of the bed. 'You have lovely hair. The colour of highbrow marmalade. Wait!' He seized a spray full of Bellodgia. 'Shut your eyes; keep still – no turn round – fine.' The room smelled of a million gardenias now, and the sun had sunk out of sight.

*

There was a little more time when they went downstairs to find that Oliver had taken Ginny to see the pool. They sat on a sofa with another drink talking about him quietly; Elizabeth explained – not again, but in the context of Oliver – how awful their stepfather was, 'The kind of man who'd almost *force* you not to settle down in case he started approving of you. Oliver simply loathes him : breaking up his marriage with May is Oliver's dearest wish,' and John sat regarding her benignly with his glasses on and not saying anything. A relative of Gustave's came and lit the candles on the dining table : instantly, moths collected for their doom : and just as Elizabeth was starting to worry about their fate they heard the others returning; Oliver's

140

voice and Ginny's little exclamations of bare incredulity. John picked up Elizabeth's hand and kissed it.

Ginny wore the smallest white dress Elizabeth had ever seen in her life. It fastened on one shoulder with a huge gilt buckle: 'She looks like someone in a Roman epic,' Oliver explained. All her nails were painted gold and her hair was carelessly piled on top of her head. When Elizabeth said what a terrific dress it was, Ginny replied that it was absolutely all she'd got.

'I think the pool's just top *dog*,' she said to John Cole during the *langouste*. 'Mummy always meant to put one in, but Jean-Claude was so *fright*fully mean and kept saying what was the sea for. He should have been stung to death by jellyfish and Portuguese men-of-war but it didn't happen to be a good year for them. I collected a whole lot in a suitcase and put them in just as he was diving off that board but he didn't even notice. I think success spoils men far more than women, don't you?'

'I'm glad you like the pool,' John said, 'I thought we'd come back and swim in it after the night club.'

'Take my father, for instance,' Ginny continued, 'oh good about the swim; Mummy said he was absolutely charming until he made that movie with her, but with just the tiniest speck of fame he became ghastly. I'm sure it's all right what *you* do,' turning to John. 'After all, you're not in the least famous are you? Just rich.'

'That's it.'

Then, just as Oliver was saying, 'Anyway, Ginny, you'd be a rotten judge of character –' the telephone rang, and after an interval Gustave came for John, who got up saying, 'Do go on with the duck – don't wait.'

He did not come back until halfway through the duck, and the moment Elizabeth saw his face she knew that something was wrong.

'That was Jennifer,' he said looking at Ginny. 'Apparently you've invited her to stay.'

'I just called her up this afternoon and told her to come on out. I didn't invite her to the Roc. I assumed she'd be staying here.'

Elizabeth realized that it was worse than she had thought when he came back on to the terrace. 'What time is she arriving?' she asked, she hoped, casually.

'Tonight. On the same plane that Oliver came on.' He met her eye with no expression at all.

That was that. They finished dinner and went to the night club. When he was dancing with her, John said, 'You know this changes things?'

She looked at him dumbly – suddenly so frightened about them she couldn't even ask what things.

'I've told the servants to move me into another room. I didn't want it to be like this. Jennifer's not – I've given her too rough a time. Damn that interfering little girl.'

There was an act at the night club whereby they collected somebody off the floor and asked them a string of questions: the trick was that you must not say 'no'. If you succeeded for long enough you got a bottle of very nearly undrinkable champagne. Ginny achieved this, and behaved as though it was really an achievement. She was unaware of tensions. Oliver knew that Elizabeth was anxious, and Elizabeth became increasingly frantic about John, who seemed to have retired from the scene – seemed hardly to know her. Oliver danced with her and said, 'Don't get so worked up. Of course she'll like you.'

'It doesn't just seem to be that.'

'What is it, then?'

'Don't know.'

He hugged her. 'Anyway – I'm here.'

'Why did Ginny do it?'

She felt him stiffen. 'I don't know. They're friends: I expect she just thought it would be fun to see Jennifer.'

She didn't answer that: Oliver was too mad about Ginny to want to understand.

Later, she danced with John and they didn't talk. Night clubs were bad for seeing anyone's face but her neck ached with staring up at him. When the music stopped, he wrapped his arms round her. Then, she said, 'Do you want me to go away?' But he didn't hear her because of people clapping the band, and she hadn't the courage to say that again.

142

Back at their table he said, 'I'm going to take you home now and Oliver and Ginny can make their way later.'

When they were well out of Cannes, he drove very fast to a small café they'd never been to before. 'We're going to have a spot of coffee and cognac.'

They sat at a small table in a dark corner, and he said, 'Of course I must explain a bit : of course I must do that. I was going to, anyway, but I thought I had much more time.

'Jennifer is – she's had a rotten childhood, of course. You know she's the same age as you?'

'You told me.'

'Twenty. Well – she doesn't seem like twenty at all. She's fearfully young for her age.'

'Where does she live?'

'She wanted her own flat in London : she shares with two other girls. She's just started at an acting school – last term, I mean. Of course it's holidays now. She's got a sort of flat in the house in Buckinghamshire. To use when she feels like it. She sometimes spends a week-end there with me, but she's always hated making plans. She wants to be free. You know.'

He met her eye at the end of this with a smile that was apologetic and also curiously urgent – as though beneath or inside his random remarks about Jennifer there was some anxious and secret message to be conveyed. She wanted to ask quite simple – probably stupid – questions like, 'Will she resent us?' or even, 'Has she any idea about us?' but she didn't ask because she felt that she knew the answers and they would be all wrong.

There was a short silence and then he said hopelessly, 'I'm sure you'll get on.'

He paid for the brandy and drove her home. Ginny and Oliver were not back. He stayed in the car and she felt another wave of fright.

'Are you going to bathe with the others?'

'Are you going to the airport now?' She knew it was far too early for Jennifer's plane.

'I might as well.'

'I shall go to bed.'

He nodded agreement to this dreary plan, and so she got out of the car and made for the house. As she reached the steps, he called, 'See you in the morning!' in a hard, cheery voice. She was nearly crying, and found that Ginny's stopping-a-bus gesture was the best answer to that.

In the bedroom – now most obviously and merely hers – she lay on the bed resenting Jennifer, needing Oliver, despising Ginny, worrying (illogically, surely?) about May, her mother, whom she had so heartlessly and gladly abandoned to what Oliver had described as a living death worse than fate, *loathing* Horrible Herbert, hating Jennifer (why on earth should *she* mind her father being happy?) wanting Oliver just to be there teasing her and making light of her feelings, wishing she didn't think Ginny was so heartless and *decadent*, feeling guilty that she had so often and so adroitly avoided going back to Surrey for weekends; perhaps May felt as abandoned by her as *she* now felt abandoned ... Perhaps it all served her right ... Then she could no longer stop thinking about John; could think of no one else and got rid of all her tears.

*

'What's up?' John Cole asked his daughter.

'How do you mean, Daddy?'

They were lying on the sea raft a hundred yards out from shore and there was no one else within range.

'Why are you making everyone feel uncomfortable?'

'I don't think I'm making *everyone* feel uncomfortable.' She started putting on more lotion from a bottle that she wore tied to her waist. Her skin was very white, and had constantly to be protected from the sun.

'Well, you're making *me* feel awful. I don't like my daughter being unfriendly to my guests.'

'Guests! Honestly, Daddy! Come off it! She's not a guest.' She wore a red linen hat with a flopping brim that suffused her face with a pink glow: it wasn't all her natural indignation.

Before he could reply, she put down the bottle of lotion, gripped her knees with hands that were so like Daphne's, and said:

'Listen, Daddy! How would you feel if I was sleeping with a man twenty-five years older than myself?'

'It would depend upon what you felt about him. And what he felt about you.'

'I'm not talking about feelings. I'm talking about the plain facts of the matter as any outsider might see them.'

'Why?'

For a moment that silenced her: she gave a deep (patient?) sigh.

'How long have you known this girl?'

'Jennifer do stop cross-examining me – not very long – a few weeks, why?'

'All I can say is that it seems very odd to me that someone of twenty – someone exactly my age – who hasn't got any money would want to risk setting up with somebody old enough to be her father. I suppose you gave her that car!'

'Why not? She hadn't got one.' But flippancy was useless with her.

'I must say that she tried to conceal the fact that you gave it to her.'

'I think,' he said with both patience and revulsion, 'that she was trying to be tactful.'

'Tactful! Why should there be any need for tact?'

'Jennifer I've had enough of this – I warn you –'

'So have I! I don't see why you should abandon Mummy simply in order to indulge some kind of Lolita complex – you're just infatuated and at your age it's disgusting!'

When she was like this, pale grey eyes protruded, chins became one, bosoms heaved, thighs quivered. To be responsible in any way for her existence filled him – as it always did – with a disgust so murderous that immediately afterwards he felt as he imagined somebody might who had actually committed a murder in a sudden fit of hatred and loathing. This was his daughter, his only daughter: if he was responsible in one way for her unfortunate appearance, it could be said that he had only himself to blame if he was unable to fall back, as it were, upon her character. She was, she must be, literally what he had made her. Poor girl, then. In the same way that he could not bring himself to speak of Eliza to Jennifer, he surely owed Jennifer the same loyalty. They must simply be kept apart. She had begun to cry now : he was afraid that her acting school had simply oiled the works where histrionics were concerned.

'There, there,' he said, 'I really can't remember when I last took a nymphet to a motel. And it's a bit unkind of you to keep rubbing in my age : an astonishing number of people regard forty-five simply as the gateway to maturity.'

But she simply looked at him with wet, resentful eyes and said, 'I do wish you wouldn't be so hard and cynical.'

Over her head, on the top terrace by the villa, he saw the tiny figure of his love. She was walking very slowly, and then, because she stood still for a moment, he imagined that she was looking out to sea, to the raft, to him. He wanted to wave to her, but knew that the gesture would be misinterpreted by both girls. Must keep them apart, he thought again.

He suggested a swimming race back. Jennifer was a very good swimmer and would easily beat him.

*

'I'd rather go if you don't mind.'

'I *do* mind.'

'I feel as though you are a bit ashamed of me.'

'It's not *you* I am ashamed of – it's myself.'

'But that's just the same for me, don't you see?'

'Yes I do. Darling : I'm so sorry about it all. But I'm sure she'll get used to the idea : it was just rather a shock.'

Silence. Then he said, 'Please – Eliza – you won't abandon me entirely, will you? Will you?' But she looked at him with that bright, trapped look of someone who was prevented only by pride from crying.

Jennifer's footsteps – voice. 'Daddy!'

'Coming!'

'Don't bother. It's only, do you think Elizabeth would mind *awfully* if I borrowed that car you gave her to drive Ginny back to the Roc?'

She shook her head then, saying, 'Of course I don't mind,' pulled the key on its ribbon over her head and handed it to him.

Their hands touched and all the other starvations shouted out. Jennifer came in and said, 'I'm sorry!'

●

Two days later she and Oliver left. It was all quite civilized: everybody told somebody else quite acceptable lies: Oliver said that their mother was not well and wanted Elizabeth to come home; John said how sorry he was that they had to go; and Jennifer said what a pity it was that she was losing her chance to get to know Elizabeth as they must have so much in common. Other things were said, of course.

'Can't you stop her?' Oliver asked Ginny.

'Stop who?'

'Don't be an idiot.'

'Jennifer thinks her father should go back to her mother,' said Ginny primly. 'It's mad, of course. People never go back to people – except in books. Look at Mummy: she's always going back to people in movies but she never does in life.'

'Can't you tell her that?'

'Oliver don't be so *dim*! It's not *really* what she thinks. She just wants her father to herself.'

'Well, if you knew all that, it was bloody of you –' And they had a frightful row which ended with Ginny saying she was going to Martha's Vineyard, she was sick of France, and Jennifer was right about one thing – young men were a pain.

●

They left on a three o'clock plane after an extremely uncomfortable lunch at the villa. Ginny came to it, but she was not speaking to Oliver. John and Elizabeth did not speak to each other. Oliver, who loathed her, ignored Jennifer, who was chattering at Elizabeth with a placating eye on her father. Nobody ate much, and in the end Oliver and John had a desultory conversation about the early winter days of the Riviera, Katherine Mansfield, and Gjleff. As soon as coffee had been served, Elizabeth, who had refused it, said that she must go and finish her packing.

'I'll help you, if you like.'

Elizabeth stopped at the end of the terrace. 'No thanks, Jennifer. I prefer to do it alone.'

Oliver said quietly to John, 'I think it would be better if we had a taxi, you know.'

'I'd arranged for Gustave to drive you. I'm not coming to the airport – don't worry.'

Somehow or other, the cases were put in the car, various farewells got through and they were off. Oliver looked at his sister. She sat rigidly, staring out of the window away from him. She was wearing the dark blue linen suit in which she had left Lincoln Street, and there was a white stripe on her fingers where the ring had been. Oliver took one of her hands and held on to it. Neither of them knew how much English Gustave understood, so they said nothing.

In the aeroplane, once they were up, Oliver said, 'Have a huge brandy.'

She looked at him for the first time, and he could tell by her thick upper lids that she must have been crying after lunch. 'That's another thing. I've only got ten bob.'

'Ha ha! I thought of that. Look what I've got.' And he pulled out of his breast pockets a bundle of notes. 'I haven't even counted them yet.

'Oh Oliver! Where did you get that.'

'Don't sound as though you've never seen a five pound note in your life before. They haven't come from outer space.' He lowered his voice. 'Loot: from that damned awful little bitch.'

'Not Ginny!'

'Of course not. I never take money from women I *have* loved. No – the real, prize, first-class, hysterical, neurotic, hideous, boring, megalomanic little bitch: Jennifer Cole. I popped up to her room after lunch and took what I fancied.'

'Oh Oliver!'

'Oh Elizabeth! I call it meagre revenge. It doesn't matter to her: I bet she just asks for and gets what she wants. She probably didn't know what was in her Hermès wallet. Let's see. Five, ten, fifteen, twenty, twenty-one, two, three – ten. That's going to keep the wolf from the door: and anybody who saw Jennifer would only have to show her to the wolf – she wouldn't need money.'

'It's stealing.'

'That's what it is. And if you asked me whether stealing twenty-three pounds ten is as bad as what that little bitch has just done, I'd say you want your head examined. Anyway.' He ordered the brandies and ginger ale. 'That's to satisfy your puritanical urge. All women feel reassured by long drinks – even if there's twice as much alcohol in them. Darling Liz. It's not as bad as you think. You've kept your watch, I see. So you must regard the situation as not entirely lost?'

'Do you think it was wrong? I didn't want to seem pettish. I left everything else, but he knows I lost my other one. I don't understand anything about it.'

'Of course you don't.' The brandies had arrived and he poured the ginger ale, mixed it up with his finger. 'There. A nice, brotherly drink. Swig it back. The situation is perfectly simple, really. Jennifer doesn't want anyone competing with her for her father's affection. How about that?'

'That part is not in the least difficult. But what does *he* feel about it?'

'Oh – there you have me. Haven't the slightest idea. Can you imagine what on earth made May marry Herbert? People are so keen on explaining every nuance of human behaviour that they fall back on the kind of invention that tells you more about *them* than it tells you about what they're explaining.

Although I'd hardly call either Daddo or Jennifer a nuance,' he added a bit later. 'Go on: drink up, and we'll have another. We've got to face Lincoln Street after I've been alone in it for a fortnight. We need a spot of blurring and bracing.'

Just before they were landing, she said, 'I do need to know what he feels, though.' She had had the two brandies, and was now simply relaxed and unhappy.

It was raining in London and looking its August worst. In the bus she cried a bit, but silently, and then, holding a bit of his coat sleeve, said, 'It would be so awful without you – you can't imagine.'

'Don't cry too much; there's nothing to blow your nose on but five pound notes. Think of me. Think of wicked horrible Ginny buggering off to Martha's Vineyard in order to get away from me. Think of my broken heart.'

'Oh yes! Poor Oliver! Do you mind awfully about her? I mean – *is* your heart broken?'

'A bit,' he said, 'but don't worry – it's smaller than yours.'

3. Surrey Blues

It wasn't until after Elizabeth had rung up that May realized how down she had been. Three or four times a day she had been telling herself that this was absurd. The weather had been good: Herbert had alternated trips to Lord's with a much keener and more practical interest in the garden than he had shown before. He treated the lawn with various chemicals, hosed it, rolled it, mowed it, and walked about it discussing its future perfection and the possibility of croquet. It kept *him* happy. He was just the kind of man to get obsessive about lawns, she thought. Mrs Green had been angelic: especially when May's digestion had been so stupidly bad that she hadn't felt like cooking – let alone eating – anything. Mrs Green had even got her nephew to repair May's electric pad because she simply couldn't get her feet warm at night. Of course she worried about Oliver – not having a proper job, not seeming to care to get on with his life – but what she had already learned from the League had taught her to despise that kind of practically dishonest concern. Dr Sedum would simply ask *who* she was really worrying about – Oliver or herself? And as it was clearly worse to worry about herself, she knew that that was what she must really be doing. Elizabeth she suspected of being in love; a perfectly natural and reassuring condition. Lavinia had said that the impression she was creating upon other members of the League was largely favourable. The few people with whom she had obliquely discussed the difficulties of living with Herbert had treated him as a chronic natural hazard – like a degree of fall-out or the build-up of pesticides. It had – reasonably enough – been a reflection upon *her* that she was allied to such a man. Quite right (she was sure that anybody who could point to any of her behaviour and pronounce it shoddy, dishonest, underhand in some sickeningly unconscious manner must be right): but the facts were that she had to go on living and dealing with what she had done. The house, for instance. The curious thing about that was that she (not forgetting darling Oliver and Elizabeth) seemed to be the only person who really hated this awful house. Herbert, naturally (it was he who made her buy it), adored the place; but, far more mysterious, Dr Sedum and co. seemed *also* to think well of it. Lavinia had pointed out that many of the rooms were ideally suited to communal activities, although she was maddeningly unprepared to say what they might be. May was in a curious position *vis-à-vis* the League. At steady intervals she was invited to a Time – in a garden flat in St John's Wood – but she could not go unless it happened to coincide with one of Herbert's cricket days. When she *did* go, she came away feeling curiously depressed. This was partly because everybody except her seemed to understand everything that was going on, and partly because, this being so, she *pretended* to understand when she did not. There were usually about nine people, one of whom was allegedly in charge and who read something and then asked other people what they thought about it. Everybody spoke in very calm, deliberate voices – as though everything was unspeakably bad but they had faced up to it. Nearly all of what people said was in the form of a question – so all the talk was like some wavering chain with an occasional bead. The reading matter was so wide, as well as high-minded, as to be (to May anyhow) totally obscure. There had been one paper where it had started with primary colours and May had thought, oh good she knew what they were, but in no time the Trinity, the Milky Way, the Three Bears, fairy stories, triumvirates, geometry, Shakespeare's plays, being-more-civilized-than-allowing oneself-to-be-presented-merely-with-the-alternative had all been thrown into the breach until the air was heavy with cigarette smoke and the whole of philosophy, and people were even pretending to want to interrupt one another. Einstein would be dismissed as clever (?) and Krishnamurti as not a realized man (?). The question marks saved everyone from noticing how far someone had stuck his neck out. No wonder May left with indigestion – of a different kind from her run-of-the-mill prosaic kind – and wondering as she took the tube to Waterloo whether these symptoms, both physical and mental, were just the result of being fifty – i.e. too old for serious mental or spiritual effort. Herbert simply made her feel older by wanting her to make a will, because, he said, things could be so difficult with step-children if it wasn't all cut and dried. When she'd rung up the only lawyer she'd ever known because Clifford had used him, he said the same thing. But when she'd told Herbert this, thinking he'd be pleased, he'd got quite shirty, as darling Clifford used to say, and said he'd got a perfectly good lawyer already, there was no need for her to go ringing people up behind his back. Sometimes it seemed impossible to do anything right, and she really felt so wretched a good deal of the time that she seemed to have no energy. Herbert, who talked a good deal about her state of health, said he was going to take her into Woking to see a tremendously good doctor, but when she suggested getting on with this scheme he said give it a few more days with the pills he'd always used in India for *his* indigestion, and the hot drinks he brought her every evening. Twice Herbert made appointments about ten days in advance, and on both occasions she felt so much better that the first time she refused to go at all, and the second time she only went to please Herbert.

All in all, she was very glad when Elizabeth rang up and said she was coming down for the week-end.

They were mutually surprised by each other's appearance. May thought that Elizabeth looked dreadfully unhappy, and Elizabeth thought her mother looked worryingly ill. Neither of them mentioned these facts. They talked instead about Oliver, who *might*, apparently, be going to get some sort of job on a London newspaper; about Alice, who was apparently pregnant; and finally about Claude, who had taken to hunting all night in muddy and dank places and drying off luxuriously in the linen cupboard to which he seemed mysteriously always to have access. He had also kept such a sharp eye on any food imported into the house not specifically for him that he no longer bothered to kill and crunch up bluebottles. 'His one asset, from our point of view, simply thrown away. He's tripped Herbert up twice in passages when we haven't had spare bulbs and Mrs

Green thinks his moulting gives her asthma. Somehow the awfulness of Claude is very consoling.'

Elizabeth looked at her mother's profile (she had met her daughter at the station in the Wolseley, which she drove with great care extremely badly). It was easy enough to imagine what her mother needed to be consoled about : Daddo and the horrible house. Apart from May's beautiful English complexion (that Elizabeth supposed she must be noticing so particularly because everyone in the South of France had been too brown to have one), her face looked as though she had lost too much weight too fast. Elizabeth felt that as well as looking ill, her mother did not seem to be happy. Nobody who thought of Claude as a consolation could be *very* happy.

'How is Alice getting on?'

'It sounds as though she is having a baby : at least she has absolutely every Victorian symptom. She writes me extremely long letters, and the moment I have screwed up the energy to reply she sends another one. Imm*e*diately. She wants to come and fetch Claude, but she says she's so sick in *any* vehicle that she dare not risk the train.'

'Perhaps I could take him to her!'

'Oh darling, that would be kind. Alice simply adores that cat, and on top of everything else she sounds a bit homesick, although how *anybody* could be homesick for this, I cannot imagine.'

They had swept precariously round the drive (May treated all corners – even gentle curves – as dangerous) until the monstrous builders' folly was in view. Oliver, who never tired of insulting it, had once said that it would be ideal for an American film producer to do a B feature on the haunted-house theme. Beams, battlements, leaded windows, nail-encrusted doors, awful, useless chimneys that looked as though they had been knitted in moss stitch, liver-coloured bricks, ill-judged pieces of roughcast (dinosaurs' vomit Oliver had also said) made the place a landmark : it was called Monks' Close, and Oliver had also said how lovely it would be if you opened the hideous front door one day and found it chock-a-block with monkeys.

Herbert was standing in front of the front door to greet them.

He wore cricket flannels, a white shirt and a panama hat and carried a syringe. He waved this last in greeting and then stood elaborately at attention as the car drew to a halt.

'Well well well well! Here you are. Welcome home, m'dear. Don't bother with the car now. I must say, Elizabeth, you're looking remarkably well. Flying the nest seems to agree with you, eh?'

Elizabeth had never known him so affable. He even made her a fearfully weak gin and tonic without being asked: but she took her small suitcase up to her room by herself. It was exactly as awful and the same. It seemed to her as though she had been away for – not a hundred, but about ten years. The thought that forty-eight hours ago she had been with John in the villa drinking Paradis and feeling so happy that she could notice *everything else* seemed extraordinary now. In the cupboard were a few outgrown, or at least outloved, clothes: they seemed both girlish and faded. The horrible bridesmaid's dress was there, too. How John would have laughed at her in that! The trouble was that she could not bear to think about John – in case it was no good thinking about him. The great thing was to think about other people: May, for instance, and even Alice. She washed her hands and combed her hair, collected some cigarettes out of her case and went down in search of her mother.

May had made dinner and to her amazement, the colonel had more or less laid the table, so there was nothing to be done.

'It's not very exciting, I'm afraid darling,' May said. 'Just steamed plaice and some baked apples. We've taken to eating very little in the evenings.'

'That's fine. I'm not especially hungry, anyway.'

'Well, Herbert is trying to keep his weight down, and eating at night doesn't seem to agree with me at all these days.'

Elizabeth watched Claude, who was crouched on the back door mat cracking drumsticks with his head on one side, almost as though he was testing for sound.

'He seems larger than ever.'

'He is. He must be: I can really hardly lift him now. That is another problem: he'd never fit into his cat basket. Darling, would you like another drink?'

'I'd love one : what about you?'

May shook her head. 'I've had my little cocktail. The drink's in Herbert's den.'

In summer, the den looked merely dingy rather than dank. It had an unreasonably high ceiling with unfunctional beams. The furniture, a nasty mixture of pitch pine and mahogany, was bilious from the evening sunlight which filtered in through the narrow, heavily leaded windows. The flat surfaces of the room were ranked with photographs of the colonel, in uniform and out of it, in various hot and cold countries, and accompanied by an assortment of animals – alive or dead – as his sense of occasion had seen fit. There were also a number of metal filing cabinets – unlabelled and locked. Elizabeth found that she was looking at each awful room quite freshly, as though it had absolutely nothing to do with her.

Herbert was sitting in his large chair with his head thrown back listening to the cricket news from a small and badly serviced radio resting on the arm of his chair. A whisky and soda lay within his grasp. When he became aware of Elizabeth, he went through the bizarre and contradictory motions of not getting up out of his chair although he knew he should : or, possibly, seeming to get up out of his chair and then not managing it because he was listening too hard to the radio. Elizabeth took advantage of this pantomime to make signs at the drink and herself, and with the barest flicker of hesitation, he seemed to agree. Luckily for her, the drink was still unlocked, but pouring a slug of gin under Daddo's eyes, as Oliver had been wont to remark, required the most artistically unsteady hand if one was to get a decent drink. There was about a third of the bottle of tonic left from her first drink. No ice : no lemon. Just as she was deciding it was worth the journey to the kitchen for, at any rate, ice, the news came to an end.

'Ha! M'dear – you should have let me do that for you.' He had switched off the radio. 'Lost without m'cricket. Haven't been up so much this season with May being a bit off colour.'

'She doesn't look well : has she seen a doctor?'

'First thing I thought of. Got her to one in the end. Bright young chap in Woking. Mark you, had to make at least two appointments for her before I could get her there. She won't take enough care of herself, you know.'

Elizabeth asked what the doctor had said, but he was hunting for the drink cabinet key on his vast and crowded key ring: he didn't seem to have heard her.

'What did the doctor say?' she asked again.

'What? The doctor? Oh – he thought she'd been overdoing it. Alice's wedding and all that. I told him the moment she knew she was coming to see him she seemed much better – much more like her old self – and he produced some fashionable twaddle about psychology – they all do it now, you know, can't stop 'em, even got it with M.O.s towards the end of my time. Personally and between you and me, I don't think *any* woman of her age likes to admit to herself she can't do as much as she used to when she was younger. I don't say it, of course, but my view is that she should rest more, settle down a bit, all this dashing up and down to London takes it out of her. Wish you'd have a word with her about that, m'dear.'

His pale blue eyes were fixed upon her face: he looked anxious, tactless – or rather as though tact was an almost unbearable price to pay for him getting things right with people – and above all, as though he needed help of some kind if only he could explain the kind ... She began her customary retreat from dislike and ridicule: it was unfair, worse than bad taste, wrong for her to laugh at her mother's husband with her brother. He was like she was; simple, not specially clever or good at understanding things, but here he was, clearly doing his best. She smiled at him (she had no idea how anxious her smile was) and said that of course she'd do anything she could. The colonel seemed tremendously relieved by what she said. They finished their drinks in an unusually companionable silence.

After supper, the remains of which were clearly going to provide an ample snack for Claude, the colonel insisted on putting the car away without help. May and Elizabeth piled the dishes on to the rickety trolley and wheeled it down the stone passage, through the baize doors that stuck and squeaked, to the kitchen. Claude emerged unhurriedly from the larder where he had had a rather unsatisfactory check-up.

'Do you mean you *still* haven't had the larder door fixed?'

'No : like so many things, I still haven't done it.'

Her mother's voice sounded despairing, and Elizabeth, going to hug her, realized that she was very near tears. 'Darling – what *is* it?'

'Don't know – feel so awful – don't tell Herbert – headache – lovely to have you here –'

A bit later, she said, 'I've had my little moan. Feel *much* better.'

Elizabeth offered her a cigarette, and she took it doubtfully.

'It might be nice; but often they make me feel sick, these days.'

Elizabeth said, 'Do you think you might possibly be having an ulcer?'

'The doctor didn't seem to think so. Herbert took me to one in Woking. And I saw someone else in London and they thought definitely not.'

'Who did you see in London?'

May had lit her cigarette and now turned to throw away the match. 'Oh nobody you would know, darling; but he was most reassuring.'

Here, the conversation was interrupted by Claude, who was sick and tired of waiting for his plaice. He stood on his hind legs and reached an arm across the top of the trolley until he'd hooked a backbone off what, unfortunately for him, turned out to be the colonel's plate – the only one of them who'd eaten all his dinner. He shook it free and tried again, knocking over and breaking a glass half full of water. This gave him a horrible fright, but this time he held on to a hardly-eaten fish and retired with it under the table.

'Isn't he ghastly?' said May fondly. 'The dustpan's over there. It isn't as though he's intermittently awful – he never stops being it.' And what with getting the fragments of glass and the sticky glue of fish bones and skin off the floor, nothing more was said about the London doctor. Later, Elizabeth made her mother some hot milk and took it up to her in bed. There she learned that Herbert, who was shutting the dogs in, had taken to doing this every night.

'He's very sweet about it. He's bought Horlicks, and Bournvita and cocoa, and I never know which it's going to be.'

'That's good.' Elizabeth tried not to sound surprised. 'I'm afraid I've just put a little nutmeg in this.'

'Delicious, darling. Now off you go to bed – you look tired and we've got the whole of tomorrow to talk.'

But somehow or other, they never did talk. This was because May was afraid of Elizabeth telling Oliver about Dr Sedum and his laughing at her, and also because Elizabeth was afraid of breaking down completely if she began to tell May about John. So long as she never said even his name to May, she could pretend that the whole situation – including having to go away because of awful Jennifer – was unreal, or at least that the going away part of it was unreal. For minutes at a time she did not think at all about it, and then, just as she was beginning to notice in perhaps a rather sickening, congratulatory way that she had not thought about it, it filled her mind; John, unhappy, apologetic, at a loss, giving in to blatantly horrible Jennifer, so that there was a kind of double pain of seeing him give in and send her away and of actually going away. Thinking about it after not thinking about it was always worse. Going to bed was, of course, the saddest time: better at Lincoln Street because Oliver was always about, but here, at Monks' Close, it was really awful. She was even glad of Claude, who turned up reeking of fish to lie on her bed. He waited until the lights were out before he began a vigorous all-over wash that shook the bed for about forty minutes. At least the maddening absurdity of him stopped her crying.

Next day she knew she couldn't bear to stay much longer. It was having nothing to do – except things that she didn't really have to do – that made it impossible to stay. By lunch time, after she had fed the dogs, gone to the village shop for some rennet to make her mother a junket, made it, talked to Mrs Green, been shown the possible croquet lawn by Herbert (she was trying not to call him Daddo any more as he was obviously being so nice to May), been offered, and accepted, a South African sherry, it seemed as though she had been back for months; and just after she had tried the sherry, forgetting and remembering how much she had always disliked it, she also had a moment of actual panic because it seemed to her that far from time making things better about John, it was making things worse. Already they seemed to her about as much as she could bear. May had tried asking her about her job in the South of France, but she had been waiting for that, and her dull answers came out so pat that they quenched the kind of mild curiosity known as 'showing an interest' that was all May thought proper with her grown-up children. The colonel asked her whether she'd been to Monte, and when she said no, told her how much nicer and cheaper it had been in the thirties.

After lunch, she offered to take the dogs out, and when she got to the village, she rang Oliver who was in.

'Goodness me, you haven't got much stamina, have you?' he said in a rather jeering voice (she had got him out of the bath).

'Well you only stuck it for the inside of one day.'

'Quite a contrast to Antibes, I bet.'

'Oh – don't!'

'Do you want me to ring you up or send an urgent telegram?'

'Ring up, I think.'

'Have you got any money?'

'Only what I left you with: minus train ticket, of course. Surely you haven't spent all that dough you got?'

'Don't say "got" in that suburban voice. Stole you mean. No, I haven't. I'll buy us a lobster if you come back in time to make mayonnaise.'

'Ring up in half an hour then. Is there – are there any letters for me?'

'Afraid not.'

So Elizabeth was half dragged back to the house by the large, dull dogs, but with a lighter, if more guilty, heart.

May accepted her going with the usual good grace: there was an awkward moment when she reminded Elizabeth of her promise about transporting Claude, but it was agreed that May should come to lunch at Lincoln Street next time she was in town, and bring Claude with her. The colonel said it was a pity she was going when she'd only just come, and Claude yawned for such a long time that she thought perhaps he had forgotten what he was doing, but eventually he shut his mouth and then his eyes very slowly like sliding doors. May drove her to the station while they reassured each other about what they had not really discussed. Elizabeth said, 'You *will* see another doctor, won't you, if you go on having this stomach bug or whatever it is?' And May said, 'Of course, darling, but it's bound to go: everybody's been having it; even Herbert hasn't been feeling quite the thing.'

As they drew up at the station, May said, 'Darling, don't work *too* hard. You don't look as though you're having enough fun. Make Oliver pull his weight.' And Elizabeth said, 'Oh – I don't do too badly. Yes, I'll tell Oliver: perhaps he's got this job.'

They kissed and Elizabeth told her mother not to wait, and May said that she'd just walk on to the platform, but she *did* wait for the train, and kissed Elizabeth again and then immediately started walking down the small platform: it was then that Elizabeth noticed how much weight her mother must have lost.

Waterloo: the bit of time walking down the platform when you knew you weren't going to be met, and you could imagine that you might have come from anywhere; you had to jazz up the departure because there wasn't enough to be said about arrival. You could only like London at the beginning of August if you knew it very well the rest of the time. She took trains to Sloane Square and then walked – with one or two rests from the suitcase.

When she rang the bell, the door of Lincoln Street opened rather slowly and she couldn't see anyone. Then Oliver said:

'It's me. Behind the door. I'm naked. I knew you'd come if I took off all my clothes.'

'Is that why you did?'

'No – you *fool*! I was just going to try out a new stuff that's supposed to turn you brown while you wait. Give it to me.'

He took her case and they padded upstairs. Oliver collected a bath towel and Elizabeth flung herself on the sofa saying, 'Anything to drink?'

'I must say high life has made you very demanding.' But when he got nearer to her, he saw that tears were sliding down her face. 'Liz!' He rubbed his face against her. 'It's nothing like as bad as you think.'

'How isn't it?'

'I've made a marvellous drink for you. And there is a huge lobster in the fridge, and I went to Buck and Ryan and bought some immensely useful-looking tools that will do for picking the best bits out as *well* as screwdriving. I bought a bottle of Pouilly Fumé – costs the earth, I must say – to drink with the lobster and a packet of Gauloises for nostalgia –'

'Oh don't, Oliver! It's only – seventy-two hours since we were there!'

'*That's* why you haven't heard from him. Oh yes, and I was out last night so he might easily have rung up if he can ever sneak away from loathsome Jennifer. Now – first you're going to get a bit drunk, and then you're going to get indigestion, but the whole thing will turn out to have been worth it when you look back on the evening – you'll see.'

'What about the mayonnaise?' she said about half an hour later.

'Do you think if I brought the ingredients here to you you could manage it?'

They'd each had three tremendously strong Negronis and Liz had just remarked that he had a lovely easy name to say when drunk.

'Standing on my head.'

'That won't be necessary. You're not at the Palladium now.'

When he had assembled everything, and she was sitting with her feet tucked up under her on the sofa stirring away, she asked, 'What about the job?'

'Which job?'

'The newspaper one.'

'Oh that. Well I've got that in a way. Freelance. As a matter of fact I've got three jobs. Haven't let the grass grow under my feet. Can you imagine *anyone* doing that in England? Rheumatism and awful metal notices telling you to keep off it, and dogs peeing and worms casting and even policemen asking you to move along.'

'What are your other jobs?'

'Well – one of them's rather silly, really. The idea is that I should do a TV ad for the people who make this instant brown stuff. And I wanted to see if you could watch it working.'

'You're brown already.'

'Not really. I'm simply not the British un*earthly* white. This is supposed to turn you Nescafé olé, as the international slogan might well go.'

'What's the third job?'

'Well that's a bit queer, and I'm not supposed to talk about it. I answered an ad in the paper. All they seem to want you to do is to watch things.'

'What on earth do you mean?'

'Not absolutely *any*thing, of course. They ring you and tell you to watch, say, 29 Pelham Place.'

'How do you mean – watch it?'

'Who goes there, etcetera.'

'Oliver! That's simply spying!'

'That's right. An immensely fashionable occupation. Not very well paid at my level, but still not negligible.'

She put down the fork in the mayonnaise bowl.

'Look here, Oliver, honestly!'

'Before you start all that, I'm going to get the lobster. You may think you're a stanchion of society, but I know bloody well you couldn't walk down a flight of stairs without help. So off I go.'

While he was assembling dinner, she sat in a state of semi-alcoholic despair about life: about Oliver: brilliant at Oxford; no fool, really by any standards, fiddling about with sleazy old part-time employment kicks. And what was she doing? Cooking for unknown, boring, quantities of people. Their father had died fighting the Second World War. May was hanging out with that silly boor in the home counties. Who was enjoying what? And what about John? What about John? What about him? *What?* Was the world ruled by Jennifers? Once it was certain that you could get no pleasure from anything, were you automatically in a position of power? Where the least you could do was to see it that other people did not enjoy themselves? What was the *point* of being as clever as Oliver if people only asked you to do silly things like watching houses and putting idiotic stuff on your back? Why should children – like Jennifer – exercise this fearful blackmailing jurisdiction over parents? Jennifer was the same age as *she* was – grown up, in fact: no longer in need of – supposing *she* had made that sort of fuss, she supposed that she (and Oliver, of course) could have prevented May from marrying Herbert. They could have made May feel so awful about it that she would have given up the idea. Perhaps that was exactly what she ought to have done. This thought quickly took hold to the exclusion of any other.

'Crying again, I see.' He dumped the tray on the coffee table. 'Everything is your fault, I have no doubt, and by the time I've reassured and comforted you about that, everything will be *my* fault. Better if we both got down to a nice dose of strontium 90.'

'What?'

'Liz, dear, do stop snuffling and blow your nose. Lobsters, as you clearly didn't know, are chock-a-block with strontium 90: not as much as crabs, but still enough to worry some people. There.' He handed her a plate on which was half of an enormous lobster, some chopped pieces of tomato and a length of cucumber. 'You've *cried* into the mayonnaise!'

'It won't hurt it.' She stirred up the bowl a bit. The lobster looked far too big. He was pouring out the pale, delicious wine.

'You'd better eat some bread: this'll taste awful after Negroni.'

On the tray were a collection of what looked like burglars' tools. While she was fingering them, Oliver tied a large tea towel round her neck.

'Now: we are going to enjoy this: you may think I'm wasting my life, but I'm not going to have you wasting my lobster.'

'What about *you* having something round your neck?'

'No point when it's just skin.' He was still bare to the waist, but had put on a pair of jeans and some vicious-looking sandals that a friend had brought back from Marrakesh.

The lobster wasn't too big, and the burglars' tools turned out to be extremely useful. Oliver was the ideal person to eat a lobster properly with, she thought: you could crunch and probe and lick and he only thought the more of you.

After the lobster there was half an extremely ripe Camembert and some crusty bread and finally half a bottle of brandy.

'It is so awful changing one's standard of living with too much of a jolt,' he said. By then she had told him about May and how Herbert had seemed to be nicer, and he had said that May would be bound to feel ill if she lived with such a bore and he, for one, did not believe that Herbert was ever *really* nicer, he must be pretending. Elizabeth argued a bit – that people surely didn't throw *up* for psycho-whatever reasons, and Oliver said oh yes they did. She had hiccoughs by then and you never win an argument with them. Oliver gave her a mediocre fright and some more brandy. Then she said,

'Now, Oliver – we've got to talk about you.'

'What are we going to say?

'Oh, *I* know,' he added, when he'd had a good look at her face. 'The trouble with me is that all my life I *haven't* wanted to be a doctor. I've got no sense of purpose. You get that with rather charming, spineless people sometimes, and with me you've got it. I simply want a tremendous lot of money for nothing. Nearly all work that people do seems to me so absolutely awful that I'd rather live from hand to mouth. I haven't quite got that sense of showmanship required for the Church, or the Bar or the stage. I haven't the senses of responsibility and greed that would make me any good at business. I only like nature in amateur quantities, so farming is out. (Also – I could never fill in the forms.) I've thought seriously of crime, but prisons are full of such *frightfully* boring people all wanting to tell you every single unfair thing that has ever happened to them. What else is there? Oh yes, the Services. Now them I wouldn't mind so much if you could choose at all where you went, and didn't get chucked out the moment you'd got any good at it and had a chance to tell other people to do the dirty work. Also they are tremendously keen on people having spines. The arts sound more fun and I might end up on that kick somehow or other, but deep down they're horribly hard work and you get your sense of dedication creeping in: I'd have to be a charlatan. I thought of running a brothel – rushing to Victoria station and saying, "You like my sister? Very clean" – what else is it they say? – but somehow that is a mixture of business and vicarious pleasure. No: I'm afraid I've simply got to marry a very rich girl and let people say what a marvellous chap I would have been if I hadn't done that. So I'm quite prepared to talk about Ginny. The trouble is, I don't think she has the stamina for marriage, and the other thing is I'm really very fond of her in between when she's not being spoilt and boring. What do you think of her?'

Elizabeth, who felt as though she'd been holding her breath without warning for far too long, hiccoughed in spite of this and said that she didn't think marriage was a way out. For a man, she added.

'What about a woman? I mean one could look at it from Ginny's point of view. It might be a way out for her. You don't like her, do you?'

'I don't have any feelings about her.'

'With you, that amounts to dislike. Well, of course she's not the *only* rich girl in the world. I don't think we ought to marry people each other don't like, do you?'

She shook her head, hiccoughed again, and held her glass out for more brandy.

'Like a Gauloise with it?'

She nodded.

'It's a pity we've got to marry anyone, really: we get on so well. The only trouble about incest must be getting yourself to feel like it. Otherwise it strikes me as a very harmless and economical arrangement. It's funny how brandy seems to make me talk and shuts you up. Can't you think of *anything* to say?'

'It's my hiccoughs. But what would we do about children?'

'Have them, of course. With your looks and my brains (I must say, Liz, that you really have quite *suddenly* got much prettier) they'd probably be marvellous. And think how nice for May not having any sons- or daughters-in-law: cutting down family friction to the minimum. I suppose I could be an amateur detective, but there's nothing I really want to find out – in that sort of way, I mean, I would love to know what we're all here for. The only people who've taken any trouble about that got so bogged down with knowing what *they* were for.'

'What?'

'Taking trouble about what we're here for, silly.'

'Anyway, I can't marry you. I don't think I'll be able to marry anyone.'

'Watch it! You're going to cry in a minute. You mean because the only person you want to marry is John and you won't be able to because foul Jennifer will bitch it up?'

She nodded, put down her glass and started looking for her handkerchief.

'He is the first person you've ever fallen in love with.'

Miserable tears had started streaming down, and no handkerchief.

'Look, darling Liz: most people have to try dozens of people before they find the right one. He isn't the only man in the world.'

'He *is*!'

'Oh dear. O.K. I was afraid of that. Because you see the course that *yawns* before me, don't you?'

She rubbed her face with the tea towel.

'No.'

'It's up to me to seduce and elope with Jennifer. Thereby getting her out of your way and remaining true to what I know would be generally accepted as a sordid ambition; but I do feel that that simply means one must exercise even more loyalty. She is awful, though. I suppose if I was drunk and always wore dark glasses I could just about bring it off. But then, you see, *you* wouldn't like me marrying someone you didn't like, would you? How will it all end I wonder.'

'You don't know how awful I feel.'

'Now then. Your situation is by no means hopeless, and the best thing you can do is think of others. That usually makes one feel so frightful that one can stand any parochial anguish. Think of Alice.'

'Oh dear.'

'You see? You can hardly bear it at once. You just think of how you can brighten her perfectly dreadful life.'

'Claude!'

'What about him?'

'I promised May I'd take him to Bristol for her.'

'What on earth made you do that?'

'You know how when you're bored you'll pledge yourself in the most tiring ways. Alice is pregnant; she can't travel to fetch him, and nobody seems to think he could go anywhere unaccompanied. So I said I'd do it.'

'You do it and then you can tell me all about their horrid little happy home.'

'You are absolutely beastly.'

'No. Just accurate. But if Alice wants Claude and you are at all sorry for her, it is the least you can do.'

4. Blue for a Boy

Alice was so excited at the double prospect of Elizabeth and Claude that on the morning of the day that they were due, she hardly minded being sick. She was usually sick about three times before eleven a.m.: once after she had fried Leslie's bacon and eggs, once after she had mopped and cleaned up after the hysterically dirty puppy that was Mrs Mount's newest token of kindness to her daughter-in-law, and once after she had obeyed Leslie's command that she have a nice cup of hot tea, or coffee. Leslie had usually gone to his office before she got to the puppy-cleaning time. Then she would go and have a bath. The cold sweat, the dizziness, the soiled disorder of her body, usually revolted her so much that she had to try not to be sick a fourth time. So far as she knew, she was six and a half weeks pregnant, and the doctor had said that many people suffered from morning sickness for the first three months. She explained that she often felt sick in the evenings as well and he said that often happened, but with most people it was one or the other. The idea of another six weeks of feeling like this was so terrible, that she simply retched and crawled through each separate interminable day. After her bath, she did the housework very slowly while the puppy yapped round her. If she shut him into any room he made a mess in it and then yapped and howled to be let out. Sometimes she put him out into what would one day be their garden but was still just a rectangle marked off by a paling fence. As soon as he found he could not get out of the garden, he yapped to be let into the house. He was (more or less) a miniature poodle and his nature was both disagreeable and demanding: he smelled faintly all the time of shit; she no sooner got rid of one set of worms than he contracted another; his breath offended her, particularly in her present condition;

169

he had a capacity for yapping that seemed almost electronic; he was hardly ever obedient, and totally undiscriminating in his affections; he ate so fast that he nearly always threw his food up; he seemed quite unable to keep any parts of himself clean and his grasping claws ruined any pair of stockings she wore. His expression was unreliable and silly and she could not get fond of him. Leslie thought it was wonderful of his mother to give her a dog – it was company, as he kept on saying: he did not seem to think that it mattered what kind. She took him shopping with her on the days when she felt strong enough and he strained on the lead, strangling himself, winding the lead round and round her until she was immobile, peeing every two or three yards, yapping at any other dog. When she felt really weak, she would leave him in the bathroom and go guiltily off without him. She would buy food for supper; things at the chemist and the ironmonger for the house; she would get herself some books from the library and occasionally she would eat lunch of some kind in a tea shop or women's café. Then she would walk slowly home, clean up and let out the dog and lie down with one of the library books. In the afternoons she did not feel sick, simply overwhelmingly tired. She would read two pages and fall into a heavy sleep. The house was still far from finished, and she did nothing at all about preparing for the baby in whom, when alone, she just did not believe. She would wake at about five, force herself to get up, and start sewing Rufflette tape on to half-made pairs of curtains, slicing french beans for supper, or marking some of the wedding present linen with indian ink and a tiny, spluttery pen. By the time Leslie returned she was just beginning to feel sick again, but gave the appearance of having been at wifely occupations all day. He would make himself a drink, switch on the television and tell her about his day in a raised voice over it, while she struggled with nausea and supper. After they – or sometimes he – had eaten, he would watch more television with another drink. He always asked her how she was feeling; he was very bucked about the baby and said several times a day that he was sure it would be a boy. Once or twice a week his family either turned up or summoned them. These were the worst evenings. Otherwise, she could get into her housecoat after dinner and read or watch television with him. At about ten she got hungry, and what she liked best was anchovies on water biscuits. When, eventually, they went to bed, Leslie left her alone which was the single best thing about being pregnant, she decided. He would kiss her forehead, pat her hand, sometimes – maddeningly – stroke her belly, but he seemed to regard sex as unnecessary.

There were terrible days when Rosemary turned up in her little second-hand M.G. and talked and talked: it was extraordinary how people telling you things could wear you out: the only hope was that one day Rosemary would have told her everything and would then stop coming. And this was odd, because nearly all the time she felt more lonely than she had ever felt before in her life. Always, before, there had been so many things to do for her father that she had not needed to bother about how she felt. She had always wanted a friend, but somehow Rosemary would not do: she seemed to treat Alice like an inversion of the radio – she simply turned Alice on as a listener.

So when Elizabeth wrote to say that she would bring Claude down and could she stay the night, Alice felt as though it was a turning-point. Things were bound to get better once Claude was there, and Elizabeth must care about her or she wouldn't go to all the trouble: Claude would not be an easy person to travel with. After she had told Leslie and he had remarked kindly that that was very nice, she started feverishly to get the spare room into some sort of order. The bungalow was tremendously full of wedding presents, and as they were mostly either ugly or useless, and often both, Alice had been dumping them in the spare room. Elizabeth had only given her twenty-four hours' notice (never *mind*) so after Leslie had gone and she was more or less over being sick, she set to work. It was lunch time before it occurred to her that Claude would be unlikely to take kindly to the puppy. He disliked all dogs intensely, and a puppy in his own house was a kind of double insult. If *only* Mrs Mount would take it back! She had a sandwich lunch (anchovy and cucumber) and finished the curtains for what she by now called Elizabeth's room. She had telephoned Lincoln Street and made all the arrangements: they were travelling by the morning train, and she would meet them in a taxi if Leslie could not let her have the car. She spent an hour or two with her cookery books trying to think of the best things for dinner: Elizabeth was such a good cook and Leslie preferred very plain food. She decided on lamb and summer pudding which she made well because her father had particularly liked it. In the afternoon she went to buy the meat and fruit and she took the puppy with her to make up for probably being horrible to him tomorrow.

That evening, because Elizabeth was coming, she realized how very little she and Leslie said to each other; up until now it had not seemed especially strange that she and Leslie talked to each other much less than she had talked with May, for instance. But now she was afraid that Elizabeth would think it very odd, and in a desperate, last-minute effort to alter this situation, she tried to chatter to Leslie. But Alice trying to chatter was so unusual, unlikely and unsuccessful, that after a short time Leslie asked her whether she was feverish, and after she'd said 'no', she couldn't think of anything at all.

The next morning, she bought half a rabbit and some whiting for Claude. Leslie needed the car, so she took a bus to the station – a queasy, but not disastrous progress. She was far too early, but it did not matter. It was a baking hot day and when she reached the platform, the station smelled of cool dirt. She sat on a hard bench and wondered whether anybody could tell, by looking at her, that she was pregnant. Perhaps Elizabeth would stay for several days – for quite a long time. Her hopes rose as the train did not come. Very few people were waiting for it, those that were had a holiday air: red-faced women in sleeveless dresses with shopping bags and either silent little babies in blue and pink nylon, like elves, or something out of an egg, or hot toddlers in dungarees, burdened with awkward and favourite possessions, who tugged at any free hand to try and make something happen.

The signals changed; a feeling of routine or professional expectancy charged the station. Two porters appeared. An old man who had been walking down the track, climbed up on to the platform. A case of carrier pigeons was moved nearer the line, and somebody cleared their throat into the loud-speaker.

She hardly recognized Elizabeth: new clothes, her hair cut differently and her tan made her look a different person – almost unbearably glamorous to Alice, who had found her marvellous enough before. She wore a dark blue linen coat and skirt and carried a small red case. Claude was surely not in that?

They kissed, rather shyly, and Elizabeth said:

'They wouldn't let him travel with me: he's in the guard's van. I did go and see him several times, but I don't think it made much difference to him.'

The guard was putting what looked like a small picnic basket on to the platform. When they reached it, Alice saw that it had a label saying, SEYMOUR, BRISTOL on it. No sound came from the basket. She bent over it.

'I don't think you'd better open it here. He might rush out.'

So she waited until they were in the taxi.

Claude, looking even larger than she remembered, crouched on his old blanket inside. He looked up at her and opened his mouth, but no sound came out.

'Oh dear. I'm afraid he's lost his voice. I'm not surprised, I must say. He went on and on about how much he hated everything all the way to Paddington and whenever I went to see him in the van.'

She stroked him, and he winced as though he was past any such attention. He went on opening and shutting his mouth and staring resentfully at her: he smelled faintly of circuses. It was lovely to see him again.

'It is kind of you to bring him.'

'That's all right. It's jolly nice to see you again.'

'You look very sunburned.'

'I've been in France.'

There was a silence. After a bit, and after thinking what to say, Alice said, 'Our house – it's a bungalow, really – is on a new building estate, so everything looks a bit unfinished.'

'I'm longing to see it.'

During the rest of the taxi ride, she asked about Oliver and May, and, finally, her father. Elizabeth was funny and animated about Oliver, said that May did not seem to be very well, and said that Alice's father seemed to be looking after her as much as he could.

After that, she suddenly started feeling very sick – so much so that she had to tell Elizabeth.

'Do you want to stop and get out for a bit?'

'It's all right.'

After a bit, she said, 'I'll tell you if it isn't.'

The road to 24 Ganymede Drive was only half made up. They lurched and jolted and dust came in through the windows, so Elizabeth shut them. As she leaned across to do Alice's window, she said, 'Are you excited about the baby?'

And Alice answered in a colourless voice, 'Oh yes.'

They opened the tricky little gate and walked up the path. Elizabeth insisted on carrying Claude's basket. The moment Alice put the key in the lock, there was a frantic yapping. The puppy, who had hurled himself against the shut door and fallen over, had picked himself up in time to hurl himself at them when the door was open. There was a heavy lurch in the picnic basket, and Elizabeth tried to hold it higher from the ground.

'Wait a minute: I'll shut him in the bathroom. Please go in the sitting-room, Elizabeth.'

Elizabeth had plenty of time to look around the sitting-room. It had streaky black and grey Marley tiles on the floor, a fireplace of the kind that Oliver had once described as Builders' Revenge, with cute little shelves made of tiles. There was a coffee table also made of tiles – rather improbable tropical fish – a sofa and two armchairs upholstered in black imitation leather, a corner cupboard of limed oak and a rather large cocktail cabinet of walnut veneer. On this stood a wedding photograph of Alice and Leslie. Alice looked as though she had just sneezed and Leslie seemed to have too many teeth. The curtains were blue linen, and Elizabeth suspected that Alice had chosen and made them. There was a fluffy rug the colour of beetroot juice in front of the fireplace. There was a reproduction of Degas's 'Dancer' in colour, and a mirror with the most serpentine wrought-iron frame. In the corner cabinet were some silver cups that she guessed Leslie had won playing golf.

She had put Claude's basket down in the middle of the room, but she knew that Alice would want to open it herself. Just as she was beginning to wonder what could have happened to her, Alice came in.

'The puppy had made another mess: I'm so sorry.' She looked rather green.

The basket was opened and Alice lifted him out, Claude turned his head from her and jumped clumsily to the ground. He then prowled slowly around the door and the windows with exaggerated caution, his belly touching the ground. When he could find no way out, he went and crouched under the coffee table. He looked dusty and disgruntled. When Alice went to stroke him, he got up wearily and crouched somewhere else.

'He doesn't remember me!'

'He's just upset. Perhaps he's hungry.'

She fetched him a plate of rabbit: he sniffed at it and sneezed.

'Perhaps he's thirsty.'

Milk was brought. He grudgingly drank some of that, and then, with a gesture that seemed to Elizabeth deliberately involuntary he knocked over the saucer with one paw. Alice had made him a tray with sand in it. He sauntered to that ('He's feeling more at home!' Alice said) and spent about five minutes walking round and over it, scuffing sand out, settling himself with his face turned towards the ceiling and a fixed expression and then changing his mind. When most of the sand was on the floor he got into the right position, his eyes became glassy and one natural function, at least, was achieved.

'Do you think he will get on with the puppy?'

'No. I know he won't. My mother-in-law gave it to me: I asked her not to but she did. I don't know what to do. Perhaps they will keep out of each other's way.'

But this, of course, was not possible in a small bungalow. After they had had lunch, Alice and Elizabeth made the experiment of bringing the puppy into the sitting-room. Claude uttered a single cry of rage and despair and tried to get under the sofa while the puppy gambolled around and fell over him. He swiped at the puppy who retreated yelping. As it was clear that he could not possibly get under the sofa, he jumped on to it and crouched there swearing continously under his breath. The rest of the afternoon was in the same key and Elizabeth realized that the situation was a crisis for poor Alice. 'You see, Leslie *likes* the puppy because his mother gave it to us. He doesn't do anything about it, but he would never agree to getting rid of it. What shall I do?'

Elizabeth did all she could. She helped with dinner: she cleared up after both the puppy and Claude. She even took the puppy for a short walk and he laddered her stockings. Taking these off in the spare room that had been shown her with such humble anxiety for her comfort, she saw how brown her legs still were and felt so miserable, so homesick for John, so bewildered by the sudden, horrible, inexplicable change in her life, that all Oliver's cheering-up went for nothing and she wept. As she was washing her face she remembered what Oliver had said about having to spend a fortnight in Cornwall with Leslie. Being in this house made that seem about like having measles compared to a life sentence. It was all too clear that poor old Alice was not happy. Why on *earth* had she done it? A mystery and as Oliver had once pointed out, many of them were horrid if you got at all close.

Leslie came back at a quarter to six, and by then Elizabeth felt as though she'd been in the bungalow a week. He embraced her facetiously, kissed Alice with more social practice, and said he'd make them all a drink. This was a good idea, but when he went into the sitting-room to do this, he encountered Claude, who, having demolished the plate of rabbit and a raw whiting, was grandiosely engaged upon the only other natural function left to him. The smell was awe-inspiring and Elizabeth had to admit that it was reasonable of Leslie to object. So Claude and his tray were moved to Elizabeth's room: she said she didn't mind a bit. (This was true: she felt she would never mind anything again.) But Leslie was somebody who continued to discuss something after it was over. The windows had all been opened; the puppy had been let in, the drinks were made, and Leslie had only just got into his stride about what coming into his home and finding Claude doing that had been like. After two gins and tonics he was still on the subject of how much worse (worse?) cats were than dogs. 'You've got a nice little pup for company,' he said over and over again. 'You don't want a dirty creature like that.'

They had dinner in the dining alcove. Roast lamb, mint sauce, rather old new potatoes and ageless, frozen peas. The summer pudding was excellent, and Elizabeth told Alice this but the poor thing was by then too distressed to eat any of it. While she was making coffee, Leslie told Elizabeth that women who were expecting were always touchy; his mother had warned him of it; he was glad of course that Alice had a stranger on the way and that he was sure it would be a boy. Elizabeth looked at her beautiful watch while he was getting his pipe. it was twenty to nine. She went to the kitchen to see if she could help with the washing up and found Alice in floods of tears. There is a curious sensation of genuinely trying to comfort somebody who is sincerely unhappy when they are utterly unused to being comforted. Elizabeth found that you quickly reach a point where anything you do feels dishonest; you are embracing or stroking a tree, not a person; any words you say sound as though you have not understood or do not care: added to this, she felt that if Leslie came into the kitchen and found them, a kind of spurious treachery would be added to the scene.

They went to wash Alice's face and to see Claude in the spare room. At first they could not find him but this was because he had gone to sleep on Elizabeth's bed *in* her open suitcase and mysteriously covered himself with her white cashmere cardigan. It was Alice who found him and who sank to her knees beside the suitcase to tell him he'd been hiding. He stared at her coldly: his whole routine had been upset and grudges were very much his line, but Alice seemed neither to know this nor to mind. 'The thing is, Elizabeth, that he *is* my cat and I can't – I don't see why I should –' And Elizabeth realized that she would start crying again if something were not done about it.

'Of course he is,' she said briskly. 'I'm sure they'll settle down together in a day or two. Don't you think we had better take the coffee in to Leslie before it gets cold?'

Alice nodded dumbly, sat at the dressing-table to powder her nose and met Elizabeth's eye in the glass. It was funny, Elizabeth suddenly thought: if you didn't say *anything* to Alice you felt she understood everything you hadn't said, but if you *said* anything at all, somehow you felt that whatever you'd said had been wrong and all communication with her got blocked. She was trying to smile now: but as Elizabeth touched her shoulder – rigid with the inexperience of being comforted – the smile somehow turned into a face that Alice was making – absurd and repelling: you had to think hard to be sorry for her.

But as soon as they were back in the sitting-room with the coffee, she felt sorry for Alice all right. Leslie put down his evening paper and started.

He didn't want them to think him an unreasonable man, as a matter of fact that was the last thing that he was, so he defied anyone to think it, but he *did* believe in plain speaking, he'd never been someone who minced their words and he had no intention of starting this evening. Everybody had got their coffee by now, and the two women were seated looking – he thought expectantly – at him. In fact Alice was trying not to hate him, and Elizabeth was trying not to yawn. What it amounted to – after what seemed like hours but was, in fact, about forty minutes – was that Leslie would not have that cat in the house. At any price, he had reiterated many times as though there could possibly be one. The third time that he said that Alice had got the puppy after all, Alice said that she had had Claude first and that she didn't really *like* the puppy. It was a present from his mother, Leslie said, thus putting it beyond the realm of liking. The argument about whether Claude was clean in the house began. Leslie said look at what he had had to come home to, and Alice said that as soon as he was settled down Claude would use the garden, but this simply drove Leslie back to square one: he would not have that cat in his house. Just as he was saying that Alice had got the puppy, after all, the telephone rang, and this was so loud and surprising that Elizabeth, at least, jumped, thinking 'Thank God' without knowing why. Leslie went to answer it (the telephone was in his study) and came back a moment later saying that the call was for Elizabeth. This seemed both to amaze and annoy him. Wondering what on earth Oliver was up to now, Elizabeth escaped to the study.

'What *are* you doing in Bristol?' said John Cole's voice.

It was John. It wasn't Oliver – it was John.

'Are you there?'

'Yes. I'm in Bristol.'

'Yes, I thought you must be. Do you want to stop being there? Because if you do, I'll fetch you.'

'Now – would you?'

'Yes. I'm at London airport. That should just give you time to pack.'

'Oh! I don't think I *can*, though. I'm supposed to stay the night here: at least. I mean I haven't even *been* here for a night yet.'

'Couldn't you explain to them?'

'Well – no, I couldn't really. Not enough to stop people feeling hurt.'

There was a pause, and then he said, 'All right: what about tomorrow morning?'

'That would be O.K.'

'Would it be lovely as well as O.K.?'

But as soon as she didn't answer, he added quickly, 'Jennifer has gone to Capri with some of Ginny's set.' Then he said, 'Oliver said he didn't think you'd mind my ringing you, but I quite see about staying the night. Would ten o'clock tomorrow morning suit you?'

'Yes. I'm sorry, I'm no good at talking on the telephone.'

'The trouble is that there's nothing else you can do on it really. Never mind. Tomorrow; ten o'clock.'

'Have you got the address?'

'I have.' She waited; there was a faint click and then the dialling tone. He never said good-bye.

She put the receiver down and walked unsteadily back into the sitting-room trying to compose her face to suit the now so distant as to be meaningless situation of Leslie versus Claude.

Leslie was definitely intrigued, as he put it, by Elizabeth's telephone call. This was partly, Elizabeth felt, because he was rather rudely amazed that *anyone* should want to call her long distance, and partly because she sensed that he had wrung from Alice some form of capitulation about Claude, and, having got his own way, was breezily determined to change the subject.

The young man sounded definitely intriguing, Leslie repeated; was he someone they might have met at the wedding? Which was absolutely ridiculous, Elizabeth thought, since he must know perfectly well that apart from the caterers everybody at the wedding had been some sort of actual or potential relation.

No, she said.

Well people didn't phone people for nothing: that was a fact and certainly not at this hour of night, so perhaps there might be another wedding that they'd meet him àt?

He was like Rosemary in plus-fours, Elizabeth thought, but even *he* could make her blush.

He was a friend of hers and Oliver's, she said : he happened to be in the neighbourhood and Oliver had suggested to him that he pick her up. Which he was doing tomorrow morning at ten o'clock. And from coldly and casually not looking anywhere, she turned to Alice with something like entreaty. Alice made an effort to smile and said that she thought perhaps she would go to bed. Would Leslie take the puppy out? Of *course* he would. Where was the poor little chap? In the kitchen in his basket. When he had gone, Alice said :

'Would you mind very much having him in your room to-night? Claude, I mean,' she added.

'Of course not. I'd love to have him.'

Alice followed her to the door of her room. 'He's very good at night : as long as he's got someone warm to lean against and you don't turn over too much.'

'I'm sure he is : I'm awfully sorry, Alice.'

They kissed clumsily; Alice's eyes filled with tears and she said, 'Just bad luck.' Then she had to go without saying good night to Claude, because Leslie and the puppy had returned.

But with Alice gone, all pity, all dismay vanished. It was almost impossible to feel really happy *and* really sorry for someone at the same time – or at least *she* didn't seem to be managing it: of course she wasn't simply happy about John – they were going to have to have a serious talk, about Jennifer and everything. It was more a mixture of tremendous relief that she'd heard from him, and excitement at the thought of seeing him, and apprehension about what seeing him would be like. 'This time tomorrow,' she thought, unable to think any more than that about it.

Claude still lay in her suitcase, but now his tail hung out and down the side of the bed like a bell pull in a Beatrix Potter story. She lifted him out of the suitcase on to the bed, and without the slightest pause he started to climb into it again. So then she lifted the suitcase on to the floor and he got out at once. He had no intention of spending his night on the floor. When she was in bed and had turned out the lights, he subjected her to nerve-racking minutes while he walked over her dressing-table hitting things and knocking them over. She called him, and after a suitable delay, he landed with exaggerated caution on her neck. He then tramped wearily over her, testing various places to see whether or not they could be expected to take his weight, until he finally settled in the crook at the back of her knees. Here he sneezed eighteen times and then got down to a thorough all-over wash. His muscular and rhythmic tongue shook the whole bed for what seemed like hours. But he did one good thing. From thinking that she would not be able even to shut her eyes, he made her long for him to shut up and let her fall asleep. Eventually, he did.

John arrived punctually at ten. Leslie had left for work, it having been made interminably clear that Claude was not to be in the house when he returned that evening. Elizabeth left them alone together and heard Alice saying good-bye to him and then the outbreak of his fury when he found himself back in his travelling basket. She had tried to do the breakfast washing up but Alice had stopped her: 'You'll leave me nothing to do.' So now she stood in the sitting-room by the front windows that looked on to the small blazing desert that was to be a garden when, as she had heard it variously put, Leslie got round and Alice faced up to it. The thought of being Alice was, at the moment, so awful, and the kind of chance whereby *she* had escaped this fate so utterly mysterious that she felt a kind of moral sadness for the world . . . She could see the car.

The bungalow gate made him look even taller than usual – turned him into a kind of Gulliver; he stopped to undo the fussy little catch, but really, he could just as well have stepped over the whole thing; she rushed to the front door and opened it before he had finished striding up the concrete-scored-to-look-like-crazy-paving path. He beamed discreetly at her, looking much browner than he had looked in France. Alice appeared in the doorway of the guest room and Elizabeth introducing John, suddenly saw her as a complete stranger might do : a large, ungainly girl, but striking in a gentle, picturesque manner, as much out of proportion and place here as, say, a Labrador in a hen coop. She was very pale, but blushed when John shook hands with her and immediately started to apologize for Claude about whom John, as yet, knew nothing. Elizabeth, who had thought that perhaps they would have to endure coffee and each person trying to think of things to say that would be all right for the other two, realized from her glazed·expression and oddly trembling mouth that she was very near breaking down again : it would be better if they left as quickly as possible.

So this they did. Claude, whose protests had settled in volume much as a long distance runner adjusts his speed to the course, was put on the back seat with Elizabeth's small red case beside him. Elizabeth thanked Alice again for having her : they kissed, and their noses bumped together painfully.

'I promise I'll take him home to May.'

'I know : thank you so much for coming, Elizabeth.'

She stood at the gate – it looked absurdly small beside her, too – and waved to them like someone who had never done it before. When Elizabeth turned back for the last time, she was still waving.

As soon as they were out of sight, John stopped the car and put Claude's basket in the boot which he propped open. 'I've nothing against him, you understand, but I want to keep it that way.'

'As long as he can breathe.'

'Lots of fresh air in that boot.'

'He loses his voice in about forty miles.' She couldn't help feeling a bit guilty about him.

'Where are we going?' she asked some time later.

'Somewhere nice: *I* don't know. Let's just – see.'

They were out of Bristol by now, into the rich green and multi-coloured country: fields of ripe corn; hedgerows overgrown with flowering brambles; cottage gardens choked and blazing, the thick, grassy verge crammed with poppies and buttercups and cow parsley . . . she thought of Alice jammed in the house Leslie had built, pregnant, and still, in spite of marriage, lonelier than she had seemed before: of her mother, doggedly frittering her time away with menial and unnecessary tasks for a bore; and of Oliver, wasting his brilliance and youth for lack of opportunity or purpose or something like that . . . She did not want to think about Oliver; in fact, in her selfish way, she did not want to think about any of them: they all added up to life being some kind of tightrope; if you were on it and didn't look down, everything seemed easy, but if you even began to look down . . .

5. One Fine Day

When she could no longer even hear their car, Alice turned back to the bungalow. It was going to be another baking day. She had planted three white geraniums in the piece of earth that she had marked out for a flower-bed, and already their lower leaves were wilting. In any case, only three plants in a whole garden looked odd and wrong, but it had been too late to sow the lawn and the man who was to turf it had not turned up. There was no shade in the garden, it was really just a rectangle of ploughed-up earth with a garden path laid at one side of it. Then there was the house with the puppy. The black dots that lay in wait one inch from her eyeballs took yet another curtain call – diminishing as though sinking to the bottom of a curtsy and then bobbing up again. She started walking up the path, trying to find things to notice that would stop the sick, empty feeling that seemed to come and go but always to come back. The puppy was alternately hurling himself against the study door and howling. The thought occurred to her that it would be possible just not to go into the house at all; she was perfectly in control of herself – all she had to do was *not* go on walking towards the front door: she could stop everything as simply as that ... But still she would have to be somewhere. She shut the door very slowly and leaned against it: breathing had become something she was having to notice to make sure it went on happening. She went into the sitting-room meaning to sit down somewhere and wait for things to get better, but the room, when she reached it and looked round her, seemed to horrible, so arranged to expose her as an alien, neither at home nor even at ease, that she couldn't sit alone there. In her underclothes drawer in the bedroom – hidden beneath the pastel Celanese and nylon lace – was the red-leather book that she had bought in Barcelona. It had thick, white paper with gilded edges. Into this she copied her poems when they were as finished as she could make them. She took the book back to the sitting-room and sat for a long time with it on her lap. Sometimes she looked at the poems: she knew them by heart, and also exactly what they looked like in her writing on the page, but it was comforting to look. They were never really what she had meant, but they reminded her of whatever that had been; it was the nearest she got to being able to tell anyone anything, and in reading or recalling them, she was able to become somebody else whom she was telling. This made it the opposite of lonely. The last poem was about the bird in Cornwall.

•

'But it said: PRIVATE ROAD!'

And John, maddeningly like Oliver, replied, 'So it did.'

They were driving through a beech wood, a chequered, green cavern – ahead was the sunlit, tunnel-shaped exit: it looked dazzling and mysterious, but then they were out and it was just ordinary summer afternoon light. On either side of the narrow road were hedge and meadow, the road curved, declined, and then straightened, and on their left, the other side of a field, and set a little above it, was a very square and pretty house. John stopped the car. It was built of stone so bleached by the sun that it was neither grey, nor white, nor cream. The shallow roof was almost concealed by elaborate stone coping, and the middle of the front was entirely covered by wisteria. John got out of the car.

'Where are you going?'

'To explore. Come on.'

'I'm sure it's private property.'

'Awful for them if it wasn't,' he said cheerfully, and opened a wicket gate. There was a wide path of cropped or scythed grass which led straight across the meadow towards the house. This, she now saw, was in fact set on a terrace some ten or twelve feet above them, that was faced with the same stone and contained a black painted door in the centre and at their level. John was striding towards this. She followed him because if he was going to get into trouble it would be disloyal not to get into it with him, and also perhaps she might prevent him from doing anything too idiotic. The door would be locked anyway, she betted. But to her dismay, he opened it easily and walked through.

'John!'

'Don't you want to see the house? I thought it was rather pretty.'

She caught him up. 'John honestly!'

He had begun on the flight of shallow stone steps that clearly led up to the terrace above them.

'It's August,' he said. 'People who live in this sort of house are always away then. Don't be such a little stickler : you know we don't mean to do any harm.'

'Gardeners,' she said : it was awful being shown up as craven and law-abiding.

'We can always deal with them.'

They had reached a lawn path hedged with sweetbriar. He picked a piece of this and held it out to her. 'Pinch it.'

'There you go – *taking* things now!'

'Where's your sense of adventure?'

'Oh – don't *shout*!' They were now only about twenty yards from the house from which there was no sign of life. Blinds, she saw, were down on the upper windows : perhaps everybody *was* away. 'What do you want to do?' She felt it would be better if she knew.

'Just have a look round.' He seized her hand and walked her rapidly up to the long, narrow windows of what turned out to be a dining-room. 'Dinner is laid for two,' he said after peering in.

'They must be somewhere about, then,' she said, trying to sound reasonable rather than terrified. But already he had gone ahead and was disappearing round the corner of the house. 'It would be worse to be caught without him,' she thought. Bees in the wisteria were making the outdoor equivalent of ticking clocks in empty houses – too loud and the only noise she could hear. She followed him, and away from the bees became aware of her heart beating.

Round the corner was a conservatory tacked on to the house. It was quite large, and hexagonal in shape. The garden door stood propped open by a watering can, and she could see that it had a black and white marble floor. There were pots of geraniums and fuchsias, a table and various garden chairs, a french window leading into the house, but what really struck her was a tea trolley laid with an elaborate country tea and a kettle actually over a spirit lamp.

'John! Honestly! They'll be coming to have tea any minute.'

But he simply went in and took a cucumber sandwich and then flung himself into a basket chaise-longue. 'If anyone else *does* turn up we can always ask for more cups. Come and have a sandwich, dearest Eliza. They're awfully good, they've got that touch of curry powder in them.'

She stared at him : he was smiling – nearly laughing.

'I own all these sandwiches,' he said.

'Is this your house then ?'

'It is, actually.'

She stared at him a second longer and then burst into tears. 'Absolutely *beastly* – you are!'

'Darling Liz – I couldn't resist it; it was only a joke –'

'Not at all of a joke!'

'You were so funny : I never knew you had such a law-abiding nature –' He got out of the chair; she was crying more; he would have to apologize to make her feel better. 'I'm terribly sorry, and I'll never do it again –'

But she interrupted, 'You couldn't! I know all your other houses.'

'Oh no, you don't. There is yet another, in Jamaica, so I could do it again, but I won't. Cheer up. Think how much better it will be to have a nice tea than be chased off the premises by an angry and righteous owner. I'm not angry or righteous.'

'You're just smug and horrible.' But she mopped up her face and sat down and made the tea for them both.

*

Leslie had felt quite upset by all the fuss about the cat. The point wasn't that Alice was unreasonable – there was no question but that she was *that* – it was whether in her condition he shouldn't perhaps have tried to humour her more?

Naturally he didn't want her to be upset. The worst thing about marriage – in its early years at least – seemed to be the terrible way you couldn't take anything for granted – had to keep on noticing the other person, making allowances or putting your foot down, not to mention changing all your social habits, it *was* taken for granted you'd do that. And what did you get for it? The cooking wasn't up to Mother's, although it wasn't bad. Company, but really when he came to think of it, he wasn't at all sure that women were much good at that side of life. He wouldn't have married a vulgar bit like Phyllis Bryson for instance, joining in the laughs at men's stories in the pub: no thanks, not for him. There was the sexual intercourse side of things, but here again, you ran into trouble. It had become clear to him by degrees that Alice didn't seem to be all that keen on it – intercourse, he meant – not that he would necessarily have thought the more of her if she had been; when you came to think of it there wasn't any way that a woman could be enthusiastic about intercourse and still be what for want of a better word he could only call decent. So it wasn't exactly that he wanted Alice any different in the dark to what she was, so much as, being a normal man, he sometimes felt he could do with a change. He supposed that when she'd had a couple of kids everything might settle down and become more normal. After all, everyone went through it. This last reflection cheered him up and he decided to phone Rosemary to see if she could pop over to Alice and cheer her up a bit.

'Down in the dumps, is she?' Rosemary's voice had the kind of cheery, professional concern that implied that this was nonsense of Alice, but that it could be dealt with by someone who knew how. Leslie explained about Claude and Elizabeth coming for the night.

'Deary me: what a storm in a tea-cup! Not to worry: I'll drop over and see if I can't take her out of herself.'

Leslie put down the phone much relieved. Rosemary was a good sort; she could be a real tonic if she tried. Alice always seemed especially pleased to see him on the days when Rosemary had been over.

•

After tea, he said, 'Elizabeth! We've got to talk. Shall we do it now, or would you rather wait until after dinner?'

'I'd rather start now.' The thought of waiting for a serious talk once you knew that it was going to happen was awful.

'I don't even know whether talking about it is going to make you understand, but at least I've got to try.'

'Yes.'

There was a very long silence. A Spanish servant had cleared away the tea and been given instructions about the car and Claude. He had asked what time they wished to dine and then padded quietly away. The silence went on much longer than just waiting for the Spaniard to go.

'Goodness! This is much worse than I thought,' he said at last.

'The thing is, I must have seemed an awful coward in France: when Jennifer came and everything went to pieces. Well, you see, I *am*: that's what she does to me. I don't mean it's just about you, any more than I mean that there have been a lot of other girls. It's really anything I try to do except make money. It's partly why I've got so much money and hardly do anything.'

'*Why* does she?'

'There are two aspects of that question. Why does she *want* to stop me having any kind of life, and how does she manage to succeed?'

'Well, start with why she wants to.'

'That's not very difficult. Jennifer, at a very early age, was deprived of her mother. Even before that, she was deprived of a motherly mother, if you see what I mean. Howling egocentrics like Daphne take up having children like archery or the harpsichord; they soon find you have to work at it far harder than the effect seems worth. Jennifer was never an easy child. When I finally divorced Daphne, she was old enough to know what was going on in a way, but she certainly wasn't old

189

enough not to look at the whole thing entirely in terms of her own loss or gain. She'd lost a mother: she'd won me as it were. I've been a kind of hostage for her security ever since. Children seem to be rather good at that.'

'But – she isn't a child now, any more, is she?'

He looked slightly taken aback: then he said, 'I told you, she's very young for her age.'

'But she still doesn't have to be treated as a child, does she?'

'I'm not at all sure that I know how *else* to treat her.'

This seemed to stop either of them having anything to say.

'We've got plenty of time to talk about this,' he said in the end. 'Do be sure of one thing. Somehow I've got to make you understand, in fact we may have to stay here until you do. Come on: I'm going to show you the house.'

*

'So having thought about it a great deal –' she corrected herself, 'as much as I possibly could – it did seem that this was the only useful contribution I could make. Even though it is only potentially useful.' And she smiled apologetically: in spite of feeling like death, she might easily live to be eighty ...

Dr Sedum seemed to clear his throat and say something at the same time.

'I'm sorry: what did you say?' It had sounded like 'furry concerns' which it couldn't have been.

But it was family considerations that Dr Sedum had mentioned.

'Oh no: that's – they're quite all right. I asked my children, Oliver and Elizabeth, you know, and they would both *far* prefer to have the little house in Chelsea. So *that* is all right.' She paused, because, actually, the rest of it – meaning Herbert, wasn't: yet.

'I shall have to discuss it with my husband of course.'

Dr Sedum nearly shut his eyes and rocked slowly backwards in his huge chair.

'It's just a matter of telling him, really. I mean – much though he seems to love the place, he couldn't possibly manage there without me. He'd be fearfully lonely and uncomfortable and he hates being either of those things. It's just a matter of telling him,' she repeated, beginning to dread the thought.

They were sitting in the sitting-room in Dr Sedum's mews in Belgravia. In spite of it being a hot and sunny afternoon, the room was do dark that May would not have been able to see to read in it. This also meant that it was difficult to see Dr Sedum's face clearly, which in turn meant that it was harder than usual to understand what he said. In the spring – the only other time she had been there – there had been lamps lit and it had been much easier. But now, although the curtains were not drawn and there were windows at each end of the room, she could see that one of them faced a quite alarmingly close, black, brick wall and the other was entirely covered by the leaves and branches of some dusty evergreen. The room smelled of coffee and stale clothes. Dr Sedum always offered people coffee and they always accepted, and a girl called Muriel who typed all day in a tiny little room by the entrance door always heated it up a bit and brought it in. There was a sugar substitute and some powdered milk in a pottery jar that you could have as well. May had had some powdered milk, as she was afraid that black coffee (which had at one time been instant and then constantly reheated) would make her indigestion worse.

Dr Sedum said something that sounded like 'evil suspense'. It couldn't be that.

'What?' she said.

It turned out to be 'legal aspects' : he wanted to know if she had a good lawyer.

'Oh, I think so,' she responded vaguely. She had thought that lawyers, by the nature of their profession, being fair and everything, must really all be the same. 'He was my first husband's lawyer,' she added. Lawyers, she felt, were not a thing in her life that Dr Sedum could expect to change. But he just smiled in a conclusive manner, and said let him know how things went, so she knew that the interview was over before they had had time to talk about anything in the least interesting. He shook hands with her at the head of the steep and narrow stairs, and Muriel met her at the bottom. Through the half-open door to Muriel's office she could see that someone else was waiting to see Dr Sedum and she wondered if they, too, had had to think up some great practical reason for the privilege of spending half an hour alone with him.

•

'You say something about it.'

'What shall I say?'

'Well you could at least ask questions,' he said – not only irritably for him, but pretty crossly for anyone, Elizabeth thought. Still, questions seemed a sensible idea: the only difficulty was that they were all very hard questions for *her* to ask.

'Do you mean that she – Jennifer – will make things awful whenever she turns up?'

'I suppose I mean that she might.'

'When mightn't she?'

'I suppose if she got used to the situation – felt it didn't threaten her: or, I suppose, she might fall in love with someone herself.'

There was a silence while these distant possibilities receded still further.

Then, using a certain amount of courage, she asked, 'Is it our having an affair that she finds so objectionable?'

'Don't know: don't think so. You mean, if we were respectably married, she'd be all right?'

'I did mean that; yes.'

'I don't know,' he said again. 'The trouble is that one can't do that sort of thing as an experiment. It would be so frightful if we were wrong about it.'

'But it *couldn't* be an experiment – from the point of view of Jennifer! I mean it simply isn't enough her business to be that!'

'Perhaps it oughtn't to be – but it is.'

'It certainly oughtn't to be,' she said feeling angry and wanting to cry. 'She's not a child; she's twenty. Like me!'

'She's not like you – at all.' He said this very sadly, and she began at once to feel less angry and more sad.

They were sitting in the window seat of his dressing-room.

Outside, the orange and violet of the sky was slowly darkening out: milky mist was rising from the meadow and a young owl was trying out his cry that sounded with sudden, juicy, jack-in-the-box ease – probably frightening even him, Elizabeth thought.

'You have to give her a chance to grow up?' she said with a slight question at the end so that it didn't sound too obvious or patronizing.

'But we can't get married to do it,' he said. 'Come on – we'd better go and have dinner.'

*

'. . . in witness thereof I have hereunto set my hand this blank day of blank nineteen hundred and blankety blank.' He cleared his throat, took a final swig of the cold tea and looked expectantly at his audience. 'I sign it of course; George Frederick Herbert, etc. etc.' He made a point of never telling people like Hilda his real surname: you never knew what that kind of woman might get up to if she was given the chance.

He had been reading for nearly twenty minutes. Mr Pinkney, that solicitor chap, had drawn up a draft according to his specifications which, broadly speaking, were that he was leaving everything to his dearly beloved wife Viola May: he had fetched it that morning, lunched at the club where he had tried unsuccessfully to interest the member who had introduced him to Mr Pinkney with the results of this introduction – the member had simply said all wills made him feel morbid, old man: so now, after a little spot of dash with her, here he was reading the thing to Hilda. He had read over the whole caboodle in Mr Pinkney's office and again over his lunch at the club, but somehow, to get the full flavour of it, it needed to be read aloud, and by God it brought out the best in him when he did. He read well – hadn't fully recognized this talent in himself – and felt staggered, confounded, positively intoxicated by his own generosity. He was leaving everything, every single blasted little thing to Viola May. Not simply his shares, but clothes, weapons, mementoes, books, the car, the dogs, a hell of a lot of snapshots of damned interesting and unusual places, some jolly good books – well he'd mentioned them, but not what they were: classics, mostly, but some pretty rare books on India as well – eye-witness accounts of the Mutiny, for instance, which some feller had had privately printed – all long before his time, of course, but after all, he'd served there, knew the country better than most, and that book was a piece of exclusive history as it were; probably highly valuable if truth were known and by no means the only rare book of the lot; then his stamp collection – heaven only knew what that would fetch ... then there was all the furniture he had bought for Monks' Close; hundreds of chairs, whacking great pictures, filing cabinets, fire-irons, his transistor radio set. All his clothes were made of far better cloth than you could buy nowadays, so even they would fetch a good bit ... his mind was crammed with these and other generous assessments (he'd insisted on Mr Pinkney itemizing his possessions in groups of catagories – otherwise the whole document would have been barely two pages) and he had to admit that the whole thing sounded very well ... He looked across the small room to Hilda again. She was sitting in the other chair – the upright one – with her feet on a small footstool, her hands tucked into her kimono sleeves, her plumpish chin resting in the vee of its low neckline, her eyes indubitably closed. How like a woman! A feeling of hatred for her surged up, made his gorge rise as the saying went, only it didn't stop but went on up to his head so that he felt that something up there was going to explode. Steady on! The doctor had said months ago that his blood pressure was up and that he shouldn't indulge in undue agitation: a nice thing if having just read his will he was to drop dead! He could see the funny side of that: nobody could say he hadn't got a sense of humour. He started to take deep, quieting breaths and just then, Hilda opened her eyes and said, 'Very nice, Bogey.'

'That seems a peculiar word to use.'

'Well, striking as well. You've got such a lovely reading voice, it wouldn't matter what you read. A really lovely voice,' she repeated. Her mouth opened in the perfect O of a yawn and she laid the palm of her hand over it before any sound could come out.

Of course she'd been asleep; he wasn't easily fooled. It had been foolish of him to ever think that she had the intelligence to be interested. He decided to be getting along. Where? The thought of tooling back to Surrey and a quiet supper with poor old May was suddenly depressing. He didn't *enjoy* her feeling so under the weather, dammit, it was just that some things could not to be helped. It wasn't much fun for *him* sitting it out week after week, but you couldn't always do things just as you wanted to – had to take a long view and all that.

He got to the door before Hilda reminded him about the money. Then she reminded him that it was an extra thirty bob – she wasn't one to forget the money, was our Hilda! He said this as he chucked her rather painfully under the chin before she shut the door. What he would do was have a spot of dinner at the club and see if anyone felt like a game of billiards. He could telephone May from the club: women always appreciated little thoughtful gestures of that kind . . .

•

'The worst thing is, you see, that I don't – I can't – I simply feel terribly guilty about her. All the time. As though the whole of her was my fault.'

They were lying in bed, both of them still and Elizabeth silent as well.

'Most fathers love their daughters:' he gave a short, unlife-like laugh, 'sometimes they're supposed to love them too much. The trouble is that I never have.

'I never meant to say any of this to you, in fact, I meant very much *not* to say it. The fact is that you only really feel guilty about people you don't love. The other thing is that if you feel guilty about somebody, something sad and knowing in them finds out *and* knows the reason why. Then there is the shady little game of trying to compensate them.'

'How do you mean?'

'Oh giving them things, and putting up with being bored or inconvenienced by them, and hating anyone else to criticize them – all that. And of course they play that game: why not? Nearly everyone settles for what they can get in the end.'

'Do they?' The thought appalled her, but she felt that she must remain non-committal.

'If she'd had a normal sort of mother I suppose the whole thing would have been less emphasized –'

'Do you feel guilty about *her*?'

'Daphne? Oh, years ago, I did; before we parted company. But I got so cross with her for always letting Jennifer down that there stopped being any *ought* about loving her – Daphne, I mean –'

'Well I don't think there should be any ought about loving Jennifer now. I can't see why she shouldn't see her mother if that is what either of them wants, and if they don't, let them sort it out on their own.'

'You think the whole thing is a storm in a tea-cup,' he said coldly, a minute later.

'I think you'll simply turn Jennifer into some sort of monster if you go on protecting her *and* letting her bully you.'

'Perhaps that is what I want. To prove that she's a monster, so that I am excused for never having loved her. That's a convincing little by-way psychologically speaking, wouldn't you say?'

'I don't know.' She sat up and swung her legs over the side of the bed. 'I don't see why you have to be so determined that she'll bring out the worst in you. I'm sick of psychology anyway and the way people keep falling back on it. I thought we were going to talk about what we were going to *do* – about – everything, not just go on and on about what you and Jennifer feel or don't feel about each other.' She realized rather belatedly that she was naked, which somehow didn't go with feeling angry, so she seized his dressing-gown and started cramming her hands into the armholes.

'Where are you going?'

'Have a bath.'

He sat up and began getting out of bed. 'It's no good, Elizabeth: girls *do* feel strongly about their fathers – nobody can get round that.'

'I wouldn't know: I never even saw mine.' She tried to slam

the bathroom door, but it shut and then swung open and he was standing there. They stared at each other : it had never been like this before and the horrible novelty made both of them speechless. But only a few seconds later, he said,

'I think we'll postpone the ugly rush to grovel.' It was going to be all right : not the same – but all right.

*

Oliver had been relieved when John Cole had rung up inquiring for Elizabeth. He had been extremely resourceful about getting the Bristol telephone number, which Elizabeth had written with her finger on the greasiest bit of kitchen ceiling just above the gas cooker without telling him that that was where she had put it (he'd worked out at lightning speed where she had been when she'd taken the number) and he'd finished the conversation with what he hoped was just the right degree of nonchalant friendliness : 'Good-bye, then : hope you find her,' was what he had said. But then, noticing that he felt relieved that *that* was all right, he began to feel slightly irritated; either he had to keep on feeling sorry for Liz, or else she was having a bloody marvellous time. On the whole, he preferred being sorry for her, partly because he saw more of her then. But what about *his* life? When anyone else asked this question, he would airily shut them up (that was one thing he liked about Ginny; she only ever asked him what he was going to do that evening) but sometimes, like *this* evening, he started to wonder about the whole business and found it difficult to stop. Bitter little tags after Housman (after all, *he* was twenty-four); famous men with melancholia; philosophy seeming to go *on* finding out that man was vile; the revolting expense of the slightest luxury; the rank bad luck of not knowing exactly what he was for; the frightful lack of saints or anyone seriously different from and better than anyone else (he could keep his discontent on quite a high plane if he tried); the feeling that though he was not particularly happy or well off things could quickly get infinitely, alarmingly, much worse; the sensation he sometimes had of peddling his own life endlessly uphill – having to keep at it all the time or at the best nothing happened; at the worst one could slide with unearthly ease into some abyss – the alternative to which certainly didn't seem to be a bloody marvellous time. Sometimes he thought it was because she wasn't very clever that Liz nearly always seemed to feel all right; sometimes he thought that perhaps he was simply living in the wrong time. In what other century would he be sitting on a cramped and crumbling balcony looking on to a dull, dusty street whose air was thick with diesel fumes, eating a Mars Bar that had clearly been kept too long, while from some open window or other a gobbled Oxford voice roved suavely round the world remarking on its chaos, and *he* wondered what the hell to do that wouldn't cost too much or be too boring? He began thinking how else it might have been at various times and ages ... Hock and seltzer with Oscar and Robbie – a delightful dinner for about seven and six (he decided not to bother about inflation : calculations about which would ruin imaginative nostalgia) ... or he might be lying in a hip bath in front of a coal fire in a huge bedroom, frequently waited on by pretty young maids with rosy cheeks and tiny waists, then dressing for the house-party dinner before the ball where he would dance with a delightful young creature called Maud or Gwendolen – in white, of course, with ivy leaves in her hair. There was a bit of a gap here, but there he was again, or could be, downing his second bottle of port (unfortified, naturally, in those days) with a group of chaps who knew a thing or two about the army, the navy or the Church, with whom he would have dined by now, before riding to drink tea with some delightful sisters called Mary and Ann and Elizabeth and Jane, whose simple life in the wilds of Hampstead had all the charm that reflects upon true elegance of mind and refinement of nature ... they would run to greet him on little slippered feet, muslin skirts flying – the youngest barely fifteen but already proficient at all the sweet and useless accomplishments that were thought proper and desirable : netting, fan- and table-painting, making pens and embroidering anything they could lay their hands on. Earlier – he was getting hazy about how much – he would be riding back from a jolly good day's hawking – a castle this time, but nice and clean – they'd only have been there about a week : the smells would be merely festive, roasting wild boar and hare, perhaps a swan or two; a serf would run to his stirrup with a beaker of spiced – ale would it be, or mead? – and up some tortuously twisting stair would be someone with immensely long hair called Margaret or Philippa, who'd had nothing to do all day except wait for him . . .

When the telephone rang, he was so physically wedged in the balcony that quite a lot of plaster fell on to the dustbins in the area by the time he got out, and he had time to get excited about who might be ringing him up.

It was May: not even a girl he wasn't particularly attracted to or had got tired of, but his mother. He snorted and she immediately asked him if he'd got a cold.

'Good God, no!'

'All right, darling; I only asked.'

'I should have thought you'd had enough practice at being a mother not to ask that sort of thing.'

'Clearly not.'

That was better. He smiled, and said, 'Where are you and what do you want?'

'Well, I thought we might have a drink together.'

'Where *are* you?'

'In a call box. Is Elizabeth there, because do bring her if she is.'

'She's in Bristol.'

'Well get into a taxi and come straight away, darling, because I'll have to catch a train – hurry up –'

'We'll never meet if you don't tell me where you are –'

'Knightsbridge tube station: don't be long because there may not be anywhere here to sit down . . .'

She was standing anxiously at the Sloane Street entrance: she looked as though she could do with a drink. He paid off the taxi and took her to a pub in Kinnerton Street. When they were both established with glasses, he said, 'What have you been doing all by yourself in London? Isn't it a bit risky to be seen after shopping hours in Sloane Street?'

She blushed faintly, but retorted, 'It has always amazed me the way the moment you have a life of your own you assume that I can't possibly have one. You behave as though I should only come to London for the dentist and Peter Jones. I might easily have friends and interests of my own, you know.'

'Oh, I doubt it. At your age I should have thought –'

'And what are *your* interests may I ask?'

'You really mustn't try to change the whole *tone* of a conversation with no warning like that. I've got no news. No news is bad news with me as you've probably noticed, and as I find it very depressing, I've nothing to say about it. It really is awful,' he went on a moment later after he had refused to meet her eye, 'the way you keep on wanting me to start something and I keep on wanting you to stop.'

They looked at each other; both knew which way the conversation was going; but the familiar challenge – the routine reluctance – was too much for either effectively to resist.

'You want me to set about almost *anything* from nine to five – and I hope you jolly well realize that at no other time in history would your maternal instinct take such a poky and squalid form – while I simply want you to stop living with such a preposterous bore. I want your life to be nicer while you seem to want *my* life to be harder – harder and even more boring.'

'You're bored because you *don't* do anything.'

'Am I?'

'Everybody has to have some sense of direction.'

'Do they?'

'After all, we all know that externals don't matter in the least.'

'Is that so? And if it is – so, I mean – why do you care whether I'm doing anything or not?' Then, lowering his voice, he added, 'I suppose you realize that everyone is so fascinated by the thrust and parry of this conversation that they're not only not talking to one another – they're not even *drinking*. I won that round. While I get us a refill, you think of three reasons why you should go on living with Daddo.'

He was quite right; it was a small bar and the few customers all had that glassy air of covert attention to someone else's business. Even the landlord put down his paper with a hearty start when Oliver reached him with the glasses. Three reasons ... But the moment there *had* to be reasons for being married to somebody there weren't any. When Oliver came back with their drinks she smiled firmly and said, 'It's ridiculous of you to blacken poor Herbert in this silly way. Anyone would think he was some kind of *criminal*. I admit he's a weeny bit – old-fashioned in his ways; staid – what you doubtless call dull, but he means well – in fact he's really very kind and protective – he *minds* what happens to me ...' To her discomforted amazement, she seemed to be crying: tears that could not have come from anywhere but her own eyes were slopping on to the drink-rimmed table and Oliver seemed enormous and blurred.

'... a dry eye in this family's a full-time job. Sorry, darling. Darling May, I swear I'll never criticize him again: if you don't stop crying you'll qualify for a short which I don't have enough cash for. So do try to stop because you know how mean I am.'

'Buy us both brandies,' she said when she was over it.

'Let's have dinner,' he said when the brandies were gone.

'Oh darling – I would love to, but I can't. Poor Herbert would feel so abandoned if he gets back and I'm not there.'

So he took her to the station and she caught the seven fifty-five. The cab passed Herbert's club where he was drinking gin and peach bitters and reading the *Evening Standard*.

•

When Oliver had seen his mother off (standing on the platform watching in case she waved, with 'Colonel Bogey' on the amplifying system) he had so little money and so little to do that he walked. On Westminster Bridge he wondered about becoming a politician, but then somehow he felt that it might seem to imply a basic sympathy with the status quo and he wasn't at all sure that he had enough of that ... When he got to Victoria Street and passed the Army and Navy Stores, the idea of being an explorer came and went. There was hardly anywhere left to explore that wasn't so nasty and difficult to be in that one wouldn't really enjoy it ... He plodded on. It wasn't that he liked not being able to think of anything to do : it wasn't even that he didn't try to think of something, it was simply that the only things that seemed to him at all nice – like living with darling Elizabeth or meeting a new, wildly attractive girl and going to bed with her long before he knew her too well – were neither of them money-spinners, and delicious meals and foreign holidays clearly used money up. He knew he was meant for better things : it was just a question of knowing which ones.

*

'What you mean is that if you married me I might *get* to want children, and then, whatever we said or did about it – everything would go wrong?'

'Something like that;' he was watching her face very closely.

'Oh.' She knew he was watching her and kept her face deliberately still, not realizing that he would notice that as much as he would notice anything else.

They were sitting at the end of a small lawn edged with yew. Behind them, on a stone pedestal, was a stone lady whose naked back was turned but whose downcast profile was visible as she looked for ever over her shoulder and down upon the lawn.

'Why are you so sure I'd want them?'

'I'm not. It simply isn't a risk I feel able to take. At the moment, I mean.'

After another long pause, she said. 'So what do we do?'

'It isn't lack of love. I can't imagine loving anybody more than I love you, but I still seem to have some of the perfect fear left over. Darling.'

A little of the strained unconcern left her face as she repeated, 'What shall we do?'

'Not part, and stay as we are together at the moment, that means nothing. We'll do nothing : just live.' He took her hand and stroked the back of it gently. 'Do you like this house?'

'Best.'

'Good. We'll spend all my spare time in it.'

'We'll not get married and not have children but stay together,' she said, but asking for confirmation.

'What do you think?'

'I don't mind about the marrying or children part: I just want to stay with you.'

Part Three: December

1. Jamaica

The trouble was that if she relaxed she fell out of the bunk and if she braced herself against the next quivering, uneven plunge, she could not get to sleep. John was all right: he was so tall that even lying as diagonally as his bunk permitted he was naturally wedged, and provided he didn't try to move he seemed to be safe and able to have long refreshing sleeps that Elizabeth quite envied. Sometimes she would give up trying to sleep and kneel upright to look out of the port-hole. The sea and the sky – an angry grey and skim milk that heaved and pounded and lurched – were so tilted and confused together that she felt quite glad to have this scene bounded by the round, brass rim. Sometimes she struggled with the giant screw that made livid rust marks on the glossy white paint until she could free it and swing the window open. Then a strong soft wind beat against her face like the damp wings of some powerful bird; she could put her head out and feel it more, withdraw, and hear the domestic creaks of wood straining against the sea and feel more sharply the vibration made by the engines – a kind of solid and busy reassurance. It was not a bad storm, just ordinary Atlantic December weather, they said; the forecast – after a day or two more – was good, they would all be sitting out on deck sunning themselves, they'd see. Elizabeth did not care. She did not feel in the least sick, and was perfectly happy. This was the third day out, the time was so packed with traditional activity that they seemed to be living in crowded slow motion, and already she felt as though they had been in the ship for weeks. The first thing was China tea at seven in the morning with the breakfast menu, as John liked to have that meal – a large one – in privacy. 'I like tea, and then you, and then breakfast.' Getting up took ages because of having to hold on to something nearly all the time, but there were nice things about it : the shower was like a scorching cloud-burst and could be salty or fresh; shoes got cleaned every day and towels seemed always to be new. On the first morning they had got themselves wrapped in rugs on deck and were given cups of steaming Bovril – called beef tea – as though, Elizabeth thought, they were really precious and had been frightfully ill. That morning they had also walked – round and round – holding hands and not talking at all. Even then she had still been worrying – had not been absolutely certain : and so the newly minted feeling of beginning, of being festive and shining and unused, had been rubbed with anxiety. She couldn't, or wouldn't, ask : it was then that she discovered how often someone may inquire about the welfare of another simply in order that – having got the right answer – they may dismiss them from their mind. Of course, *she* didn't want to do that, but if she asked, he might have to lie and that was something that he shouldn't have to do – with her at least. So they walked until he said, 'That's enough to earn us a drink,' and they went in to the large saloon where the tables and chairs were screwed to the deck and she found that he had ordered a bottle of champagne and wondered if that, too, didn't smack a bit of going through the motions until he had said, 'I asked for this because it was our first drink – do you remember?' and when he smiled at her she remembered the first time he had ever done that and the extraordinary difference it made to his face.

'You're smiling a great deal,' he said.

'Am I?'

'Every time anyone looks at you.'

'Oh. Oh dear.'

'They're all loving it. It's an excellent thing, really, because a good many people with fringes look rather stern in repose. Dear Mrs Cole.'

The first lunch time the saloon was fairly crowded; the wind was freshening, but only enough for people to make jokes about it. The menu was enormous, the tables elaborately set with linen and silver and flowers : stewards charged skilfully through swing doors and rushed about with a high degree of bustling order. The captain sat at a round table with seven such hideously boring-looking, although otherwise assorted, people that John and Elizabeth (alone at a table for two) spent most of the meal trying to think what they could all be. In the end they settled for a sociologist, his wife, who wrote children's books, an ex-mountaineer who'd made a belated fortune out of windproof garments, and *his* wife who bred Afghan hounds, and a bucolic man who'd always been a baronet with a woman who'd always been just a wife. That left one lady whose appearance was so ambiguous that it was far from clear what she could ever have accomplished. A widow of one of the directors of the line, they decided weakly.

'Poor captain.' On this particular day, Elizabeth had been disposed to think everyone more unfortunate than herself.

After that first lunch, she had slept for three hours and woken to find John sitting by her bunk with tea.

'In case you are harbouring the slightest doubts I'm really finding being married to you much nicer than I thought.'

Later they played backgammon and drank Planter's Punches in the bar. That night it began to get rough and now here it was, just about as rough as she felt she could manage. Already, quite a lot of people couldn't manage it. The captain's table had shrunk to the ex-mountaineer, minus wife, and the captain. Tablecloths were damped, the ledges round the tables were up, but still whole tablefuls of glass and china crashed to the ground. The stewards charging through the swing doors often lost the contents of their trays before they reached the few stalwart passengers who continued to appear for meals, but morale seemed high, the ship was excellently run and the large jovial captain exuded efficiency and good will. Walking round the deck was out of the question now : they ate and read (backgammon was no good as everything slid about too much) and had drinks, made love a great deal, and John slept while Elizabeth dozed and dreamed.

The wedding had only escaped being awful by its shortness. She had spent the night before it at Lincoln Street with Oliver. 'At least you're not having to put up with me in pink net. Or Daddo making speeches,' he added after a time. They were both sitting on her bed; Oliver was polishing her shoes and drinking

Guinness which he said made his spit more nourishing to shoe leather. John had particularly not wanted family about (the Jennifer situation) and Elizabeth, with reasons none the less violent for being indefinable, seemed absolutely determined on keeping the colonel and John apart. They had met very briefly when Elizabeth and John had returned Claude to Monks' Close: they had arrived without warning at the innocuous hour of tea time, but this had so enraged the colonel that May had thought he was going to have a stroke. They had 'broken in' on him when he was in the greenhouse mixing something up for the lawn; no common courtesy left – he'd looked up from measuring something because he thought he'd heard a sound behind him, and there was this giant stranger without so much as a by-your-leave standing over him – enough to give any honest feller a heart attack. He'd lost his temper: not for long, but enough to make everyone feel intensely embarrassed; then he'd stalked off to find Elizabeth's mother. Poor May had made the mistake of offering them tea, which was accepted, and this had made the colonel stalk even farther – down the drive in fact, with a clashing of gears in the old Wolseley. May had had such an awful time with him afterwards that she had collapsed – in tears – and the next day had gone so far as to suggest that perhaps she and Herbert were not really suited ... but he wouldn't hear of that ...

So in the end only Oliver and McNaughton, the charming Scottish chauffeur who had brought a bunch of dahlias grown by himself, had come to the registry office. They had all waited in a small, ugly room until called into a larger ugly room where the ceremony was performed. After Oliver and McNaughton had witnessed the certificate they went back to the first room, already full of the next wedding party; people staring at their own white shoes and the gap between their hands on their dark blue serge knees; people speaking so quietly out of shyness and discomfort that in the end they said everything again much too loudly. It all looked a bit like having a collective tooth out, Oliver had said. They had packed into the Rolls and McNaughton had driven them to Claridge's where John had taken a room. McNaughton parked the car and joined them for a drink or two and then left them. Elizabeth had wanted him to stay to lunch, but John had said that McNaughton had been quite firm about that. You could drink' with anyone, he had said, but you couldn't enjoy a meal outside your own class. He'd fetch them at three. They were driving to Southampton, to catch the boat for Jamaica. As soon as McNaughton had gone, Oliver had said that if they didn't mind, and even possibly if they did, he didn't think he would come to Southampton: he'd feel too awful for too long coming back. The other two immediately said of course not and how much they understood, but everybody was a little dashed by this: Elizabeth had begun imagining him going back to Lincoln Street by himself until he said don't worry, he was going to a smashing party that evening. They had a very delicious lunch beginning with oysters and ending with crêpes Suzette. Outside it was raining and there was an east wind, and when she hugged him, Oliver said, 'You can always tell if she's healthy by the state of her nose: ice-cold at the tip – even in August. Just like a dog, really.' Then he and John had shaken hands and John had shivered and said, 'How I hate saying goodbye to people.' He looked as though he was surprised that he'd said that.

Elizabeth had watched Oliver waving and then turning away before (of course) they were out of sight. 'People shouldn't do that,' she said aloud but really to herself.

'What shouldn't they do?'

'Turn away while you can still see them doing it. It doesn't sound as though they don't care enough; it sounds as though they don't care at *all*.'

'Look, or looks. I see what you mean. But it's supposed to be bad luck to wave someone out of sight.'

'I bet it isn't. I bet that was just invented by someone very lazy at seeing people off.' A tear bounced on to the car rug and then sank greedily as though into moss.

John took her hand. 'I know what it is.'

'What?'

'You're so happy, you need the luxury of a small grief. We'll ask him to stay if you like,' he added.

She shook her head. 'Much better for him to try to get a job.

You're quite right about luxury and small griefs. It wouldn't work the other way round, though, would it? I mean if you are really sad or miserable something nice but small isn't the slightest good.'

'I know,' he said, but when she looked anxiously at him he said, 'If you start worrying about me I'll get your passport out and show it to people in the ship.'

The Customs and Immigration men seemed quite unmoved by her picture and handed back both passports as though John was not married to and taking abroad a dangerous criminal lunatic. When Elizabeth pointed this out, he said, 'Oh yes, they did. They notice everything. But they're very patriotic, you see. They realize it must be good for England.'

In their cabin had been a bowl of shop roses with a card from Alice. 'Wishing you every happiness,' she had written in her upright childish hand. She must have gone to some trouble to get the card sent to the Southampton flower shop. There were also some orchids from Lady Dione Havergal-Smythe and Mrs Potts, whose name was spelled Fopps (Lady Dione's had come out perfectly). By the second day out the flowers had to be put in a bucket and wedged in the bathroom, and they died very soon after that.

The fourth day it was fine; not smooth or hot enough to fill the swimming pool but good enough to go out: the sea was the steely blue of some roads – the great diagonal shoulders of water were still capped with creamy feathers, and above, the sky was boisterously blue and white. They walked, round and round the deck past rows of people swaddled in rugs on long bony chairs looking like Channel-crossing jokes in *Punch*, past the sardonic-looking sailor who was greasing staples very slowly on steel hawsers, past the officers' quarters (a little above them) from which came snatches of curiously sedate jazz accompanied by whiffs of coffee and bacon, to where they could look down upon the bows of the ship ploughing vigorously towards the horizon: round to the starboard side (no sun and so no passengers except for a pair of earnest table-tennis players), past a cabin – one of the two really grand ones – from whose open window they could hear an angry lady explaining why she

212

preferred flying everywhere: for six rounds they found her in full spate. Eight rounds were supposed to be a mile, but any kind of repetition makes things seem longer, and they stopped, by mutual consent, at a mile and a half. It was extraordinary how much they seemed to agree with each other, Elizabeth thought.

The next day it was perfectly fine and there were flying fish – like small silver darts – that shot suddenly from the sea to stream their arcs through the air before they vanished from sight. The pool was filled – with sea water; Elizabeth, who had said that she wanted to bathe, got into her bathing dress before she had changed her mind.

'Why have you?'

She was standing in the middle of the cabin before her dressing-table. She looked at him crossly and he knew she was anxious.

'I just don't want to.'

'But why not, darling?'

'*You* know perfectly well.' And when he was silent at this, she said, 'You can *see* why not. I'm portly.' She looked down at herself with distaste.

'Oh. Well *I* can't see anything portly about you at all.'

'You can. You're just pretending. Of *course* you can.'

'I really can't you know.'

But she interrupted almost triumphantly. 'That shows you'll mind when you can. You wouldn't sound so consoling if you didn't secretly mind. You know perfectly well I'm portly now and it's going to get much worse.'

He put down his book, took off his reading glasses and put on his ordinary ones. 'Ah; you're not crying. You have a fearful capacity for sounding as though you were, and then, on the other hand suddenly doing it when you haven't sounded like it.'

'Stick to the *point*. I thought it was women who were supposed to be so bad at that.'

'It is, but I am as well. Women and me.'

'You're nearly laughing! It's no joke, I can tell you, having to face the prospect of my whole relationship with you being ruined just because of any old Tom, Dick or Harry or whoever's inside me.'

He did laugh then. 'Oh I do think you ought to know that. I mean, if that's what you're facing, I do think you ought to know who's making you face it.' Without the slightest warning, he picked her up and carried her to his bed. 'Now Elizabeth. Now then,' he said, raising his voice to prevent her interruption, 'why on earth you should feel that having our child will ruin our "whole relationship" I can't think –'

'Of *course* you can!' she said, or this time cried, again. 'It's obvious. I'll look more and more awful until even you can't love me. A lot of people's teeth and hair fall out.'

'Nonsense.'

'Well they have millions of stoppings,' she amended sulkily, 'and some people's hair goes all dull and greasy.'

'Heavens, how horrible!'

'And supposing it's a hideous criminal or simply a terrifically dull child. People do have them.'

'I know. Look at Jennifer.' He met her eye easily, and she flung her arms round his neck. 'It's all right, darling. Jennifer *is* dull : and seeing that – being nasty *about* her as you would say – makes it much easier to be nicer *to* her.'

'You really don't feel guilty any more?'

'Yes, I do, but I can manipulate it : the acme of success in middle age. Arrange your guilt to suit your means. Thanks to you, I've done that. Don't worry. This new Cole won't be dull : at least, not to us and that's what counts.'

A bit later, she said, 'Well – even if it starts all right, I may be such a rotten mother that it immediately grows up awful. Nearly everyone says that they had something frightfully wrong with their childhood which proves that it must be a jolly difficult thing to get right so I bet I won't.'

'Won't what?'

He had been stroking her neck absently : she was curled up against him but he was so much larger that he could look down on nearly all of her.

'Get the childhood right and stop it turning out to be a wicked monster.'

'If you really hate looking after it we'll get a nurse: then it will grow up with all the old-fashioned neuroses instead of the fashionable ones.

'Oh no! I'll do it. Other people might get it even wronger.'

He smiled then, perceiving that she was now enough re-assured.

'It's marvellous the way you aren't sick. How do you feel?'

'Perfectly all right. Goodness knows, I've *had* the being sick part. Nearly three months of it. It's extraordinary: I don't feel anything at all. Except a bit important,' she added after thinking about it.

•

Alice lay perfectly still: after a second or two, the puppy whimpered, came up to her and licked her ear and a piece of her forehead. The thin dark ice that she had not seen at all on the crazy-concrete paving was now splinter-cracked into a huge clumsy star. The air was so cold that it still made her gasp if she even started to take a deep breath, so she decided she'd better not try again. It was so cold, that not only were her face and hands icy, but when she touched her smock it was just as bad – like clothes on a dead person. But she wasn't entirely cold because there seemed to be a kind of hot spring inside her that was gently welling up and keeping her legs – or at any rate her thighs – beautifully warm: she had at one and the same time a feeling of disaster and a sense of comfort, and it seemed a pity to change this by moving or having a thought – or anything at all. The puppy was irritating: kept coming up to her with its little frowsty breaths and complaints – disturbing the peace, which indeed it had always done. Her ankle hurt: this discovery was of course a nuisance and should also have been a relief; it wasn't though. By turning her head rather uncomfortably she could see that the jigsaw gate was hung with icicles: it was cosier to turn back to her own open front door. The house must be getting cold, and just as she found that she couldn't help wondering how long she had lain on the path (after, it was obvious of course, tripping somehow and falling on the ice) she had suddenly – but thank God gently to start with – a pain that was like a skewer, or an enormous long butcher's knife stabbing the bottom of her spine and then probing, feeling the best place and way to split it. The pain – so intense for the apparent gentleness that at first it seemed as though it ought to be a laughing matter – accelerated without warning into something past the beginning of a scream. It was like missing a bus; hopeless too quickly for screaming to help. Then, just as she was wondering who *was* screaming, it all stopped – or seemed to – turned into a bit of pain, discomfort, and then nothing again. The funny thing was that as soon as it was over the whole thing seemed like something she had read in a book : 'a dreadful pain like a sword pierced her back with mounting waves of agony,' that kind of stuff : rather dull and nothing to do with her at all.

It wasn't just her ankle – it was a long way up her leg. She shifted to see if she could see any damage; she was of a size that made looking at any part of her legs difficult and it seemed to her ages since she'd seen her feet when she was standing up. But after twisting a bit she could see that she had a horrid graze from her ankle bone nearly up to her knee. Her stocking was rent, but bits of it were sticking to the rather dirty and clotted-looking wound. When she tried to reach the stocking to pull it away from her leg – perhaps take it off if she had the energy – a piece of paper slipped out her hand. 'Half a pint of double cream today please,' it said. *That* was what it was. She had been going to put a note on the gate for the milkman, and the puppy, or dog it was really by now, had suddenly shot past her in the doorway and she'd lost her balance. It always behaved like that – rushing out the moment you opened a door as though it had been imprisoned all its life, but once out, it had no sense of adventure. It had come back to her again, sniffing the graze on her leg, and now, with its head turned away from her it was intently licking the path : licking up the bits of ice? she wondered, and then it moved a bit and she saw that what it was licking – almost lapping up – was blood; very dark red, and surely far too much to have come from her leg? Nausea, terror, had hardly a chance before the skewer interrupted with total efficiency : this time she could not imagine how she had stopped

216

feeling what it had been like last time. After it, she was possessed by a sense of irritable urgency: she had to do a lot of difficult things before it happened again (which she now knew it would) but she didn't know what they were. Well, she'd have to move; she couldn't do anything lying on her own front path like that. When she finally got to her feet, and started to lumber back into the house, she realized that it certainly wasn't blood just from her leg and it wasn't even only blood. As she almost fell into the chair by the telephone in Leslie's study she thought – quite easily – 'I'm losing the baby, then,' and like her first feelings about the pain, she could have been reading about it in some magazine story, without much interest.

•

Lavinia could be awfully tiresome: even when she was a child, she had displayed what May – having just been wretchedly subject to it – now called arrant curiosity. It was really not, or, at any rate hardly, her business what May so urgently wanted to see Dr Sedum for; if she was any kind of sport, she would simply have accepted May's word for it and just driven him down when May told her to – or perhaps suggested, was a better word. Heaven knew she didn't want to dictate to Dr Sedum, but the circumstances did seem to add up to a kind of emergency and May always felt at her worst in those. In any case, one false step, spiritually or practically, and she might be cast aside like old gloves or a petty sin. No – she had to see Dr Sedum, and due to her rotten health Mahomet was going to have to come to the mountain (whenever she faced that phrase there was the fear of getting it the rude way round for the other person). And the only member of the League (that she knew) who could drive Dr Sedum down to Monks' Close was Lavinia. So why couldn't she just *do* it, and stop asking niggling, maddening, *pertinent* questions? She didn't at all seem to understand that (a) it was always alarming using the telephone when you weren't quite sure where Herbert was, and (b) that he went through all the toll calls with a tooth comb and would be sure to ask what this one had been. Why on earth not ring people up in the cheap time, he would demand, not realizing, of course, that he and the cheap time most unfortunately co-incided. He was *always* at home in the evenings unless he was actually in London, but since she'd been feeling so awful, he had stayed at Monks' Close. This was both kind and tiresome of him : fearfully kind if you didn't want a life of your own, and a tiny bit tiresome if you did. Anyway – after it taking far too long (from the toll-call-in-the-morning point of view), Lavinia had agreed to drive Dr Sedum down for the afternoon. (Herbert, with even less reason than Frank Churchill – he had far less hair – had gone to London to get it cut. He was going by a late morning train and would try to get something to eat at his club, he had said.) The moment that he was gone (the old Wolseley was audible for miles), she began to get up. One of the most frightening things about her these days was the way she often couldn't properly feel her feet – swinging them over the side of the bed, she sometimes didn't realize when they hit the floor. This morning she watched carefully and – perhaps because she was watching – she thought she could feel them a bit better than usual. This morning the fears that she pretended to herself were nameless seemed not so much to be that as without other substance; everybody thought they were dying of some fatal disease at one time or other in their lives. She had a slow, hot bath and put on her warmest jersey with her blue suit. The day had begun with frost and fog; the latter had cleared but the sky was leaden, without either cloud or sun : it was a typical English December day and Herbert had remarked (as he always did when it was either cold or wet) how homesick he had been for weather like this when he had lived in India. This seemed to May extraordinary and Oliver had agreed – had remarked that the Indian equivalent of *that* kind of homesickness would be missing cobras very badly and must therefore, except for a very small minority largely made up of other, immigrant cobras, be nonsense. Oh dear, she did miss her children : she didn't want them to be younger or smaller again, she simply missed their frivolous company. She lunched off a large glass of milk and tried to think about the Absolute so that she would be in the right frame of mind for Dr Sedum. Even with months of practice and Help in the form of Times galore she did not feel

that she had got any better about this — in fact she often felt
that she had actually got worse: it was extraordinary how trying to hold on to one thought was like trying to hold your arms
over your head, or even stretched out like poor Jesus: she
hoped He hadn't been expected to do both things at once ...
There she went, thinking about the difficulties of doing something rather than the thing itself. The trouble was that she was
really dreading the interview with Dr Sedum (although it was
always, of course, wonderful to see him). It would be less wonderful to have to see him with Lavinia, but, on the other hand,
Lavinia would probably understand the horns of her dilemma
and possibly help.

She felt too weak to do all the scene-shifting required to use
the morning room; the den, or study, would have to do. She
dragged in a second comfortable chair — for Lavinia — and collected a second electric fire: even so there were simply two
small areas of scorching heat in an otherwise freezing room.
Mrs Green — whose days at Monks' Close were yet further reduced by the quiet but inexorable decline of her bicycle, was
not about: it *was* one of her days but she couldn't come. She
arranged a tea tray in the kitchen and put the huge kettle on
the kitchen range: in spite of it, the kitchen seemed very cold
and the passages were so icy that she had taken to travelling
about them in her oldest overcoat. She filled a hot-water bottle
with water from the tap for a foot warmer and sat in Herbert's chair to wait. As there were two electric fires, Claude sat
with her.

They were late; it was nearly half past two when the dogs'
barking warned her of the car. Those poor dogs! Nobody took
them out now that Alice had gone.

Dr Sedum wore his muffler and Lavinia had a fur coat: they
were both smiling, which they went on doing without saying
anything while May helped them off with their coats and led
them to the study (as she always called Herbert's den when he
wasn't there). Dr Sedum sat in Herbert's chair and she put Lavinia in the other nice one. Claude took one look at them and
then slunk out of the room as though they were infectious and
it would be very dangerous for him to stay even a moment.

Dr Sedum stopped smiling, leaned slightly forward and exclaimed 'Now!' rather as though he was starting a race.

'It's about the house; this house.' If she had thought Dr Sedum had stopped smiling before, she must have been wrong. He really stopped now. 'Herbert – my husband – seems to regard it as half belonging to him anyway. And when I pointed out – I had to try and make him see that I had bought it, he said it was the only thing he really cared about. So I don't see what – I simply can't think how to –'

'Are you trying to say that you want to go back on your word?'

'No – of course I'm not!' It was much easier to talk to Lavinia even if all you were doing was trying to shut her up. 'But can't you see how awkward it is? I mean it means practically leaving it to the League behind Herbert's back!'

Nobody answered this. After a moment she said, 'It seems rather shabby to me.'

There was a pause during which she noticed that Lavinia looked knowingly at Dr Sedum, who, while he did not return the look exactly, did not snub it either. Then he cleared his throat softly and spoke about one's image of oneself for a long time, at the end of which she felt both confused and ashamed. She could see that it was awful either to do or not to do things simply because you minded what other people thought of you: it was, or could be, a sickening kind of vanity and she had little doubt that this was probably what had caused her dilemma. She *wanted* to leave Monks' Close to the League, but Herbert would mind this and she minded Herbert minding. Yes – but *oughtn't* she to mind? (Him minding?) Or was it (she knew that often one's feelings were exactly the opposite of what one supposed them to be – it was so lucky and calculable that they should be *exactly* the opposite) that perhaps she *didn't* want to leave the house to the League but was afraid of what they would think of her if she didn't and was therefore sheltering under Herbert's alleged feelings? Or was she cold-bloodedly using the house to see who would give her the most attention and interest – Herbert or Dr Sedum? She wondered which of these possibilities was the worst: if she knew *that*, she probably – almost certainly – would know which she was culpable of. It was amazing, she thought, how Dr Sedum could show you in a moment how worthless you really were ...

Lavinia suddenly, surprisingly, offered to make some tea for everyone. May, very gratefully, explained that she'd got a tray ready, showed Lavinia the beginning of the way to the kitchen and returned to her uncomfortable chair opposite Dr Sedum. Lavinia wasn't such a bad sort after all.

'I'm sure you're right,' she began; 'one's motives are nearly always suspect, aren't they? At least, I don't mean *your* motives, of course,' she felt herself blushing at the idea; 'I mean mine, of course. It's partly because I'm rather stupid – have never been able to think clearly about anything at all – that I couldn't think what to *do* now, you see. And I haven't been feeling too good lately, either, which hasn't helped.'

Dr Sedum lit his second cigarette, and then, as a gigantic afterthought, offered her one. It was likely, he said, that her poor health was due to her sense of conflict; nothing was more exhausting than Wrong Imagination and Wrong Imagination was something so many of us suffered from. It often prevented events from taking their natural course, speaking of which, at what stage had things got blocked, as it were? He seemed to remember that she had mentioned some lawyer in July ...

'Oh yes! I've done all that, I went to him very soon after I saw you. But you know how long everything takes. It wasn't my *lawyer's* fault,' she quickly added, 'it's just that I don't get up to town as often as I should like, and when I do only half the things on my lists seem to get done. He did a draft and sent it to me but the envelope made Herbert so curious that I didn't like – I felt I couldn't – so anyway in the end I told him to keep the actual will until I could get to London, and even then, you see, I have to think of a reason for going to London – it really isn't at all *easy*!'

Dr Sedum said something stern about easiness and she hastily agreed because she wanted to ask him something else.

'Dr Sedum! Do you think that perhaps there is a possibility that I *am* ill – that I am *not* imagining it?' She looked earnestly at him, in case – only out of his extreme compassion – he might soften the blow. He smiled, and she realized immediately that it *had* been a silly question, but he answered at once with what she recognized was his most indulgent kindness.

There was *always* the *possibility*, he said, that she was not imagining what she thought to be her state of health : anything was possible, and everything was conversely improbable; it was essential that one consider one's own nature in the light of events, but for most people this kind of consideration was a life's work with no knowledge of how to go about it. This was what the League was partly for or about. He was sure that as she understood better how to use her life for the glory of the Absolute she would find that minor anxieties dropped away like so many dead leaves ... Before she had finished thanking him, Lavinia arrived with the tea trolley. Tea was quite gay : Lavinia poured out and generally was so much at home that May felt as though she was a guest at a delightful small party. Of course Lavinia knew Dr Sedum – really *knew* him – and was also a senior member of the League, often standing in the centre of the Circle at Times.

After they had gone, she reflected that Herbert had taken her to that doctor in Woking whom he said was so good and that when she'd taken the powder stuff prescribed she had seemed to be getting slowly better. The prescription was repeatable, and she decided to get some more.

Lavinia and Dr Sedum encountered the colonel three-quarters of the way down the drive, which was generally too narrow for two cars to pass one another. Lavinia made one of those coquettish gestures of despair that most middle-aged women would do well to outgrow, but the colonel lifted a majestic hand and then backed noisily and damagingly to the entrance gate which he nearly rammed. As it was, he parked so that it was very difficult for Lavinia to edge the Bentley past him : she wound down her window and leaned out in an attempt not to graze his wing, calling cheerfully, 'How do you do! I am a cousin of May's and we have just been paying her a visit!' In League language this was being adroit; to the colonel it was plain worrying. He drove slowly up the drive in first with bits of broken rhododendron dropping from the luggage rack, wondering what on earth May had been up to.

'What on earth have you been up to?' he asked as soon as he could.

'How do you mean? Oh! Lavinia! She dropped in to see me. My cousin: she married a man in Texas who's dead – I mean he died last year.'

'Who was the feller she was with?'

While May was wincing at the idea of Dr Sedum being described as a feller, he went on, 'Looked like a doctor, to me.'

'Herbert, you really are extraordinary!'

'What on earth do you mean?' While she might be delighted by his perspicacity, he was too alarmed for complacence.

'Well – he *is* a kind of doctor – in a way.'

'What do you mean – in a way?'

'I don't know actually.' She did not want to discuss Dr Sedum too much. 'He's not a *medical* doctor at all. But there are hundreds of other kinds, aren't there? I just know that he is one. He's called Dr Sedum: a friend of Lavinia's.

'I know what,' she said as she trotted after him into the hall. 'He's a doctor of philosophy. I bet you that's it.'

'*I* don't mind what he is,' he rejoined, now that he no longer did.

Neither of them wanted to explore Dr Sedum in depth.

2. Ginny

Oliver woke up remembering quite clearly how awful he'd felt when he went to bed and looking forward now to having slept some of it off. He opened his eyes very carefully; it was still dark, but then it nearly always was these days. He rolled his eyeballs gently and swallowed. It was no good pretending that it was just a hangover any more: both movements made him wonder if he was at a not too distant point from death. He tried to shift his legs to sit up, but they seemed immovable. Just as he thought, 'God! paralysed!' he remembered the vast and weighty Labrador who was a temporary P.G. at Lincoln Street. She was a noble and resigned creature, hell-bent on loyalty, and given the absence of her owner she turned all her attention on to Oliver. Now her tail thudded against his ribs that he realized were actually aching – as though bruised. She got to her feet and stood on and over him (her nose was refreshing, but her tongue felt like his – hot and abrasive): then, with a heavy, faintly artificial, sigh, she cast herself anew upon some more of his aching and bruised bones. With his free arm he knocked over the glass by his bed and turned on the lamp: he'd drunk all the water anyway. It was ten to six; as he registered this, the Labrador heaved herself up again, jumped or fell to the ground and firmly scratched some more paint off the door. She wanted to go out, and that meant both of them, whether it killed him or not. When the father of a friend of his had offered him ten shillings a day for keeping and looking after Millie, he had, on accepting, jolly nearly said it was too much, but he hadn't and it wasn't. He wrapped himself in his eiderdown, crammed his feet bare into outdoor shoes and padded down the steep stairs. His head throbbed in a way that made him feel as though it was one stair behind the rest of him.

Millie had not yet worked out which way the front door opened and there was some bulky confusion before she finally made her way to the street, casually bringing Oliver to the ground in her progress. It was freezing cold and Oliver's teeth immediately began to chatter : Millie, on the other hand, no sooner reached the fresh air than she began to amble. He gave her one chance which luckily she took before calling her back into the house. Upstairs he put on another jersey, took the last three aspirins and got back into bed. Millie had managed to get her fur icy in those few minutes but her stomach was warm and on the whole he was glad of her company. Together they fell into stupor.

Oliver was working at Harrods, for December anyway. He was doing this because he found that life at Lincoln Street without Elizabeth was more expensive as well as being far more uncomfortable, and he had chosen Harrods because he hoped to see some of his friends there buying their Christmas presents. So far the friends part of it had been a dead loss; a woman who'd taught him not much French when he was about ten who looked just the same and just as nasty, and who immediately remembered him with shrieks of Gallic hypocritical surprise, and someone he'd never liked whom he'd known at Oxford and to whom he owed five pounds. Still, he'd only been at it a week – selling ties and handkerchiefs to desperate women – it was certainly the only time of the year to sell in the men's department, but on the whole the crush and rush was such that you never got to know anybody ... By Thursday, he was feeling pretty fagged, but he put that down to the ghastly hours he was having to keep. He got up at seven in order to give Millie a decent run before going to Harrods. He walked there, but took a bus back in the lunch hour in order to take Millie out. Back in the evening and she would greet him with overwhelming vigour but clearly expected more exercise. Her horse-meat meal nauseated him so much that he hardly needed dinner, but he would take her to the pub where she behaved beautifully and everyone would tell him what kind of dog they had or had had. On Friday he woke with a sore throat and a headache, but it was pay day so he struggled through and had a rather longer session at the pub than usual, partly because it was so cold outside and partly because after a couple of whiskies he felt so much better. But the feeling-better wore off sharply on the short, but agonizingly cold, walk home and by the time he went to bed he felt very ill indeed but pretended and hoped that it was because he'd drunk too much. By ten to six, however, he was trying to tell himself that he'd only got 'flu.

At eight o'clock the telephone rang. It was Ginny.

'I thought I'd call you,' she began, 'because I've run out of money and I thought you'd be the least bad-tempered about it.'

He took a deep breath and said, 'That doesn't sound as though you have a genius for friendship, I must say.'

'For God's sake, Oliver, don't try to be clever: I've been on an aeroplane all night and I'm bushed.'

'I've been under a Labrador all night and I've got 'flu. At least,' he added, 'that's the least that I've got.'

'What's your cash situation?'

'Approximately twelve quid.' He was just starting to say but he needed it, when she said (far too loudly: it hurt his ear) 'Oh goody! London here I come!' and rang off.

'She's got a nerve!' he said – several times – to himself: trying to work up a sense of pure indignation (that worthless little chit turning up just when it happened to suit her) to counteract the spurts of excitement and fury that were already stopping him thinking clearly. He hadn't seen Ginny since that – very necessary – quarrel about her getting Jennifer to Cap Ferrat, although they'd had one or two horrible conversations that had begun with her apologizing nothing like enough, showing that she didn't really care about having ruined Liz's holiday, and him telling her this, whereupon she instantly stopped apologizing at all and simply said in the same breath that she hadn't done anything and he was an idiot to mind the tiny thing she *had* done. There had been two conversations exactly like that. 'She's got a nerve!' he said again as he realized that his fury was not because she was coming, but because he was feeling so awful when she was. There were two things he could do, he told himself. One, get up as quickly as possible and just not be here by the time she came, and two ... but in the middle of not being able to think what two was he absent-mindedly swung his legs over the side of the bed and sat up. Instantly he felt so frightful that he lay down again. There were two things he could do: one, was to keep absolutely still until he either died or recovered however long either condition might take to achieve ...

The door bell was ringing and Millie's broadsword tail was lashing his Adam's apple: she was out of bed facing the door with her back to him; she knew perfectly well that bells meant that people had to answer them and this meant that she, Millie, had the chance of getting the hell *out* of wherever she might be – her chronic wish.

Ginny stood drooping on the doorstep looking even smaller and more fragile than usual in a stiff, felty coat the colour of mustard (English, not French or German).

'It's four pounds ten,' she said. Then she jerked her head backwards in the direction of her driver who looked quite frighteningly like Prince Philip and added, '*he* says.'

A typical Ginny way of getting out of it; announcing the price and then putting it all on to someone else. He'd left the money upstairs oh *damn* because if he sent Ginny for it, she might give away all he'd got.

'Well, that seems rather a lot to me.' His no-nonsense smile was being ruined by chattering teeth.

The driver straightened up from a fulsome exchange with Millie.

'It seems a lot to *me*, sir,' he said cheerfully, 'but there it is.' Then he added, 'It's the time of day, you see, sir.'

'Oliver do hurry up: I'm simply freezing!'

Then, while words were failing him, she cried, 'Oh darling – it's so marvellous to see you again, you've left your wallet upstairs I bet, I'll get it for you.'

Millie bounded after her into the house. It was easier to let her get the wallet – he couldn't, he thought, *manage* another trip to the top of the house and down again. 'It's in my jacket,' he called. It was going to be tough bargaining with Prince Philip when he was wrapped in an eiderdown. Still he'd *earned* those twelve pounds; they were damn well going to slip through his fingers the way he wanted them to. The driver was unloading Ginny's luggage – black-and-white striped canvas – and carrying it piece by piece to the bottom of the flight of steps up to the front door. No tip, thought Oliver viciously. Just as he was thinking that, Millie bounded out of the house again with the wallet in her mouth which she tenderly laid at the driver's feet. Her tail was wagging gently and she had an expression on her broad face that was both creative and benign. By the time Ginny had appeared, Oliver had given the driver five separate pounds and was thanking him profusely for the filthy ten shilling note produced as change.

'There we are, then,' said Ginny after he had staggered up the steps for the last time with her luggage. She hadn't offered to carry any of it, but when he tried to look at her morosely, so that she would ask him what was the matter and he would tell her, everything went dark and a stair or a banister or something struck him across the face. When he came to, he was flat on his back.

'.. oh Oliver!' She sounded distraught, and without much effort he kept his eyes shut to hear some more. Just then, she dropped an ice cube into a sort of niche above his collar bone. He sat up and it rolled down to an even more private place. He glared at her. 'Oh God! Honestly.'

'Don't worry; it'll melt in two ticks: you've got the most ghastly fever. A tear went on your face just now and it sizzled like a drop scone.'

'Have you been crying? Have I been out for ages? Can it be that deep down you care for me?'

But she answered with disarming truth, 'Don't be silly: you know perfectly well I haven't *got* a deep down. But yes, you have been just lying there. Long enough for me to look up Dr Garth-Elwyn-Garth's number, anyway.'

'Who's he?'

'He's the most eminent gynaecologist in England. Mummy swears by him.' And when he burst out laughing, she said crossly:

'Oh shut up! I don't *know* any other doctors in this country. It would be easy if we were in an hotel – you just ring up and say you want one and he comes. Why don't we just slip off to Claridge's? They've got everything there.'

'I thought you'd run out of money.'

'I have. You have a bill, stupid.'

'But you have to pay it in the end, idiot. Thanks to you, I've now got seven pounds ten. And thanks to you, he added most unfairly, 'I've probably lost my job.'

'It'll probably bring out the best in you.'

'What on earth do you mean?'

'Nearly every great man has been poverty-stricken and diseased at some time or other.'

'Nearly every kind of man's been that. There's absolutely no guarantee of what it brings out.' She was sitting cross-legged on the floor in front of him. The black fox beret she was wearing made her face look unbearably fragile.

'I must go to bed,' he said.

'I must have a bath first, darling – I've been travelling such ages.'

'I didn't mean bed with you: I'm much too ill,' he said and immediately wondered whether this was in the least true.

But in fact Oliver really was quite ill and Ginny surprisingly stayed and looked after him, proving fairly efficient in some – exotic – ways. She ordered food, for instance, not just from Fortnum's, where her mother had an account, but from the Star of India and Fu Tong as well. She used what she called her hocking diamond which travelled everywhere with her in a dented Elastoplast tin and got what seemed to Oliver a fantastic sum from the pawnbroker. With this she bought some clean sheets and sent all the others to a laundry. She bought Aristo-dog for Millie so there was no horrible horse-meat to cook, and bought muscat hot-house grapes for Oliver that he worked out cost about one and ninepence a grape. She bought mimosa that lasted only a day but was worth it, and Campari and champagne that she mixed with a shot of Pellegrino. She bought him paperbacks and L.P. records and a transistor radio and a pair of pyjamas from Harrods. For herself she bought sixteen different lipsticks for her collection and an auburn wig. When Oliver got better, she wrapped him up and took him in taxis to the Curzon Cinema and the Starlight Club and the Reptile House at the Zoo: Just 'nice, warm, cosy places,' she said. Once she cooked him the most terrific dinner. It took her all day, and even the day before she was abstracted and snappy thinking what to cook. But it *was* a stupendous meal: Oliver ate until he was bursting but there was a lot left. 'Marvellous!' he said. 'Better than Elizabeth?' 'Different,' he'd answered shortly. Liz was not a good subject for them because of the Jennifer incident. 'What will you do with all the remains?' She was setting aside a good deal of a cold goose stuffed with cherries in a rather dismissive manner. 'Oh we shan't eat any *more* of it. I'll find someone: a tramp or some of a movie queue – they're usually so bored they'll eat anything – what shall we do? I feel boredom coming on.' She was wearing a lilac-coloured Pierrot suit with large, watery black spots and a huge white frilly ruff round her neck. 'Couldn't we have a party, or something? It'd be a good idea, really, because I've got to go to Dublin in a minute.'

'*What?*' She'd never said a word about Dublin.

'You know. For Christmas. I only stopped off here for Christmas shopping. I'm meeting Mummy and Roderigo there –' she looked at her watch, 'the day after tomorrow, actually.'

She looked so very pretty and unreliable that he felt he must have a serious conversation with her.

'Ginny! We've got to talk.'

'No, we haven't. No need at all.' She looked nervous and lit a small cigar.

He thought of how she had been the last five days: domestic – in a way – efficient: she had not minded ringing up the right person at Harrods and explaining the situation (which meant, of course, that he had lost his job) any more than she seemed to mind his feverish sweats, the dirt in the house, the persistent quiet problem of Millie but above all, the fact that he was – or had been – literally in no state to entertain her in any sense whatever. Except for going to bed, of course.

'*I* need to.'

'Talk, then.' She looked away from him then, as though it would be rude to watch anyone doing *that*.

He was lying on the battered old sofa in the sitting-room and she was curled up in the only serious chair.

'Well, I thought it would be an awfully good thing if we got married. There you are: as beautiful as the day, and rich and young and tremendously needing a stable background –' but she interrupted, 'What ghastly cheek of you to say that! I must say!'

'Ginny, it wasn't meant to be. But you can't want to spend all your life flitting from one hotel or villa or rented house to another doing nothing but try to amuse yourself.' As he said this, it sounded like something anyone could easily go on doing, but it was also something that almost everyone who had never done it decried, so he went on, 'I mean, it was all very well when you were a child and dependent upon your mother and all that –'

'Never been that! You don't know Mummy! You can't be dependent on her! Anyway, the sort of people who talk like you, dreary old Oliver, wouldn't at all approve of me marrying like that – as a kind of escape. *So?*'

He sat up. 'I should have thought you would have wanted your own life, at least –'

'How would marrying you make any difference to that?' She lay back sideways in the chair with her legs swinging out over one arm.

'Don't be dim on purpose. I mean having your own house –'

'Don't *you* be so silly. You don't have to be married to have a house and lots of people who *are* married don't have them. I don't see the connection. If you are going to go on being so boring I must have a drink.' She got up – almost leapt up – and prowled over to a Fortnum's carrier bag from which she drew a bottle.

'Are you always so rude to people who propose to you?'

'Yes. Now you'll have to wait while I get some salt and glasses.'

While she was gone, he shut his eyes frowning and trying to think why things were going so badly. Something to do with her neurosis, he decided, and he'd touched some raw and painful bit in her.

She brought very small glasses, an eggcupful of salt and a saucer of cut-up, very small, green lemons.

'Tequila,' she said. 'Help yourself.'

He watched while she filled a glass to the brim, put a pinch of salt on the edge of her hand, ate the salt, knelt to drink, and then squeezed the lemon juice down her throat. This was the kind of thing she did in a manner both practised and dashing. When she was licking her fingers, he said:

'I can't take neat lemon juice.'

'It's lime; much nicer than lemon.' She had another shot as quick as lightning and then said, 'Now – you can go on.'

'Being boring?'

She shrugged her shoulders so that the frill hid her ears.

'It's not difficult to bore you: there's no challenge there.' But even that didn't seem to move her, and she remained frozen in the shrug.

He tried the tequila minus all the salt lime nonsense and it was like a small, disgusting explosion at the bottom of his throat.

'People who are most easily bored are usually the most boring.'

'If you think that, why on earth do you think you want to marry me then? You're silly not to have salt and lime.'

'Because it's not the only thing about you.'

'I'll tell you something.'

'What?'

'Let's both have another swig first. You may find you needed it'

In silence, he waited while she poured the drinks, put salt on what she described as the lockjaw bit of his hand and got the limes handy. Then she said, 'Right,' and they went through the ritual. He began to see the point of tequila, and was just about to say so, when she remarked,

'It's time you knew, I think, that I don't have any money.'

'What do you mean?'

'I mean I'm not in the least rich – any more. I used to be, but now I'm not. Not a peseta, not a cent, not a threepenny bit. That's why I called from the airport. I'd run out.'

There was a silence while she watched him and he tried to think what he thought. Ginny bored but with money was not an easy proposition, but Ginny bored and without a sou made him feel really nervous. And the economics of the thing : living with Ginny was more a case of two could live as cheaply as about seventy-four ... even if they both worked like mad at Harrods from morning till night ...

'Why did your mother do it?' he asked.

She shrugged again. 'Mightn't even have *been* her. The only time my parents actually liaise is when they think up something nasty for me. They always seem in complete agreement over that.'

Oliver drank some more tequila a bit too fast. This made him choke and Ginny laugh.

'Is it fury you're choking from?' she asked when he could hear her.

'No, but it will be if you go on like that.'

'Well, isn't it my money you wanted to marry me for?'

'It's funny,' he said, 'I thought it was. And I can see it's a completely different proposition –'

'You mean you *don't* want to?'

'Stop pouncing! No, I think I *do* want to, and I'm only saying 'think' because we're back at the dreary old problem of what to do with me to get me earning some money. Clearly I can't marry you without a job. You'd have to get one, too.'

'Any minute now you'll suggest that we both go *trudging* off to Harrods every morning to earn our married livings.'

This made him angry, as something of the sort had just begun to cross his mind. He shifted nearer the table in order to reach the bottle as she went on, 'Rush hour every morning and evening – worn to the bone, both of us and nasty little married crush hour every Friday – or is it Saturday? – night. Besides, we could never go anywhere decent – our holidays would be too short. Surely you can see?'

He took another drink and said, 'Why did you stay here then?'

'Because I wanted some money and then, even when I found you hadn't got any much, I was sorry for you.'

'Well, I started by wanting *your* money, and now I'm sorry for *you*.'

'What on earth for? *Are* you?'

'Yes I am!'

'No need to shout! I just wanted to know. And do you honestly think you love me?'

'Considering how awful you're being without putting me off, I must.'

She poured them both large drinks.

'Well I don't love you,' she said calmly. 'Sorry, but that's that. And before you can start telling me that I might get to, I'd better tell you that it isn't just you – it's anybody. I just never get to care enough. I used to think it mattered and tried awfully hard with people, but now I know I'll never change so I don't bother.'

She twisted in the chair and leaned forward over the table with one of her sudden, but entirely controlled, movements, and began cutting up some more limes. He thought of her during the last few days – and nights.

'You seemed to me to have been bothering with me.'

She looked up from the lime cutting. 'It is the easiest way not to be rude to people, really, isn't it? Of course I didn't want to hurt your feelings.'

'What do you think you're doing *now*?'

'*You're* making me have to do that – *probing* away and trying to change everything. And I warn you,' she added, 'tequila often makes people madly quarrelsome, so you'd better be careful.'

Before he could reply, the telephone rang, and seeing that she seemed eager to answer it, he felt determined to thwart her. This was easy, as the instrument was on the floor by the fireplace, much nearer to him, but he hadn't realized that she'd left a tray on the rug at the end of the sofa until he'd stepped into and tripped over a bowl of braised celery. 'For God's sake!' he said just after he'd picked up the receiver : she seemed bent on humiliating him; there seemed to be no end to her horrible, appalling behaviour ...

'Darling – it's me.' It was May, sounding apprehensive and miles away. 'Oliver? Was that you sounding so angry just now?'

234

'Not with you, though.'

'If you've got people I –'

'Nobody who matters,' he said with what felt like vicious smoothness.

'Oh well. Because I don't want to interrupt you –'

'You're not. What is it?' It must be something: she regarded even toll calls rather like brandy – only to be indulged in in an emergency.

Ginny had got up and was clearing away the remains of dinner except for the tray he had trod upon. The moment she opened the sitting-room door, thin far-off howls could be heard from Millie shut up in the spare room above.

'... so extraordinary – I felt quite frightened.' May was saying. The line now seemed to be crossed, because from even farther away a woman's voice said, '... all over the back stairs – so Tuesday would be no good.' Her voice faded suddenly and Oliver quickly asked, 'What frightened you?'

'I told you, darling; but it's so unlike him that I expect it's just because I don't feel too good anyway that I'm imagining it.'

'... five miles there *and* five miles back and I've never known her finish what's on her plate –' and another voice, astonishingly like the first said, 'No good suggesting anything to *you* on a Wednesday –' both voices agreed that it wouldn't be. Millie howled again and Ginny hissed, 'Shall I let her *out*?'

'Do what you like,' Oliver shouted – into the telephone by mistake.

'Darling, you're obviously having a party and I wouldn't have rung you but I've never felt like this before –'

'Like what? I'm sorry, but I didn't hear the beginning part –'

'So frightened. Somehow, it's the most awful house to be alone in, so I wondered whether you could possibly –'

'Where's Herbert?'

'I *told* you, darling – he's gone *storming* off in the car. So *could* you – just for tonight?'

At this moment, the other voices broke in; a crossed line, they said with muted umbrage: it was funny how some people listened to other people's conversations ... May started to apologize; triumphant barking could be heard from Millie, and Ginny came to lean against the architrave of the open door in a Petrouchka-like attitude. A wave of retrospective humiliation swept over Oliver at the sight of her.

'I can't possibly come down tonight; I've got appalling 'flu,' he said more loudly than anybody else who was talking. There was silence for a moment. Then May said:

'Of course you shouldn't dream of moving then, darling. But would you mind very much if I caught the last train up and came to you?'

Panic assailed him. Except for feeling that she mustn't come – not *now* of all times, anyway – he was paralysed. If she came, he *knew* that everything with Ginny would go wrong, and what's more she'd *see* it go wrong. The crossed-line voice was now saying that it was the *second* Friday in every month that she went to Mr Worksop.

'No,' said Oliver; 'don't do that: not tonight, anyway. Look, I'll ring you in the morning when things are a bit more settled. How would that be?' he added when there was no reply and then May – she sounded miles away again – said she didn't know; she expected it would be all right.

'It's hopeless on this line, anyhow,' Oliver said trying to sound bluff and calm instead of guilty and panic-stricken.

'Good-bye, darling. It was nice to hear your voice.'

'Good-bye.' He put down the receiver and ostensibly glared at Ginny who was now sitting astride Millie.

'That was your mother you couldn't be bothered with, wasn't it?'

He ignored this. 'You *can't* have meant what you said just now.'

'I bet I did, but what was it?'

'About not – about simply not hurting my feelings in bed – about not caring about me, in fact.'

'Oh that. Mmm. 'Fraid you're wrong.'

'Women can't pretend to that extent; it's an absurd exaggeration – just because you don't want –' but she interrupted him:

236

'They can pretend and most of them do. And most of them get away with it. You can always get away with it, in fact, except in one situation.'

'And what's that?' He thought he was speaking calmly and merely folded his arms to stop himself shaking.

Ginny had got off Millie now and was back in her original leaning position in the doorway. 'If the man is really, honestly, completely in love with you, you couldn't cheat,' she said, 'it wouldn't work and you wouldn't want to anyway. There'd be no need.' Her voice went back to what it usually was. 'But oh brother – it's the way to find out whether a man loves you. It's the – big – infallible test. It always works.'

'You mean you pretend, and if he doesn't catch on it means he doesn't love you?'

She gave a little nod, and then slid slowly down with her backbone against the frame until she was sitting on the floor. Then she said again, 'It always works.'

Whether it was her pretty, clownish clothes, or her disconsolate position, or feeling that she meant what she said – and more, that what she said meant something – he didn't know, but he had suddenly a quite different feeling about her; as though she was Elizabeth, or a child, or somebody in some way poor who needed affection and protection and pity . . .

'Ginny, now you've said all this, couldn't we try again –'

'Oh don't say *that*! Let's both have another drink quickly before I have to tell you something else.' She sprang effortlessly to her feet and dodged round him to the tequila table. When she'd helped herself, she said, 'The test, you see, is that the other person doesn't know they're being tested. If they knew, then all that would happen is that we'd both be cheating.'

'But if you found someone who passed the test – would you marry them?'

'Oh that. I don't know. I never have found anyone and it's a private rule not to cheat about the test.'

'But surely – that's the point of the test, isn't it? That you'd marry them if they passed?'

She took another glass of neat tequila and then threw her

head back to squeeze drops of lime juice into her mouth. At last she said,

'If you swear – I mean seriously swear – not to tell anyone, I'll tell you something.'

'All right.'

'No – seriously.'

'I am serious,' he said – sounding merely peevish as people do when pressed on this point.

'I couldn't marry you – or anyone. I *am* married.'

He stared at her while she composedly selected and lit one of her small cigars. When, eventually, he said, '*What?*' she went on as though she had always been going to : 'My father fixed it when I was fourteen. He disapproved of my mother's morals, you see : she got sort of custody of me and he was afraid I'd get like her. Whenever she "knows" any man in the Old Testament sense for more than a few months she *always* marries them : my father says that she is incurably middle-class in this way, so he decided to queer my pitch in that direction which what with money *and* my mother has been a godsend.'

'Who are you married to?'

'Oh – some boring old man on my father's estate. He's about a hundred years older than me so my father said he'd probably die about when I got sensible. I only saw him that once. But my father keeps an eye on him, of course.'

'I'm glad to hear that.'

'You're rotten at sarcasm. You mean, you're shocked. You're British to the backbone – except for about an eggcupful of Scots blood I'm not British at all. My father's hacienda is about the size of Ireland.' She thought for a moment : 'Well – perhaps not the size of Northern and Southern Ireland – just Eire.'

'So what? There's no point in showing off about that now. I'm clearly not going to profit by it.'

That made her laugh. 'Good for you. I wasn't showing off. What I meant was that on his land my father is a kind of king. He can do what he likes. But he's *not* been beastly to José at all. I promise. He gave him a house and enough land to grow food for his huge family and he more or less bought José a much younger and prettier woman than he'd ever have got on his own. Of course he made José mark a document saying he'd always leave me alone and had no claims on me and all that. But I promise you he likes Lola and she's all right because he's got more of everything than anyone else she might have taken up with –'

'But supposing they want to get married!'

'Oh Oliver! They wouldn't want to do that! It's far too expensive – hardly anyone does. Extraordinary the way you *harp* on marriage! I warn you, you'd better not meet my mother, she's taken to marrying people younger and younger than she is and she's just about got to your age –'

'I don't care about your mother!'

'Well I often think that I'm tremendously like her so I bet you're well out of me. Look – if I'm going tonight, I simply must pack.'

'*Are* you going tonight?'

'It's too depressing staying after one of these conversations, I find.'

'You do, do you,' said Oliver hopelessly, but she had already vanished upstairs. In a messy, multi-horrible way he'd never felt worse in his life. The whole evening had been a bit like being at the wrong (receiving) end of some major character's revelations in a play of Shaw's. It wasn't that his heart was broken, exactly; there was little or no good clean misery about it: he felt angry, sad, disgruntled, shocked (he called that astounded) a bit miserable, a bit humiliated, rather anxious, considerably depressed, slightly overwhelmed: his pride was hit, his self-confidence dented ...

'What will you do if you never meet someone who passes the test?' he asked when she staggered down with the smallest black and white suitcase.

'Never marry,' she answered with such weary practice that he had to go on:

'Am I *exactly* like everybody else you've ever met?'

'Not abso*lutely exactly* like everybody I've ever met.'

Which was really only half withdrawing the barb – and twisting it to boot.

He brought all her other cases down at once, partly not to

prolong the agony, and partly to show her, but she didn't seem to notice and he broke a banister. 'My taxi should be there,' was all she said. She had changed out of her Pierrot clothes and was back in the mustard coat.

He stared stupidly at her: the whole thing was getting worse than a play and more like some boring – and fairly bad – dream.

'I ordered it while I was packing, silly.'

'Where are you going?'

She was trying to open the front door and did not reply.

'Claridge's, I bet.'

And when she did not say anything to that, he seized her by her spiky little shoulders. 'It wasn't true about the money, was it?'

'Oh – Oliver!'

'What about the other things?' He shook her slightly. 'The being married and not caring about anyone – all that?'

'Oh Oliver! You are a fool! It wouldn't matter, would it, whether it was true or not. The point is I've *told* you. Even *you* ought to be able to understand *that*.' The bell rang and in surprise, he released her. As she opened the door, she said, 'I honestly think you are one of the dimmest people I've ever known.' A lightning, feathery kiss on the side of his chin and that was that. Helplessly, he watched the taxi drive away (she didn't look back or wave). In the house the stairs smelled of her rich rose scent, there was more washing up than the kitchen would hold and Millie was guiltily cracking goose bones. One of the dimmest people she'd ever known. He went slowly up the scented stairs in search of the tequila.

3. An Old Devil

The reason that the colonel had 'stormed off', as May had put it to Oliver, was that he had mistakenly thought all day that it was Tuesday. The naked, incontrovertible truth had dawned only when – long after dark – there was still no sign of the dogs' weekly (and inadequate) consignment of horse-meat. The moment he started to complain about this – which of course he did to May, there being no one else to complain to – she told him that it had come yesterday. 'It always comes on Tuesdays,' she had added.

'I know it does. And it hasn't come today. That's what I've been trying to say.'

'It's in the fridge.'

'Why didn't you simply say it had come then? No need to make a damned mystery of it.'

'Herbert, don't be absurd! Of course I'm not making a mystery. It came yesterday, like it always does, and naturally I didn't rush to tell you. I couldn't have; you were out.'

'How do you mean 'like it always does'? You said just now it always came on Tuesdays.'

'I did! It does!'

'You don't mean to tell me it's Wednesday!'

'Of course it's Wednesday.'

He would not believe her until he had looked up a radio programme for Wednesday and tested that it was actually in progress. And even then he didn't seem pleased: rather more furious than ever, in fact. He became suddenly panicky about the time and wouldn't believe her about that, either: just snapped at her.

'Are you going out?'

'Of course I'm going out. Why on earth do you think it matters what blasted day it is?'

She said nothing to this, but eventually tracked him down – or up – to his dressing-room where she found him fumbling irritably with his ties. It was half past seven : fear – now familiar – at being left alone in the house with her evening pains coming on induced her to make one of those gestures which are vaguely in a self-preserving direction but none the less more often cause damage. 'Herbert, I really think you might tell me more what you are doing. I really think it's a bit much to be left suddenly at this time of night. Just because you've forgotten something.'

'You do, do you?'

'Well, yes. I mean – you didn't even believe me just now about what day it was. And then you sound as though it was all my fault.'

'I never said it was your blasted fault –'

But she had fatally interrupted, 'Couldn't I come with you?'

Of course she couldn't. And not only could she not come, but why on earth had she asked? Was he to have no vestige of privacy – have every little thing he did – or wanted to do – or, as in most cases *had* to do – interfered with, probed into? It was time she realized that he gave up far more of his life to her than most husbands did to most wives, but it was his personal and bitter experience that if you gave any woman an inch she asked for an ell. By now he had changed his tie, brushed his hair, arranged a new pocket-handkerchief and apparently whipped himself into a state of such general indignation that it would have been hopeless for her to attempt an answer to any specific charge. He decided that he wanted to see how much money there was in his wallet but not, of course, in front of her, so he sent her off to his den to look for his car keys. But she had hardly got down the stairs before he called out that he had found them (nine pounds ten and his cheque book). Then, because he really couldn't face her again, he shouted, 'Off now : shan't be late,' and scarpered down the back stairs. He was almost smiling as he let himself out. A bit of an old devil, that's what he was ...

May found it very difficult to be angry. She was not an unemotional woman, she simply found *anger* difficult; perhaps confused would be a better word for her feelings round about being angry. To begin with she so often felt that any unfortunate state of affairs was the result of something she had done (and since Dr Sedum, *been*): to go on with, she could far too often see the other person's point of view. It was therefore almost impossible for her to fix upon the reason for an object of anger. Being told to find Herbert's keys at once made her forget why he wanted them, and not finding them before he did made her feel (very faintly) guilty and inferior. As she heard one of the many back doors slam behind Herbert, her main feeling was of desolation. 'It was too bad of him' was as far as she could get about her husband leaving her without warning and for no reason at the beginning of yet another long winter evening. She decided to bolt the back door after Herbert before she began thinking about any of it. But by the time she had done this (the back door was at the farthest possible point from Herbert's study) her mind was too full of the emptiness of the house to sustain what had seemed like a straightforward state of indignation with her husband.

Her feet seemed to make too much noise on the uncarpeted passages, and the varnished pine floors had an institutional and discomfortingly unfurnished air that in turn gave the house the feeling of being barely, even uncertainly inhabited. She paused in the kitchen, but the thought of supper made her feel queasy and tired. This was not what Claude felt about it: and he rammed her thoroughly with all his firm and furry bulk until it was clear what his requirements must be. She fed him and heated herself some milk while he ate. When the milk was hot, she longed for a little whisky to put in it: the chances were that Herbert would have locked up the drink but perhaps it was worth going to look. Claude accompanied her as he never slept in the kitchen in winter if he could help it. She was glad of his company through the creaking baize doors that swung and creaked so long after one had passed them and decided that if there was any whisky she would shut them both in Herbert's study with as many electric fires as possible.

There *was* a small drop: it was so small that he hadn't bothered to lock it up. Unexpectedly, there being some, and it being so little, started to make her feel angry with Herbert again. It really was monstrous that he should go off as he had done, without warning, to goodness knows where leaving her entirely alone in this awful house that she had really come to hate. And if she hated it so much, why on earth had she let Herbert bludgeon her into buying it? Why wasn't she living in Lincoln Street with Oliver – leading entirely his own life, of course, but *there*? The whisky wouldn't be locked up *there*. She had got used to far too much: had been taking bad things for granted which must surely be even worse than taking good ones ...

Claude, who had been sitting on her lap, tried once more to like milk with whisky in it, but the filthy taste was too much for him. He shook his head violently, and beads of hot whisky-milk flew from his chin and whiskers and landed all over the place. He was going to have to wash his face to get rid of the smell, and as he could never manage this unless he was on a really firm base, he jumped heavily off May's lap to the floor where he found that her legs were taking up all the hot room in front of the fire. 'How affectionate he is,' she thought as he butted impotently against her until she made room for him. She wasn't entirely alone while Claude was about. It didn't seem to make much difference moving her feet from the fire to make room for him, as she couldn't feel them anyway. It must be a very cold night. This made her remember that the fire was not on in the bedroom, which would be icy, and then she began thinking of the awful trek upstairs, feeling for and turning on the half-a-dozen light switches – and then, without warning, she began to feel frightened. She was almost at once too much afraid to consider what she was frightened of: she simply knew that she did not want to have to make the journey upstairs and down again; did not even really want to have to leave the comparatively small and bright room. This was when she telephoned Oliver. While talking to him she managed to discover and thence to explain that in fact Herbert going off in this sudden manner had frightened her; she couldn't very well just say that it was the house, but Oliver sounded very busy and there were some other people talking so she wasn't sure whether he heard properly or not. Then he said he had 'flu and then something else he said made it clear to her that he didn't really want her. She knew she was going to cry, so she said something pointless and sensible to put an end to the conversation in time. Crying left her feeling rather sick, but, she told herself, relieved in her mind. The whole thing showed what a beginner she must be about the League, because she tried several times to think of higher and better things and didn't in the least succeed. But she *did* remember afterwards that something had been said about making use of what material was to hand, and clearly Herbert came under that heading. She had *married* him, after all. Why? She had to think very hard about him to recall the first impression he made upon her ... Chelsea Flower Show – the last day. Marvellous weather, too hot, in fact, to march about in one's best clothes; but they had met wearing them, both in search of a good shrub rose to buy when the show closed. The circumstances weren't the point: what had he been *like*? Very frank and straightforward: simple, in a way, but chivalrous: obviously, she had thought, a man who liked women: he had a keen way of looking at you as though he was interested because he immediately understood you so well. He had been modestly reticent about himself – he didn't want to bore her etc. – but he had been an awfully good listener and it happened that at that time she particularly needed one. Oliver had just come down from Oxford; not, as she had fondly hoped, with a brilliant degree and a dedicated determination about his mission in life, but with a Second, the general reputation for not having done a stroke of work and the expressed intention of enjoying himself. This was when he needed a father, when even uncles, she had felt, might have stiffened up his moral fibre, but alas, there were no uncles. Clifford had had a sister but she had never married: she herself simply did not know a single man of approximately her own age except her lawyer and her dentist, neither of whom she had felt would be really right for dealing with Oliver. So this large, military-looking, interested and courteous stranger was an open blessing. They had had dinner together, at the end of which she felt better about Oliver than she had for months (they had spent most of the dinner over him, neither Alice nor Elizabeth proving to have the sheer staying power as a topic of conversation that Oliver seemed to have).

In the end (when they had got to Grand Marnier and coffee) the colonel – as she already thought of him – had leaned forward and said how much he admired the gallant way in which she had for years shouldered burdens clearly meant for men. When she explained how much easier everything had become since Aunt Edith in Canada had died, he said money be damned, excuse his French, it in no way lessened her *moral* responsibilities. And May, who had never really thought of relations with her children in those terms, instantly began to worry about *why* she hadn't, since this kind and upright gentleman seemed to do so. What she now should do was stop worrying about her son, realize that he was – to all intents and purposes – grown-up, and start to live her own life a bit more. Get out, make new friends – enjoy herself. At the time she had simply agreed with this agreeable advice : afterwards she had interpreted it. What he had really meant – only he was far too kind to say so – was that in spite of all her secret vows about it, she had imperceptibly become a possessive and stultifying mother : living her life vicariously through her wretched children. This was wrong and at all costs must stop at once. With her new friend, the costs did not seem to be at all high. They started to spend every Saturday together : Kew, Richmond, the river-boats to Greenwich, Queen Mary's Rose Garden in Regent's Park, Hampstead Heath, and then invariably home to tea or drinks and supper at Lincoln Street. Quite soon, she had realized that Herbert was not a monied man and she had used the utmost delicacy to avoid his having to pay for things . . .

One thing she realized about her life was that through some initial piece of cowardice (masked, at the time as not wanting to hurt other people's feelings), she kept on landing herself in awkward situations. The present predicament was really due to her having given in over buying Monks' Close in the first place. Now, having got it, she wanted to leave it to the League in her will and Herbert wanted her to leave it to him. Really, the fairest thing to do would be to sell the place and leave or give them half each of the money. In the case of the League she would give it to them: in the case of Herbert they could buy some small but comfortable place to live in that would suit whoever outlived the other. Darling Elizabeth seemed to have married someone with almost too many houses, and Oliver, of course, should have Lincoln Street. It all seemed so simple when she thought of it by herself. In one way this solution got easier as time went by, because, as Herbert had predicted it would, the house was steadily increasing in value. Agents wrote to her – not often, but regularly – asking whether she would consider putting the house on the market, and the last sum quoted by them (Herbert always made them do that) was the astronomical one of twenty-two thousand pounds. Surely enough to go round? Yes, but plans of this sort, or indeed any sort, did not take into account the possibility of her dying before she had accomplished them. Herbert was also right about making a will. She must not dally any longer, and whatever he might feel she could not now go back on her promise to Dr Sedum. If she died, the League would get everything: otherwise, she would share it out. Tomorrow morning she would ring Mr Hardcastle and get him to post her the will to sign.

A sound outside – a car in the drive? – and some of her fears returned; it was horrible to feel nervous in one's own house. She decided to pull herself yet further together; to go and make her bed-time Horlicks and take it straight up with her. Claude could easily be got to come too as he adored Horlicks and benefited from her hot-water bottle.

Upstairs – Herbert insisted on the windows always being open – the bedroom was as dankly cold as a railway station in an east wind, and loneliness overcame her. Elizabeth, in Jamaica, was unspeakably far away. She decided to ring Alice, who after all would be far the most likely to explain that her father often rushed out in the evenings (whenever Herbert had seemed to do anything eccentric, Alice had been in the habit of saying that he was often, or even always, like that). But Leslie answered the telephone: sounding, May thought, as though he was a little drunk. Alice was in the nursing home, he said; she'd got pneumonia and lost the baby, but she was perfectly all right. May sent shocked and affectionate messages, but she wasn't sure if Leslie took them in: he kept saying, 'Well, I'll tell her you phoned,' in a sort of heavy, final way and then not putting down the receiver so she said good-bye firmly, to stop the conversation. Poor Alice! She was the only person May had ever met about whom she felt continuously protective. She would write to her tomorrow morning. Claude had drunk the first half inch of Horlicks, but hating cold rooms even more than he liked hot milky drinks he had got right into bed in order to be next to the hot-water bottle. She got into bed with him and composed herself for sleep by remembering Herbert as he was when she first met him. His frank kindness: his simplicty: many people with these old-fashioned virtues were sometimes the weeniest bit boring ...

•

'. . . look at me like that, I feel as though you've known me for years.'

'I wish I had.'

'That's a nice thing to say.'

'Not nice, m'dear: true.'

'Some trifle? Or would you prefer the cheese board?'

'Which are you going to have?'

'Well – I shouldn't really, but tonight I'm going to spoil myself. A little trifle. I ought to watch my figure really.'

'Nonsense! A little of what you fancy, eh?'

'That's what my husband always said! *I'll* watch your figure, Myrtle, he said, *you* enjoy yourself. What about you? Two trifles, please, Ramon.'

They were the last in the dining-room, and their table, if not the best, was the most secluded. The tables round them had already been laid for breakfast; the Muzak, like the Tyrolean sconces, had been turned low: they sat before the unearthly cheeriness of a Magicoal which cast endless speedy reflections upon the horse-brasses each side of the huge brick fireplace. Myrtle Hanger-Davies owned the hotel: at least, she had inherited it from her husband, Dennis, who had clearly died from obvious forms of over-indulgence at the early age of fifty-six. Myrtle had been much younger than he when she married him and although they had been married for some time before he died (last September) there was no reason to suppose that she had caught him up. She had spent dinner telling the colonel these and other salient facts, and, frankly, she had not enjoyed herself so much for years. The great question was whether she should continue to run the hotel, or whether she should sell up and go abroad – possibly to run something or possibly just to retire. What she had felt was that on the one hand, she did not want to feel lonely, as she might in somewhere like Majorca with nothing to do, but on the other hand, she'd seen a lot of human nature. She sighed. The colonel expected that she had and agreed that it was something of the devil and the deep blue sea. The trifles arrived, and Ramon, who was certainly trained in some things, had brought a jug of Bird's custard *and* a jug of cream. Myrtle had quite a lot of both, and so did the colonel.

'When in doubt always do nothing, Dennis used to say. What do you think of that? As a maxim?'

'Lot of old-fashioned truth there –'

'Excuse me one moment – what will you have? With your coffee, I mean.'

He decided on Drambuie and she a Tia Maria. The conversation came to a halt while Ramon was getting these things. The colonel gazed at her. She was blonde and very well covered, both of which he liked: tonight she wore a tight electric-blue woollen dress with a high neck, so she was well covered in that way too. At her shoulder she wore a poodle brooch that was made of real diamonds with ruby eyes. Her hair had been done that day and so had her nails – it was a damn good thing he hadn't gone on thinking it was Tuesday . . .

'. . . look at me like that, what are you thinking?'

He laughed challengingly and said, 'You'd be surprised.'

'Would I really?' she asked, hoping not.

'I was wondering if you'd ever been to Portugal.'

'Never!' she said. He certainly wasn't predictable – you never knew what he would say next.

He gazed at her a moment in silence, 'Ah well,' he said in the end. A little blazing shiver began at the bottom of her spine and travelled right up to the back of her neck. At this moment, Ramon returned with the liqueurs and coffee. When he had gone, she raised her Tia Maria and said, 'What shall we drink to – a Merry Christmas, or a Happy New Year?'

He picked up his glass,

'Let's start with a Merry Christmas.'

*

John had been watching Elizabeth watching a humming bird. The bird was feeding from a bottle of honey and water. It was so small, and so amazing in colour, that even when it poised itself to siphon up the nectar she could hardly believe that it was really *there*. The expression on her face was serious: she was almost frowning with attention and pleasure. It was Christmas Eve; the sun was beginning to drop like a huge, round, red-hot stone into the sea, palm trees were turning darker than shadows and the mosquitoes had not yet started their night assault. The humming bird left; Elizabeth, who had been sitting on her heels, linked her hands behind her neck and stretched – in the middle of which she became aware of John.

'Did you see?'

'Yes.'

'Only feathers are that colour – or those colours, I suppose you'd have to say. Flowers aren't; jewels aren't.'

'Silk?' he suggested.

'It tries to be. Doesn't work, though, because there's always too much of it.'

'Butterflies,' he said, sitting beside her.

'Of course.'

'And tropical fish.'

'That's one of the things I like best about you.'

He waited.

'How you go into things. There are far too many things that a good many men don't think it worth talking about.'

'Is that so?' One of the things he noted with amusement was the way in which her generalizations about men proliferated as her confidence grew about their marriage.

'Yes. A lot of men would think it was silly to discuss humming birds at all. A lot of men –' she stopped as she saw his face.

'I married you for your experience, Mrs Cole. It was a woman of the world I was after –'

Here the telephone rang, which it all too often did. The only way in which John could leave England for so long was by letting people telephone him whenever they felt like it. He had explained this at the beginning, and she was very good and always read a book while he was talking which meant that she neither fidgeted nor listened. When he was finished he saw that she was starting *Bleak House* which he knew she had read.

'It's the fog,' she said looking up as he bent to kiss her. 'The contrast to here is so terrific.'

'It must be. Now. What would you like to do this evening? A terrifically vulgar man has asked us to a party –'

'What kind of party?'

'The kind that starts off very pompous with too much of everything and ends with people getting thrown into the swimming pool.'

'What else might we do?'

'We might go to Negril and have a hot-fish beach picnic.'

'Can't we do both things?'

'We'll do anything you like, my darling.'

'Don't you care at *all* what you do?'

'Not if I'm with you.'

The sun was almost touching the sea: the palm trees, relaxing against the sky, were black and silhouettes.

'I can't ever have been in love before,' he said, 'because I know I've never felt like this. And I'm pretty sure it's what people always do when they're in love. I wouldn't have known before; but I do now.'

She waited, wanting to see if it was the same.

'*You* know. My God, I hope you know. It's finding that you're very simple : that you don't need anything at all except the presence of the person. That scrambled eggs, or going to bed early, or it raining the whole day, are all enhancements: anything at all can make you think you are happier than you were

251

before. It's feeling that everybody else must be better than you thought, and that whatever they are you mustn't be against them because perhaps somehow, they've missed it –'

'It *is* the same for everybody,' she said. 'I mean – you couldn't stop thinking of enhancements, but basically it's the same.'

The sun was sliding down out of sight. 'It looks as though there was a sort of slot for it – just beyond the sea and before the sky begins.'

In the end, they didn't go anywhere, but stayed by their own pool, and drank Daiquiris and swam and had supper and talked, as John later remarked, as though they had known each other all their lives but hadn't met for a year.

'We might as well be in a basement in Fulham Road.'

'Oh no we mightn't. There'd be no oxygen and you'd have too many clothes on.'

She was wearing one of his shirts over her bathing dress.

'God, money, sex, how to bring up children, birth control, democracy, education, socialism, looking after animals and things, boarding schools, homosexuality, good names for boys, how much we *agree* about things – oh dear, I've just thought –'

'What?'

'We've never had a serious quarrel! Do you realize that?'

'Nor we have. Do you want one, particularly?'

'Oh *no*! Of course I don't! I was just thinking how awful it would be when we do.'

He was bending down to lift her off the sofa.

'Perhaps we shall just not find the time,' he said.

4. Christmas Eve

Ten days after his pleasant little meal with Mrs Hanger-Davies it was Christmas Eve, and from first thing in the morning, nothing seemed to go right. To begin with he woke up with indigestion – or something that felt damn like it. He'd taken a couple of Alka Seltzers with his morning tea but before they'd had a chance to work, May had started nagging him about the house – they'd-have-to-get-rid-of-it-it-was-far-too-large-for-them stuff. It was some time before he realized that she was serious: even shouting at her didn't seem to shut her up. Then, when he'd slipped out for a quick drink at the pub, he'd suddenly had a feeling that he ought to ring Myrtle: funny – he really had a sixth sense or something. She said she was so glad he'd phoned, because all his talk about Portugal (he'd only mentioned it for God's sake, he hadn't talked about it at all) anyway, she had said that all his talk about Portugal had given her ideas. She was going on a cruise to the Canary Islands. When? Next week. A *cruise* of all things. Everybody knew what occurred to middle aged widows on *them*. He liked a lot of time to arrange things in – he hated being rushed – but that was what was happening to him, and just when he wasn't feeling up to scratch. Having told Myrtle three or four times what a splendid idea he thought the cruise was, he asked whether he might pop in for a spot of tea. Had he really got time for that on Christmas *Eve*? Myrtle had always understood that that was when most gentlemen did their shopping. Had she now? (Damn good thing she'd reminded him.) Well, from this point of view, at least, he'd like her to know that he was no gentleman. He'd laughed a good deal when he said this to be on the safe side. He'd rung off and rang May to say that he wouldn't be back for lunch because he'd suddenly remembered his Christmas shopping. That put the lid on it. He'd go to London and kill two birds with one stone: pop in to the lawyer (he'd written to Mr Pinkney asking him to prepare an appropriate version of his will – recently signed with a flourish in the presence of Mr Pinkney – for his wife to sign): then he'd have a spot of lunch at the club, then he'd nip along to Selfridge's where they often had bundles of slightly imperfect handkerchiefs at decent down-to-earth prices – back to Waterloo – train to West Byfleet (Myrtle's nearest station); Myrtle – and then May. Bit of a marathon, especially when he wasn't feeling quite the thing in the first place. Still – he was never a man to shirk his duty, which was what he called anything that he wanted to do enough to decide to do it. He headed the Wolseley towards West Byfleet; it would be madness to take the car to London on Christmas Eve.

It was madness to try and get about London at *all*: there were far too many people milling about all over the station, far too many children and parcels – you couldn't move without falling over them – and there was such a mob on the stairs to the Underground that he decided to walk to the Strand and Mr Pinkney's office. It was bitterly cold and the sky looked as though there might very well be snow later. He paused on Waterloo Bridge because walking seemed to have a bad effect upon his indigestion – he'd been walking fast to try and keep the cold out. The river looked damn bleak: they said nowadays that there was no need for a man to go down three times before he drowned, he'd be dead anyway by then from the effluent. He couldn't for the life of him understand somebody throwing themselves off a bridge in any case, but then suicide had never been in his line.

At the lawyer's it was very tiresome. Mr Pinkney was engaged they said: he had someone with him. When he objected to this, they asked whether he had an appointment. Of course not; he'd come all this way simply to pick up some papers that Mr Pinkney should have ready for him. They went away again and after what seemed a positive aeon came back and said would he like to wait just a few more minutes, Mr Pinkney *would* like to see him. Eventually Mr Pinkney did. He was full of breezy bonhomie, which meant, the colonel knew, that he was not going to do what he had been asked. So as soon as they finished agreeing about the possibility of there being snow, he fixed Mr Pinkney with his frankest look and said he'd simply no idea that one was supposed to make an appointment when one was just going to pick up some papers: then before Mr Pinkney could reply, he added that of course when he came to think of it, he could see that chaps like Mr Pinkney had to organize their lives pretty carefully – it was damn foolish of him not to have realized that before. Mr Pinkney said well, there it was.

He'd happened to be in London for a spot of Christmas shopping – Mr Pinkney doubtless knew what store the ladies set by Christmas – and so his wife asked him to pick up her will ... His voice died away and he leaned slightly forward in his chair in order to fix Mr Pinkney more firmly with his simple, expectant gaze.

Mr Pinkney also leaned forward and cleared his throat very gently. Possibly the colonel didn't understand that generally speaking affairs of this nature could not be conducted in this manner. But the colonel did not look as though he understood what Mr Pinkney meant. What Mr Pinkney *meant* was that if Mrs Browne-Lacey wished to make a will, it was up to her to communicate personally with him or any other lawyer whom she wished to direct in the matter. Mrs Browne-Lacey had not been to see Mr Pinkney –

His wife was far from well. Not up to doing her own Christmas shopping in fact. Besides, like most sensible women, she expected her husband to deal with all that sort of thing –

Perhaps she would care to write to Mr Pinkney with instructions –

She wouldn't have sent him to fetch the papers if she'd wanted to write – she wasn't *well*: he was only trying to save her any extra trouble –

Mr Pinkney entirely appreciated the colonel's attitude, but he was afraid that in this particular matter he really was unable to act without personal instructions. He leaned back in his chair rather firmly, as one closing this interview.

It seemed to him quite amazing – all they wanted to do was

leave things to each other – that so simple a matter should be made so complicated. No doubt Mr Pinkney had some expert, technical reason for feeling as he did, but for the life of him, he couldn't see what it could be.

Mr Pinkney sighed; if they weren't interrupted he might well be let in for trying to explain to the old boy. But luckily (though late) Miss Scantling came in with the stock bogus message (used on relatively few clients, it was true, but on them with jaw-aching regularity).

'Your call to Rome is waiting.'

Mr Pinkney started to his feet. Forgive him, but he must take that call. Perhaps Colonel Browne-Lacey would discuss matters with his wife and let him know after the holiday what was required. Mr Pinkney would be happy to go down to Surrey if Mrs Browne-Lacey wished. The colonel must excuse him – all the compliments of the season . . .

The air was raw, and seemed colder after the stuffy warmth of Mr Pinkney's office. The colonel's thoughts for the first few minutes in the Strand were positively murderous. Damm the man! Pompous, pretentious, pedantic, pettifogging little cog in the wheel. It was people like Mr Pinkney who were responsible for the decline of this country. Bureaucratic bores, intent on some letter of a minor law at the expense of getting anything whatever done . . .

Lunch would be heartening. He'd get a bus in the Strand to his club. He got the bus all right: simply because the traffic was solid: you could step on to a bus any time, and people were constantly doing this and stepping off again. After ten minutes of being stationary and crawling forward the odd yard, he got off too and walked. One certainly got on faster walking, but still not fast enough. It was half past one by the time he reached his club only to find that the luncheon room was full. He enjoyed his first drink, however, but after two more his indigestion seemed worse. At least, funnily enough, draining his glass and suddenly remembering Pinkney leaning back in his chair, he had the extraordinary sensation of something slamming against his rib cage, his gullet, the back of his throat or the top of the front of his head – a kind of weak banging that hurt and was very bad for him without making any vital difference ... Afterwards he felt distant and relaxed; as though something momentous had happened that nobody else could possibly understand – like his heart stopping and his blood changing direction, a difficult and dangerous thing to do. It was not easy to put the glass on the table and he couldn't even think clearly about it not being easy. He'd simply got too much on his plate. A bit later when he'd almost had a doze, and they'd told him they had a table for him, he summed it all up. Filthy weather, Christmas, bureaucrats, the wilful unpredictability of women – he'd got to simplify things somewhat. His spirits rose at the sight of the menu when Doris finally brought it to him : it was nearly two and he was starving. He decided upon hare soup, grilled sole and treacle tart. Henry came over, and the colonel told him he was busy today and how about half a bottle of his usual, and Henry smiled admiringly at the colonel's acumen and everything seemed all right for a minute or two.

But when it came, he didn't really enjoy his lunch; left most of the soup to leave room for the sole, but then found he didn't seem to fancy the sole. He felt tired, somehow, and he'd clean forgotten what treacle tart did to his dentures, so he had a drop of coffee, signed his bill and made off. Getting to Selfridge's was so bad he nearly gave up, but by the time he felt like that he'd shouldered and tramped three-quarters of his way there, and he couldn't think of anything else to get, or, come to that, anywhere else to get it.

He had a bit of luck in Selfridge's. They were selling small, white handkerchiefs with a nice bit of lace on them and embroidered initials in bundles of a dozen. This was when he realized that both their names began with M – a considerable saving. He bought a bundle and got the girl to divide them into two lots of six and then to wrap them up fairly well in flat boxes with robins on them. He was in and out of the shop like a dose of salts. It then took him – he timed it – nearly an hour to reach Waterloo. Nothing but queues when he got there : he couldn't even buy a platform ticket because the machines he went to had all run out or broken down or something. So then of course he had to go back to the bottom of the ordinary ticket queue again. He just caught a train, and that meant standing in the draughty corridor for the whole journey next to a man, who, as he planned to tell Myrtle, was definitely not using Amplex: also, he hadn't brought his muffler, and had the uneasy feeling that he was getting a stiff neck. He sometimes wondered whether he took enough care of himself.

The Wolseley wouldn't start – at least, not until he had totally lost his temper, got out the handle and had a go at turning her over. Icy gusts of station air eddied unerringly round the gap between his socks and his trousers as he bent despairingly over the machine, at the same time as he felt trickles of sweat edge their way from behind his ears to the top of his collar. He was late for Myrtle already, and what on earth was he to do if this infernal engine wouldn't start? Just then it did – gave a convulsive heave in a forward direction (he'd left it in gear) and died again. But it *had* started.

All the way to the Monkey Puzzle Hotel he tried to think out what he was going to say to Myrtle, but he was driving along a road he didn't know at all well and he was worried about being late – for the second time running with her. Also, the snag about rehearsing conversations was that people – women, at any rate – simply did not say whatever it was you'd planned they should say; so the whole thing was thrown out pretty well from the start.

He was certainly right about things getting thrown out. When he got to the Monkey Puzzle, first he was told that Mrs Hanger-Davies was not in, had gone to hospital or some such gibberish: then he was told – none of the blasted servants spoke decent English – that Madame-very-work-not-see-at-all stuff. He brushed aside the feller who said all that; he was a little chap and fell against a huge wreath of real holly that stood on an easel in the entrance hall – in fact he was such a little runt, that he nearly fell through it. The colonel couldn't help seeing the funny side of that. He pushed open the door to Myrtle's private sitting-room-cum-office without ceremony and went in.

She was there, of course, but in the middle of some interminable telephone call. She looked upset and abstracted and not even specially glad to see him.

It was minutes after he had tip-toed with an elaborate panto-mime of not disturbing her that she stopped her monotonous performance of listening for a long time and then saying how sorry she was and then listening again. Then it turned out that the chef – cook chap – had dropped dead that afternoon – heart, or something.

'It was his poor wife I was talking to. Poor thing; two kids *and* she's a foreigner. He was only forty-six, she says. Really – I seem to be haunted by it : first Dennis and now Antonio: you can't help wondering who the third will be. There's no rhyme or reason to it *and* the holiday coming on and all. He was only halfway through the turkeys and they say there's going to be snow.' She blew her nose for rather a long time – ending up by wringing the end of it while she was still blowing which the colonel found a bit much.

'It sounds as though a nice cup of tea would do us both good,' he suggested hopefully; there was no sign of any other refresh-ment.

'Out of the question – for me, anyway, I'm afraid. I must be off to the kitchens. I could have a tray sent through to the residents' lounge if you're very keen.'

'Oh, come – surely you could spare a few minutes m'dear. It's Christmas *Eve*, after all.'

But she had got to her feet and was tucking her handkerchief in the pocket of her emerald green cardigan. 'You wouldn't realize as you've never been in the business, but it's just *because* of the holiday that I must keep on the go. I've spent all after-noon trying the agencies for a temporary but of course they've got nobody and they close early, and then it took me a long time to get hold of his poor wife, and we're nearly full right through over next week-end and one way and another I just don't know which way to turn.'

Controlling his rage he asked about the cruise.

'Oh I cancelled that first thing. I couldn't possibly go away now for ages. If I do get a replacement for Antonio I'll have to break them in, and if I don't, the cooking will have to be done by yours truly. Is that for me? How nice; I'm always short of hankies. I'll keep it till tomorrow to open. Shall I ask them to bring you some tea in the lounge?'

But he said he thought he would be getting along, he mustn't be too late. They wished each other a Merry Christmas and he stumped out to his car that had had ample time to get freezing cold again.

In the car he nearly cried: well – actual tears came to his eyes. Damn it all! He'd keyed himself up all *day* for this meeting with Myrtle: he'd planned that it should be important – cosy, intimate, but definitely epoch-making. Just as she seemed to like recalling how funny that they should have met in the same railway carriage three weeks running, she was to have remembered tea on Christmas Eve ... Well, she wasn't off on her cruise: one had to count one's blessings. On the cold, slow journey back to Monks' Close he tried to do this, and Alice, his only daughter, came suddenly – and for the first time since she had left home – into his mind. She had always been an attentive housekeeper; warn room, hot meal, no-questions-asked type of thing. An admirable stopgap, that was what Alice had always been, and for the first time, here he was, going to have to manage everything without her.

•

Alice had spent the afternoon having a rest on her bed as Mrs Mount had insisted she should. She and Leslie were spending Christmas with his parents: it was one of those large plans that Alice didn't think about too much when it was first mooted and then realized later that the reason she hadn't was that she would have dreaded it so much. Ever since her miscarriage – and that seemed weeks ago now – she had found it very difficult to care about anything. This was not, as Leslie and his mother seemed to think, because she was so heart-broken at losing the baby – she wasn't and hadn't been that in the least. She'd wondered when she woke up the first night in the nursing home whether she'd lost someone she might have been able to talk to, but the thought had simply crossed her mind and left no wake. Probably not, was the answer she had given herself at the time. What she had found unnerving was how much everybody else seemed to expect her to feel, and what a lot they seemed to know about it. She'd spent ages listening to the various things that Leslie, Mrs Mount and Rosemary told her she was feeling. When they weren't there she simply lay either staring at the ceiling or with her eyes shut. She'd had pneumonia as well as the miscarriage, and for a few days people hadn't talked so much – had just brought flowers, which she had liked. The nurses had been very kind all the time; they kept telling her how she was *going* to feel, but they did not commiserate or describe any similar experience. She was a very good patient, they told her, and she certainly never complained or asked for anything, but this was only because there was nothing she wanted. It was not until she was more or less over the pneumonia that she began to notice that there was something wrong with her – that she was, or had become, a sort of gap or void. She did not mind being like that very much but she felt that everybody else would mind if they noticed, and she became increasingly afraid that they might. With them her face ached with trying to smile and respond generally, and when she was alone she found herself listening – to see if anyone was there – to see whether she could catch herself out existing, or not existing, as the case might be.

Alice had always found communication with anyone difficult, although up until now she had been able to talk to herself. But now there was the sort of silence inside her, as though it was too dark to see at all, and there had been a heavy fall of snow so that all ordinary sounds of people had ceased, some general and complete eclipse of the senses that would be mysterious and awful if one had left any sense working that could know that. She did still seem to have, albeit precariously, some small, critical stronghold that intermittently sent out a series of S.O.S.s of a disapproving nature. The results of these were useless. On one occasion, the chaplain looked in on her during his rounds and asked if there was anything he could do for her, and had only halfway withdrawn his head from round her door before she had said yes. When he was sitting down, his initial expression of alarm fading to goodwill, she tried very hard to tell him about this non-existence feeling and ended by asking him what he thought it meant. He had replied, after not much hesitation, that it was clearly a case of body being so debilitated that mind – he let alone spirit – could not function properly, if at all. She would feel miles better, he said, when she had recovered from the effects of the antibiotics and benefited from whatever tonic he was sure she was getting. When she was up – a bit of a change – the sea, perhaps, and she would be a new woman. He'd pop in again before she left them, he had added when on his feet, which he was sure would be *soon*. The next time, she had asked her doctor whether people who had had rather bad miscarriages and pneumonia often felt that they did not exist. Of course they didn't he had answered at once: it was all in her mind: women often felt run-down and nervy after a miscarriage and that set them imagining all kinds of things about themselves. There was nothing the matter with her; she must simply not give way to hysteria. He had no doubt that she'd be pregnant again in no time and Bob's your uncle. She gave up after that.

So here she was, in the Mounts' spare room having a rest so that she would be all right for their party that evening. Mrs Mount had been cooking and/or assembling food for days: Rosemary had asked several men and Sandra was having her best friend; a number of Mount relations were attending – they would be thirty-eight in all. Alice had never been good at parties (in fact she'd been to very few), but the Mounts' parties were the worst she'd ever tried to be good at. Everybody seemed to know everybody else extremely well: there was a great deal of public badinage, and when – as experience had awfully taught her it invariably was – this was directed at her, she was struck dumb, paralysed, utterly done for. There were always too many people for the room: the large dining-room table loaded with food took up a good third of it. It was also very hot, as Mrs Mount imported fires and put them all over the place so that the room was alive with scorching culs-de-sac and perfectly airless. None the less, Mounts and Mount guests managed to eat and drink and think of things to say to one another for hours and hours, and Alice, as a quasi-Mount, was in agony. Sometimes, late in the evening, they played terrible games that drew attention to people and, she felt, particularly to her: 'games' being a kind of cynical synonym for torture. The worst feature of these social nightmares was the feeling that everybody was enjoying themselves except her. It seemed so unfair: like being colour blind or tone deaf or not being able to smell or something. 'Relax!' people would cry; 'not to *worry*!' 'She's shy,' someone would inevitably, but publicly, confide – as though she was, not tone, but stone, deaf. The last, awful thing that Alice had noticed about the Mount parties was that they were all exactly the same. Since knowing and marrying Leslie, she had been subject to several and she could not find anything different at all about any of them. After hours of refusing more and more food (people always pressed refreshments upon you if you didn't talk much) and trying desperately to talk at all; escaping sometimes to 'powder her nose' – really to go somewhere where she could open a window and breathe – she would return to find the hard core of the party plotting some awful game where you were sure to have to stand up in front of everyone and pretend to be somebody or do something while everyone else shrieked with laughter at how funny you were and how badly you were doing it. She had begged, first the family generally, and finally Leslie, to let her off this particular part of the festivities, but they wouldn't: Mrs Mount took the view that the less Alice wanted to play games the more good it would do her to play them, and Leslie always said that he simply didn't understand what she was talking about. He always said that. At this point it occurred to her to wonder whether she got on worse – or less – with Leslie than with any of the rest of the Mounts simply because she saw so much more of him? Because really things had reached a point where even half hours in the nursing home with Leslie had been a peculiar ordeal. At least Rosemary and Mrs Mount did most of the talking: but Leslie expected her in this, as in most else, to be like his mother and sister. Some part of her had been making kind of emergency allowances for how everything seemed to her – being in the nursing home, staying at Mount Royal as the house was unlaughingly called – but now, considering Leslie, she inevitably thought of their bungalow and going back there alone with Leslie to live. For a few moments she thought carefully about each room there; the black glass and black Formica in the bathroom that showed every mark, even water looked shocking on them, the bleak prettiness of their bedroom (at any moment now, marital relations were to be resumed, according to both the doctor and Leslie: it was like some ghastly weather forecast), the sitting-room or lounge that never, whatever she did in it, seemed to be inhabited, seemed just to tolerate pieces of furniture, and sometimes people as well, being there: it was actually filled to the brim with Mount wedding presents – the cocktail cabinet (Mr and Mrs Mount), the coffee table (Rosemary), the corner cupboard (Aunt Lottie), the black armchairs bought with the Albert Mounts' cheque and the beetroot-coloured rug that Leslie's best friend's mother had made for them; and finally, the spare room – Leslie still called it his study – that Elizabeth had actually stayed a night in with Claude ... 'I do know something – because of loving him,' she thought gratefully. She thought of the windswept and scarred piece of ground that was to become a neat little garden (no shade for years, because there were no proper trees on the whole estate), and then she simply thought, 'I must put a stop to it – all of it,' and the next moment she was out of bed and dressing quietly and sensibly in her warmest clothes. She packed her small suitcase with a nightdress, her kimono, some slippers and her sponge bag. All the time she felt not the slightest excitement or fear; nor did she think about what she was doing – she simply got on with doing it. Her purse contained only fifteen shillings, but then in the wallet was the five pound note that May had given her on her wedding day – her very own money, and enough. Getting out of the house was easy: everybody was shopping or at work excepting Sandra, and she was immersed in a bubble bath with Rosemary's transistor going full blast. The danger was meeting any Mount returning, not so much just outside the house, as she could hide in the laurel bushes, but in the street itself. It was five o'clock and the lamps were lit: they would recognize her easily if they saw her from a car or a cab. She turned down the street away from the main road; it would be better to walk round the block. It was all quite easy, really, and in fact, suddenly got even easier. A cab set down a woman laden with shopping bags: the driver was pleased to pick up a fare at once and take her to the station. In the cab it occurred to her that she had left no letter, no message, nothing. Would they, would Leslie, perhaps, wonder what had become of her? They would think she was mad; but would they actually *mind* her disappearance? Not awfully, she hoped; she didn't want to cause them any trouble. By the time she reached the station she had decided that she had been quite right to leave no note; if she had, and they had found it at all soon, it was just possible that Leslie would have come to the railway station in search of her. This thought unnerved her so much, that after she had bought her ticket to London, she hid in the Ladies until the train came in. She would write a letter from Lincoln Street.

•

The only good thing that happened to May on Christmas Eve was that she got a telephone call from Elizabeth – all the way from Round Hill, Jamaica. It came through in the afternoon while Mrs Green was still there, and she having, just that minute, witnessed May's will, was very pleased: events of this kind were what she went out to work for.

'Yes – it is really me,' Elizabeth was saying.

'Oh – darling, how lovely.'

'How are you?'

'I'm fine,' May lied; what else could one possibly say? It didn't matter anyhow, it was each other's voices they were after, not what either of them thought or said about anything. Mrs Green was going round the den shutting the narrow, gothic windows with the utmost meaning, although May couldn't think why.

'How's Jamaica?'

'It's almost more like one imagines than I thought it possibly could be. Tremendously beautiful and worrying. Is Oliver spending Christmas with you?'

'No, darling – he doesn't seem able to make it. He seems rather low. Depressed,' she added: the full luxury of talking to her daughter was beginning to penetrate: she knew she would remember everything they said all day. 'How is John?'

'Well, he's very well: only his daughter is threatening to come out here and she never seems to have a good effect upon anyone. That's the only thing. How is Herbert?'

'He's fine,' May lied again. What could she say about him? Pride, unhappiness, years of protecting Elizabeth and months of not wanting to be possessive or get in her way stopped her crying out, 'He's awful! He's turned into a quite different person. I think he even hates *me* some of the time. I'm miserable and a lot of the time I feel so ill I think I'm going to die.' None of this came out: there was simply a short, and, Mrs Green thought, an unbelievably expensive silence. At *last* Mrs Browne-Lacey was behaving like a lady: sitting about and wasting other people's money in unusual ways.

'When are you coming back?' It would be lovely to know that: something to look forward to.

'I don't know. Well, I do, really. By the end of January, anyhow. Did you know I was having a baby?'

'Oh *good*. When?'

'May.'

'Yes?'

'I'm *having* it in May you idiot.'

And just as May was thinking that in that case, she must have been having the baby for quite a long time, Elizabeth said, 'What I most wanted to say was, I'm sorry I sort of got married behind your back: it wasn't exactly not wanting you to be there –' her voice tailed off.

May said, 'Darling, that's *quite* all right – of course.' Indeed it was far more than all right, she thought, after they had said good-bye. Both of them knew perfectly well why Elizabeth had behaved in this way; what they had both needed was for it to be made clear that the exclusion had nothing really to do with Elizabeth not wanting her mother. No need to go further.

Mrs Green was simply waiting about in the hall outside the den.

'I shut the windows because of the noise from the birds,' she said, 'as soon as I realized where your call come from.' She waited, expecting news.

'Elizabeth is having a baby,' May said happily. 'Isn't that lovely?'

'Oh madam!'

But that was all about the day that *was* lovely. Mrs Green went just before lunch. May then realized that she had not bought enough bread to make bread sauce for the chicken that she and Herbert were to celebrate Christmas with. This meant walking to the end of the drive and half a mile to the crossroads for the bus into the nearest place to shop. It was extraordinarily cold: people kept looking at the still, congested sky and prophesying snow. She was frozen by the time she caught the bus, and never got warm again that day. The only bread left in the shop was the much advertised pre-sliced Sorbo rubber so she bought one or two other things to make the whole journey feel more worthwhile. Then she longed for some tea or coffee before waiting for the bus back, but the only place had a queue of people waiting for a table, there was only one bus back, and she had to give it up. It was nearly dark by the time the bus set her down, and she plodded back along the road, up the drive, her exhaustion tinged with slight, persistent, humiliating fear. The dogs barked on her return: they had no discrimination, and were, in any case, bored to death. She knew that the first thing would be to feed them.

One way and another, by the time Herbert returned – much later than she had thought he possibly would – she was feeling thoroughly overdone and worked up, and longing for a cosy drink and chat.

She knew Herbert was in a bad temper before she even saw him, as he did not call out, 'Here we are, m'dear; all present and correct.' He didn't call out at all, but she heard him crashing about in his den, swearing in that peculiarly savage way that alarmed her enough to make interrupting him a minor ordeal.

'Why the devil didn't you light a fire in here?'

She had forgotten. At least, it hadn't been worth lighting before she went shopping because it would simply have gone out. And since she'd been back she'd had so much –

'Give me a box of matches.' He fumbled angrily with shiny, purple hands.

She had turned on the bigger electric fire just before lunch –

'I can see that. I'm not a complete fool. It may be easier for you to use the electricity in this irresponsible manner, but it costs far more than lighting a good, old-fashioned fire.'

'Really, Herbert, I told you I had to go *out*.'

'What on earth did you have to do that for?'

'And anyway, good, old-fashioned fires have to be cleaned out and re-laid. They're not necessarily cheaper – just nicer in some way. Let's have a drink –'

'What are we having for dinner?'

'Well – I didn't know what you'd feel like –'

He sat slowly back on his heels. While he turned his head slowly towards her as though he had a stiff neck and it was painful to look at her.

'Didn't know what I'd feel like,' he echoed, 'I see. So I come back frozen to the marrow after slaving away all day to a cold room and no food at all – in order to have the pleasure of choosing which tin you will open –'

Here without either meaning to or being able to help it, she burst into tears. At once everything got better. While she was crying and explaining, more or less incoherently, that it wasn't just tins, she'd laid the fire specially to save Mrs Green – they'd run out of bread and what with waiting for the bus both ways you couldn't leave the fire and she was sorry she was such a hopeless housekeeper but she felt so rotten – he, making loud clucking noises, had helped her into (his!) chair and put her poor feet that she couldn't feel on to a footstool and found her a paper handkerchief and a cigarette and said that what they both needed was a stiff drink. So while she worked the bellows on the reluctant fire, he fetched glasses, unlocked his cupboard, and for once gave her a whisky that was quite dark brown. He put her Christmas-present ostentatiously on top of his roll-top desk and she told him about the little mixed grill she had planned for them. They listened to the seven-thirty news and then, just as he was getting himself a second drink and she was talking of going to the kitchen, the pains began. They had never been so bad: appalling stomach cramps that doubled her up and made her sweat with pain, until she knew that she must vomit somehow or other. He supported her upstairs, put her in the bathroom and when, gasping, retching minutes later, she was fairly sure she had finished, he practically carried her to bed. He said he would fill her a hot-water bottle and call the doctor (the only telephone was in his den). She lay for what seemed a long time, shivering and sweating in bed: the nausea was dying down, and she felt thirsty and frightened. She knew she ought to undress, but felt too weak to make the attempt. The question 'What *is the matter* with me?' recurred urgently in her mind and perhaps what frightened her most was finding that she was afraid to think at all of an answer. It was awful feeling this kind of fright, and at the same time feeling too tired to bear it: she cried a little and couldn't find a handkerchief and snuffled quietly against the sheet. She tried to think what Dr Sedum would say to her in these horrible despairing circumstances, but nothing either useful or comforting came to her mind. It was cowardly to be frightened like this: but she mustn't make too much fuss or Herbert might get fed up with her, and she was utterly dependent upon him. 'Like this, at any rate,' she thought. Her teeth were chattering and she felt clammy and squalid. She could hear Herbert's measured tread on the stairs and then in the passage and tried to smile at him when he came in with the hot-water bottle.

'Not much of a Christmas Eve.'

'Can't be helped. Here you are, old girl.'

'I'm dreadfully thirsty.'

'Always is after one's been sick.'

'Could you get me a glass of water? Oh – and what did the doctor say?'

He was tucking the eiderdown round her legs and did not immediately reply.

'Herbert?'

'What? Of course I'll get you some water.' He went off to the bathroom and seemed a long time there.

'Don't drink too much at once or you'll have it up again.'

'What did the doctor say?' she asked again when she had had a few sips.

'Said I was to put you to bed, keep you warm, and he'll be along first thing in the morning.'

'Not tonight?'

But he repeated, 'First thing in the morning.'

'Herbert, I don't want to fuss, but I think I *am* rather ill.'

'If you must know, it's my fault for giving you such a stiff whisky. A drink like that on an empty stomach – I'm prepared to bet you didn't have a proper lunch, did you now? Thought not. A drink like that on an empty stomach, and yours has been in a delicate state lately – see what I mean?'

He had been fidgeting with things on the bedside table, now he straightened himself and passed a hand over his hair which she knew he did when he was embarrassed.

'I think we ought to get you into bed. Do you want me to – er – ?'

'No thank you darling, I'm sure I can manage.' She wasn't at all sure, but she didn't want to embarrass him, besides she felt so squalid and miserable after being so sick that she wouldn't really want anyone to help her.

'Right. I'll pop down and make your hot drink.'

'Did the doctor say whether –'

'Yes, yes, he recommended it. Settle your stomach and warm you up. I'll have one with you.'

As he was leaving the room she called, 'If you see Claude, his food's on the top shelf in the larder. I couldn't find him anywhere earlier when I did the dogs. He must be ravenous.'

'Right.'

'And Herbert?'

She had wanted to tell him how kind he was being, but he had already gone. After a moment or two, she sat up and slowly pulled her jersey off over her head, but this simply made her feel so cold that she could not face taking off any more clothes. She reached for her bed-jacket, and then her woollen dressing-gown. When they were both on, she felt warmer, but more tired, and lay down to have a little rest until Herbert came up with her drink. He had had nothing to eat, poor dear, so she hoped he was getting himself something.

She became awake quite suddenly: one moment her head was on the block and the guillotine knife was coming down with its inexorable force, and the next moment her eyes were open, the alarm clock was ticking away and she was herself, in bed with the bedside lamp on. She remembered that she had been ill, and that Herbert was fetching her a drink – she must have dozed off. As she sat up, she realized that she still felt pretty awful, and looked to see whether she had any water left.

Then she got a bad shock. The alarm clock said twenty to four. She found herself staring, wondering how on earth it could say that – that would be – that meant that she had been asleep for *hours*! She was still wearing her dressing-gown. Except for the clock ticking, the room was very quiet – much of it shadowy with only one lamp on, but it looked as though her door was ajar. Herbert might have brought up her hot milk, found her asleep and not liked to disturb her. Then where was the milk? Herbert might have brought up her drink, found her asleep and taken it away again. But then where was Herbert? Herbert might have brought up her hot milk, found her asleep and not liked to disturb her *so* he had taken the drink and gone to sleep in another room. He'd left the door ajar in case she needed him. This final conclusion seemed sensible and likely, and she wondered why it did not make her feel less anxious, but it didn't. She did not want to go and look in all the rooms for Herbert in case when she found him she woke him up, which she knew would make him very cross indeed. But on the other hand, she did need to know that he was *there* – where he was, she meant, of course. It would be too awful if he had just got tired of her being ill and simply gone off somewhere as he had been doing rather a lot lately. Other considerations took over. Her stomach, which felt as though it had been repeatedly kicked, warned her that another attack of diarrhoea was imminent; she'd have to get up. She got to the bathroom all right, but it was horribly cold there, and she found that she had to walk very slowly because the ground seemed feathery and uneven as though she was walking in a dream. This feeling was increased when she pulled aside the passage curtain and looked out on to the drive and lawn and shrubs. It had been snowing heavily : everything was thick with it and, even in the dark, luminous. Very large flakes were still slowly slipping down and casually coming to rest. It crossed her mind that she was actually dreaming. In a dream she would go – no, float – downstairs to something amazing. Obviously it wasn't a dream; none the less she was going downstairs, that was the thing to do. She pulled her dressing-gown up round her throat, clutched the banisters with one hand and started down.

She went straight to Herbert's study because she saw that the light was on there. It was one of those glaring lights, a naked bulb topped by a shallow glass shade – it did nothing to soften, let alone conceal what she found.

Herbert was dead. He seemed to have opened a window just before he died as his hand was still clenched upon the casement catch, and he lay with his arm, its shoulder, and his head upon it, half out of the window. It looked a very odd position, but then she realized that in fact he was jammed there; as he had fallen, the width of his shoulders had stuck in the narrow window frame. The rest of him was sprawled over the low stone window seat and the floor. Snow had fallen against the open casement window and his head and clung there, making his white hair look like dirty ivory, and he was so cold to touch that she knew he was dead. She noticed all this without feeling anything, but it seemed to her that everything was happening so slowly, like people said about films and things, that for all she knew she might have run into the room, seen all this and any minute now would give a shriek – it was just that she hadn't got to the shriek. She never got to it. There was more to notice in the same slow, minute and passionless manner. The fire had gone out, but in the hearth lay a document – stiff paper, red ribbon and seal – that she recognized as the will that had arrived from Mr Hardcastle and been witnessed by Mrs Green – this, no yesterday, morning. The paper had been slightly burned – quite burned at one corner – and it lay just below the grate as though where it had ceased to burn it had dropped from the fire. She tried to remember where she had left the will. Elizabeth had telephoned just after Mrs Green had done her bit on it, and she had put it on top of Herbert's bureau to dry while talking to Elizabeth. Then, she had forgotten it. On the edge of the bookshelf by the top of the bureau was a wide tumbler about a third full of what looked like Horlicks. Milk was spattered about the shelf and even as far as the bureau, and she knew what that meant. Oliver had suggested giving Claude milk goggles for Christmas as he seemed to blind himself with spray when engaged upon drinking. It was Claude who had had the Horlicks. She tasted it but it was not at all nice cold, and was anyway no good for quenching thirst. By the Horlicks were her cigarettes and she took one and lit it. It reassured, at the same time as faintly nauseating her. The room was icy. Even the telephone felt cold to touch. She dialled the operator but there was no more or different sound. She tried two or three times but nothing happened: the line, she decided, was dead. Like Herbert. The cigarette was making her feel very sick. Herbert was *dead*. He must have had a heart attack or stroke, or something like that, and had been trying to get some air and she had been too far away to help him. She felt she ought to try and get him out of the window because it looked so uncomfortable, but when she tried to pull him in by the shoulders he did not move at all – was quite horribly rigid. So she simply brushed the snow off him, and that was when she saw the marks of Claude's paws on his collar. She stopped bothering with the snow after she had uncovered the part of Herbert's face that had been shrouded by it. His eyes were open and his expression made her feel uncomfortable to the point of fear. He looked as though he had been stopped in the middle of some violent resentment, and that, in turn, made her feel that at any moment his resentment might suddenly resume . . .

She was frightfully thirsty. Whatever she ought to do – and she had not thought what that might be – she needed to drink something first, and she decided to make some tea. She must have got very cold without noticing, as one of her feet seemed to have gone to sleep; when she started to walk she simply could not feel where the floor was, and so, in fact, she literally stumbled over Claude.

He lay just by the swing baize door to the kitchen quarters, and he, too, was dead. He was not stiff but his fur had that impersonal feel to it that was retrospectively unnerving. Poor Claude! As she was getting to her feet, she saw the pool of vomit. She turned on another passage light: all along the passage near the wall were the marks of Claude's final misery. He must have come in through the open study window, drunk the Horlicks –

What she thought then was so monstrous that she felt the distinct urge to lose consciousness – in vain. It was as if she had suddenly looked behind her and caught the glimpse of a hideous cloven foot in the door: her mind made some frenzied but too faint resistance and then fell back against the force of some horrid explanatory and voluble crowd. The Horlicks had been made for her. She had been feeling very ill. A whisky had also been made for her earlier. For months, drinks of various kinds had been made for her. She had been so ill this evening that she had thought she was going to die. Claude was dead. Her children were away. She had been mysteriously ill for ages. He had had two other wives. They had both died. He had made her buy this house and had changed from seeming to care deeply for her to seeming sometimes actually to hate her. If she had drunk the Horlicks she would be lying dead. She might have been very sick, but she would still have died. An agony of horror that anyone in the world could be like that; she did not feel personal about it: simply, she would never have believed that there could be such a person unless it had been proved – as it now seemed to be – in relation to her. Claude must have suffered, she now knew, great pain before he died instead of her. She knelt down again to take him up in her arms: Alice had loved him and he deserved proper obsequies. (Alice!) But he had watched her, afraid, in pain, knowing all the time what was to become of her, indeed, arranging her eventual death – for what? She stumbled with Claude in her arms to the kitchen where she laid him in the cardboard box in which he had often slept. His eyes were open: they were going dull and she tried to shut them, but they would not stay. She put on a kettle and began to make tea without thinking at all. She would drink the tea very slowly, and time would pass, and in the end it would be morning and the doctor would come ...

After the tea she got up from the kitchen table: if the doctor was coming (but perhaps, that, too, had been a lie?) there were things she must do. It meant going back into the study, and she discovered that she dreaded this. It was as though she was more afraid of the stiff, wicked thing jammed in the window than she had ever been of the living creature whose cover had been that of being a bit of a bore – but none the less a straightforward, kindly man ... There were things she *must* do.

So, shivering, wretchedly ill (she paid another visit to a freezing lavatory) she none the less carefully put away her will (he must have read it and had a fit of rage at its contents) and then dealt with the tumbler of Horlicks. When she tipped it away, she saw that there seemed to be a good deal of sediment in the bottom of the glass and that was when she wondered weakly what poison he had used. She washed out the tumbler very carefully, wondering whether she was going to die in any case, or whether she had been sick enough to escape. She would also have to bury Claude. Everything took ages because she could hardly walk. She opened the heavy front door: the snow had stopped, but it lay about five inches deep in the drive and that meant that there would be drifts. In any case, she found that under the snow the ground was iron-hard from previous frost and that she could not dig it with the study coal shovel. This made her cry, and once she had begun, she could not stop at all.

She wanted everything to be tidied away before the doctor came: she did not want poor, gentle Alice to have to know what her father had been. This idea – that had occurred when she had been putting Claude in the box – had grown to the exclusion of any other, and she kept explaining to herself why it would be terrible for Alice to have her father posthumously dubbed a murderer. She might realize that her *own* mother had probably been poisoned: 'slowly fading health' which was how that poor lady's demise had been mentioned had now an ominous sound to it. And then there was her step-mother, whose mysterious ailments had also culminated in death. If Alice were told anything, she could hardly fail to guess a great deal more;

more, certainly, May felt, than she could bear. So of course it was awful that the ground should be so hard. Indeed, after a rest in the kitchen (she had turned out the light and shut the door of Herbert's study) she put on a coat over her dressing gown and carried Claude out for a second attempt. And this was where, at six in the morning, Alice had found her.

5. Oliver and Elizabeth

The call came through at five in the morning on Christmas Day, and to Elizabeth it seemed hardly to have finished one ring before John had turned on the weak and yellow electric light and was propped up in bed on one elbow listening to the operator.

'Yes,' he was saying; and then, after a pause, 'I said – I accept the call.'

She thought then from his voice that it was Jennifer, and moments later, when his look of speculative affection dissolved to a courteous blank and he settled down to listening she knew. No good going on sleeping, or even pretending to sleep.

After a very long time, John said, 'It certainly sounds like rather a muddle.' There was another pause while he listened. Then he said : 'Oh *no!* Why? You really ought to know why by now. We've come all this way in *order* to be by ourselves. Honeymoons aren't usually attended by close members of the family. I realize that. Yes – you told me.' He listened to another long speech. 'Well – we'll have to see. Wait a minute.' He groped for a pencil. 'Next time, you might work out the hours before you call.' He wrote something down. 'All right all right. I was simply telling you. Yes – I'll see to it.' He put down the receiver and turned to Elizabeth. 'Oh dear, oh damn. That was Jennifer.'

'Yes.'

'She has contracted some sort of alliance with someone who sounds like a *joke* – they're so awful.'

'Is she in love with him?'

'Love?' He looked startled. Then he said, 'She's only known him ten days; he's married and he's just got through a cure. He's also a Catholic so he really is married –'

'Goodness.'

'She is also pregnant – she says.'

'How can she be, if she's only known him ten days?'

He shrugged. 'Some sort of remote lack of control. But why does she have to come here?'

'She's *not* coming here!'

'That's what she rang up about.'

Elizabeth threw herself back on her pillow in mock horror to conceal the real kind.

'She's bringing him with her.'

'How long for?' she asked much later when they were having breakfast.

'Nothing was said about that.'

'When, then?'

'This afternoon. I'm meeting them at the airport.'

'I don't want you to.' She was trying to sound sulky because she was frightened.

'Darling, don't be silly.'

She burst into tears which faintly shocked both of them. He thought of course she was pregnant; she wondered why on earth she should seem to hate Jennifer so much. After a few seconds ineffective struggle, she rushed off the terrace into the house. He, in turn, sat battling with the murmuring pangs of guilt that had become noticeable, like indigestion, when her tears had brought his attention up against them. In the end, finding he could do nothing about himself, he went to comfort her.

She was sitting on the edge of the bath, sternly combing her hair.

'You asked me last night whether I cared at *all* what I did. Remember?'

She went on combing her hair. 'You said, "not if I'm with *you*."'

'That's right.'

He took the comb out of her hand and threw it on her dressing-table. 'I want *you* to feel like that,' he said and took her hands. 'I want you to feel that you could have 'flu or break your leg or embark upon an evening or a week with some of the world's greatest bores, or be shipwrecked or anything awful you can think of, and that you'd feel all right about any of those things because you were with me. The only thing *I* couldn't bear would be to be without you.'

'The only thing *I* couldn't bear.'

'So however awful Jennifer is – and I expect she'll be that one way or another – she won't make any real difference to us. See?'

'I warn you,' he remarked when he had finished signing the letters the secretary brought in before lunch, 'I warn you that all this engagement business is probably just a bid for my exclusive attention. And I'll have to go through the motions of considering the match and advising her against it. *That'll* mean a few heart to heart talks.'

'I'll come with you to the airport?' she suggested after lunch.

'No – it'll be bakingly hot, and you went to bed far too late last night. Have your siesta and I'll come back and wake you up with tea.'

But he never did come back because on his way home from the airport the car went at a great speed into a bus that was travelling in the opposite direction, and thence through some fencing into a small ravine. The bus driver said that he thought the car was completely out of control, but the whole thing happened on a corner and so quickly that it was difficult to know for certain. The police said that the steering was locked and that an inner tube had blown, and that either or both of these things could have caused the accident. John, who was alone in the car, died almost at once, but nobody in the bus was seriously hurt.

*

It was Oliver who fetched her from Jamaica. By the time he got there the worst of the arrangements were over or had been made: the lawyer and accountant had flown out and gone back, the inquest was done, reporters dealt with – even the packing was finished. Oliver arrived one morning and took her back to London that afternoon: she did not want to stay; the sun was out too much, she said. There was only one road to Montego Bay and the airport and so they passed the ravine with its broken fence. She asked the driver to stop the car, and got out, and Oliver knew that she did not mean him to come too. When she came back, she said, 'She made him go to the airport for nothing. Didn't bother to call and say she'd changed her mind – just sent a cable letter that afternoon. I wish I could stop thinking about any of that.'

He did not know what to say. She seemed to him to be either stunned or oddly restless – as when for instance, she completely repacked a suitcase in the plane. But everything about her – even the restlessness – seemed to be stiffened with a kind of dignity that he had not known she possessed. She slept in the aeroplane and woke with tears on her face, but she went away at once and came back without a sign of them. He could not help feeling slightly afraid of her and hated himself for this feeling, because it could be no use at all to her. When they were being given dinner and she was pretending to eat, he asked her where she wanted to go, and she said at once the house in the country.

'Not ghastly old Monks' Close!'

'No : John's house.'

'Do you want me to come with you?'

'Of course I do.'

McNaughton unexpectedly met them at the airport. As soon as they had been cleared by Customs, there he was immediately. She clearly had not known he would be there : she called his name, and took his hand in both of hers, and for a second he saw a look of such desolation in both their faces as though exactly the same thing had hurt them in the same way at the same moment, and then she – his sister – stopped it, said things, made them do things with the luggage and get through the next few minutes somehow.

They spent the night in an hotel at her request, and the next day, Oliver drove them down to the house in the country in the same white car that she had been given in France. On the way, he told her about May, and Herbert, and Alice, ending with the extraordinary and awful time he had had with Alice, when she had poured out all her terrible suspicions.

'Never known Alice talk so much,' he said – seeing that he had really caught her attention. 'You know how she doesn't seem able to tell you anything that she wants you to know? Well, this time she couldn't stop. She walked out on Leslie, planning to go back to the old Close, but she caught a rather late train from Bristol so she tried to spend the night at Lincoln Street, poor little thing. I was out. It was an appalling night, so off she went to Waterloo and caught some sort of milk train or whatever they're called because she was afraid she hadn't got enough money for an hotel. When she got to the station it was nearly five, of course no cabs so she walks – through snow-drifts and all. And when she got there, she found him dead, and poor darling May weeping with a torch and a coal shovel in the garden because she couldn't bury Claude.'

'What had he died of?'

'Herbert? Rage, I should think. But the thing is – you were right about him.' She was silent, and he was afraid that he'd lost her again. 'Because what do you think Claude died of?'

She shook her head.

'Arsenic, my dear: a hell of a lot of it. Meant for May. That's what I mean. He was such a screaming bore, I didn't think he could be wicked as well – but that's what he was. A monster. Alice said her mother *and* her stepmother. She took poor old Claude to be analysed because she was so worried about May. She thinks May doesn't know and it would kill her to find out.'

'What does May think?'

'She thinks Alice doesn't know, and it would kill her to find out. That's why she was trying to bury Claude.'

'Poor May! Poor Alice!'

'Well – in a way. But they've decided to look after each other – because they feel each other have had such an awful time. So they're going to live in Lincoln Street and go to frightful meetings where nobody can say what they mean because they don't mean anything. It suits Alice because it makes her feel more like other people, and it suits May because it makes her feel worse than everyone else which is what she feels is right.'

She asked more questions about her mother; indeed, the subject lasted them almost until they arrived. He knew when they were approaching the house, because she fell silent except for telling him which way to go, which was not the quickest way, she said, but the way she had come before. The morning had been grey and overcast, but as they drove through a beech wood the road became a lattice-work of shadows and sunlight, and the bare trees ahead turned fox-coloured. Then they were out of the wood and a few minutes later she told him to stop. 'That's the house,' she said. 'Will you come with me now?'

They walked through a wicket gate across a field towards the house which was set on a terrace above them. There was a black painted door which she opened to present them with a flight of steps. They walked slowly and in silence up the steps, past a little thorny hedge where she stopped a moment, and then on to the house itself. At the dining-room windows he saw that the round table was laid for two. Elizabeth was ahead of him now, walking round a corner of the house which had bare snaky branches growing round its windows. When he joined her, she was standing in front of a conservatory, its windows misted so that one could not see clearly inside. She tried the door and it opened. Standing on the black and white floor in a huge tub was a camellia growing up to the roof, twelve, fourteen feet high and encrusted with flowers and buds of pale red flowers. She shut the door behind them and said: 'He promised that my best Christmas present would be here,' and then she made a sound articulate only of sheer misery that ended, 'Oh Oliver! What shall I *do*? How do I bear it,' and stretched out her hands blindly to find him.

Much later, when she had finished crying, for that time, she said some of the things that she had to say once – to someone. 'It's the first time I do something – anything – that I last did with John that's so difficult. I keep on making myself do them – in a way to spoil things – to try and make things I remember with him *unholy*, and then, even that seems wrong and feeble. Do you know what I mean?'

'Yes,' he said – really trying to. But nothing had ever happened to him, he knew, that could ever approach making him feel as she was feeling, and as he wondered whether it ever would, he noticed a pang of humble envy.

'It changes,' he said. 'Time changes people always whether they like it or not. You've got that baby to have and bring up. And if you go on wearing that black velvet mac, you'll end up looking exactly like an outsize mole,' and was rewarded by the first, watery smile. But she said :

'I feel like black. I know now why people wear it. But after I've had the baby, I won't, of course. Babies prefer yellow or red.'

'Shall I stay with you – till you have it, anyway? Not happily ever after or anything, but just as a sort of stopgap?'

'It's what people usually are to each other, isn't it,' he went on after she had agreed and he'd thought that she might be going to cry again. 'Except for people properly in love, of course,' he added out of kindness to her feelings. 'And I can't imagine being that.'

'Of *course* you will. I've had mine, but *you* will.'

They looked at each other in a way that they had always done whenever each had thought the other wrong or stupid ('she'll find another love; of *course* she will'), and both were aware of the familiar state of affectionate challenge that on this single occasion neither had the slightest intention of taking up.

The Light Years £4.99

Home Place, Sussex, 1937.
The English family at home . . .

For two unforgettable summers they gathered together, safe from the advancing storm clouds of war. In the heart of the Sussex countryside these were still sunlit days of childish games, lavish family meals and picnics on the beach . . .

Three generations of the Cazalet family. Their relatives, their children and their servants . . . and the fascinating triangle of their affairs . . .

'She writes brilliantly and her characters are always totally believable. She makes you laugh, she sometimes shocks, and often makes you cry'
ROSAMUNDE PILCHER

'Vivid and compulsively readable'
THE SUNDAY TELEGRAPH

'A superb novel . . . strangely hypnotic . . . very funny . . . surpasses even the best of what Elizabeth Jane Howard has written'
SELINA HASTINGS, THE SPECTATOR

'The creation of a vanished historical world . . . engrossing'
VILLAGE VOICE

Marking Time £4.99

Home Place, Sussex, 1939.
The English family at war . . .

The sunlit days of childish games and family meals are over, as the
shadows of war roll in to cloud the lives of one English family. At Home
Place, the windows are blacked out and food is becoming scarce. And
a new generaion of Cazalets takes up the story . . .

'Elizabeth Jane Howard's incomparable imagination, insight and craft
have achieved a work of solid and fascinating reality – and beauty. I
read on with admiration and joy. In due course, this chronicle will be
read, like Trollope, as a classic about life in England in our century'
SYBILLE BEDFORD

'A charming, poignant and quite irresistible novel, to be cherished and
shared'
THE TIMES

'Vivid and compulsively readable'
SUNDAY TELEGRAPH

'Evocative and gracefully written, this is Howard at her most
bewitching'
COSMOPOLITAN

'She writes brilliantly and her characters are always totally believable.
She makes you laugh, she sometimes shocks, and often makes you
cry'
ROSAMUNDE PILCHER

Mr Wrong £4.99

'Miss Howard has a gift for tilting our sense of reality . . . wry humour
and elegant perceptions'
THE GUARDIAN

A family Christmas, a picnic, a house-party in France . . . the subtle
tensions of relationships, from flat-sharing to adultery . . . a haunting
journey into the macabre . . . Funny, perceptive, spine-tingling,
Elizabeth Jane Howard's nine delightful short stories will entertain you
with their style and delicious wit.

'As polished, stylish and civilized as her many devotees would expect'
JULIAN BARNES

'Each of these stories may be read again with real pleasure'
DAILY TELEGRAPH

All Pan books are available at your local bookshop or newsagent, or can be ordered direct from the publisher. Indicate the number of copies required and fill in the form below.

Send to: Pan C. S. Dept
             Macmillan Distribution Ltd
             Houndmills Basingstoke RG21 2XS
or phone: 0256 29242, quoting title, author and Credit Card number.

Please enclose a remittance* to the value of the cover price plus: £1.00 for the first book plus 50p per copy for each additional book ordered.

*Payment may be made in sterling by UK personal cheque, postal order, sterling draft or international money order, made payable to Pan Books Ltd.

Alternatively by Barclaycard/Access/Amex/Diners

Card No.   □□□□□□□□□□□□□□□□□□□□

Expiry Date   □□□□□□

_____

Signature:

Applicable only in the UK and BFPO addresses

While every effort is made to keep prices low, it is sometimes necessary to increase prices at short notice. Pan Books reserve the right to show on covers and charge new retail prices which may differ from those advertised in the text or elsewhere.

NAME AND ADDRESS IN BLOCK LETTERS PLEASE:

....

Name _____

Address _____

_____

_____

_____

6/92